YOUR ENEMIES DO KNOW YOU BEST

- A CIA NOIR -

BY L. DEANE TANNER

*"Light is man's love, and lighter is man's rage;
his purpose drifts and dies."*

W.B. Yeats

Printed in the United States of America
First Printing, 2017
ISBN 978-0-9980761-4-0
Cover by Vanessa Mendozzi
Published by Book Counselor, LLC
www.BookCounselor.com

PROLOGUE

It was a grey, cold and pocked sidewalk that coughed up leaden applicants at the entrance to the United States Embassy in Bogota on the last Friday before Christmas. My baseball-capped taxi driver, sea captain of his dented and droning taxi, yapped above its chugging engine all the way from the airport about the coming year being the last for his country. The taxi gave a final wheeze and came to an awkward stop. He looked at me imploringly with my money in his fist, hoping that I would not ask for change. Several people on the sidewalk took sour notice of the whole transaction.

I walked past a few thousand well-dressed Colombians who stood in a morose line that circled the whole complex—all more or less with that sinking feeling they would probably be calling each other comrade in a year or so unless they could get a quick ticket out of the country.

Those people knew all about Caguan, the government's attempt to show good will to an implacable Communist insurgency by means of a gifted demilitarized zone the size of a decent New England state. Its inauguration was only a week away, and the fall of the country perhaps only a few months beyond that. So, the downtrodden stood day after day hoping for a modern miracle, a last-minute tourist visa to the United States that would allow them to leave hell and death and horror behind for the other guy to worry about. It was the last embassy working day before Christmas, and I doubted whether half the ground-floor staff was still in the country.

The gate guard pointed me out to two marine escorts who walked closely beside me as soon as I squeezed through the quickly-opened main gate all the way through the brick courtyard and into the embassy building. They stayed with me in the elevator up to the third floor, peeling away after I knocked on the right of two large double doors, which opened for me quickly.

I felt ill at ease for several reasons, one of which was that I had to leave my backpack and the tools of my trade—gun, binoculars, wire, knife, and cash—in a hiding place in the woods outside my condo in Cali. We were both better off if they had no physical evidence of my use of any of those tools over the previous few weeks.

Another reason for my lack of aplomb was that I was still weak from the serious illness and several minor injuries that I'd battled before arriving here; in fact, my doctor told me that under no circumstances should I fly up to Bogota until good health had a chance to take hold in me.

I stood before about eleven angry men and Doctor Susan Appleman, who, until recently, was either my runner or the runner of the people who ran me out of the embassy. Having become a net provider of trouble to that accomplished officer of the CIA, who now glanced up from a pile of papers at the head of the long oval table when I walked toward her, it was not at all a sure thing that I would walk out of that building a free man. She rose and embraced me tightly, almost passionately, as if I were going away and would be fondly missed. "You look like shit, Tommy," she said, stroking the back of my head.

I had agreed to report to the meeting as a gesture of good will, not as a guilty man, at least in their sense of the word. I knew that the American side wanted to put me in a locked room until I modified the essentials of my story. The Colombians, however, did not care what story I told, since several years in a dungeon-cell would give them ample time to teach me their version of events for easy repeating to a judge.

The mix of stone-faced and perturbed American and Colombian brass at that table eyed me like a bad fish, one worthy only of being chopped up for chum. I turned back toward the door, but Dr. Appleman took my hands in hers, holding them securely between us like she was about to cuff them, before she led me to the empty chair besides hers. She introduced me to three men, one of whom was from the Green Berets, judging from his chiseled build and chin, and clean-cut look. The other two were in-house analyst-types from the CIA. She also introduced me to a General from D-2, the Colombian Army Intelligence Division, and an assistant to the Secretary of the Fiscalia in Bogota. The rest of the crowd were assistants and adjutants, who looked at me with bewilderment, as if Tommy Connolly in person did not seem to represent such an intractable problem, one that a single bullet would solve behind any nearby building.

For the benefit of the table, Dr. Appleman made a brief inquiry about my health.

"How would you rate your own fitness, Tommy?"

"Fit for normal, but not extraordinary duties, Doctor."

"In your line of work, what would that entail, exactly?"

"I can make a mean chicken salad sandwich."

There being no laughter in the room, I continued. "…I suppose it means that I can undertake light duties on a limited schedule."

"How limited?"

"We have to work that out, I guess."

"If we could somehow placate your doctor, do you wish to continue your work for your country, Tommy?"

There it was again—nationalism or bust—either I succumbed to the glory of the flag and accepted the horrors that followed, or I led a life of quiet desperation and suburban boob tube watching. Far below the rhetorical flourish, which the Colombians surely saw through, there was a far more sinister blandishment struggling for air. The underlying question was, "Isn't the cash we have recklessly thrown at you for the last two years enough to buy a little more of your loyalty?"

I would have been more comfortable with that question; at least, it would have been honest and would have displayed probative power. Did I owe them anything more? I was ridiculously overpaid; from the beginning, they either stuffed money in my bank or looked the other way while I helped myself to (in their world)piles of small change. I arrived in Colombia—according to Nando, since I was not there at the time—with six-hundred dollars in my pocket, and now had somewhere between eight and nine million dollars.

But in the depths of my heart, they could never compensate me fully. I was changed, deformed and certainly lessened as a man. There was also a little matter called command responsibility, a doctrine that we turned upside down and shook until it was impoverished of meaning, stripped of dignity, and finally left in the archives to rot. You can never pay me for that, Dr., I thought. I knew that we would never have that conversation, since the essence of my job was to forget everything I saw, and everyone I met, and carry out their instructions without unreasonable delay.

"Of course, I wish to be of service to my country, Doctor. I just have less enthusiasm though about performing tasks that could lead to greater risk or injury, considering my present state."

"Do you consider yourself 'injured' right now?"

3

"I consider myself taking an extended rest to recover from a state where I dealt with some life-threatening situations. You might even say kill or be killed."

I paused then to throw a cheeky glance at my Colombian counterparts.

"I consider I deserve the rest."

"You are referring to your recent experience in the San Lucas Mountains. You were missing in action, maybe even KIA."

"Yes," I said, but wanted to shout,

"You have no fucking idea...."

"How long do you expect this leave of yours to last?"

"I expect to flesh that out constructively within the course of this briefing, Doctor."

"Alright, Tommy. Let's begin at the beginning. Walk us through what happened out there."

Depending on your propinquity to Tommy, and your understanding of his efforts to several causes, there were a lot of beginnings from which I could choose, like picking up a slip of paper from an audience member at an improv-comedy show, and starting a routine based on the suggestion the paper carried. The Dr. was interested in only one particular event, however, one that mattered greatly to her host country and its assembled guests.

Unfortunately for them, we all knew they had nothing on me that they were willing to introduce in a court of law, and the CIA would not allow them to try me in one of their military courts. I began to speak in the detailed graduate seminar fashion I learned from them. As I spoke, the group-particularly the Colombians—read from a briefing paper based on a CNP debriefing, which they perused for the usual omissions or inconsistencies, all the while nervously readjusting their collars and tight-fit military uniforms that had suddenly shrunk a size.

So, I told them as much as they needed to know and not a word more. The Columbians were losing their country by the square mile every minute to the FARC insurgency; the civilian population was petrified, and if this is how they wanted to spend a Friday afternoon before Christmas while their country was under siege and their capital surrounded on three sides, well fuck them and their national honor. They were getting what they deserved. They were also getting on my nerves. I had earned my stripes and did not feel called to the manor in front of the bi-national assembled "brass." Let them squirm.

CHAPTER ONE

Nando's hard pushes on my shoulder in the barracks bunk wobbled my head around until I came back to wakefulness. Whatever I had been dreaming at that moment was unmoored now, and unresponsive to my attempts to ignore Nando and return back to sleep.

"Marika—get up! We have to go now. You are leaving Colombia."

I muffled some type of response from the limbo between my dreams and Nando's sudden jostling of my shoulder.

"Yes, the Colonel thinks you are well enough to travel."

"And where does the Colonel suggest that I travel?" I yawned at him, slightly raising my head off the pillow.

"We are going to Aruba. The Colonel is paying for a flight there. After that, you can return to the United States or stay there and surf."

"So, the Colonel has decided all that for me?"

"He thinks it is best for you to leave now."

"I don't want to disappoint the Colonel."

"Yes. That is very true."

"Ok. Give me a few minutes to shower and pack."

"I already packed for you, including your passport. You can shower in Aruba or Miami or wherever."

"Why so early, Nando?"

"Five minutes, marika!"

Jeans, tennis shoes, leather jacket, pain pills from the bathroom cabinet, and water in the face: I beat Nando by about 17 seconds, which pleased him micro-emotionally. His outheld hand had three pills, two of which were blue, and the other white, a newcomer to my pill regimen since I arrived in the empty barracks a few weeks ago.

"What is that white one for?"

"For flight sickness. We are not flying commercial."

I drank them down with a cup of water, which Nando was quick to snatch back from me and put back in its place atop the sink in the barracks bathroom.

Nando held onto the lapel of my leather jacket to push me out the barracks and down the gravel path in almost total darkness. Apart from a single lizard who scampered along the wall of the barracks at night, there was no one who visited me, and therefore no one to whom I could say a farewell. There was only Amelia, who by now began to live more or less in my dreams, where paradoxically, she had a more consistent form and voice than when she appeared during my attempts to summon her image while I lay on the bunk in the evenings, trying to sleep.

At the end of the path was a Range Rover with civilian plates. I caught a glimpse of a suitcase in the back seat, and perhaps a duffel bag or two in the rear compartment. Nando unlocked the passenger door and opened it widely, helping me into the seat as if I were still hospitalized. I pushed in with images of exile in my mind.

It had been about four weeks since Nando delivered me into my spare, cavernous existence in the empty barracks, set at the far end of eight identical long and green Quonset huts, which I counted each time the driver took me back from physical therapy sessions. Nando, seldom visited me or shared information one might think vital to me, such as the reason I was held under guard in an empty barracks, or why I needed pills and physical therapy in the first place. But he had been my sullen minder since I left the sweet breath of Amelia and the comforts of the fourth floor of the hospital.

I resented him from the beginning for his cold dismissal of my attempts to elicit information from him, but mainly for having taken me away from Amelia so abruptly. After I wrote the farewell note to her, Nando picked me up in a jeep outside the hospital at the same spot where Amelia would smile at the security guard assigned to me, so that he would lag behind some distance while she wheeled me carefully down the shaded paths through the hospital garden during my recovery.

We drove me across the base to this small, green hut, which had enough beds and showers for a small company of soldiers, but no one other than those authorized to deal with me—Dr. Howe and Nando— ever entered the barracks.

Breakfast came to me on a tray at the front door, and a jeep came for me at noon to take me to a gym. The few times that I opened the door of my place of confinement, there was always a guard beside the door, but evidently he was not allowed to converse with me at all, or even to look at me. Left alone within the barracks without books or newspapers or even simple conversation, I watched lachrymose telenovelas—and news accounts of ambushed army platoons or images of dead narcos—on a small black-and-white TV someone set up on a stool near my bunk.

Once, while walking on a base road between the gym and my barracks in an attempt to gauge whether I was capable of exertion for more than a short walk, I saw the hospital in the distance, but the guard turned me back when I began to walk toward it. Doctor Howe, my brain surgeon, who had been the one who also planned my recovery, put me through a series of stimulus-response exercises to measure my reflexes, and shot the usual mini-flash light beams into my eyes. Like everyone else, he would not answer any questions about how I chanced upon major damage to my back and scull, or why I was kept in isolation during my rehabilitation.

Nando stopped by every few days in the evening to speak to the guard on duty, often not even bothering to enter the barracks and speak to me. He avoided unnecessary chatter with me as if I was a carrier of something he dreaded. At night, I listened to the cicadas between sprays or shrieks of rain, and thought of Amelia and her beautiful face. I thought of her disappointment with me, and my heart ached like someone had battened it down with tightly-bound rope during a torrential storm.

By the time Nando reached the base perimeter, his little white pill had tricked me down to sleep, but not until I saw Amelia again, standing over my hospital bed, kissing me softly on each cheek before she spoke: "Good morning, Tommy!" Her voice and her smile jolted me into one last attempt to stay awake and alert, so that I could turn my head back toward the hospital. Finally, my head fell down, my limp body held in place by the seat belt Nando had fastened tightly around me.

In the beginning was that smell, that sweet woman sweat smell in my muggy hospital room. Even the rig workers who drilled downward behind my right ear in eight-man teams paused to take a look at Amelia. She was lovely—like a 1950s Italian movie actress, all shimmering black hair and natural curves and forthright carnality.

"Welcome back, Tommy." Amelia comes to my left side. She takes my hand. I can make it twitch now.

"Tommy—do you understand me?"

I twitch. "My name is Amelia… Do you know where you are?" Twitch. Twitch.

"You are in a hospital." Twitch.

"Do you remember what did happen to you?"

Twitch. Twitch.

"Are you in pain?" Twitch.

"Does your head hurt?" Twitch.

"Can you talk?" Twitch. Twitch.

Do you know who I am?" Twitch. Twitch.

"Do you want me to stay with you?" Twitch. She kisses my hand.

"Ok. Go to sleep now, Tommy!"

I am all joy for a moment when she lowers her breasts onto my chest and kisses me on the cheek. "Sleep now, Tommy."

I opened a blurry eye to the first light of a bulbous red sun above the horizon line of the sea.

"We are landing soon, marika. Prepare yourself."

Instinctively, I looked out the window toward the sun, which blindingly replied to me with its first fierce rays as the plane headed towards it. We banked, and flew downward to the east, coming down straight onto a narrow road that seemed to arbitrarily divide the vastness of the desert in twain.

We came down quickly, and landed with a few hops, an excellent landing considering the narrowness of the road and the dimness of the light at ground level. The pilot turned the plane around on the dry, rocky ground and bumped the plane back onto the beginning of the runway where the plane stopped and its engine sputtered and rested with tinny pings. A Range Rover was parked nearby in front of an abandoned flat-roofed building, but otherwise, there were none of the essential features of a working airport.

There was no depressurizing, or instructions from the cockpit, or orderly deplaning by aisle and row; Nando and I were the only passengers in that plane. He and I just pushed onto the pavement from an open hatch, stretched a little, and led by Nando, went behind the building to relieve ourselves. I needed water, badly. Beginning to heave and tilt under a tremendous heat, even at dawn; the last thing I remember before falling over was that the heat was enough to bake you from the inside.

Nando rolled me over on my back, not to check on my condition, or give me much-needed water, but to grab me under the armpits, so that he could drag me toward the shade of the plane. I felt a trace of a new headache emerging behind my right ear. "Nando," I motioned toward the plane, "I need my pills." Nando nodded, and the pilot re-opened the hatch, which Nando shot through catlike in seconds.

I put all the remaining pills in my front jeans pocket, and handed Nando the pill bottle, which he smashed below his foot and then scattered the shards in the wind.

"Ijuepuutaaah! Que calor!" said the pilot.

"Where are we?"

I ventured.

"La Guajira, near Venezuela."

I knew this to be the most desolate part of Colombia, a place of dry, scorched landscapes and huge distances without towns, roads or water, or police of any sort.

"Nando, I am going to sleep for a while."

"You do that, marika!"

I am awakened by some low murmurs and several eye clicks. "Good morning, Tommy." I open my eyes. It's a café now. A guy who looks like the Buffalo Nickel guy is in a corner chair. A doctor, his hand holding my eyelid up near my forehead, leans close to me and smiles. "Todos afuera, por favor." I got that.

"Everyone outside!"

The Buffalo Soldier stands and walks out. Amelia follows him. Another nurse enters. She closes the door. There is a bed pan. My first smell. The new nurse lifts it and sets it down somewhere. Circles on my back. Cream? Most likely. The nurses chat as they work. No, cleaning. My back, thighs, feet, down below. I am flat again. Neck, shoulders, and arm pits. A motor starts and I am pushed up. It stops. I am at the top of a Ferris Wheel. I bump the bar and lean forward. The old nurse has nurse scissors. She puts one hand on my chin. New nurse is on the window side now.

There is a new smell; it is rotten flesh, apparently mine. Behind my right ear, the two nurses work as a team, cutting bandages, or maybe dead skin. When the nurse comes around the bed in front of me, I see red and yellow gauze at the end of her tweezers. Now the Doctor grabs my finger and holds it.

"Tommy, can you hear me?" Twitch.

"My name is Doctor Howe." Twitch.

"You are much, much better now." Twitch.

"I think you are going to be awake much more often." Twitch.

"You probably have a lot of questions." Twitch.

"For now, you need rest and just a little stimuli." Twitch.

"So, no rock concerts for this week, ok?" Twitch.

"OK, my friend. I will come back tomorrow. Nice to see you."

He has a nice, friendly, professional manner. His optimism seemed like real stuff, but he has seen the gauze pile, too. He seems confident. Suddenly, I want to eat: a cheeseburger. A Coke. A chile dog. Fries. "Tommy's Burgers has sixteen locations in the greater LA area." That was on the radio once. Some pasta primavera?

"Tommy, leave some of the lemon slices for me," my mom would say.

I feel myself swallow. How did I eat? Who feeds me? Old and new Coke—nurse—leave. The door is still open. Buffalo Soldier guy and Amelia enter. He's a cop? He has a brown uniform and holds a cop hat in his hand. No, his shoulder has those eggs, the scrambled ones. He is an… officer.

Amelia has crept from behind him as he goes to the window side of my bed, and is now in his place. She is beautiful, as if a mad scientist somehow mixed Sophia Loren and Maureen O'Hara. A gym girl. Young, like upper class Latinas in the L.A. gyms. She holds my hand and smiles at me. "Loca enfermera esa!" Crazy nurse. She walks behind the bed. The Ferris Wheel goes slowly back down in reverse. Stop. She takes the cream. She takes off my blanket. She rubs my legs, my feet, my thighs. She stops where the fun starts. She gets some scissors. She cuts some hair. She cleans my ears, at least the left one.

What does she see behind my other ear? Does she move quickly to get away from the smell? She stands again. I try to look at her, but my vision has that old movie screen shape, the wide rectangle thing. She senses something like that. She moves down, and I put eyes on hers. She moves in and kisses my cheek. Buffalo Soldier guy looks away.

Nando woke me again, this time with a nudge of his foot that was not so purposefully mean. I had no basis for the insight, but it seemed that he had softened since we left the barracks the night before or perhaps he ventured that if he pushed me too far, I would die, and that would leave him with an even bigger problem.

We drove down the movie back lot air strip and onto a dirt road, all the while trailing a tight swirling flame of yellow-orange dust that would have made surveillance almost impossible. We drove slowly over ruts that made the undercarriage of our car beg for mercy, finally rising onto the rear gate of another military base. This one appeared to be abandoned too, so that birds had by then pecked away at all its signs. We drove along its perimeter for about a mile before merging onto a highway and speeding off toward Venezuela.

Through the tinted windows I made out a welcome sign for the city of Maicao. It was flat, dusty and unusually prosperous for an indolent little town that was tethered to nothing of apparent value for over a hundred miles. It was probably as far from Bogota as Colombia extended, which was probably the way the locals liked it.

We stopped at a typical roadside restaurant and sat near the street at a white plastic table under the only tree that cast shade.

"Tres frias, mi amor!" The lithe teenage waitress scampered away.

"Could I have some water?"

Nando nodded, and a new member of our group went back to the Range Rover. Before he came back, I had taken two more pills, and then drank them down with water from a canteen that Nando carried with him. The new guy looked at me oddly, so I wiped the top of the canteen with my sleeve. "Mejor?" Better?

Their beers arrived with little twirls of napkins flowering out of the top of the cans. I could not remember the last time I had a beer, but Nando let me know with his glance that I was not going to drink one that day, or under his watch. "Una picada, mi amor." Nando got up abruptly after ordering, walking back onto the street, and quickly disappearing from view. I lifted my left arm to get the attention of the waitress. She came with a smile until she saw the bandages behind my ear, after which she trained her eyes to the other side of my head. "El bano?" She pointed around the back.

With a nod the pilot told me that a bathroom trip was permitted. Inside, I took off my t-shirt and soaked it in the sink water. There were no towels, so I wrapped toilet paper again and again around my hand, and then let water soak the bands of cheap paper into a compress that I applied with my head resting on the edge of the sink.

There was a noise behind me, toward which I abruptly turned. The waitress entered the tight space between the toilet and the sink, almost squeezed against my back. "Excuse me, senor. I brought this towel for your head."

"Gracias!" She handed it to me, hovering (perhaps to see her first live gringo or from earnest compassion for the wounded). "Where are you from?" she asked.

"Are you a guerrilla?"

"No, senor—I hate the guerrillas!"

"Then from the United States."

I soaked the towel completely in the sink.

"Very far from home, no?"

"Si." The towel weighed down on my head, and I heard little after that.

After I cleaned myself, I looked in the mirror. Handsome Tommy Connolly was now a thin, beggared, and pale camp-survivor. His shoulders were droopy and pointed toward each other; his right eye was seconds behind the left. His shiny black hair was wild and matted with blood, and stubble sprung up from a gaunt, haunted face that only hoped for no more pain. The towel was now on the floor, with small drops of blood on it from the reopened wound behind my ear.

How could Amelia ever love that face?

Nando paid in cash from a small paper stack of bundled Colombian money that he pulled out of his wallet. As I prepared to return to our vehicle, the waitress reappeared in haste at my side. Touching me lightly on the arm so that I did not fall over, she handed me a small bag. "Buena suerte, senor." Surprised and touched, but too tired to express proper gratitude, I muttered "Gracias, Nena!" I walked out to the street and followed Nando and his crew to the Range Rover. The heat of the day was reaching its tropical zenith, so Nando put the air conditioning on full blast.

Inside the paper bag from the waitress was a new toothbrush, a half a tube of toothpaste, a fresh towel, and a cross. They were her obviously her own personal items, a gesture she could probably ill afford. She had shown pity for me, the only emotion my current condition could inspire in anyone, apparently. The cross was not one of victory or redemption, or any of the hopeful messages of the risen Jesus. It was a cross of pity, a talisman to prevent the approach of any more demons, the only cause she could think of to explain the ravages my body and mind had endured.

As we drove around the bluff to the landing strip, we saw the airplane in its position at the beginning of the air strip, but an old truck had parked nearby. Through the dust I could see a man in a white hat on the door rider of its shaded side. He stood as we drove through the dust clouds, stopping just short of the lone building. Nando approached the man without hesitation or thought of security.

"Quibo, Nando."

"Quibo, Hector."

"Two hundred should be enough."

"Claro."

"Cerveza?"

"Gracias."

Nando nodded at one of his crew, who went back to the Range Rover for more beer.

"Do you want it all in the plane?"

The pilot spoke now.

"It can hold 225. I should need about 80, maybe 90, but there is always the chance that we will need more."

Nando added, "Yes, fill the tank, and the auxiliary tanks. We will not carry a lot of weight."

Hector, evidently another member of the team Nando put together for this so far unnamed operation, looked at me without interest, as if I were a horse in a travelling trailer.

The beer arrived; Hector, one hand steady on the gas nozzle, which filled the main tank, drank his beer in one straight gulp, crumpling the can and handing it to Nando instead of tossing it away.

A tremendous heat now bore down on us; even in the shade, it compressed and then baked me from within.

"Nando—water, please."

Almost as soon as I handed it back to him, my head fell back on the ground under the plane, and I slept.

A nurse comes in to my room in an unusual coolness of morning.

"Hola—Tommy! Como estas, pelao!"

I can shake my head a little.

"Necesitas algo?"

She notices now the sweat on my cheek.

"Esta un poco caliente el cuarto?"

"The room is a little hot for you?"

I moan. I can moan now.

"Ok. Sacamos esta manta. Me voy por una toalla para ti."

She will ditch the blanket and get me a towel. The blanket comes down. She comes back and towels my cheeks and my forehead. She lifts up my back from the bed and feels the sheets.

"Estan mojadas las hojas, Tommy! Ud. esta sudando mi Corazon!"

The sheets are wet from my sweat. She is careful and thorough. I am not in a position to complain. She could leave the sheets wet and no one would know by morning. Instead, she carefully takes off my gown and cleans my back.

She presses a button to make the top half of the bed rise until I am leaning over near the top of the Ferris Wheel, like my first ride alone at the fair that summer when my mother, almost apoplectic below, screamed at the carny to save me.

She is kind to me, and even a little flirtatious, but I listen only to the lute of Amelia, whom I wait for every day.

The next morning? Three days later? Six years later? Late the next week? I wake after a sound sleep. There are male voices outside. "Gracias, mi Colonel!"

The Buffalo Soldier and Amelia walk in, quietly, like they are on their way to take the wafer in a Catholic Church. He leads, even more distracted. I sense he has more pressing business than to visit his least favorite pet Gringo, the sick calf on his huge ranch of command and responsibility. He comes to the edge of the bed and gives me a brief glance; apparently satisfied, he turns and goes outside.

Taking his departure as a cue, Amelia comes from the rear wall and stands close by my bed on the right side. She pushes the tray back so she can stand closer to me. Her backpack appears on the chair near the window. It is yellow, with a water bottle in a side pouch.

She speaks in accented English.

"Good morning, Tommy!"

She leans toward me and gives me a slight kiss. A little gold star on a chain at the tip of her necklace slaloms down atop a drop of sweat until it plows into the side of her breast and stops.

"You look so much better today, Tommy! Do you feel better?"

I moan, consonants and vowels mashed down into a vocal poultice.

"Tommy, you speak!"

She kisses my other, far cheek. I feel a moment's breast breathe on my nose.

"You want some water?"

She takes the plastic cup from the tray and fills it from the plastic container. She puts a straw inside my lips.

"Now just a little bit, ok?"

Grunt. I suck the water upward. She chokes off the straw half way. I feel the water go down my throat. She is softly rubbing my cheek with her handkerchief, tinctured now with her perfume and smell.

She picks up my hand and holds it between her two.

"The doctor is very happy with your progress! He said that soon we can go in the wheel chair and leave your room. Would you like that?"

Back to basics: Twitch. She drops my hand and lets the sheet down to my waist.

"You are gaining weight, too, Tommy!

The doctor also said that soon you can hear music and I can read to you. Would you like that?"

I start to grunt, and she drops her finger into my hand. Twitch.

"Good! You will tell me what you want to read, Ok?" Twitch.

"I will go and get the nurse now. I will be back in a moment."

Another really unearned kiss on the near cheek. She walks out. And I fall fast asleep.

It was apparent since I awoke to several mentions of the word, that they were delivering me to someone in particular in Aruba. Since I awoke in the hospital, no one had even bothered to tell me which month, or even year it was. I did not know what day we left the military base, or how long our flight had lasted. Neither did I know what awaited me the next time the plane stopped. Nando, the keeper of all my personal data, treated this as a simple snatch and grab mission, though one with some traces of captive-captor friendliness. His orders were becoming a little clearer to deliver me alive in Aruba, according to some terms he treated almost like state secrets.

Hours later, under the tiny spangles of distant stars, the plane prepared for its next takeoff. Nando stood up on its side, instinctively grabbing me by the shoulder so that I would not walk into the propeller. "Before we leave, I will need water and the flashlight to clean my head, Nando. It is bleeding again."

"Ok," he said as he turned toward the plane to fetch a canteen. Expecting him to offer assistance, but not receiving any, I blurted out,

"Nando, where the fuck are we going?"

"I told you, marika. To Aruba. You can go home from there."

He got into the plane and quickly returned with the canteen and a medicine kit.

I stretched out my arm to take the canteen, but he shook his head, leading me with an arm holding firm to my shoulder away from the plane. "Let's go down around the building. I don't want to leave blood on the tarmac, especially gringo blood." I said nothing, mostly due to surprise at his compassionate gesture.

Behind the building, which at the point of Nando's flashlight looked like the mini-mart portion of a small gas station, Nando wetted some gauze, which he daubed behind my ear. I took advantage of the moment to take two pills from my pocket and swallow them with a slug of water. I handed the canteen back to Nando, and then bent over in the college boy's puking position.

"Pour the water slowly on the right side of my head."

"I know what to do, marika."

Nando came close and pointed the flashlight onto my head. Without a word, he poured the water carefully, so that it dripped down the slope of my head, and front to back. I stood up and put the cloth towel on the wound. Reaching into the first aid kit, he concocted a poultice out of some antibiotic cream and some cotton. "When I place it on your head, hold it there with your finger."

Nando wrapped tape around my head a few times and then sealed it with white football tape, making me look like a rugby forward inured to bone-crushing injury and a concussive understanding of things.

"Thanks, Nando. You have missed your calling as a gifted nurse."

Nando was not given to cheerful responses to my jibes. He wanted me alive, but beyond that, he wanted to place tremendous distance between us, which I did not begrudge him at that moment.

We weren't friends, nor were we enemies. I was merely cargo for him, but cargo he took pains to deliver in a certain condition. The hospital stays, the physical therapy, and now the late-night exfiltration: there was an implied agreement, to which he was a party, that I was to be returned with a certain level of health and wellbeing to a party or parties unknown in Aruba.

"Tomorrow morning in Aruba, take off everything and dry your head in the sun. That should be sufficient.

"Let's go now."

"I have to pee. I'll be there in a minute."

Pissing in a jug on a plane was hard enough for someone with a fully functioning skeletal system. When Nando turned to leave, I decided to take a chance on his good mood.

"Nando…"I started.

"What month is it?" He looked away.

"It's May, marika."

"Fuckin' May!" I said in English. I braced myself against the wall with my head sunken downward. Ordinary time-—measurable, recordable, memorable—had stopped for me the last month of December, 1996. Based on the time I had spent with Amelia, and then in the barracks, it was clear that I had been asleep for almost two months, awakening only to Amelia's voice in a strange hospital. Nando spoke English to me for the first time.

"Let's go. You have your family and the rest of your life to recover from your injuries. My job is to get you there."

His English was surprisingly good, and contrasted with the martial indifference I had encountered in him thus far in Spanish. I took a chance.

"But why Aruba?" It was a wrong move.

"No more maricadas! Let's go!"

Commanding again, Nando took my arm and swung me once more in a safe arc away from the propeller and wing. After strapping me into my seat, Nando swiftly closed the hatch and locked the door, calling out to the pilot, "All good—let's go!" The plane, in the complete quiet and stillness of the desert, pushed back into its furthest crouch where the road trailed off into desert scrub and rock. It then shot forward for about twenty seconds in a smooth, controlled lift, veering to the right, rather than gaining an even higher altitude. We were within radar of at least three countries, but not if we flew only a thousand feet off the ground, a level we must have maintained the whole trip. At the quick gain of altitude, as well as the banking to the right, my stomach lurched upward. For the first time, I felt feverish, and welcomed sleep when it came within minutes of our low hard charge through the dry desert air to the east.

There is a loud boom outside my window, which shakes the hanging plasma bag, sending Amelia into my room. She tightens her jaw for a moment, and then she releases it. "Ijuepucha! There are many bad drivers out there today! I am glad we are not on the road."

"Quite." A word comes out, naturally!

"Tommy! You speak!" I can feel myself smiling, which I also did not preplan. She bends over and kisses my cheek. I want to move my neck and kiss her, but I am too deep in my pillow. "The doctor is going to be so happy when I tell him!"

She wets a towel in the sink and returns to me to cool my arms and legs and torso. But she keeps the sheet over my midsection.

She speaks again: "Tommy, you come from California? Is that true?" She is at my feet, so an "Uummn" slips out. "That is a long way from Colombia." Suddenly, she wants me to know that. Someone has told her to insinuate a few facts into our conversation. I am in a secured hospital in Colombia. I am under the protection of a military figure. He does not care for me personally, but he wants me to stay alive. I am wounded in the head and now, from the tightness I feel when the nurses turn me over to clean me, it seems my back. My injuries are severe. At one point they must have been worse. Perhaps my nice doctor saved my life, or was important to keeping my alive during a bad period. Two bombs went off today in the city where I am. Colombia.

Are the bombs connected to my injuries? Why? Amelia is looking at me. My eyes must have been down in repose. Now, I look up at her. She wants to know if I remember anything. I repeat "Colombia." She smiles, but it is weak and passes soon. I look at the clock. It is 11:55. She looks, too. "The heat of the day is coming. Let me ask the nurse if we can keep the sheet at your waist."

"Ok."

Booooommm! Amelia rushes to my side to reassure me that things are alright inside my room. "You are in a safe hospital. Your doctor is excellent. My father, he studied at the University of Michigan. He has taken care of you since the beginning. He thinks you will have an excellent recovery—that you were too stubborn to… stay so sick.

She means "to die." She has tact and manners; she catches her errors to protect me from knowing too much before I am able to endure the truth. Her father: Buffalo Soldier is her father. That explains their common visits. "He is a soldier."

"Who?"

"Your father. He is a soldier?"

"Yes. He is an officer in the National Police."

"He is tall."

"Yes. Men from his part of Colombia are tall." She takes down the sheet to my waist. She daubs at the lint that has gathered in my belly button. She rubs cream on my chest. She tries to roll me on my side until I wince. "Sorry, Tommy." She slowly walks back to the tray side of the bed.

There are no sleeves on a blue and white striped shirt.

"Do you want me to go now?"

"Claro que no."

"Tommy—you can speak some Spanish!"

"Yes. But my head hurts more."

"We will speak English for now."

"You speak well."

"Oh, thank you. I assisted at a bilingual school in the south of… my city."

"Water?"

"Of course."

She fills the plastic cup and dunks the straw. She bends it as she carries it to my face. The straw finds the mark, but my eyes lock onto her breasts. I lurch down the water, but cannot swallow. My coughing blows it out my nose.

"I am sorry."

"No, Tommy. The doctor said that you need practice with many things. That you need to remember how to do some things. Let's try again."

She puts the straw back and squeezes it in the middle when it is full. This time only a trickle goes down my throat, and there is no gag reflex. "That was better." She takes the straw and cup away.

"Do you want some music, Tommy?"

"No, I need talk."

"Ok, we talk then."

"What is your name?"

"Amelia Hernandez. Your name is Tommy Connolly."

"Yes."

"Where are you from?"

"I am from another city in Colombia—it is about six hours from here."

"How old are you?"

"I am 21. You just turned 25." I cannot remember my birthday.

"What is the rank of your father?"

"Why do you want to know that, Tommy?"

"Please."

"He is a Lieutenant Colonel."

"He is busy."

"Yes. He has important responsibilities."

"Is this his hospital?"

"No, but it is a military hospital."

"What city?"

She leans over and kisses me on the lips and then my cheek. She paints my lips with Chapstick. Next, she kisses me again. "You are tired now, Tommy. You need to rest. The nurse will be here soon."

"Don't go."

She kisses me again. "I will be back soon, Tommy. You rest now, ok."

I am glad Amelia is here. She is all I know about the world so far, and I need more knowledge. My room is not exactly swarming with flowers in vases. I only remember Amelia, Buffalo Soldier, and a guy in Creased Pants so far. Sleep.

I awoke again as the small plane banks and plows downward to the ground. Unbuckling himself as the plane nosed toward blackness, Nando dropped forward to the cockpit curtain to give the pilot some final instructions, I guessed. The left side of the island was fully lit along its edges, but we were flying toward the dark side of the island to our east. Out of complete darkness—apart from the mast lights of a few pleasure boats—lights appeared along a straight line on a mesa near the shore, and we hurtled down toward them as if every action from that moment forward required rapidity rather than accuracy.

Seconds later, we bumped onto a thin paved road with its own street lights, apparently another informal landing strip, one without buildings of any sort, even in the distance. After the propeller stopped, all was still and dark until Nando stood up hurriedly, shouting out to the pilot, "Good job—this will just take a few minutes."

My head had experienced too many compressive and decompressive events since Nando slipped me a pill about twenty-four hours prior. Small drops of blood began to ooze out of my head wound again, and trail down behind my ear. My fever had not abated; instead, it was consolidating its dominance over the whole of my scull.

"What time is it, Nando?"

"It's certainly not time for maricadas, marica!"

He compromised for the sake of command cohesion, or perhaps just speed. "It's about three in the morning." There was nothing to see or observe out the airplane windows, so I quickly followed Nando out of the plane.

We stood on ground that quickly warmed the bottoms of our feet and did our own little stretches. Being outside their country, Nando and his pilot moved and acted a little more quickly, giving darting looks up and down the runway. "Mission complete, Nando!" the pilot nearly whispered, his voice hinting to Nando that he wanted to leave as quickly as events would permit. "Ok—give me a minute."

Nando went back into the plane through the open hatch. There were ruffling noises from within that broke the cicada, silence of the night. Nando and the pilot went to work pushing duffle bags out the hatch and onto the tarmac. Nando reached into one of the duffle bags and took out some bundles of money, which he handed to the pilot. "Count it before you leave."

After he finished counting his money in the light of his plane seat, the pilot returned. "Listo, Nando! Gracias!" He extended his hand, which Nando grasped warmly. He was showing signs of being human, at least with members of his crew. "I'll be in touch. You should be back in bed with your negrita by dawn. You can take the plane back to Cali in a couple of days."

"Ciao, gringo!" the pilot waved at me. I nodded slightly, but did not extend my hand. He gave me his cap though, which was kind of him, especially since he wanted to leave quickly, and would never see me again. "You will look more like a tourist this way, gringo!"

"Thanks." He walked with the bundles of money in his left hand and opened the cockpit door with his right.

The pilot only turned on his lights when he was pointed back down toward the eastern sea, and only seconds before he began to speed away from us. I heard a final "Ciao, Nando!" and a wave from the cockpit window. The pilot gunned the throttles at that point and was airborne about half way down the runway.

"He is a good pilot, no?" I queried Nando. Nando answered me in English for extreme emphasis. "Excellent, and you never met him or that plane. Clear?"

"Quite," I answered.

Nando took four duffel bags toward a lone shed at the end of the runway with the hard strides of someone who wanted to stamp down on some kind of uncertainty that had crept into his plans for that night.

Sweet-smiling Tommy Connolly had been successfully exfiltrated from an abandoned Colombian air base to a clandestine Aruban runway. The operation entailed a professional pilot, one used to evading radar and landing on short, bumpy runways in near darkness. From that perspective, the duffel bags could be as important to the operation as T. Connolly, class of '94. Since Cali, Nando had shown the duffel bags considerable duty of care, never placing unnecessary distance between himself and them, even during the drive into Maicao.

It was Tommy Connolly who made no sense in this operation. I did not have an intelligence background, or wish to know any matters involving state secrets. I had never held sophisticated views of political matters; hell, I did not even read newspapers, which my mother viewed as the "stable boy gossip of the establishment." Someone paid money for this operation, which was obviously undertaken by intelligence professionals—at least in the case of Nando. That someone contracted multiple parties to get me out of the country safely and quickly, but quickly if all else failed. Who was I to these people? Why the urgency and the desert air strips in the dead of night? My exfiltration was nearly over, but I had not picked up any more clues about its real purpose, nor did I expect Nando to suddenly explain events to me.

Who had I crossed or benefited to justify this strange treatment?

My life, or at least the intermittent recollections that came to me in the barracks, had been—by inclination and circumstances—well under any possible radar. My single mom raised me in a comfortable double-wide trailer community of truckers and itinerant agricultural workers in Lindley, California. I grew up with Delta breezes that carried the smell of walnuts—lots of them—into our home each night.

As a child, my friends and I popped them under our bicycle wheels. Freshly fallen from the tree, walnuts' green outer skins were more slippery than banana peels. In middle school, we made mounds of them, under which we placed improvised 4th of July explosives to watch them explode. In high school, we took to parking deep in the groves after Friday night football games. There, I touched my first breast and drank my first beer. I graduated and went to the university in Berkeley. I did very well with women, befriended a group of sympathetic professors, and produced grades ample for further study in doctoral programs.

But first I wanted to work in the Foreign Service for a few years after graduation. I moved to Los Angeles where, after working with Hispanic immigrant youth during the day, I studied for the Foreign Service exam at night. The closest I came to intrigue was a year-long affair with Yolanda Perez, the school principal where I worked, who placed a lock on Tommy Connolly's sexuality during his stay in her high school.

My acceptance letter came late in the school year for a posting the following January. It was for Bogota, Colombia, which I knew little about, and cared even less. Yolanda had resolved matters so that we spent most evenings and weekends at her house, where I arduously provided her with orgasms, but little else, since my tastes outside the bedroom were less important than my duties within. Before my Christmas departure, our groupings became more frantic, as she openly lobbied for my sperm to find its way inside her, instead of its chump's ending in the condoms I always brought with me to her house.

She let me go reluctantly, hoping to the last that she could snag a much younger husband and finally produce a child. A few days after Christmas, I got on a flight to Cali, the only flight I could get into

Colombia during the Christmas holiday. I had two days to make it from Cali to Bogota, which I figured could not be longer than a bus ride from Los Angeles to San Francisco. All my memory stopped there, and did not begin again until Amelia leaned over and coated me with her cool, sweet breath one morning after I awoke in the military hospital.

It was not the sort of life that would have attracted the attention of anyone like the Colonel or Nando, especially someone with the power to exfiltrate duffel bags and human cargo between countries. In various forms though the question had defeated my limited ability to form abstractions since I awoke in the hospital; why was so much intelligence wherewithal being brought to bear to hide and remove Tommy Connolly, United States Embassy clerk-trainee?

CHAPTER TWO

Nando, having whistled for me to join him at the end of the runway, put two of the duffels against the small shed and bade me to sit on one of them.

"Nando, I would like to pee." He reached inside his backpack and gave me a flashlight.

"Go behind the maintenance shed. There are trees," he said in Spanish. I walked around the shed and lit up flashes of brush, soda cans, and emerging around the corner, scabs of cement between dirt, oil, and dried grass. A canopy of tree branches hung over the far corner of the lot. Beyond, I saw a few lights from isolated homes in the distant hills. I went up this bank and into a small grove. There was a lasting silence. The lapse in the hum of the plane engine made orientation in space a task once again. I grasped a tree branch above me while I urinated.

My scalp felt too dry and tight. I needed a good mechanic who would unscrew the bolt a few turns to relieve the pressure on my scull. I had no desire to eat or shit. I dug into my pocket to make sure there were sufficient pills, and there were.

Nando was smoking a cigarette when I arrived, causing me to cough deeply and uncomfortably after I sat beside him. He took a last drag and put it out under his shoe. I poured water on my head, which loosened the tightness a little, and dried it with the bloody rag. The near complete quiet, not suggesting forward movement along the axis of Nando's so far carefully-timed plans, unnerved us both.

I swallowed two pills with water.

"You have a new plan, Nando?" I finally said, breaking from several minutes of total silence in the hot desert night.

"Si."

"Does it involve my exchange, delivery or death?"

He gave me another of his looks of impatience.

He began with a dismissive smirk.

"You will meet a consular officer in a few hours. You will be in a nice hotel in Florida this evening."

"If you are not a kidnapper, why did you not release me to the U.S. authorities in Colombia?"

"That is a long story. I cannot tell you anything about your time in Colombia."

"And Amelia?"

"What about her?"

"Was she real?"

"She is a real person, yes."

"She visited me in the hospital many times, no?"

"She was there every day, marika."

"But she stopped."

"It was necessary to move you, and she could not come to see you."

"I was not able to say goodbye or thank her. Did she ask about me?"

"I don't know. You sound like a girl... it was for the best."

"Do you know her, Nando?"

"Yes, a little."

"Please tell her that I will look for her."

The smirk returned. "Of course, marika. I will be happy to." A long silence only interrupted by water gallon chugs came back. I was growing impatient for the first time, since little in our isolated outpost in the rocky hills of Aruba suggested a speedy turnaround of our immediate fortunes.

"Nando, is your plan still in action?"

"Yes, marica." A few more minutes of quiet ensued. This was getting annoying, the silence and uncertainty, and increasingly the tightness in my muscles and dry, parched mouth.

Just then Nando stood up suddenly, grabbed the duffel bags, and ran around the back of the shed. At the beginning of the road, where our plane first touched down, the lights of a car slowly turned toward us. Coming back, he lifted me strongly, causing me to heave the pills back out of my mouth. "Leave the water, marika. Let's go! If I tell you to get off the road, or lay down flat, do it quickly."

"Change of plan, Nando?"

"Yes. It seems so."

"Would you like to share what you know, or is this classified too?"

Nando smiled. "Fortunately for all of us, marika, your adventure ends tonight. Se lo prometo!" I promise.

We walked only a kilometer or so before I could not continue without a rest. The car had come to a stop where we had rested, but there was no movement of flashlights or voices. Nando carried only two of the four duffels from the plane. He had hidden the other two for a later retrieval behind a group of rocks close to the main road along the crest of the ridge.

The sun was rising grey-green from the east, illuminating in the faint light the white-concrete road and, ahead, pink roofs, which would be bright orange-red in a few minutes. Brush on each side of the road was sweet in the mist of dawn. There were many groupings of granite rocks, atop and leaning on each other on the interior, high side of the road.

Nando stopped ahead of me. "It is not much farther, marika. You can rest ahead."

"What is the name of this place?"

"I think it is Santa Cruz. We are south of Paradera. This is a small, quiet village."

"How do you know?"

He gave me his disappointed look. "Marika, A few of the houses were lighted, but there were no street lamps. Someone had done his homework."

We had been walking only about twenty minutes, but a storm was gathering inside me. I felt the lack of those last two pills, my head warming steadily and uncomfortably in the first noticeable heat of the day. Suddenly, the toil of the last hour had begun to catch up with me in earnest. I began to feel fever heating up my skin beyond my head, and headaches returned behind my ear. I tried to take the rag out of my jacket and daub my face, but I kept missing and wiping the air around me.

Nando watched all this with amusement until, satiated with laughter, he turned and walked onward toward the small village down below us. In a few minutes we headed down the final stretch of road onto a street with a few stores. Nando, not having handed me off at the air strip, needed a phone, even a pay phone, to get instructions from someone on the island.

We passed small grocers, a florist, and a few tourist estaderos, all either closed or boarded up, and looking like they were in no hurry to reopen. At the next corner there was a fast food restaurant.

"Is it open?" I yelled out to Nando.

"No, not yet. But there is a phone in the parking lot. Wait for me in front." He moved quickly forward, while I moved more and more slowly toward the planter curb in front of its entrance.

I noticed for the first time that I did not see the remaining duffel bags with Nando. Sometime, probably before dawn, Nando chucked the other two bags into some brush or behind some rocks. This made sense, as we looked more like vagrants or fugitives than tourists or honeymooners, and could not have explained whatever was in those bags to the local police. I saw the front entrance of a McDonald's and sat down in front on its steps.

My throat was dry, my lips painfully chapped. At some point along the road, I had begun to sweat. Maybe I could sleep for a while, I thought.

Same day, I guess. The sticky heat lingers, but without so much reach into my room. I sigh to fill my lungs with more air. Amelia stands up. I did not see her down below the cones of my feet under the bed sheets.

"Hola, Tommy! I was sleeping too—on the chair."

"Hi, Amelia."

"You took a long nap, today."

"I feel better. I spoke Spanish a little with the nurse this morning."

"Yes, she told me. You asked many questions from her."

"There is much I don't know."

"You know; you just cannot remember. You will start to remember soon. The doctor said that in the next few weeks your mind will see again. Does that make sense?"

"Yes."

"But there is no hurry. You need to rest, get strong. Is there anything you need?"

"Steak and lobster?"

She laughs. "For now, they feed you through a tube. But I will make sure your first real food is steak, ok?"

"Medium rare, please."

"Do you want some music?"

"No, thank you. But could the nurse take off the gown. The sweat makes me itch."

"I can do that. The nurse lets me do some of the basic things."

She laughs.

"I know what you are thinking. No, I let the nurse take care of your other needs."

She laughs again.

"But I can remove your gown if you want."

"Yes, please."

I look up and see that the fan is not spinning. Amelia looks at me: "The doctor said, 'No' Tommy. I am sorry."

"It is ok. The air feels nice. Can I stay like this for a moment?"

"I think it is ok, yes."

She leans me forward again and massages and cleans my back. It sounds like she is crying a little.

"Amelia, what happened?"

"Nothing, Tommy. You are much better. I am glad for that."

"But you cry! Is it because my body is ugly?"

"No, Tommy. You are strong. I am being a silly girl, Tommy. Please ignore it."

"Don't cry, nena. I…."

I cannot complete the thought. She lets me back down and covers my chest with her body and holds me tight. I want to wince, but grit my teeth a little instead.

"It's ok, Amelia. Things will be ok."

Amelia. Is it true? You come to visit me every day?" She cries more.

"Si, Tommy."

"But why?"

"Because I want you to get better."

"And I am, Amelia. And it is all because of…"

She places a finger over my mouth, preventing me from saying more. I don't think we knew each other, but we met before this. I feel her love, which is more than pity. She has not taken on my case because she was my girlfriend, but I want it to be so.

A few days pass, I believe. It is morning, and Amelia is back at my side, now pushing me down the corridor in a wheel chair. Many people stand in the lobby at the strange sight—the white invalid pushed through glass sliding doors by the most beautiful woman most of them have ever seen. Amelia slips some sunglasses over my eyes before she pushes me out slowly, as if over a speed bump, which knocks the glasses off my head, and onto the ground.

The doors having swung open for us, Amelia is directly behind me and my sentry off to the right. His radio buzzes, which draws more attention to us, but it sounds like a shared frequency, and he makes no effort to respond.

I am out into the world, still in circumstances that bedevil my attempt at putting the small clues together. The brightness is too much at first, despite the sunglasses clinging to my nose, but I am quickly reconciled to natural light, some soft breezes, and the smells of plants around me. Light, as much as it signifies life, as much as it proves that I am back in the world, brings pain, at least for now. Amelia stops and crouches next to me:

"Tommy, are you alright? Do you want to continue?"

"Yes. I am fine."

She stands off to my side to make her appraisal of my first reactions to natural light and sound, after which she wipes my face with a handkerchief before we push on. We take a path to the right that leads away from the main entrance toward more lush plants beneath the odd shapes of light and shade on the curvy path away from the hospital. There is a pond with swarms of small bugs that surround us, even though we are parked far from it. Amelia blows them away from my face, having noticed that my arm got stuck in midair on the way to shoo them away.

In the distance I hear a jeep squeak its brakes to stop. The sentry stands back and leaves Amelia and me to talk. "It reminds me of MacArthur Park in Los Angeles. There are palms and a big circular pond. There are also plants near the pond."

"Did you live there?"

"I lived nearby. In a small apartment a few blocks away."

"Did you go there?"

"No, it was a park to buy drugs mostly. It was different before."

"So, you lived in Los Angeles?"

"Yes. Before I came here, I lived there."

Eventually, we go deeper into palms and plants into a deep shade that is suddenly cool. "This is a nice place. The sun will not make you too hot." I hear more cicadas and a woodpecker on the palm trees above us that brings more confirmation that I am alive, and that Amelia is real and has not left me. I move to scratch my nose, but my arm falls down half to my face again.

"What is it, Tommy?"

"My nose."

"Do you like it here?"

"Yes. The light is not too bright. You have been here before?"

"Yes, when you sleep, sometimes I come here."

"You are very kind to me, Amelia. Don't you have classes?"

"I am not taking classes. I did not want to study this semester."

"I see. So you take care of a gringo with holes in his body. I guess the other students got the best internships."

"What is an internship?"

"Work by a student for no salary or a small one... to gain experience."

"Oh. I see. Yes, it was the only job I could find!" In the distance, more distant than before "Boooomm!"

"Asi es Cali?"

"Asi es."

Amelia has brought some towels from the hospital room, which she uses to wipe my forehead and eyes, and then my neck.

"Don't you become bored with your gringo-caring job?"

"No. It is easy. He sleeps most of the day. He is not bovo like most gringos. His favorite nurse takes care of him... most of the time."

"Favorite?"

"She likes you. She makes me leave when she cleans you."

"That is just nurse policy, no?"

"But she closes the door, and I can hear when she talks to you."

"We both follow the Asian financial markets. It is a hobby we share."

"I am sure about that!"

"What do you know about me, Amelia?"

"I know that you are brave but silly, and that too many nurses visit your room."

"You need to find peace with the nursing profession, Amelia. Should I push you for a while?"

"Como no, Tommy. Como no!"

She stands up now—there is real concern on her face, which she does not want me to see—and goes back behind the wheel chair, twisting her head away from me. She pushes me quickly back onto the cement path without caution this time, so that the low, hanging branches scratch my face as we pass through them. The sentry sees us approach and falls into a loose formation beside us, lending a sense of discipline to the sudden silence between Amelia and me.

Nando awoke and lifted me at the same time. He spoke to me in English again. "Marika, we do not want to bring attention to us. We will have transportation in about a half an hour. We need to get off the street—now." We walked around the back of the building where there was a series of garbage cans in the far corner of the parking lot. We sat next to them, Nando alert to any sudden danger on his own horizon, Tommy beginning his circling down a long drain.

My head burned beyond mere annoyance; unable to stay awake, I laid it down and slept for what seemed like just a few moments. Nando pushed me in the back, exciting the holes in my back, and I lurched forward. His own knees braced the fall. "Easy, marika. I am just waking you up. Our ride is here."

I saw a blue sedan pull into the parking lot and stop in front of us. A thick-set, strong-necked man with black hair and cold eyes got out. Standing squarely in front of Nando, he spoke in English, but with an accent I could not place, even continentally. "Hey, Buddy! I am sorry. We got the call from one of our guys in the VDA even before you called."

They shook hands, agreeably, but somewhat warily. Nando hesitated before he spoke. "Who tipped off the VDA?"

"It was probably the DEA in La Guajira. Anyway, the VDA convinced them that the intelligence was bad, and they went away. We got the call to stay away, though. Anyway, you're here and safe."

"Are they looking for us?"

"The DEA is still poking around, but there is nothing on the police radios about you. They found a few pills next to the shack, but that doesn't mean anything."

"Alright. Alright. Please keep listening. Let's get down to OrangeTown and conclude our business."

"Sure, friend. Does your associate there need any help?"

"No. Just the room I asked for."

"OK. I just don't want the guy dying on me."

He started to laugh, but Nando was not laughing at all. He looked at the sedan with impatience, and then at me like the prize was almost not worth the effort involved in this mission.

"We have to stop to get the duffel bags. After that, we can conclude our business."

Below the littoral lights of OrangeTown presented themselves below like a strip of Christmas lights, and the red morning sea clouds of the South Caribbean began to replace the last few night stars.

"Where to…?"

"To the hotel. I have to get my friend freshened up a little." The swarthy guy pointed down toward the coastal lights.

"OK. I got the key already."

My forehead now was hot to the touch, and sweat retraced last night's routes down the sides of my head. My throat was still dry and burning. My back, in the fierce clutches of some kind of ogre, held me erect, as did the man next to me, who let me know with shoves that I could not fall over and sleep. Old but familiar pains—the tremendous ones from the first weeks after I awoke in the hospital—were returning to the back of my head, and I felt dizzy and faint. I could not reach the pills in my front pocket, even squeezing my hands into my pocket. At that moment, I must have fainted again.

In an instant, the door swung open, and a black man looked directly at me and gave me a smile that he could not sustain. He quickly looked to someone for guidance.

Nando spoke. "I got him. Thanks."

Nando's counterpart in whatever deal was afoot gave the valet some money, and pulled him close. He whispered in the black man's ear."

The duffels?" I asked Nando.

"Todo bien, marika."

Like a protected witness at a mob trial, Nando led me into a limestone and pink David Hockney lobby in a swoosh of movement. Holding me strongly by the elbow to keep me upright, he asked the front desk clerk without breaking stride, "Elevator?" The attractive young woman pointed ahead of us in our general heading. I looked back, and she confusingly glanced first at us, then security, and finally her phone. When we were out of sight, Nando took a key card out of his pocket. He pressed and quickly an elevator opened to us. I could no longer stand.

Nando shoved me into the elevator corner, where I crumpled downward onto the ground. Luckily, these were not glass elevators, nor were there any stops before we reached our destination.

"Nando, I think I am out of fuckin' pills. I must have spilled them in the desert."

"We'll get a doctor. Hang on, marika. You are almost there. You can sleep and eat, and a car will take you to the airport tonight, or if you want, tomorrow."

"Pills, fresh clothes, fuckin' McDonald's, new shoes, underwear, cologne, and a professional shave."

He gave me his Nando sneer-sniff laugh.

"This is the Las Cabanas resort hotel. These things are possible."

I tried to give him a smile of appreciation, since he was my only source of human—if not kindness, at least understanding, but it must have seemed awkward to him.

He slid the key card into a door and opened it with a "whuuummmph!" I stooped to take off my shoes, but Nando grabbed my arm and led me into the bathroom. He sat me on the toilet, and while bracing me with one arm, reached in with the other one and turned on the hot water. I fumbled with my shoelaces. Nando kneeled and in short order had me naked and pushed down into the shower.

My clothes, rumpled in a pile, gave off a terrible stench. "Nando, burn that shit, please. Check that. Tell the concierge my sizes and then burn that shit."

"Marika, you did not have to ask. I have been waiting since Maicao."

I was almost free of Nando, of uncertainty, of reckless care, and invisible conspirators. I celebrated by passing out.

CHAPTER THREE

A few days, perhaps a week, pass without a cheerful morning visit from Amelia, during which time I become, without official permission, ambulatory. I leave my walker outside the bathroom door and have managed to urinate inside the bowl. I turn triumphantly to go back to my bed, and I suddenly see Amelia, who is looking at me fiercely.

"Tommy!"

"Good morning, Amelia!"

"What are you doing?"

"Chi Chi."

"Standing up?"

"Yes."

"Come here, Tommy. You are not ready to walk around."

"Amelia, I have been going to the bathroom by myself for a week now."

I actually smile in the expectation of her approval, but Amelia does not seem interested now in my little victories over dependence on others or mastery over myself.

"Tommy, Dr. Howe determines your activities. He has not approved you for walking around and doing your chi-chi by yourself."

I walk by her and crumple over onto the bed. She completes the roll and settles me in the middle.

"Amelia, I used to bench press 225. I could run eight miles. My body fat was 12%. Dr. Howe has his medical knowledge, but I know some things too."

"You will not get better by following your own ideas."

"I just want to recover and get my body back."

She turns and walks back to the far wall and stays there a lingering moment, petulantly, with crossed arms although she has looked out that window a hundred times by now.

"Amelia, come here please!"

She walks to me, but stops at the foot of the bed. I lift up my hand and suspend it in air. Although she wants to be cross with me, she comes to my side to put her hand in mine. I squeeze her hand, firm and tight, in a demonstration that I am no longer helpless or dependent.

"Thank you." I kiss her hand and rub it on my cheek. She extracts it and caresses my other cheek with soft and careful caresses, while she wipes away a tear with her other hand.

"Are you happy that I am better, Amelia?"

"Que pregunta, Tommy! Of course, I am happy."

I take her hand again and bring it and her to me. Her lips come to mine, but she pulls away after a brief kiss.

"I am sorry, Amelia."

"No, Tommy. It is ok. It is not time for that."

"Can I kiss you when I am strong and can leave the hospital?"

"Perhaps. But maybe they will move you to a different type of hospital, one with strong, male nurses and locked doors, instead of medicine."

She is pulling away from me for reasons she will not share with me, even though she does not seem to endorse them. Not knowing what plans they have for me, there is little I have to work with.

"Amelia, when I leave here, where will I go?"

"I suppose you will go back to North America."

"And you will go back to your university?"

"I suppose."

"So, when I am well, you will go back to your life?"

"I will try."

"So, if I stay here for five years, you will be with me for five years more?"

"No, I will let the nurses have you after two years."

"You could come with me."

"Now you sound like a typical Gringo."

"Is that a bad thing?"

"Tommy—why you never ask if you had visitors?"

"Because, I don't know people here, and no one I know has a security clearance for this place. I don't have much family."

"You have a family, no?"

"I have a mother. But she may not know what happened to me."

"She knows."

"Who told her?"

"I did."

"And your father knows."

How did she know about my father? "He is not exactly my father."

"I don't know what that means. He knows. He came here."

"When?"

"About a month after you… came to the hospital. He stayed all day. He asked many questions. My father spoke with him. They made some agreements so that your father knows of your condition."

My father was in the room with the Colonel. He was the man with the Creased Pants. Amelia probably does not know that I met him only four to five times in my life, and only for a few hours each time.

"Did you talk to him?"

"A little. He is a very reserved man. He thanked me for taking care of you."

"Did anyone else come?"

"A girl tried to visit you. She called the embassy in Bogota and asked about you. They would not tell her your condition or where you were. She has asked her Congressman to help find you. She thinks you have been kidnapped."

"Is her name Morgan Taylor?"

"Yes, I believe that is her name. Miss Morgan Taylor… did you know her?"

She meant of course did I know her well and were we intimate. "A little. We became friends in a gym in Los Angeles. We ran around Hollywood together at night. She is a young, poor actress, but not for long. She will be a big star.

"Why does she care about you so much—more than your other friends?"

"We had some fun. Kid stuff. We went to the clubs for the not-so-famous crowd in Hollywood. I gave her acting advice."

Amelia looked at me dubiously.

"You know something about acting?"

This was trivial conversation, tilting toward bitterness, and not clarifying anything, especially in a way that would make Amelia want to stay with me, and not leave me alone. Suddenly, for Amelia I was selfish and immature; worse, I was fickle in my relationships with other people, and perhaps even cold. I was running out of time, but I could not possibly explain my life to her on the basis of her questioning.

"Do you want that I invite her here? I could make the arrangements."

With that comment, I could tell that I had lost Amelia.

"Do you want to know how is your mother?"

"I imagine well."

"And your father?"

"Amelia, why do you want to know about my family so much? For someone whom I barely know, why do these things matter to you?"

"I just want you to know that they are well. That is all. Loco Gringo Ijueputa!"

"I understand that, you know."

"You should. You will probably hear it a lot in Colombia."

With a wrapped towel covering my lower body, I walked into the room where Nando stood close to a tall, thin white man, to whom I was anxious to speak in English.

"Did I mention a comb, Nando?" He looked at his companion.

"This is Dr. Hilliard. He is the hotel doctor. He will examine you. I am going out. I will be back in an hour."

"My clothes?"

"It's all on the bed."

It was a feeling kindred to Christmas for me. In the double-wide, where my mother would ply me with all the latest toys, though our modest circumstances did not square with such expenditures, I would take in for a moment the extent of the packages, and then quickly rip them open and release my new toys.

Shopping bags—small and medium—piled on the hotel bed next to me. Dr. Hilliard seemed to agreeably take in the pathos of the wounded boy and his gifts.

"Dr. Hilliard, would you give me a moment to look at these things?"

"Of course, old boy. Of course."

I opened the shopping bags—probably from the lobby stores. Fresh replacements: jeans, loafers, socks, a belt, a new leather jacket, underwear, toiletries, a belt, and handkerchiefs, which instinctively I picked up to smell, my mother being in the habit of spraying them with strawberry or lavender perfume after she ironed them.

I wondered if Nando had hired a common decency consultant for the occasion.

I grabbed the toothbrush and toothpaste cartons.

"Dr., could you open these for me?"

"Of course, young man. Meanwhile, let's slip this thermometer in your mouth."

He took the toothbrush and paste out of their cartons and took them into the bathroom. He took a moment to thoughtfully observe my attempts to brush my teeth, which resulted in blood from banging the hard end of the brush against my gums. He came back and opened the master closet, pulling a hotel robe off its hanger, and draping it over his arm. He also took the rest of the bags and put them on the sofa table.

He came back to me with more concern on his face, which a quick grin could not fully encase. By this time the thermometer had been in my mouth long enough. "102.5. Uncomfortably high. Let's put you in this robe and into bed. I will call room service for some tea, orange juice and bread. I will have to give you a complete medical examination. That includes drawing blood. By the way, young man, when was the last time you had a bowel movement?"

"Four days, I think."

"We are going to have to remedy that, too."

"Coffee sounds good."

"Not for that particular problem, no."

I had been delivered at last, apparently beyond hospitals and barracks and desert planes. Things were clean now, and the friendliness and concern of Dr. Hilliard were sincere and human. I did not know if this was a rest spot between nightmarish visions, but it felt wonderful.

After breakfast, which Dr. Hilliard had to ladle to me, I went back to bed, and began a deep sleep. In short order, the doctor awoke me with a few drug store bags. He sat down on the sofa and gave the prescriptions a final look until he felt inclined to pick them up and bring them to the tableside bed.

"Take these, please."

He imitated, mouth opening, and dropped the pills in my mouth.

"My advice is that you remain in this room—or one similar—on this island for the next thirty days."

"How is my fever? It can't be that bad?"

He looked at me with a mixture of surprise and pity. "You have an infection, or better yet, a reinfection in your inner ear. This has probably affected your balance, vision and appetite. You have some sore rib muscles, you are malnourished, dehydrated and in danger of arthritis in your back. The wounds on your scalp were healing until recently. The bandages there now should have been replaced 24 hours ago. I don't know your line of work, young man, but its present course will take you to an early grave."

My line of work—I had not thought of attributing my loss and grief to that.

"Thank you, Doctor. I should probably slow down. Can you tell me about the medicines?"

"Your description of the pills you have been taking leads me to believe that it was a drug to prevent seizures. The frequency with which you took the pills is similar to post-trauma patients with seizure risk. You also need a blood thinner and some antibiotics for two weeks."

"Do you have the resources to stay on the island for about a month?" I hesitated. No reasonable response emerged for a few moments.

"I can take care of the expenses, Doctor."

"Good, because they will add up quickly. You will need a nurse to change your dressing daily, and I will need to see you daily for the next week, and then less often after that."

"Is all this clear to you?"

"Yes, Doctor. One more question—when can I fly?"

"Like I said, you have no business leaving this room for at least two weeks. Alright then, the concierge has my phone numbers. You can reach me through them. Now, let's take care of that dressing."

Nando woke me again about noon, this time with a kinder and gentler shake of my shoulder. Standing behind Nando was the boss-man from this morning's rendezvous up in the eastern hills. He stood near the door, slowly making his way toward the foot of the bed to take in my weakly-voiced words.

"Marika, I promised you a luxury room and a flight home, didn't I?"

"Yes, you did, Nando."

"We have one stop to make, and then I'll bring you back here, ok?"

"What's the hurry?" I thought. I explained to Nando the report from Doctor Hilliard in particular, the overhanging consequences for travel. He clenched his jaw and swung a look over at his black-jeaned and white-t-shirted companion.

"Fucking Hell! You got some problems here, friend!" the swarthy type said. Neither of them looked like they were willing to modify their plans to the degree necessary to obey either the letter or spirit of the Dr. Hilliard's instructions.

"Can we get another doctor?" asked Nando.

"He is the official doctor for tourists at the Las Cabanas hotel, and better than most, but...."

"But what?"

Nando interrupted. The pills from Dr. Hilliard had lowered my temperature a little and righted my verbal ship. I was beginning to enjoy the room and its comforts, and the beach and its proximity, though I had not yet used them. I already felt myself an honored guest.

"What risks?"

My mind began to fly upward on the wings of Dr. Hilliard's little fun pills.

"In order to procure medicines from a licensed pharmacy, he wanted my full name, occupation, address, passport number, arrival and departure dates. I was only able to tell him my name." I let out a friendly giggle, probably inappropriate in those circumstances.

"Fuckinnng Hell!" the local guy repeated. Nando went out on the veranda. Things do not arrive at impasses for intelligence professionals, I imagined, there being a premium on swift action to avoid knots of events such as this morning represented for Nando.

Nando could see the inevitable: an investigation of a badly-wounded American who knew nothing more than his own name, who arrived without papers in a luxury hotel with South American minders, and who could not account for his employment, history, or source of income, who appeared to have participated in violent activity with insufficient medical care, and who knew nothing about how he arrived in such an awful state.

For Nando, it could get even worse. He was a military officer who arrived in Aruba on a clandestine air strip without alerting local authorities. His passport was not stamped either.

"Nando," I asked.

"What is the VDA?"

"Dutch Intelligence on the island."

"Why?"

"They probably monitor unusual island illnesses."

"Thanks for the reminder, marika."

Nando seemed willing to travel a certain distance with the immediate risks.

"Just put him on the plane and let the gringos worry about the details."

"And if they start to look at hotel surveillance photos? Or talk with Dr. Hilliard?"

The local boss gave a quick look toward the balcony. Nando stood, walked to the terrace, and brought back the coffee tray. He put it on the sofa table and poured three cups.

"Marika, are you strong enough for one little trip? It will take us about an hour. After that, you can come back here and recuperate— for as long as you want. A day or a month. 'All expenses paid,'" he closed in English.

"Sure, Nando. I'll get dressed…" I started to swing out of bed. He waved me back.

"Coffee first. Then we go."

The new blue pills from Doctor Hilliard were not like the ones in the hospital in Cali. These new ones provided a joyous choir of emotional contentment I had not felt since I took some of my mother's anti-depressant pills in high school. My emotions were speaking freely. My back was becoming softer and more pliant when I felt it at all. My headaches had subsided to a little corner down below my right ear, underwriting new thoughts that grew in confidence and trended toward a great love of all peoples and races and creeds. I felt a warm, fraternal trust of Nando and worried about his happiness.

"Why are you smiling, marika?"

"I don't know; it must be the pills."

Nando went to the dresser top where Doctor Hilliard left them.

"Ijueputa! These are not the same pills as before, marika."

"I did not remember the name of the pills, so the doctor made his own diagnosis."

"These will not help you remember, marika."

"You can help me, then."

"Fucking Hell," said the perturbed boss man to no one in particular, though Nando felt the weight of his concerns.

"Drink up, marika, before you start singing love songs."

I got dressed in my fresh clothes. The shoes were the right size and the jeans fit well, but the shirt hung on me like slackened sails in a full breeze. We walked down the hallway to the elevator and from there to basement parking. We got into the same car as before, a long sedan with dark windows. Without being instructed, I got in the back with Nando.

"Are we going shopping?" The laughter started in the front seat, and even Nando could not hold it in.

"No, marika—we have a business appointment. You don't have to say much."

"I have to go to the bathroom though—is that a problem?"

My comments were now like the jokes that prompt studio laughter during the filming of a TV program. I sat back, not having felt this good since I awoke in the hospital in Colombia. We drove down a California coast scene for a minute or two, and then pulled into an orange, pink and yellow extravaganza. It was as if the Dutch Burghers had commissioned Peter Max for their storefront facades. To the left there was a huge docked cruise ship and several of the large, luxury chain hotels squatted on the better sea views.

"Could I have some sunglasses, please?"

That one got huge guffaws from the audience. I almost broke into "It's a Dutch World after all!" but I kept the remaining shards of my wits to myself. It only took a few lefts and rights moving inland as we went, and we pulled up in front of our destination.

Inside the lobby, it was all grey, from the small receptionist shell to the long leather couches. The lighting came from chandeliers that hung far above us. A strong cooling blast also came from above. There being no elevator, stairs in the rear curled up greyly to a second floor balcony. With no receptionist to begin the rituals, the boss walked me to the corner of the near sofa and helped me down into the cushions.

Nando, meanwhile, stood and waited. Once, he went back to the front door and looked through the spyhole. I saw a box of Kleenex behind the receptionist's half shell desk. I stood up, wobbly, which drew the boss man's attention, and made a run for it. I hit the corner of the clear glass table and fell on the ground, bruising my forehead against the table leg. He came to pick me up.

"I just wanted a Kleenex."

The boss sat me back down and grabbed a handful of tissue sheets, which he handed to me, hoping to avoid further commotion and embarrassment from my antics. Suddenly, blood began to trickle down my scalp and down my nose.

Hearing a back door open and seeing a woman approach, I tried unsuccessfully to sit up against the couch. She was rangy, with a wide face, but with pretty, small lips that I felt I had seen somewhere before. She wore sandals, men's frayed Levi shorts, and a t-shirt tied into a knot. She walked toward me with a legal folder filled with documents in her hand.

"Is this a dentist's office?" I asked. The boss man and Nando ignored me now. She stopped close to me, kneeling down close to me when all of a sudden she put a hand on her mouth.

"Tommy? Tommy Connolly?"

"Yes, is it my turn?" I giggled again.

"Tommy, it's me, Chiara."

I looked up at her, at first unknowingly. Taking out a few Kleenexes to daub my forehead, she looked down at me with a cringe and then looked up at Nando with cold fury.

"Chiara? Is that you? Holy shit, it has been a long time. The last time I saw you was in… Berkeley, right?"

"That's right, Tommy.

It was a few years ago now."

This was the space when she should have uttered a commonplace about how well I looked. But instead she looked at my head scar, my lazy right eye, my drug addict's physique, my new forehead wound, and deduced the rest from my new, compliant young child's mien.

"Chiara?" She squatted down to my level.

"Yes, Tommy?"

"I have to go to the bathroom real bad."

"Sure, Tommy, I'll take you."

I stood up and reached out for her hand, which she used to pull me off the couch.

She looked sharply at Nando. "What the fuck is going on here?" He spoke in English again.

"Miss, I can explain, but we need to hurry."

She looked straight at Nando, and then more fiercely at the boss man.

"Sal, what the fuck have you got yourself involved with. You have about five minutes to get your stories straight. I know this man. This boy is not that man. I am not going to waste five hours of my Saturday separating a few millions worth of 20s and 50s into stacks for some Colombian dirtbag kidnappers. Fucking Hell, Sal!" She took me by the elbow.

"Come with me, Tommy."

"Olay," I thought.

Chiara walked me down the lobby to the rear door, which she opened, and led me through several dark corridors until she opened a bathroom door for me.

"Do you need help, Tommy?"

"I'm ok, Chiara." I struggled to make her see me differently.

"I'm not like this. The doctor gave me a new pill this morning, and things are different.

"It's ok, Tommy." She helped me position myself inside the men's stall.

"Tommy, do you know those men?"

"Nando brought me here."

"You mean to the bank?"

"The bank, yes, and the hotel and the island."

"How long have you known him?"

"He took me from a kind of hospital—maybe a few days ago."

"Do you know the other man?"

"No. I met him at dawn in the desert behind a McDonald's"

"Tommy, listen closely to me: how did you get to this island?"

"A small plane that landed in the hills."

"Do you know why you are here?"

"I thought it was a dentist at first, but this is a bank?"

Loud defecation sounds broke out.

"Sorry," I said.

"It's ok, Tommy." More ensued.

"The doctor gave me medicine so I will…."

"Like I said, it's ok. Tell me about this doctor. Is he here in Oranjestad?"

"What's that?"

"This city here—where we are now."

"Yes, his name is Dr. Hilliard. He works at the Las Cabanas Hotel. He gave me new medicines."

"One more question: Do you know how you got those injuries on the side of your head."

"No, I just woke up that way. No one was allowed to tell me."

"Ok, Tommy. By the way, what year is it?"

I shook my head with a polite smile.

"Tommy, can you wait here a moment?"

Chiara left the bathroom. I shat a few more times, managing the toilet paper ritual and washing my hands, but with declining strength as the pills began to wear me down. I saw my face in the sink mirror, sweaty and bright pink in the faint bathroom light. I put my hand on my head. It was hot to the touch. In an instant, dizziness sent me down into a little spiral, and then everything went black.

I woke up on the grey couch. There was a cool towel on my head, from under which I saw Chiara on the sofa seat next to me. She closed her file and turned to me, taking off the towel from my forehead. I sat up and took a few seconds to gain some immediate orientation.

"How do you feel now, Tommy?"

"Better. The effect from that pill is mostly gone."

I spoke with your Dr. Hilliard. You are right. He is mostly a hotel doctor. He treats tourists in the big hotels. Sunburn, bad sea food—that sort of thing." I tried to stand up, but Chiara pressed me back down.

"Where is Nando?"

"I chased him off the island under threat of capture by the local police. If he is smart, he is already on his way back to Colombia by now."

"And his friend?"

"Business associate at best. They just met on this trip. He's a local. He is good at helping take things out of planes and boats, not very good with medical issues."

"So, what do I do now?"

"Your fever is down a little, but Dr. Hilliard said you have some serious health matters. I am going to take you by taxi back to your room. You are going to take a long sleep and call me when you wake up."

I slept naked under a thin sheet next to an open window where the trade breezes lightly tapped the curtains on their way to filling my room. I slept all that day and night, and into the next afternoon. I remember someone lifting my head and putting pills in my mouth, and returning again to repeat the same actions later that night. The same hands administered a thermometer and turned me on my side to change my dressing. Since I also awoke with an IV in my arm, I could not leave the bed until a nurse arrived. When I was finally able to stand, I called Chiara to tell her I was awake. My next call was to housekeeping since over the last thirty-six hours I had apparently wet my bed.

I was dependent once more on nurses, but I was happy to be through with intelligence types, rendezvous points, and botched exfiltrations.

For the next few days, Amelia stayed away from the hospital. The staff, which at that time had dwindled to only two nurses and a single sentry, would not tell me if she had visited me or made any plans to do so. I began to walk around the floor of the hospital, which did not endear me to the sentry, who looked like he feared serious repercussions due to my unauthorized mobility. Finally, the tubes taken out of arms and the monitors removed from the room, two new sentries filled a duffel bag with some "personal" items. They handed me my cane, shutting down the room where I came strangely back to life, but according to someone else's plan and terms.

The sentries seemed to have instructions to move me quickly and efficiently out of the hospital. Stopping suddenly, I hobbled my way to the nurse's station. I believe I am left-handed, but I could only make my right hand function with fine-motor precision. The nurse gave me a pen and paper, upon which I wrote words meant to raise me again in Amelia's esteem and express all I could say at that point.

"Amelia, thank you for your care of me. You made me stronger. I will find you again. Please believe me and wait for me, Tommy."

I folded the note and handed it to the nurse. I told her to give it to Amelia, even if it takes her five years. Give it only to her and tell no one else. Promise? Then I walked to the elevator. The sentry gave me a dry smile and pressed the down button.

I couldn't chisel Amelia out of my mind. She was a real person— after all, Nando told me so.

CHAPTER FOUR

Chiara Manso visited me several times during my first week at Las Cabanas. She habitually checked the dresser and bathroom drawers to make sure I was adequately provisioned with clothes. Dressed in the skirts and tops that probably represented island banking casual, she would then take my hand and walk me around the hotel grounds like Amelia had wheeled me through the hospital gardens in Cali.

It was obvious she had briefed the staff that I was a special needs VIP customer. Everyone held their smile a little too long in my presence, waiting until I was nearly passed to sneak a look at my head-taping; or they would stop in their tracks unnaturally to let me pass, or make sure I maneuvered myself around the pool without falling in. Still, it was care and humanity and generosity way beyond my previous duty post in the humid, empty barracks in Cali, or within the semi-brutal clutches of Nando in the deserts of La Guajira.

A note arrived from a bellman poolside one day—or rather, the perpetual shady side of the Las Cabanas pool—that contained an invitation. Chiara invited me to dinner at the hotel steak house that night at 19.00. So far, following Chiara's request that I think of Las Cabanas as my home, and equally that I not think of money, I had filled my hotel room closet with sandals, swimming trunks and sleeveless shirts, a belt to accommodate my new reduced physique, tennis shoes, and handkerchiefs. Anywhere on the grounds of Las Cabanas, like a Disneyland pass, my room number had been sufficient guarantee for anything I could contrive as a necessity.

I did not know whether my secret benefactor had arranged these expenses as well, but I felt no reason to forego the odd modest extravagance, or room service meal, since the unaccompanied walk down to the lobby restaurants was still a precarious voyage at times.

That night, however, I walked into the steak house without help and in the best clothes I had. I told the maître d' Chiara's name, which issued a closer inspection than I expected. Even with a scientific diet, daily nursing care, and poolside girl-watching, I was still thin and little spooky looking with bandages on the side of my head.

The host led me to not just Chiara's table, but Chiara's and the boss man from before. He was built like a weight lifter from the waist upward, but lithe as he stood up to shake my hand. A kindred gym spirit, I thought.

"Tommy! Welcome. Let me get your chair." He was in expensive black jeans, well-shined shoes, and a thin cloth white dress shirt. He made it to my chair before I did and motioned for me to sit. Instead, I stuck out my hand to his.

"Tommy Connolly."

"Sal Manzo."

Chiara was not coiffed, but someone in a salon had trimmed and styled her hair to make her prettier. She was in a black sleeveless cocktail dress with nice round white earrings. I answered her queries that my recovery was greatly assisted through the agencies of Dr. Hilliard and my physical therapist, which she seemed to calculate as good investments.

Soon the waiter arrived. Sal asked for another scotch and rocks, and Chiara a Manhattan. Having committed their orders to memory, he now looked to me. Chiara spoke for me, "He'll have an ice tea." It could have been a residual sunny spot in my spirits from Dr. Hilliard's medicines, but Sal looked at me more fondly than the situation warranted. I tried to return his smile periodically, but his rested upon me uncomfortably, and without apparent reason. Drinks came, and then menus, punctuating nice, trivial conversation about the hotel, my routines, and adjustments.

This was a soft sales call. Sal saw some kind of opening, possibly as a result of Nando's bad luck upon our arrival in Aruba, or perhaps because Chiara told him to act that way. Sal was very comfortable when I spoke, and encouraged me with innocuous questions. Chiara, evidently not anxious to close any kind of deal with me, sipped her drink and looked at me occasionally.

It was Sal who introduced the topic of Berkeley.

"How did you guys meet?" Chiara looked at me to begin the story.

"I was working at a Café near campus. Chiara was a regular at night. I had seen her there for as long as I had the job."

"So, you worked during college?"

"I had a scholarship, but not for pocket money. So, one day I took a break and sat at the table next to hers. Chiara was looking through the course catalog for a spring class." Chiara gave me an assist.

"I needed a class outside my major to graduate."

"I just made some small talk. I said it is tough to find classes that fit one's schedule." Chiara came back in with another prompt.

"Tommy told me about an easy class in the Classics Department for three units. He said it could be an easy A. I needed at least a B to graduate with honors. Below that could land me in second-tier MBA programs."

"So, you two took the class together?"

"Kind of," I added. "Chiara didn't show up to too many lectures." Chiara stamped her straw down into her drink playfully.

"I went to a few."

Sal, having heard the story before, but not during a convivial dinner chat, pressed forward with his faux cross-examination.

"So, how did she get her A?"

Chiara looked to me again to explain. "I was never in a fraternity, but I knew some guys at a certain frat house. They have file cabinets in the basement. They keep records on the quizzes and final exams for a lot of the lifer professors. They go back decades for some of them. Chiara needed two ten-page essays and some help during midterms."

"And you got all that for her?"

"Yeah. She needed the help."

"And what did you get?"

Chiara was a little cross with her brother's insinuations, which doubly breached both of our personal privacies.

"Sal! Be nice!"

"Nothing. She paid for the essays and quizzes from the frat house for a few cases of beer. As far as I know, she never opened a book. But she graduated with honors."

Sal liked the story.

"It's true. She is on her way to Harvard for an MBA... first one in our family to go to Harvard."

I looked over at Chiara, who gave a little mini-clap of glee.

"Congratulations, Chiara. That is great news."

"Tell me about the system, Tommy."

"Well—before midterms, I went to the frat house and looked at the files. The midterms were short answer and never changed much from year to year. I could rehearse good answers with Chiara. But there were also a number of multiple-choice questions. I noticed that she would not have the depth of knowledge since she missed the lectures and readings. So, we needed a system to transfer answers from me to her without the professor getting suspicious."

"Ok."

Sal was actually interested in my thinking as much as my little innocent college cheating scheme. "During the midterm exam, Chiara sat behind me. I knew that there would be about twenty multiple-choice questions and five short answers. There were about ten topics from which five would be chosen. Chiara studied the ten answers from the frat house files. During the midterm, I gave her the answers to the multiple-choice questions in code."

"What kind of code?"

"First, I cracked my knuckles to orient her to the first question. There was a tile floor in the classroom. Each corner represented A, B, C, or D. It was spring and I wore flip flops, which I took off. So, if the answer was A, I rubbed my toe on the upper left corner of the tile. B was upper right, C was lower left, and D was lower right. After the initial knuckle pop, I would scratch the back of my neck to start each subsequent question. So, for example, I would trace a 2 or 7 or 12 on my neck to prompt Chiara. I needed time to study the questions."

"Sure," Sal threw in.

"I got a respectable A-, while Chiara actually got one of the highest grades in the class."

"Bravo!"

"How did you come up with that kind of system?"

"I didn't think about it much. A tile has four corners and a multiple-choice question has four options. Easy stuff. Students always stretch and crack knuckles—teachers are used to that. There was no reason to suspect cheating from someone who was already doing well in the class." Sal was impressed with the dual simplicity and complexity of the scheme, which I do not remember spending more than two minutes to develop.

After dinner, coffee arrived, and buttressed by the comfort derived from spending a nice evening, Sal finally delivered his pitch. "Tommy, we are grateful in my family for your help with Chiara. Because of your arrival here, we are in a position to show you our gratitude." Sal Manzo sounded too heavy and Sicilian and old country in his approach, which seemed to make Chiara uncomfortable. But he was clearly the senior partner between them, as well as her big brother.

"That's ok, Sal. It was fun."

Sal raised his hand to retake the floor.

"I work in an official capacity at the InterCaribe Bank. Your Colombian associates made an appointment to utilize our banking services. We were prepared to assist them with their financial situation. And we were ready to conclude our business when Chiara recognized you and your... incapacity. We asked your associates to explain your arrival in Aruba, your condition, your future plans, or their plans for you."

Sal looked around the restaurant unconsciously and returned to the theme. Even though he spoke in the plural at all times, he was really talking about Nando, and his Aruban bad luck.

"We were not exactly satisfied with their explanations. They could not account for their relationship with you. They made several references to Colombian national security that they would not explain. They said that they were keeping you from danger, but could not explain any details. Nothing added up. That left us with a dilemma. We could take their claims of national secrecy at face value and conclude the deal and in that manner gain a new client. But in that way, we could not guarantee your health and security. Or, we could ask them to go away, but they could still take you with them. Part of the security they requested was that you stay in the hotel during our business, so it was an easy handoff from their control of your person to ours."

This guy could be dangerous to cross, I thought. He felt comfortable assisting Colombians with an exfiltration based on a handshake, and then turning on them without much concern about their powers to exact revenge. Guys like that live in protected fortresses, which I learned over time was what Aruba represented for him. He had guts: he decided to keep their money and send Nando off the island, keeping me as some kind of collateral, which he was paying to fatten up and learn more about Nando and his crew, or at least I thought.

Chiara tried to soften her brother's explanation. "We even got a phone call from a distinguished Colombian lawyer in Miami. He vouched for the national security implications in this matter. He said he would be able to provide explanations at a later date. He could not tell me anything about you, or the manner of your safe conduct, however. I merely listened. After careful thought, we arrived at a solution, Tommy. If they want the money, they only have to satisfy a single condition. That is, they have to ask you for the money. At present, the money is attached to your name."

"Me?"

"Yes. The gentlemen claimed to be associates of yours, and acting on your behalf. However, due to your incapacity, none of that could be proven. So, they can easily prove it to your satisfaction, and at that time, you can transfer funds back to them if and when you feel comfortable."

"How are they supposed to prove their bona fides?"

"They can come here and you can sign the money over to them, or part of the money, over to them."

"So, the money is in a checking account or something?"

"Not quite. You can come to my office this week, and I can explain to you the details."

"Chiara, I don't know Nando, or why he would take an interest in me. I think he was hired to get me out of the country, but I don't know why I was in the country in the first place. They could tell you any kind of story, and I would not be able to refute it."

At this point, Sal Manzo took a shopping bag off the floor and handed it to Chiara. She stood up and took out the items. There was a small wallet, the kind meant to be worn in one's front pocket. Sal took a credit card out of his pocket and handed it to me through Chiara. "This is linked to the funds, Tommy. You don't have to worry about paying any bills unless you do some serious shopping at a Mazarati dealership or something." Chiara put the card into the wallet. She also put Sal's business card there. "There are a few papers to sign, but we will take care of that later this week."

It may have been unseemly, but the question burped upward.

"Sal, I don't mean to be forward, but how much money are we talking about?"

"Oh. About three million dollars U.S."

"Oh, shit. That changes things," I thought.

I had three million dollars, some or all of which belonged to a Colombian intelligence officer, his patrons, or narco associates, all or some of whom lost the money due to unforeseen coincidences and complications during my exfiltration. Men like that did not chalk up their losses to experience and return to their rose bushes. Their particular disappointment was directed toward a guy named Tommy, who was hiding out poolside in Aruba at a gangster's hotel under his protection. That would be enough to send out killers and torturers who knew how to get the right answers.

While this aggravated me, I don't it troubled Sal Manzo for a minute. He might be a good friend to make, I thought.

Sal and Chiara really encouraged my Aruban Life of Reilly. My lean, blond, divorced Dutch physical trainer let me know that we could continue our therapy in other formats if I wished. She would grasp my butt with little squeezes in the pool, or rub sun lotions on my arms and legs and up around my chest until the grounds staff, and even the other poolside couples, took notice.

She also encouraged therapy sessions in my room. In these, I would often lay on my back while she straddled me from above, either to flex my limbs or massage the soft tissue. Her scent in the room was palpable. But the pills blunted the connections between too many critical wires. I could see small hairs poking through her bathing suit, and see her nipples when she leaned over near me, but it did not invoke the whole power plant of sexual response it would have before my head got crushed by someone.

There was also Amelia. I went to sleep with her image from the hospital: her soft kisses on my cheeks, her golden skin, the little streaks of sweat down her breasts; her pride and her decency; her simple elegance and Olympian beauty; her smell and her breath and her scent and her lips. She was all royalty. Not that I was in any credible position to negotiate, but I wanted Amelia Hernandez or nothing; I wanted another chance to show her I was a man, not a cloying, anxious boy who could not explain his own past. I wanted Amelia to see me tall and strong, and capable and firm. And virile. Yes, I wanted her to see me that way, too.

The phone call from the Miami lawyer, which interrupted my normal afternoon nap, was somewhere between a polite reminder and a subtle warning.

I could not tell whether the receptionist was from the hotel or beyond. I held. The thought of another doctor joining the team was welcome.

"This is Dr. Oviedo."

"This is Tommy Connolly."

"Hello, Tommy. I am Rafael Oviedo. How are you, sir?"

"I am fine."

"That is great news. It is my understanding that you have been through quite an ordeal."

"I am enjoying my recovery, sir."

"Please call me Rafael."

"Dr. Oviedo, could you please tell me in which field you acquired your doctorate?"

"Law. I am a graduate of Yale Law School in the United States."

He was not a specialist that Sal Manzo enlisted to hasten my recovery so that he could close some kind of deal with me. He was the man to deliver the first warning, gentleman to gentleman.

"Thank you, Rafael. And how can I help you today?"

"One of my clients, associates, is also an associate of yours."

I cut him off. "Here on the island, Rafael?"

"No, it is an associate of mine and yours in Colombia."

"Is this associate of yours known to me?"

"If you will give me a moment to explain...."

That is precisely what law school and legal practice and intellectual pomposity had trained him to: capture, surround, and subdue a conversation like a small calf in a rodeo. "This seems to have great import for your client." Three years of law school following probably four years of indolence in a Bogota university. And in this corner, Tommy Connolly with half a brain, but a degree—diligently pursued—in the classics.

"Yes, it is a matter of importance to you both."

"Then, please tell your client that Aruba has an excellent airport with daily flights, and I would welcome the opportunity to associate with you both."

"There are certain matters whose clarification could be handled more expeditiously between us."

"More than likely, Rafael. It is simply a model of conducting business that does not fit my mood these days. Thank you for calling though, Rafael. I will be certain to send a small check to Yale in appreciation of your intervention. Good day." He had not expected any of that—neither the derision, the haste, nor the spleen.

"Wait. My client insists on the clarification of certain matters."

"Rafael, while I do not have a lawyer at present, and during my recovery I am not at all able to protect my interests from a professional point of view, I would suggest that you address your associate's concerns to a young man named Sal Manzo at the InterCaribe Bank. I believe he is a Princeton grad. He is handling my affairs at the moment."

"Tommy, my friend, let us approach these matters with a view toward an equitable solution."

The pirates rushed out of their cove behind my ear and onto the beach with swords and muskets in their waving arms. I tried to calm them, at least until I could think a little more. I had the money, they had the threat of violence, and in the middle was Amelia.

"Capital, Rafael. Let me start with one of my concerns. You have in your possession the telephone number of the hotel. Let's endeavor to arrive at an equitable solution to this problem. I want to speak to Amelia Hernandez. I want to speak to her on the phone, privately—without minders. Make that happen—soon—and I promise you that good things will follow for your associates. Once I verify that she is free to speak to me, and in good spirits, we can resume this conversation. Good day, Sir." I hung up.

I wasted no time in pressing button three for room service.

CHAPTER FIVE

It felt good and right, poking that pompous legal cyclops with a lit stick of threats and buffoonery in his eye, but it probably ruined my last chance of ever knowing Amelia Hernandez, goddess of my morning constitutional routine, Helen of my recovery of new-mindedness. There was space to squeeze into some kind of reasonable accommodation with Rafael, probably at a loss of about two million dollars, but I could not bear his credentialed bonhomie a second longer. As long as I shall live, I will have to bow down to people who do not deserve even a hand shake, but Rafael Oviedo was an overpaid errand boy who sized me up as a nuisance to his clients.

My heart was beating too fast, an anxiety that exfiltration could not cause, but the thought of losing Amelia produced to a frightening degree. I wanted out of that room, its off-white color scheme and tropical charm. Downstairs, instead of heading left to the pool, I went right to the bar to rightsize a growing rage among my scull pirates. Luckily, the hostess was on scull-left, the scars were on scull-right, so that I passed through the entry with a smile, and headed straight to the barstool.

"Whiskey, please."

At this point in my recovery, the scull taping was a small, around patch, and not scull-circling, or evidential of anything more than a minor pool accident, or perhaps the result of a skirmish with coral or drunken pool artistry. The bartender did not hesitate to serve me, but just in case, I drank it in a single gulp. It burned down nicely, and then pleasingly raced back up. I could imagine Rafael Oviedo on his satellite phone with Nando in Colombia, explaining how the last time he endured such cheek, he fired the particular house maid.

The pirates sniffed the air, seeing their bloodied foes swimming out to sea. "Another, please." It arrived, and I gulped it, too.

Unfortunately, the bell captain spied me in the bar at the same time I spied him in the bar mirror.

"Tommy, old friend. How are you?"

"Good, Herbert."

"Tommy, the doctor said you are not permitted to drink alcohol."

He made a throat-cutting motion to the bartender.

"Just one more, Herbert."

"Tommy, let me help you back to your room."

Without hesitation, he grabbed my arm, almost lifting me up off the bar stool in a single—for me—wrenching motion, and led me back to the elevator, and up to my room.

That kind of authority did not come from a hotel manager on duty, or a snap decision from a bell captain, but from the offices of Sal Marzo himself. While made to feel a special guest throughout the resort, this was my first taste of confinement, which linked Sal at that moment at least, with Oviedo. The drinks were enough, as I passed out in my room, and slept until the next morning when light and hope came back to me.

The phone call—the opening pitch of baseball season, the first daffodil in a snowy meadow—that wondrous throaty voice came the next morning when I was still in bed.

"Tommy?" It was Amelia, my Helen.

"Amelia! Is that you?"

"Hello, Tommy. I am so glad to hear your voice again. I did not think it was possible again."

"I told you I would look for you."

"Yes, you did, but that is the way gringos talk."

She would talk that way, but I knew she did not believe it.

"Did you get my note in the hospital?"

"Yes, I came to the hospital the next day. The nurse said that they took you away back to the United States."

"No, they took me to a military barracks on the other side of the base. I was there for about a month."

Amelia cursed and laughed, possibly quite used to the stratagems of her father.

"Ijueputa mierda esa farsa!" What a fucking farce!

"What's the matter?"

"They told me that you wanted to go back to the United States as quickly as possible."

"No. I never said that. They made all the decisions. A sentry moved me quickly in the early morning after I saw you the last time. I only had a moment to write to you, like putting a note in a bottle."

"I still have your note. I like to read it."

"Amelia, how long has it been since you last came to visit me?"

"About seven weeks, I think."

That would be late April, about two months after I woke up, the time in which she cared for me almost every day.

"Did your father tell you anything?"

"He said that you needed to see specialists in the United States. And that your father wanted to… eh…supervisor…."

"Oversee."

"Yes, oversee your recovery."

"I have not even spoken to him."

"Well, by some miracle we are talking again."

"I have waited to hear your voice… I think about you all the time."

"Nando called me last night, and told me that you were in Aruba. How did you get to Aruba?"

"They brought me here in an airplane. It is a very long story. Most of the details make no sense to me."

"How long have you been there?"

"Since I left Cali."

"You have not been home?"

"No, I have not left Aruba. I was very weak when I arrived."

"What do you do?"

"I am getting stronger. I walk, I go into the pool for therapy. I am starting to ride the stationary bike in the exercise room. I eat good food and rest. I am growing fond of afternoon naps."

"Good for you, Tommy. You deserve a rest."

There was some gap—of credibility, of will, of purpose—which I had to fill quickly, if I wanted ever to see Amelia again.

"Are you in school, Amelia?"

"No, I did not go back to study after Christmas. I lack two semesters to graduate. This summer I will stay at home with my mother."

"How is she?"

"She is fine. She worries about me too much."

"Amelia, listen to me. Please, just listen. When I saw you the last time, I did not think it would be for the last time… do you understand?"

"Yes, Tommy."

"Amelia, can you get a ticket?"

"What ticket? What are you talking about?"

"A ticket to Aruba. To come and see me."

"Aruba? Loco Gringo."

"Amelia, listen. Please. I found you again. This is my only chance. I am not wanted back in Colombia. I don't think your family will ever let me get close to you again. You know that. I have never forgotten you—not for a day."

"After my therapy at the base, I wanted you to come through that door to see me a better man. I have gotten stronger so that you would see me like I really am, not a crippled boy in a hospital."

"I know how you are, Tommy."

"No, you don't. I am stronger now. I get terrible pain from the therapies here, but still I work so that someday you will be there at the end of the day, and you will like what you see."

"But, Tommy, we are not... comprometidos."

"And if we do things in a normal way, we never will be. Your family will now allow it. And we will never know if we do not try. I cannot come to Cali. But you can come here. Please come, Amelia. This is our chance."

"Tommy, es dificil."

"Will you be satisfied not trying to see me again? Will you be happy if you don't try at least once to see me? You can leave the next day if you are not happy with me. I would never pressure you to do anything."

Amelia began to cry in little murmurs that threatened to deepen into a torrent.

"OK, loco. I will come."

"Listen, give me your phone number in Cali. The hotel concierge here will call you. She will have the details of your flight. For God's sake, get your passport ready! You don't need much here—a swimming suit, some shorts."

"Tommy, are you sure this is what you want?"

Heck, Paris, are you sure that girl from Troy is worth the trouble?

"Yes. I am sure, Amelia. I am sure that you are supposed to be with me. I think that you kept me alive so that I would come back to you. Well, I am back. The rest is details."

"Ok, Tommy. My father will kill me, but he will have to wait for my return before he does."

"I am going to the lobby now to talk to the concierge. She will call you in about an hour. Her name is Fleur. She will take care of everything. Start packing, Amelia."

"This is really what you want, Tommy?"

"Yes, Amelia. This is what I want. You are what I want."

"Ok, Loco. Bye."

I plopped down the phone and went down to the concierge desk where Fleur wrote down my instructions without questions or suggestions.

I was on dangerous ground, adding enticement and kidnapping to my current charges of theft and illicit enrichment since I was burning through someone's money week by week in Las Cabanas. I knew I was under the protection of Sal Manzo, but that was protection from people who had lost money, not a daughter, especially one as beautiful as Amelia Hernandez.

But I wanted Amelia more than I feared death, or torture, or Rafael Oviedo's high-class hectoring; for me, it was that simple. They all held no fear for me. After I tasted her kiss, they could drown, shoot or behead me. I would come out the winner.

It was Lukas, a Dutch bellman, a coed slayer, the most daring of the young surfer-bellmen in Las Cabanas, who had offered me marijuana during our beach jogs, and, despite my rejections, passed me another roach as we settled into the town car for the trip to the airport. Obviously not a close confidant of Sal Manzo, he felt sorry for the ersatz little rich boy with the bump on his head who needed help to remember his way around the grounds of the hotel, or to remember his room number when he signed for clothes in the lobby.

Fleur had reported back to me within a few hours of my conversation with Amelia. The flight was to be in two days with a late afternoon arrival. I told her that I wanted a straight Cali-Bogota-Aruba flight—nothing routed through Panama City or Caracas. It seemed like the whole of Las Cabanas changed to a matchmaking service. Fleur actually came up and arranged my new room herself, putting on the cleaning woman's elbow-reaching gloves to scrub around the bathroom. She arranged my personals on the far side of the right sink, pushed my clothes into the bottom drawers. She ordered flowers for arrival in two days. She also had a basket of female mists and soaps and creams delivered. Lukas put a few condoms under my underwear in the drawer—with a knowing, professional wink. Cologne and mouth wash suddenly appeared on the bathroom sink the day before she arrived.

For my part, looking in the bathroom mirror at night at a thin man with a slug-slow eye and slow responses to things around him, I did double sessions those last two days with my personal trainer and bicycle routine. To the disgust of the tourists, I sat near the pool with my scar toward the high sun around noon. That night I also bought suntan lotion and two beach towels.

I had forgotten what color she was, our rendezvous in Cali being in the dark hospital room or under the morning equatorial glare in the hospital gardens. Finally, I was currently eating six hamburgers with fries each day, only after a four-egg with bacon breakfast.

Lucas knocked on my door about an hour before the scheduled arrival time of Amelia's flight. The hotel Lincoln was in its space in the basement parking lot, but Lukas told me to wait at the valet parking in front of the hotel. I double-checked that I had my wallet in my front pocket. I put on a fresh layer of cologne and some cream. I could not do anything for my scar, but I had nothing to hide, so I ditched a tourist hat.

Before we left, Lukas put on the smallest bandage that would cover my scar. He pealed onto the coastal route, and within minutes we were cruising in front of the ocher-colored façade of the rather tiny airport. He whipped out a final-offer joint.

"Dutch courage?"

"I think not—Sexual Beast, American Girl-devouring Dutch Man."

I waited as he sucked down about half the joint in one puff and put the roach in his uniform jacket pocket.

"OK, Tommy. Ready!"

I had lured her out of her country after taking three million of her clan's money. But I wanted her, in flesh and spirit.

We walked out of the parking and into the crowded lobby. We were only a few feet into the building when Lukas swerved us both into a nearby bathroom.

"Dogs, Tommy! Fuckin' Dogs! This is my last joint."

After a moment's delay we moved out and set up post outside the customs and baggage check counters. Lukas, zigzagging through the crowd on the way to the airline counter, returned as if with a battle report from Thermopylae.

"The plane landed about ten minutes ago, Tommy. Customs is very fast." He pointed to the nearest flashing arrival/departure screen. "It already landed. Get your dick out. Joking, of course." Lukas paced and smiled and jerked around a corner once or twice when a dog barked, and he feared imminent capture. I endeavored to stay upright and alert and not slobber, and to think straight and act normally, and not slobber. There was a new kind of pounding in my head that started from my heart. There she was. It was Amelia—tall, Olympian, graceful, perfect. She wore white shorts, a sleeveless blue cotton shirt, and a white hoodie tied around her waist. She was resplendent that day, her hair fiercely-black, her green eyes mesmerizing, and her skin a cinnamon-copper mix. She walked in a line with the other passengers, but purely by accident, as if she had come down from Olympus, and merely by accident landed among mere mortals in the deplaning line.

"Jesus! Good work, Tommy," said Lukas. She walked up to me with a sudden tremulous look, which she quickly replaced with a wide smile. I did not speak at first, so she crept forward more.

"Hello, Tommy."

"Hello, Amelia."

Lukas stepped forward and grabbed her suitcase off the ground.

"Hello, miss. I will take your bag for you. Do you have more luggage?"

"No. Just this one."

"In that case, I will meet you outside on the curb near the baggage carousel. Welcome to Aruba!"

She moved even closer to me. It was nearly too much to endure—an impossibly beautiful women so close to me, and here on this island as a result of my declaration—implied, but declared—of love for her. My hand shook, but I lifted my left arm anyway to embrace her, but she ducked under it and onto my chest to spare me the effort. She put her arms around me lightly, so she would not hurt me, and rested her head on my shoulder, smelling my chest, which she would have remembered as the only bit of eroticism permitted by the nurses in the hospital.

She kept that repose for about a minute, it felt, during which I smelled her hair once again, relighting fires in my brain from that time.

"We are both standing up, Amelia! First time." She understood what I meant.

"You look great, Tommy."

"Really? Not too scary...to look at."

"No, Tommy. Not at all."

She was with me now—damn all other calamities that Nando or Rafael Oviedo could throw my way.

I took her by both hands and slowly brought her back to my chest, where once she felt me near, she started to cry a little. She bolted her head back and put her hands behind my neck and kissed me with passion.

"My handsome, loco Tommy!"

"My beautiful, morning girl, Amelia."

Holding my hand and purposefully walking on my right side, we walked outside to the sidewalk and were greeted by Lukas's beeping of the Lincoln's horn as he pulled in front of us.

Back at the hotel, Lukas performed his final task for us by placing Amelia's suitcase on a stand in our new room, a surprise gift from Sal Manzo, and quickly retreating without further comedy. It had two beds, a couch, and a glass-topped table, but looked directly out on the pool and the palms on the edge of the beach. Amelia wanted to use the bathroom, so I took the opportunity to read the card tucked within the flowers.

"Enjoy the new room and your company! Sal Manzo."

Sal had gone beyond acts of gratitude towards me, or even salesmanship. He was clearly a criminal, which I had been raised to rightly scorn, but I had no reason to look down upon him or not to trust him so far. Actually, he was looking out for my interests better than I could myself.

Not able to bear more nervousness, I went out to the balcony—the trade winds swayed and dropped the palm branches above the grassy lawns and the pool outside my window. Beyond was the bobbing turquoise sheet of the sea.

Amelia came out in a logo t-shirt and a pair of jeans shorts, all flawlessly featured in light cinnamon skin and bright red lipstick. She stood behind me and put her arms around my neck, which sent new jolts through the tightness on my back and my scull, causing me to shake a little. She knew the arrangement of the scar tissue and released her grip quickly. She needed to see it for herself, though.

She bent over and kissed my cheek.

"It's lovely, Tommy."

"I hope you enjoy it."

"What do you usually do at this time of the day?"

"Just this. My therapies are in the morning… my doctor only comes once a week now."

"You have gained much weight—you are not so white like in the hospital." I pointed at the scenery around us. "All this has helped."

We both became silent, but I was deep in conversation with the smell of her body and the feel of her hands on my chest, so I just held her close to me, needing to know that Amelia was really by my side.

"Do you want to see the hotel?"

"Yes."

We walked around or ducked under the blue parasols near the pool and took the sand path between palms to the beach. The late afternoon sun was low enough to strike my eyes from the west. Amelia sensed things and took my arm, walking toward the dry frond-covered bar stools near the beach.

"How do you feel, Tommy?"

"I'm fine, Amelia. Do you like it here?"

"Of course, silly—what do you think?"

"It is better than your last internship. Tomorrow we can swim."

Amelia saved her smiles for me, but when not looking my way, the smile dropped away quickly. She grabbed my hand to take me away from the beach.

"Let's go. Too much of this heat is not good for you." We walked back into the hotel.

At night, in our room, as Amelia made herself even more lovely and fragrant in the bathroom, I took off my clothes and put on the white hotel robe. I knew that the pills would not let me take her with any sort of force or passion, which seemed like a cruel joke from the Gods, having delivered Amelia to my side, and rendered me unable to be a man to her. Amelia came out in her bathrobe, too.

"Tommy, I feel sleepy. Can I go to bed now?"

"Of course. I'll be back in a moment."

I went into the bathroom to examine late-therapy stage Tommy Connolly. My right eye was slightly askew, but the features were reasserting themselves, unlike the bloated, expressionistic ones from my time staring in the barracks mirror in Cali. My face left a less severe impression upon the casual observer, but Amelia did not fall under that category. She knew more about me than I could glean from the almost non-existent memories of my life before I first heard "Good Morning, Tommy!" that first morning of wakefulness.

As I brushed my teeth, the image of Amelia—naked, long-legged, pubescently-scented, smooth-breasted, and sweet-mouthed—arrived like a runaway perfumed freight train through my senses, but did not bring much ardor. I put on cologne anyway.

She was sitting in the bed nearer to the balcony, the covers only to her waist, her breasts silhouetted by the moonlight outside. I switched off the light, and stood still in the darkness, listening to the light spill of the waves and the calm poolside chatter.

"Tommy. Why you are not in bed with me?"

"I did not want to rush you, Amelia."

She got up and came to my side. "My Tommy is very silly sometimes."

I had to tell her the truth. "Amelia… I… ugh… the drugs make me…."

Amelia put her finger on my mouth. "Tommy, I know about that. I am here beside you because I… want to be with you."

Amelia took my hand in hers and led me to bed.

I can forego the rest, I thought. I have kissed Amelia, smelled her neck even, and listened to her soft, appealing voice. I have made her happy and content in my arms.

"I missed you so much, Tommy. I thought you were gone forever."

"I'm back now, I think." She laughed a little before succumbing to sleep. I kissed the beautiful woman next to me tenderly on her back before falling asleep too.

I woke up earlier than Amelia, who slept deeply, even after the leaf blower was below our open veranda. I had a therapy session to attend, so I wrote the second note of my life to Amelia: she could shop and eat in the hotel on the room account; that I would be finished by noon; and, that if she bought a new bikini, my recovery would prosper, to which I added a dopey smiley face in pen.

Later, after a grueling session in the gym, during which I pushed myself on the treadmill for half an hour, I spied Amelia lounging under a blue parasol, the rest of the guests awestruck by her perfect beauty. I could see a large paperback with Emile Zola on the bottom of the front cover, which hid her face. "Ah—light comedy. Perfect for an Aruban vacation." She laughed and grabbed her things, putting them all in a strapped bag, which she hoisted onto her shoulder. "I never knew you were a cultural critic too, Funny Man."

We walked to the frond-covered bar stools at the edge of the beach to change into our swimming wear. "I have a surprise for you." she teased.

"You have a penis?"

"Sinverguenza usted!"

She took off her shirt and shorts; beneath and now commanding my attention were black, yellow and pink blocked sections covering only her breasts and pubis. Her tummy was flat and fuzzy and lighter than her legs and newly-exposed torso. I was starting to feel it.

"Lovely, Amelia. You are really not a bad looking girl, sometimes. Your reading habits are a bit dreary, but you have some good qualities."

"Take off your clothes, funny Irish man. We are going into the water." I did. Amelia reached into her bag and pulled out a baseball cap for me.

"I hope you like the Cubs of Chicago."

"Chicago is a good baseball town. I have no problem with that hat." She put it on my head. Somewhere a Lieutenant Colonel was calling an old associate at Interpol.

The sand was hot, so Amelia grabbed my hand to propel me down to the water in large, light strides atop the burning surface. There was no cold sensation in the water when we jumped in, and I doubted that that water had been cold for a million years. We floated further out to about the mid-chest level where the spent surf was breaking far from shore. Amelia came close to me. I kissed her deeply this time with two hands on her butt.

My body cooled suddenly though the water temperature was no different than the ambient one. The pain in my head went far back into its ear cove, and I was for an instant headache-free. I also felt stronger, so I held onto Amelia as a sudden big wave crashed into our bodies, but I did not fall. Instead, I held Amelia strongly around the waist to support her. With Amelia in my arms, and my body withstanding an elemental force of nature for us both, I felt like a man in that ocean. More waves came through us, but I held onto Amelia and took in more kisses as rewards.

Suddenly, she broke away from me, holding onto my hands, but floating away from me with a wry smile.

"How was your therapy this morning, Tommy?"

"Good. I have been doing double sessions for about a week now."

"I see. And what kind of exercises?"

"Pulling, lifting, stretching, bicycle riding, carrying weights in the pool even." She reached down below us.

"Hhhhmmm. I compliment your trainer."

"Why?"

"What kind of exercise can explain this?"

She was holding my erect penis. I turned, so that she was facing the beach, hiding it from the lifeguard in the tower and the couples on the beach that had gathered to see Amelia enter the sea.

"I swear. I have never seen him before. Should we call resort security?"

"No, I know how to handle this type of… intruso."

"I would be very grateful if you would, miss."

We kissed again and walked back to the gazebo, Amelia quickly wrapping a towel around my waist. A waiter ran out to us to take a drink order. Amelia spoke. "No, thank you. We are going back inside!"

In the room, Amelia put her things down and went into the bathroom. Unlike her previous insistence on complete privacy in the bathroom, she left the door wide open. I heard running shower water that I envied for its total access to Amelia Hernandez. I took off the towel and hung it over the balcony fence. "Tommy Connolly, come in here right now!" I went into the bathroom in an instant where Amelia peaked from inside the shower.

"Y que ud. se lo lleve el intruso tambien!" And bring the intruder with you. I took off my shorts and got in the shower.

She stood naked now in the hot steam of the bath: tall, lithe, proud-breasted, browned, salty, her patch forming a perfect, brown triangle below her flat belly. She reached down and stroked me and walked in to kiss me. "Now, what was that little trick you did in the ocean?" She had a new kind of smile now.

Amelia spent a few extra minutes in the bathroom until she came out like a bronzed Venus from the sea, except that the sea breezes now came ashore to caress her face. Closer, with no clothes at all on her body as she stepped toward me, she was Ava Gardner in the poster from The Naked Maja—only far more bewitching and lovely. She took me by the hand and led me to the far bed near the shades, which she closed with a quick flick.

Amelia had also been the chalice from which I hoped to take a ceremonial sip, but that day in bed with such a woman of nonpareil sensuality, my brain and senses went slightly mad.

"Life can be so beautiful, Tommy, no?"

"Or course, Amelia."

She held me close to her afterwards. "Stay with me, Tommy! Promise you will stay with me!" I felt greatness, and power, and pride, all brought to me by being with Amelia, a pleasure afforded to few men this side of Mount Olympus.

But while not at that moment, I also knew that Amelia Hernandez would attract certain furies, which would hover above my life until the propitious moment arrived to inflict harm for daring to love her. I was still slow-minded and pill-addled, but I was learning to compensate: to think slowly and carefully, to observe as much as I could about those around me, and to take minimum action for maximum affect. I hoped that that would prove to be enough.

After we made love for the first time, she looked at home and content in our room, curled on her side, smiling and beckoning me to hold her, and take her again. She put her hand in mine, and we fell asleep. But before drifting off, I couldn't help but ponder: what did it all mean? What should I do next?

I had now taken three million dollars and the only daughter of a powerful man, one with recourse to Miami lawyers, hidden landing strips, and powerful associates. This could end gloriously for me, which I put at about fifty-to-one odds, or in a ditch, which I put at about six-to-one.

But I had made Amelia mine.

CHAPTER SIX

At my next appointment, Dr. Hilliard agreed to halve my dosage of anti-seizure medications, giving me more and more acuity. I didn't use those powers to solve crossword puzzles; I made love to Amelia several times a day, skipping my self-imposed schedule of physical therapies until Amelia made me return to it after a few days.

It was perhaps a week into our time together when I asked Amelia how we initially met. The question came out innocently, not as a way to insinuate that she was keeping anything from me, but Amelia knew exactly what I wanted to hear. We sat on the balcony enjoying the slow hand of the trades when I put the question to her.

"How long have we known each other, Amelia?"

Amelia looked at me calmly; there was no reason for her to deny me any further, yet she still stared at me a moment to size up some quality I still might have lacked in order to withstand whatever she was going to say.

"You really want to know, don't you?"

"Yes. I want to know."

She stood up, stroking my face a few times, then walked inside our room to the phone. She punched a number and spoke. "A bottle of red, not blush—something stronger. Yes, two glasses. Thank you very much."

She minced her way back outside with her hand tucking her hair behind her ear in a prolonged fashion. Outside on the balcony, looking out at the sea an uncomfortably long time before turning to me with a grim look, she spoke without the forward thrusters that launched her feelings about most things.

"Tommy—are you sure?"

"Yes, I lost six months, Amelia. It is nothing personal. I need to know why. though."

"Ok. But tell me to stop if you can't take any more."

She meant that I should stop her if she could not take anymore, if she could not bear to revisit—even from this remote and tranquil vantage—something that provided her as much horror as it left me without peace.

"I promise."

Amelia stared out at the sea, only occasionally glancing at me, telling our story in heavily-breathed phrases that bore no similarity to her normal style of speech.

"It was a Saturday night between Christmas and the New Year. I was in a bar near Avenida Sexta in Cali with my friends Paola and Susana. We sat in the back of the bar against the wall and drank beer. Susana liked this place because it played New Wave music. We drank our first beers before you arrived there. You came in with a suitcase. You were so arrogant, like a typical Gringo, we all thought. You gave your suitcase to the bartender—like he was your servant—and you explained something to him and went back outside like a little prince. You came back with empanadas from the street and drank your beer and ate them by yourself at the bar."

"You saw me in the mirror, and you turned to look at me sometimes. You smiled at me like you expected me to get up and run to your side like a gringo movie. My friends noticed you right away. They laughed at me that the gringo noticed me first. They joked about big hands, big feet, and that sort of thing. You bought a round of beers for us and turned toward us on your bar chair with a big smile. There were many tables in front of us. I am sure they noticed. You wanted to come sit with us, but I would not let you. My friends told me that I was mean to deny you a seat with us. Eventually, you turned away, but you still looked at me in the mirror from time to time."

"Then a short little Indian in a mask came into the bar. He moved toward our table with his gun pointing at us. It was so fast, Tommy. The sicario suddenly pointed his gun and fired off several shots very quickly. Susana and Paola were shot and died immediately. They didn't even have time to fall over. Their heads just fellow over and stayed there. I looked to you. I don't why, really. Everyone else in the bar was on the floor with their heads covered. But you didn't move, Tommy...you were so calm. You picked up a chair and hit the sicario right over the head. Not once, but several times. The chair broke and you still had a piece in your hand, and so you hit him again and again."

"His blood was on your face, but you did not care. You looked up because another sicario ran into the bar. He saw you standing over his socio on the floor. You saw something, sensed something. You ran to me and covered me with your body. You spoke to him in Spanish. You said something about you represented the American embassy and that I was a protected person. He laughed. You grabbed my hands tightly.

'Don't be afraid,' you said to me. I trusted you. Then you squeezed my hands hard inside yours."

Amelia began to cry, her voice chords now working through the sorrow of her sudden tearing up.

"He fired into your back two times, and then into your head. You wanted to fall, but you would not let your legs collapse. There were the whistles of the police outside next. He got scared a little and left. Everyone was still on the floor. You fell down then. Blood was like a spray from your head. It flew out against the wall. I covered it with my hands, but it was shooting between my fingers. The bartender gave me a towel to stop your bleeding. He looked at me like you were going to die soon, anyway. You tried to talk, but only bubbles came from your mouth. You still held my hand on the floor. You were turning cold."

Amelia began to cry in earnest, first in a weeping manner, but eventually in a torrent of tears.

"There was nothing I could do to help you, Tommy."

The door knocked, and I went to answer it. I came back with the two glasses first, and went back for the bottle. Amelia was a little more composed, but tears fell from her eyes again.

"You had no color, Tommy. You were almost dead. You coughed from blood in your lungs. I whispered in your ear, 'Stay with me. Stay with me,' in English."

Amelia began to cry again. "I took out your licensia. It said Tommy Connolly from California. I whispered again in your ear, 'Stay with me, Tommy. Stay with me.' You went unconscious at that moment. You almost stopped breathing. I did not know what to do to save you. The ambulance came. My towel was still on your head. The ambulance men saw a wound on my hand, so they took me too. They put tape around my hand in that ambulance. Two paramedics worked on your heart so it would not stop. They wrapped your head in tape and put tubes in your nose. Your heart was so slow. I thought at any moment it will stop and you would die. At the hospital, they took you away. They said you would probably die, but that I must take care of myself. They took my purse. I told them to take you to the CNP hospital. That I would pay."

This was not my story, not one in which I would play a principal role. I was afraid of fire works as a child; my mother always sat as far away as possible from the explosions on the 4th of July, so that I would not cry. My mother would not let me watch cop shows on TV for fear that I would see a gun as a valid solution to a problem. I was timid and friendly, always talking myself out of fights, and running when I had to. In college, I never approached another guy's date or made sly suggestions. This was someone else. It was not Tommy Connolly. This guy frightened me.

"My parents arrived later with Nando. I told them about Susana and Paola, about the sicarios and about you. My father left and my mother and Nando took care of me. 'How is the gringo?' I asked. They did not know anything-even your name. The emergency room nurse gave me a shot, and I went to sleep in a hospital room. When I woke up, I asked about you again. A nurse told me you were still in surgery. My father came back in the morning. He wanted to take me home, but I wanted to stay close to you. He took us home, anyway. I did not see you for a few days. They kept me in bed at home under...."

"Sedation."

"My arm was in a big...."

"Cast?"

"Si, cast. My mother gave me pills to calm me because I was calling the hospital all the time. My arm hurt very much, but I did not think about that. I asked about you, and they always told me 'no change.' Finally, I told my mother I would go by myself if she would not take me. My father said ok, but not until Nando arrived."

"Who is Nando in your family? He's a relative, right?"

"He is my father's son from his first marriage. He does not live with us, but he is still my big brother. We all came to the hospital. You were still in the ICU. My father got angry when he saw your hospital room. The next time there was a guard on your door. He never explained the reason. The next few days I went to the... entierro of Paola and Susana. All my friends were there. I did not know what to say. I went back to the hospital a few days later."

"You were still in the ICU. I could barely see you. They kept you in the darkness and in complete quiet—like you were already dead. You did not move at all. The bandages covered your head and eyes. There were tubes in your nose and mouth and arms. The nurse let me enter the room just for a minute since they did not expect you to live. "You can say goodbye, but do not touch him."

"I whispered in your ear, 'Tommy! Stay with me. Everything will be ok.' I repeated it over and over until the nurse made me go away, but before I left, I kissed you on the cheek. I came to see you every few days, whenever Nando was available to take me. Each time I said to you 'Good morning, Tommy. I am so happy to see you.'"

"I did not return to school. I did not care about it then. Every day I was afraid that the hospital would call to tell me you were dead. My father wanted me to stay away from the hospital and to see a psychologist, but I refused. There was nothing the matter with me."

"In March sometime, you opened your eyes for a few minutes. Nando told me. I got a cab the next day. You were asleep, so I held your hand and put cool towels on your arms. The nurse let me do that, but not to do anything involving the tubes. This is when I met Dr. Howe. He said that he had spoken with your father. He told me that you would not be having visitors, and that you needed human contact. He said I should be gentle and patient, and speak to you slowly. He said that I could come anytime, but not after dark."

He probably said that so the rest of her family could get some rest.

"I asked Dr. Howe when you would wake up. He said they were keeping you asleep with drugs. That if you woke up too soon, you would have a heart attack or a brain seizure. He said I could call the nurses for… ("updates"), yes, updates. I called every day. There was not change for a week. The next time they said you opened your eyes briefly. I went early the next morning. I gave you a kiss. I said, "Good morning, Tommy! It is a beautiful day! Wake up now, Tommy!"

"Did I wake up?"

"No, you smiled though—like you knew my voice. I started to go every day after that. Nando was upset, because he had to take me on his way to work. Around the beginning of April, I think, you began to wake up and stay awake. You could not move your head, but you saw things. You noticed me too. I talked to you now with your eyes open. With those tubes, you could not talk. You were sweating a lot. I told Dr. Howe your room was too hot. He was a great doctor. He saved your life. Anyway, one day I arrived in your room. Your father was there. He wore a dark suit. His shoes were so...."

"Polished?"

"Yes, polished. He sat next to you. My father sat at the foot of the bed near the window. They watched you slowly."

"My father introduced your father not as Mr. Connolly, but as Ambassador Michael Faraday. Your father was being very polite with me. He asked me how I was recovering since somehow he knew that I was injured, too. The Secretary said that you were making good progress, and he thanked me for taking care of you."

"He and my father left the room at that point. I saw them talking in the gardens from the window. I came back about a week later. My family took a vacation to Cartagena then. I was so jealous when I came back. You were speaking in Spanish with the nighttime nurse. She did not let me enter the room when she cleaned you. After that, I could not get to see you for a few days. The local police interviewed me. They wanted to know if you attacked the sicarios. I wanted to scream at them. I told them I could not remember anything. The next time I saw you, you were already speaking. I spoke to you in English."

"I remember: you saw me in the bathroom and got angry."

"Yes. That happened in this time. I began to sleep in your room. There was always a guard, so it was safe. The night nurse was too nice to you. I did not trust her."

"You cried one time, Amelia."

"Dr. Howe told me that you would be leaving the hospital soon, and no one knew where you were going. I wanted to be there when you left. So, I walked with you in your wheel chair and spent more time with you. That was when I went to your room and saw you in the bathroom. I was silly. I got angry with you and left. When I came back the next time, you were gone. My father said you had gone back to the United States to a hospital there. I heard nothing for almost two months, and then suddenly Nando gave me your phone number. When I heard your voice, it was like a Tommy I did not know before, but still recognized. You spoke now without the druggy sound to your voice. You showed me that you really remembered me, and that I was important to you."

"I was surprised that you were in Aruba. Nando and my father still will not tell me what happened. They never will. I packed my bags quickly, but did not tell my family. I took a taxi to the airport. Like you said, I only had to show my ID. I called my mother from the airport. I told her that I wanted to be with you. She said that she understood. I have not spoken to my father. He will probably kill you and then me. I have spoken to my mother a few times since I arrived here. She knows that we are in Aruba, and that I am with you. I told her that you are stronger, but you still do not remember many things. She told me not to be scared. That is the story, Tommy. You went to the wrong bar, and acted the gringo for the wrong girl. It almost cost you your life. But you did not die... I tried to keep you alive in the hospital."

Amelia broke down in an anguish long pent-up, and then suddenly released. I held her, her tears rolling over the hand that tried to wipe them as they fell in one after another.

"Do you still want me, Tommy?"

"Yes, of course. Do you still want me?"

"My Irish boy is very silly sometimes, but I forgive him."

"Get used to having me around then, Amelia."

Amelia cried again deeply after that. I held her in my arms, wiping away her tears with my handkerchief. Her paroxysm returned, convulsing her came from deep within her scared little heart: the instantaneous, brutal murder of her friends; her own wound in her arm, which I had never noticed before; her lubricious bathing in my blood on the bar floor; her anguish to see every day the shrunken, scull-wrapped, tube-fed-version of her hero. She had guts, my girl.

There was nothing there that needed improving upon, either, through psychological remedies or a pill regime. She sought something that therapeutic technique could not touch upon or provide for her. She had seen it up close—death, evil, blood, and was changed for good. What she wanted was a shield from the evil that men can do, and someone to wield it at the proper time and against any possible return of danger. Danger had taken the form of fast bullets that entered her friends breasts and stilled them forever. She had seen my face turn blue as the final breathes seemed to escape my mouth. Too proud, too pre-modern for conventional remedies, she needed to believe that Tommy Connolly would make things right for her, and keep them that way. It was a romantic notion, deep and impenetrable, while her parents wanted ongoing psychological treatment for her during sessions that made no vow to protect her. It was a clash of visions separated by at least a century and a continent or two.

She knew that a psychologist would try to wipe away the lingering effects of her trauma through novelty and effacement of the bad things, including Tommy Connolly, so she avoided school, previous attachments, medicines, and familial advice. That was implicit in her plane ride to Aruba. She chose Tommy Connolly and irrational, heroic love to a rational, orderly recovery.

Yolanda Perez in Los Angeles saw me as a big-dicked man-child, ladling me vaginal fluids in her bed and giving me parking privileges in the faculty parking lot. Especially during her ovulation, when she would peak into my classroom with unannounced visits, she thought I needed full-time protection from the big bad world. "Stay with me, Tommy! You are just a child. I can take care of you, here. It is too dangerous for you out there. We can make a little baby together. I will take care of you both. You can get a real teacher's license. Then, I can pull the strings to get you your own principal's job." I declined her generous offer, and took the first available foreign posting in Bogota, about which I knew very little.

What did heroes have? Hector was not episodically or vaingloriously courageous. He would have impaled the first shooter on his pike and threw him in a dumpster. He would have calmed all three girls, lifting his head shield only when he addressed Amelia. While everyone in the bar would have patted him on the back, he would have been friendly with all who approached him, patiently posing for pictures with the bartender and the waitresses. He would have left the bar with clunking metal strides with no promise to return. Achilles would have impaled both men on the same spike, sullenly demanding free beer for the rest of the night. Odysseus would have known the shooter would arrive, and set a trap for him into which he would fall while Odysseus escaped.

I responded way too late. Two girls died before I picked up a chair. But why did I pick up that chair? What made diffident little Tommy Connolly bring death to that teenage gunman? The thought occurred to me that perhaps I was not a hero at all. Perhaps I was that deformed offshoot of the hero making its way in mass formation across the world. Maybe I was just a thrill killer. It would help to see morgue photos. There is a difference between a scull with a serious crack, and one in egg shells in the red yoke of its own blood. In her description of the killing, she emphasized that I hit him again and again, supposedly while he was prostrate and dying on the floor.

I was not there for the event; so far, Amelia was my chief publicist for the heroic thesis. Amelia did not share any of my secret doubts about my culpability for the violent death of the first shooter. For her, Tommy partook of the heroic, and that was enough to raise him in her esteem above all others. Tommy entered the bar like Achilles—brash, uncouth—and left like Hector—loyal and noble, struck down only after the mightiest blows befell him. He killed without hesitation to defend her life, without reaching a quorum among varying impulses, and suffered near-mortal injuries.

The now recovering modern-day hero slept a long time until his maiden's voice woke him up. "Good morning, Tommy." She felt these mythic notions strongly, and consequently had no quarrel with the fact that I was capable of hyper-violence. *Good morning, Tommy!* Those were the sweetest words that I would ever want to hear. They put an end to my neurotic prattling like a gavel in a rowdy court room, but only from her voice and in our castle would they continue to tamp down on my unease.

After Amelia told me the truth, I gave little thought to my newly-discovered darker impulses. We made love differently after that, almost partaking in ceremonial rites to celebrate the joy of life and nearness of death. She did not like to be apart from me, so I scheduled my therapy and training for the early mornings while she still slept. When she awoke, I was there to give her her first morning kiss. We never spoke formally about individual plans, or even a small separation in order to work out plans. We had rejoined, in flesh like our first time on the bar floor.

I told Fleur to book a return flight to Cali for two, not one.

Before I left, I accepted a lunch invitation from Sal Manzo. As I expected, he asked me to come alone. I left Amelia in the room one afternoon, and took a cab to Sal's bank. He greeted me at the door with keys in his hand. We shook hands warmly, and he gave me a big hug, testing my bones and muscles inside his massive squeeze. He stood back to take in for an extended moment the recuperated Tommy Connolly. This one was in white slacks and shirt, dark glasses, and leather shoes.

Sal, looking like he had been waiting patiently for his arrival, had plans for that guy.

The purpose of the meeting became clear after the unforced leisure of lunch on the Aruban coast. He told me that he needed to explain some of the details of the previously discussed financial matters. The three million dollars were in short-term U.S. government paper. Due to the current rates, I had already earned about $22,000.00 in interest.

"That should cover my hotel bill!" I joked.

He told me that I enjoyed the corporate rate for the bank's premiere clients, which included discounts on food, liquor and medical care. He said $10,000.00 should suffice. He said that he wanted to get the money in motion, as there were investment opportunities on the island and off that would pay a return far more than U.S. T-bills.

I told him that I was grateful for the bank's particular attention to my case, and its patience with my recovery. But it would be premature for me to move money around that may leave my control within the week. He asked me if I intended to return to Colombia and clear up any providence issues. Sal Manzo knew more about the source of those funds than I did, but banking ethics—even among the crooked—did not warrant any spilling of details to me.

"Amelia and I are leaving in a few days."

"You'll be fine. Perhaps we will see each other down the road." There was less doubt in his voice than the question implied.

Sal gave me another of his cards, writing his private number on the back. "Call me when you get back. The account is set up so that only you can make changes, and only in Aruba. That was Chiara's idea. She thought your relationship with the Colombians was... unbalanced. She wanted to protect your interests. If anything happens to you, your mother gets rich, but the Colombians get nothing."

That made sense: they could pressure me, but unless they wanted to sit with me in Sal's bank, and force me to sign, no transfers could take place. Sal really had no fear of those guys at all. I wondered if Sal let them know about the terms as well.

The next day, Amelia and I bought a second suitcase, and made our hotel rounds for the last time. When we checked out, it was at the concierge's desk. Fleur handed over the bill with a wink. It was for $10,000.00. I added five hundred each for her and Lukas, though with some qualms about putting Lukas behind the wheel of the hotel sedan with even higher-quality marijuana in his brain. Fleur had to remind me that I could pay with my bank credit card, which she swiped at her desk. After I signed for the whole stay, she stepped around the desk to hug Amelia and me.

I was going back to Cali, the city of which I knew nothing more than blood, immobility, isolation and then expulsion. But I met Amelia, and it was time for me to stake my claim to her hand and her life. Amelia told me about the night of blood and the months of immobility. Still, I went back with more questions than answers about the other things that happened to me there.

CHAPTER SEVEN

Sal Manzo's last favor to a new promising client was to procure for me the hotel rate which owners such as himself extended to others in the Caribbean. I settled into the seventeenth floor of the Hotel Inter in West Cali, at a price people paid at flea bag motels beside the interstates back home.

Amelia returned to her home each night by taxi, but the days belonged to us. She wanted me to know the city with a fondness not warped by the bloodiness in the Liverpool Bar; it was, after all, her home town. She also wanted to overcome her fear of the outside world and the types of people who lurked within it. We took to eating lunch at a new restaurant each day after my early morning workouts in the hotel basement. Each afternoon on our big hotel bed, Amelia would place her head on her boyfriend's growing belly—a source of pride for her—atop which she would order action movies from the hotel TV until she slept.

We were "comprometidos" now, unofficially engaged, but anxious for an occasion where we could make a formal declaration to her family. Amelia told me that she would contrive an occasion in which we could all meet together, so that she and I could carefully explain our plans to her parents. A phone call did come from her father, or rather, the office of her father, but not one to meet with her family, as I had expected. He was asking for my appearance in his office—without an explanation.

A young adjutant asked me in slow Spanish if I could be available in two hours for a meeting with the "Lieutenant Colonel." I should have felt suitor's nerves, but half-suspecting the Colonel as the source of the three million dollars, those feelings came and went like panic over a leaky roof during an earthquake. The Colonel had other things on his mind.

Amelia gave me that look when I told her about her father's phone call. It was the look that gave me wide berth to cut and slice my way through the world, the one that said Tommy would figure out the problem, and solve it, brutally or otherwise. Though I felt strongly that Amelia should go home by sundown, she decided to stay in the hotel after I left for my meeting, a turn of events that struck me as quizzical, as if Amelia wanted to give me a reassuring hug after spending an hour or so with the big, bad Colonel.

I had saved his daughter's life; let him bring what he must, I felt.

I left her there and met the jeep and driver in front of the hotel about 18:00. The adjutant drove in silence through the central spine of the city, and then south toward the pined hills that sloped upwards at the valley's edge.

A sentry saw us through the main gate of the base with just a wave. We sped through a complex of barracks and parked in front of a four-story building with antennae and dishes on the roof, but otherwise identical to others around it. The driver escorted me into a wide and long reception area clothed in military drab. The adjutant picked up the phone and dialed four numbers. He announced our arrival, listened and then replied, "Si, mi Colonel!" He showed me the way down a dark corridor, which we took the length of the building.

I walked in at my full height with the most serenity and presence I could command. Who was I kidding? There was the Buffalo Soldier, a man with bearing, elegance, and gravity; he belonged in purple tunic, rather than ill-fitting military khakis. He was the very one from within the cartoons my mind played at the beginning of its second infancy in the hospital. He was easily 6'4". He was not massive, but angular and smart in movement and poised while at rest. This was not to be a meeting of minds on any sort of equal basis.

He stood up behind his desk, and walked around it to greet me. His tie was loosened and his sleeves rolled up to the elbow, evidently pausing from deep involvement in command issues to deal with an apparent scofflaw of drearily predictable intentions. His glasses hung on his shirt from a lantern like they had asked to be relieved from the duties he placed upon them. He put out his hand briefly and took it back from me quickly, not quite sure what to do with it at the completion of the ritual.

"Lieutenant Colonel Aurelio Hernandez."

"Tommy Connolly."

"Please sit down, Tommy."

The choice was between two green washing machine-colored couches that shared a view from different angles through the window slats to the training field outside. I had an impulse to run out there and do volunteer push-ups while he watched from the window. I said nothing at first, since he had called the meeting. Oddly, he also did not speak, or tighten his tie, or put his jacket back on, all plausible ways with which to sever uncomfortable silence.

Finally, he spoke, in excellent English. Perhaps by habit, but his tone was that of someone giving an intelligence briefing toward a non-command figure. "Thank you for having come on such short notice. I have been aware of your presence back in Colombia. However, my office has many responsibilities involving matters of national importance. I am sure you understand."

"Completely, Colonel."

"Good—can I provide you with something to drink?"

"Perhaps an iced Coke." He picked up the phone and relayed an order for two iced Cokes to the adjutant.

He resumed in formal tones, delivered in a hard voice, one searching for a reason to soften itself on this occasion.

"I would like to thank you for saving my daughter's life. As you have come to realize, I would have lost her were it not for your actions that night."

I began to speak, but he pushed back with a palm in the air. "I know that your wounds have not completely healed, and may never heal satisfactorily for you. But you have my personal gratitude, and that of my family."

"You are welcome, Colonel."

It was the formal expression of gratitude he was obliged to make. But it did allow me to introduce my knowledge—and its source—about that night. "Amelia and I have spoken about that night, Colonel. I had no previous memories of that event, or any events in Colombia. Amelia has been able to help me reconstruct what happened in the Liverpool Bar, and the following months. Her version is that I took an appropriate action to save her, but was not lucky enough to save myself from danger."

"From the records, that would appear so."

His professional coolness was unnerving. He could have easily convinced me to confess membership in the Rosenberg spy cell at that moment. "Perhaps you are correct. You nearly lost your life. The problem is that your case has much greater scope than you or Amelia realize. I am not at liberty to explain why I took certain actions, particularly those that affected you. I hope you understand."

He lit a cigarette and smoked for a short while in silence. And then, for some reason, he changed his mind. He took his arms off his desktop and reached into a drawer. Carefully, he pulled out a file and placed it on his desk. "These are classified materials of the Colombian government. I cannot show you its contents, but.…"

His phone rang. "Excuse me." He picked up the phone and listened. "Si. Si. Bueno. Esta consigo? No, entonces donde? Quiere que? Ihueputa. Le llamo hace un ratico? De Donde? Ihueputa! Si, esta aqui. Si, Si. Todo con calma. Si. Conmigo. Ok. Hablamos entonces." Is she with you? No, then where? What does she want? Oh, for Christ's sake! Yes, he's with me. Everything is ok. He's fine. Ok. We'll talk later."

He was on the ropes during the length of the conversation; it was a phone call from his wife.

She was with Amelia, and they wanted something from him that vexed him. The adjutant came in with a green, chipped tray. He poured the Cokes and left them on the edge of the Colonel's desk. The formality, which modulated his severity, slipped down from eight to two. He put the Coke in front of me, reached into another drawer, pulled out a whiskey bottle, and raising it in front of my eyes for approval, poured us each a shot into our Cokes.

He got back on the phone, stamping down on a single number to reach the adjutant outside while he looked at his watch. "Traigame todo de el de esa noche. Si, el video tambien. Le explico despues." Bring me everything about that night. Yeah, the video too. I'll explain later.

He smiled his most wan smile. I took my first sip of whiskey in a very long time. Never a fan, I had to admit it had a unique calming effect on my nerves. The adjutant brought in a two-level stand with a VHS player and TV. He turned them both on and slipped in a tape. He handed the remote to the Colonel. "Gracias." The adjutant closed the door and left. "Since you are naturally curious, why don't we take a look at that night."

"How is that possible, Colonel."

He brought his hands together on the table, and looked from me to my glass, waiting for me to take my first sip. "To understand that night, we should start with the basic facts." Some urge, or rather some reassessment of factors known only to him, to share intelligence had come over him. He did not strike me as a man to whom fits of recklessness came frequently. He ran his hands through his head again. He tried another smile, but this one missed the greens too.

He wanted me to watch the tape; he was examining me as surely as if I were a patient on his couch.

"You arrived on an American Airlines flight from Houston. The terms of your employment at the U.S. Embassy began on January 1, 1997. Your employment was on the ground floor of the embassy in matters of visas and immigration. You were made aware of the security situation in Colombia and the need to avoid actions that would place you in harm's way. Despite that, you arrived a few days early, and in Cali, rather than Bogota."

For an intelligence officer, this was not a slight, forgettable error.

You took a taxi directly into Cali from the airport. The taxi driver suggested a stop on Avenida Sexta. You then asked the taxi driver to stop and let you out. You paid cash, crossed the street, and entered the 'Liverpool Bar.' You still had your suitcase, which you gave to the bartender. You ordered a beer and went back outside to get some empanadas, since you did not eat on the plane. Are these facts correct?"

"Yes." So far, none of this veered from Amelia's recollections.

He stopped and turned on the video. "These are video images that capture what happened next." It was a split-screen scene of the bar interior. The first image, from the rear corner, showed six to eight tables of couples and friends, perhaps twenty people in all. Amelia and her friends were absent, as they were against the rear wall. The image on the right, taken from the front of the bar, showed the groups of tables, and Amelia and her friends in the rear. I was midway down the bar, facing toward the bar, but occasionally glancing at Amelia.

The Colonel hit play. A skinny teenager in jeans, white t-shirt and a bandana entered the bar. The right image showed him from behind. He had a pistol in his hand. He slip/slid between three rows of tables, whose clients all hit the floor upon seeing the pistol. No one yelled "Asesino!" Amelia and her friends were unaware of any danger, quite happy with their beer and jokes and holiday vacation time together. The young, skinny shooter stopped across from me and raised his pistol. He shot from left to right, putting several bullets into the first friend before Amelia realized something was amiss.

Freighted with the horror of that night, Amelia was slightly off in her recollection. Actually, I grabbed a bar stool after the first girl was shot. I was not wild-eyed or terrified at all; in fact, my eyes narrowed like countless cowboys on dusty, backlot movie sets during the climactic duel scene.

The stool was made of heavy varnished wood. I lifted it up over my head in a relaxed manner—more like a caddy lifting up a golf bag than an adrenaline-kicked rush to get the motion started. By then, he had put a single bullet into the forehead of the second girl. His gun recoiled a little. During his third or fourth shot, I turned towards him, and began a roundhouse motion with the bar stool. It ended with the seat of the stool hitting the back of his head—low and square, expelling him forward and down onto the floor. He went straight down, unconscious and already bleeding onto the wooden floor from his neck.

The gun skidded away out of reach for either of us. My second blow was more like a miner's strike with a pick. It came crashing straight down on his head, now held in place by the floor below. He breathed out his last. I crashed the stool down on his head two more times. Blood flowed out now, unimpeded by the integrity of his scull, spreading into a large circle around him.

Amelia was immobilized by fear and panic, and the dread that she was next. At first, she seemed terrified of me. A second gunman entered, whom she saw before me, and alerted me with a lunge of her eyes back towards me. In the video, I looked down for the gun, which was too far away for me to recover. I immediately looked toward the approaching gunman, who was not expecting me to be there, or to put up a credible fight, as he wore no mask.

I ran over to cover Amelia as the gunman lined up his shot. There were now subtitles on the bottom of the screen in Spanish. I faced the gunman and said, "This bar is now under the protection of the U.S. Embassy. This woman is now a protected person under U.S. Embassy control. Leave now before U.S. authorities arrive."

The gunman laughed and extended his arms for a shot. I turned around and covered Amelia, closely like romantic dancers, to cover the width of her body within my own. I put her hands inside mine, and extended them upward. There were police whistles blaring outside. The gunman swayed his arm from side to side to get a clear shot at Amelia, who was well within the shell of my body. For the briefest of moments, we were locked tightly together. The shooter re-straightened himself and fired directly into my torso, concluding that I would drop, and he would have a free shot at Amelia.

Two bullets ripped into my upper right torso. My knees bent, and I slid a little. My lock on her hands brought Amelia down with me a little way down the wall. The gunman had a moment's chance at a head shot. At this moment, Amelia ripped her hands from mine. She put one on my waist to hold me up, and covered my head in a thin horizontal band with the meat of her elbow and forearm. The gunman shot at her darting head and missed. Some voices began screaming "Asesino! Auxilio! Auxilio!"The next bullet went through Amelia's arm and somehow into my head from behind my ear. My head jerked wildly to the left, and then fell on its right side, limp.

I managed to remain standing somehow, just as the gunman had turned and left, but I quickly weakened and crumbled downward. Amelia let me fall to the floor gently. Blood spread out around my torso and shot out in little flumes from my head. Amelia looked like one of the Trojan women in the dirt at her slave auction, her hair and face lined with the blood that slowly flowed down my head and onto the floor beside her. She put her hand on my head to stem the flow until the bartender brought her a towel.

She never once looked at her dead friends, who observed the whole scene like ghostly companions.

Turning away from the video player, I looked for a moment at the Colonel. He had to be thinking: how much easier if he had just died a real hero's death. At least, I would still have three million dollars.

I finished the rest of my drink in a single gulp.

The Colonel, from what I could tell, took a keen interest in his daughter's actions during the aftermath. She never screamed or attended to herself, and used her arm like a tool or a board, since her right hand fell limply and futilely, unworkable after the bullet smashed through her wrist. The blood from her arm fell onto my face as she frantically tried to stop my own blood loss. My head rested on her lap; I looked upwards toward her voice with closed eyes.

The Colonel stopped the video with a jabbing flick of the remote with his non-cigarette hand. "That must be very difficult for you to watch. But unless we start your story here, the rest of what I have to tell you will make no sense. You obviously know something about Colombia, but not enough to stay alive here under present circumstances. My intention was to remove you from the country and for you not to return. It was urgent to get you out of the country. It is in your interests still to leave Colombia."

"You had better tell me more then, Colonel."

"I will, but not now. You and I have an appointment."

"Does it involve small aircraft?"

He smiled, looking once again at my glass, which I grabbed in order to take a big gulp this time. "Not tonight. No. My wife—Amelia's mother—called. I have to take you back to the hotel. We are dining there at 8:00. Amelia's request." The word 'we' seemed to cause him significant grief.

"Colonel—one last question. Have you placed a security detail on Amelia and me?"

"Yes, Tommy. Since you arrived back in Cali."

He knew then that we were practically living as a couple out of that hotel. I looked at the frozen image of Amelia's unimaginable horror on the bloodied floor of the Liverpool Bar; it reminded me of the girl on the grass from the Kent State shooting—a girl with a good heart and strong character, but overmatched by a horror she could not fit into any scheme of things.

The video showed me as Amelia's valiant hero, but also as a cool, competent killer. Any criminal investigator would see the two separate actions: my cold dispatching of the first shooter—with all of its precise excess of force that was not necessary beyond the initial blow—took place before I realized there was a second shooter. My decision to take death to save Amelia would not excuse my earlier actions, at least as far as lex naturalis went.

My series of pick-axe thrusts into his sleeping brain on the bar floor split his scull in pieces. It was quick and clean: I counted four blows to his head, three of which occurred when he was probably already dead. What must the Colonel think of this first part of the video? This was the man who had spent a month in an Aruban resort with his only daughter. This was Tommy as killer. I looked toward him several times during the video, but he ignored my glances throughout.

The heroic thesis only found support after the arrival of the second gunman. I moved quickly over the body of the dead boy and in front of Amelia in a brief timed movement. My actions made this a tough assignment for the second shooter. He was not paid to shoot a gringo, or skilled in taking out a shielding bodyguard.

When I turned and covered Amelia's body, I must have known shots were going to cut me down, possibly down to death. My hands were tight on Amelia, her head down below on my chest, my nose taking a last smell of her raven hair. The two shots came quickly together, but I did not fall as he expected. I flexed outwardly and then crumpled downwards, my locked knees preventing a full collapse.

The Colonel excused himself from the room, at which point I began to feel the effects of the adrenaline from the video session; my head began to throb, and I reached into my pocket for a pill that I no longer had.

There were two men in that video. Was I the only one to see them both?

The Colonel returned with the same air of command in a grey suit and tie.

How many Tommys did you see, Colonel? I wanted to ask. Which one would you want near your daughter?

"This way." He pointed toward the anteroom door. I got up and led the way out of the building.

The Colonel and I got in the back seat of a green Range Rover. He had had several decades of adult life to ponder and weigh and to reconcile himself to his strengths and shortcomings—as father, professional, and man. I had no trajectory in an established career, no wife or children, no great sorrows that I had overcome, and from which I could gain some wisdom. The little I knew about myself was now completely painted over, and the new canvas was Janus-like, on the left, hero, on the right, assassin.

We drove mostly in silence with a lead and rear security detail. Only after the guards positioned themselves outside the hotel, and in the lobby, did we walk into the hotel. Amelia and her mother were on the low, sleek couches in the middle of the lobby, Amelia resplendent in a black, sleeveless dress. The Colonel did not seem to know how to mince his strides. It took almost a canter for me to keep pace with him.

I was sweating, uncomfortable, and short of breath. Nearly overwhelmed by so much truth delivered so efficiently through the video captures, I wondered if the Colonel wanted me this way at our first family gathering, or simply supposed that a man should see for himself his good works, manage his feelings calmly, and not fret too much about the strange twists of fortune.

Amelia stood and strode up to us. She suppressed a desire to hug me and gave her father a kiss instead. She did stand next to me and hold my hand as we walked toward her mother. Her mother stood up—short, red-haired and white-skinned, oddly enough.

"Buenas noches, senora." I shook her hand.

"Hello, Tommy. Nice to meet you at last," she said in lightly Southern-accented English. I looked at the Colonel, who remained inscrutable.

"Nice to meet you as well, Ma'm."

"You look good, Tommy. You have made a nice recovery."

"Have we met before, Mrs. Hernandez?"

"No, but Amelia described you pretty well."

"I would have liked to make your acquaintance, Ma'm." She laughed.

"You had other things on your mind at that time." Yeah, like bullet fragments, I thought, uncharitably. The Colonel took a timely look at his watch. "A las ocho, verdad?" He turned toward the lobby elevator, and we followed.

The view from the 20th floor of the hotel was spectacular at night. We looked east and south over the near high rises on the west side, and then out toward a sparkling carpet of houses and streets on a glistening, electrical grid.

The Colonel sat with his back to the window with a security detail of two men standing near the elevator, and two more at our sides.

The Colonel asked for Johnny Walker and soda, his wife a Manhattan, Amelia a Coke, and I sputtered in my response. "White Russian," which raised not a purr from the Colonel, but did not sit well with Amelia.

"Tommy—not yet, mi amor," she whispered to me. "Te helado," she said directly to the waiter.

The Colonel neither expected nor granted much conversational quarter that night. He had seen that film probably a dozen times, and now met the star in person, whom he treated like the outcome of a poor choice of casting. As a group, he looked at us from time to time, but mostly into the distance between and beyond us, or after signaling to one of the guards, he would whisper an instruction, which sent them scurrying out of the room.

The atmosphere was not leaden. Mother and daughter seemed less resigned to than practiced at lifting up the mood of a lifeless dinner with the Colonel. Neither did he meet my gaze for any masculine rapport or common cause. I fell in with the feminine tambourines then, which were pleasant, and still gave me moments to think about what the Colonel had decided to show me in his office. There was lively chatter about the mosquitoes near the river, the shopping, the electrical storms, and the rude taxi drivers in Cali.

What did the Colonel see that night?

The waiter came back with a wine menu that he passed to his wife, who handed it off to me. "Tommy, you are from California—why don't you help us with wine?" I picked up the wine list and looked at the California selections, which would have distinguished a tub of college sangria, but not a formal dinner. This being a steak house, I ordered an Argentine Bonarda and a Chilean Carmanere of recent vintage.

"Don't want a California wine?" asked Mrs. Hernandez.

"These suit the menu more than the California wines."

And in case of attack, the bottle makes a handy blunt instrument.

The waiter poured out four glasses from the first bottle after he took away our salads. With an assist from the noble grape, their conversation eventually poured over its banks and onto the common areas.

"How did you like Las Cabanas, Milly? Your father and I never stayed in Aruba before."

"Mama—it was like a palace. The view from the room was divina! The balcony overlooked the pool and the ocean. The breezes came every afternoon. We ate our meals by the pool most of the time."

"How did you like the hotel, Tommy?"

"It was… valuable for me. The service was excellent. There were many things I could not do at first. The hotel staff had to help me a lot."

"What do you mean?"

"At first, I could not walk across the street by myself. Someone from the hotel had to take me shopping. I would forget my room key card, and they would have to open my room for me. If my head bled, and the doctor was not there, the staff would have to help me clean the wound...."

Amelia kicked me for embarrassing her father since Nando had effectively abandoned me there, and returned to Cali, though admittedly with a prompt from Chiara Manso. "Later, I was able to enjoy the facilities of the hotel more and more." Mrs. Hernandez gave a peeved look at her husband, as unsecured details of my unsteady, solitary recovery in Aruba, which she must have determined were under her husband's control, became common, family knowledge.

When the waiter came with the dessert and coffee, Amelia brightened and spoke to him directly. "We would like a bottle of champagne." The Colonel did not respond to this enthusiasm, either. I did. The charm of his company had failed to make its mark on me. He was a legend in intelligence circles in Colombia, but as a dinner partner, he would have been aptly placed in one of those photos of members of the Soviet Politburo observing a May Day parade.

"Great idea, Amelia."

While we waited for the champagne to arrive, Amelia held the floor with tidbits of "Tommy and I..." this and that, concerning events of the last few days. Finally, the champagne arrived, popped, and settled. We took our glasses and raised them. Amelia stood up, holding her glass in one hand and mine in the other.

Throw the guy a softball, Amelia. Keep it light and not too sentimental. Don't force him to embrace me too early—I could still get traded on to another team.

Unconsciously, she put her hand on her stomach. "Here is to the next generation of the family. I'm pregnant! Mommy, Daddy—I am going to have a baby!"

Oh, God! He hasn't worked out whether I am a grifter or a killer, and now we're family.

I tried my best to smile. How could one not welcome this news without utter joy? Well, if you had just watched yourself crack a boy's scull into small pieces, and take three kill shots to your head and torso, you might not be oriented toward the higher, more soul-blossoming emotions.

The Colonel gave a wan smile that signified nothing but evasion. He must have been livid. Just because I saved his daughter from death, he must have reasoned, does not mean that I should presume to knock her up and marry her. He chose not to intervene in Aruba, and by the time we arrived in Cali, Amelia was already pregnant. It meant for him that he had lost almost all control over his daughter to a young, uncouth grifter, one who took advantage of his daughter's tragedy to insinuate himself into her bed and his family. It was, for the Colonel, a situation that would require careful thought—and management.

But it was Amelia's night. The Colonel and I both knew this. We agreed in a single instantaneous glance to let matters between us stay below the surface for a while. This was, after all, another way in which Amelia had chosen to close her mind to the past, so I put on my best smile and grabbed onto her hand, kissing her on the cheek and whispering in her ear that I loved her. Her mother looked at me with comical feigned bother.

Amelia's mother stood up and approached me, placing her hand on my shoulder to assert some physical acceptance of me. She bent over to hug me and whispered in my ear, "It will all be ok, Tommy. We are a family. We protect each other." She smiled, grazing my cheek with her hand as she walked back to her seat.

I leaned over and kissed Amelia again on the lips. I directed my comments to her, so that her parents would not construe my feelings as a follow-up speech. "That is the most wonderful news I have ever received. I will try my best to be a good father to our baby, and… " I meant it, but wondered at the same time who was speaking at that point.

Her mother called the shots from that point onward in the conversation.

"When did you find out, Milly?"

"Yesterday, Mommy! I went to a clinic, and they did the test. It was positive."

"How far along are you?" If she would have stopped there, there would remain a few salt shakes of ambiguity, enough for me to deal with the Colonel by jumping from pad to pad atop our little pond.

It quickly crumbled. "He thinks about a month." Another way of looking at the calendar would be Aruba, week one. I gave the Coronel the sort of smile one gives to a neighbor when he notices that you have chopped down his prized rose bush.

The Colonel drank the rest of his glass.

"Daddy, say something!" Yes, like your initial impulse to let me bleed out in the emergency room. Or, using your police contacts in Aruba to take me on a short boat ride. Or, having my visa revoked in Colombian customs. A theater in the round of lost possibilities must have tormented him in that moment. But his silence on the matter could just have easily indicated that he was just mulling on-going operations against a powerful drug clan.

"Amelia, I think that is wonderful news. I am so happy for you, sweetheart." There was no mention of me, a fact that raised the eyebrow of his wife.

"Tommy, congratulations!" She raised her hand to get the waiter's attention. "Let's get another bottle!" Amelia seemed to get the differentiated responses she wanted.

The Colonel looked at his watch and finally put an end to our merriment.

"Amelia, you should drink less now and sleep more. Let's go, shall we?" He stood up.

"Tommy, I'll send a jeep for you tomorrow about 08:00."

"Daddy, tomorrow is Saturday. Let him rest!"

"We have many things to discuss, Amelia."

He transferred his look to me.

"Is that alright, Tommy?"

"08.00 is fine, sir." Mrs. Hernandez got up and put on her sweater, but Amelia made no move to stand, so I whispered in her ear.

"My love, go with your father."

"No, Tommy. I want to stay with you. We are a family now."

"Amelia. Please. Go with him." She stood up gingerly and walked to the other side of the table near her father.

I gave them about a five-minute lead, and then headed for the hotel bar in the lobby. I needed Gerry Mulligan's Prelude in E Minor; or, a twelve-pack and one of the bluffs where we sat and drank after Friday night football games along the Delta. I settled for a double whiskey, scanning the bar now and then for the guy with nothing to do that night but watch and report on Tommy C.'s more pertinent activities.

CHAPTER EIGHT

A military jeep stopped in front of the hotel entrance a few minutes after 08.00. It was Nando in the driver's seat this time, smiling at people who crossed the jeep to enter the hotel, all the while gleefully aware of my discomfort since he was more or less in control of my movements once again. We had not seen each other since my episode of infantile glee in Sal's bank, so I did not imagine that Nando wanted much to renew ties with me, at least under conditions he could not ultimately control, which that morning's agenda suggested was a possibility. But his money was now in my hands, so he had to accord me some civility, however forced.

He looked smart in aviator glasses and a polo shirt, quite out of uniform, but still sheathed within a military bearing that would have driven women away in an American bar, but impressed the locals. I got in the jeep without much enthusiasm. This time Nando put out his hand to shake mine, smiling snidely. He started in colloquial Cali Spanish. "Good morning, marika. Nice to see you again."

"Likewise, Nando."

"You look good. First class hotels agree with you."

"Amelia and I will invite you over sometime."

He drove the familiar route down the tree-shaded riverside roads of West Cali to the central trunk and then south to the edge of the city. We parked and took the long walk down the dark corridor to the Colonel's office. I hazarded the guess that the Colonel preferred to work while standing, as he was behind his desk in full uniform, looking down at an open file on his desk in deep thought. Peering up at our approaching figures, he closed his working file and walked around his desk to greet us.

"Good morning, Tommy."

"Good morning, Colonel."

He motioned me toward the rear couch, while he and Nando grabbed the two green chairs, and pushed them toward me in identical flanking movements until they were on each side of me. This time there was coffee and china on a tray on the table.

"Coffee, marika?"

"Yeah, Nando." He poured three cups and handed one to me. I helped myself to the cream. And just like that, the Colonel began.

"Tommy, since the shooting in the night club, life has changed for all of us. Due to your prolonged rehabilitation, you are the only one who does not realize how much. I want to take you back to that night, if you don't mind."

Of course, I wanted to know all those facts that Amelia could not tell me, or could not deduce from her father and Nando's actions up until now.

Not sensing reluctance on my part, he continued.

"It is the real starting point for our discussion. Permit me to retell the story of that night from a different perspective. Amelia was spending a night out with friends from her high school. They all attended different universities in Bogota, and seldom saw each other there. She called me from home at this office to tell me her plans. You have seen the tape, Tommy. The sicario walked calmly past many tables and only shot at Amelia's. He was paid for a specific target. He attempted to kill all three girls, so that the investigation would have been much more complex for us. He could have shot everyone in the bar, but that would have taken much more time."

"The night of the shooting, I saw Amelia at the hospital. She was in shock. She was unable to provide me with important details about the event, so I returned to the bar with Nando. The local police were already there, and in the midst of their investigation. I told the officer in charge that there was a national security aspect to the crime scene. He handed over the security tape, and we began the process of formally interviewing witnesses and gathering evidence. The statements of the witnesses agreed on the essential details."

"I also looked into your background. It only took about an hour to trace your movements in Colombia and your destination at the U.S. Embassy. On that basis, I got in touch with the desk officer in Bogota, and explained the situation. They took over the task of notifying your family, including Ambassador Faraday. The embassy agreed on the need for secrecy about the crime, its details, and your involvement."

"Pardon me, Colonel, but I don't understand. Why the need for secrecy?"

The Colonel looked at Nando and resumed. "The U.S. Embassy is by nature the most powerful building in any city or country in the world. Especially, in a small country such as Colombia. It would lose credibility—it would invite repeat attacks even—if the world actually knew how easy it was to assassinate an embassy employee. You were not the target, but the world would not see it that way."

Nando, who had listened thoughtfully to his father, continued, also in English. "A lot of groups, especially the FARC, would use your death as propaganda value. They would claim ownership of the event, and try to drive a wedge between our governments. There are a lot of pending deals at all levels between us right now. This could have been a distraction, or it could have caused real trouble in your Senate and ours."

The Colonel resumed his narrative. "The next morning, I spoke with your father on the phone. He understood the need for secrecy, and asked me to personally handle security for your person. I told him I would be glad to do this. We spoke almost every day for a few weeks. You were in a coma, and we had no knowledge if or when you would ever come out of it."

I would have died alone, in other words.

"During that time, our investigation deepened. We followed several tracks. One, the target was Amelia. We still do not know why. Two, at least one sicario was local and hired by the second shooter for the job. There are at least several narco or guerrilla groups who would wish to harm me, my family, and this institution."

We all have our problems, Colonel, I thought. "Why was it necessary to rush me out of the country?"

The Colonel resumed his analysis after my hasty interruption. "Your involvement in the shooting began as rumor and became factual for a great many people. Of course, we tried to contain any knowledge of your whereabouts and condition to as few people as possible. But a hospital is a large place with many people who knew about your stay. On the other end of things, we interviewed all the people in the bar and asked them not to speak to anyone in the press about the incident. We were thereby able to keep it out of the newspapers and TV news."

"We started hearing interest in you from intercepted FARC communications, what you call 'chatter' in English. They discussed the idea of raiding the hospital so that they could finish their initial strike against imperialism. No one would dare dispute their ownership if that occurred. They even offered money for information about your whereabouts. We moved you to a safer part of the hospital as soon as we received permission from Dr. Howe."

"Your father fully understood the political and security rationale and agreed with our decisions. We did not want him to come to Cali, but he wanted to see you. I understood as a father, but unfortunately, his presence confirmed your importance; it also put his own life in danger. There was a real possibility in the first few weeks that you would die. Your brain swelled up. You had infections in your lungs and ear canal. Your back wounds did not heal well, since the doctor ordered minimal movement of your body. During your coma, follow-up surgery would have been impossible, so all the major surgeries took place in the first 48 hours. Ultimately, your father agreed not to come until you were clearly out of danger."

Translation: no longer likely to die.

"Your scull could barely contain that big head, marika," Nando said, chuckling at his own well-timed joke.

The Colonel resumed. "He stayed for two days. There were more intercepts about his visit. The FARC determined that you were his son and this deepened their interest. It became an issue of dead or alive. Dead, you provided propaganda value; alive, you were an ideal kidnapping victim: sedated, disoriented, and immobile."

He paused to gauge how much of this information I was capable of accepting. "There is a thread here Tommy that you must see. All the information about the shooting, your participation, your movements were sold to the FARC. That information was in government hands, either within the walls of the hospital, on this base, or within the walls of your embassy."

"It leaked out either for profit or to support the FARC's political and military goals. When I received credible information about an attack upon your person, I acted."

"Why not just hand me over to U.S. authorities?"

"Because no one knew about your whereabouts, including your side. The U.S. embassy leaks, too. There are quite a few Colombian civilian employees with pro-FARC beliefs. Your father agreed with my approach. One benefit of this experience is that we are following several leaks from the embassy and this building."

Nando cut in once more. "The morning after you left the hospital, we actually staged a fake hand off at the Cali Airport. We found a mono about your height and dressed him in bandages. We walked him across the tarmac and flew him to a base south of Bogota. Sure enough, marika, the FARC knew about the flight. They thought you were now in the United States. They stopped seeking information about you."

The Colonel read my thoughts adequately. "Tommy, the best intelligence operation is in one's own backyard, as an American would say. You control all the variables. The exfiltration of you into Aruba was an operation in neutral territory. We had little time to prepare. We have few contacts and limited local knowledge there. And to be honest, Tommy, you were one of several operations we ran simultaneously. We landed with the cooperation of local intelligence officials. However, the DEA found out and decided to accompany the local police on an interdiction that the locals never intended to undertake. When the DEA found out they had been duped, they were not happy."

"They demanded a briefing, which would have undermined the secrecy we had maintained for several months. Our intention was to clean you up in the hotel, take you to the bank, and then drop you back at your hotel with a doctor and a guard until U.S. officials came for you. Once more, we could not control all the variables. The doctor turned out to be a… a tourist hotel doctor. The drug he gave you was one whose properties a head surgeon would have known and avoided. Instead, he gave you a strong dose. You became delirious."

And Sal Manzo smelled a rat and stepped on it.

There was a huge hole in his description of the operation. "But why didn't you leave me with the guard? Why did you have to take me to the bank?" The Colonel took command again.

"Because, Tommy, we had two objectives. The first was to deliver you safely to U.S. authorities in Aruba as agreed. The second was to open up a bank account in your name and signature for one million dollars."

I stood up, now looking down at each of them with real anger in my voice. "Are you joking? Did I ever ask you for money? Is that how you see me?"

Nando shot up as well, easing his way toward me until our noses nearly touched, and finally speaking in a near whisper. "You would be well advised never to speak to the Colonel that way again, Tommy."

I looked right into his eyes as well. "You would be well advised to stay the fuck away from me, Nando." He stepped back but remained closely on guard in case I erupted again. I felt sure that my face at that moment was eerily similar to the one just before I crashed a bar stool down on a young street killer's head.

Nando learned something at that moment about me, while I saw that Nando had never killed or probably even harmed a guerrilla or a narco in his life.

"The money was to show you our appreciation for what you did for Amelia..." He put his cup on the table. "... and to pay you to forget about Amelia and never return to Colombia."

I dropped my cup. It landed on the green-yellow carpet and poured out. The spoon was left orphaned in my left hand, an image which Nando seized on immediately, though he did nothing. "What the fuck? Money? In a foreign bank account?" I cast a hard gaze at Nando, daring him to wave his little yellow caution flag at me again. The Colonel's gaze was indifferent upon me, as if this was just another bit of impertinence during a routine interrogation.

Nando, unwilling to take up the challenge of my anger once again, tried to soften the impersonality of all their explanations with his own colloquial English. It was a weak performance by many standards.

"Tommy, it was nothing personal, hombre. We honored your sacrifice—your health, your career. The embassy is not going to pay for your future care. But we had to think about Amelia, too. She needed treatment for trauma, not to take care of you. She was becoming obsessed, man! She threatened her own security by staying at the hospital. She disappeared from school and all her friends. She only wanted to take care of you. It was not normal, marika."

I pulled out a handkerchief and cleaned my shoe. There was a tear in my eye that I could not remove in front of them, so I turned and wiped it away. I looked directly at the Colonel at that moment.

"This is the result of your intelligence analysis of me, that I would take a million dollars and leave you alone?"

Nando continued to assist his father. "Tommy, it was a million for saving my sister's life. The understanding between men was separate. We could not explain all these details in your condition. You would not have understood that your life will never be completely secure in this country. You barely understand now. You are not in California, hombre."

I ignored Nando, my gaze never leaving the Colonel's almost placid face.

"Did you have us followed in Aruba, Colonel?"

"No, Sal Manzo did not answer our calls," Nando continued. I continued to press for answers from the Colonel. The DEA looked at you a few times until your father told them to back off."

"I probably have a DEA file now."

"My gardener has a DEA file. Big deal," snarled Nando.

"So we were not tracked or followed, and you did not attempt to rescue Amelia?"

"We are not the mafia, marika... we are a family. She only spoke to her mother at first. There was more than a little understanding between them. Mrs. Hernandez realized you were not a threat to Amelia, and that Amelia was happy with you. It is not the first time a woman in her family had run away with a handsome stranger."

Nando tipped an obsequious and silly hat at his father.

The Colonel gently worked his way back into the conversation, appearing reluctant to speak about his feelings concerning Amelia. The thought came to me in that moment that throughout all these events, he acted like a Lieutenant Colonel, but he also experienced things—brutal and mean—as a father. "She would not speak to me until I promised her I would not interfere."

The Colonel stood up, apparently seeking a break from tawdry details of individual human emotions, even those of his daughter, thereby declaring the current flow of conversation to be boxed and ready for shipment. "Let's go get some breakfast."

Only one million of that money was intended for me. The Colonel had the wherewithal then to gather one million dollars for me, and another two million dollars for account owners unknown, or known by Sal Manzo. Did my father know about this? Was he the source of that money? Did he suggest or acquiesce to a cash payment to his son, both for his noble sacrifice and hasty departure?

I knew at that moment the whole truth about my injuries, isolation, and exfiltration; it made me angry and small. My father, the Colonel, and Nando: they had each made correct decisions in a timely fashion under conditions of personal and command duress. That was how the report would read, even if I was its reluctant author. They protected my person, and only at the end of my personal safeguarding, they were sloppy in Aruba, which personally cost me nothing more than a month at a luxury resort free of charge.

My only quarrel then was with the million dollar payoff, but I was not yet a father, and could not know the anguish of the Colonel since last Christmas in the Liverpool Bar.

Amelia did not know about anything we discussed that morning; she could never know. We all had an interest in never disclosing these terms to her, especially the Colonel, who, after a series of lies to her, tried to buy off the father of her children so that he would not ruin her life. Still, it was unseemly. The Colonel could have set up a medical trust fund with that money. He could have given it to my father. Instead, Nando walked me dumbly into a bank so that I could sign for it and leave on the next flight.

They did a good job of keeping me alive; and in the end, I finagled my way back to Amelia, winning her heart honestly. Still, humiliation was becoming my brand around these people.

This also explained why Nando had never brought up the subject of money until now. I had absconded with only part of their family fortune. I knew roughly what a Lieutenant Colonel brought home in the United States. It was enough for Amelia to study at a first-class university, but not enough to fill four duffel bags with rubber-banded stacks of U.S. currency. How did the Colonel find three million dollars in cash? Who put him in touch with a savvy money launderer like Sal Manzo? I knew it was tainted money; the only question was from whom, and for performing what kind of timely services.

Things began to go click in my brain at that moment.

I looked at each of them, individually, and then as a team; their glances bore back into me, issuing a friendly warning that I should direct my curiosity about their side businesses elsewhere. They had insulted me with their cash-based dismissal of me, as well as their fraudulent concern for Amelia's psychological well-being. Their position as men in their family had weakened; it wasn't too late to walk away with their cash—I could stand up and turn around and get Amelia on the next plane to Miami.

But I didn't. I was still short on facts, but I knew something about those two, something they would not want Amelia to know, not now or ever. If I was not a match for those men at that moment, then I would be later. Their business—or businesses, for all I knew, would cause them to protect their secrets, but they would not kill me. My plans changed at that moment. I earned that money and intended to keep it—all of it. If it was the product of honest effort or savvy investing, they would have asked me for it by then, but I knew that they did not want to have that conversation.

We parted after breakfast outside the mess—Nando and I heading back uptown, The Colonel returning to his office—without any immediate plans to meet again.

I went back uptown and stayed there for the next few months, ignoring for as long as I could Nando's attempts to reengage me on a personal level through lunch appointments, or minor real estate deals for which he needed a signatory.

Instead, I kept my appointments and got to know the city. Amelia showed me the schools she attended as a girl, and—Cali being Cali after all—the mansions of the mostly-deceased leaders of the Cali Cartel. I imagined that Amelia had extraordinary beauty even then, causing her father to cloak her with security between home and school, on the curb outside birthday parties, or trailing behind as she walked in a mall with her mother.

An eye surgeon said that the bullet fragments had bumped up right next to the nerves behind me eye, enough so that I could see at distances decently, but not focus on written materials for any length of time. In other words, I was then—and probably would be forever more—a headlines reader, someone who had to get things right the first time, or not at all. Doctor Howe was pleased at my progress during my bi-weekly visits, since by then I was swimming daily in a club pool, and lifting weights seriously about three times a week, but not at all pleased that I had skipped out on my pill regimen without his approval. I never mentioned the hotel bar.

I was moved by his concern. He still considered me his patient, with all the attendant privileges to medically examine me and to hector me for perceived lapses from courses of behavior which he assumed, from our brief discussions in the barracks, I would carry out in good faith. I could not tell him that my flight to Aruba was involuntary, but I did tell him about Dr. Hilliard's tenure as my physician, which left Dr. Howe with a low opinion of hotel doctors.

He ordered me not to fly for three months under any circumstances, or even to go to Bogota, which after all has an elevation of about eighty-five hundred feet. He put me back on pills; if I planned to drink, I would have to skip them for a few days. At the end, he asked to speak to Amelia in private, which rather shut down any possibility of gaming his efforts to ensure my continued recovery.

Amelia, loved by the Gods even during pregnancy, did not show any baby bump, and even lost weight during her second trimester. She carried twin girls, quietly forming at a slow, relaxed, and medically-impressive pace in Amelia's abdomen.

We even had our first argument during a rainy afternoon at the movies in a midtown shopping mall. Amelia, inured by careful cultivation as the princess of a man of public honor, was content to accept the official version of most things. She could see the rottenness all around her, but felt that a great distance lay between her family and the gangsters that ruled the fringes of Cali.

The movie, sentimental, held aloft by an intrusive soundtrack and resort to the same joke repeatedly told with only minor changes throughout the movie, was greatly entertaining for Amelia, who easily followed the English and the story, and was content to take the story at face value. I left about half way through, only coming back to greet her when it was over.

"It was just a movie, Tommy, you are just supposed to laugh and have fun, not write a review in your head as you watch it!"

"It is a classic example of a director who thinks he is making one statement, when he actually makes another… Forrest Gump was an exculpatory tour through modern American history."

"What do you mean, Tommy?"

"He represents—whether the director planned it that way or not—an American innocence and lack of culpability for our actions. We did not kill two million Vietnamese under a dubious pretext; after all, we simply stumbled in as poor, slow-thinking idiots and made a few mistakes. Every wrong thing we do is ok since we are just big-hearted hillbillies at heart. It was offensive, Amelia, sorry."

"Tommy, sometimes you think too much. Not everything has hidden meaning—it just does for you. I think you are wrong. Forrest had a good heart—a pure one—that is all the director was saying. That you need courage to succeed, not intellectual gifts."

"I hope so."

Not winning the argument, not sure of my point anymore, and sensing that Forrest Gump bothered me for other reasons, ones having to do with Tommy-Forrest similarities, I changed the subject to baby clothes.

"You know, we haven't bought the girls any baby clothes." Amelia, still peeved at me, too well-mannered to turn her victory into a rout, rerouted the conversation.

"Tommy, have you thought anymore about where we will live?" Of course, I had. If Doctor Howe had not grounded me for three months, I probably would have slipped away to Miami by then, letting the Colonel know by phone call from the Miami airport.

The security situation in Colombia was deteriorating, not only in the far mountains, but on the streets of Cali, where narcos had taken to shooting up night clubs again after the decade-long truce during the rule of the Cali Cartel. It made bile rise in my throat to merely think about it, but we needed her family.

"Amelia, I want you to stay near your mother. These are your first babies. You will need her help. She will not want to leave Cali for the United States. I like Cali. I have started my new life here. I am not scared here. If you feel unsafe, we will go to Aruba, or Miami or New Orleans; I will work for the Bubba Gump Shrimp Company. Otherwise, we will stay here. Is that ok?"

"I am always a little scared here, but I don't think that will be different in Aruba or Miami."

"So, let's buy a house near your parents, or a condo up in the air." She smiled so innocently at the thought, perhaps thinking that money came from a settlement with the State Department or some existing life insurance I carried.

"Ok, mi amor."

It was really no more than that—we wanted a place to have babies.

The next day Amelia and I were the first customers at the Range Rover dealership in Ciudad Jardin. I assented to a Black Range Rover with a modern control panel of gadgets and a cup holder large enough for a beer can. What I held in confidence between the salesman and me was the repaneling of the windows with bullet-proof glass. About a week later, it was ready for Amelia, who drove a car whose windows and wheels could both withstand bullets fired from close range from someone with the completely suicidal notion of ever bringing harm to Amelia Connolly.

The next week, I took a chunk of the three million dollars and bought a high-rise condo in San Antonio, in the luxurious hills above the fog line in the western part of the city. It looked down from twelve floors in an Olympian manner on most of Cali. It had views in four directions on its two floors, and a sweeping staircase to our huge bedroom upstairs.

We filled the place with obscenely expensive furnishings. After I set up the grotesquely sized TV, we sat on our new couch where I clicked it on. The television news reporter was about fifty miles north of Cali; evidently, there had been unusual killings of bus drivers and gas station workers for the past few weeks.

"What's goin' on, Amelia."

"Just the bastards from the Cartel del Norte. They are clearing their zone."

"Huh?"

"If there are no busses and no gas, then no one can travel there. In that way, they can run their cocaine laboratories and no one will bother them."

The reporter stood quietly for a moment, having cued the pre-recorded part of his investigation. He talked about an escalation of murder between two narco gangs that vied for the remnants of the roots, laboratories, and cash of the Cali Cartel.

"It's madness, Tommy, they just shoot people because they have the guns and no one else does. Without cocaine, these people would be selling chatarra on street corners. They were the lavaperros for the Cali Cartel. They were not paid to think—just wash the dogs of the capos. Now, they are billionaires. There were sixteen bodies found last week in

Cali. We knew one of the men they killed. His name was Bustamante. He was a prosecutor in Cali—he was crooked, like most of them—and went to prison. As soon as he got out, the goat-fuckers from the North of the Valley kidnapped him and then tortured him until he died. I played with his daughter when I was a girl."

"Why?"

"For what he had in his head… they probably thought he knew the location of the remaining caletas of the Cali Cartel."

"What is a caleta, mi amor?"

"A hiding place for money. They rip open the walls and stuff them with cash. Only the capos and one man know the address of the caleta. With so many dead now, the goat-fuckers probably thought he knew."

I switched off the news at that point, making it a point not to go back to the habit. Amelia had the means now for a significant return to happiness: a bullet-proof car, a palace high in the sky, and a husband who was not on steady ground in many respects, but knew he would kill to protect her.

The whole valley of earthly troubles was now below Amelia, unable through any means of entering our fortress to further trouble her. After she had our babies, only I would have to attend to the viciousness of life below, while I would tell her sweet lies about whatever I had to do to make a living down there.

"Why don't I connect the video player to the TV, mi amor. In that way, you can practice English and learn a few things about life in the United States.

"Ok, Tommy. The news here is not good for the babies."

That settled, I proposed to Amelia formally at our favorite restaurant on the bend of the Cali River the next day. We married on a damp Christmas morning in between services in a poor Catholic church parish.

The Colonel was not shy about using his influence to take over half a restaurant or an entire beach to meet the security needs of his family. His influence with the church—at least in our case—was no more or less than an average citizen. I was not a Catholic; nor did I agree to take Catholic rights during the ceremony. This, as well as the lack of social significance in Amelia's choice of groom, precluded our union in the major churches in Cali.

A Catholic priest in a small church agreed to allow the ceremony in his church for a healthy fee, one that would allow him to tend to his poor parishioners with money from the political oligarchy he apparently despised, Che appearing next to Jesus in the photos behind his office desk.

Amelia required modifications to her dress. She was now about six months pregnant and showing an ample bump about the stomach. We exchanged rings and kissed, and then after a dinner with her family, which included wedding presents from Ambassador Faraday and his wife, we returned to our condo in the clouds as Mr. and Mrs. Thomas Connolly.

We had no plans beyond bringing our babies up to the tower with us and living peacefully.

On one of the last days of 1997, Nando woke me up with an early morning phone call and told me to be downstairs in the lobby in an hour. "Asshole," I thought. Then, I went.

CHAPTER NINE

Nando shook my hand without much genuine interest beyond testing my physical strength.

"Good morning, marika. Get in."

"Where are we going?"

"You are going to get a haircut. It was the Colonel's idea. We can't have a lice outbreak near his grandchildren."

He always checked his teeth in the mirror of his car after the consummation of—in his estimation—a clever remark.

We drove into the center of the city, and then out towards the church where Amelia and I married only a few days before. After a few blocks of circling the same streets, and checking for tails, Nando took a sudden right, parking in the middle of the block, in front of barber pole on the right side of a glass door.

"Ok, marika. Off you go. Ask for Stevenson." Nando, after shouting at a store keeper to bring him a beer so that he would not have to leave his jeep, peeled away from the curb without further instructions.

I walked into a classical, three-stool barbershop, one that could have been on Main Street in thousands of small towns or Norman Rockwell paintings. In my town, it was on Wright Street and had six chairs that faced each other in teams of three. Old Man Banner was the name boys gave to the barber who shaved the heads of the boys when I was a child. In this one a short, squat dark-skinned man awoke from his nap in one of the barber chairs. Smiling away his embarrassment, he stood up quickly to the ringing of the door's entry bell. He wiped down his white smock as he approached me.

"Good morning, Sir."

"Hello, I would like a haircut."

"Of course, Sir," he beamed, pointing me toward the center chair. He cut and clipped about my scalp for about ten minutes, all the way trying to engage me in conversation about my business in Colombia, which reminded me that so far, I had none. My hair was thicker now; he would have had to take off all my hair to see the scars that were now the beginning of a pink zigzag behind my ear. The grand finale was a few minutes of hot towels and a single-blade shaving of my face; he even rubbed oils through my hair.

I gave him a tip about twice the amount of the haircut. "Is there anything else I can do for you Sir?"

"I would like to speak to Stevenson." His bright smile became slightly forced, as if I came with ulterior motives rather than the enjoyment of his noteworthy service and bonhomie. He pointed at a door to the right of a sink in the rear of the room. Seeing him reach for his broom, I walked to the door and knocked.

"Come in." I slowly opened the door into a dusky, smelly room with a single ceiling fan and a military surplus desk with file cabinets. On the wall behind the desk was a map of Colombia. There were no books or plants or photos, nothing to connect the occupant with a family or profession or even a hobby. In his desk ashtray the butts of about twenty cigarettes lay like the crumpled dead.

A man in dark polyester slacks and a striped shirt approached me as if for a donation for his own treatment. He was light-skinned and narrow-faced; his wire-rimmed glasses rested about midway down his nose. The bald spot on the crown of his head gave way to a stubble of grey hair. He extended to me a bony hand with fingers dyed yellow with nicotine.

"Shall we speak in Spanish?" I nodded back.

"You must be Tommy. I'm Stevenson."

I shook his hand firmly. "Nice to meet you, Sir." He unfolded a chair from between the two file cabinets, and placed it in front of his desk.

"Would you like something to drink?"

"Maybe some bottled water." Stevenson went swiftly to the door in quick strides to shout out an order for two bottles of water and some cigarettes.

I looked upward at the single light bulb and the ceiling fan, which gathered upwards the rank tobacco smoke hanging above his desk and dispersed it along the ceiling and then back down the walls, so that the fetid air actually had a white, hazy form. I felt queasy before he lighted his first fresh cigarette.

Stevenson spoke Spanish with the more formal Bogota accent, which next to the informal twangs of the local Cali accent, gave the listener the feeling of being called to chambers. "How are you getting along these days, Tommy?"

"Fine, Sir."

"You look healthy. Any lingering effects from the bar incident?"

"Once in a while, but they are manageable." He did not start off with conversational niceties or the slow sales approach. He began the conversation as close to his topic as he could reasonably begin.

This was almost like a request for a fitness report, so he knew the history of my recovery from the hospital to the present day. He was, more than likely, either engaged in off-the-books military intelligence, or retired and kept abreast of events by the Colonel. I looked at his yellow skin and bony limbs. He looked to be about the same age of the Colonel, but his desiccated skin made him look years older.

"Are you taking medication?"

"Yes…" He waited for me to continue.

"I take pain medication for my back and a blood thinner."

The barber knocked, and quickly entered the room with two bottles of water and a pack of cigarettes. Stevenson took the last cigarette from his present pack, lit it, and threw the previous pack away in a small garbage can under his desk. He paused to carefully formulate his next question.

"A little under three months ago you had an appointment with your doctor, is that correct?" This sounded uncomfortably close to an interrogation, having now entered the realm of private matters between Dr. Howe and myself.

"That is not a matter for discussion, Sir. If you asking that particular question, you already know the answer, so why don't we just skip over the formality."

He tried again, and from an equally uncomfortable perch just beyond the obvious prerogatives of my private life.

"Tommy, have you made any long-term plans?"

"Not as yet, Sir."

"So, I take it you have some free time these days."

"Yes, I guess so."

There was a hint of malice in his interest in my livelihood. Nando, the Colonel, Stevenson: these were all men who commanded others; it was elemental in their world that I find myself in some kind of complementary, civilian command, one where I would report to a location and undertake specific tasks toward an overall objective. My trips to the gym and dinners with Amelia were hardly the stuff of directed duty for these guys.

The new flow of tobacco smoke from Stevenson's lungs floated across the table and, being sucked up into the fan, sideswiped me on its way toward the nearest air pocket. I was beginning to feel nauseous.

"Tommy, I want to discuss a proposition with you."

I wiped my dry eyes, wincing to induce some moisture into them.

"Go ahead, Sir." With my handkerchief in my hand, I poured some water onto it, which I rubbed onto my face and into my eyes. Stevenson, his cigarette held aloft by his elbow on the edge of his desk, looked at me oddly.

"I want you to think about working with me."

"Here in the barber shop?" He laughed suddenly, causing him to cough deeply in his lungs.

"No, we are not accepting applications in the barber shop at present." I fell back on a charm that held no interest for Stevenson.

"Pity, Sir. It is a trade where I think I could make a contribution." He put out his cigarette atop the mound of butts in the ashtray.

"That may be true, Tommy… however, I was thinking about a transportation company." I took another sip of my water. This was the formal beginning of his pitch.

"I'm listening, Sir."

"Air transport—from Cali and Medellin to the islands. Standard stuff—fill planes with goods and fly them to a destination for a fee."

Of course, it was nothing so simple or elegant or honest or aboveboard; otherwise, we would be meeting in a hotel on the west side near our condo, and not in furtive conditions in the rear of an unsuccessful barber shop. Further, I was not a pilot, nor had I any notion about airport protocols or plane maintenance.

"I am not a pilot, Sir," stating the obvious and expecting the conversation to peter out amicably.

"No, but the Liverpool Bar incident was over a year ago. The medicines you described do not suggest that you are unable to fly as a passenger."

"Why would I need to fly as a passenger, Sir?"

Stevenson took another tack. "Tell me about your friend, Sal Manzo."

"He is the crown prince of Aruba. You probably know his family influence on the island—newspapers, land, sports teams, hotels. He has friends in the island security police, the airport tower, and runs his own bank. He does whatever he wants on that island."

"Is he willing to work with you?"

"Sal? Sal Manzo won't get out of bed unless he can make at least a hundred thousand dollars."

"But if he could make a hundred thousand, would he cooperate with you?"

"I spent a month in his resort. He was a busy guy-we did not hang out much, but we talked a few times. He told me that he would like to do business with me, should an opportunity arise."

Sal Fucking Prescient Manzo. He practically prepped me for this meeting during our lunch at that restaurant before I left Aruba. He knew that someone would put our names together and reach the smart conclusion that Tommy could easily fill Sal's banks with dirty money on a semi-regular basis, and at manageable risk for nearly everyone involved.

Did the Colonel put it together and hand the task to Stevenson? Or, did Nando—counting every dollar I had spent from Aruba to Amelia's wedding ring—insist upon my positive action toward refilling his depleted bank accounts of the Hernandez clan. It would make sense. Nando would need the Colonel's approval, however, and the Colonel would want to place at least one layer of separation from the unfortunate business practices of his son-in-law and the rest of the family.

Stevenson had bad lungs and did not wear a wedding ring, nor did he look like he had expensive habits, particularly at those levels of material comfort that required offshore banking accounts and wall safes full of cash. Who knew? Maybe he had a favorite niece, or like so many crooked Colombians, a daughter in a Miami university. Or maybe that money was going outward as capital flight, and coming back as arms and expertise. That was a compartmentalized operation—I simply would be better off without that kind of knowledge.

"How would this company be incorporated?" For Stevenson, having endured trivialities thus far, it was my first noteworthy question. He lit another cigarette, revving up the smoke circulation system in the yellow shack once again. I doused my handkerchief before he took his first full drag.

"Tommy Connolly as the owner of an Aruban corporation, flying an Aruban-registered plane in and out of the Aruban Free Trade Zone." I finished the sentence for him in my mind. "and every once in a while by way of Aruban desert landing strips in the middle of Aruban nights handing the goods off to Aruban muscle."

The outline was rough, but I had already actual experience in the small, unmentionable details: it would be my company, whose single asset would be a small plane. It would fly between Cali and Aruba, with possible stops in Medellin, I gathered. Sal would be our only customer, for now. That would double the protective layering between the Colonel and myself, since the mischief would begin and end in Aruba, and not require any possible assistance from the Colonel to affect its nefarious ends. Stevenson, for a fee, would collect the monies and write out the banking instructions for Sal Manzo.

"It is an interesting offer...."

Stevenson blew out more smoke, stabbing his cigarette this time while blowing smoke directly toward my face. Stevenson did not wait for my thoughts to weaken on the vine. "Here is what you need to do." He pulled an envelope out of his desk, handing it to me with a downward chopping motion. "Give this envelope to Sal Manzo. He will put you in touch with plane brokers. Get a newer, small plane with a minimum cargo of fifteen-hundred pounds."

"Should I call you from Aruba?"

"No..." He wrote a telephone number on a piece of paper. "Call this number—only if you sense immediate danger—don't return here in person until you get clearance from Nando or me. Do you understand?"

"I do. But I want to talk about fees." I made my second intelligent comment, judging from the slight pause with which he lighted his next cigarette.

"Oh, yeah. Fees. Sal Manzo will want 1.5% as his counting fee. You will get 1.5%, out of which you will pay all costs, including your pilot. This office takes one percent. 3.5% total." I had no idea if that was a reasonable fee for money laundering directly into a respectable foreign bank.

"Any questions?"

"No, just a condition: I don't want any drugs on my plane."

"It is not that kind of business, Tommy. Your value is your island contacts. We are not engaged in narco-related operations. That is the extent of your involvement…" His voice tailed off, and once again I found myself completing his sentence in my mind. "…in the drug trade." It struck me how he described the venture as an operation, rather than a business.

He looked at his watch. "Tommy, I have to leave now. Wait in the barbershop. A car will come for you shortly."

I suppose in the parlance of the Colonel's world, Stevenson was my handler. The Colonel, at the end of my three-month honeymoon, had struck, choosing a light criminal vocation for me that would keep his daughter on the twelfth floor of our mansion with a positive cash flow, instead of a slow leak of money from his family, or perhaps clients.

I could not completely blame the Colonel—or Nando through the Colonel—for arranging the meeting with Stevenson. So far, I liked being Amelia's husband but had not achieved much toward securing her welfare since the Liverpool Bar. I was only drawing down about two thousand dollars a month from the account in Sal's bank, but I was publicly idle out of the starting gate of my marriage. The Colonel, after all, was a member of Cali society, and even a semi-criminal son-in-law was preferable to an indolent one.

Real estate seemed to be the preferred career endeavor of Amelia's family; Nando had driven me out to several rural areas where Cali was likely to expand. He had explained that my role would not have to extend beyond taking ownership of raw land for short periods of time, for which I would be richly rewarded. But I always passed on his offers.

"Take me to the Colonel." It began as a thought. I deserved to know whether the Colonel, if not profiting from this joint venture, at least knew of its details and intentions.

"Sure, boss." The driver pulled away from the curb and swung a quick right back toward the center of Cali.

The driver pulled up in front of a brick high-rise neighborhood in the center of Cali about fifteen minutes later. "That way, Sir." He pointed with his radio toward the security desk beyond a holly-framed wrought iron gate. "We will tell the portero to buzz you through. Do you want us to wait, Sir?"

"No, I will go home after I speak with the Colonel."

The gate jolted open. On the far end of the portero, a tinted glass door dulled the brightness of a pool in the central square of the building. It was about noon, and being a few degrees north of the equator, the sun stuck straight downward, allowing no shady place around the large blue pool for a few women and children. The security man put down his phone. "Sir, please wait here. A guard will take you to the person with whom you wish to speak." I walked closer to the tinted glass opening.

On the left side of the pool, standing on the balcony of a second floor condo, bare-shirted and with unkempt, pool-messed grey hair, was the Colonel. A young woman of about twenty-five—unusual for her Nordic whiteness—stood slightly behind him in a towel wrapped over her breasts, her arm around his waist, while she whispered in his ear. The woman unclasped him with a kiss to his cheek and turned away from the Colonel. She playfully picked up an inflatable beach ball and tossed it back in the condo. Then she began to hang her bathing suit from a circular clothes drying bar. The Colonel looked down at the water momentarily, his arms stretched out in a strong yet relaxed pose.

The woman put up another bathing suit, this one in two small pieces like that of a little girl. I took a closer look at the balcony. The Colonel looked back over his shoulder to talk to someone in the condo. A guard in dark sunglasses rushed onto the balcony and whispered in the ear of the Colonel. He looked toward the tinted door, and I stepped back a few feet from the window.

Someone had made a terrible mistake. The Colonel had probably never bothered to say that under no circumstances should a member of his family be brought to this location. It did not need to be said. I doubted whether Nando knew about this place. No official business takes place at your mistress's apartment. Mistresses were left alone; you could kill a man's family, but for some reason, they spared the mistresses.

My head began to clear from the acrid cigarette steam bath my brain had endured in Stevenson' office. And then the pieces came together for me. Of course, the guards would grant my request to visit the Colonel, since they viewed it as the second part of my business with Stevenson. They must have felt that I was here to brief the Colonel on my meeting at the barber shop, a meeting that they knew about, since the

Colonel must have informed them that it would take place. Stevenson called them for my pickup, rather than a taxi, since ultimately I came from the Colonel. It was only the Colonel who would be surprised by my request for a personal interview, which did not come to the Colonel's attention until the driver at the curb radioed the condo with the alert about my arrival.

The two off-duty policemen were still at the curb. I put my hand on top of the car and leaned almost inside the front cab. "I changed my mind. I don't want to disturb the Colonel on his day off."

"Do you want us to drive you home?"

"No, I have some things to do. You gentlemen have a nice day."

This would change things. The Colonel knew that I knew he had a mistress, likely one with a child. I was now the holder of a significant secret about a powerful man. Even though that man was my father-in-law, it still made me his secret accomplice, and him my secret culprit. Among the hierarchy of unnecessary complications that this news represented, it was not a major one, but an ugly one, which could bring a schism between Amelia and me, a small codicil to my general agreement not to let any harm ever come to Amelia.

CHAPTER TEN

Sal Manzo thought of it first. "Maybe they are in your blazer?" It was at that moment that the memory came back. Amelia, seeing them on their new case on the bed stand, put my new glasses in the inside pocket of my blazer. The heat being prohibitive and the company indifferent, I had not used that blazer outside an airport since I bought it. It was a protective but naïve impulse on Amelia's part. She hoped—with total disregard for my eye surgeon's solemn diagnosis—that my eyesight would make a delayed and spectacular recovery.

They would not improve my ability to read the photocopies of plane specification sheets before me-even if they made sense to me, which they did not. The plane broker—a mid-30s Dutchman named Michael Roepper—was glad to repeat details, or point out features on the fact sheets. In lieu of the careful, deliberate due diligence an experienced aviation consultant would undertake, I had Sal Manzo along for the ride.

I gave Sal Stevenson's envelope while we huddled together in his office within the protective din of heavy metal music in his office. Even an island prince takes eavesdropping precautions; our knees nearly touched in the space between our leather chairs within the pounding crang of Motley Crue coming from his speakers. Sal leaned back in his leather chair, rubbing his chin, and taking an occasional sip of whiskey while he read Stevenson's two-page letter carefully. All he said to me was, "I like it, Tommy. We'll go out looking for planes tomorrow." I thought about asking to see the letter, but after he finished reading it, he locked the letter in a drawer behind his desk.

We had spoken in his car on the way to the executive airport of the better manufacturers of planes, engines, and radio systems. Sal, as always, had a thread of analysis dipped in a tincture of illegality, but not criminality.

"Tommy, planes die like moths in the flame in the South Caribbean. The margins are so great that a plane is as disposable for a narco as a razor to you or me. What are these gonzos flying? B-18 Bolos, B-25 Mitchells. And why do they prefer these planes? High speed? A little. Long range? Maybe? Disposability? Now, you're on to something. You can pick one up from collectors and have it down here in a week. On the way, though, you fly it out of Miami and enter the probable narco smuggler list of every DEA office in the Western Hemisphere."

Sal was slowly building up to an important point, which had so far completely eluded me. "So, why stand out? Hmmm? Why drive the cherry red Mustang when the Ford Sedan will take you to the same place? True story, Tommy. I was driving around Hollywood one day, checking out the stars' homes. We drove around the windy streets North of Wilshire. They were huge, Tommy, fuckin' huge. As we approached Wilshire, there was a small little post-war shack at the corner. 'Poor fucker' I said. 'Why doesn't he sell out and go the desert?' My pal looked at me seriously. 'Sal—he has more money than the rest of these houses combined.' You have to pass for something, Tommy, and the worst thing you can do is to look and act like just another narco. Your plane will help you create a cover that will make sense… under moderate scrutiny, at least."

Sal Manzo was far brighter than he looked, or wanted people to know.

Sal favored the Piper 28 series. It had, perhaps in an attempt to capture a greater share of the narco-market, increased its fuel tank significantly since the era of Pablo Escobar. It was not a performance demon—it would not soar sharply, and was a little stingy with fuel. However, a good plane, as Sal explained, does not need to outrun a bigger plane, something no small plane can do; nor does it need to outrun a hurricane, an endeavor only an idiot would attempt. "The flight from La Guajira to Aruba is one hour over calm seas most of the year. The flight through the central valleys of Colombia could be uncomfortable due to heavy rain, but not enough to blow a small plane off course. Your main concern will be to stay consistently under radar for hours at a time. That is not a high-performance concern. That is just cautious route-selection."

The Piper fit this need well enough, according to Sal. "It earns its keep by never stalling. In the Caribbean, there is a lot of water, and not a lot of land. Go with the Piper, Tommy. It will never drop you on your ass unless you want it to." I did not know how much we could trust Mr. Roepper with trade details, most of which Sal explained to me on the way over. We needed 7-8 hours of steady flight times between refueling. That would work from Cali to La Guajira, but not always from Cali to Aruba.

I had done some research in the university library where Amelia had planned to return to her studies. The plane would also need to carry its own weight in cargo. It would need easily removable seats and room for extra fuel bladders. It would also need reinforced wings and struts due to the added weight and the pressure of landing 1000 pounds over specifications.

"It's doable, Tommy." Sal looked at the specification sheets for about 10 planes and then handed over three pieces of paper to Mr. Roepper. "Let's take a look at these, Don." Roepper directed us toward his BMW, and drove us to a sort of plane lot. It was within and around a small hangar beyond the express mail hangars. I had never heard of a used plane lot before.

"We get a lot of people who fall behind on their payments, or need to leave the island quickly and for a long time. There is an auction, and they resell to the public. Those kinds of guys don't come back looking for their plane. That is usually the least of their problems."

Roepper pointed out the three planes Sal recommended. They were all Pipers. I followed Sal around as he went inside all of them. Sal measured the seat area, and the added cargo space we could extrapolate from their removal. It looked like about 150 cubic feet of cargo room. With a maximum cargo hold of 1500 pounds, we had the possibility of transporting 10 pounds per cubic foot. That seemed like a lot of cans of paint. Sal agreed. "Let's go back and discuss the Turbo, Don."

The plane, the Piper Turbo IV from a few years ago, came to Mr. Roepper through auction, and he could vouch for its provenance but not its past use. Sal asked Don if we could send someone around to examine the plane. He had no problem with that.

"If the plane passes its inspection, are we looking at a deal here?" Sal looked to me to do the talking.

"I think most of the details are settled, Don. Let's talk again after Sal's people have a chance to examine the plane. We may have to modify our agreement based on our... findings."

Don stood up and extended his hand. "Tommy, ok. It was great to meet you. I hope we can close this deal soon."

Back in his office, Sal grabbed a remote and turned on the stereo again at eaves dropping-impenetrable volume. He poured two drinks and carried them to me at our little conversation pit between the two large sofa chairs.

"Tommy, even the DEA would not dare to bug our bank. We have it swept regularly anyways. But the club is fair game. We know they run agents through here, they bug it, and they break into it. But there are some things I am more comfortable discussing here, instead of in the bank. Capisce?"

"Ho capito."

"I am a banker. I run several businesses with my family on the island, and we have investments in New York and Canada. I run the island more or less for my family. I have the feeling you are going to be sending a lot of money back to Aruba in your new plane." Sal would not talk this way unless that letter had some pretty favorable terms for himself as well.

He held up his hand. "I am not asking you to give away any of your business practices; in fact, I wish you would not. Of course, I would like you to consider our bank as your banker. I think we have developed a rapport, an understanding." I did not interject, so he continued. "You have seen that we can handle large quantities in cash that come onto the island and need a home. That all takes time and effort, and unfortunately represents risk. The government here is very good about not asking questions and looking the other way. That takes money. There has been a lot of DEA heat on this island this past year. Some of our Lebanese clients have made too big of a landing on the island, and Aruba is starting to tilt. Your government doesn't like that, and they don't like looking stupid. The Yanks can close the tourist spigot off in a minute, and then we would all be selling fruit near the highway."

"It sounds like you want to discuss a fee structure with me, Sal."

"Yeah, I'm coming to that. Tommy, our family does not run the airport, but we have a certain amount of influence there. We work closely with what we can call the 'fixed wing' airplane community."

I started to laugh.

"It's true, Tommy!"

"I get it, Sal."

"Anyway, there are certain fees which are attached to one's membership in the club. First, you have 24-hour landing rights; you have free use of a cargo holding warehouse in your company's name; you have a gasoline credit card."

"What company?"

Sal paused and then explained. "Since you have a plane, you will need a business to explain its comings and goings. You will not need to declare island revenue; in fact, the bank can loan you money, and your company can consistently lose money and therefore pay no island taxes. You are occasionally going to need to store things in a bodega, Tommy. That's just the way things work around here."

I asked Sal if he had already incorporated a business here for me. "No, I need your permission and I need the paperwork on that plane. We'll take out a loan for the plane at the bank, which your company will pay through ongoing earnings. It is a proven system, Tommy. It has worked that way on the island without Dutch or American interference for a few decades now. I don't expect things to change either."

"Tell me about the fees, Sal."

"Right. The basic transit fee is $1000. If you fly in from Miami, refuel, and continue on to Colombia, for example, that fee would apply. The take-off fee for cargo-bearing flights is $2500. That will not apply to you so much, but there it is. For flights beyond the island with no cargo, the fee is $1000. The cargo-bearing landing fee is $5000. The landing fee with no cargo is $2500. That is 24 hours a day with no dog inspections, no customs, and no import tariffs. On a load with $2 million in value, that is less than 1%. Good luck getting that kind of insurance anywhere else in the world."

"Actually, Sal, that sounds entirely reasonable. But how can they guarantee no DEA interference?"

"I'm coming to that, Tommy. Let's talk about fees first. The bank will charge 1.5% of the gross amount for any cash-based deposits. That's the 'counting fee'. That will take your duffel bag and turn it into a legitimate deposit in a personal or an anonymous corporate account for yourself and your clients."

"That also sounds reasonable, Sal."

"So, on a million-dollar value import through the airport and into the bank, you will incur only $7500 in processing fees. Your pilot will want from five to ten thousand a flight, I imagine. That represents fixed costs of about $20,000 per million dollars, or 2.0% of your gross cargo value. There are some airport Christmas gifts as well, which we can discuss later. So, remember those figures before you quote a fee to a client."

Aruba—from its crooked tower guys at the airport, to the dirty cops who would make sure we were not bothered, to Sal Manzo—would cost me two percent. Stevenson and I would split the rest. I paused to let all the fixed cost figures fall away from the 3.5% we planned to charge our roster of customers.

"Every business has fixed costs, Tommy. You will also have to pay to upkeep your plane. The only figure that will show up on your Aruban tax statement, however, is the monthly loan payment for your plane, and some small earnings we will arrange for you on the island.

How does that sound to you, Tommy?"

"Good, Sal. I am with you so far."

"In that case, on to the last hurdle."

"You will have to negotiate with vendors, Tommy, and make contracts, and above all, answer fuckin' questions. You may be prepared to answer those questions, but I promise you a time will come when you are not so prepared—or inclined. You want to be walled off from trouble when the shit hits the fan."

"I never thought about all that, Sal." It was entirely true. The idea of requiring legal help did not make sense if my business was intentionally fraudulent.

"You are gonna need yourself a good lawyer."

"Do you know anybody on the island?"

"Leo Huff."

"Is he your lawyer, Sal?"

"No, but he is probably my lawyer's lawyer."

"What makes him of such value? I mean my contracts will be simple and straightforward and not require a lot of billable hours."

"You're thinking small, Tommy. What you should be thinking of is well-managed intermediation and not just financial. Contracts are a small part of what these guys do. They keep their mouths shut is what they do. They do it against pressure from the Dutch, your Justice Department, and especially those fucks from the DEA. Your lawyer is an important part of your shield from those assholes on this island—the other parts are my friends in Dutch security on the island, and the banking rules that my family wrote into Aruban law. There are going to be times when you need to urgently speak to him—in confidence, across continents, sharing potentially incriminating information. Can you put a price on that kind of confidence? Or do you want the guy who is so cheap he stamps his own documents at the court house?"

"Alright, Sal. I get you. Set up a meeting with Mr. Huff. Now, let's get the fuck out of this dungeon."

"One last thing, Tommy—and this includes wives and girlfriends—never tell anyone what I do or how I do it—from the hotel, to the casino, to the counting room. Capisce?"

"Capito."

That was the only time Sal ever gave me a direct warning, even though he said it without any sharpness in his voice—like a boss showing a new worker on the floor how not to get burned.

Sal and I clinked glasses and then headed out to dinner at a steak house at a point up the coast. From the hostess to the bartender, everybody knew Sal Manzo, and reached out without any wasted or hesitant motion for the cash he threw everyone's way. We did not talk about business anymore. He was a pirate prince on the island of Aruba, but he was a normal guy, and lot of fun once he had a few drinks in him.

The next day at 10:00 I met Mr. Leo Huff, Esquire. He was overly tan, plump about the gut, pony-tailed, with copious outgrowths of grey hair on his knuckles and in his ears, a pelting that probably did not make life in the tropics comfortable at all for him. His office was actually quite small, like a rear bedroom in a double-wide that was used by a ham radio hobbyist. During our introductions, it became apparent that he was Dutch, had limited amounts of patience, and spoke English better than me.

"Tommy Connolly from California and now a resident of where, young man?"

"Cali, Colombia."

He looked up from his desk to give me a subtle re-analysis.

"Ok, how can I help you?"

"I am looking for a lawyer to handle my corporate affairs and some personal matters."

"And what are your corporate affairs?"

"As soon as you could set up a proper import-export firm under the auspices of the Aruban Free Zone, I will have a corporate account. Once that is in order, I would like you to oversee the financial details of the purchase, renovation and local licensing of a plane I intend to buy, declaring the plane as an asset of the corporation."

Leo wrote none of this down, and only stared at me occasionally, his hands looking for occupation as he sat back in his chair. I knew, however, he was taking it all in, from the timber of my voice to the folding of my hands on my knee. "That sounds like a straightforward series of tasks. I would need the names of all parties to your transaction, and your guidelines for transactions with each of them."

He handed me a piece of paper. "Signing this document gives me power of attorney to negotiate terms on your behalf regarding the purchase, any renovations you wish to have undertaken, and to register your island corporation."

"Any and all transactions?"

"Those contracts and agreements for which you have clearly expressed your consent. This conversation has encompassed the establishment of a duty-free company, the purchase of a corporate asset, and its declaration as an asset in your soon-to-be-declared company. Is does not give me the right to purchase a McDonald's franchise in your name, or to dispose of any asset you possess without written consent." Like Stevenson's haste, he had his own way of punishing silly questions.

He handed over several other documents that made him my attorney. The last was the front page of an application for the Free Zone company. He already inserted the name of the company for me.

"Tomlinson Investments, Ltd."

"Yes, it is a good name. Waspy and trustworthy and a little boring."

"Do you require a retainer or a deposit, Mr. Huff?"

"Your handshake will do for now, Mr. Connolly."

He rose to shake my hand. "Enjoy your stay at Las Cabanas. I will call you when I have any developments to report."

I slept deeply that night, since away from Cali and Amelia, I was a social whiskey gulper, and not a prescription pill taker, with wonderful effects on the depth and duration of my sleep. A knock in the late morning on my door brought me back to the relaxed, tropical version of this vale of tears.

At the door was a young man about my age or younger. In his chinos, white polo shirt, and deck shoes, he could have come directly from a tropical wear summer catalog. We were about the same age, but he had taken the light, casual approach to the opportunities that came his way, rather than my steep and sinister rise to prominence—I was, after all, on a first name basis with and non-paying guest of the biggest gangster on the island. He seemed happy to be working for Leo Huff, rather than angling for something bigger that he was setting up for himself. Maybe, he was just glad to be out of the cold Dutch winter.

"Can I help you?" I asked.

"I am here for you, Sir. I am Leo Huff's driver. There is a car waiting downstairs."

"Your name?"

"Call me Mike."

"Call me Tommy, then."

"I don't recall requesting a car, Mike."

"Mr. Huff felt that maybe his calls were not getting to you, so he asked me to check on you." They had; I had slept through them.

I opened the door for Mike to pass through, whereupon we both noticed I was in my underwear. "Yes. I just woke up. Can you amuse yourself for a few minutes, Mike, until I am ready?" I tossed him the TV remote.

"I will be alright here, Tommy." He was polite and supple, not in possession of any quality that would bring him to the attention of anyone. He was Tommy C. before the three bullets and the awful recovery.

"In that case, can you call down to room service for some coffee and whatever you want?"

"I will do that, Tommy."

A shower, shave, and dressing took about twenty minutes, after which Mike and I drank coffee to some cable news about the United Nations and Bosnia.

"You follow this stuff, Mike?"

"I was supposed to go to Bosnia, but I came here instead."

"Smart call."

Leo came out and greeted me in the waiting room of his office about an hour later.

"Hello, Mr. Huff. Thanks for seeing me."

"Right this way." We went into his office.

"Coffee?" I was already suppressing coffee shakes.

"Maybe a sparkling water." Leo picked up his phone and breathed my request into it.

Leo handed me a pen, and then a series of thin folders—all with typed labels starting with "Tomlinson…"—that I pretended to peruse carefully from behind my black-rimmed glasses. Leo had arranged the light on his desk so that, with my head bent over the documents, he had a clear, well-lighted view of the scars behind my right ear, which he took note of several times as I signed my name at the bottom of several pieces of paper.

In only a few minutes' time, I signed corporate, Free Trade Zone, Piper purchase and financing, and an enhanced power of attorney form, so that I did not have to leave Cali just to sign more papers. Leo shook my hand. "That settles things, Tommy. Sal Manzo has the keys to your plane. Don't fly too close to the sun; I don't like losing good clients to unfortunate accidents."

I taxied back to the hotel and squeezed in a shower before I sped off to meet Sal in the disco next to his office. At the entrance, one of two big doormen walked me through and around the perimeter of the disco and up some steps. He had a small pocket flashlight, which he pointed at a door guarded by another large type. The door opened for me as I approached it.

Inside were Sal, Lukas and about four slinky Euro brunettes and blondes, their pale legs vying to be entwined with those of the dark-suited men in powerful poses on large sofas. A low glass table in front supported several bottles of champagne, glasses, and from the smell, some type of salmon, which had some cocaine crystals on its flank. Sal stood up, leaving his cigar in the ashtray on a small lamp table next to his chair. "Tommy, Buddy! Come in! The champagne is still cold! Lukas! Go to the office and bring the other chair!"

With the particular grace of the alpha gangster in his own hidecut, Sal picked up a bottle and glass and carefully poured for me, his eyes equally split between not wanting to dribble champagne on the lines of

YOUR ENEMIES DO KNOW YOU BEST

cocaine on the table below, and his leering nods toward the prostitutes on the table.

I looked out at twenty or so dancing couples and more at the bar. Island casual was evidently not permitted in Sal's nightclub. The men wore after-hours business casual with slacks and loafers and open business shirts. The women were in mini-skirts almost uniformly. Sal not only made me pledge to absolute secrecy about his business operations, but let me know that I could never go beyond this point, which I took to mean that the counting room was nearby, probably on the other side of the private members' club.

We clinked glasses with our arms careful not to extend over the table. "This is a good place to relax, Tommy. It is a one-way mirror. One of the few on the island." One of the girls leaned forward with one hand holding her long hair in a fist, and the other curled around a half-straw. She put her head above a silver tray and lowered her nose and the straw onto the surface. She drained two thick lines of cocaine, and cut some rock on the corner of the tray into four new lines. Sal lifted his glass towards mine.

He bade me welcome to the pirate's life.

"To the English gentleman known as Tomlinson. Long may he prosper on our island."

"Chin Chin," I offered in return.

Lukas came back with another large black leather chair, which he positioned to enable more private conversation between Sal and me. Lukas spoke some Dutch with Sal, and left out the main door. Seconds later, he was walking through the crowd to the exit on the other side of the disco, speaking to someone in a walkie-talkie. Sal, meanwhile, motioned for one of the girls to refill our glasses. Another girl handed me a glass tube, but I shook her off with my palm, and looked at Sal.

"Doctor's orders, Sal. Thanks, anyway."

"No problem, Tommy."

The girl handed the tray on to Sal, who drained two lines and gave her back the tray. Another of the girls came and sat on the thick raised side of my chair. She put her hand on my neck for a moment, and then rested it on my back. It felt nice—a little too nice. The arm was connected to a tall, thin brunette in a dress that permitted a view up a smashing pair of legs.

I smiled and leaned forward, taking her hand off my back and depositing it back on her lap. "Maybe later. Thanks." She smiled weakly and returned to the silver tray.

"You will bring us lots of good business soon, Tommy!"

I had the feeling that as soon as I returned to Cali, it would not be necessary to contact Stevenson. I had only been on the island for four days, and the business was already operational. The plane had its own parking spot at the executive airport with the privileges of executive membership therein. Local mechanics, chosen and instructed by Sal Manzo, had already modified the struts, and connected the extra fuel bladders to the main tank. Someone on Sal's end had already test-flown the plane to Sal's satisfaction, including landings with over a thousand pounds of cargo, which Sal ingeniously placed in the cargo hold by combining a generator, a bunch of paint cans, and some sections of a palm tree that fell on the property.

It only required a pilot, which I felt sure Stevenson had already contracted and flown to Cali, awaiting only my arrival to quietly launch Air Tommy.

Sal shook me out of my reverie.

"Are you sure I cannot interest you in some of our island pleasures."

"No, thanks, Sal. The champagne is delicious though."

He had seen Amelia; he knew the comparison between her and his island hookers to be an absurd drop off in quality. Amelia was raised to be the First Lady of Colombia; these girls had missed everything that mattered, from family bonds to basic safety, and were inured to grasping men like Sal and smoky rooms like this. As soon as I took a sip, a slinky blond would top my glass for me, trying to be serviceable, and thus called back for another night into Sal's little private playhouse.

One of the girls came to his seat, where gregarious Sal Manzo was more welcoming, and understanding of her desire to be put in play for reasons of his pleasure. He put her on his lap and fed her cocaine from the tray, rubbing the remnants left on the tray onto her nipples. The other girls sat glumly and nervously. They obviously wanted more from life than this moment, but at that moment they just wanted to make the cut.

Sal seemed to settle on two of the girls as his night's companions. The brunette sat on the other puffy side arm rest and rested her arm around Sal's neck. She looked at me plaintively, as if we each had one last chance to salvage something pleasant from the evening.

The last girl of the four, not currently in demand by Sal, had also taken on the role as the group's cocaine monger and doubled her earnings through cocaine consumption. Sal had so much cocaine on that tray that her frequent assignations with the straw and tray bothered him not to the slightest degree.

I had not formed a criminal identity yet—one where nights like this were as normal as an evening brandy for a corporate manager in a high-rise hotel lounge; nor had I gotten into this business in order to live Sal's version of the good life. Sal and I were now in business together, and there was still much to learn about the modern pirate's life, so I stayed and watched the girls fight boredom back with heavy drinking and watch checking until closing. But I brushed it off even before I was back in my room. I needed my wits to see beyond the choppy waves in these parts. Big things—even for a guy like Sal Manzo—were afoot, and I was in the middle of them.

Besides, I loved my wife a lot.

In the lobby the next morning, I saw Lukas. He was parched and hungover, carrying his shoes across the tiles of the hotel lobby.

"Good morning, Tommy!"

"Hey, Lukas! Nice night?"

"Yes. I hope I did not catch something."

"Or transmit something. I suggest an appointment with Dr. Hilliard at your earliest convenience."

"Thanks, Tommy. He and I are on a first name basis as it is. Where are you going?"

"To Cali."

"Ah, yah, that beautiful wife of yours. I would be in a hurry, too. Have a safe trip, Tommy!"

"Get some sleep, Lukas!"

"Yah. Yah." He yawned and waved at the same time. I took the hotel Lincoln to the airport. I was home in the condo in west Cali by late afternoon.

CHAPTER ELEVEN

I returned to Cali, a young businessman in the area of aviation consultancy. For anyone observing closely, such as the DEA, I was a known associate of a major island criminal, the money-laundering partner of wayward Colombian intelligence types, and below the level of prosecutable intrigue, an anxious son-in-law, just trying to pay into family accounts, rather than draw them down lower and lower.

There were no messages from Nando or Stevenson when I arrived—that pleasant fact alone presaging a few pleasant days with Amelia in our new home in the Cali skyline. The condo was quiet and still; Amelia napped peacefully to the sound of light rain through the open balcony window. I gave her a small kiss on the cheek, beholding her daffodil smell and classical, imperious beauty, not at all dulled by the transformations of pregnancy throughout the rest of her body. My Helen of Cali still could hold in thrall any serious student of beauty, even with two babies in her pouch.

She was about nine or ten weeks from childbirth and becoming more alive to activity within her abdomen than to the squalid and disordered world below the 12th floor. We had sworn off the news. Amelia had prepared a room with two beds for the babies; I saw pink dolls and empty picture frames ready for the girls' first smiles. She had had the walls painted pink as well, and had begun to store cases of diapers in the closet.

There being no beer or alcohol in our house except for my nocturnal stash, I went back to my club to uncoil my back muscles in the pool, after which I sat with some of the other members who—like Tommy—did not keep regular hours in any particular place of business. I could sense then with much more informed instincts who was a part of my world. At least two of those guys were retired narcos. Their attempts to explain their businesses and lifestyles invited, rather than deflected questioning. I wondered if my legend was so obviously constructed.

I had been going to the gym since I left the Hotel Inter. They all—the narcos and the wealthier members--spoke somewhat freely around me, sensing that I had been there too long to be a DEA plant. While the Colonel completely locked down the event in the Liverpool Bar, he made no attempt to hide the fact I was his son-in-law, and therefore someone who could be expected to know a thing or two about police and narco matters, which I shared freely with them.

The ex-narcos never spoke about their own business with the Cartel, but their regrets about the decline of Cali were almost like children lamenting the closing of the county fair. No one then seemed to have money in Cali—the loci of the cocaine business having moved with the goat fuckers way to the north of Cali. The high-end shops and restaurants in Ciudad Jardin were struggling now that the leaders of the Cali Cartel were now in jail and no longer paying off judges, generals, and mayors. Somehow, the Colonel abided quite well.

That day, their conversational lamenting had moved on to something called the Clinton List, which was the equivalent of the Hollywood Black List for serious narcos and their associates. The impetus for the law was to confiscate the ill-gotten riches of the important narcos, the reduros. As I listened to their wistful conversation, their imagining of Cali in the era of the Cartel as a city in its golden age, another part of the law loomed ahead like a Viking mast coming out of a dawn mist toward my little raft: it punished any American citizen who dealt with narcos with a ten-year stretch in prison.

In the aftermath of the Cartel's disintegration, the national police, particularly in Cali, was in disgrace. The DEA dealt with them reluctantly. Somehow, as before, the Colonel floated above the wretched prospects of those who took money from the Cartel. This law would not harm the Colonel, who had his own methods, and so far had not suffered the new style of shame in Cali: the posting of one's name in national newspapers as a recipient of Cartel money, or a prolonged squat in the basement of the Fiscalia in Bogota.

It was a razor's edge for me. I was not an employee of Tomlinson, Ltd. of Aruba. I was its sole proprietor. If individuals on the Clinton List held bank accounts that I proffered to Sal's bank, I would be daddy-fugitive with my children in Cali, while I hunkered down in a small hut somewhere on the banks of the Amazon River. Sitting in the sauna, I set about to answer my own pressing questions for once: Stevenson and Nando had to come clean about their client list before the Piper ever lifted off the ground. And they would pay more: the new price was 5.0%, of which Tommy took 2.5%.

Felicitously, Nando left a message for me to meet him for breakfast in the ground-floor restaurant in the Hotel Inter the next morning. He sat in the rear, far from the other customers who were grouped closely together on the far end, causing the waitress to make a special trip to his private corner booth whenever he raised his arm for more service.

"You look good, marika."

"I feel better, Nando. Amelia is safe and content. We love our new home…."

"Marika, please! You sound like a model in a new condo development brochure. How did things go in Aruba?" There were, apparently, limits to his intelligence reach; I had just established a few of them since he knew nothing of my activities over the past week in Aruba.

"Sal is onboard with the operation according to your—pardon, Stevenson's plan. The plane is licensed to a Free Zone company I control… it is an asset of my company in Aruba."

"Are you able to fly in and out of the Aruba airport freely?"

"Yes, and without interference from any authority who would have an interest in watching the airport. Informally, they call it the Aruba Airport Club. I am now a member in good standing. The tower tells no one when I arrive or depart, or alerts police to unusual activity."

"How is your security?"

"I have an Aruban lawyer. All communications with him are privileged. If I need to speak to Sal, I send a coded phone message to my lawyer, and he sends a runner to Sal, who responds by sending the runner back, and another coded message comes back to me. He is close to the Manzo family, so there is no possibility of infiltration. I get the feeling this sort of thing is not very new to him."

"For an amateur, that is impressive, marika. You are not as dumb as you look, but only by a close margin. Now, tell me about the plane?"

"I bought a 240 horse power Turbo Piper and upgraded it to 320. We took out four seats to increase the cargo space. I added twenty-five more gallons of fuel capacity to increase the range to over eight hours. We can carry a maximum of about two thousand pounds."

"That will limit you in the armaments market." Nando had never mentioned armaments before.

"Yes, probably."

"Still, that is a good start."

My coffee arrived, so we abruptly stopped our chatter during the time it took the waitress to deposit little china basins of cream and sugar, time Nando utilized to size her up for ancillary duties. He asked the waitress for steak and eggs, and I asked for sancocho, a modest chicken broth soup, enlivened by a few vegetables.

"You need to fatten up, marika. Sancocho is for starving peasants, not a business owner." He watched the waitress walk to the far end of the restaurant before he called her back, giving him enough time for a few more points, and to smile at her during her catwalk back to our table.

"Still, good job, marika. I expect there will be a lot of business in the next few years. The country is changing quickly. The Medellin and Cali Cartel decline and fall is over. New cartels are asserting themselves; the country is filling up with fresh money that wants a safe harbor." The information about the Clinton List still grievously impinging on my thinking; I told Nando what I thought about his new clients.

"Please tell me that we are not in business with those kinds of people, Nando."

"What kind?"

"Extraditable to begin with."

The arrival of the waitress suspended his otherwise look of disappointment with my concerns. He smiled up at her, pointing charmingly at our coffee cups, and making a gesture of regret that she would have to trudge back across the room to fill our almost topped off cups.

"Have you ever seen a billion dollars, marika?"

Nando had evidently given the matter considerable thought, and could not wait to share his findings with me.

"No, of course not."

"It takes up an entire train car, to the ceiling. You could fill the walls of a family house with only about fifteen to twenty-five million dollars. That means forty houses to hide a billion. Pablo Escobar kept a wall safe in almost every property he controlled. It was how he stayed solvent; he always knew where to find money. He would factor in 10% yearly loss from rot and mice." He laughed. "Imagine that. One hundred million dollars a year ran out the assholes of some dirty rats."

"Fine, Nando. You spend twenty years in a federal supermax prison for dealing with members of the Clinton List. I'll tell you where the plane is parked in Aruba. I don't need this shit. You make sure that there is a huge gap between me, my plane, and the new narcos you have befriended."

"Cool down, marika. The money enters your plane anonymously. You will never know who your clients are—even if you wanted to know."

"I don't think the DEA will see it that way—they view things holistically—they use words like conspiracy, not unwilling partner."

I was not a lively opponent for Nando that morning. His usual subtle insinuations about me did not seem worth my time to follow down the rabbit hole. Instead, I let each one pass along without the slightest interference on my part, and enjoyed the times in which he did not speak.

"Have you never heard of the 'nesting syndrome,' marika?"

"In the animal kingdom, yes."

Our breakfast arrived. "Bon appetite, marika."

"Likewise." The waitress again stopped on the far end of the restaurant, but immediately looked over her shoulder for Nando's next importunate request.

"Amelia is nesting, marika. She is up on the twelfth floor of your mansion, building a nest. Instead of a suitable tree and the best sticks to make her nest, she wants a house, a big car, and a live husband."

"The last I checked, she has all three, Nando."

"The problem is that she will want to talk to you ten times a day about insignificant details that mean the world to her."

"We can have fewer, but more detailed discussions then."

"Marika, do you know anything about women?"

"What do you mean, Nando."

"She is starting her 7th month now, right?"

"Yes."

"Do you think she will be satisfied with weekly discussions in the 8th month? Do you think she will be pleased hearing from you every five or six days? Or, knowing that her husband—who is not fat and distended like she is, and handsome in a gringo sort of way—is floating around Aruba with money and nice clothes, with a scent of danger about him?"

"Probably not."

"So, marika. One flight a week maximum for now. We will pack your little plane like a train car for now. Sleep as many nights as possible in your new home beside your wife. You look pale, marika. Eat your campesino gruel."

After breakfast, Nando and I drove to the barber shop in the late morning under a drenching Cali rain. I raised my points early: my concerns about the Clinton List did not fall upon unsympathetic ears, since they were engaged in extraditable undertakings as well. They agreed that the risk premium was greatest for me, as the linkman between the international banking system—with its hundreds of thousands of bank branches, clerks, investigators, and Treasury hounds—and the so-far unnamed clients. They would not budge, however, on the issue of the identities of the individual clients, and their proximity to the new cartels,

Stevenson, more respectful of Nando's lungs than mine, did not reach for a cigarette during the whole of his discourse. "Tommy, it is a matter of operational compartmentalization. Do you know what that means?" I nodded in agreement. "In your case," he continued, "it is best that you do not know the names of the clients...."

I spoke up. "But Sal Manzo will know. He could also be called to testify."

"Not quite. Your banking contact, whose name you do not have to repeat by the way, will receive a manifest of coded names and account numbers. He builds new accounts and fills them up with our money. You come back to us with passwords, which is the only thing that connects us with those accounts."

"In that case, I have to trust you both that we are not dealing with Clinton Listers?"

"I promise that we will declare any individual or firm on the list to you, and that you have the right to withdraw consent."

We both looked at Nando to intuit his willingness to play by this new rule. Nando did nothing more than wipe some lint off his trouser and smile. I smelled a ruse. They did not even present a mild objection to my insistence to raise our fees to 5.0%. I could have said 8%. The kind of people for whom there was not a difference worth parlaying between the two figures wanted money out of the country desperately, and in large sums. We were not talking about Cali dentists.

That was the first time Stevenson had told me I would be carrying coded account numbers. Someone—a rival narco, the DEA, a local hood—would eventually find out, and take an interest in Tommy's comings and goings between the airport in Cali and our twelfth floor castle. That kind of danger I was beginning to understand, and learning to accept. I had taken bullets to the soft tissue of my brain; I could deal with gunfire. Still, I pitied the fool that thought about bringing harm to my wife.

The first flight was scheduled for the next afternoon. We shook hands and departed, putting myself down for 2.5%, which on ten million dollars, would be over two-hundred thousand for me, about a third of what I had spent from the money Chiara Manzo signed over to me in Aruba. That would be enough to allow the Hernandez Clan to forget about past losses and look forward to significant earnings in the future—that is, if I did not fall out of the sky.

That night, Amelia did not leave her bed, except to roll off it, and over to the bathroom in a slow, hulking manner. I brought her a tray with soup, which she sipped while watching American movies from a stack of videos on the stand next to the television I set up at the foot of our bed. Pregnancy had not rendered her subject to strange eating habits, as much as alarming viewing ones. If it blew up, or got shot by a cop, or exploded, or defended America from sudden peril, Amelia had to watch the movie, hushing me in case I should interrupt the climatic, or heaven forbid, anti-climactic scene.

Finally after a sip of brandy, I turned off the lights and, setting her on her side, began to induce sleep with soft kisses to her cheeks. She grabbed my hand, pulling me down beside her to lull herself to sleep with my arms around her.

That night I told Amelia the expurgated version of my new air transport company, which included my irregular travel schedule.

"Tommy, wait—are you staying with me for a while?"

"Yes, mi amor."

"Do you love me, Tommy?"

"Yes, I do, Amelia. Very much."

"I love you, you know."

I kissed her cheek softly to seal the exchange of intimacies.

"Are you scared when I go away?"

"Not in this building. There is so much security here. The portero likes you. He is very protective when you are gone. He does not let anyone come to our door. He takes the deliveries himself, and calls to warn me before he arrives."

He had better, I thought—I pay him enough.

"I will only be gone a few days a week…we can go out places when I get back. We can even hire a guard if you want."

"Actually, I was thinking of a maid, Tommy—the cleaning service is fine, but I will have to cook and clean and take care of the babies in a few months."

"You are a real pioneer, Amelia."

"Please, Tommy?"

"I'll think about it."

She savored this promise while I continued.

"Do you still have nightmares, Amelia?"

"Yes. The sound of the bullets in your back and your blood. But not so much anymore."

"Probably due to your careful selection of videos." She laughed, but that went away quickly.

"What about you, Tommy? What are you afraid of?"

The running list, nearly all of which I could not discuss with Amelia, included the second gunman; the possibility of a fragment of bone in my brain causing further damage; a small plane crash; a DEA warrant; and long imprisonment because Stevenson and Nando cared less about the Clinton List than a few tens of thousands of dollars more for their accounts. There was also something I had not yet identified as a tendency or a one-off event: that I split a man's scull in pieces with a barstool in a display of unusual proficiency for a first timer.

"I don't have nightmares. When I awoke from my coma all that went away. Until your father showed me the videos of the bar, I had no memories, except for what you told me."

"What? There were videos? You saw them?"

"Your father showed me the videos from within the bar. After the shooting, he and Nando returned to the bar to take control of the crime scene. He did not want your name to be in the newspapers or in a police investigation. I killed the sicario, Amelia. I almost broke open his head with the chair. He died instantly."

"Good, the motherfucker. You did the right thing. You should never feel badly for killing a cockroach, Tommy."

140

"Your father asked the local police to stand down, and his men took the tapes and did the official interviews of the witnesses. The murder now is only a rumor. The witness list is gone. My name is nowhere in the files. Your father made the whole thing disappear."

This is not what Amelia wanted to talk about; there was something deeper she wanted to know.

"Tommy, during your stay in the hospital your father came to see you, but not your mother."

"They are not married, Amelia."

"I know. I spoke with her on the phone."

"How did that go?"

"She was concerned, Tommy—I could tell. But I did not think she understood what I was saying."

"She understood the meaning, but no so much the implications."

"What do you mean?"

She understands facts, but she is losing the ability to place a meaning to facts."

"Is she brain damaged?"

"Not with a disease. She has something organic."

"She raised you by herself?"

"Yes. I grew up in a small agricultural town. It was safe and never changed, and people knew her, and she never harmed anyone, so they let her raise me. A social worker visited us once in a while."

"How did she meet your father?"

"My mother was always taking courses at the local college. One day she saw a poster for a speaking engagement of a visiting diplomat. He was on a lecture tour around small universities and colleges—the State Department tried to bring foreign policy to the common man. My mother sat in on one of them. She sat in the front row and went to the reception after the lecture. I think it was in Stockton, a city near our town. During the reception after his speech, she stood near him and acted like his Girl Friday."

"What is a Girl Friday?"

"A woman who handles the details for her boss."

"I see."

"She just got in the taxi with him and went back to his hotel.'

"He was a conservative Georgetown bureaucrat in the State Department. She was a lovely, slightly mad Irish girl. For him, it was the closest thing to bedding down a groupie he would ever have. It probably seemed risk free for him. Unfortunately, she got pregnant and had me."

"Did he visit you?"

"Not at Christmas or birthdays or during the summer, no."

"How did you see him?"

"I saw him once or twice in San Francisco. He would be on business, and we would spend a day in the Golden Gate Park and maybe have dinner in Chinatown."

I continued to rub her ankles and shoulders to induce sleep.

"What do you remember of him, Tommy?"

"He was formal and succinct and reserved. We mostly walked. We did not play baseball or throw a Frisbee. He wore a business suit every time we met. He would fly out the next day, and we would drive home."

"Did he continue his relationship with your mother?"

"No. After that night, they were never together again."

"Did he support you?"

"No, my mother made enough money as a teacher. She teaches reading. We lived in a small town and did not need a lot of money. We had a little house, and she had a car, and we lived alright."

"What about the university?"

"I had scholarships from the city and the county. I worked some jobs in college too. I never suffered any hardship."

"Did you talk with him in those days?"

"We met a few times in San Francisco. It was the same thing. We would meet at his hotel and have lunch in the City."

"What did you talk about?"

"Mostly politics. He was at a level above the politics that show up in the newspapers. He did not give me State secrets, but we discussed things from a higher level than the media reports."

"Was he interested in your education?"

"He liked the fact that I studied the classics. He thought a 'classical grounding,' as he called it, would help me in any profession I chose."

"Did you discuss your future with him?"

"He told me that he would help me if I wanted to work in the State Department or Treasury or on Capitol Hill."

"Why didn't you take a job there?"

"Mainly, I did not want his help. I wanted a job in diplomacy as a means to a career in academics, but not through nepotism—even nepotism one degree removed."

"What did you do then?"

"I spent a year in Los Angeles studying for the exam for the civil service."

"How did you earn money?" I was going to be a substitute teacher part-time, but a school in a Mexican neighborhood offered me a job full-time."

"What did you teach?"

"I taught literature to high school students who barely spoke English."

"Only in America."

"That's right."

"And you took the exam?"

"I took the exam in June in a hotel in downtown Los Angeles. I passed but continued the job until December."

"Why did you choose Colombia?"

"I spoke enough Spanish so that I did not need to go to a language school or pass a test. They posted me to Bogota with a January, 1997 start date. I continued at my job until Christmas vacation and then flew to Cali."

"Did you tell your father?"

"No. I took the exam under my mother's and my name, Connolly. My father's name is Faraday."

"Is that Irish, too?"

"Yes, he is Kennedy-era WASP Irish."

"The White Anglo-Saxon Protestant."

"Yes, the Irish's upwardly mobile cohort."

"So, he did not know?"

"Unless he monitored exam passing results, he did not know."

"And your mother?"

"I called her and told her, sure."

"What did she say?"

"'That sounds like a grand idea' she called it."

"Did you go and visit her?"

"No. I just left."

"My future husband arrived all alone in Colombia."

"Kind of, yes…" I felt her forehead. It had become warm.

"Amelia, you have a fever." She ignored that comment.

"Thank you for telling me your story. That was not easy, was it?"

"It is a bit Gothic, Amelia."

"I think I understand."

"I love you, Tommy. Do you understand?"

"Yes, mi amor."

"Stay with me for a while."

I undressed and got into bed beside her, feeling her breathe, and imagining our girls growing bigger and bigger in her stomach.

Like so many nights when I came home from the field, sleep was fitful for me that night. I had not told Amelia of the dangers and illegality of my new endeavor; from an operational point of view, she could not possibly know; even small details were in violation of my promise to Sal not to breathe a word about his laundering operation; and I did not want her to know that there was any possibility that her troubles were far from over. Our tower was a safe place for Amelia—that is all she needed to know.

That night, still a long way from dawn, I sat on the balcony with a bottle of brandy, which I hid in a shoe box marked "cool jazz" in my side of the closet. I put Gerry Mulligan on the cd player downstairs at low volume, and drank glass after glass above the gunfire and filth and future goat fuckers of greater Cali.

It was humiliating to tell Amelia these stories of small-town eccentricities, compared to her careful grooming as a Cali debutante. There was much I left out, like the parties my mother had along the banks of the delta with her hippy friends, in which, believing they were the reincarnation of the Bloomsbury writers, they would sit on lawn chairs in a circle, acting out plays, and couple late at night, whilst I slept in my mother's car.

There was no shame in single-mother childhoods where I grew up; in fact, they were common in Lindley, since local boys often decided to grab something more from life in another part of the country—usually through military service—after spending a few months working at low-pay farm jobs, and burping babies back to sleep in the middle of the night to the sound of rolling railway stock on the edge of town.

But even by prevailing, local standards, mine was a ridiculous entrance into the world, at least due to its lopsidedness, my mother with Asperger's Syndrome, almost a ward of the community, and my father a distant figure somewhere within the pantheon of mortals who made mischief—or so said my mother—with the Gods of War.

My mother always told me: "You come from the Gods, Tommy. You are the son of Irish Kings and an American Diplomat. You have nothing to be ashamed of. You have greatness in you."

Would I have ever completed my plans? Would I have entered a doctoral program after a few years in Bogota? It seemed unlikely now. More likely was a slow rise through the lower levels of the State Department, and an eventual rapprochement with Ambassador Faraday in Washington, D.C. He would have placed me on a path I would never have achieved for myself, and I would have accepted it.

First, I would marry a pushy, super-achiever in Washington, D.C. and indulge in non-stop cleverness during dinner with carefully cultivated friends in high places. We would love the idea of shaping the nation and have horridly conventional sex. I could never get back on that path, and frankly, I was glad.

Instead, I was thrown ashore in this strange, bloody land, where only a few miles to the west, high in the mountain villages outside Cali, FARC guerrillas enjoyed home cooking from petrified local peasants under threat of murder; or where military officers went to sex parties with all expenses paid by the leaders of drug cartels; or where a reduro could pay a million dollars for a night of sex with a famous actress; or where for fifty dollars you could find a shooter who would enter a bar and kill young women.

My mother told me that I was beloved of the Gods, but not necessarily worth anything to men. Beyond the Greek stages of my mother's hallucinations, the Gods were very far away and fickle with their heros, but shooters and DEA agents could come from around any corner in Cali.

CHAPTER TWELVE

A few days later, at a small municipal airport in Jamundi, about twenty-five miles south of Cali, Nando and I drove through a side gate and directly onto the airport's small runway. I recognized the pilot; this time he wore a Red Sox baseball cap. He was considerably more open and friendly this time, likely since I was now his boss and traveling companion, and possibly fellow cellmate, whose succor he might greatly rely upon at some point in our relationship. We shook hands like conventioneers who had met the previous year, but did not want to chat about that event.

Nando used a walkie-talkie to communicate with the tower, which gave us an all-clear to proceed. Nando shook hands with Red Sox and slapped a large manila envelope against my chest. "Marika, some light reading for you! Don't let us down!"

That really was the essential question: who was 'us'?

The plane was now pointed directly toward Aruba. We took off without much drag, easily gained altitude despite a few thousand pounds of cargo, and flew steadily at about 125 miles per hour. Without recourse to a map, Red Sox maneuvered through passes and down the Magdalena River, and then out toward the northeast corner near our private strip outside Maicao.

This time we knocked on the front door.

We arrived about 11:45 at night, rocking gently down to the runway with the winds that came ashore and pushed us lightly on the way to the landing strip. There was no communication with the tower in Aruba beyond a brief landing instruction twenty minutes beyond Aruba; it was an unnerving experience to touch down without any sort of local guidance. Red Sox landed heavier and with a little undue bounce with the added weight, but there the plane held together, and we taxied smoothly back to spot F-12.

As soon as Red Sox turned off the plane engine and lights, another set of lights came on. It came from a van that swung behind us and placed its lights on the rear of the plane just long enough to get an idea of our general location, whereupon they went out. Red Sox, not having moved from his chair, or used a bathroom jug during the previous eight hours in the cramped cockpit of the Piper, cracked his neck and opened his door, sliding out onto solid ground and stamping his feet on the solid cement below.

I opened my door—my legs and neck stiffened by inaction—and slid down the wing to the ground. There were quick looks of recognition, and a few brief greetings between Sal and me, but we kept our comments plain and short, while we stared at Sal's men going to and fro with an economy of movement, even in the darkness between the Piper and the van.

The whole transfer only took about two minutes, during which Sal, Red Sox, Lucas and I began to pile into the van.

"Lukas, make sure the rear door is locked." Red Sox and I hopped in the back of the van through the side door.

"Hey! Tommy! Not you. You go in front!"

I hopped in the passenger side of the hotel van for the short ride up the coastal strip to Las Cabanas. We split up in the basement of Las Cabanas: Red Sox walked out of the building for some place unknown, while Sal and his men filled hotel laundry carts with the duffel bags, and wheeled them toward the resort casino, where I expected the count to take place.

Without pills, and with a whiskey from room service, I slept like a king that night in the same room where I first made love to Amelia. I had three million dollars then, but no real future. Now, I had a little less than three million, a pregnant wife, an avaricious brother-in-law, and an imperious father-in-law; I was also an initiate in the secret society of money-launderers, the modern South Caribbean pirate class. I was going to make a fortune, I knew; Stevenson had told me that there was a billion dollars waiting to leave Colombia among the narco and corrupt government classes. I thought of Nando's train car, and soon I slept.

The next morning in his rear nightclub office, Sal Manzo placed a small table between our two sofas to accommodate platefuls of bacon and eggs and toast, as well as operational security. The black and purple swollen bags under his eyes proved to me he took the count seriously; he probably never left the counting room all night.

We commenced yelling across the table to one another within the din of head-cranging metal music that shook the yokes of my eggs. Sal handed me a piece of paper, on which he had written "$150,000." I rolled up the piece of paper and ate it, followed by a solid gulp of coffee.

"I just credited your account, Tommy. I knew we would do good business together!"

"Sal, you got any pepper?" I joked.

"It won't always be that big, Tommy, but it will add up. Just watch! You are on your way!"

I flew back to Cali commercially a few hours later. Leaning back in my seat, enjoying sparkling water, which I took with one of Dr. Howe's blue pills, it all seemed too easy. I did not have to scout for the clients or their money; I did not have to fly the plane or empty out its contents; I did not have to stay awake all night placing U.S. currency in counting machines, and daubing each note to detect a fake; I did not have to undertake the falsification of bank documents, so that it appeared that much of this money flowed through Sal's night club and casino; I did not have to send the money on its crooked path through offshore banking havens to some unknown final resting place. I just stood between crooked men with a smile and a wink, and coordinated their greed.

Whatever it was, whichever skill I brought to bear in the whole of the operation, I became good at it; even when other opportunities presented themselves, I always considered myself a friend and associate of Sal Manzo, who got the first crack at any sum of money Stevenson could raise. But as much as the pirate life was fun during short cruises, it was not for me. The cocaine, the whores, the black flag of illegal gain— none of those things struck me as more than lucre, which I backed into because of a series of mishaps during my exfiltration. My mother, my father, and now Amelia: they all felt that I could put down stakes in enterprises greater than petty crime.

If not a pirate like my friend Sal, what then was I?

There being no magazines with large pictures on the plane, I remembered Nando's package. Taking it out of my backpack, I ripped it open and took out a bundle of about fifty pages of paper. The top page was a note in English from Nando: "Marika, we got these from Amelia's email server. They are from her ex-boyfriend. This series begins a few days after the Liverpool Bar. The last email is from last week. We can talk about this more after you return from your sales trip."

I shuffled through the pages. Each page, in photocopy form, contained an email from Amelia's boyfriend from college, and her subsequent reply. Preceding each one was a header, which gave the day, hour, minute, and second of transmittal. Putting on my glasses, I tried to read in small stretches until my eyes watered up, and I had to wipe them away to continue. I knew that Amelia loved me deeply, and I had felt nothing close to a bruiser's inability to accept her previous relationships, but it was not a series of innocent letters.

"Hola mi amor. When are you returning to Bogota? Give me a call at my parent's house. They will be in Miami for a few more days, so we will have the house to ourselves. Un beso, Ivan."

Amelia responded tersely a week later. "Ivan, thanks for the note. Things are difficult here. I am going to stay at my parents' house for a while. Ciao, Amelia."

"Amelia, Why don't you answer the phone? What is happening there? Your mother was tight-lipped about things there. I want to come and see you. I know that something is happening. Please call me! Ivan."

Amelia waited a few days before replying. "Ivan, I am sorry. Please do not come here now. I am not going to Bogota this semester. I will be with my mother in Cali. I cannot tell you more. Amelia."

I was deep in an induced sleep in January, the time when these exchanges took place. Amelia told me that she had been sedated for several weeks after the Liverpool Bar incident, and wore a cast on her right arm. She had been to her friends' funerals as well.

Ivan wrote back the next day.

"Amelia, please tell me what is going on there! Is someone ill in your family? Has something happened to you? You can tell me about that, if it is the case. I need to know if you are all right, and when I can come to see you. All your friends are asking about you. Yours, Ivan."

Amelia responded again in a dry, vague manner the next day.

"Ivan, I need some time to myself. Please understand me! Finish your school year. You should concentrate on that for now. Don't worry about me. Amelia."

That exchange took place when, according to Dr. Howe, in a noiseless, darkened room, my brain firing silent electrical storms across a dry plain of consciousness, I was closest to death. Amelia knew none of that, of course, but she could easily intuit the even probabilities of my eventual recovery or sudden death as she sat near my bed all those days in late January.

I skipped forward to April, when I was awake and able to speak to Amelia.

"So, the rumors are true. Paola and Susana were killed by sicarios, and you survived. There was nothing in the news, and my father has not been able to learn anything about the event. This is the Cali way, I guess. Your father never even spoke to my father, who is surprised that your father has not called us. What happened down there? Now, I understand your distance from me. You were in shock—too deep for you to return to school and your normal life. I understand now. Have you been talking to anyone, like a psychologist or counselor? I will wait for you here until you are ready to come back to Bogota. With a kiss, Ivan."

"Ivan. I cannot talk about what happened. Rumors are just that— rumors. If I go back to school, it will be next September. For now, I will stay here with my mother. Please do not use your father's office to investigate rumored events here in Cali. I must insist upon that. Ok? Study and finish university soon. You have a wonderful future ahead of you. Amelia."

My eyes began to weaken, filling up with liquid that seemed to ooze out of the fractures behind my right ear. I had only read about five minutes, but the small print and weak cabin light worsened my normal incapacity for sustained reading. The next page had a header from August, about the time Amelia announced her pregnancy, and we began our engagement.

"How is that possible, Amelia? You fell in love with a gringo? What? You hated gringos and 'GringoLandia', and the gross culture and imperial designs they have inflicted upon the world. What happened to make you change the course of your life? Weren't we happy together? I thought my love for you made you content. The week we spent together in my parent's house in December was the happiest of my life. I imagined our lives together in a nice house, with our friends and someday children. I still love you with the passion I felt for you before your life—or your thinking about life—changed. I wish you never left Bogota for Cali last Christmas. No, Amelia-this cannot be. I cannot accept that a vile gringo is the man you wish to be with. Just because some gringo has used black magic on you, I will not accept it."

Amelia replied the next day.

"Ivan, please respect me, my fiancé, and my privacy. You and I are not a couple anymore. We are not in a relationship or on intimate terms with one another. I love him very much. He makes me happy and that is all I have to say—to you or anyone. I am so sorry that this makes you suffer, but isn't it time to move forward with your life, to find a new love, and make a new happiness for yourself? I made my choice and my decision—I am happy with it. Show me the respect you supposedly have for me. Please leave me in peace, Ivan. Amelia."

A headache had consolidated behind my right eye, which was a stern warning from my brain that severe pain lay ahead if I continued to further abuse my limited privilege of reading. I pulled out the last page on the bottom of the stack. It was dated six days ago. A stewardess brought me a whiskey that I did not remember having ordered.

"So you are 'Mr. and Mrs. Tommy Connolly' as the gringos would say. Your marriage is a public record now. I heard you had to marry in a squalid little church in the east of Cali. Did you have to bribe the church to allow the gringo on church premises? It will take a little effort, but I will find out a little about your gringo-husband. He cannot be worthy of you, Amelia. In your heart, you must realize this. Your fineness and strength and dignity cannot have a match in some gringo you met in a hospital. It is not too late to admit a simple mistake, mi amor. It would not besmirch the high regard for you shared among your friends, professors, and of course, my family and me. Please think about this, mi amor: gringos come and go in this country—they are never who they seem; they take their pleasure the way they invade countries; nor do they keep promises they invent upon a moment's notice to acquire the things they want. They usually get their way and then move on to the next girl, or global market, or war... You will not be able to count on the gringo for much longer. You will regret having met him. Ivan."

This guy was starting to bother me.

"Ivan, you are scaring me. Please leave me alone. My husband and I are happy together. You know nothing of my husband and should not make ignorant comments. Go away, Ivan. I beg you. I am changing my email address. Please forget me and allow me to forget you, and live in peace. You know nothing about me, Ivan. Anyway, my husband will always protect me from danger. Please know that before you do something stupid, again."

She spelled it out for him clearly, but from a common, lovelorn fanatic in the first emails, he had declined to an unstable, puerile brat by their end. This, not pregnancy discomfort, brought forth Amelia's fever the other night. She wanted to know that none of Ivan's accusations had the merest basis in fact, not to know more about my upbringing or college life. She wanted to know that I would shield her from threats and dangers—and guard our fortress with my life, if necessary. I had forgotten that my wife had taken a blind walk of faith, too, one far away from what she expected her life to become, and one that she had obviously not fully convinced herself was truly the right one.

It was at that exact point of Amelia's insecurity that Ivan decided to drop anchor.

This was not the threat to our family that I expected. This was not why I spent sleepless nights pacing my condo in search of solidity in my role as husband and man. Ivan was not a street-tough sicario with sapient, hissing disregard for living things that could explode suddenly in death and blood.

I had taken from him the card which would complete his suite of being young, rich, talented, and successful. He was so close— the right university, the plumb government job, and the beautiful, desirable girlfriend, whose hand he would hold on the grandstand before his maiden political speech, or upon whose cheek he would plant a light kiss before thanking the crowd for their support in his first election victory. I had taken only a piece, but I knew that for Ivan the whole structure now would not stand.

Amelia had the fear again, all pathetically cultivated by her ex-boyfriend, and possibly stoked by her brother. Something unwanted was circling like African buzzards above our little safe haven in the sky, but she could not say, "Tommy! Take that fucker down!" I drank down the whiskey in a single gulp, its burn filling my stomach and spreading outward to my limbs and my brain.

I wanted to bang on the cockpit door to speak to the captain for a simple request to reroute the plane to Bogota.

Nando intercepted my attempt to step toward the back of the taxi line for my ride back to San Antonio. "Mar—... ," he caught himself.

"Tommy, I have a car in the parking lot. This way," he said while slipping the backpack off my shoulder, and hoisting it on his own, thereby securing the envelope with the coded account numbers close to his breast. I shook his hand.

"How are you doing, Nando," I said to him in English.

"Good man, it's this way."

With his hand on my shoulder, he led me through a series of aisles of cars, finally opening the passenger door of his Renault in a spot close to the airport exit.

"Home, James," I tried to joke. Nando switched back to Spanish.

"Yeah, alright, marika—but first let's talk about your trip."

The details being few, and mostly occurring outside my scope of reference or expertise, I had finished my briefing before we left the airport. Nando only asked me about the security at the airport, which was adequate, being far from nearby roads, hilltops or other such places where the DEA could park and take pictures, and dimly-lit, which would make it nearly impossible to know the real purpose of the congress between our small plane and an unmarked van. "Good, marika—and the plane?"

"Parked in Tomlinson's spot, F-12. Fueled and ready."

We drove in silence for a few minutes. "I read some of the emails, Nando. Maybe four of five. My head began to hurt after that. I read the last one, though. Thanks for giving me the package." Nando said nothing, possibly disappointed that his cleverness had designed a scheme to make a devastating impact on me, but my incapacity had almost trivialized the matter.

"What do you make of this guy?"

"Amelia and Ivan were a couple since her first year in university. His father is a senior official in the Foreign Ministry in Bogota. The Colonel knew of the relationship and approved of it. It would have been a good match, marika."

And never will be again.

"How well did you know him?"

"I met him a few times in Bogota with Amelia. He was obviously crazy for Amelia, and treated her well. She seemed happy with him."

Nando realized that he was portraying a version of young love whose conclusion was my superfluity, so he pulled back a little from his implicit endorsement of their relationship.

"You never know, marika. Maybe Amelia had planned to drop him before she met you."

"Has anyone talked to the guy?"

"About you?"

"No, about backing off and leaving Amelia alone."

"No, he obviously has sources of information in Cali—not the Colonel—Amelia told him to stop talking with Ivan and his family last August."

"Then based on your knowledge of the guy, why is he doing this?"

Nando thought for a moment. "I think he cannot imagine that he lost Amelia, especially to someone he would not consider a rival. I think his pride is hurt pretty badly."

"Does Amelia know that I know?"

"Hardly. I made up an excuse to get her to change her email address. She doesn't want you to worry about this guy, obviously."

"How can I find him, Nando?"

"Now you are talking like a man, marika!"

He pulled a piece of paper out of his front shirt pocket.

"'Ivan Michael Moreno Quevada—that's quite a name."

"Try to meet him in public, marika; he works for the Fiscalia after all. If it comes down to his word against your word, you are as good as in jail."

"Ok, I'll let him suggest a meeting place… any other advice?"

"Don't take any shit, marika; you are Amelia's husband!"

The next day, I called Ivan Moreno's office to ask for a meeting with him in a public place in Bogota. His secretary called me back about an hour later with a time, a place, and a date. The place was a bistro called Bar Sevilla, which Nando told me is close to the complex of government buildings near the Capitol, popular with the government and finance workers in the area.

Amelia only knew that I had some unnamed business in Bogota, for which I wore my light linen suit. She gave me a kiss as I left. "My Irish boy is so handsome when he dresses well. Hurry back to me,

Tommy—ok?" Pregnancy had not given Amelia the shakes half as much as Ivan had.

I cupped her face in my hands. "I'll be back for dinner. I promise." I left to the image of a swollen, tired, and scared Amelia, who locked the door behind me. On the way outside the building, I gave the portero a big tip to continue his security precautions, and report back to me any unusual events pertaining to the twelfth floor.

The mid-morning Cali to Bogota flight left me ample time to catch a taxi into the center of Bogota. A few minutes after our appointed meeting time, I presented myself to the hostess at the entrance of the Bar Sevilla, within which there were the few remaining customers who did not have to rush back to their offices. "Ivan Moreno. He is expecting me."

"Yes, sir. Right this way, please." She took me back to a rear table, where Ivan was finishing his lunch.

I stopped close to the table to take in this new type of chill. It was petty and class-based on the surface, but surly and immature and, unfortunately, quite sure of itself, inside and out. Ivan felt no obligation to stand, nor did he reach across the table to accept my outstretched hand. "May I sit?" Instead of speaking, he pointed to the chair.

I looked down at a man about Amelia's height with bony shoulders and a plump waist, the inverted V-shape that upper-class young men in Bogota often displayed in tight polo shirts that conformed to their lazy and soft builds. Ivan wore a charcoal grey suit with a conservative blue tie. He had brown hair and dark eyes with a mole on his right cheek. He had discolored smoker's teeth, and was lighting a cigarette as I sat down. I could hear his mind adding points to his side of the ledger based on appearance alone.

Ivan had set up the occasion not as a lunch, which suggested equality between participants, but as a hearing, in which he was the hearing officer. He had finished his lunch, leaving the plates on the table before him to show me that I was not granted the right to eat with him. I sat down quietly.

"My name is Tommy Connolly."

"Ivan Moreno."

"Thank you for agreeing to meet with me."

Ivan merely nodded, once again to suggest that I should make haste to present my petition and hurry away.

"As you know, I am Amelia's husband. We married last Christmas Day in Cali. Amelia will have twin girls in a month and a half." I left a pause, a chance for Ivan to say something conciliatory or at least earnest, but he stuck to his pose with an added smattering of lawyerly pomposity.

"I am aware of these facts."

At that moment, I wanted to slap his face Bogart-style until he cried for his mother.

A waitress came to our table.

"Would you like a menu, Sir?"

Ivan gave a snide smile, and rushed to take the first puff of his cigarette, the crowning of his ongoing slights towards me.

"No, just bring me an ice tea, please."

Ivan blew smoke off to my side, but the ceiling fan took it and blew it up and around my head. I suppressed a reflex to cough out loud, but ultimately sent a few light coughs into my handkerchief. Ivan seemed amused.

"Where do you work, Ivan?"

"In the Fiscalia—the equivalent of your 'Justice Department'."

"Do you like the work?"

"Yes. I will be going off to Harvard in a few years for diplomatic legal studies. And you?"

"I am a business owner."

He made no response to my comment, unwilling to prolong my stay any more than an amount necessary to make my case, a point he reiterated by stubbing out his cigarette, and placing his cigarette pack in his coat pocket.

He gave me a contemptuous smile, which I weighed and measured, but did not return with anything he could bag as evidence of my character or intentions. I reached into my pocket and took out a single sheet of paper, the last email he sent to Amelia before she changed her email address. I handed it to Ivan face upwards. He would not take it, so I let it rest on his entrée plate.

I began with low-toned university earnestness into which I hoped my real threats would become known to him. "This has got to stop, Ivan. Amelia is having a difficult time in her pregnancy.

This is increasing her stress. She has made her wishes known to you. As a gentleman, I am sure you understand what I am saying." I made my case, simply and politely, leaving plenty of room for Ivan to back away from his shame.

"Is that what you came here to say?"

"Yes. That is all."

Ivan reached into his coat pocket and took out his tobacco assemblage again. He lit his cigarette, and took his first drag, savoring it a moment before he began to speak.

"Amelia was mine, gringo. We were a couple. She will always be mine. I don't know what kind of magic you did to entice Amelia into your bed, but magic shows get boring for someone with as much class as Amelia."

"I understand how you could view the matter that way." I choked back every threatening thing I wanted to say to Ivan, who was, after all, a lawyer. What I said next further enraged Ivan, though I meant to pacify his anger through a distancing of our claims. "Until I read this email, I never even knew of your existence, Ivan. I never set out to destroy your relationship with Amelia. But we are married now, and I am asking you to please cease these emails, which are upsetting Amelia."

Ivan, seeing the waitress approaching our table, crumpled up the piece of paper, and handed it to her before she could put down my drink. He held onto his anger until she turned and left.

"How did you meet, anyway? No one seems to know anything about you. Tommy Connolly does not seem to have left any footprints in this country. You are obviously not a narco, but you are certainly no businessman. What can Amelia possibly see in you? Gringo charm? 'I don't see it, pal,'" he ended in English.

Evidently, Ivan had already begun his preliminary investigations.

"Those matters are between Amelia and me, Ivan." I was running out of reserves, even spying a bar stool and fixing my eye on it a bit too long. Ivan followed my gaze, which meant nothing to him yet. He seemed to bristle at my use of his name, a familiarity he had tried in several ways to sever. "I will never ask Amelia for details of your relationship with her. I only ask for the same respect about our privacy."

"You intrigue me, gringo. And no, I will not show you respect in any manner or under any force of compulsion. It will be fun to find out who you are and what you do in this country. A lot of fun." He wanted this to be a particular kind of personal vendetta, one that matched his strengths to my weaknesses, his ability to tap into innumerable government databases, or ask for special little favors from the other security departments of government, against my limited ability to project an aura of possible danger.

"I understand you have connections and resources, but I assure you that your time would be spent better following other suspicious characters. Amelia and I will be leaving Colombia in short order, anyway."

"Then I had better get started, gringo."

Ivan stood up quickly, reached into his wallet, and placed some money on the table.

"Ivan, please—let it go. Find someone else and be happy."

He looked his most angry and pathetic, again partially owing to my ill-chosen words, which condescended to Ivan a therapeutic remedy to the anger that had intensified and maligned his personality. I remained seated while he put on his jacket.

"When you are where I intend to put you, I will still be here, and Amelia will be here too, 'Mr. Connolly.'"

"You don't have to do this, Ivan. It doesn't dignify either of us." Ivan turned and left.

I had kept my anger in check, but the damage was done. Ivan was a spoiled delinquent in possession of an enormous petulant rage and a new purpose, ancillary to his previous one of delivering Amelia from her tragic mistake. Now, he would expose the real Tommy Connolly, and in this endeavor he could rely upon the investigative powers of the Fiscalia in Bogota, and more than likely in Cali.

So far, he appeared to know only that Amelia suffered injury in the Liverpool Bar, and that her friends died there. He could subpoena all the records for the shootings, but Nando had assured me that the Colonel had scrubbed the files down to a minimum of factual matter. Without a witness, one of the twenty or so in the bar that night, he could make no connection between me, Amelia and the Liverpool Bar.

But as I was learning fast, this was Colombia—life and information both came pretty cheap.

There was not much I could do except to wait for Ivan to make his move. If I beat him to a pulp, which he clearly needed, he would add criminal charges to whatever he was cooking up in the basement of his ruined and spoiled ego. The Colonel, his institution discredited and being picked apart by revelations of bribery by the Cali Cartel, could only push back against Ivan so much. Amelia's ex-boyfriend was in this game for a significant victory. Tommy, befuckinware.

That night, Amelia wearily enjoying the soft breeze of an early Cali night, I placed a special order for empanadas and green chile sauce from our favorite restaurant on the bend of the Cali River. Afterwards, I put on a new cd and Amelia and I danced to Ray Charles "I'm Movin' On!" She kept one arm around the bottom side of her plump belly, and tried to move in tune, her added weight notwithstanding. I knew that dance therapy would not calm her fears, but it made her feel happy, and that was worth something.

Amelia had never heard music like that. Next we spun to "It Should Have Been Me!" which Amelia understood word for word. She laughed and kicked her legs to the subtle naughtiness of the song. I brought her close and kissed her face and cheeks. "I love you, Amelia. I am your man for as long as you want me. I will always protect you." I kissed her again.

Amelia threw her arms around my neck and cried. "Thank you, Tommy. I know you will." I pulled away, and we danced to "I've Got a Woman." Afterwards, I took her to bed and rubbed her feet until she fell deeply asleep.

Again, as was becoming customary for me, I walked down the staircase in the middle of the night, and after ritualistically checking the locks and window jams of the condo, sat down on the balcony on the south side of the condo. It was still and breezeless, except for the occasional pop of fireworks, signifying that someone's deal had gone down right. The city was coiled tight—the FARC was getting closer, and the city streets had fresh narco blood on them again. Upstairs, mercifully, Amelia and the babies slept deeply, the stillness on the second floor giving me some satisfaction that thus far nobody with a pistol or a subpoena had managed to penetrate our front door.

While listening to the morphine-slurred voice of Chet Baker, I had my first and most vital premonition about Ivan: that he would not cease, and that I would have to stop him.

I'll be your fuckin' Valentine, Ivan.

That he held the higher ground was obvious—superior knowledge of the law, the ability to surveil me, and even suborn witnesses if his case was weak. His petty sense of preeminence, animating all his actions toward me thus far, had become a little engine that knew little rest. Agitated and needing some project to take my mind off Ivan, I went to the basement garage. Amelia had not been kind to the Range Rover; each of several little dents and scrapes was a reminder of how little Amelia had ever done for herself before that night in the Liverpool Bar. In our storage unit, I recounted my piggy bank. There was still fifty-thousand dollars of "I'm outta here!" money.

Having enemies was new to me; after the seventh grade, I never got into a fight, or snubbed another kids so that I could be momentarily supreme. But then again, smuggling money across borders in a small plane was also new to me, which I accommodated into my life without much psychic displacement. I went back upstairs to sleep nearly at dawn, having placed the problem of Ivan somewhere for quick retrieval, but I had more pressing matter that required my immediate attention. After all, I was an aviation consultant businessman.

CHAPTER THIRTEEN

The next morning Nando called me again to meet him for lunch at a steak restaurant in midtown.

Nando was already at a rear table when I walked in. He had a newspaper flat on the white tablecloth. I took a good look at Nando in the bright afternoon light. He was lighter-skinned than Amelia, with strawberry blond hair, and a constant tan that gave him the appearance of being a white who lived in the tropics full time. He now had a stricter military haircut than the last time I saw him. His dress khakis were sharply creased and an open collar was the only departure from military dress formality. His sleeves were rolled up to just below his elbow, which he instinctively rolled up one more time on each sleeve when he saw me, looking up and grinning as I entered and refolding the newspaper back to the front page.

"So, how was your meeting with Ivan?"

Keeping narrative elements to a minimum, I tried to present Nando with the basic facts of our meeting and exchanges and farewells.

"It sounds like you did the best you could. I never saw this side of Ivan before. But then again, you never expected to kill a man with a bar stool."

"What about his threat to expose me?"

"It is credible, but he has no evidence, and there is no evidence to be found."

"Including certain real estate transactions we have profited from?"

"There were no illegal maneuvers, and we did not deal with any narcos or Clinton Lististas. Pay your taxes, marika—I will keep a close eye on Ivan." Before we parted, Nando gave me the departure and arrival details of our next flight.

A few days later, Red Sox and I took off on a rainy night from the airport in Jamundi. Due to the implications of Ivan's threats, Nando decided to depart at night, which would make long-distance cameras with telephoto lenses a sucker's game. It also meant that I was away from Amelia for two days instead of one day, since the counting in the basement of Las Cabanas would take place during the day, leaving me without a flight out of Aruba until the following day.

Nando gave me an envelope before I left.

"Happy Birthday, marika."

"Is this about Ivan?"

"Yes, it is. But it is actually your birthday, marika. Didn't you know that?"

"Must have slipped my mind."

"Ohhh, marika."

The job paid about seventy-four thousand dollars. On the return flight, after ordering a preambular whiskey, I opened up Nando's envelope and pulled out a single-page letter from Ivan to Amelia. I began to read Ivan's assessment of our meeting and me.

"Dear Amelia,

You have not responded to my last three emails. I suspect this is the result of your gringo's interference rather than your own preferences. He went so far as to call and demand a meeting with me, which I concluded this afternoon.

The poor man is obviously not in good health, and I doubt he is in possession of a sound mind. A little tobacco smoke in the bar sent him into paroxysms of coughing, and throughout our conversation he needed a handkerchief to keep saliva from falling from his mouth. Since he is obviously not an ex-soldier, I have to wonder how he fell into such a state so early in life.

He was not raised to be your husband; in fact, he must have found some stratagem to raise himself in your esteem and gain an entry to your life. Otherwise, I cannot imagine circumstances in which your lives would intersect normally.

He is obviously ill-educated and relies upon a charm that, while sufficient to seduce a maid, is not enough to charm a woman such as you. Do you want this uncouth, unformed gringo to accompany you through life, raise your children, and support your ambitions? When the charm begins to fail, on what will your illusions about him subsist?

I have spoken with your father. Sadly, he told me that he will not interfere in your life or otherwise persuade you to bring this rash bit of fun to an end.

What happened to you, Amelia? What caused you to suddenly throw away our passion for that shallow, slow-eyed gringo? I know about your pregnancy. I would gladly raise those girls with you if you could see that this thing with the gringo cannot and will not end well.

With deepest love for you,

Ivan"

I could have killed Ivan with my own hands in that moment. Instantly, I regretted the calm demeanor and the underlying caution with which I endured his teenaged taunts. He needed more than a good beating. He needed to know that Tommy Connolly could ruin his life by himself—without statutes or investigators. He needed to know that Tommy would be coming for him, and that he would suffer to the marrow of his flabby self. I could have squeezed his neck muscles down into a handful of gristle. His tremendous presumption to speak this way, as I pondered his words, almost forfeited his right to his silly, mewling life.

It was shameful for me that I had to fear him, based on nothing more than his advantageous protection within the tentacles of the Fiscalia. But his type—spoiled shitticus connectedius—was all over Bogota, and could rely upon a superstructure of school associates and party members to bring down a landslide of legal problems for me, and for Amelia.

As a man, he was not worthy of my fear, or a hesitation to act against him with violence. If he took a punch at me, I would return it with glee. But he would not. All he could bring was harassment from his little lawyer's toolbox of mischief, buttressed by the smug satisfaction that no one would come after him unless the attacker could contend with his family and his position deep in the government classes of Colombia.

And I couldn't. I was a blunt instrument, and tested in extreme violence, but untested in anything that could cause Ivan Moreno concern.

I could not bring myself to go home with such rage in my mind. Instead, I called Stevenson's barbershop from the Cali Airport and demanded to speak with him. There was no management workshop to acquire the "tools" to survive in this place, and I needed to know some things before I ended up in a cell.

I was also tired of being on the short end of Nando's sneers, and now Ivan's contempt due to their insider's knowledge of how government agents skimmed all the good stuff from society, and then brought down any man they wished. I was perfectly capable of discerning—and acting upon—different customs; this was something more noxious. There were camps in this country—the CNP, the Army, the Fiscalia—lead by strong men, and one fell in line behind them to make corruption a safer course and more rational matter than doing something right with one's power. None of them seemed to want Tommy as a permanent member. Stevenson agreed to an 18:00 meeting, which left me with an hour to spend until I would need to take a taxi back into Cali.

The second floor airport bar beckoned. As I trudged up the stairs, I saw Ivan, all petulant smugness and the tyro's bravado, blowing smoke into my face and smiling at my discomfort, tracking in minute detail each delay of my right eye. I ordered a whiskey and watched a few evening planes land.

There were two narco types milling behind me. They had all the trimmings: the flashy suits, slick hair, loud shirts, and the cockiness of those who had amassed a decent fortune by their late 20s. They had made the first cut, neither killed by their own people due to bad luck or honest stupidity, nor killed by an enemy for an "ajuste de cuentas," the famous adjustment of narco accounts that was the official police explanation for most of the unsolved murders in Cali.

They were of a specific type Colombians called gomelos. They had more handsome than normal features, and an ongoing concern for their hair coiffing that was off-putting to other males due to its effeminacy, until one also gave them their due as cold-blooded killers. They were all over Cali these days, like master-less Ronin, waiting for someone else to recreate order among the new drug gangs of Cali, and offer themselves to the new capo.

They walked a little closer to me. I began in Cali Spanish.

"Gentlemen"— I made my opening move — "is there something I can help you with?"

"We would like to invite you to share a drink with us."

"That is a kind offer. But I have a flight to catch."

"You just landed."

"You probably confused me with someone else."

They looked at each other and laughed. "No, senor. We are quite sure." One gomelo looked at the other, and taking the floor from his associate, looked directly at me.

"Senor, we are here to discuss an important matter with you. Please come with us."

"I don't want to. We don't know each other. Sorry, but that's my answer."

"Senor—we are here to discuss a matter of business. There is no need for hostility. We are not here to harm you."

"Fellahs, I don't know you, and I don't get into strange cars. Somehow, you learned about my schedule. That's a point for you. You can do a lot better if you identify yourselves and make an appointment to talk to me. Take this message back to your boss—'show some fuckin' respect.'" I signaled the bartender for another whiskey.

My instincts were correct, as they were only drivers. They lost some of their gift of patter at that point. They did not know how to handle impertinence from someone they knew better than to strong arm. "Senor, please consider our request."

"I have and it is rejected. I am sorry. It is my birthday. I want to get back to my wife. Can you understand that? Can you see that maybe I want to spend time with my wife and not your boss? Did they teach you that in gomelo school? Are you allowed to concede that small fistful of decency in your line of work?"

Or is deadly menace the whole of the man, I thought, dismally.

The alpha gomelo spoke up. "Perhaps you are right, senor. Please excuse our interference. Happy Birthday, Sir." I tilted my glass to them in appreciation of their momentary infusion of kindness into our conversation. I downed my whiskey and, splitting the two gomelos, headed out of the bar.

This was a fresh crack in the wall of security, a failure on the part of Nando and Stevenson, who had to find and vet clients, and then persuade them not to get greedy and attempt side-deals with the guys in the planes. Or it could be something worse: a car ride for me that comes back with one fewer passenger.

It could have been on Sal Manzo's end, the result of a careless conversation on an unsecured line that Tommy C. was the guy in Cali to move easy money out of the country. That did not figure, though. Sal did not chat on the phone, or reveal business practices to anyone outside his family. He had never invited me into his counting room or opened up his bank's books, or taken me on a tour of the exit routes into legitimate accounts for my money. There seemed to be a breach, and I would bet it was here in Cali.

Now, knowing that gomelos were able to locate and trap me in an airport bar, I would have to practice some of the standard evasions that Nando had taught me. I took a taxi to a shopping center, ran out the back, and found a taxi there. I repeated this a few more times until I arrived at the barbershop about twenty minutes late.

Stevenson accepted the news of the gomelos calmly. "Tommy, did you take precautions on the way here?" I outlined the maneuvers I took to arrive without a tail.

"Listen—Stevenson—we have a breach—it is not on my end."

"Don't worry about those guys—they are not what they seem."

"Do you know them?"

"They're harmless."

"Stevenson, they followed me around the airport and into the bar. They confronted me in a public place and expected me to follow them. If they were shooters, I would be dead."

"You won't see them again."

"How can you know that?" He looked at me like the rookie who doubted the play-calling of the senior quarterback.

"What's on your mind, Tommy?"

"I—I think I deserve some deep background. I know you can't tell me operational details—I get it. But I am operating out there without much direction… without much knowledge about the players and their teams."

"What do you want to know, Tommy?"

Stevenson treated me like I was shooting marbles, so I decided to grab my biggest marble and send some others flying out of the circle. "Tell me about my father-in-law, Stevenson. How did he become a legend? Whose side is he on? How is he connected to our little side business? Let's start there."

Stevenson stamped a cigarette onto the top of his desk and then lit it. "For fuck's sake, at least pour me a drink if you are going to blow that shit in my face." Stevenson made a side grin and picked up his black desk phone to call the local tiendacita for some beers. Discovering courtesy, he set up a floor fan to blow the tobacco away from me before it landed.

"What do you know about your father-in-law?"

"He has a huge brain and his own code of justice. No one can catch him at whatever he does. He can keep massive amounts of information in his head without spilling a drop. He loves his daughter. He indulges Nando. He tolerates his son-in-law. Not much else." Obviously there was another fact, which Stevenson knew well, but he gave me a challenging look—to spill a cardinal secret of the Colonel—and then lit another cigarette.

"Your father-in-law was born dirt poor in a small village in the north of the country. It's called Manati. It is dry, isolated and poor. He had no formal schooling as a boy... no brothers or sisters to teach him anything. He worked his father's small farm—chickens, rabbits, a fish pond, some fruit trees, a few sickly cows. After Sunday church, he would ask the priest to help him learn letters and some words. He taught himself to read. The priest in the village gave him simple grammar books and taught him some math. Your father-in-law did the rest. He learned how to read and write at night, under the nearest streetlight. Eventually, the church prevailed upon his father to let the Colonel study formally. It all took place on Saturdays—the rest of the week he worked—hard."

"When he was thirteen, he went to Barranquilla to study at a church high school. He was already six feet tall. He mastered Latin, higher math, and some Greek. At nights, he washed car windows for tips in a restaurant parking lot and sent most of the money to his father."

There was a knock on the door. Stevenson got up and jerked some money through a door opening wide enough to permit the handing off of a bag of beer cans. He turned and tossed one to me. As soon as he sat down, he resumed.

"His scores were so high in high school that all the major universities accepted him on scholarship. He studied in Bogota. In three years, he finished his university studies. He wrote his thesis in Latin. Since there was no one at the university to approve it—they had to find a priest on an archbishop's staff to read it. He had his choice of careers or government ministries. For some reason, he chose the National Police. No one knew why. He could have walked into an embassy or a Congressman's staff. He also acquired a girlfriend—she was the daughter of a high government official. He was only nineteen years old."

"He was too young to receive a commission from the police, so for two years he worked as a uniformed policeman in intelligence operations against smuggling gangs. When he was old enough, he was commissioned as a Captain. He spent five years directing squads of policemen against the new scourge of drug exporters in Cali and Medellin. He had major successes, and gained several promotions. He also made powerful enemies. When he got bored, he asked for a transfer back to Bogota to study law at night. At twenty-eight, he had his law degree, a beautiful blond wife, and a son, Nando. He rejected a job in a ministry that his father-in-law wanted to arrange for him."

"What did he do next?"

"He went back to Cali and resumed his police career. The Cali Cartel had begun to consolidate its preeminence and its influence. They became the economy and political class of Cali. They managed the valley for their own benefit and made a generation of poorly paid government officials rich beyond their imaginations... or abilities. Their wealth began to purchase judges, generals, mayors—whomever they needed to achieve a strategic objective. The Colonel, though, did not take their money."

"Did he cause them losses?"

"Undoubtedly."

"On his thirtieth birthday there was a party in his honor at a Cali restaurant. He was too drunk to drive that night, so his wife drove for him. A few blocks from the restaurant, sicarios shot up the driver's side window of his car—his wife died instantly. The Colonel was asleep at the time of the shooting. It was tragic for the Colonel, well beyond his ability to forgive himself. He lost all interest in his work. Nando was only eight years old. His mother's brain matter and blood were on his face in the back seat. The Colonel was not able to solve the crime, or even develop a theory of the culprits."

"Eventually, he went to the leaders of the Cartel, personally, in their own home. He asked them to swear that they had no part in the murder of his wife. They swore that they had not commissioned the assassination, even though he was costing them millions of dollars. A bargain of sorts began that night, Tommy. An agreement between men. The Cartel found the murderer of his wife. It took them three days. They handed him over to the Colonel, and the shooter and the driver disappeared from history. No one asked any questions. Then or now."

"The Colonel was not under any obligation to the Cartel, but he remembered their help. They arrived at an agreement, at least in principle. It was an agreement that lasted for twenty years, during which the city of Cali prospered like it never had before. He insisted upon certain rules. No bodies dumped in the city, no harming of innocents, no extortion of the commercial classes, or kidnappings for profit of non-narcos. In turn, they gave him information on crimes in the city that the police could not solve. They did their business on airstrips and on highways. The Colonel let them do their thing."

"Jesus."

"Yeah. After a few years, he got bored again and requested special training in the United States. He had taught himself English by that time. There was a program for policemen in anti-insurgency strategy at an army base in the state of Alabama. Nando stayed in Bogota for six months with his mother's parents. The Colonel was the star student and became fast friends with a Lieutenant Mackenzie, an instructor at the college. The Colonel was a great admirer of Mackenzie's. He considered him as a friend until Mackenzie died a few years ago."

"One night, Lieutenant Mackenzie invited the Colonel to dinner at his house. The Colonel was thirty-one years old, tall, potent, brilliant and heart-broken. His blame and guilt were poisoning him from within. In the Lieutenant's house were his wife and a twenty-two-year-old wild girl that the Lieutenant had taken on as his maid. His own children had begun their adult lives.

She was fair-haired and had a reputation in town as too big for her Irish britches, but Lieutenant Mackenzie managed to settle her down somewhat. She served the tall, dark, impeccably-mannered man dinner and fell so far in love that she would not sleep or work until the Colonel returned to ask her for a date. Lieutenant Mackenzie gave his consent. They dated for three months until it was time for the Colonel to return to Colombia. Of course, he graduated first in his class."

"Amelia's mother was already a month pregnant. Lieutenant Mackenzie did not judge the Colonel; he respected him. He knew about the Colonel's loneliness, but he insisted that the Colonel take responsibility for Kathryn's predicament. Amelia was born eight months later in Cali in a new house the Colonel bought for his bride in the south of Cali. There were rumors that the house was a gift from the Cartel, but out of respect for both of them, no one ever asked to see papers. The

Colonel worked in Medellin, Bogota, but managed to return to Cali, where he raised Amelia and Nando."

I had guzzled down about three beers during his summary of the Colonel's life. "Quite a story, Stevenson. Where do you fit into it?"

He looked at his watch. "You are tired, Tommy. Let me get you a taxi home, alright?"

That was my second humiliation of the day.

I turned twenty-six or twenty-seven that night. Amelia was too weak to dress herself for dinner or manage the trip to the basement parking lot and into the car for a birthday dinner. We had pizza and beer sent to the house and watched Amelia's insipid hyper-violent movies. How could I be glum next to the most desirable woman in Cali, a certain winner of Miss Colombia had she chosen to enter the pageant? Pregnancy had not diminished her beauty, but added a blue luminous aura of fresh loveliness like additional lines to a beautiful sonnet. She had beaten back the fear for a while, but it was out there, circling.

Amelia laughed with me and held my hand on the couch, enjoying my deluxe massage of her feet, and her ankles, replaying scenes from an American movie over and over to catch up with jokes or other bits of dialogue. She placed my hand on her stomach and told me that she loved me and regarded me as big, strong, tall Tommy Connolly, who would be there if bullets flew or neurotics lurked outside the window of our lives, or if some massed force we could not imagine crashed our party or threatened our safe, little home in the sky.

There was no way back and no other route to take. I embraced fortune, but thought seriously about shooting lessons.

CHAPTER FOURTEEN

$56,000, $84,000, $92,000, $59,000, $126,000: the amounts were not overwhelming, but consistent, and taking only two days a week, I had more money than I would have made in twenty years of teaching college. My accounts were back over three million and climbing, which meant I was free and clear of financial debts to the Colonel and on route to clear over a million dollars that year.

That was dream-on money for Tommy Connolly, the boy who scampered under the bleacher seats early on Saturday mornings after Friday night football games to pick up enough small change—fallen from fans' pockets when they stood to cheer—to buy Cokes and candy bars, or a new bicycle wheel.

I kept track of it, but otherwise did not understand it or know what to do with it. Guys like Sal Manzo knew how to spend it, foolishly and broadly, on prostitutes in even numbers, or farms in upstate New York and Canada, or as tributes to old guys back in Canada. They liked knowing it was in their pockets, or stacked nicely in their wall safes, or in banks they would never enter.

It had not touched me yet—I was still diffident Tommy Connolly, and even though I had a growing legend as a guy who could make certain things happen in Colombia, that was some other guy during moments when I needed to square the real accounts with T. Connolly. I was married to the most beautiful woman I had ever seen; how could I ever place a cash value on that?

I accepted the terms of a flight eight days before Amelia's due date in early April, with Amelia's blessing. At about four o'clock in the morning, as I was settling into bed after a few hours with Sal in his night club, there was a loud knock on the door of my suite in Las Cabañas. "Fuckin' DEA!" I thought, an irascibility that heretofore only Nando could bring out in me. I opened the door for a night shift bellman who handed me a note.

"Marika, Amelia is in labor. Get your ass back to Cali. Nando." Shit. Shit. Shit. The count would not be done until the early afternoon, and Red Sox—even if I could find him—needed rest before beginning another long flight back to Cali.

By the time I arrived in Cali, two new lives would be brought forth from streams which do not often cross.

On my side, we have Cromwell-hating Irish immigrants who ran bars, smuggled liquor and otherwise marauded through California for a hundred years until their spark ran out and their days wound down, a decline finalized by a pure-blooded Irish single mom with a mental disability who settled into a trailer with a small son. This son was a solitary boy who grew up versed in Yeats and the Easter Uprising, and improbable family sufferings at the hands of Indians, or the Los Angeles police, or Japanese soldiers in the Pacific, or if all else rhetorically failed for my mother, Oliver Cromwell.

On Amelia's side, the Colonel brought black, mestizo and Italian blood, and an intense hatred of poverty and laziness to the DNA mix.

It was our policy that I did not call home from Aruba, so I had not been able to speak directly with Amelia since Nando announced her labor. She had taken a taxi to the hospital by herself late last night and slept through the early hours of her labor. She did not know where I was or when I could return. My plan was to take the afternoon flight to Bogota, and one of the hourly flights to Cali from there, which would allow me to be with her by sundown.

Sal was slovenly with his women, but he respected Amelia. After I told him the news, he promised that he would speed up the count, but still did not allow me near the counting room. He only quickly added that he would give me the return envelope at breakfast in his office the next morning.

The plan—from Aruba to Bogota to Cali—was working all the way onto the coastal highway until Lukas dropped a roach down his collar and hit a taxi a few miles from the airport. The police arrived, and noting the "Las Cabanas" labels on the door panels of the Town Car, gave Lukas the option of returning to Las Cabanas after they finished their accident report to avoid the inevitable drug test.

Lukas was wildly animated with fear and guilt. I had to grab him so that he would not slug the taxi driver, who was screaming that he needed a complete police report to save his job. He would not take cash and decided upon the dangerous course of demanding a drug test from Lukas. I had to throw Lukas in the back of the Town Car and keep him there, so that I could reason with the guy without Lucas threatening to slash his tires.

I looked up and down the road for a taxi, but our accident had stopped traffic for miles behind us. One of the policemen called Sal, who promised him a free night in the VIP section of the club if he would get me to the airport. I got in the police car, and we drove with the siren successfully clearing our path straight into the departure's terminal, arriving about ten minutes late. I called Sal to thank him, and to ask him not to punish Lukas for the accident, even though he desperately deserved a slap to the back of the head from someone experienced in the maneuver.

I missed my flight. There being no more flights into Colombia from Aruba the rest of that day, I had to take the only flight into Panama City left, where I could get the quick hop along the Pacific Ocean coast to Cali. With nothing else to do, I called the hospital.

Amelia had awoken and was asking for me. Nando, in the hospital with his own security team, was not sympathetic to my description of events, and my remedy. "Why didn't you take the Piper back to Cali, marika?"

"Something called mission protocol, Nando. Listen—when is the approximate hour of the birth?"

"There is not such concept in nature, marika. It just sort of happens—maybe about four more hours."

"Shit! Shit! Nando—I will still be in Panama City. I'll talk to you then." After a three-hour wait there, I caught a late-night flight to Cali, all the other flights before mine being full. I got through customs about 01:00 in Cali, and made it to the hospital about 02:00.

I opened the door after a timid knock. Amelia was in a blue gown in her hospital bed, with a hospital robe loosely around her. Her hair matted to the sides of her head, her mother had applied some makeup to her eyes and lips to restore as much beauty as the shock of childbirth would permit. She looked up from her bed when she saw me enter the door with eyes that instantly cleansed themselves of doubt and worry.

"I thought you were not going to be able to come, Tommy, come here!"

"That was never in doubt, Amelia."

I bent over the bed and kissed her, letting her release a quick torrent of tears that subsided into hiccups and kisses, muffled by the pair of arms that held me around the neck and would not let me rise for breathe.

"Thank you, Tommy."

I stood up, silently holding her hand, giving her my profound thanks for being my wife, and now the mother of our children.

Behind us, Amelia's mother stood with her father, whom I had not noticed before, there being no security outside the door. I broke the embrace to kiss her mother on the cheek and to shake hands with her father.

I did not have to mention anything about where I had been and why I was late: this was a family that knew there was no reason to engage in small talk about things that happen while out in the field. I was learning to fill those gaps with phrases that lent verisimilitude to my concocted stories.

"I have been out of communication for a few hours. I am sorry for that. There was a problem with the plane. I can't tell you how relieved I am to be back, though."

Amelia's mother spoke to me in slightly southern English. "Don't you want to see your girls, Tommy?" Kathryn took me by the hand to an incubator on the far wall. I walked near and then saw Bonnie and Claire in little white bundles. They each had black hair, little button noses, green and hazel eyes and full lips. Their hands touched each other as they slept peacefully.

The shock was severe; I had been close enough to death to know how wonderful was the renewal of life. I put my hand knuckles-first into my mouth, trying to tamp down on deep-seated emotions until Kathryn noticed blood on my hand. I returned to Amelia and put my head close to hers so that only she could see me cry.

"So beautiful, Amelia, and we have two." I whispered in her ear. I could barely get out the words in English.

"Yes, Tommy. We are blessed."

"We made beautiful girls, Amelia."

I lowered myself to her face again for another kiss when the door flung open. Nando appeared with a bottle of whiskey and plastic water cups. I turned to him with teary moistness still in my eyes.

"Marika, please! You will scare the babies that way. They need to see their father is a man, not a proud gay man."

Amelia's mother laughed and told Nando that he was terrible.

"Come on, Pop! A toast to the juevon who owns an aviation company and couldn't catch a flight to see the birth of his own daughters!" The Colonel guffawed at the joke, passing along a cup of whiskey with a friendly pat on the shoulder.

I returned my gaze and my hands to Amelia's. She was suddenly asleep, so we moved the party out to the hallway, where inside a cordon of two guards whom I had not noticed before, Nando resumed his joking about my misadventure in Aruba with invented details, since it was not material to anything that my hotel driver was stoned. The Colonel offered to get me a hotel next to the hospital, but reversing the format of our courtship, I slept on the couch until Amelia awoke early the next morning. I positioned Bonnie and Claire on Amelia's chest until suction was achieved on Amelia's breasts by both girls, and sang little lullabies to them.

It took a few days for the semblance of an ordered household to appear in the condo. That entailed three nightly feedings, morning baths, cradling with Mom, Dad and Grandma, and of course the ungodly cleaning chores. I sent myself out for diapers—and brandy—on day three. The reckoning of a month's supply of diapers was off by one baby. At our current rate, we would not last ten days. Like Amelia, with whom I shared the feeding of the girls in the middle of the night, I was peevish from lack of sleep and overall disorientation. Capping my bad humor, Nando called to tell me to be out in front of the building in an hour. "I need to get some diapers, Nando! This has to be fast."

"Anything you say, marika."

Instead, we drove the familiar route down the spine of Cali to the general's headquarters.

The office of the adjutant was empty, so we strolled down the corridor, and knocked on the Colonel's office door. "Entre!" I recognized the Colonel's voice. He was in his dress khakis, but with his sleeves rolled up and a cigarette hanging from his hand. On the table, there was a bottle of scotch and two glasses.

"Should we wait outside, Colonel?"

"No, Tommy. You are just on time. We have a visitor." I did not see anyone else. Nando pushed the door wide open and sailed past me into the room. He went straight to the bottle, poured himself a drink, and otherwise comfortably settled himself into a chair.

"Can I get you anything to drink?" asked the Colonel.

"Just water, thank you. It will go nicely with your scotch if you can find another glass."

The Colonel went out into the adjutant's office with a light smirk and came back with a bottle of cold water and another glass. He put his cigarette out in the ashtray on the table, so that he could properly mix our drinks. The scotch burned deep into my stomach and rose back up as regenerated calm after a few days of sleeplessness and nearly-blown nerves.

We sat and talked about the babies, unnervingly chatting about his granddaughters until the mystery guest arrived. Well into my second drink, the door opened and a man in his late 40s, grey-suited and blue-tied, walked in with large strides to the center of the room.

His shoes shone brightly, and the crease of his pants was outstanding in this climate. Like so many diplomats and academics, he had the ability to control his sweat in torrid tropical heat. His hair was thinning and greyed and oiled from front to back. I stood up to greet him. He extended his hand and introduced himself.

"I'm Martin Fuller from... the U.S. government."

"Tommy Connolly, Sir."

"It's a pleasure to meet you at last, Tommy."

The first drink improved my constitution, and the second my humor, but it also—for better or worse—loosened my tongue.

The Colonel spoke in Spanish now. "Dr. Fuller has come from Bogota to address some issues regarding your government service." Dr. Fuller switched to Spanish as well.

"I won't take much of your time, Tommy." He didn't, really. He reviewed the national security interest of my treatment at the hands of the Colombian National Police. I assured him that the treatment was of a high quality and that they had my respect and gratitude. He assured me that the State Department had briefings on my care and my whereabouts at all times and that there was no reason to interrupt the plans of the Colombians in light of the security risks involved.

"Tommy, due to the exigent nature of the shooting and your medical recovery, we found that we had to cancel your embassy contract. I hope you understand, Tommy. You were an excellent candidate, and you likely had a great career in your future."

"I understand, Dr. Fuller."

He returned to English for the next patch. "Technically, you did not follow your site-country arrival protocols. Your taxi drive into central Cali and your entrance into the Liverpool Bar were in violation of the security precautions required due to the security situation in Colombia. The U.S. government therefore does not take responsibility in a legal sense for your injuries, and has voided your employment with the United States Department of State. That is the fine print, Tommy. We are deeply sorry to sever ties with you on an official basis. I want to say, personally, that your conduct displayed the highest degree of bravery, and the State Department recognizes your valor in saving the life of Amelia Hernandez."

This was almost bizarre. He was talking about events from sixteen months ago like he was just now reviewing the file on them. I listened to his strange explanation of events from a life before my present one, and none of his explanations mattered much to me now. There was no urgency to inform me of my lack of employment at the embassy, certainly none that would cause a mid-level bureaucrat to fly to Cali and relate to a young prospect the utterly obvious news that his career would not ever happen.

The scotch breakfast was also discordant. It was apparent that Dr. Fuller was familiar with the Colonel, and felt comfortable enough to sit in his office and share anecdotes and observations over drinks.

"Certain doors have closed to you, officially, that is. But we will always be available to you unofficially, if that is your wish." I looked toward the Colonel.

"Could I have your card, then?" They both laughed.

"I must have left them in Bogota. The Colonel will be more than happy to serve as an intermediary."

Dr. Fuller stood at this point, and I followed.

"Tommy, I wish you good fortune, especially with your new family."

I almost felt that I should walk the poor, disoriented man to his rental car, like walking a deranged man off a movie lot sound stage after he delivered an otherwise excellent take. "Thank you for the kind words, Dr. Fuller. I will always regret that I am unable to serve my country in an official capacity."

He smiled at me. "I think you will find a way to be of value to both causes, Tommy." Dr. Fuller returned to Spanish to say his farewells with the Colonel and walked out.

I sat back down and finished my scotch. I did not speak and the Colonel did not listen. He did drink, however, savoring the scotch until his glass was empty. What cause was he talking about, and why would I need the Colonel as an intermediary in order to deal with him? I shook my empty glass at Nando, who poured three more.

"Colonel, I need to get some diapers. Amelia is waiting for me." There was no subtle way to engage the Colonel on the question of why I needed to listen to a truncated, official release from duty speech that was about a year late. He looked at Nando with a slight loss of patience, as if preparing himself for something almost distasteful.

Nando almost threw his glass at me. "Don't be such a marika, Tommy. Do you have any idea what is going on in this country? There are some things more important than baby diapers, or don't you follow the news?"

"I do, but thanks, Nando."

"Do you know how many operations are underway at this moment that the Colonel is leading? If he calls you here, it is not to discuss your family preparedness!"

"I get it, Nando. Sorry."

The Colonel waved off Nando as well. "Tommy did not know the import of Doctor Fuller's appearance here, Nando. Besides, he hasn't slept much lately."

The room needed to regroup and cool down, so the Colonel indulged in a little personal nostalgia.

"Tommy, my favorite event when I was in the United States was the Army-Navy football game. I flew up to Philadelphia as a guest of Lieutenant Mackenzie. It was bitterly cold in Philadelphia in December. I was in my Colombian police uniform, but without a jacket. General Hargreaves from the U.S. Southern Command let me use one of his jackets. We sat on the Army side near the center of the field. It was a glorious day. There were about 100,000 people in the stadium. Both teams were playing with a great intensity and for the honor of their institutions and the traditions they carried forward that day."

"I thought that this was American society at its finest. Passion for national service wedded to an equal passion for individual glory. My thoughts turned darker only brief moments later. I thought what if this game was in Colombia? Here, loyalty would conflict with duty, and solidarity would conflict with bigotry. In Colombia, half of each team would consist of infiltrators from the other team. The referees would take money from both coaches. There would be rules in the game, but no one would follow them, and the referees would not notice. After the game, the players would drink and go after putas with the players from the other team. There, they would plot to kill their coaches."

I took a deep gulp of scotch, jealously eyeing the remaining finger or two in the bottle. Nando continued with his usual levity, "The losing team would kill the mascot of the winning team!" He and the Colonel laughed.

"At this moment, my office is investigating at least 225 narcotics-related murders. The total since 1995 is over fifteen hundred. The streets of Cali and the little towns in the valley cough up over twenty bodies a weekend. Why such stakes? The yearly revenue of the Cali Cartel was over $8 billion annually! That is all up for grabs now. In the north of the Cali Valley, they are attacking rival gangs with helicopter gunships. In the jungle, occupying over half the land in this country is the FARC. They are close to each major city and slowly closing a ring around Bogota. They intend to topple our government and install a Maoist-style dictatorship."

"Our main line of defense is not our own infantry, but groups of psychopathic self-defense forces that want to be narco-gangsters too. But out of chaos there is coming an emerging order of sorts. Your government has declared to the world that Colombia is a 'failed state.' We are The Mouse that Chokes on Cocaine. So, billions will flow into Colombia in the form of planes, electronics, spies, used equipment, special forces, and no doubt a legion of pacifist Quakers."

"Like you, marica!" Nando almost spilled his drink at that one.

"Tommy, I have over 500 men under my direct command. Half are engaged in actions that are taking out the intelligence, logistics or financial operations of the remnants of the Cali Cartel. This is not your war, Tommy. You are not obligated to do anything more than take care of Amelia, which you can do from Arlington, Virginia or Miami, or California. You are a father, a man now. You can go back or stay. If you stay, your stay will benefit by knowing the rules. The only people whom you can trust, and who will never betray you are in this room. Whomever you do business with will sell you out to save themselves, and the most duplicitous characters you will ever meet will be government actors. So, you can sell Cadillacs in Miami and raise orchids with Amelia on weekends. I will respect your decision and leave you alone. You started your career as a..." he stopped speaking English, and directed himself toward Nando in Spanish. "Los que estampillan a los documentos en oficinas del gobierno. Como se llaman en ingles?"

"No se. Un... que 'Stamper'?"

"Yes, Stamper. That is how you presented yourself. A document stamper. You have a second chance now. You can go be the best stamper in Miami..." Nando laughed until the Colonel cut him off. "or you can work with Colombia and the U.S. to end all this mierda de drogas y violencia. You are in a unique position, Tommy. Your father can provide you with contacts and resources in Washington, D.C. I can open doors for you here in Colombia. You know the country well; you have stakes here, Tommy; you can make a real contribution."

The Colonel was reaching the summation of his speech. "But you have to live with the betrayal, savagery and insecurity of this country, Tommy. It is the rhythm of life here. As soon as you have something in this country, someone appears who wants it more than you do, and usually is better at taking it than you are at protecting it. You have to be fully determined to succeed in your work."

"What work?"

He paused for a swallow of scotch. "Dr. Fuller is from the CIA, Tommy. He knows your father. They both think that you are suited to carry out intelligence work here in Colombia."

Nando cut in again with more uninspired jocularity. "Code name: Stamper!" The Colonel looked back towards me patiently, aware of the abrupt nature of Dr. Fuller's visit.

Dr. Fuller's mawkish appreciation of my defunct career in the embassy made sense now. Dr. Fuller was finalizing his pitch to the Colonel when I walked in. I was not meant to engage with Dr. Fuller, but rather to listen to the Colombian version of the pitch, which the Colonel intensified through his parade of Colombian horrors.

The Colonel appended his own messages to the basic pitch: that this was dangerous work, for which there was a real possibility of death; that there would be no rules or formal training; that betrayal could come from any direction and at any time; and that albeit with a much lower estimation of my worth as a man, we would still be in the same family if I did not take the job. He threw down the challenge softly, but it landed on my cheek, twice-recently humiliated, like a boxing glove with lead inside.

After all, I was in reality a document stamper, collegial, reliable and charming, but lacking the skeletal virtues of fortitude, discernment, and guts, ones that separated the commando from the stamper. The Colonel in effect was telling me at that moment that I had to make a decision: to take on my fair share of the blood sports in Colombia, not just take a percent off the top in the safe confines of my work with Stevenson; or go back to Miami, so that the real men could get on with their work.

There was no one with whom I could discuss the offer, even if I had not made up my mind immediately. Amelia would never know, but she would understand.

At that point, my funds were well over three million. I could probably stretch out the sale of our house in Cali for a few months, increasing that amount by almost half a million dollars. Amelia and I could start businesses and live a smart social life in Miami. Occasionally, I would undertake a criminal deed on behalf of Colombian intelligence and their allies for extra money in Miami, and to keep somewhat in the game.

But I would always be a Stamper in their eyes, counting and stacking sheep hides inside the walls of Troy, while the real men stopped the invasion beyond them in bloody warfare, from which only some of them returned each night. I would be diminished by having missed my war, and quite possibly for Amelia as well as the years flowed by comfortably in Miami.

Intelligence covered a lot of undertakings—from renting cars for spies to putting bullets in brains. I wondered how far along the spectrum my father, Dr. Fuller, and the Colonel placed me. I poured my own drink.

"What kind of work do they have in mind?" Nando went over the specifics in a vague manner.

"Air supply, mostly, but also intelligence collection on the ground. They are pouring a lot of money into the anti-guerrilla fronts. They need an objective assessment on their return on investment." I looked over at Nando, who had the good sense to realize that I was on my own now.

"They being the CIA?"

"They being agents from your government or their contractors."

"Tell Dr. Fuller that I accept his offer, pending my Aruban lawyer's approval of their offer of employment." I moved to the Colonel's desk and wrote Leo Huff's name and phone number on a pad. "This is his contact information in Aruba. Once they work out details, I will be happy to begin."

I finished my drink, placing it gently back on the tray on the Colonel's desk and shook the Colonel's hand. "Thank you for your serving as an intermediary, Colonel. I know you are busy. I will take over from here." The Colonel rose to shake my hand, only slightly relieved, since this was probably a small matter compared to the Cartel civil war in the north, and the constant subversion of urban guerrillas in Cali.

I turned my attention to Nando. "Nando, let's go!" Outside the building, I spoke close to his ear. "Tell Stevenson to be ready in two days, and prepare a big load this time."

$72,000, $96,000, and then $107,000, as if Stevenson knew I would be otherwise engaged for a while. There had not been a nod in my direction from Ivan so far. His ego would not remain patient for long; he had resources—it was only a matter of time before he decided to call upon them. But the gates of Troy had opened for me briefly in the night so I could escape to the shores, while Ivan seethed within them. I was going to war.

A few weeks later, after settling the details of my milk run with Sal Manzo, I sat comfortably in Leo Huff's office, having informed him that I wanted to be part of the contractual discussions with Dr. Fuller only during the final iterations that addressed the contract's finer points. Leo Huff was dressed in a Hawaiian shirt, not unusual for a Saturday morning in Aruba.

"So, Tommy. I got a phone call and then a fax from the office of a Mr...."

"Doctor Fuller."

"Yes, he is from a department of your government that does not like to refer to itself by name. I had to remind him that contracts are not valid if one party is not in a position—and in our case that means having a jurisdictional name—to sign the contract. We had to dance around that question philosophically several times. In fact, the discussion of that term is probably longer than the contract itself."

"Based on your knowledge and experience, Leo, does the contract put me in any danger?"

"Tommy, working with the CIA is not clerical in nature. Of course, there is danger. It may come through a U.S. Senate subpoena, a leak about your participation in a secret mission that appears in the Washington Post, or plain ethical issues about right and wrong. That is a short list of a long volume of possible risks. These risks, however, are manageable. The CIA has an interest to use your services as a conveyance company. You should ask yourself—or perhaps you already have—why the CIA is interested in a young man without experience in flying, conveyance, or certainly espionage. That is your business to ponder. The contract is straightforward. You are contracted to perform conveyance duties through Tomlinson Ltd. of Aruba of cargo deemed vital to furthering the interests of the United States, that you are not responsible for its contents, but that the CIA will not avow your working relationship in case you wind up in the wrong hands. The bad guys certainly will know that you are working for the CIA and size up your market or hostage value appropriately. That is the unwritten part of the contract.

"And the drugs?"

"Tomlinson will not agree to take possession of any item which contravenes U.S. narcotics laws."

"Good. Does it mention pay?"

"You always come back to that, don't you?"

"Sorry. Tomlinson is a business, Leo."

"Yes. They will pay you a standard rate unless both parties change on a case-by-case basis the terms of a particular conveyance. I gather the idea of risk has to have a floating value in this type of business."

"As my lawyer, do you see any legal reason why I should not sign this contract?"

"No. It protects you financially, it will hide your identity from most subpoenas, and you can leave it at any time without penalty. You are not allowed to talk about your role in any of its aspects for the rest of your life, though. To anyone."

"You are in a separate category, though."

"I am your lawyer, Tommy. Not your favorite bartender. You tell me things to further my understanding of a problem that you need to solve, and no more. Ok?"

"Yes, Leo. I got it."

"In that case, you can sign this document 'as is,' and I will send it off." I signed the contract and Leo walked it out to his secretary for fax transmittal to a military base in Tampa. Leo asked me to wait in the reception area while we waited for the exchange of faxes.

Leo's secretary smiled at me occasionally. There were no magazines in his office, and I had forgotten my reading glasses, rendering of little utility the bookcase of thickly-bound volumes in Dutch, German, Italian, Spanish and English. Sparkling water did little to make the time pass faster. Eventually, the initial bars of an incoming fax hummed. In the room beyond his secretary's desk, two pieces of paper fell onto a tray. She picked them up and carried them into Leo, who moved the papers around to the lilt of Vivaldi. A few moments later, the phone on her desk rang, and she waved me into his office.

He handed me the fax. There was no cover page, nor did it mention a sender or me. The addressee was Tomlinson Ltd of Aruba. The next line was the address of Leo's office, which was, I gathered, Tomlinson's corporate address. The next line said "Personal and Confidential: not for distribution." I turned to the next page. Holy Shit. Tomlinson accepted the contract to convey cargo from the Aruba airport to a set of coordinates in Colombia. Tomlinson would take possession of the cargo at midnight tomorrow night, and proceed in a direct fashion 'without unreasonable delay' and arrive at the coordinates indicated by noon the next day."

I had only accepted a commission. The actual contract was at a Panamanian base in someone's safe until I arrived there to sign it. The CIA likely felt that the guarantees codified in a contract were less than the higher law embodied in my duty to my country.

It was another place of potential havoc, but it was out there—beyond my refuge where my daughters were learning to crawl and my wife not to succumb to sudden panic. Having absconded with Helen of Cali, somehow I thought that we could live a peaceful life with our children and family far from the Achean invaders. Silly Tommy. Silly country fuck.

CHAPTER FIFTEEN

Leo Huff did not look pleased at all with my uninvolving synopsis of our upcoming voyage through Colombian airspace. "Problem, Leo?"

"It is your first trip, and a night flight through the central spine of Colombia, with a landing point that is not referenced by an airport. I may be out of touch with modern airplane technology, but that seems quite risky to me."

"The pilot will know the territory, Leo. They have been night flying since Laos. The CIA knows our flight path, and will alert the Colombian Air Force and local authorities to stand down."

"It is flying over a jungle, Tommy, with all that that entails." We left matters at that impasse, Leo content at having made clear his objections, and thereby having fulfilled his formal duty of counsel, and perhaps issuing some words of wisdom that he could not justify in aeronautical terms.

Amelia, as a consequence of being her father's daughter, of having felt throughout her childhood that he participated in the day's headlines without ever being able to ask him a direct question, did not mind that she knew very little about my strange comings and goings. Things were taking form and shape in my life; though she knew better than to cross over—however indirectly—to my side through even the most innocent question, Amelia felt that her husband was involved in important things, which would bring him either more money or greater acclaim, both justifying his long absences from her. She kissed me deeply when I left early for Panama that first morning.

"I know you can do anything, Tommy! Come home safe for me, ok?"

The next morning, a black sedan took me from my Panama City airport hotel, a short distance across empty lots with soggy and steamy tire mountains and tilting concrete slabs until the creamy white block letters of "United States Air Force Howard AFB" came into view. In the distance low hills stood down a protrusion of orderly rows of buildings, avenues, and geometric lawn patterns.

We drove a few miles above the modest base speed limit about a mile down the main entrance road and took a simple right turn into the second of a row of three-story cream buildings. The sentry, younger than I, but inured to visitors with normal business on the base, walked me into the main reception, where the guard checked my passport against a visitor's log on a clipboard. He took me down a long, white-tiled corridor to a large brown door marked "Major Randall Keuken." The sentry knocked and waited until we heard a low-sounding and gruff "Enter."

He pushed the door open and then stepped back for me to enter. Behind the broad desk sat a broad, blond man in his 40s. Even though there was no air conditioning in his office and the temperature was already in the low 90s, Randy Keuken wore his collar buttoned and tied, only accommodating the intense muggy heat by rolling up his sleeves to just below his elbows.

As he stood, a small plane without military insignia snuck downward in its approach toward the tarmac behind his back in almost total silence.

He approached me and extended his hand with plain, masculine economy.

"Randy Keuken."

"Tommy Connolly."

"Come on in and have a seat, Tommy." He seemed strong and dependable, quite able to handle the ambiguities of overseeing CIA plane-support on the base, I thought.

Keuken asked me about my flight and my stay, calmly settling into a comfortable pattern of exchange by which we established a handle on one another. After a while, he approached our matters directly.

"Tommy, I have a package for you. It is marked personal and confidential. I have not read it, nor has anyone else on this base. You are the addressee. Please take all the time you need to study it. It needs to be signed before we can continue to the next part of your visit with us." A quick hint of awkwardness appeared on his face; etiquette required I be offered a beverage. "Can I get you a coffee, Tommy?"

Leo told me to sign the document, but not to appear in too much of a hurry.

14. I understand that the purpose of this agreement is to implement the responsibilities of the Director of Central Intelligence....

I told him that I would love one with cream, if possible. I opened the package, which began with a cover letter from Dr. Fuller. It explained the contents, which were the terms of the agreement between Tomlinson Ltd. of Panama City, Panama and the Central Intelligence Agency. It was simple and thorough, though I knew that if things were straightforward, they would not have hired me.

My obligation was to transport, using my own corporate assets, conveyances of the United States government. These shipments had starting points among about five bases in Panama and "installations of a military nature" within the country of Colombia. There were clauses wherein I was not to take title to any of these shipments, and would have no further obligation for them once I obtained a signature on the receiving end. My fee was $25,000.00 per flight. Interestingly, the CIA had the right and obligation to find a pilot for any conveyances over 5,000 pounds, while I possessed the option to provide my own plane and pilot for any conveyance under 5,000 pounds.

That had to be Leo's work, I thought.

10. I understand that any breach of this agreement by me may result in the Central Intelligence Agency taking administrative action against me....

I waited for Randy Keuken to return so that he could unofficially witness my signing. I sipped some coffee and asked him for a pen. I signed three copies of the document, one of which I kept. Randy got on the phone and dialed four numbers, before taking a sip of coffee and wiping some sweat off his upper lip. Randy, who seemed comfortable at dealing with the CIA as an almost silent partner, could tell that I was not.

9. I understand that nothing contained in this agreement prohibits me from reporting intelligence activities which I consider to be unlawful or improper directly to the Intelligence Oversight Board....

"This is Major Keuken from Executive Transport... I'll hold, yes." He leaned back and took in for a few seconds the view of the empty runway below. "This is Major Keuken. Is the room ready?" He looked at his watch. "That will be fine. There will be two of us... with Tampa, yes... Alright, then. We'll see you then." He hung up the phone.

3. In consideration for being employed or otherwise retained to provide services to the Central Intelligence Agency, I agree that I will never disclose in any form the following categories of information...

Randy Keuken did a decent job of reading my mind in that moment.

"Tommy, I assume you have heard of Air America?"

"The private plane company that flew supplies in and out of Laos during Vietnam?"

"Yes. That is the basic model of ownership and provenance in your case. You will fly loads in to target locations, and we will maintain all planes—yours and ours—here, or at one of the other bases. They will gas it for you—you gas it up on the other end if necessary with a bag of cash or a corporate credit card that you will fly with—plus a generous tip. These are short flights, though. I cannot imagine the need to refuel unless you curl around Lima and head back." He smiled at his own wisecrack.

"Tell me about the plane, Randy."

"It dates to the Korean War. In those days it was the Douglas D-26 Invader, a light attack bomber. Its class was officially decommissioned, but actually many of them went back to the Douglas workshop. In the Air America days, it gained electronics. That generation has been sitting around jobless for a while. Some got the full Douglas treatment, but were never used. It weighs about 25,000 pounds and can fly at 35,000 at a maximum 365 mph. 40k is pushing it. That will put you in Tolemaida in about an hour and a half and the Amazon region in about three."

"Who is going to pilot that size plane, Randy?"

"You'll meet him later this afternoon. His name is Cody Pryor."

"Agency?"

"Are you?"

"Point taken."

It would behoove me, I thought, not to ask that sort of question ever again.

He looked at his watch, and suddenly alerted to our appointment, slapped the edge of his table. "Let's start spending some of those 1998 appropriations for anti-drug fumigation equipment sales to Colombia!" I smiled. Already, these guys were a little too blasé about misleading a distractable public for my taste. My mother used to tell me that the last great U.S. President, Eisenhower, was wise to people like that.

"Lead the way." He grabbed his jacket from a closet in the corner of the room, and led me out to the parking lot behind the building, where it awkwardly met the angles of two other buildings in a massive orthogonal failure. We both put on sunglasses. "Let's take my jeep, Tommy."

We made our way out to the boulevard and drove another mile under almost crossing rows of tall palm trees. Randy hopped out of the jeep, only taking a moment to properly adjust his officer's cap before striding up to the door of the two-story building. I looked up at four or five large satellite dishes fighting for their place in the sun on the roof.

Minutes later, Randy addressed the soldier who sat at a desk outside the satellite room calmly. "We are here for the Tampa hookup. This is classified. You can leave as soon as we have established a handshake. We should be a half an hour or more. Can we get some coffee?" Randy looked toward me. "Water would be good, Randy." We sat down at marked spots on the side of a rectangular wooden table, a microphone on a stand between us, a blank screen in front of us.

I was almost soaking wet, a condition whose cause I could not distinguish between the humidity of the base, and my growing apprehension that I was about to embark upon clandestine activities with people whom I had never met before, and who seemed to treat espionage as a series of technical problems, rather than ethical issues.

The technician placed a console in front of us and proceeded to test some volume levels. Soon the large screen against the wall went blue, displaying numbers on the bottom before becoming alive. On the other end we saw an empty room, similar to our own. A few more seconds passed when Dr. Fuller sat down and made himself comfortable in the remote location. The sentry brought us coffee and water, after which he quickly left us in privacy with our live video feed.

"Randy! Tommy!" Dr. Fuller gave us a cheerful salute.

"Good to see you again, Dr. Fuller!" I said. Obviously a frequent participant in these types of secretive briefings, Dr. Fuller leaned close to the microphone when he spoke.

"Tommy, welcome to the exciting world of executive air transport consultation services!"

"I couldn't be happier with the opportunities that await me in this burgeoning industry, Dr. Fuller." He laughed.

"That's the spirit, Tommy!"

Someone on Dr. Fuller's end brought him a glass of water. Randy spoke up. "Tommy has signed the documents, Marty. We have spoken about some of the unwritten clauses. He understands the 'business needs' behind them."

Dr. Fuller rubbed his hands together playfully. "Good. Let's talk some good old-fashioned COIN then. Tommy, you may remember a conversation we had in Cali some months ago. The matter of Colombia facing 'failed state' status is not something we take lightly. We have serious doubts whether Colombia will be a democratic state in ten years. It has weak democratic roots to begin with. Their Congress makes ours looks like a collection of Solons by comparison."

We laughed heartily at that one. It was a horrid thought, though— my wife and children in a nation-state that had a termination date unless we took direct covert action.

"While the central government is weak and unreliable, the FARC are like a business growing at a compounded rate of 20% a year. Right now, they operate as tax collectors in their territories toward those who want to make a dishonest living in the narco trade. They are too smart and ambitious for that, though. In ten years, they will have a yearly cash flow of a billion dollars. Let that sink in a moment, Tommy: a guerrilla army with a billion-dollar yearly budget. Mao would have given up young girls for half that! By regional comparison, they will be the best-funded army in Latin America. The world has not seen something of their size and sophistication since the Viet Cong."

That did not end as well as the Dr. Fullers of that age reckoned if I remembered my Modern U.S. History Course.

"This time they're not the home team, though," Randy added. "Quite true. But they have intimate knowledge of the terrain and more or less control of the high ground."

"What's the plan, Marty?"

"For the sake of our young friend, Randy, let's start at the beginning. There are 41 dedicated military intelligence centers in the country, though most of them are still using tin cans and wire to transmit. We are treating them to an upgrade as we speak. They will communicate amongst themselves, as well as trade information with local, friendly sources. For the first time, they will share intelligence across the country in real-time, something the FARC have probably been doing for ten years now."

"In terms of COIN, we have placed the entire country on a grid. Each intelligence unit has responsibility for a certain number of them. We are training their intelligence personnel at a high level—mostly in Bogota—and at times we will be training at a low-level. Grid-by-grid, we are going to flip the square from guerrilla to friendly and then to government."

I had no idea what he was talking about. He sounded like he should be in a rabbit suit in a high school production of Lewis Carroll.

"Who is going to handle the low-level stuff, Marty?"

"Mostly Green Berets. Some of our contract people. Some ex-Desert Storm and even Contra vets. The other pillar is supplies. This is a completely under-capitalized Army. It can't project military force more than a mile outside their bases, and the FARC know it. They can set up shop outside army mortar range, and dare the army to leave their forts and attack. Its other problem is lack of professionalism. We will teach spit an' shine as well."

The water arrived, which gave me something to do with my mouth as Dr. Fuller continued his brief overview of our intervention.

"But our master plan is that Colombia be the most mechanized and capitalized army in Latin American in ten years. For every FARC dollar, we will spend two. Of course, each time we take a grid, we are taking money out of their Chairman Mao and Minney Mouse wallets, which will peeve their little Red hearts."

"We are talking about a top to bottom operation of heavy metal thunder, as you likely remember from your church choir days, Randy. The Air Force will get the good stuff. They will also have Special Forces units that could steal Lenin's Tomb on May Day. We are looking at a billion-dollar investment ourselves over ten years. The appropriated stuff will dwarf that someday, but for now we have to dip into our own accounts to get this operation underway."

I wondered exactly who had control over 'our accounts.' Only the reference to my name jolted me out a pleasant retreat to memories of the last time I was in bed with Amelia.

"That is where your little operation comes in, Tommy. We are not interested in a fair fight. In ten years, the FARC will be selling tacos to quartermaster their army, while the Colombian Army will be in the supersonic age. Ultimately, victory will come about on a grid-by-grid basis, and that means classical counter-insurgency."

So, that was COIN.

Randy spoke up. He was insistent upon making clarifications about the training of different kinds of soldiers, which did not seem to be the thrust of Dr. Fuller's remarks.

"So, the low-level training you spoke about concerned regular army and marines."

"That's right, Randy. The training of the friendly forces is a separate track. It is, however, equally vital to the success of the re-stabilization of the country. It is our little patch of grass, Tommy and I. There will, of course, be some overlap. People tend to bump into each other in crowded military theatres. Beyond the three of us, and a few support people, no one is authorized to receive briefings or ask questions about our little operation."

"We'll keep things quiet around here, Marty."

"What about security on the Colombian side, Dr. Fuller?"

"My next topic, young Tommy. At the top is a Colombian Central Intelligence Command, probably out of Tolemaida. It will be us at first, and then they will take over when they learn how to turn the knobs on all the new machinery without frying the whole network. The 41 intelligence teams will split up the country and run things at the level of intelligence command and control. At the ground level, there will be only one guy. He will be the only link between the paramilitary forces and Central Command. This will insure maximum security."

I spoke up next. "Dr. Fuller. The 'guy on the ground.' Is he military or paramilitary?"

"Good question. We are taking a good look at their files up in Tolemaida and Bogota MOD right now. The guy we are looking for is retired or near retirement. He has had advanced training in counter-insurgency and a few seasons in the big leagues. He speaks at least two languages, he is self-motivated, and he hates Communists like 'Liberace hates cooze', as you Presbyterians like to say, Randy."

"Took the words right out of my mouth, Marty."

"He is out on point and for at least the medium-term. He is therefore adaptable and patient, and has natural leadership ability. He has to recruit, organize, train and quartermaster overlapping grids of paramilitaries who do not see the benefits of cooperation, installment-payments, and the monumentally-delayed gratification of our WASP ancestors. He has to turn a blind eye to a lot of nefarious actions. But he is ultimately the key player in our little oil-spotting venture."

That was not an answer to my question. I would be spending a lot of time with these guys; I had a right to know if they were active-duty or paramilitary. I let it pass, though.

That last reference was new to me. "Oil-spotting?"

Randy answered. "It is a counter-intelligence term that comes from the French Algerian campaign. You drop a spot of oil on paper and watch it slowly spread. That is the growth model of an effective counter-guerrilla campaign, Tommy. You slowly, methodically take back territory and hold it until the national regime stabilizes. That could be months or years. But while you are holding it, he is trying to take it back. He may have help from 5th column politicians in Bogota or a change of heart from the central government. Or the local population finds out the new boss is just as exploitative as the old one."

Dr. Fuller put things in ideological perspective. "Tommy, we have to convince his communist pea brain that he has nothing to gain by attempting to retake the lost ground, and that maybe he can negotiate his way out of sudden death. He may decide though to go out in a blaze of Marxist glory in one massive counter-attack. It is high-risk stuff, Tommy. You have to see the big picture and keep your nerve out there."

That sounded suspiciously like an instruction, a harsh one for an aviation consultant.

"Dr. Fuller. If I may: I have a plane that can hold a big cargo and needs a long runway. Isn't my job rather simple? I fly into Tolemaida or San Juan de Guaviare and drop off about 10,000 pounds per day. It sounds like a six-month job, tops."

"Quite, Tommy. And you can call that phase one, for which we do not need someone with your background. We need a qualified pilot and a flight pattern. You will, however, learn a lot during this phase, and establish yourself broadly across bases and theatres. These guys are not the most trusting of Christian souls, Tommy… they don't survive in their world without some doubt about the Christian nature of their fellow man. Anyway, I see Phase Two starting by this summer."

I did not even bother to ask how phase two would distinguish itself from its predecessor.

He paused for a drink of water. "Tommy, remember, this is a country where no one controls the highways by night. You cannot move cargo more than 100 miles without multiple escort vehicles and anything over 500 miles has a success rate of only 56%. Hell, the FARC gain intelligence just by watching the flow of military trucks. They know most of the frontier is unguarded, and act accordingly. There is also the matter of their intelligence services. The FARC have infiltrated all branches of service in Colombia. They know the Colombian army better than we do. They are usually about a half hour ahead of any significant military maneuver."

They would know about me then, my flights, and in due course, my role in the build-up.

Dr. Fuller rowed slightly ahead of my next question. "They will know if routine flights enter Tolemaida from Panama every day. That we can live with. Keep 'em guessing. Ambiguity is good for the communist soul. We cannot tolerate that they know what we are delivering at the Brigade level, since a whole lot of stuff is going to that level in the next two years' care of little aviation companies like yours. We are going to have to supply and resupply locally, and that means local relationships. It also means shorter runways and more hazardous conditions. Your father-in-law's name will open doors for you. You know how to shoot the shit with these guys in their own language. But— (and here he paused slightly for effect) most importantly, we would rather have conversations with you in this office then rely upon local... idiosyncratic intelligence sources. No one on the Colombian side will have much incentive to tell us the unvarnished truth. If it sounds good, it will probably have been fabricated and agreed upon amongst all parties. If it is bad news, you will not hear about it until it is too late. We will not have eyes and ears on the ground unless we pay for it. And as our Lutheran friends have learned to their dismay, 'it's no good if you have to pay for it.'"

"Amen!" said Randy, chuckling.

What he was proposing placed me closer to the 'guy on the ground' than the types who had Geneva Convention protections.

"Dr. Fuller, will you want me to supply local brigades on a national basis?"

"No, clearly not. It will make sense to feed the grids on the Eastern plains from Bogota. Tolemaida will make the runs south into Putamayo and the Amazons. We will take care of the south of the country using other agents. We are thinking of the area from Medellin to the coast. It is an area larger than California by half, over which the government at present has about 50% control. It is where the first grids will turn back to the government side, Tommy. It is our where we want to make a big splash. We expect the FARC to take that personally. For degenerate communist pederasts, they are not bad at strategic and tactical thinking themselves. They can move their troops through dedicated jungle trails for nearly a thousand miles in coordinated attacks. It is also where the paramilitary leadership lives and feels comfortable, and where you can learn the most. We strike hard in the north, Tommy, fast and hard and ruthlessly."

"I can't tell you much more than that, Tommy. The local, division and Brigade-level intelligence links are just becoming operational. Some don't even have offices and equipment, yet. They will of course when you arrive. Things will come into greater focus by summertime. I expect we will get some fresh orders from local paramilitary units by then as well. Simple stuff. They will need uniforms, medical equipment, medicines and guns. We'll throw in the rubbers for free. And, hopefully lime. I understand that in Antioquia alone we are looking at over 100 paramilitary units. Then, there are Cordoba, Magdalena, Boyoca, Santander, and Uraba. Fun stuff for COIN-types, such as Randy and me."

He made it sound like the shared arcane knowledge of model airplane hobbyists.

Dr. Fuller, petering out at that point, left much unsaid, which is the way these operations were discussed. There were no on the ground instructions since my job was only to report on what I had seen, not to bend events toward one particular pole. But I would be in the middle of these unspoken matters.

"Tommy be fucking quick," I thought.

"So, young Tommy, bring your deodorant, and most importantly be courteous and alert. Try not to turn down a drink. Pick up checks whenever possible. Your marital vows are your business, but for mission success, you may find yourself in uncomfortable situations, if you know what I mean. Make the most of them, to the extent possible. It goes without saying: never repeat to anyone what you see or hear until you get back to this room. That includes your pilot, dentist, brother-in-law or wife. Give my best regards to your father-in-law and your wife, Tommy. I am going to sign-off now. 'I Love Lucy' is on in about twenty minutes and crosstown Tampa traffic is a sour-faced bitch at this hour. I wish you the best of luck and Godspeed, son."

"Thanks, Dr. Fuller. I will be in touch as circumstances warrant."

"Randy, keep that plane well-oiled for our young friend."

"As you wish, Marty. Signing out, then!"

"Signing out."

Randy looked over at me. "So, there you have it."

"Simple design, but thousands of moving parts," I added.

"This is a whole new order of events, Tommy. This could be a model of military-led nation-building or a tremendous clusterfuck of overly-ambitious cross-intentions. We are bringing the four horsemen this time: CIA, Army, Marines, and our Contractor friends. We are going to create a modern army and fight an anti-guerrilla war at the same time, all under cover of Congressional darkness, and under a big false flag that says 'Anti-Narcotics Only.' And you are our main eyes and ears in the North when the first ink stains drop."

I had signed the papers already. There was nowhere to run, even if I could find a way out of that base.

"Randy, quick question: why would the paramilitaries need lime?"

"So, that when they bury bodies in a pit, they dissolve quickly and there is less chance at DNA matching."

I was stunned. They were not tipping the balance of power between government forces and FARC guerrillas. This was a hostile take-over of the country's institutions of war to refashion them for all out counter-insurgency across the whole country.

An entire country was in play; this was CIA-sponsored mayhem.

"Let's get some lunch, Tommy."

So far, they had not mentioned my activities in Aruba, which I had no intention of disclosing—at least until Leo advised me otherwise. Those flights—like a weekend pilot's trips to his country house by comparison—would continue, and I doubted that there would be much opposition to my side jobs from Dr. Fuller. I would be risking my life for these guys; in fact, I was CIA-connected, soon to be going in and out of secured areas of military bases, shaking hands with commanders, and discussing counter-insurgency with Green Beret trainers.

The DEA could go take a flying fuck compared to those kinds of credentials.

I was slipping out of normal, regulated life and into history like the guys in Laos and El Salvador, or the Bay of Pigs and the Berlin Airlift, unknown to the history books, but consequential to the life or death of a whole nation.

Randy Keuken told me to stay near the telephone in the hotel. He wanted to "front-load" the operation with the big armaments, the guns and rockets that would make an early impact on the ongoing, feeble skirmishes between guerrilla and Colombian armies that had not significantly tipped the country considerably toward one side or the other for the last twenty-five years.

"This time they will hear the bomb that kills them." Randy explained that normally things do not move that quickly in the military, especially when appropriated from Washington, but since the CIA was using its own funds, ones no further than your local Panamanian bank, there was no excuse for lack of speed and initiative.

I got the phone call in my little hotel room the next afternoon: the target date was five days away, so I took the next flight up the coast to Cali.

CHAPTER SIXTEEN

Stevenson was not opposed to taking a few weeks off. From the myriad of wall baseboards, cellar barrels, vacation home mattresses, country farm pasture caches, or wives and nephews' bank accounts around Cali, there was plenty of cash looking for a reputable home outside Colombia, and not a lot of competition for the terms that we at Air Tommy could offer.

I was suddenly someone to reckon with.

The next morning, I looked for clothes that would support a flight in a slightly-heated plane, the purchase of which, in shopping malls only four degrees north of the equator, was not a sure thing. I was enjoying a coffee on a terrace café in a midtown shopping center when I saw a face for at least the second time. I had seen only seen it recently: the first time was in the Cali airport last night on the sidewalk when I left the airport; this time, the same figure—a short, fat mestizo in jeans and tennis shoes and a red shirt, naturally sloppy and indolent under the canopy of his baseball cap—was looking into the window of a men's store across from me. Whenever his eyes stupidly locked onto mine, he jerked his head to the side at a passing pretty girl.

Having the jump on him, and watching him wriggle about uncomfortably under the hot noon sun; I lingered slowly over my coffee. It was hard to get a read on his understanding of things. If he knew that I had detected his surveillance, he would move away, and perhaps the next time, there would be a completely different crew forming a circle around me. If not, he had poor spy craft, since he had made no effort to move for several minutes. I stretched the minutes in long, slow sips of my coffee and unnecessary glances at my watch.

Having finished the coffee, I walked with my bags into a nearby sporting goods store. From the back of the store, behind the curtain of a changing room, I saw that he had taken up a similar outpost in front of the window across from that store. Two things were apparent: he was not a pro, nor was he part of a team. He had not signaled to anyone, nor had he moved from his position by even a few feet. He walked in front of a new store, but he kept the same pose in front of a new storefront window, and used another window to dumbly wait for my next movement.

My surprise was only mild. There were several organizations that took a close interest in my movements: Stevenson would want to know if I was making side-deals with his clients and cutting him out of commissions; the Colonel, had he known about possible threats against me, would handle the matter without my knowledge; and the CIA would want to ensure that I was not a traitor or compromised in some manner. All of these groups or individuals, however, would use the services of a professional team of rotating agents, not a guy who learned it all from a correspondence course.

The other side of the ledger included only the FARC or Ivan.

I bought a baseball bat.

He was still in his awkward, window-shopping pose as I exited the store. At a brisk pace, I went down the central mall escalator to the street level parking. Pulling my Giants cap low on my forehead, I walked the length of the parking lot, and swung open the door to the lower parking levels, checking as I swung my arm onto the railing at the first step that he was still there. He was, skipping along and closing. I ran down two new levels of stairs and waited outside and to the left of the door. I could hear the dull ping of stairs under his heavyweight force.

The door pushed open, and when I saw a leg appear, I swung right at its knee cap, causing the corpulent figure to fall over without the support of one leg, and land with his face away from mine. In an instant, my hand was on the back of his neck, which I used to drag him back into the stairwell, shutting the door behind me firmly. I rolled him over. He held his knee and puked.

He had fat features, a few sprouts on his chin and very bad teeth; he was quickly losing his facial structure to panic as the fissiparous pressure of intense pain reached his brain. He held his right knee and rolled to his side in pain. I whacked the bat down on his raised ankle, causing another volley of watery vomit. He sat up, heaving downward on his shirt. "I'll be brief, friend. Nothing is broken. The next time I will start breaking things. You have one minute. Tell me who you are, who sent you, and what are your orders. Go."

"It was fucking Ivan Moreno! That asshole sent me!"

"Why?"

"He told me to find out where you go and who you meet with."

"How did you know I would be in the airport?"

"Ivan can trace your phone calls and all your credit card records."

Randy Keuken would want to know about that.

"How long has he been following me?"

"Since last night. We just started surveillance."

"Who do you work for apart from Ivan Moreno?"

"I'm a cop." That was difficult to believe, as he did not evince enough intelligence for even basic police functions.

"What does that mean? How do you know Ivan?"

"I don't really. He called our office and asked us to open an investigation of you."

"What was the cause?"

"He said you were a smuggler... that there was a big chance we could catch you with cash or drugs or stolen goods. He said you had contacts with the Cali National Police, so he wanted the investigation to take place without their authorization."

"Did he also mention that my father-in-law is a Lieutenant Colonel in the CNP?"

"Mierda! Please don't kill me. Mierda!"

"Exactly. Listen, you don't know what this is all about. I'm not a bad guy. This is a vendetta, something of a personal nature. I am not involved in any crooked business, but I will break both your fuckin' legs if I catch you again. Ok?"

"Si, senor."

"Shut down your investigation. Wait a few weeks, and report that you only saw me go straight home from the airport and occasionally to the gym. Report that my only hobby is to look at old books and shop for diapers." He spoke in a mewling English.

"Ok, mister."

"Now repeat these instructions."

He understood the gist of what I wanted from him, and for a slow thinker, unable to lie logically and creatively upon a moment's notice, his story made sense. The Cali Fiscalia was as compromised as the CNP, their reputations in tatters, and many of their go-getters were in the same prison levels as their CNP counterparts. Still, although the Colonel was a remnant from the ersatz Golden Age of Cali, he was still a formidable figure in Cali. He would know in a matter of minutes if Ivan passed along a hot tip about his son-in-law.

Getting behind him, I lifted his wallet out of his pants. "Gregorio Antonio Palanco. That will be easy to remember, but I will write it down as soon as I get to my car. You're going to be limping for a while. It happened by falling down the stairs. Ok? That will be in your medical report. If it is not there, you have not taken to heart the message I have tried to send to you. Do you understand? Stop your fuckin' investigation, and put in the file that there is no basis for further surveillance. Do you understand?"

He went back to Spanish. "Si, senor."

"Listen carefully, Gregorio. You will meet me in two weeks at the café here in the shopping center. I will give you five thousand dollars in cash. You will bring me a copy of your surveillance report, and any other requests Ivan Moreno makes in your office, or anything else you learn about him. If you double-cross me..." I crushed his drooping ankle in my fist until he howled.

"Understood?"

"Si, senor."

"Two weeks. Clean report. Fall down stairs. Close file. Long, happy fuckin' life."

"Si, senor."

"Don't try to move; I will tell the portero that you need medical attention."

"Don't fuck with me, Gregorio."

"I understand, senor."

I could only guess that this was how it was done—Gregorio whimpered all the right things, but he could be more motivated than ever to deliver good news to Ivan. A criminal outcome, oddly, was the least of my worries.

I looked at my watch.

Nando would need to know the full story. I would have to tell him about the assault, which was within video range in the parking lot. He would reach his own conclusions. I satisfied my own evolving standard of secret agent decorum; I was formidable with a minimum of violence and a regard for Gregorio's life. Besides, I made an effort to win him over to my side, which was a much better place than an ally of Ivan.

I snapped off my cell phone as soon as I finished dialing Nando's phone number. Fuck! I had to be more careful now. Ivan was listening, as well as tracking my movements and credit card usage. That alone justified a phone call to Nando. There were coins in the Range Rover, so I called Nando from a gas station on the way home. He was not surprised to hear about Ivan's budding investigation, but did not consider it to be a substantial threat to any of my current activities. "He'll have to back down, marika—let him have his fun for now."

For how long? Nando said I should focus on my new job, and leave Ivan to his personal sorrow. I could imagine Ivan waiting quite a while until I had to come to him.

CHAPTER SEVENTEEN

Cody Pryor walked like he was on a pair of bent stilts when I met him a few days later at Howard AFB. His wobbled on thin legs beneath a right hip bone that had apparently never healed properly. He was bereft of hair atop, except for a single line that started at his neck, and fell to the side before it reached the top of his head. He wore blue jeans and a parka and carried himself with unnecessary distinction, like everyone's least favorite middle-aged graduate student in a guest-only seminar course. He reeked of cheap cologne atop the usual smells of alcoholism. It was 05:45 and already hot and humid on the tarmac at Howard Air Force Base, executive jet division.

Up close, he appeared about fifty-five years old, but in poor health and doing nothing to remedy the several serious maladies he seemed to carry with him. He carried a backpack over his shoulder and ambled toward me with a momentum as if it was difficult for him to stop. We shook hands.

"Cody Pryor. I'm the pilot."

"Tommy Connolly. I'm not sure what my title is."

"You'll have to work on that. In this business, it helps to have your legend straight."

"Good point. Air cargo consultant."

"Pretty good."

Cody also bent forward with a crooked back and spared his legs their full walking burden by dips and slides in lieu of strides. He looked up at the plane and scratched his chin.

"Nice to meet you, Tommy, agency?"

"No, hired for the job like you."

It was when he stepped close that I noticed the permanent alcohol stains in their various forms and hues. There were tiny red veins on his nose, and blue ones through his cheeks, and yellow streaks on his eyeballs. He had probably suffered from a tropical disease before and given up on his teeth years ago.

His next look was to me.

"All right. It's a full circle then… Tommy, have you flown before?"

"I can't offer any details, but I have flown about 25,000 miles." He snapped back sardonically,

"And still in your twenties, are you?" He gave a weary smile that suggested he had been through this ritual too many times.

"Come on, Tommy! What do you say we get out of here?"

"So far, so good for this creaky old bitch."

"You sound like you knew each other in the past."

"My grandma would have flown the original. Douglas got the contract to convert these in the 50s. Ever since then, they have been looking for a war or a COIN operation to use her in. Bitch never got properly humped during her heyday. It's basically a WWII misfit. She couldn't cut it as an executive jet. She couldn't cut it as a bomber. It's tough to be in the shadow of the B-26. It would make anyone neurotic. I bet most of her brothers and sisters are ditched on a spike at the entrance of an air force base somewhere."

"So, they want to see if she can cut it as a short-haul cargo plane?"

"More likely they are trying to see if the Colombians are stupid enough to buy it." He made a "my lips are buttoned" motion and flipped a few switches. Tapping his finger downward on a few buttons, he gunned the engines forward on its first few furlongs toward the runway. After picking up sufficient speed, we climbed quickly out over the Atlantic side of Panama in just a few minutes. She ran smoothly. Cody seemed to find the ride comfortable and sank deep in his chair with the look of a man who had looked but failed to find reasons to doubt his newest horse.

Within minutes, we were approaching Colombian air space. Cody looked at his watch and gave some codes over the radio, which I did not understand. Ground control from somewhere wished him a happy flight in heavily-accented English, which would be the last radio communication until we requested landing instructions.

"About two hours is all, Tommy. I got a coffee thermos in the back. When we level off, go on back and pour us some coffee, will you son?" I gave him the thumbs up. We crossed over intensely green littoral patches. These turned to green bluffs, and we climbed higher over duller green pastures and hills with some lines of brown river water. "Going over Uraba on the way to Antioquia. Guerrilla territory. Don't want to get shot down there! If the guerrillas don't take you, the smugglers have even less use for you." I wondered if he knew that it was my next duty tour down there.

It felt good in the cold cockpit after the unrelenting humidity of Panama and Cali. The plane being pressurized, but not heated, my fingers slowly turned blue at the tips. Cody still had on his parka, but I went with my leather jacket. We leveled off before the rise of the two Cordilleras before us. "This old bitch can't go up to 15,000 feet, so we need to slide between the cordilleras. Luckily, we have the river to guide us. After Medellin, we'll have to climb a little, but she will hold. She won't cut it as a cargo plane, though. Too many of the young planes can carry more load with less fuel. That is not a narco concern, but it matters to a young 'aviation consultant.'"

It was a few minutes past 08:00 when we touched down on a long, cement runway between straddling plateaus of cold, dry rock. An officer with a clipboard and two soldiers approached us. I stretched out a few muscles and limbs before they reached us, while Cody just stood with a slight hunch. "Teniente Miguel Saavedra!" He extended his hand to both of us.

"How was your trip from Panama?" I looked to Cody, who looked back at me.

"Smooth the whole way."

"Good—welcome to Tolemaida Air Base. We will commence the unloading soon. There is no need for a debriefing, but we have arranged for you to have a nice breakfast in the commissary. Is there anything I can get you?" Cody spoke up.

"How about a Coke?"

"Yes, Sir. We will take care of it."

"And you?"

"Is there a telephone I can use?"

"This is a closed base, Sir. And this mission is classified in both our countries."

"Ice water, then."

Saavedra returned as we were enjoying a quick breakfast. He told us that the inventory was confirmed and the plane unloaded and refueled. "Twenty-six minutes!" he added, smiling, and looking at his clipboard. He said they checked the fuel levels, and that we could easily reach Panama. "Gentleman—you are free to return now. We will see you

tomorrow at this same time. Please have a safe flight back to Panama."
He walked us back to the hangar by means of hallways and courtyards,
and left us alone with our plane.

"Easy money, kid."

"For how long?"

"At 10,000 pounds a day? Until they realize this plane will not
service a national army in a country three times the size of California.
Let's hope Douglas makes a sale, or they stay unhip to the skip, eh?"

"And now?"

"We debrief with Keuken and hit the greens or the bars. Panama
has both. No women on the greens, though. Bad luck." We walked
toward the plane hatch of the evidently moribund Douglas jet.

The next two days we flew loads into the Air Force Base at San Jose
Del Guaviare. This was in hostile territory, with known FARC jungle
commands only 25 miles from base itself. The base officers were elated
to see 10,000 pounds of armaments come to them in an American jet
that would come over and over again until there were enough bombs
to kill every FARC soldier twice.

Cody took a few Colombian Air Force officers up for a test flight
on the second day. This was not in our plans; Cody said he knew nothing
about a test flight, and therefore, we did not have that flight in our fuel
budget. The base being closed during our time on the ground, it was not
possible to contact Randy Keuken or Dr. Fuller for the authorization of
the additional flight. I had the implied authority while on the ground,
especially since it involved plane sales, and therefore a way for the CIA
to make easy cash.

I gave them permission, paying for the additional fuel charges with
my Tomlinson credit card. While Cody test-flew the Douglas for a few
commanders, I ate lunch in a full commissary, where I was joined by
about two hundred soldiers.

An air force captain escorted me to my table. His name was Captain
Guillermo Campo. He was only a few years beyond graduate studies
at the University of North Carolina and thrilled to use his English in
an official capacity with me. All the personnel in the commissary stood
when he entered the room. We headed to the chow line, where about
ten soldiers dished out soups and breads and fruits. Among them was

a tall, thin boy in an army uniform assigned to hand out bread at the end of the line.

He looked at me nervously when I entered the line, bobbing from side to side, and wiping his forehead like he wanted his face to suddenly vanish. He was looking behind and around for an exit, which he could not will into existence through frantic gesturing. I smiled to attempt to calm him with eye contact and a smile. But he bobbed and sweated more. I was about 10 feet away when he shouted, "Eso es una ijueputa fantasma!"

He took off his apron and ran back into the kitchen before it came to rest on the sneeze guard of the chow line. We heard another door slam, and then the clutter of metal in motion on tabletops and service trays, and competing voices reasserted themselves.

Captain Campos looked for a duty officer and called him over. "Go and find that soldier and bring him back here. I want to know why he has shown such a lack of courtesy to our North American friend."

"I will, Captain," he replied and went back into the kitchen. The duty officer returned in about ten minutes. "Captain—he has disappeared. We are searching for him now. Should I seal the base?"

"No, but let perimeter security know about the missing soldier. Brief me in my office."

I did not think more about the incident. He was young and had probably hated his military service and the United States.

Cody was gone about two hours. He said the Colombians wanted to fly fully loaded, so when they arrived, we still had to wait another hour to unload and refuel. I was angry with Cody for keeping that detail from me—a D-26 explosion with a belly full of ordinance would cause a tremendous explosion and mean international headlines and a heady success for the FARC. It also would have sent Tomlinson into liquidation.

The next day Cody and I flew up the Magdalena River, past Bogota, and split the difference from Tolemaida before turning toward the Eastern llanos of Colombia. We carried our last load. When we came to a stop in the hangar, we popped the hatch and exited the plane. Cody opened the cargo bay as well. I took out the invoice and stood still there until Captain Campos arrived. He moved toward me and shook my hand. "Good morning, Guillermo."

"Good morning, Tommy." I held out the invoice.

"I have special instructions today. I am to oversee the unloading. It is a time issue, Guillermo. The agency so far has no idea how long it takes you to unload a full plane belly. They want you guys to unload in a normal fashion."

He was not happy, but he was not authorized to challenge a suggestion—from his perspective—from an agent of the CIA. He walked to the nearest hangar wall phone and spoke briefly. Cody and I peered into the cargo bay. The boxes were not surreptitiously marked. We saw crates marked M60, M60E3, M14, M16, and M79, and one just marked "Mine ordinance." Cody stepped down when we heard others gathering around the side of the plane from which the plane was unloaded. Four airmen were there with a dolly and a long platform with a push bar. We stepped aside, and they went to work.

Each crate weighed a few hundred pounds, I imagined. It took two of them to wedge the crate to the bay ledge and two below to carry it to the ground. They repeated this about 50 times in about 20 minutes. Seeing the array of "goods" now in their position, we both now realized that these weapons were offensive weaponry.

"Sign here, Guillermo." He signed the bottom of a two-page invoice. "For my taxes," I joked.

"Tommy, before you leave, could I talk to you?" He walked a few step nearer to the crates, and I followed.

"Do you remember that soldier yesterday? The one who panicked when he saw you in the commissary?"

"Yes, how is the poor soldier? Has he recovered his wits?" Guillermo did not seem to understand the expression. "Has he recovered from his attack of nerves?"

"He disappeared. He is not on the base. We sent out search parties into San Juan. We think he took a bus to Bogota. I just thought you should know."

I was not about to show an officer with whom I had no history that I was overly concerned about the boy, but it was a piece of information worth storing away, one that might make sense in another context. While everyone in the United States had an agenda, everyone in Colombia seemed to have an angle. I thought no more about the young soldier or his panic attack for the rest of the mission—after all, Cody and I had a schedule to keep.

"Thanks for the tip, Guillermo."

"Have a safe flight, Tommy."

CHAPTER EIGHTEEN

After delivering one-hundred thousand pounds of guns, missiles, and mortars over several days, Cody finally parked the Marksman back in its spot at Howard AFB for five days of well-deserved rest. I was anxious to get back to Amelia and the girls, but Cody demanded a boys' night on the town. Having finished on Friday afternoon, I napped in my hotel room, granted conditional absence by Cody, but only under the condition that we rendezvous later that night at his favorite whorehouse. I paid a nervous cabbie triple fare to induce him to drive in that neighborhood at night.

Cody—in a ridiculous red Hawaiian shirt that featured eighteen holes of exciting mouse golf action—limped over from the bar towards me, until almost gasping, he slapped me on the back and then leaned on my shoulder for support. He presented me to a curvy, spangled ribbon of skinny, Indian girls with numbers painted on their shoulders who sat along the wall and onto the bar stools. "My associate Tommy, girls! Not a toothless old git like me!" He pressed me forward to the table nearest the dancers' stage.

"On the house, young Thomas, so don't be shy!" Soon, there were four companions and six beers on the table. An outer ring of girls, hoping to gain notice or at least a dancer's drink, stood nearby. They had paintings on their cheeks like little girls at a suburban birthday party. Some had not even developed bodies that could hold up their bathing suits. Soon, Cody—a regular and probably part-time resident—grimaced through the pain of supporting one girl on his lap and another on his arm.

These girls had come straight out of their school girl-uniforms from the outer villages of Panama to this place, where they made nightly sums of money that fed their families and paid for the siblings' tuition. There was genuine innocence in the looks and gestures, their flirtatious tugs and cheek-kisses to bring a man to want them a little more than the next girl. I felt slimy—the girls qualified as victims of imperialism; I had been repeatedly drilled at Berkeley to recognize such injustices, but it just felt wrong to press-gang them into sexual mysteries in such a dreary place.

They toyed with their beers to avoid drinking them. Cody told me I should dance with one of the girls, an offer I sheepishly declined. I also did not want an arm around my neck, or soft little kisses on my neck from a fifteen-year-old girl, or palm brushes across my chest, all of which I politely rejected.

Cody looked at me like I was a new breed of agent—perhaps a Mormon—that looked down on bars and hookers, and by implication the men who frequented them. I tried to compensate by drinking more and listening to his war stories. I put down two whiskeys quickly and raised my hand for another. Consequently, it took only a few minutes until word got around that I was not seriously in play, and the girls slipped away from the table.

Cody took another poke at male bonding announcing to the table that I had become a father. He leaned toward me and whispered, "The girls like fathers as customers. They think you will be more gentle with them, and tip them more." He winked at me slyly. The remaining girls all clapped and gave me kisses on the mouth and cheeks.

Cody toasted to my fatherhood, yelling out to me, "Tommy! It will take the most from you in all your life. It will also make the most man of you. I wish you sincere luck and happiness!" He was almost in tears, a surge of emotion I was not able to reciprocate, especially in the manner he expected from a comrade in arms. But I was born after Laos, and missed the good times in El Salvador and the Panama Invasion.

"I appreciate it, Cody!"

Pounding his glass down on the table, he put one girl over his shoulder and gimped hand-in-hand with another girl up the stairs to the private rooms. The other girls, except for one, had all drifted away. The last girl was younger and shier and less vulgarized than her bar mates. She wore a bathing suit top that held up a little bit of breast flesh. We spoke for a few minutes about life in Panama City until I excused myself to talk to the bartender. "Is it possible to get a taxi down here?" I asked him.

"You'll have to pay at least double, but… " I gave him $20 and asked him to take care of it for me.

I walked back to the table. She stood sweetly, like a girl waiting for a nice American boy to cover her with his coat, and then walk slowly away from her troubles to a better life. She evidently thought my conversation with the bartender concerned my purchase of her body and time. I sat her back down on the edge of the table. Holding her little hand in mine, I told her that she was beautiful and sweet, and slipped $50 into her hand, rolling it up into a fist. Instead, she took me by my shirt neck and poured herself onto my torso, her full weight wriggling to create some greater seal upon me, until she slid her legs upward and wrapped them around me. She pierced my mouth with her tongue and sucked her lips deep into mine. She was probably fifteen years old.

I pulled myself off the chair. She sensed a fading possibility. "Another time, perhaps?"

"Yes, another time."

"Promise?"

I turned toward the door, and I actually paid triple to get me out of that neighborhood quickly and back to my hotel.

The next afternoon Nando and I entered Cali from the northern airport entrance during its intense, smoky maniacal rush hour. At a stop sign, Nando signaled a street vendor for two beers and handed me one.

"How were the flights, marika?"

"Everything took place on schedule and ran smoothly. That is about all I can say."

I took a long swig of beer. "Shit. I forgot to ask. How are the girls?"

"The little gringitas? They will have your gringo nose and their mother's lips. The rest is 'to be determined'," he concluded in English.

I changed topics to my recent surveillance in the shopping mall. "Nando, did you scoop up all the surveillance tapes from that day?"

"Yes—we have it all. You are really a bastard; you know that by now, don't you?"

"A bastard would have broken both his legs, Nando. Study your favorite American gangster movies a bit closer next time. I bruised his knee and gave his ankle a light tap. The vomit was really a bit of method acting."

Nando shook his head at me and laughed. Approaching the northern limits of Cali, he stopped on the side of the road for two more beers.

"Gregorio Antonio Palanco has realized that he does not need friends like Ivan Moreno, Tommy. It is not necessary for you to meet him. He will drop his investigation as a display of friendship with our family. He is content with that."

"I promised him five thousand in cash, Nando."

Nando waved off the remainder of the theme of Gregorio Palanco. "Marika! He is just a poor, stupid cop. Don't make him into something more than he is."

"It shows that Ivan has not given up, Nando. He certainly has other options than a city cop… what if he reaches out to the DEA next?"

"Ivan will have to step back. The Cali Police will also issue a formal complaint to the Bogota Fiscalia for interference and political pressure. Ivan wants a political future. He can't afford to make enemies among whole institutions."

That seemed to settle the issue for Nando, but I knew that Ivan would be back to reconcile the greatest loss of his life, and that the next venue would not be a shopping mall, nor would his instrument of choice be a young and sloppy city cop. Nando seemed to be playing some kind of twisted intermediation between Ivan and me; his reading of Ivan was not at all close to the inner hostility of the man I had seen in Bogota.

Nando drove us to my house, where the family gathered for the return of the conquering hero. Amelia, having several weeks of intense workouts in the gym under her belt, and eating almost nothing but rice cakes and yogurt since she began to reform her body, had nearly regained the figure from our first summer vacation in Aruba. Much to Nando's disgust, she ran across the living room to kiss me, leaning on me so much that I lifted her in the air and swirled her several times like in old dances with girls in hoop skirts. After several kisses, I sang to her, "I've Got a Woman!"

"And I've Got a Man!" she belted back.

I shook hands with the Colonel with Amelia by my side and kissed Mrs. Hernandez on her cheek.

"This is a nice house, Tommy. It will prove to be a good investment."

"Thank you, Sir."

"How did your business go these past weeks?"

"Smoothly. Point to point without any issues."

We spoke as we moved toward the living room couches.

Nando brought us cold beer.

"Happy days are here again, marika ijueputa! Imagine, Pop! You and I are the only non-Irish in this family now! What is happening to our country?"

"Indeed," the Colonel deadpanned for his wife.

"Marika, where is the remote?"

"What?"

"The remote, marika! Cali plays tonight." I pointed to the drawer under the TV.

"Perfect."

"There is champagne and beer on the table."

Nando sat down on the reclining sofa, and popped open his can. We too took a seat and were content with drinking beer and analyzing soccer strategy for the first half of the game.

At half time, for some reason I remembered the event at the Aipay base. I had given it little thought and figured it wouldn't hurt to mention the incident to someone. I told the Colonel and Nando about the strange occurrence with the youth at the commissary—how he had behaved as if he'd never seen a foreigner before, or as if I was a ghost; how he took off his apron and ran away when he saw me; and how he then disappeared from the base. The Colonel became a piece of stone; Nando sat still. Their reactions startled me.

The Colonel then asked me if I remembered anything else.

"No, sir. This morning the base liaison told me that they searched the base and found nothing. They expect he took a bus to Bogota."

The Colonel dropped his plate on the sofa table and walked to the door. He stayed out in the hallway for about ten minutes.

"Nando, what's the matter?"

"Oh, marika. How many people in this country have reason to believe that you are dead?"

"Just one."

"Poor marika. How are you ever going to survive in this country?"

"Where did your father go?"

"He is making a phone call to have that security tape delivered here 'asap'."

Looking over at Amelia's long, sinewy legs, her puffed up breasts, and the salacious licking of her lips she shared only with me when her family was not looking, I thought: this was not the sort of homecoming that I had wanted. Motioning Amelia into the kitchen, I told her that I would be busy for some time with her father and Nando.

In the living room, the large TV showed the players entering the field for the second half of play. The Colonel was back on the couch with a beer in his hand and seemed to regard the game as the most important matter in the room. Nando examined the VHS player under the TV. I opened the drawer and took out that remote.

"Is there another television?" Nando asked.

"Yes, the guest bedroom has a television." Nando disconnected the VHS player and carried it there.

The Colonel calmly ate his snack foods and shook an empty beer can at me.

I came back with three more beers, bringing the last one to Nando in the guest room.

"I think it will work. I just need a tape to test it." I went back out and picked out one of the rental videos that Amelia had accumulated. Nando put it in and after a few button presses on the remote, gave me a thumbs up.

"I like this movie—it has that new American blond in it." We went back outside and watched soccer.

There was a knock on the door near the end of the match. Nando went to the door and saluted a figure in the hallway before returning with the tape. The Colonel did not wait for the match to end. He took the tape from Nando and took it to the guest room.

"Nando, manage this thing for me."

Nando pressed fast forward.

"How far, Pa?"

"To the last part, outside. The tape whizzed forward. Nando made some forwards-backwards corrections, and then stopped the tape at a frozen image of a tall, thin boy with a gun in his hand a few feet from the Liverpool Bar entrance.

"Is that him, marika?"

"Yes. Shit! It's him."

The Colonel stood up and walked out of the guest room. A few moments later, the front door opened and closed harshly. Nando stood up as well.

"Let's get a beer, marika." We stood with beers on the patio in front of the view of the lights of Cali to the South.

"We were all wrong, marika. Don't feel too stupid. You lost much of your memory of that time, and you only saw the tape once when you were heavily sedated."

"I hope the Colonel feels that way." He smiled.

"We got it all wrong, marika."

"We have been looking for evidence within the Cali gangs, marika. We thought we could establish a chain from the dead shooter to a contract to a figure in Medellin, in Escobar's world. We interrogated his whole gang, but they didn't know anything—and believe me, they had every reason to talk. We didn't bother to examine a military angle. We have to reexamine that tape now from a different angle."

"I can't help you much."

"No, but you need to watch that tape again."

We heard the front door open and shut and the Colonel walk in. We regrouped in the guest bedroom and continued. Nando had to rewind to the beginning. There was Amelia—radiant, charming, unconcerned—and her once again dead friends. I am at the bar, cheeky and awkward on my first night in town, entranced by Amelia and her beauty. Her friends giggle at my forwardness, my nerve. Amelia gives me the slightest glance and whispers in her friend's ear. They giggle in chorus at a naughty thought, unaware of the rest of the bar. A short Indian boy in a dirty t-shirt enters and raises his arms. I look to him and my eyes widen. He gets off two shots, and I stand. He gets off a third shot, and I pick up a chair. He gets off a fourth shot, and I sling the chair over my shoulder. He turns his head to me and keeps his arms outstretched. The arm and the pistol at its end wheel toward me like an old wooden mast. I crack the chair baseball style across his temple, and he falls forward. The gun slides across the floor toward the rear bathroom hallway.

The Indian boy scratches the floor blindly and, with blood beginning to seep out of him, waves his arms in search of his gun. I step to the right and bring the chair straight down on the back of his head. His hands flatten and his motion stops. I slam it down two more times in the same place. His scull is wide open, and blood is flowing out. His bandanna is soaked red but unable to stem the flow of blood. I drop the stool.

Amelia is beginning her shock, recasting her face into a horrified look that occasionally reappears when we hear a car backfire. I turn toward the front of the bar. "Stop the tape there, Nando!" the Colonel demands. "Why did he come into the bar? Was that the plan? Did he sense a problem? This was a simple two-sicario job. He should have stayed in his car and waited. But he was in the bar only seconds after the four shots. He could not have known that the other sicario was not coming out, or that the job was not complete."

Nando spoke next. "He had his gun out before he entered. Entering the bar was part of his plan. It would not be efficient to be some kind of support shooter, in case the original shooter messed up the job...."

I cut him off. "Actually, that scenario would make sense if there was a third person — a driver. In that case, his entry in the bar could be to make sure the job was complete."

"That is too complex. Three people make security much more difficult. They went after Amelia in a bar in a good neighborhood. I think there were only two," said Nando.

"That could mean then that the second shooter intended to kill the first one. But why in the bar?" The Colonel did not speak, so Nando continued the tape. I ran toward Amelia and held her in place behind me. I spoke to the gunman who is mystified by his first ever encounter with a gringo. He gives a shooter's grin and raises his arm. I turn around and cover Amelia like a wall side romantic clutch in a dark dance hall. My hands cover hers and extend toward the ceiling, our hips rubbing together.

There is a crack and a second crack. I am hit twice on the back, and my right side shakes and my hands—with Amelia's inside—slide down the wall. My knees began to buckle and slide outward. Amelia releases a hand and puts it around my waist, pulling me upwards. She peers out at the shooter. He takes aim where he last saw her head. Amelia covers my scull with her wrist. Crack. The bullet goes through her wrist and into my scull. I fall out of her grasp onto the floor. Amelia falls down to my side, screaming in anguish. Apparently, for the shooter, the job is over. I am on my back, and blood spurts upward out of my scull and cascades down with my heart's fading rhythm.

The shooter turns and runs. Amelia holds her hand to my head to stop the bleeding. She raises me onto her lap. Someone gives her a towel. She looks on the floor for pieces of scull like Jackie Kennedy in Dallas. My blood is on her arms and shirt and face, like war paint that contorts her face in the depths of a savage battle. She never looks toward her dead friends at all. The blood is thick now, around my head and on my back and in a pool around me. Amelia looks like she does not know how to stop all the blood, and feels me going into blackness.

Nando stopped the tape again. The image is one of Amelia's contorted anguish, La Pieta in the midst of the aftermath of the shooting. "He could have run for several blocks, put his uniform back on behind a building, and walked out calmly as a soldier. From there, he could have taken a cab to the bus station, or ridden a motorcycle to another town. Or, he could have gotten into a car and changed clothes there."

The Colonel listened to Nando carefully. "We will know a lot more when we find out how long was his leave and under what circumstances it was approved…."

The Colonel spoke up when Nando did not finish the matter. "Tommy, this stays among us. Please do not take the lead on this investigation. We will ask the questions from our end. It is important that you not make any investigations yourself. At least one shooter is still out there, and he knows you are alive. He has already told his bosses you are alive. They will draw the appropriate conclusions. He will use his resources to avoid capture at all cost. If he is desperate, he will strike. We will tell you what we find out. But please. Do not discuss this matter with anyone, including Amelia, is that clear?"

"Yes, sir."

Ivan Moreno, meet Ghost Killer; Ghost Killer, meet Ivan Moreno.

I spent four sweet days with Amelia and the girls but left with my worries having doubled. Amelia, having seen her husband go behind closed doors to discuss matters of state with her father as an apparent equal, was mad for sex that week. She knew in some sense that her husband was not just a small-time vendor to the U.S. government, but part of the huge build-up that was taking place on military bases around the country. She delighted in the fact that I could not tell her about my work, and that I returned at times in need of peace and calm, and after caring for the babies, she carried me softly into her body and then into sleep.

We also discussed serious matters during that particular home visit. Amelia decided, based upon my growing commitments in the build-up, that we were not going to leave Colombia in the next, and probably not in the subsequent fiscal year. So, she decided to finish her studies in one of the universities in Cali. I agreed. She knew the risks involved, but favored those risks to a few years of hiding in our house, and waiting for my work to end. A woman like Amelia would lash out eventually if kept in a high tower for too long.

On that basis, and utilizing the security resources of the Colonel, we hired Consuela, who would take care of the twins and give Amelia time to attend classes and study at home. I got the Range Rover ready, too; I had a pistol placed under the driver's seat and told her to call Nando about firing lessons. Lastly Amelia took possession of her first cell phone. She kissed me goodbye in bed before I left the house with a "Fuck someone up, Tommy!"

"My God, Amelia, where did you hear that?"

"One of the videos—I thought it was a great Americanism."

"A bit vulgar, but I guess it has gone global now, mi amor."

I could not talk to anyone about the ghost shooter, or Ivan Moreno. But I could make money.

CHAPTER NINETEEN

Before arriving in Panama for my next week's work, Red Sox and I made a run into Aruba. Arriving around midnight and apologizing to Sal Manzo for missing out on the nightclub fun, I went straight to bed. The next morning, I took a taxi to Leo Huff's office. Leo handed me a bank statement from Tomlinson's local business account. There was a deposit for two-hundred and seventy-thousand dollars.

"What is this all about, Leo?"

"Your nameless friends are paying you for your first month's work."

"Isn't that a little steep—or, at least suspiciously off contract?"

"It does seem that way, yes."

"Should we leave it at 'someone up there likes me,' or inquire about my good fortune."

Leo told me that he would handle the matter, and try to get an answer for me before my flight to Panama, which was to leave in about four hours. I went back to Las Cabanas and napped. In two hours of near dreamlessness, there were two knocks on the door. The first was a Las Cabanas bellman, who handed me two sealed envelopes. The first was for Stevenson, and the second had my name on it; inside was a slip of paper that read "$27,000.00," a tenth of my CIA payday.

Stevenson did not do a lot of cold calling among the goat-fucking narco community to the North, I thought.

The second knock on the door was a messenger from Leo. I lay back in bed to read a lengthy explanation, which Leo artfully compressed into a few lines:

"Tommy, I managed to reach my counterparts in Tampa. The lengthy explanation involves state secrets and business practices that neither of us is privileged to know. The short answer was somewhat inferable from a ghastly Venn-diagram of stop-and-start explanations from a new lawyer in the office, your Mr. Fuller being in Washington, D.C. this week. It turns out that there are such things in your new employment called 'manufacturers commissions,' and they are payable to those most responsible for realizing a sale to a customer. Sales are evidently way up among certain arms vendors with a Panamanian retail presence. However, it seems that many of the men and organizations with whom you deal in Panama are not legally able to accept vendor commissions. You, however, are. So, enjoy your bounty and another favorable day at the roulette wheel of fate that seems to be governing your life in this moment. Cheers, Leo."

Randy Keuken, Steve Dubrinsky, and Cody Pryor—too close to command to risk another investigation like Iran-Contra.

While Stevenson and his Colombian clients paid me well, the CIA was paying me too well. The former had strictly business reasons for the prices they were willing to pay, while the latter could not care less about strictly business concerns, at least the ones that benefited Tomlinson, Ltd. Of OrangeTown, Aruba.

In the context of the rebuilding of Colombia, this money amounted to a cup of water in an Olympic-sized pool of falsified accounts, shell companies, false invoices, and bogus vendor contracts. We were, ostensibly, helping Colombia to eradicate coca plants with contractor pilots, chemicals, and planes. From Tampa on down the line, we all knew otherwise. Money was shooting out of hoses held by roid-raged firemen among the friends of the CIA in Colombia. So, I was getting a little wet. Like Amelia intoned in her Cali accent, "Fuck someone up, Tommy!" It was hard to place a number on just compensation when only the speed of the build-up had common value.

On the return from our next milk run, Cody Pryor and I flew from Aipay to Howard AFB at tremendous speed northward to avoid landing during a hurricane that was approaching Panama. We landed under soft, light rains that came in thin sheets and washed over us lightly on the tarmac, and then started to lash out directly into our face and eyes on the jeep trip down to Randy Keuken's offices for our briefing.

Steve Dubrinsky was there when we entered the comms room. I never figured Steve out; he looked like the local high school teacher rushed into costume for any number of Norman Rockwell paintings— the turkey-carving father, the worshiper, or the hopeful air ward captain during the World War II blackout. He was a captain in Air Force intelligence, but he had a security clearance no less than Randy Keuken, from what I could detect. His knowledge of clandestine programs emanating from Panama was much more extensive than mine, but he had a modesty that suggested a small, almost clerical role.

We were not fast friends, but we had established some sort of understanding. He was always willing to help me with the odd insight about the scheduling of our flights or the importance of a particular class of weaponry. Today he was more interested in leaving Panama for a week in Tampa with his wife and child than hearing yet again the details of our daily milk run. I repeated the details of the run for Doctor Fuller, who was probably in CIA headquarters I surmised, since our video exchanges did not have captions showing our exact locations.

He appeared to be pensively reading some notes below the screen shot we had of him during my short explanation, after which he had no questions, nor did he seek an opening for a clever rejoinder. Something rare was afoot.

Fuller looked up without his trademark half Marx Brothers-half nightly newscaster grin. "Great, Tommy. We are reaching the half way point in our inventory-buildup efforts. Many thanks to all of you for filling Colombian stockings so assiduously this holiday season. You are a credit to milkmen everywhere. That concludes our formal session for today. However, I would like Steve and Tommy to stay behind for a few minutes. Cody—you are dismissed, old sport. Much obliged."

Without speaking, Cody stood up and quietly left the room, his squeaking sneakers fading after he shut the door behind him. Dr. Fuller waited for a nod from Steve, who checked the door handle, before he resumed our meeting.

CHAPTER TWENTY

The jokes did not take off that afternoon. After Cody had left the room, Dr. Fuller began to speak without recourse to the notes in front of him. "Tommy, we have a situation—an urgent one that needs a solution in the nearest of terms. The weather in Tampa and P.C. has riven the normal tropical good will between Florida and Panamanian travel routes. We cannot get a plane anywhere near your parts, nor can we get vital parts to land in Tampa. The long and the short of it is that we need a man of your approximate height and weight for a…'project' that is up and running, but not able to reach fruition without someone who can quickly get on a plane."

"I am all ears, Dr. Fuller." Before he could answer, Steve Dubrinsky placed a matter out in the open.

"You located him, Marty?"

"Yes, Steve. He has been… incautious."

Dr. Fuller then proceeded to deliver a new kind of pitch to me, far afield of anything I imagined as suitable employment for Tommy C.

"Tommy, there are vendors on all sides of a war. The industrious ones will service both sides if they can…" Some sort of gravity had broken through his bonhomie, at least for a moment, or maybe a draft just entered his room through a ceiling fan. He sneezed with a quickly-drawn handkerchief before he put it back into his seat pocket. "The FARC is well aware of the dimensions of our build up. Evidently, they read the Congressional Quarterly out in the Colombian jungle. There are…" He sneezed again.

Steve Dubrinsky eased his way into the discussion at that point. "Tommy, there are certain weapons systems that can neutralize others— sometimes for pennies on the dollar of our expenditures. The FARC are always in the market for that kind of 'gamebreaking' weapon. Most of the time, we are able to convince the vendor to turn away from the sale before any sort of transfer take place. We have been watching a particular arms dealer. He shows no signs however of heeding considerable warnings on our part."

Dr. Fuller leaned closer to his microphone. "Tommy, we found a very misguided merchant, but we have a very short window with which to bring him to his senses. We know the departure point for his cargo, and we have his location pinpointed, but without a convincing argument from us, he is unlikely to turn back his cargo en route."

"Who is he?"

"His name is Felix Rabinovich."

"Jewish?"

"Russian-Jewish, with a Ukrainian Mafia star rising."

"Where is he holing up?"

"He has a meeting with representatives of the FARC in Geneva in eighteen hours."

"To exchange bank details?"

"Righto, Tommy," said Dr. Fuller.

"It seems there is not a lot of trust between them."

My next questions were more to the point of the mission.

"What is the takeoff point of the cargo?"

Steve Dubrinsky looked at Dr. Fuller before he spoke; I was, after all, just a contracted agent.

"Peru, Tommy. From there, it will travel up the Amazon River where the FARC will take possession."

"This dealer—so late in the game—what makes you feel he will take you seriously this time?"

"Marty?"

"Go ahead, Steve."

"Tommy, your meeting will raise the stakes a little for him."

"In what way?" Retracing his earlier steps, Steve exercised his privilege not to level with me that time.

"Tommy, all you have to do is deliver a letter to him. You will call his hotel room from the lobby and identify yourself as one of us. You only have to hand him the letter and give him a reasonable amount of time to respond. Then, you leave."

"What if he refuses the visit?"

"He won't. He will know you are in town and expecting his attention and courtesy."

"It sounds neat and risk-free, but obviously it's not, Steve, is it?"

"We will be in all over the building, Tommy. And he will know it. The letter will make clear you are operating as a messenger who expects honorable diplomatic treatment."

"Let's hope he sees it that way, Steve. So what are the real stakes here?"

"We have about thirty-five contract pilots involved with eradication efforts over FARC-controlled areas. They fly at low levels and sometimes come back with holes in the fuselage of their planes. There will be no more pilots if this sale goes through. There is also the issue of your own flights into the Brigades."

"Saving my own ass, then."

"Quite possibly."

"Do we have eighteen hours?"

Steve Dubrinsky looked at his watch.

"If we can get you out of here in two hours, we can get you in the hotel two hours before the FARC delegation arrives."

"If you push it?"

"Three and a half tops."

"So, do I check into the hotel?"

"No, but we will alert Swiss intelligence to your presence. We will also have our own men on the ground."

I looked at my grey hoody, jeans, and sneakers.

"In these clothes?"

"We know your sizes, Tommy. Your clothes are ready."

I thought about Amelia, Ambassador Faraday, even the Colonel and Nando. For fuck sake: I had not even bought life insurance for my family, though I imagined the resources of the Hernandez clan would accommodate a young widow. This was a new type of danger: they would find my body in an alley in a bad part of Geneva with professionally-placed bullet holes in my forehead and chest. There would be no note, nor would anyone take credit for having administered revolutionary justice. Amelia would never know why or where, and there would not even be a star for me in the lobby of CIA headquarters.

"Does anyone else know about this mission, Dr. Fuller?"

He read with sufficient depth my real question.

"We will be all over the building, Tommy. He will not dare restrain or harm you physically. He loves his children."

"You guys don't do that kind of stuff."

"We have the odd friend, Tommy."

"Cody?"

"He can handle a few days of milk runs by his lonesome. We will throw a bonus his way come payday."

I had run out of questions. They chose me for reasons I was not supposed to know, and that would be cowardly for me to ask. This was not a paid gig; it was, rather, for the interests of my country, broadly understood. I was no longer a vendor, making fast cash in the service of my country, but putting my life in play—regardless of their claims of total five-star hotel lock-down status—to neutralize a credible threat in a weird nation-building operation, one that did not catch the public's fancy or even warrant a name.

The Colonel had told me that I could choose manhood or orchids. Somehow, based on what they had seen or heard about me, they all knew I would not—or could not—back down from this. I looked over at Steve, who was anxious to get me showered, shaved, and buckled into a jet seat.

"OK, Dr. Fuller. Let's aim for departure in an hour. Steve, power the plane. Where is the nearest shower?"

Steve slapped me on the back.

"I'll call the tower. Marty, are things ready on your end?"

"An embassy rep will hand it over to Tommy on the tarmac. Let's remind our Jewish friend of some of his holier obligations, hey Tommy?"

"I got to get prepared, Dr. Fuller. Over and out." We smiled until we saw the blue screen.

"You sure about this, Tommy?"

"You've told me everything, Steve?"

"Everything operational, yes."

"One hour, Steve."

I was surprised to see that Steve Dubrinsky had also dressed for international corporate business travel, which I felt would probably be his choice of travel and occupation someday. "It's August in Washington, D.C., Tommy. Even the agency assets like you have gone to their second houses."

"I didn't say anything, Steve."

We were looking at an eleven-hour flight with a brief gas stop in Bermuda. Our plane was an eight-seat executive jet with a rear bedroom, which Steve insisted I utilize to better portray the role of the rested, confident governmental emissary. Having slept nearly to Gibraltar, Steve gave me a nudge. "Tommy, it is time for your briefing." I shaved and dressed, after which an attractive female air force intelligence officer cut my finger nails and polished my shoes. With a buoyant smile at me, she affixed a microphone to my cuff link.

"Felix Rabinovich was born in 1946. He is the son of Russian Jewish 'refuseniks' who were denied exit visas to Israel due to their activism. They were able to smuggle Felix as a teenager into Israel through Hungary and Yugoslavia. He is a father of three girls, all of whom live in Israel with their mother. He has a degree in engineering from Israel and speaks Russian, Hebrew and English. He broke into the big leagues of arms dealing business after 1989. He leased a fleet of planes that emptied out Ukrainian air bases and sold their contents in several African countries. He has friendly relationships with Russian intelligence and several African governments. He carries Israeli and Ukrainian passports. It is believed that he lives and works out of Tel Aviv and Geneva."

"The Israelis put up with this guy?"

"So far, they have not stepped on each other's toes. We assume that his intelligence is valuable to them, especially in Africa."

"Does he have any enemies?"

"Besides African guerrilla groups who are being pounded by his artillery, none that we can confirm."

"For an arms dealer, it sounds like he knows how to take the path of least resistance between hostile foes. So, why suddenly take on the FARC commission?"

"You might ask him that when you meet him."

We were in the middle of the Atlantic when Steve closed the book on the life and times of Felix Rabinovich. "So, that's it, Tommy. He is an extraordinarily able man who suddenly threw caution to the wind."

"There's always something more than that, isn't there, Steve?"

"What do you mean, Tommy?"

"That is the briefing for... I don't know what you call it—a non-vetted asset like me. Langley probably knows the full story. Someone probably told Felix Rabinovich they had his back in case of trouble. As a matter of secrecy, that would not make its way into the briefing book."

"Maybe, but that does not change the qualities he possesses, which you need to know before you encounter him." Looking out over the Atlantic as we sliced through it at tremendous speed, I said nothing.

"What's on your mind, Tommy?"

What could I tell him: why me and not you, Steve?

Why are you sending the guy from AA Topeka against the Yankees? Has Tommy become expandable or redundant in Colombia? "What kind of agent am I, Steve? I mean, you guys have different classifications of agents, right?"

"Technically, you are an agency asset. You do not have deep cover or non-official cover, like an embassy employee. You are contracted to perform services for the CIA. This trip is not breaking your contract-you volunteered to perform this service for your government, Tommy. It is more like the Israeli model—you wait for a coded phone call and you follow its instructions. It takes a lot of money and time to create an identity for a spy, Tommy: a fake life history, education, career highlights, marriage. Langley reached the decision to send an informal emissary, someone who will not make Rabinovich feel cornered and make him act upon any more irrational decisions. On short notice, they needed someone close who knows the theater of war, and the stakes involved in stopping this sale. That's all there is, Tommy. You are just a messenger. No one expects anything more than that from you."

"Thanks, Steve."

"No problem, Tommy."

So, there it was—a little bit of truth like a few gold flecks in a pan full of iron pyrite.

CHAPTER TWENTY-ONE

We landed about four hours later in a Swiss airfield about twenty miles outside Geneva, one much hotter and muggier than post cards had led me to expect. Steve and I shook hands with an embassy official, who handed Steve a large, flat pouch.

"I don't suppose there will be an embassy briefing when this is over?" Steve grinned.

"We should be back in the air in three hours. We are lookin' at a quick in-and-out. After that, we will be out of your hair. Tampa will tell you more."

"Ok. Good luck, you guys. Stay safe."

This was, my life with Amelia notwithstanding, the biggest day of my life, and I did not have any sort of plan in mind. Felix Rabinovich was a self-made player who could commandeer Russian aircraft for delivery in over ten African nations. Ultimately, Steve's briefing on Rabinovich proved about as helpful as a Tokyo subway map to a foreign tourist. Rabinovich had thought and planned his way toward the pinnacle of his success, while I had taken a shower and memorized a few facts about his life. We had nothing in common, including relative merits as agents of espionage or observers of the dark world where we both practiced our arts. We both rode in planes; that was about it.

It should have been simple enough, as he had likely bitten several hands in his career, and knew the pain that the principals in his deals could deliver. Now, he bit one that would end his life in a matter of hours if he did not roll over and then fetch the stick they threw.

An embassy car drove us to the entrance of the Kempinski Hotel and drove off. Steve checked into the hotel at the front desk, while I walked over to the concierge, who gave me the dismissive look he must have kept in reserve for approaching Americans.

"Good afternoon. Would you please put a call through to Mr. Rabinovich's room? Tell him an American friend from Tampa is here to talk with him." Looking at my suit and tie, which was superior in cut and fabric to his own, the concierge put through the call, and putting forth only my question, waited without speaking until he issued a final "very well," and hung up.

Steve, satisfied that no one was watching us in the lobby, continued en route to the CIA listening station in one of the hotel rooms above us.

"Mr. Rabinovich will send someone down to see you."

I remained standing near the desk until two men approached me.

"You are the man from Tampa?"

"Yes."

"Follow us."

Once the elevator door closed, they began to pat my legs, chest, and back in a thorough manner, one that lasted until the bell rang for Rabinovich's floor.

I walked out of the elevator first, pausing for directions, which came as a soft hand on my back, directing me down the right hallway.

One of the men knocked on the door, which quickly opened to a large room with luxurious couches, tables, and a bar on wheels. "Have a seat." While the two men talked in Russian or Ukrainian, I looked out at Lake Geneva. A soft breeze wafted the curtains open momentarily, where I could see the silent arcing slices of pleasure boats on the surface of the lake. Geneva was a lovely city, I thought. After a few minutes, the door opened again, and Felix Rabinovich walked into the room with two more men. He handed his jacket to one of his men, who took it back to the bedroom, and walked toward me.

"Felix Rabinovich."

"Patrick Brewer." We both sat down on opposite couches. "I know that is not your real name, but it sounds nice… So, 'Mr. Brewer' what can I get for you to drink?"

"I would be happy with a whiskey, Mr. Rabinovich." He looked behind him briefly at one of the men standing at the entrance to the master suite, rather than the man who was close to the liquor stand, but guarding the door. Rabinovich wore European blue jeans and a white linen shirt with expensive leather shoes sans socks. He did not wear a wedding ring, but he wore a gold collar around his neck with the Star of David.

He was shorter than I was, and thicker throughout, either a runner or a gymnast; but on the other hand, oddly, he also looked like he had never taken a punch in his life.

His calmness, though, was a completely manufactured product, a matter of rigid self-control rather than appreciation of some unseen harmonics. On top of all that was a sudden jauntiness, a feeling that the CIA sent their bat boy, and that the message would be pro forma.

He asked me about my flight from Panama.

"It was Tampa. We left just before a typhoon hit the area."

"Yes, Tampa."

He had already spoken with the FARC, it seemed. He smiled, and looked about the room to stretch time until our drinks arrived. One of his men approached him, and Rabinovich whispered instructions into his ear. After taking a healthy sip of the whiskey, I put down the glass on a napkin on the expensive table in front of me. A telephone rang, which prompted one of his men to speak to him. Rabinovich waved him off.

I took advantage of the interruption to restart our encounter.

"Mr. Rabinovich. I have come here as an emissary from the United States government...."

"What—like Kissinger and the Shuttle Diplomacy?" He laughed, which his men picked up and repeated behind him.

"No, certainly not at that level of governmental authority. However...."

"You have a message, which makes you a messenger."

"If you prefer that term, sir. I would like to...."

"How old are you?"

"I am twenty-six."

"You speak like an even younger man, almost like a boy... who do you work for?"

"For purposes of our business today, I work for the United States government."

"Yes, but you do not work for them. You are not State Department or Agency."

He said something in Ukrainian to his men, which caused them to laugh at me much more deeply that time.

Now, I had several pairs of eyes watching me with bemused, almost jovial scrutiny. This was not going particularly well. "My credentials can be established with a phone call—but you know that already, sir."

I paused to let that last comment, an attempt to put an end to his banter, bring him back to the topic I had thus far failed to present. "As I was saying, I am here as a messenger to deliver a confidential message to you." I reached into my coat carefully, and even more slowly slid out a large envelope, which I placed on the table before him.

"Tell me about this letter, Mr. Brewer."

"I have not read its contents, Mr. Rabinovich. It is confidential and relates to you, not to me. It is—in the customary parlance—'for your eyes only.'"

"So, you do not know what is in the letter?"

"My commission is to deliver the letter to you. Not to discuss its contents or wait for a response."

I took a deep gulp of the whiskey, putting the glass back on its spot on the table.

"Another drink, Mr. Brewer."

"No, thank you." He waved his hand upward, and his man went back to the rolling bar and grabbed a new glass, and filled it with ice.

"But Mr. Brewer, you are aware of the matters involved with the letter, and surely you have some notion why they sent you here?"

"I have many notions about many things, Mr. Rabinovich—none, however, about the contents of that envelope. It is a message from my government to you of an urgent nature. They request that you read the letter and give immediate consideration to its contents."

I glanced out the window, as if I knew the exact moment the sky would burst in explosions.

Another drink arrived on the table, which I ignored. Rabinovich stood and walked to the window, opening the glass door wider to permit the entry of more fresh air. Wiping some sweat from his brow, he sat back down, rubbing his hands together, slowly, to work out his next tactical delay.

"You are an only child, aren't you? You are not used to all this," he spoke with his hands gesturing at the splendor of the room and the hotel. I sat mutely. He was reading the headlines of my appearance and mien, but that was all. He looked down at my glass and up at my eyes, focusing on the lagging right one. "You are kind of second rate—you never expected to be in circumstances like this. It was an accident. Now, they don't know what to do with you. Your people like to take care of you because they find your diffidence is charming in an American way."

He was trying to goad me into an impropriety, one which he could use to justify throwing the letter back in my face, or physically remove me from the hotel, and thereby delay his reckoning with the Americans until after his deal with the FARC was complete. Although I was the only one who knew that this meeting was being recorded, Rabinovich seemed to be the one playing to the cameras.

"The letter is for you, Mr. Rabinovich. If you have any confusion about my role here, I will be glad to repeat it. But what I need to impart to you...."

"Yes, your letter... you know, when I was your age, I was a veteran of the Six Days War. I had seen combat in the Sinai as an intelligence officer. I led interrogations of Egyptian prisoners who were twice my age. I looked into so many pairs of eyes—mean, scared, defiant, even psychotic. There were only about ten minutes available for each prisoner. The Egyptian officers had all abandoned their uniforms and put on the ones from dead soldiers. It usually took me only a few questions— sometimes I only had to serve them tea—the officers would look around the hut for cream or sugar—instinctively—and use the spoon in a refined manner. I managed to locate seventeen officers in only two days."

You are judging me on how I sit on an expensive couch or sip whiskey? I took two slugs in my back, and one in the brain on a lark, while you listened to the whimperings of broken men in a Quonset hut! I thought. My eyes narrowed with the jolt of good whiskey in my brain.

"I imagine that skill helps a man in his career, Mr. Rabinovich." He talked right through my attempt to retake control of the helm. "It was different in '73. I was in general headquarters outside Tel Aviv. The war was not going well. We had to beg Nixon for arms, which were delayed and delayed as our young men were cut down—just because Nixon did not want to drive the Egyptians and Syrians deeper into Russian arms. Finally, the spare parts arrived, and we pushed the Arabs back from our lands."

I could not make out his strategy. Humiliating me was just a futile attempt to try to find a way out of his predicament. I was not the subject of discussion, and he knew this well, as I had told him in several different ways. He had made a stupid error. The question he faced was whether it made better business sense to betray the FARC or anger the CIA. He also knew the answer to that rather simple question, so his snide animadversions did not gain him any ground.

"What is your business, Mr. Brewer? You are not a diplomat or an analyst, and I doubt you are a career agent." I looked down at the envelope and up at Mr. Rabinovich.

"I am a businessman, probably not far removed from your business. I bring buyers and sellers together for a fee… I hate to waste your time with tedious detail, but…" I held up my hands like a salesman making his last reasonable offer.

"What do you think is in that letter, Mr. Brewer?"

"A reasonable offer from people who feel that you are reasonable and will act reasonably, Mr. Rabinovich. I imagine the English is direct and the statements are straightforward. In my experience, these fellows do not bother with subtext, or 19th century British prolixity."

I took a look at my watch. His position was deteriorating by the minute, and he had not decided what to do. The FARC would arrive in two hours to conclude the most significant arms purchase they had made in years, one that could nullify tens of millions of dollars of crop-dusting planes, pilots, and ground crews. If the CIA did not get the response they wanted, they would declare war on his person and his livelihood, and drive him into hiding for a decade or so; or, they would make him do some dirty deals for them until he had no reputation anywhere and an empty bank account. His daughters would never shop in New York again—if that meant anything to him.

There was no reason for him to be afraid to open the letter in front of me, but I asked to use his bathroom anyway. Two men accompanied me to the bathroom and back again to the suite. For several minutes he enlightened me about the deficits in the American character and the erroneous features of its foreign policy. I looked out the window several times, each time checking my watch, while lazily dreaming about rowing Amelia—in a white dress with a red belt, and under a parasol—across the lake under a late spring sky. Amelia would have adorned the 19th century well, I thought.

It was obvious he could not make up his mind, and that I needed to leave, so that he could prepare the next stage of his defiance. I rubbed invisible lint off my knee.

"Mr. Rabinovich, could I borrow your telephone?"

He nodded for one of his men to bring me the telephone, thinking that I was actually in a position to change his luck through a chat with someone in Langley or the Swiss Embassy, or foolish enough to order a strike against him while in his company. I smiled at him blandly.

"Concierge desk. Thank you." I waited for the few seconds it took for the call to go to the concierge desk. Rabinovich looked at me with unexpected concern, but I looked once more out toward the lake.

"Great. Look—this is a bit unusual, but I have to fly out of Geneva in about an hour. Question. Who makes the best hot dogs around here... no the real thing—a real deli-quality hot dog where they make their own buns and sausage. Right. And do they deliver? Excellent. Do me a favor." I suddenly stood and walked to the balcony. "Call them and get me about twenty-five premium hot dogs with kraut and mustard."

I cupped the phone, whispering toward Rabinovich. "There's a lot of guys involved in this. I don't know half of them, but hey--a guy's gotta eat."

"That would be great. I'll pick them up in the lobby in about an hour... I'm not sure about that. We may eat them here or on the road. We're kind of deciding that now. Put down twenty percent for yourself. I'll pay you cash in the lobby. No, in cash—don't bill Mr. Rabinovich's room. Look—would a twelve-pack of Heineken be out of the question? Super. Really appreciate it. Great. Bye."

I placed the phone gently on the table, placing it near my drink, which I lifted and carried back toward the window. "I have never had a real German hot dog. The least I can do is to get hot dogs for all the guys." After that, he looked like he would welcome some kind of guarantee before he opened that envelope, one that would give him the confidence to it and accept its inevitability.

I took the second whiskey and downed it in a quick gulp, after which I took out my handkerchief to wipe my chin. "Great whiskey. A guy could get used to this kind of life. You know, Mr. Rabinovich—it seems to me you have planned your life exceedingly well, better than I ever could. You escaped Communism, you rose to the top in your new country and became a successful businessman. These men who sent me—I don't know them too well. We work together sometimes, but we are not exactly close friends. They golf; I prefer spending time with my wife. But I get the feeling that they are willing to excuse one mistake—a little betrayal, a little side-deal with the enemy. It is almost like they expect that. After all, you would not be where you are now if you did not take some significant risks."

"And you, Mr. Brewer—you have taken such risks?"

"My story is not as interesting as yours, Mr. Rabinovich. I am here because of dumb luck, not talent or daring or perspicacity like you. This is not a personal appeal, but some sound business advice, if I may. Open the letter. There is always a way out of things like this. You will still be on top after this is over." I paused, and then put my empty glass back on the table.

"Ok. I have performed my duty here. This is my first time ever in Europe, but I cannot stay for long. I really would like to take some of the lake before I have to leave. If you have any questions, I will be out back near the beach."

I stood up and approached Rabinovich. "Good luck to you, sir. I have certainly enjoyed our visit. I wish you good health and my best wishes to your family." I shook his hand bone-hard and walked out of the suite.

According to Steve Dubrinsky, he read the letter as soon as I left his room, and he checked out fifteen minutes after that. By the time we landed in Tampa, Peruvian customs, acting on our tip, boarded a plane upon landing at the Lima Airport. They found twenty-five surface-to-air launchers and one-hundred tubes. In FARC hands, they would have nullified our helicopter sales and put an end to our eradication flights. They would have spared one for T.P. Connolly as well.

Our CIA jet had a small refrigerator, which Steve and I filled with authentic Swiss hot dogs. Unable to sleep, anxious to get back and find out the results of our intervention, Steve and I watched Hollywood movies and helped ourselves to Heineken, which we shared with the female officer on board. Steve came to his summation after a few beers, which I gathered from the way he responded to alcohol was not part of his Panama experience.

"That was some seriously weird shit you pulled with that guy, Tommy."

"Send a pro next time, Steve. Otherwise...."

Reheated in one of the base cafeterias, and given out to a room full of agents and analysts in Tampa, we enjoyed Swiss hot dogs during the two-hour debriefing. I answered the same or similar questions about five times. It was awkward to hear my own voice, even though the quality was poor. They all wanted to know how I managed to drop a cuff link, which allowed them to continue to listen to Rabinovich after I had left. All I could give them was a bland smile, since I did not remember dropping it. "It will be in my memoirs, boys."

I could understand Rabinovich better now. Even when rested, I still slurred my words slightly—it was almost like they sent Aldrich Ames after a five-martini lunch to negotiate for them. Steve was quite the gentleman about l'affaire hot dog. He told the briefing audience that I improvised a credible yet subtle threat to his physical person through a contemptuous combination of haste and indifference to Rabinovich—one that shook him out of his dream of arms sales to enemy forces without consequence, and back to the agreed-upon rules of the game.

That night, after filing his report to Langley, Steve stepped out of the building to see his wife and child; as a bonus, Steve, he who interfaced with the Gods, told me not to report back to Panama for another week, which I spent with Amelia and the girls. There was no one I could tell about my first spy mission; the only people who understood its significance were in Tampa and Panama and Langley, and they were quite good at keeping even the smallest of secrets.

The Gods were looking down with favor upon Tommy P. Connolly. Still, the idea of being a year-over-year contractor, rather than an agent like Steve, sat well with me. Having fewer things to entangle me as a contractor, not having a boss or a schedule, it meant that I could take my family away someday and retire to a new life of my choosing and not look back. Silly me. Silly Patrick Brewer.

CHAPTER TWENTY-TWO

A few days later, as I was parking the Range Rover, I noticed – I forgot the type of shape from elementary school geometry—a bright light along sharp angles projecting onto the floor at the rear of our condo parking garage. Walking toward it, I could see our building superintendent was outside the door at the end of the lot—, on a ledge that sloped down to a fifty-foot retaining wall. The ledge gave way to a trail that entered a hill of thick shrubs. He told me that he was no longer permitted to smoke at the portero's desk at the entrance of the building, or around the pool. I asked him where the trail led.

"It leads to the condos on the other side. It is about a ten-minute walk." After he finished his cigarette, I asked him to step back inside the darkness of the garage. With some haste to be back at his duty station, he produced a key from his pocket and locked the rear door from the inside. Back at the portero's desk, I took a pen off his desk to write a sum of money on the palm of my hand, which I held up to his face. "I would like a copy of that garage door key."

"For that, senor, I will get you ten."

Before I met Gregorio Palanco the next day, the key arrived under my door in a large manila envelope. There being no cameras in the garage, I know had my own means of early escape into a few square miles of thick bushes. Using my new key, I walked up that trail and into the woods, emerging near the entrance of another high-rise condo, where I took a taxi to an open-air mall with little bars arranged like kiosks on its ground floor. Gregorio, attempting to disguise himself with a baseball cap and dark glasses, was drinking a beer when I nodded my head toward the street entrance and slowly walked towards it. "Finish your beer. Follow me down the street."

We stood at a street corner during the late afternoon rush hour in front of a laundry string of soccer jerseys. The car honkings would make any surveillance worthless.

"The investigation?"

"I am no longer on the case, but it is still active."

"How do you know?"

"My buddy in the department is part of the team."

"Team?"

"It is only a two-man team, and they are not working on the case full-time."

"Do they have any evidence yet?"

"They have your flight information from Aruba to Cali and Panama to Cali. They know your plane lands in Aruba, but that is all. They cannot get your other flight destinations without U.S. government help."

I did not worry that a couple of Cali policemen would discover our irregular flight schedule, or be stupid enough to pass that information to anyone in their department. That was the kind of information you buried, or sold back to the owner. There was absolutely no chance of cooperation from the U.S. Embassy, which knew about my travel rotation and its purposes. Nando would need to know, however, and it would feel good to wipe his nose in his preemptive dismissal of the intelligence value of Gregorio Palanco.

"If they learn anything more, you tell me right away."

"Tranquilo, senor."

"What else have you learned?"

"They are interested in a place in town called the 'London Bar.' For some reason, Ivan wants to collect all the files from the local police on a shooting there."

"Do you mean the 'Liverpool Bar'?"

"Yes. That's right. I'm sorry."

"Ok. Continue."

Out of his league, but not out of his depth, Ivan was mounting a shotgun investigation so far. There was no connection between the Liverpool Bar and my business with Stevenson and Nando. It was the type of investigation that hoped to find evidence of wrongdoing, if only they looked long and hard and wide enough for some pattern of malfeasance. Ivan knew something, though. He would not take on the Hernandez family, and all that entails—alienation of political supporters in the Valley, loss of campaign money, heat and pressure on his own campaigns in the future—unless he was pretty sure where the investigation would take him.

"There was a shooting in that bar a few years ago. Some college girls got shut up. The National Police took over the case quickly, so we have next to nothing—only some finger prints of one of the shooters and a witness—I think he was the bartender."

Ivan probably had the bartender under lock and key already. He—even reluctantly, which would present no hazard to a speedy prosecution for Ivan—could place me in the bar with a stool in my hand and a dead guy under me. From there, and without other witnesses, Ivan could invent a scenario: young college students got in the way of a drug deal between us that ended with his death and that of two innocent college girls. The deal could have gone down when I left the bar for snacks, and concluded badly with bullets spraying out badly from the gun of an enraged street dealer.

There were several other scenarios that would make sense during an initial hearing. Ultimately, it would all fall apart. But in Colombia, without habeas corpus, it would be enough to keep me in jail for three or four years while Ivan sat on the investigation and grinned to himself, and then tried one more time to bring a young, naïve bride back to her better judgment.

Eventually, Amelia would find out about the whole investigation. Ivan would have power to subpoena her testimony under oath, which yoked her jeopardy with my own. Her father would not be able to protect her from a subpoena from Bogota. Ivan had a good plan, and it would likely have worked out well for him. Amelia would have to testify that I killed a man, and that she lied in her first police interview.

I took my leave of Palanco with a promise of more cash—much more cash—for high-quality information, but that all our future meetings would take place outside Cali. He put the envelope of money in the front of his trousers like a cheap gangster and shuffled away.

On the way back to the Range Rover, I could feel a slick, sour bile rise up in me. It was probably how I felt when Amelia looked at me with so much helplessness in the Liverpool Bar. I had come to know that feeling; it came from that place that artfully conjures up bad things for dubious people in a pinch. It was reaching my throat and causing the pirates behind my ear to sharpen their blades and head to the beach in a tight formation. Maybe beneath it all, Felix Rabinovich, who had met all manner of men in his life, could see it, too.

I was probably looking for a bar fight when I entered mall parking, brought back to a more subtle perspective on things with the realization that I had forgotten to buy diapers for the girls.

On my last day in Cali, Amelia took pictures of the girls and me on the shallow steps of the condo swimming pool. Bonnie and Claire were too fair for much exposure to the sun, which was potent until it fell behind the other condo buildings in the late afternoon. I carried them both on my chest with my arms around their backs into the shallow end of the pool. Amelia made a video of the girls and me, and then joined us in the pool, so that we each had one girl, which we glided on the surface of the water.

I saw the portero at the edge of the pool, nodding for me to join him in the lobby.

"Amelia, I have to sign a paper in the lobby. Can you take Bonnie from me?" I put on a shirt and followed him toward the lobby door.

"Senor—this looks like the sort of trouble you do not need so close to your home."

"Should I bring a gun?"

"No, it is not that kind of trouble."

Inside the lobby—in jeans with some kind of jewel in her navel, her long, blond hair topped by black sun glasses, her arms folded over her sleeveless top—was that girl—the Colonel's girl. She took off her glasses as I approached. Her eyes were sky blue, and her figure meant no harm to the sort of man who could walk away from it quickly.

"Are you Tommy?"

"Let's start with your identifying yourself and work toward who I am." She put out her hand.

"I'm Laura—Laura Benitez. I think you know who I am." Of course, I knew who she was. The question was how she, a motivated, aggrieved woman, but not an intelligence professional, was able to find me. I stored that question for later retrieval.

"How can I help you?"

"Can we talk?" I looked at the portero, who looked Laura up and down.

"Senor, you can use the office in the back."

We both sat in guest chairs in the cramped office. "I know who you are, Laura, but yours is not a situation I want to be involved in. I have not told anyone what I saw. I don't even know if the Colonel saw me that day. It was an accident; it is none of my business."

"That is partially why I am here, senor. What you saw was not what you think."

"I saw you with your arm around the Coronel. There was a little girl's bathing suit hanging from the balcony ceiling. You gave him a kiss on the cheek."

"Yes. The bathing suit was for Cecilia, my daughter."

"Like I said, your secret is safe with me—but don't involve me in this matter."

"Coronel Hernandez is not the father of my daughter. He is her grandfather."

The story she told me was rich in the folkloric detail of the Cali narco underworld. The Cartel leaders wanted to show their appreciation for the cooperation among officers of the SAPOL, the air wing of the Colombian National Police, who could fly around Colombia at any given hour, or facilitate other flights in and out of Colombia without customary tracking records. So, they rented a country finca and filled it with champagne, seafood, and opulent presents. The Cartel also recruited beautiful college girls from Cali to entertain the corrupt and ambitious officers during the five-day fest.

Laura, a college freshman, and already unable to pay her bills, decided that ten thousand dollars cash would be an acceptable price to pay for an action that did not feel right to her, but would not have to be repeated.

Nando sized her up in her bathing suit when they displayed themselves in the style of beauty queens on the edge of the pool when the officers arrived. Nando stayed with that same girl for five days at the finca, unwilling to share her with any of the other officers, as was customary on a rotating basis, or move on to the next girl. After the feast, he relocated her to a larger apartment, and continued to pay her bills until she dropped out of college to have Nando's baby. By drips and drabs, she had continued her education.

All the facts came to me then like a loose, mountainside boulder that was suddenly jarred from its precarious repose, and released for as long as it could tumble downward. She came for money, that money, and to defend the honor of the Colonel. But she had to win my sympathies first. Nando could string out this girl for years before cutting her loose. I had a good feeling about her. She did not ask to get entangled in the Hernandez Clan any more than I did. There was no way out of her predicament through Nando's sense of mercy, so it made sense to roll down the line toward me. For the first time, I looked forward to my next lunch with Nando.

"Listen Laura, we can't finish this discussion here and now. I know where you live. I can come there, and we'll talk, but you can't come here again." She leaned closer to me, wanting to take my hands, but faltering.

"I know you have a family—and that you are dedicated to them. But when can we talk, senor?"

"I don't know. How can I get a message to you? Do you trust the portero in your building?" Of course, I meant whether the porter would keep her secrets from Nando, not prying neighbors.

"He will deliver a message to me."

"In that case, wait for my message to arrive, but do not come here again."

"Thank you, senor; I will wait for your message."

A few hours later I flew back down to Panama.

CHAPTER TWENTY-THREE

After Monday's flight, Steve Dubrinsky, Randy Keuken, Doctor Fuller and I sat down for a lengthy debriefing, to which Cody Pryor was apparently no longer required to present himself. Doctor Fuller explained that we were two months away from beginning phase two of our operation, in which we would use a smaller plane to service the shorter municipal runways in local towns close to the local army brigades.

"The system is now hard-wired. 41 radio teams from the Amazon to the Caribbean are talking to each other, and giving neighborly advice to our friendly forces. The ability to engage in crosstalk has had the proper tonic effect. The friendly forces I hear are establishing territorial pissing rights amongst themselves in the hopes of getting the best goods. Once they establish top dog-little queer arrangements, we are going to be doing some serious grid-flipping starting around Christmas. So, get your shopping done now gentlemen, cuz we are going to turn our paramilitary players loose on the local Commie-loving establishment this yuletide season. That's it, gentleman. Make sure that phase one ends with bulging armories, and prepare your teams to immediately implement phase two. Tommy, could you stay after our briefing. I have some special instructions for you."

Randy Keuken handed me a sealed envelope and a pen. Attached to the receipt for services rendered on nine flights was a check for $161,000.00, representing my salary for the month of July. I wondered how much I earned in Panama and how much in Switzerland. This check was from an account in a bank in Panama, which meant it would be easier to cash in Panama than elsewhere. The CIA, after all, liked to keep track of every known fact in the world, including my banking habits.

I had not yet caught the money bug, but a wormier feeling that my outlays would continue to increase—increased security for Amelia, local police bribes, and probably expensive criminal law advice by next year—until all that I had may not be enough. Criminal greed made more sense to me now. There really was never enough money to forestall all the ways someone greedier could take it all from you.

Beyond my problems, Nando was trying to slide his paternal negligence to my side of the ledger behind my back. I would need that money and more to emerge in some other country with enough to take care of Amelia and the girls, and fight whatever rearguard battles were necessary to maintain a life free and clear of the Cody Pryors, Doctor Fullers, and Ivan Morenos of this world. They were not talented amateurs, but rather pros in their own way, with the right sort of nerve, ambition and reach.

Doctor Fuller's private request to me was indicative of the greater role he foresaw for me in his COIN operations, but it would likely finish my business and good times in Aruba. I remembered what Colombians had so often told me: there is always someone who wants your money more than you do. The same supposition held for your car, property, and woman. Not able to think my way out of this new box, a drink with Cody Pryor somehow met my mood that night, and I accepted his invitation to drink and "shoot the shit."

I met up with him in his favorite puteria in Panama. He was at the bar with two dark and skinny girls in barely butt-covering velvet.

"Hey, Cody!"

"Hi there, master Tommy! Pull up a chair."

The bartender was about to call for two more girls, but Cody waved them off. I ordered a Manhattan and settled in. The reverb from the speakers was annoying, but Cody just took it all in like distinctive parts of a 60s day-glow poster. I waved Cody toward a side table that was farthest from the speakers and the strobe lights, and the lascivious darting glances from the girls. He unclasped himself from his girls and followed me.

Cody dropped his drink on the table and spoke before his butt hit the chair.

"What's up, Tommy."

"We are going to start supplying local brigades—ones in critical regions. They are kind of splitting us up. You will drop me and a cargo load and then a few days later pick me up there or at a different landing site."

"Will I fly in the interim?"

"Yeah, you will continue supplying the big bases. Your part is classified, too. That's about all I can say."

"Master Tommy is moving up in the world! He leaks secret information to his favorite rummy pilot and then tells him the rest is classified." His comments, while suffused with puerile indignation, were more or less correct.

"Fuller told me that I could tell you about the new flight plans."

"And I am to make the same shitty money?" I looked around.

"As if you would spend it wisely anyway, Cody!"

He looked at me coldly and steadily for a few moments, while a new Cody, who had been waiting patiently offstage, suddenly made an appearance. He yelled out to the bartender. "More drinks! Young Thomas is going to pick up the check—the cheeky little gentleman." We both stared straight ahead for a few minutes.

Across the dirty, cigarette-littered floor about ten girls slithered moodily on the raised platform, offering me a private dance with a tongue roll or a small kiss.

"Ya fancy?"

"No, thanks."

"That's right—no exotic pussy for you."

Cody signaled for his two favorite girls from off the stage. He stood up and grabbed a chunk of their butts in each hand, and to their squeaks and squeals, led them up the stairs and down the dark hallway.

It was clear now. Cody appeared no more to me than a mean, disappointed drunk. He could not hide his ill-temper for long; his subordinate role in Panama, his health, his lack of plans—it had all finally broken through the surface where it could provide common cause with his growing disdain for me.

The skinny girl from my previous visit came down the stairs. Making straight towards me, she gave me a kiss on the cheek, and entwined her hand in mine on the bar.

"Here. This is for your taxi." I reached into my wallet and gave her one hundred dollars.

"I'm not ready to leave yet."

"Ok. When you decide to leave, then." Her fingers took my hand and placed it on her breast, so that she could kiss me on the lips with more cover fire than before.

"Bye, bye, 'pretty boy'." I went back to the bar to drink another Manhattan.

Cody came back about twenty minutes later; his mood having risen above its earlier meanness. "Refreshing... some of the best I've had since 'Nam.'" Having to spend perhaps another year in a cockpit with this guy, I did not want things to end this way.

"You flew that far back?" He looked at me sullenly.

"Get me a drink, bed-wetter." I obliged Cody with a beer and a whiskey chaser. "Seriously, you have been flying for... them for that long?"

"I was active duty in 'Nam'. I flew supplies from theater to theater. The helicopter pilots moved the grunts around. I spent most of my time in Saigon."

He looked around moodily, but sentimentally. "In places like this, Tommy. Those Vietnamese girls had the smoothest skins and sweetest pussies in the world."

Welcome to Red Neck Global Adventures—I am your host, Cody Pryor!

"I would spend three days in bed, sober up for one, and fly for a few days. That was my war. I got to know most of the 'Air America' guys in Saigon bars. They would bring heroin with them from Laos. They were looking for customers... they didn't want the additional risk of shipping it back stateside. We got to talkin'. I told them to give me a few hours, and I would meet them in their hotel room. I knew a lot of the bartenders in Saigon. There were thousands of GIs on leave that needed more and more thrills to forget the horror of what they were going back to. Even Gook pussy and watered-down beer didn't calm down their nerves. I walked around town. By the end of the day I had oversold their supply by fifty percent. They made ten-thousand dollars that day. That was big, fuckin' money in those days, Tommy. These days that is lunch money for some Wall Street fuck, but in 1968 that was a house where most of those guys came from. We got a system up and runnin'. That's all it is. That's the money part—just set it up and let the salesmen do the work."

"In three months, we were one of the major heroin distributors in Saigon. After a few months, we were flying heroin to the bars around the other bases. We got on well. They got me transferred into Air America at the end of '69. I flew that route for over a year—scariest fuckin' year of my life. The runways were shit, indefensible—we took huge losses in planes and pilots. The gooks knew what we were up to. They let loose when it was Air America. Two things gooks hated most: white dick in their girls and Air America carrying away their heroin. In that time I made over a quarter of a million dollars."

"That's huge bank, Cody! How did you get it out?"

"I walked out with about a hundred grand left."

"Where?"

"Home was Eugene, Oregon. I bought some acres, but blew most of it on my first plane."

"You wanted to get into business."

"No, I just wanted to be able to get out of there on a moment's notice."

"Were you married?"

"Kinduh. I knew she was fuckin' around while I was gone. The thrill was gone by the time I got back. We had a daughter, but after that, I cleared out."

"Where did you go?"

"I flew for a regional airline for a while—up and down the gulf coast and into Louisiana."

"Was that fun?"

"Sure. The flyin' was good. The money paid off, and women always like a pilot."

"You didn't settle into that kind of life?"

"I got a phone call from some of my old Saigon partners. They said there got special instructions for some flights in Central America."

"What year was that?"

"Around '82… maybe later."

"You are talking about the Contras."

"I am talking about the never-ending full hard-on fascination of the CIA with drug-financed counter-intelligence operations."

"You could have called it 'Air Central America.' We had about ten planes, modified fuselage, extra fuel tanks, and gallon water bottles to pee in. From Panama to Mena, Arkansas—we were the air kings in those days."

"Mena, where the fuck is that?"

"That is above your pay grade, young Tommy—it could also get you killed. Let's just say present and past presidents knew about it, profited from it, and will never speak the word. It was the final dumping point for our cocaine. I flew mostly Panama into Costa Rica and Honduras. Other pilots took over from there. We took product from Cali or Medellin—we didn't care—someone else took care of that. I made about twenty-five grand a month. I had more hair and more pussy than I could handle."

"I think I know what happened. Someone got the brilliant idea to send a bible and a birthday cake to Iran. The CIA folded up the operation, eliminated some risks, and burned a lot of paper." Cody turned cold again.

"I knew some of those men, Tommy. They were good and true. They had served this country since the Bay of Pigs. They had families… children in Florida schools."

Cody took a big drink and wiped his chin.

"See you tomorrow, Tommy boy."

"No. I am away on business for a few days. You fly solo."

"Classified—right?" He gave me a spurious salute, got up and left. I ordered another taxi. I paid triple fare again.

The next day I met with Leo Huff in Aruba.

"The level of secrecy will be much greater. There will be less tolerance for lapses of security in this new assignment." Leo listened calmly to my side of Dr. Fuller's recent dictum.

"The CIA has given me some strict, perhaps we can say, guidelines." He again did not interject any comment, so I continued.

"They want me to unwind almost all my operations and contacts in Aruba."

"I see, please continue."

"They want me to sell the plane as quickly as possible. They want me to limit my contact with Las Cabanas, and they want me to almost exclusively conduct business through Panama."

"They told you this in person?"

"Dr. Fuller explained the new project and guidelines. They… Dr. Fuller showed me some surveillance pictures from the airport. They were long-distance shots of me, the plane, and some of Sal's men. We were loading duffel bags into a van."

"You personally?"

"No, I was standing off to the side. Sal's men did all the work, but we got into the van together. I am sure they have shots of that, too."

"I see. It is undoubtedly local security police helping out the DEA. So, they have established a tenuous link between Tomlinson and Las Cabanas. It is quite a weak one, and under the auspices of the CIA, a plethora of sins are forgivable. Still, I can understand the caution of the CIA in this case. They are not so much as protecting you, as themselves. You could easily leave a trail of crumbs that could lead to one of their operations."

"I will also need a new plane. They left that in my hands. How long do you think the sale of my plane and a new purchase will take?"

"Don't count on using the Piper sale as a down payment on your new plane, Tommy. The second-hand market for planes is worldwide and moves slowly. It may take 6 months to a year to unload it, unless you sell at a significant loss."

"I think that is what the CIA had in mind, Leo."

"In that case, we can sell it back to the broker for a pittance, and let him find the next buyer."

"Could you make that happen in the short-term, Leo?"

"Yes, I can. What's next?"

"A question. Right now, Tomlinson has assets spread around banks in the Caribbean. Do I have any money in Aruba?"

"You have a small account in Sal's bank to pay your local bills." I cut him off.

"They don't want a paper trail between my accounts and the airport—they were as close to explicit about that as intelligence people can be. I am out of the airport club. If anything happens in the future, it is a la carte. Is that manageable?"

"Yes, it happens frequently. People change domains all the time. I will see to that as well."

"Great, Leo."

"Anything else?"

"Yes, Dr. Fuller hinted that the Dutch will be cleaning up the island. He said to expect indictments by summer of this year. Are you aware of any of these activities?"

"I am. My understanding is that the major targets are a Sicilian clan. Luckily, they are not clients of this office. In fact, I can tell you with certainty that no clients of this office are currently targets."

"What about Sal?"

"He is not a client of this office."

"But he is aware that he is under investigation?"

"Of course. He is well aware of the photos at the airport. That is probably why he has not contacted you."

"Is he penetrated?"

"I honestly do not know, Tommy. Sal is one of the more resourceful members of his family on this island. He runs a small, carefully planned operation. I can tell you that some photographs of vans unloading in a free-trade zone are not the foundation of a criminal indictment; nor are they the stuff to inspire great fear in Sal Manzo. Tommy, let Sal take care of Sal."

"Is there anything else you can tell me about your new operation?"

"All the flights will begin and end at Panamanian military airports. The targets are the Colombian brigades that can easily push arms out the back door to the paramilitaries."

"Ok. Continue." I was still anxious to understand whether the CIA was being normally cautious, or had some particular reason to invoke the shut-down notice on all my Aruban activities.

"They did not attempt to curtail my other businesses as much as shut them down insofar as they extend to Aruba, Leo, which surprised me, since they represent a potential security breach. I mean, they left the option open to continue my flights into Panama."

"Why do you think it is true?"

"They want the flights to continue; or, they have an agreement with Colombian officials for the flights to continue; or they are taking a piece of the action."

Leo smiled, as if I had brought home a third place spelling bee ribbon. "Of the three theories, I like the second. If they wanted the flights to continue, they would hire another pilot to perform those flights, and pay him a pittance. He would be used only for flying—not thinking—and would be easily indictable or disposable. So far, they have not treated you this way, nor would your father or father-in-law allow for such treatment. The third theory is not consistent with the CIA I have come to know. This sounds like a big budget operation, Tommy. As in tens of millions of dollars. They do not need to make side money, as they did in El Salvador under Reagan. They have regained their footing with your Congress and public opinion since then. I do not know anything yet about their new project in Colombia. I do know—as anyone with sense in this part of the world knows—that Colombia will not be a state in ten years unless drastic actions are taken. They are losing ground to the FARC ideologically. As a state, they are penetrated and weak. The oligarchy seems content to hold Bogota and pay the FARC for the right to govern the other major cities. They have almost written off the countryside."

"That is essentially the analysis that Dr. Fuller offered last month."

"It is basically correct. I expect they will run twenty planes without U.S. military marking to different parts of Colombia. Have you any idea where they intend to send you?"

"My father-in-law said to expect dealings with some of Escobar's killers, Los Pepes."

"Medellin. Antioquia. Well, that is not far from home. You could be home for dinner."

Leo looked up at his clock and continued.

"I will certainly take care of your requests. We will need to stay in touch about plane specifications. The rest I can take care of. Did they mention a start time for this project?"

"No, but I got the idea that time was of the essence."

"Ok. Let's concentrate on finding a new plane. It is a question of proper scale. If they want a cargo capacity 10 times greater than your plane, they should supply the plane. Make that quite clear to them. Right now you have a cargo maximum of what, about 2000 pounds?"

"Then, I think we should think about a new maximum of around 2500 pounds. 5000 pounds is a lot to lose, and small planes do come down without prior notice from time to time. 2500 is a good number. It almost lets you choose the mission. If they want to fly missiles, they should use their own planes, which I suspect they realize. If they want to send a shipment of rifles or mortars to a brigade on short-notice, they call in you, which is probably the role they have cut out for you."

"What kind of plane does that suggest to you?"

He paused for quiet thought. "It will sound like a narco cliché, but the Cessna-310. You can get its weight without seats down to 2500 and its cargo with reinforcements on the struts to about 5000. You probably will want your upgrades performed in Panama. You will need to talk to your father-in-law about that. My advice is to spend some time among

Panamanian brokers and your friends in the fixed wing parking lot there. You will find some plane brokers there. You should not have to look further than the Caribbean for what you are looking for."

"Is there anything else?"

"Yes, two things. First, sound out Red Sox. I may need more than one pilot. If he is out, I need to know. It won't be easy to find a replacement on short notice. Second, I am concerned about probate issues, Leo. I want to make sure that in the case of my early demise that the transfer of assets is smooth and quiet."

"I imagine you want your wife as your sole heir."

"Yes."

"In that case, I will draft a document that is DEA-proof. It will transfer Aruban Tomlinson assets to Amelia, and only Aruban assets."

"What about the other bank accounts?" Leo laughed a little.

"They are numbered accounts. They belong to whoever has the account name and a password."

"You have the names and codes?"

"Of course. You have never asked for them."

"Has anyone else?"

"There have been no official or private inquiries."

"Then what is the code system?"

"It is simple, really. Pardon me a moment." Leo opened his desk and took out a key. Turning toward a cabinet behind him, he put the key in the middle drawer, and took out a file, which he opened on his desk. He motioned me closer, finishing the gesture by turning the second light of his desk lamp.

"Do you want a copy of this document, Tommy?"

"No, I want to make sure that it goes directly into Amelia's hands if I die, and that she knows how to deal with it."

"Tommy, you are a history buff, I gather. In the left column are bank names and addresses. You see that there are eight accounts spread among three Caribbean banks. The middle accounts are the names. They are nothing more or less than the years of office of your first eight U.S. Presidents. You see it is 4301789-341797."

"Washington."

"Correct. All the way to Van Buren, the most Dutch of your Presidents."

"So, in the last column are the passcodes."

"Yes, random series of numbers that have no meaning."

"And this is the only copy?"

"No, there is another in a safe place but I'd prefer not to tell you about. If it were ever stolen, I would have the accounts frozen through my contacts at the various banks. I have been a customer myself for a while now. Would you like your own copy?"

"No. Let's keep it here. Are my instructions clear, Leo?"

"Yes. Please keep me informed of the Colombian and Panamanian end of things. I smell a significant counter-insurgency operation afoot. I can advise you better if I know more detail."

"I will, Leo, but only in person."

"I understand." I stood up and shook his hand.

"Take care, Tommy."

CHAPTER TWENTY-FOUR

It seemed to me then that the CIA wanted me to continue my side jobs, which they probably knew had the blessing of CNP intelligence. They just wanted everything routed through their friendly banks, rather than hostile Aruban ones. Sal Manzo had the longest successful run in the Caribbean of open defiance of Dutch authority and CIA interference. Neither was ever able to penetrate his operations, or crack into his bank records, with more than risible results. Perhaps they were concerned I would pick up some bad unsocial banking habits.

It must have ran seriously counter to their understanding of the proper working of things—I ran money into secret accounts that they could not control, or use to bring a tax case against anyone. They encouraged speculation; it was much cheaper than paying for information. They just could not accept successful corruption behind their backs. So, they wanted to enter as a senior partner into the operation that Stevenson had invented to take advantage of the Colonel's well-placed son-in-law. And they expected Tommy to follow the flag and turn over my duffel bags to their front banks in Panama, who would control the entry point—and therefore the journey—of purloined funds around the banking centers of the world.

The decision I faced was reducible to pretty simple terms: I could turn away from my sinful Aruban life and financially break even after paying off local cops, mounting a legal defense against Ivan's rush to judgment, and financing my plane expenses and Amelia's personal security team. On top of that, I was looking at another two years of diapers for the twins. Or, I could continue with Sal at moderate to great risk, and build a small fortune that Amelia and I could take away after she graduated from university in total secrecy. It was quite possible that I was thinking too much, or reaching errant conclusions, but I needed to run this and other matters by Sal Manzo before my head exploded.

I had made Sal enough money that he accepted my phone calls, and pushed other matters aside whenever I called.

"Tommy, Christ man! Look at you! My God! You are fully human now!"

"Thanks, Lukas! From the man who caused me to miss my own children's births."

Lucas grabbed his forehead, unfortunately using his drink hand. "Oh, shit, man! I'm so fuckin' sorry, Tommy. Your coat and all. Come on in! Let me get you a drink. What do you want?"

"Is my credit still good for champagne?"

"Of course, man! Grab a seat. Girls, make room for my friend, Tommy!"

Lukas dialed four numbers, and a few seconds later the bartender picked up his phone.

"Tommy—what the hell, man! I am running this place now."

"Congratulations, Lukas. How long now?"

"About a month, man! It is crazy! Ordering liquor, hiring people, dealing with inspectors."

"Nothing you can't handle, Lukas. Besides," I looked toward Eva and Tina, "the fringe benefits are wonderful, I imagine." He laughed.

"They change nightly, Tommy!"

Lukas had put on weight and his face had turned florid—not as the white man in the tropics, but as the budding alcoholic with skin that had not time to recover between nightly sessions of alcohol and cocaine. He was starting a drinker's gut as well. He loosened his tie.

"Where are those drinks, man?"

"Lukas—is Sal coming tonight?"

"Yeah, Tommy. Sure. He said he would be here around ten. We have time for a run up to a suite, if you'd like."

"No, thanks, Lukas."

"Oh, yeah, Tommy. How is your wife doing? Man, she is so hot, Tommy!"

I let the comment and the question both dribble away from the conversation.

"And you, Lukas," I looked around at the prostitutes and the cocaine on the table. "You have established something here on the island, I see."

"It will be my ruin, but you only live once."

The door opened and a waitress brought in a bucket of champagne bottles in one hand, and four champagne flutes dangling between the fingers on her free hand. I could see Sal running up the ramp and into the room. He burst open the door with a big smile, quickly moving to envelope me in a big, old world hug, thereby lifting me off the floor.

"Tommy—look at you! You're human now!"

"That's exactly what I said to him!" Lukas threw in.

"It was so easy to lift you that time. When I found you in the bathroom two years ago, it was like lifting up a little girl. How are you buddy?"

"Good, Sal. Great. How are things on the island?"

"We are holding up well here, Tommy. The hotel, the casino, the nightclub. We are making money in all three." I pointed over to Lukas.

"I see you got new manager."

"Yes, he has a talent for this sort of thing, so I promoted him. He is starting to look like a vampire, though!" We all laughed.

Sal loosened his tie and bent over the cocaine tray. There was the nasal inward spritz of cocaine—twice repeated—and then Sal stood up. He wiped his nose with one hand and signaled to Tina to make room for him on the sofa. He lay back and stared at the ceiling. "Fuck, Tommy! It is good to see you, man! How is everything?"

"Sal, can I talk to you in your office?" He seemed to get the idea.

"Ok." We went through the far side door and into Sal's office.

"Can you lock the door, Sal?"

"Sure, Tommy." He pulled his thick leather desk chair beside its matching guest chair, and then reached over to grab the remote off his desk to turn up the music pumped into his office from the dance floor. We leaned forward in our chairs.

"Sal, I got new instructions from the CIA. They want me to relocate in Panama. I have to get a bigger plane and fly between Colombia and Panama at their request." Sal did not respond or move his head.

"Can you hear me?" He nodded. The CIA does not want me in the airport club or even going to the airport."

"Ok, Tommy." Sal had not taken issue with anything I said, but it did not seem to register with him that I would no longer be his Aruban little buddy.

"They showed me surveillance photos of me, Lukas and your men at the airport. They had a photo of me getting into a white van." Sal nodded his head up and down.

"I understand, Tommy. I hate to lose you as a client, but you are still VIP around here. OK?"

Why was everyone so keen either to please or avoid displeasing the CIA?

"I appreciate that. Here's the thing, though. I don't want to be that much under CIA control. I told them that I would significantly reduce my activities here. I did not say I would end them. We just need a new way of doing business. Here is the thing, though, Sal: I am drawing heat, maybe for you."

Sal laughed heartily. "Tommy—my family is the most powerful political and economic force on this island. We decide how and when it heats up or cools down. The DEA has had a presence on the island for over ten years. Do you know how many arrests they have made? Zero. Tommy. They cannot get a wiretap without our security police cooperating. Do you know who wrote that law? My uncle. They have no physical assets and need our security assistance for the most minor of operations. Do you know how long it takes us to find out? About five minutes. Do you know what kind of bank regulations we have on this island? I don't either. I have never submitted anything beyond a p/l statement."

"Good, Sal. Then why are we shouting over loud music in your office?" He stood up and went to his desk, poured two whiskies into tumblers and returned in one cocaine-fueled, frantic motion.

"Sal, you know it is easy to penetrate an organization such as yours. It is like herpes. It happens to the best of men." Sal laughed.

"The CIA knows something. They told me to expect arrests by this summer. Is there anything you want to tell me?"

"They are going after the Sicilians more than my family. We are not going to crumble on this island."

"Then let's think of a way where I come onto this island and leave without telephoto thank you notes from the DEA, Sal. I don't want the CIA telling me whom I can play with. If they are steering me to Panama, they have their own selfish reasons."

"You got that, right. Tommy—I don't see demand going down for your services. The CIA is funding a lot more than counter-insurgency. There are buying anyone who needs encouragement to see things their way. The new narcos are still buying cops and airport guys and state governors and—pardon my rudeness—national policemen. If you can get the money to me, we can charge seven and a half now. The Colombians will be lining up to get a spot on your plane at that."

"Sal, I think we are back in business."

"Tommy that was the shortest fuckin' retirement from organized crime in the history of the Caribbean. Now, drink up and go out there and kiss a few titties and pretend to like my whores."

The next morning, I left a message with Leo Huff—move the money and accounts, and buy the new plane, but leave the old plane in Aruba. Tommy had a family to feed and some bills to pay.

CHAPTER TWENTY-FIVE

A few weeks later, I walked onto the brick patio of an Italian restaurant only blocks from Miguel Rodriguez's estate in Ciudad Jardin. Nando sat like the cool young professor on campus under a white parasol with labels of an Italian beer company. After just a few hours of sleep the night before, I had just thrown on some jeans and a t-shirt that morning, and looked disheveled.

"Nice Range Rover, marika. But it no longer suits you. You need a car that matches your growing heroin addiction."

"Eat shit, Nando. Oh, and by the way, the babies are fine. Thanks."

"I know. I already spoke to Amelia this morning."

"What are you doing so far south, not that I know where you work."

"I can always make time for my favorite 'brother-in-law,'" he said, stretching out the words in English for maximum annoyance.

Just then a large armoured vehicle, such that I had never seen before, parked next to my Range Rover. It was black and solid and contour-less, heavily-grilled and menacing. It looked designed by NASA for use by the Russian Mafia. Parked so close, it looked like it could eat my Range Rover whole. "Nando—what the fuck is that?"

"They call it the Hummer. It is dual-use. You can take it deep to jungle laboratories to drop off ether, and pick up groceries for your wife on the way back."

The door opened and a short, young Indian boy in black slacks and a pink shirt hopped out onto the ground. Three other flashily-dressed young Indian boys plummeted to the ground from the rear doors. Nando and I, likely seeing the same image of young traquetos skydiving out of their car, howled in laughter at the sight. All four clutched cell phones in their hands and moved as a surly squad toward the entrance, up the stairs, and past us, bumping our table without apology.

They wore thin black jackets with obvious bulges at their hips. Not grasping the role of a hostess, they took a table in the shade behind us, starting their expletives even before their phones settled onto their table. "Gomelo ijueputa! Mariconcitos!" Nando could not stop laughing. I did not carry a gun in Colombia, nor could I tell if Nando had one, or a concealed sharpshooter nearby. These types of gunmen, easily replaceable by the end of the day, tended not to think through the actions.

They gazed at Nando and me with more and more menace, though after seeing them parachute out of their behemoth car, it was difficult to accord them valid narco status. Nando began to imitate a jumping motion with his hand from the parasol down to the table.

"Behold the future, marika—a midget version of the Cali Cartel," he said, (thankfully in English) as he pointed at the table.

This further raised the ire of the driver of the Hummer. He stood up—his chair scooting back and falling over—and charged toward Nando. He came with his hands at the sides of his jacket, reaching for the pistol in his waistband. Nando waited until he was a few feet away and then stood up and faced him.

"How can I help you, traquetico?"

"By fuckin' dying, gomelo ijueputa."

Nando raised his hands upward and slowly put his hand down the open front of his shirt. He pulled out an id badge. "I know you cannot read, little pirobo, so let me explain it to you. This is an id badge from the Colombian National Police. It gives me the right to examine your person or—" Nando pointed at the Hummer, "your little midget tank. If I were to find a gun during either search, I could impound the vehicle and place you and the other lavaperros in jail. If I felt that any member of your table was acting suspiciously, I could take you all to our anti-narcotics interrogation center. By that time your boss, traqueto, would realize how incredibly stupid you were and replaced you with another illiterate burro fucker, you would be dead ten steps outside jail. And we would not give a fuck about your miserable life and well-deserved death. So, shall we begin again, little pichurria?"

The little narco signaled palms downward that his tablemates should remain calm. Nando put the badge back inside his shirt, and smiled at me while the little narco said nothing. Nando reached behind the narco's waist and pulled out his wallet. It was so thick with money that it would not reclose. Nando pulled out all the money and gave the traqueto a small amount. "Here—enough for sodas and cookies for you and your lavaperros." The traqueto signaled for his group of narcos to follow him back down the stairs.

Nando returned to the table, glowing with satisfaction from having dispatched the narco wannabes so easily. He got right to business. "Marika, tell me about your little business. Are you still active in Aruba?"

"Since my move to Panama, I have not flown into Aruba. I got another plane. This one is parked in the 'executive lot' at Howard AFB. It's a Cessna-310 with the proper modifications. I have had it test-flown. It checks out. The Piper is still in Aruba, but Tomlinson no longer has airport privileges there. I told Sal that the DEA was following our movements at the airport. He still wants our business, and I have no intention of cutting off business with him, but...."

"Good," Nando interjected.

"We are going back to that old abandoned suburb near the Eastern shore of the island," I continued. "There is too much interference at the Aruba airport."

Nando all this time listened thoughtfully. His Bolognese arrived and I paused, which allowed him to put forth another question.

"Marika, is it your impression that the CIA no longer wants you to fly into Aruba?"

"Yes and no. My impression was that they did not want Tomlinson assets in Aruba, since Tomlinson is now one of their clients... or vendors."

"Did they tell you to sell the Piper?"

"They suggested the upgrade. I probably left them with the impression that I was going to sell it to buy the Cessna."

"I see. But the Piper is still a Tomlinson asset in Aruba?"

"Yes. I also keep a small business account there. I am Gold-carded at Las Cabanas. I have never seen a bill."

"Have you done any Tomlinson-style business in Panama?"

"No. We have always flown back empty. I have no 'clear through' there, Nando."

"Explain. I don't understand that expression."

"In Aruba, I have a protected path with no CIA or DEA interference from the airport runway to the bank vault. I have no such path in Panama; if I leave Howard with a duffel bag, it would be in a CIA van going to a CIA-allied bank with CIA oversight and a CIA ride back to Howard."

"That is true, marika."

"Besides the Cessna, do you have any assets in Panama?"

"Only a small checking account for Tomlinson to cash my pay checks."

"Good. Your caution is correct in this instance. They are trying to make you a quasi-CIA employee. They want you to sit around in the whore houses of Panama until they call for you, and make as much money as they feel you need."

"Maybe they want to keep me out of trouble that they can't protect me from."

"Performing the same acts as they do for divergent reasons—that is how they would define 'trouble,' marika."

The waitress, without instructions from me, brought me a hamburger and French fries. "The challenge is to stay off their radar and obey the spirit of their benevolent requests. The best thing is for you not to enter Aruba in a Tomlinson asset. The CIA has never prohibited you from employment in Colombia, have they?"

"Frankly, we never discussed it. The Cessna is a Tomlinson asset too and will operate with Colombian government knowledge within military bases."

"Hardly. The Cessna will be landing on country roads and hard clay runways. Nobody at the brigade-level wants your plane tags on their base, marika-they only want what you carry inside."

"But with some level of Colombian government cooperation."

"Correct. We will allow you to run silently through restricted air space during prearranged time-slots and in specific corridors—and then to leave in the same manner."

"Can we leave Colombian air space and re-enter it with their cooperation?"

"That is more tricky. There is no reason to go to Panama by way of Aruba." He smiled after a moment's reflection, quite happy to solve a problem of his own solution. "If the plane were go stop for gas in say Uraba or Maicao for repairs, it could easily get lighter there, couldn't it."

"You are talking about handing off materials from the Cessna to the Piper?"

"You could never do that with the cooperation of my pilot. He is career CIA."

"But the Cessna is a Tomlinson asset, no?"

"Yes."

"Then you choose the pilot for those runs."

"Do you really think that Red Sox will want to touch down in Uraba for the CIA and make a quick run to Aruba for Tomlinson?" He twirled and ate some Bolognese.

"He could be induced. Talk to him. He is a restless guy. He does not like to sit around at home."

"Red Sox will make almost risk-free money in Uraba. There is no reason for him to quintuple his risk for the same money."

"Then pay him more. That reminds me: Sal feels that in light of supply and demand, we should charge 7.5%. He is raising his fee to 2.0%."

"That should not matter much to your clientele. Half of them are desperate to get the money out of Colombia, and the other half wouldn't understand the math, anyway."

"We'll discuss scheduling after my first few flights into Uraba."

"Good then. Stevenson will be glad about the new fee structure, and I will ask Red Sox if he would accept double his normal fee for flights into Sal's abandoned suburb in the east."

After some light chat about family matters, I wanted to talk about something more pressing.

"I had another meeting with Palanco."

"Hmmmm. And?"

"Ivan knows about the Liverpool Bar... Palanco said Ivan has testimony from the bartender."

"Did you pay him?"

"Yes."

"Much?"

"Yes."

"From now on, deal with his boss, Captain Duarte. You shouldn't give so much money to a desk clerk." You mean a Stamper, I thought.

"I know Duarte, marika. He will be in a better position to give you information in a manner that will help you understand better."

"What is there to understand?"

"Ivan's strategy, of course. What he intends to do and how he intends to do it."

I kept my knowledge of Laura Benitez to myself. There was no need to complicate relations with Nando, especially since my institucnal knowledge of the levers Ivan could pull to legally subdue me was almost null. Somewhere out there was the Liverpool Bar killer, and Ivan. They both could not, due to the logic of revenge and death in this country, just go forward, get some therapy, and walk boldly to some happier place, but they each had to peel backwards for another look, and another shot at me.

I enjoyed a few days with Amelia and our girls. My babies were almost identical, but little differences were forming—Claire's chin dimple, Bonnie's lighter hair, diverging eye colors--but starting to see things for themselves. Amelia and I were able to see some movies, and enjoy that local money-laundering wonder, the Japanese-style love motel. They probably had three customers a week, but reported so much income that they would have to rent their rooms every twelve minutes around the clock to earn that kind of reported income.

On my last morning, Amelia came back to our room at dawn from a baby check, shuffling and snapping her fingers to her favorite Ray Charles song. She scooted out of her panties before she approached the bed while I was still pinned down by Cali's pink haze of dawn. She put her finger under my nose and shot her scent into my brain like the putas in Sal's club shot cocaine up their addled nostrils. She cackled wildly.

She was formidable again, tall, proud and leonine, nearly ready to leave our tower, and walk among the sinister elements below. This was how I imagined her personality before the shootings in the Liverpool Bar. Four months after the births of the girls, Amelia could laugh out loud again, and walked naked with only a towel on her head out of the shower and into our bed. She was soft in the pleasurable spots, and athletic around the fringes.

Amelia wheeled the girls around town in a bullet-proofed Range Rover with a hidden gun and her new cell phone, chatting away with her mother, above and beyond concern like a carriage princess above rutty, dirty English streets. She was a cut or two above, and she had no egalitarian neurosis about being tall, smart, and Homeric in beauty. She had returned to school but was already thinking beyond it.

"My Irishman is going back on the road? How long this time?"

"About a week, maybe ten days. This is important stuff, Amelia. It won't be for much longer. I promise." She sat up and acted out her favorite movie line, lowering one breast onto my mouth in suckling style, while grabbing onto me from below. "'Fuck someone up, Tommy! Do that for me, ok?' She cackled again.

"I just love how that sounds in English."

I put Amelia down on the bed, my face quickly brought down there by custom and desire, so that Amelia could slowly wiggle and sway, until she brought me her honey mead wine like an Olympian goddess would give her favorite warrior the tonic he would need for another voyage out among the crooked, cruel, and cunning.

That night, there was an empty seat next to mine on the flight to Panama that a man importunately filled after a brief discussion with the stewardess. He was tall, gangly and with glasses, but looked like he could be fierce in many ways. He ordered an orange juice and vodka as soon as the stewardess made an appearance.

"Mark Robinson."

"Tommy Connolly."

"It looks like we will be bunk mates all the way to Panama."

"For the next hour and a half, I guess." The name Mark Robinson did not seem to fit the man. It was like an agency cut-out name or a clumsy attempt to Americanize on short-notice. "Do you take this flight frequently?"

"A few times a month, I guess." I did not reciprocate the question and picked up an airline magazine. He tried again. "Do you live in Panama?"

"No, I don't live there." This, for an American, was bordering on rudeness, so I gave him a pleasant rudimentary social courtesy.

"I live in Aruba."

"Aruba. How nice. The beaches, the night clubs, the painted houses in O-town. I enjoy it there."

Social courtesy again should have prompted me to ask more about his life and times in Aruba, but I did not care.

I left a sated Amelia that morning and was not looking to make a fast friend. I heard some words, but not because I sought them out or listened to them.

"Pardon?"

"You must enjoy your stays at Las Cabanas." The mask dropped off suddenly.

"I don't understand, Mr. Robinson."

"You must enjoy your stays in the hotel and casino of your friend Sal Manzo." I said nothing back, so he gave me his card. It listed in descending order "Greg Robinson... Deputy Field Agent... Drug Enforcement Agency... blah, blah, blah, Miami."

I put it in my inside suit pocket.

"Thanks, Mr. Robinson."

"I will keep it in case I need it someday." I went back to reading. "This is just a courtesy call, Mr. Connolly. I..."

"I appreciate the courtesy, Mr. Robinson."

"I think we will run into each other from time to time, so I wanted you to be able to match a name to the face."

"I look forward to our next exchange, then." I put the magazine back up in reading position.

"You have not been out to the airport lately. Is there a problem with its service or its location?"

"I am sorry, but I do not discuss my personal business with strangers."

"That is discrete, and probably a good idea from your perspective." We were in the early stages of a sterile ritual. He would prompt me with annoying remarks that intimated deep knowledge of my business until I lost my temper. Then, he would establish control through some combination of superior temperament and implied threats. "Thank you, Mr. Robinson. I think so."

"By the way, your pilot says 'hello.'" I did not reply.

"Juan Carlos Fuentes Ojeda. 38 years old. He lives in Maicao. He owns a little restaurant there. His pretty little wife runs it when he is away. I don't know how he keeps a son in private school and his poor daughter in and out of orthopedic clinics, with that one leg shorter than the other."

I continued to read. "And your brother-in-law. You had lunch with him this week, didn't you?" I gave him my blandest smile. "My organization has a growing file on him." I thought that Nando could take care of himself, but I said nothing.

"And your father-in-law. Is he well? He is hauling in the narcos left and right these days, now that his hands-off policy toward the Cali Cartel is defunct."

A stewardess walked by. I spoke to her in Spanish. "This gentleman would like to go back to economy class now, please."

"As soon as I finish my drink I will go back, miss." He also spoke in Spanish. "Where were we?"

"Mr. Robinson—I am a little confused. Have I pissed on your side of the property line? Have I taken something that you consider yours? Have I interfered with your duties? Because I am sure I haven't. Whatever I do, it is agency business. You can take up any concerns you have with them or my lawyer."

He took a sip of his vodka. "You know, I am a big fan of airport perp walks. They always dress the narcos in clothes no self-respecting narco would wear. Then, they walk them on the tarmac—sleep-deprived, unshaven and sometimes with those headphones on. The young ones— they know they will be back someday. They still have hope in their eyes. They get broken in the holding cells. We try to send them to New York because of the cold. The middle-aged ones—that is what makes my puny little paycheck so… rich. The pure hopelessness in their eyes. They know that they will leave their SuperMax cage an old, broken man. Time will have passed them by and only their enemies will be looking for them. Meanwhile, we chip away at their bank accounts and bankrupt their families."

"That's quite a story, Mr. Robinson. I will be sure to pass it along to my contacts at the CIA." He finished his drink.

"Nice to meet you, Mr. Connolly."

"Have a nice day, Mr. Robinson."

The abrupt rudeness—it was all well-practiced schtick to entice me to get "rattled" and make "a slip." Greg Robinson had nothing and knew nothing. Sal was several steps ahead of the DEA, and increasing his lead. I just needed to stay close to him. But it also made sense to buy some anti-DEA insurance.

CHAPTER TWENTY-SIX

Cody and I landed in a small municipal airport outside Puerto Berrio under a light fog on a late Monday morning. As we slowed down after landing, we could see at least twelve paramilitary gunmen waiting to encircle the plane. Throughout that flight, I had had to amiably redirect our intermittent conversations back to basic civility. He seemed to treat most of my ideas as ones lacking a basic element required to form a nucleus of sense. Football season was approaching, and I had not a care or reflection; neither had I thought much of ongoing Clinton political scandals, or the wisdom of bombing Serbia, the CIA's other reclamation project a few time zones ahead of me.

It was the last topic that seemed to set him off. I had no quarrel with Serbians, or Slavs for that matter. I had spent summers in camps with Serbian Orthodox children in the foothills beyond the Delta. We had Serbian baseball players, trumpet players, state senators, and insurance salesmen in our town. Serbia had been enduring allies during World War II, while the Croatians had been willing adepts of Nazi death camp administration. The Serbs never asked for history and NATO to dismantle their country and leave them with a nearly land-locked rump state and three new enemy states on their periphery. I guess I lacked savvy in these matters.

Cody, as a contractor, who probably was keen on Bosnian whorehouses before he retired, continued to pester me with details of Serbian gross violations of human rights. "Cody, these people can recall what you call violations of human rights back to Attila the Hun. Human Rights is our pet peeve. For them, it is not a simple trust walk to continue to do business with a Bosnian or a Croat. It is possibly dying horribly or losing your village or never seeing your wife and children again. We stepped into their history not really understanding what these events mean for them, and rerouting their destinies like the proverbial spy at a railway switch. There is plenty of slaughter on both sides, I am sure. Anyway, if we all hate the Serbs—on cue, and based on horrific media images—it is probably because there is a Russian or an oil angle. I'm sorry, the whole 'the Serbs as pure evil' ploy seems invented by an intelligence service. If the whole news media, the government, and—yes, the CIA—sees unalloyed evil in the Serbs, then maybe this whole Serbs as evil has been produced for your viewing pleasure."

He looked at me like I was one of them, the Communist, or worse, the café free thinker, from whom our country had largely been spared during its critical epochs by the efforts of men such as him. "You really believe that shit, Tommy?"

"I believe that the national interest is the sum of hidden interests that we are not told about, or allowed to question openly. Some of them may be valid, but some may be not at all in our interests."

"So, why are you doing this work then?"

"I'm saving for dental school."

Even Cody could not suppress his laughter at that point. "You are fucked up in the head, you realize that, Tommy Boy—don't you."

Cody continued to maneuver conversation so that I would divulge personal information, or at least some gleanings about the young punk who made much more money than he did, and from apparently much less patriotic capital. There was little I could tell him about my life since that night in the Liverpool Bar that would not be a security breach for someone I knew. So, as smug as it must have seemed to Cody, I kept my mouth shut.

Still cross with his wayward trainee, he shut down the engine and turned to me with his usual ironically-mocking look of professional deference.

"Do your business, Tommy." A large, green-canopyed truck circled and parked on my side of the plane. A young officer jumped out and came toward me with a clipboard.

"Ud es el senor del Panama?"

"Si, senor. Y ud es?"

"Teniente Campo, Sr. A la orden!"

"Bueno, teniente. We have the bill of lading documents for your examination." I handed over the shipping documents.

"Esta bien, Sr."

"The plane leaves back to Panama soon. And the offloading?"

"Nos vamos pa atras, Sr."

I walked over to Cody's window.

"He wants us to go down to the end of the runway."

"You asked him for his papers, right?"

"No. Is that customary?"

"He could be a guy with a stolen truck, Tommy."

"Wouldn't those be easy to fake?"

"Yes, but he expects you to ask the question."

I walked back to Lieutenant Campo.

"Sr., que pena pa ud., but could I take a look at your papers as well.

"Por supuesto, Sr."

He reached into his wallet and took out his Colombian Army ID.
It looked legitimate.

"Gracias, Teniente." He and I walked toward the end of the runway.
The truck and then Cody in the Cessna followed behind us.

"You are North American, senor?"

"Yes, Lieutenant."

"Your first time in Colombia?"

"No, Lieutenant. It is not my first visit."

"What other parts of Colombia do you know?"

"Pardon me, Lieutenant, but I am not at liberty to discuss those
matters. I am sorry."

"Don't sweat it, Sir. I understand… welcome to the 14th Brigade.
We have lodging for you on the base."

"Thanks, Lieutenant. Do you have a crew for the offloading?"

"In the truck, senor."

"Campos guided the truck to the right side of the runway, and
waved Cody toward the left. "Soldados—adelante!" Four tall Indian
boys filed out and stood at attention at the side of the truck.

"Thanks, Cody. I'm not sure about communication channels, but
we'll work it out." He rolled up his window without reply. I got into the
truck with Campos while the boys loaded it from behind.

Like so many military bases I had come to know—and would know
in the next few —years, we drove through a thicket of trees into a flat
parade ground. This one was grass, since the rains came nearly every
afternoon and hard. On three sides were the facades of one and two-story
administrative buildings. The truck proceeded along the south side of
the grounds and stopped in front of a one-story lodging. A soldier took
my luggage and carried it inside. The truck sped away forward until it
was under the canopy of distant trees.

Campos asked me in Spanish, "Do you need to get settled Sir, or can we proceed with our schedule?" I was more intrigued by the idea of a day's observation of their treatment of our funding than a cafeteria meal.

"Let's proceed with the day's schedule, Teniente."

"Excelente, Sr." He led me across the parade grounds to more low-slung buildings. This one had no lobby and no sentry. It had two long hallways. Campos lead me down the left one, quickly opening the first door we came to. A uniformed officer stood beside a projected wall image with a cue stick in his hand. Campos and I sat in the back of the room. There were about twenty young boys—none of them in uniform—in white plastic chairs. On the board in Spanish were the words:

"FARC... Strategy... Tactics."

The teacher was shorter than I, but broader and thicker in blue jeans and a white polo shirt. He still maintained a military-style haircut.

"The average FARC soldier makes twice the salary of the Colombian soldier. Think about that. They make twice what you make for destroying our nation as you made for defending it. If they were a corporation, they would be the 3rd largest in the country. They control more territory than our own government. How have they achieved this? By terror. That is their ultimate advantage. We must obey military rules of engagement in every battle with them, while they do not. They can use illegal arms or not wear uniforms. They do not honor agreements or keep promises. You all probably know someone in your village who disappeared one day, and later you found out they became FARC. They are prisoners, now. Even if they want to escape, they cannot. They will die in the FARC."

He wiped some sweat from his brow, and backpedaled toward his water bottle off to the side of his slide presentation.

"So, how do we equalize the battle with the FARC? We bring the terror right back to them. Those that hunt become those that are hunted. Your new orders are to hunt and kill. They may seem to you cruel or unnecessary. They are not. Those that gather intelligence in this region know who is a friend of the FARC, and who resists them. Even though a soldier of the FARC is not in uniform, he is still a traitor to the country. You will be well-paid as a paramilitary. You will make as much as the FARC soldiers. You will not train with wooden rifles anymore.

Each of you will have a gun—the same ones used by European and North American soldiers. But you will still be in a military command."

He took another swig of water. "We will begin training shortly. Each of you will have a paramilitary uniform and a rifle. We will conduct this training at separate bases in Santander. It will last several months. You will receive additional coursework in communication protocols; in the principles of counter-intelligence; in FARC strategy and tactics. From this day forward, you are members of your local CONVIVIR, but you are also members of a paramilitary unit. As such you are soldiers with a forward mission—to take territory back from the FARC and hold it until national government control returns. We will hold you to a high professional standard. It is for you a new standard. You must never betray your command or your fellow soldiers. When you talk with family, friends, or an investigator, you belong to your local CONVIVIR and do not communicate or follow the battle plans of any paramilitary unit. Your paramilitary unit ceases to exist the moment you leave you unit. Is that understood?"

He walked slowly within the rows of desks to the back of the room and then back. "Is that absolutely clear? I repeat: your family, friends, girlfriend, priest or policeman will never hear from you that your paramilitary unit exists, or that you are a member. Paramilitarism does not exist. That is one of three reasons you can be shot by your paramilitary commander. The second is to betray an order from a superior. At times, you will act independently in small groups. At other times you will join the National Police or the Army in joint operations. Even during these operations—when you are fighting alongside old friends from this brigade or others—you must never use your name, the name of your commander, or the name of your unit. You are to deny these exist until the day you die. Before we begin this course, is that absolutely clear?"

He paused. All of the boys yelled out their answer in the affirmative. "We will take a small break now. You can smoke outside the building. We will reconvene in fifteen minutes. Understood?" They all shouted their affirmation in an even louder manner before leaving for the courtyard.

Campos and I stood and approached the instructor. He waited until the last recruit closed the door and then extended his hand.

Campos spoke first.

"This is our instructor of paramilitarism, Comandante Miguelito." The instructor began in English.

"It is a pleasure to have you here, sir."

"Thank you for allowing me in your classroom, Comandante."

"We are honored to have you here, sir. What is your name please?" Campos spoke. "He is called Stamper."

"That is a strange nom de guerre," he said with puzzlement.

"It began as a family joke… and well, there it is."

"Ok. Stamper. Have you made plans for lunch?"

"No, I have not."

"Great. Would you please dine with me after the am session of our classes?" Colombian chow hall food made me envy Cody's quick landings and departures.

A-4 was at the end of the wing. It was the same size and layout as the previous classroom. A few men took notice of my entry, but the men in this room represented older, more seasoned military leadership, and took less notice of an American in their midst. They had left successful military careers behind them, yet enticed by the chance to refight their country's civil war with new rules of engagement, unlimited budgets, and threadbare concern for military justice, they came back in droves.

The instructor—a man about 50 with a slight, elegant build and gray curly hair—pointed at an empty chair along the right wall. The title of the lecture was "Principles of Communications Command." Below, chalked on the white board, were four subjects: (1) Theories of COIN; (2) Communications and COIN; (3) Internal Security Protocols; (4) External Security Protocols; (5) FARC communication protocols. He looked over at me and placed a ruler on the number two. I nodded my appreciation.

The analysis was appropriately dense, and followed—as I came to understand later-the written works of Dr. Fuller.

"COIN is a machine that moves more quickly if it is fed the right kind of gasoline; that gasoline of course is valid information. The intelligence officer collects and distributes before he analyzes and acts. Why? Information that is irrelevant in your theater may be vital in the carrying out of commands in another theater. You have been selected to these positions due to your technical expertise and your ability to analyze theater factors quickly and take appropriate actions. But those are not essential to your success in this command. We will operate under a centralized command structure. Intelligence command will oversee 41 intelligence units. They may be marines, army or navy. It does not matter. You will all have the same equipment and command responsibilities. Central Command will be the repository of all information across intelligence divisions. You will send all relevant information to them and receive specific intelligence in return. The determination of which incoming information is actionable—and in what manner it is actionable--is a matter between two agents: one will be your brigade liaison; the other will be the commandante for your sector."

He is out there alone....

These were the lonely boys that Doctor Fuller described. The ones who knew all the secrets, who would sit as an equal with brigade intelligence officers in a secret meeting, and then slip out the back door to give a kill order to the paramilitary bosses. They had to keep everyone's secrets, and it would behoove the brigade or paramilitary captains to deny ever having known them when the COIN caravan moved on to the next country.

They would live the high life for a few years; there would be no rulebook for the coming counter campaign against the FARC, and they would send men, women and children to their deaths in areas as big as states. There would be wine, women, and sacks of cash. The CIA would see to that. But there would be no U.S. visas or photos with visiting Generals, only the occasional meal with a guy named Stamper who picked up meal checks, and distributed thick envelopes once in a while. When the COIN caravan moved on, we would deny them sixty-seven times before dawn. But they didn't know that.

That afternoon, Miguelito, Campos and I took a helicopter ride out over the Magdalena River Delta, a big, flat sludgy brown pond where the river slows down, shits out industrial effluent, and waits for more rain to push it all down river. Miguelito pointed out the petrochemical plants of Berrancabermeja to the north, and in the distance, the Sierra Nevada of San Lucas, the ancestral home of the first generation of angry, petulant intellectuals from Bogota who formed the FARC.

"We started moving south along the river about six months ago. We stalled here, Stamper. The FARC are not fleeing like in other areas. They have decided to stay and fight. They have been bosses around here for thirty years. The locals need to see that we are serious about retaking these villages before they support us. The FARC rely upon the Magdalena for communication, supply and of course transportation. They own the other side of the river at night—nearly everything north of Puerto Berrio. We attack, and they take it back the next day. We need it all here—more men, communications, weapons, intelligence."

So this was my role, and it was frontline stuff. The FARC knew I was there; I could almost see them peering out of the jungle on the other side of the river.

Cody came two days later. We rode back together in a sullen manner to Panama. Cody drove himself off base, while a driver took me to the communications center for an audience with Steve Dubrinsky and Dr. Fuller. I described their request for bases on the other side of the river, and the minimum requirements that Campos and Miguelito described to me in subsequent conversations. Steve Dubrinsky told Dr. Fuller that the actual budget would arrive in Tampa the next day. I briefly described the base funding request.

It was a huge financial and logistical commitment made more precarious by its fixed location in the proximity of the San Lucas Mountains. "Assuming we decide to fund, the natural supply route is to fly into Barrancabermeja, utilizing the local airport, and helicopter our loads across the river to the new bases. It is much shorter than from Puerto Berrio. The army has the sites selected—they just can't protect them right now."

Dr. Fuller interjected as the tempo of my analysis slowed down, and showed no sign of having taken the bait. "Ok. Tommy. Keep stocking the shelves there for a few days and head up to Cimitarra. Three or four days should suffice. Let Cody handle the airport work—you poke around the base and get a feel for how up to the task they are about killing FARC nancy boys. Then, rest up a few days in Cali and report back here. There is mischief afoot elsewhere, which we can discuss next week. Cody can stay sober long enough to drop off supplies in Cimitarra in serial fashion for a few days and return here. We need to start flipping some of these major grids—so far we haven't been able to turn anything more strategic than Mayberry, RFD. Tommy, since I will be up on the Hill justifying your malarial travel junkets, let's do everything we can to clear the Reds from the Magdalena. As they say, 'We either hang together' or we end up working the local frostie machine separately someday."

After signing off, I sat still for a few seconds.

"What is it, Tommy?" Steve asked.

"The army—through the paramilitaries—are telling the FARC their days are numbered. I mean—look at their plans—it is like a spa and resort twenty miles from the FARC's oldest bases."

"You are correct, Tommy—it has an element of psychological warfare. The FARC have plans to take Bogota, while we draw up plans to take their homeland. But it is also strategic. The 'friendlies' have to take control of the Magdalena to end the war... everyone knows the stakes."

"It's gonna be savage, Steve."

"Something like that, Tommy. Something like that, indeed."

CHAPTER TWENTY-SEVEN

A few days later, I lounged on our bedroom floor with Amelia and the babies in the cool aftermath of a late night deluge in Cali. The lightning strikes that rocketed down from the mountains always woke up the girls and sent them into frantic crying fits. The girls in dire straights, I took the rare night off from fretful worry. Anyway, Amelia needed an introduction to Otis Redding.

Laura Benitez, whom I had avoided for the last month, was an issue that I delayed at considerable risk to the happiness of my family life. The porter in my building told me that she had stopped by to see me, and then quickly left. That showed respect both for my work and my marriage, but an impatience that could cost me dearly if I avoided her much longer. I owed her a visit, so I went down to the lobby pay phone and told her to expect me the next morning.

That night, the low hum of the air conditioner played base to the high drone of the cicadas in our room after the girls finally slept. It was one of those nights when a jet engine could not dislodge the swampy feeling in Cali. I sat on the couch and sweated. Amelia listened to my expurgated stories of chow halls, one-runway airports, and special meetings with intelligence officers—all the while applying cream to her thighs and arms, handing me the jar and rolling over on her back.

"Thank God Daddy was never stationed in those places... so terrible... it is so backward—all those small river villages filled with putas and guerrillas and cholera. I hope you don't have to go back there again."

"I think I will be going there a lot—they will need uniforms and guns and equipment."

"I hope they are paying you for all the hazards they inflict on you."

"They don't see it that way; they see it as my duty. But yes, the money is quite good. You will never lack for violent American videos again in your life. I am thinking of buying you a new remote in fact."

Amelia kicked her legs up and down like a teenage girl. "Tommy, Daddy wanted me to tell you—we are spending Christmas at Lago Calima this year. So, try to finish up your work by the end of the year."

"They told me to expect to work through the holidays."

Amelia turned to me and winked. "They can find other people to work over Christmas, or you will just have to fuck someone up a little quicker this time, ok, mi amor."

The next morning, utilizing a few anti-tailing tricks that I explained to Amelia as missed turns, I drove her to school with a constant eye in the mirror behind us. My security firm let me get outside of their range of vision, knowing where I would show up to close the circuit back to Amelia's university. "I'll pick you up this afternoon, mi amor," I promised. I ditched the Range Rover in a midtown mall, and took a few taxis out to Laura Benitez's apartment. She greeted me at the door of her lonely apartment, and after serving me coffee on a turquoise tray, retreated to the sofa chair closest to the sofa where I sat. She was more beautiful in her own place, which did not have bars and a hallway watchman, but was definitely a cell.

"Thank you for coming, Tommy—that is what people call you, right?"

"That's fine, Laura. How is school?"

"I will finish this year, God willing." That was Amelia's plan too, but I made no mention of it.

"That is good news." I looked around at her place of confinement, which had leopard skins and African themes and thick rugs, but had lost all charm for Laura a long time ago. I could imagine Nando hectoring her from the furniture store lobby after he decided to place her in this apartment: "Just pick out what you need. They will deliver the stuff, no joda!"

"Is your coffee ok?" She had not had guests apart from Nando, I guessed. I took a quick sip.

"It's fine." A little tear formed in her eye.

"The Colonel is the only person who comes to visit me. Nando was going to send me to Miami two years ago—he kept promising me, and then he just stopped. He told me he would pay me to finish my education here. He kept that promise, but I don't know what will happen after I graduate."

"Why Miami?"

"I don't want to stay here—Nando will never marry me or be a father to my daughter. So, why not start fresh where I can have a good life away from him."

"Don't you think he will want to have a relationship with his daughter?"

"Nando—he comes here late at night when he knows she is asleep. He has seen her maybe four or five times since she was born."

The Colonel would not want to lose contact with a granddaughter, but he would respect her wishes—to the extent that they did not interfere with Nando's prerogatives and his formal plans for marriage with some more socially-suitable partner.

"My daughter will be three soon. She will speak and want to know about her family. She deserves a real father." It had never been that simple, and never would be for some children, but so far this was a matter best left to Nando. "Nando has a real girlfriend, doesn't he—I mean, someone he intends to marry?"

"Laura—I want to be honest—I don't know whether he has a girlfriend or not. He is very careful about the information he tells me. You know how he is—if you need to know he will tell you...."

"He talks about you, though. He told me about saving his sister's life."

"In detail?"

"No—just that you saved her life. You married her, didn't you?"

"Yes, I did."

"Life is like a fairy tale for some people."

"Laura—if you knew the details, you wouldn't say that. I married her for love, though."

"That's so sweet."

"You are not like Nando describes you... you are more thoughtful and patient. Nando says that you are sitting on a volcano most of the time, but that you think rain will take care of everything."

"He's quite the poet."

This dialog was achieving some sort of mutual trust, but I did not know how I could help her beyond kind words.

"Tommy, I got the impression that you have Nando's money—the money meant for me and Cecilia."

"I have never taken money from Nando. He is my brother-in-law, but that is it. We don't do business together..." Laura smiled shyly.

"If you say so, Tommy." She knew something about my dealings with Nando, but I was not going to recognize indiscrete pillow talk from Nando, or confirm any trade secrets with someone close to the Hernandez family, but still an outsider.

"How can I help, Laura?"

"I am afraid of staying in this apartment forever. Can you talk to Nando for me? All I want is a visa to the United States at this point. Forget about the money. I just want to get out of here."

She began to cry. I leaned over her with my handkerchief, which I placed in her hand. She pulled me downward by my outstretched hand and held onto me, crying with an awful release of grief onto my shoulder. Her arms went around my shoulders and around my neck. I took them off me, pulling away back to the couch.

"Laura, I'm sorry—it's not...."

"I'm sorry, too. You are a good man, Tommy. This is not your problem. I am just so lonely here."

I put the handkerchief back in her hand, but from a distance this time. "I understand, Laura—I'll talk to him. Does Nando have you followed, or prevent you from going out?"

"I don't know—he is capable of a great lack of respect for women—I guess I am just afraid what he would do."

She began to cry again. This time, I put her on the couch beside me, and held her. I could not blame her giving in to a sudden desire for a different sort of man. Nando had kept her for over four years now, in which she missed all the normal experiences he had taken from her—a nice, thoughtful boyfriend, a job after college at night, cab rides through the city with her friends, waking up late with a special boy, smoking a few joints and dancing in her apartment: Nando seemed to be cultivating her descent into a brittle neurosis, with a view to even further deterioration.

"Laura, what would you most like to do during Christmas? Is there something that would make you extremely happy?"

"Take my mother and father to Cartagena. To have a hotel near the beach so that my father could play with Cecilia in the ocean."

"Tell me about your father"

"He is a mechanic; he works on school busses, but not here."

"Could he and your mother join you there?"

"Yes. There is no school at the end of the year, but he does not make much money."

"Laura, I want you to write down all your names and cedulas, and the nearest airport to your parents, ok? Put it in an envelope and take it to the portero in my building. I will take care of the rest. But don't say anything to Nando. Promise?"

"That would be wonderful, Tommy. I cannot ever repay you, but ..." She gave me a smile to disarm my defenses, whereupon she gave me copious kisses on the cheek.

"Take a lot of pictures—I want to see a happy family on that beach!"

She deserved a little respite from Nando's psychological incarceration. He was forcing Laura to live in form and detail the miserable years of his childhood—with only one parent, feeling cast off from both families, and dependent upon the uncertain good will of others. It was petty, mean, and as I had come to realize, fully Nando.

CHAPTER TWENTY-EIGHT

Cody and I shook hands dryly and muttered mutual Merry Christmases outside the hangar at Howard AFB late on the evening of December 23rd. Randy Keuken left for the next ten days in a family outing in Montana. Dr. Fuller was with his girlfriend in a chalet in Vermont and unavailable except through a special number that would probably go unanswered in Tampa. Steve Dubrinsky went back to the Midwest with his wife and children for a week at his parent's house. That left Cody and me and a skeleton crew of airplane gnomes, who filled the plane with cargo and gas and scampered away lest we get a good look at them, or them at us.

Cody consented to two flights per day to Cimitarra and Puerto Berrio for a week. Sitting in a plane cockpit with him was nearly unbearable, more so spread over eight flight hours per day. Since we flew the same routes, and at about the same speed, I took to dismally calculating the hours, miles, and days until I could part company with Cody Pryor.

We kept hot-topical conversation to a minimum, thereby achieving a modicum of agreeability that made the week almost bearable. To the extent that the second phase of the military buildup was only a week away, and that Cody would fly alone on the short-hauls to the coastal grids, it was almost like a final parting. We would not be sharing cockpits on a regular basis, and we would be spared the company of one another.

I slipped him twenty-five thousand dollars in cash at the end of the week, which was far short of the quarter million-dollar bonus—on top of my monthly check— I made for achieving all the "metrics" Dr. Fuller imposed for the mission. "Mighty white of you, Tommy," Cody conceded. There being no one to receive a briefing from me in Tampa, I left Cody in the Cessna's far flung hangar at Howard AFB, and took a jeep from the entrance of the base to the airport.

I imagined that Cody's favorite haunts in Panama City would be open for the holidays, although most of the prized young girls went back to their villages with presents and cash for their large families. Cody had nothing to complain about, though. That money might last him a few months, drinking and whoring in his favorite cat houses, or betting fifty dollars a hole on the golf courses, but he made his own decisions, and I felt no guilt about leaving for a family Christmas, while he drank the holidays away. I had been generous with him. Even the Cessna got a Christmas present; I had ordered an engine overhaul and new tires weeks ago, paying a healthy premium for work to be performed in a Heavily-Catholic country during holy week.

I drove Amelia and the girls—strapped into the back seats of the Range Rover—to Lago Calima on Christmas Eve. It was my first Christmas as a bonded member within the Hernandez Clan, and the first time we met on somewhat even terms, since my account was now a million dollars above the original "seed capital" bestowed on me in Aruba by Chiara Manso. There was also the fact that, while I could not prove anything, nor would I ever dare to do so, the Colonel, Nando and I were all engaged in various and common criminal enterprises.

Outside a huge, two-story cream-colored mansion near the lake, there were two other cars in the driveway. Nando through the large bay window waved me away, cautioning me not to park behind them. One was an official black sedan, and the other was a new silver Mercedes Benz.

The Colonel stood up when we opened the door with a few of our many packages. The Colonel was casually dressed in khakis and a French blue polo shirt. We shook hands like men who occasionally meet on a golf course.

"Nice to see you again, Colonel."

"Tommy, you look rested," he added in his precise English. Amelia's mother gave me a deep hug.

"How are you, Tommy?" she asked.

"I am fine, senora," I offered back. She squeezed my hand before letting it go.

Nando and I went out to get the rest of the bags from the Range Rover. Walking back toward the house, I could see two armed security guards on each end of the house. There were likely two more upstairs in a communications outpost, which kept the Colonel involved in intelligence matters during all his vacations.

We all settled into the living room on various plush green couches, the women anxious to hold babies, the men eagerly eyeing the liquor cart. I shook hands for the first time with Nando's fiancé Monica. She was dark-skinned, small-breasted and thin-hipped, and not particularly lovely. Her eyes were sunk deep in their sockets, as if she never regained robustness from some tropical illness that afflicted her long ago. She was in no sense in the same company of beauty as Amelia and Laura, but this was a marriage that evidently united families, the sort of marriage the Colonel envisioned for Amelia before I rerouted the fortunes of the whole family with my impertinent act of gallantry in the Liverpool Bar.

Monica had attended a top university and was successful in the DAS, Colombia's FBI, whose building Pablo Escobar had leveled with one of the largest terror bombings in world history. She had lost friends and mentors in that blast; personally, she took a few shards in her torso, and lost a little hearing.

Amelia brought beers on a tray for all of us, while the Colonel, holding two small babies in his arms, was in a content mood. He waved his daughter to his side to close the circle of his happiness. She obliged by sliding under one of his occupied arms.

I hoped that Laura was enjoying something similar in Cartagena with her father. They were staying at a nice hotel near the beach for a week with enough spending money to pay for new bathing suits and nice meals and beach cabanas.

After dinner, there was soccer on TV for the men, while the women chatted in the next room. At halftime of the game, Nando shouted out suddenly, and for no apparent reason. "Ok! Everyone, come back! Here it comes." The preliminary TV commercials before the nightly news had ended, and a young, suited news reporter stood in front of a mansion I recognized from Cuidad Jardin in the south of the city. Behind him, with rifles posted, stood armed policemen from the CNP. The reporter began with a summation that an "elite squad" from the CNP raided a mansion belonging to a high-ranking member of the Cartel del Norte del Valle, the demented, blood-thirsty offspring of the gentlemanly Cali Cartel, who were refilling Cali streets and night clubs with grotesque battle scenes of spilled blood and dead bodies.

Police officers carried unmarked boxes out of the house and behind the back of the news reporter. He paused to let the video portion of the story take place. It described the early morning raid and the quantity of cell phones, computers and cash retrieved in the raid. There were images of police busting down the front door and rushing into the house. They played in a loop while the reporter described the find as perhaps the beginning of the end of the Norte Del Valle Cartel.

The TV announcer went live again, standing next to the Colonel, who was in full dress uniform, Augustan above the interviewer's upraised microphone. From the room came a gathering applause upwards in volume until Claire started to cry, whereupon the room quickly muted. The Colonel stood up and carried her away for a new burping.

On TV, the questioning began. "I am speaking with Lieutenant Colonel Aurelio Hernandez, commander of the Cali anti-narcotics force of the Colombian National Police. Colonel: what was the purpose of this raid?"

"This raid was the product of months of slow and careful gathering of intelligence by the dedicated members of our task force. It was carried out early this morning acting upon information that led us to this location. We found materials that will lead us to the location of more high-level leaders of the Cartel."

"Colonel, do you believe that this represents the beginning of the end for the Norte Del Valle Cartel?"

"We are confident that soon we will make major announcements concerning arrests of Cartel leaders and the seizure of Cartel assets, and the further disintegration of the integrity of their operations."

"Thank you, Colonel Hernandez!" The camera moved away to the reporter and the resumed rush of men out of the mansion.

"Thanks to the efforts of the anti-narcotics task force, the end of the Norte Del Valle Cartel appears to be even closer...."

There was soft clapping in the room. Nando looked proudly at his father, who stood at the entrance of the room.

"Pa, why didn't they announce the names of the suspects in the house?" Amelia asked.

"We do not want to announce their names, yet. There is more intelligence value if they have to find out what we know. The media cooperated in the operation very well." Monica stood up and turned toward everyone.

"If you are ready now, dinner will be served in the dining area."

With Nando playing Santa Claus to the Colonel and his wife and his legitimate grandchildren, while Amelia, Monica and I sat on the couch, we opened our presents at midnight in the large living room without the familiar touch of an American-style Christmas tree. Afterwards, The Colonel and his wife took charge of the girls so that Amelia and I could sleep without interruption.

Christmas day was light and festive, with brandy and sweets and videos of even more violent American movies, until Nando shook two cans of beer at me and pointed toward the front door. We walked along the edge of the common sloping lawns that curved down to the private docks. Bereft of speed boats on the most holy of days, the waters of the lake were still and calm.

"Most of these houses are in some way part of the narco-economy, marika... Mierda! They may not be able to get into the private clubs, but they can buy a mansion next to the aristocracy along the lake. The narcos understand the meaning of that! In the old days, an army lieutenant could borrow a cup of sugar from the narco next door. These days the narcos are leaving town like Nazis from a burning Germany. They are all scared of extradition. They want a deal with the DEA and to keep some of their fortunes."

"Most of these houses were purchased with cash, and they will be sold for half that!"

"What did you say, Nando?"

"A lot of people want to move their money out of town right now. It is a good time to buy, marika." Nando was leading me toward a discussion of much greater import for him.

"Yeah, if you have that kind of money." Nando eased out of his default rug merchant's grin for a moment.

"Marika, we have never pressured you about the money you took from us." I felt the bile rising in my throat. I wanted to mention Laura's claim to that money, but it was not serve any purpose other than to momentarily cause him to loose composure, and to let him know that I was collecting my own intelligence behind his back.

"Us? Who is 'us' exactly, Nando?"

"The money was not yours to take, marika."

"I never claimed it as my own! It is family money. And it is still in the family—safely tucked away in a foreign bank, and a lot larger now thanks to my efforts." I paused to open my beer and take a large first gulp. He was apparently stumped by a formulation which posited me as a guardian of family riches.

"By the way—that mansion on the news last night—everyone knows that it's been empty for six months now. Those boxes didn't leave that house and no narcos were hiding out there—you guys brought them to the house and then walked them out for the cameras. It was a nice show. You wanna tell me what the show was all about?"

Nando made a semi-circle in front of me, his eyes narrowing on me and the water below.

"People " ("Traquetos," I cut him off.) "…need favors from the Colonel's office, marika—either a document that gives them CI status and a reduced sentence… or maybe some intelligence on an enemy, or some lost paperwork. Especially now, a lot of people would like to drift away for a while… perhaps, forever. It is a service to society that they do go away. But there is a… fee to walk away, or face trial in Colombia rather than the United States, or face the DEA with a plea deal rather than a twenty-year sentence. That sort of assistance requires some compensation. Sometimes, it's a voluntary surrender at an agreed-upon location, or it's a tip where we can find bundles of money in a country barn or a Ciudad Jardin mansion… that sort of thing. Right now, we are facing a deadline of January 1, 1998."

"Why so soon?"

"When people don't trust each other, they insist upon deadlines… it's that simple."

"So, how am I involved?"

"The plan is pretty simple. We need to move about $30 million to Aruba—Stevenson is in for about half, and the other half is…."

"Goatfuckers from the Cartel del Norte Del Valle who want to declare only half of their cash before they hop on a DEA plane in bad clothes and without sleep."

Nando was surprisingly without words.

"That is not simple, Nando," I replied.

"It is far from simple. Firstly, depending on the type of paper, that could be between 3000 to 3500 pounds. That means multiple plane runs, or two planes to lessen flight risks. That doubles my risk. The CIA has told me to stay away from Aruba. They made that pretty fuckin' clear."

"They will not complain if you take your wife and kids on a vacation there."

"I am not going to put Amelia in the middle of an operation with all that jeopardy."

"Ok. Sorry for suggesting that, marika."

"Then, there is the matter of the DEA. They have been cracking down on Caribbean banking since Clinton got virtuous in 1994. I haven't spoken to Sal Manzo in a few weeks. Who knows whether he is still looking for thirty million?"

"He is. There is no indictment pending on his end. He is not the panicking type. I have my sources too, marika."

"Marika, use that cunning brain of yours; we need to move that money. We have a short amount of time. You have no CIA work until early next year. Your family needs you." I gave him the sort of look he usually monopolized during our lunch-time conversations.

"I'll need a budget—a big one."

"Submit it to me in Cali when you get home."

"When do you want this to happen?"

"Within four days."

"You're kidding me. That's just not possible."

"These deals take time to cultivate, but they need to close quickly. Besides, you Yankees get sentimental this time of year—everyone knows it—there will be fewer watchmen in the tower in Aruba."

"You know the DEA and probably Ivan's men are following me, Nando."

"That's their job. They are pretty good at it, but they are not going to follow your plane. They will wait for a tip from us or the CIA. But there won't be a tip. You only deal with Sal and your lawyer—neither of them are going to give you up, and you are not going to give them up, so why the sudden need for feminine hygiene products? Shit! Your lawyer wrote you a good contract. You are a CIA vendor. They can't touch you. Be a fuckin' man already!"

"Half the pilots and transport companies from the Contras era went to prison, Nando. The CIA allowed them to make money crookedly, and then turned them over to the DEA for prosecution."

"You sound scared, marika. It worries me. Are you sure you can handle this type of life? Have you been studying books on orchids again?"

I could have slugged him at that moment, but he was not far from the truth: I was scared. He was slyly shifting enormous risk over to me, a maneuver whose justification was the dubious notion that I was somehow obligated to the family for money I decided to keep in my accounts, rather than return to them.

"Yes, I'm scared. What the fuck is the matter with that? Somewhere in this country a shooter knows I am alive and may be looking for me. He may have friends in Cali. Life is cheap here."

"I should have dumped you in Florida, marika! Your shooter joined the FARC. He is several jungles away. He doesn't know you and has no intel to share with them… he only knows that he shot you in a bar and that he thought you were dead. You have to relax, marika. You are not going to a U.S. prison."

"I will do the job, Nando, but tell me the truth: Is there FARC communication about the 'Stamper'?"

"A little, yeah. From the villages around Cimitarra. It's only light chatter—at best." I took another swig of beer to wet my throat for what I wanted to say in a clear and convincing manner.

"Two million dollars."

"What?"

"Two million. That's my fee. And you pick up all expenses. You can charge your traquetos ten percent, or you can move some of your family money to my side of the books. You choose. Two million."

"Will you stop your whining, then, and enjoy the holidays like a real brother-in-law instead of a soap opera gay?"

My hand formed a fist, but soon I saw images of Laura, in sunglasses and a sexy bikini, next to a proud grandfather with bent black fingers, his first time under a beach cabana in the Caribbean, along side an indulging grandmother, with her granddaughter on her sandy lap. Both of them were absorbing the waves that crept up to them, witnessed by an ecstatic daughter, with all of them returning at the end of the day to a thirteenth-floor suite and flush with a few thousand in spending money, and a new camera for Christmas. My hand went limp. I gave Nando a hug.

"Merry Christmas, Nando!"

CHAPTER TWENTY-NINE

Randy Keuken had made known his intention to be out of range of modern communication while in the wilds of Montana; Dr. Fuller told us that since communications were uncertain in his chalet in Vermont, it would be better to reach him via Langley or Tampa; Steve Dubrinsky went back to his family on the cold, flat plains of the Midwest. I gave Cody a lot of incentive to stay drunk and unflightworthy for at least a week. There having been no calls from SoCom command in Panama, I called back and told the duty desk at Howard that I would be with family through the holidays and into January. That left me five days to make some magic happen in Aruban airspace.

Nando expected a plan from me soon, which made me pensive the rest of Christmas and the next day. Nando having explained my acceptance to the Colonel, the next day was actually quite pleasant in that house. We parted with heartfelt hugs and handshakes, especially between Nando and me. We each bore down on our handshake like we were trying to squeeze out a diamond inside our hands.

Amelia kept my plastic cup filled with brandy on the drive back down to Cali. I could not ask her to take notes on ideas that arrived, flirted, and then flitted away. I tried to order them in categories so they would stay corralled until I could get to a pen and paper. There seemed to me three parts, or separate operations, at least two of which would require Nando's local knowledge and contacts. It was complex—it would require a whole team, but it would provide me with evidence of hostility among at least one of my current enemies, and that was at least worth something, if not two million dollars.

After settling Amelia and the girls into the condo, I drove over to Alameda and tucked myself inside one of the small restaurants down the street from the seafood bodegas. I wrote down details on three separate pieces of paper, each receiving a timeline and a budget that Nando could peruse as separate pieces. The final form was a three-page description of the operation, the various timelines, and the required resources.

After ordering a celebratory beer, I called Nando to tell him I had a plan. He said he could be there in 45 minutes. I told the waitress to hold my table so that, a few blocks away, I could place a person-to-person collect call to the personal number of Sal Manzo, who was evidently still manning the conning tower at Las Cabanas during the holidays.

"Hello, champ! How are you?"

"Of few words, these days. Will you be in the resort the next few days?"

"Affirmative."

"Expect a courier. Take his envelope. Be a gentleman. That's all."

"Ok, champ. Bye, now."

I went back to the restaurant. Later, Nando pushed his way toward my table, nearly evaporating the good will between my favorite waitress and myself through his preemptory demands for beer before he could be bothered to sit down. He had a small gym bag in his hand like a country doctor on a house call.

"I'm glad you called, marika. 'Time is truly of the essence,' as you Northerners like to say." I took my notebook out of the backpack and pulled out the papers, which I handed to him.

"This is it." Nando put on glasses and took out his pocket-sized notebook. He read until the waitress and his beer arrived, whereupon he turned over the papers and closed his notebook. Once she retreated, he returned to his reading and note-taking. He read to the last line, returned to the first page—his chin deep in the palm of his hand for several minutes— and then handed the papers back to me. He took off his glasses and returned them to his pocket.

"That's a lot of putas!"

"The question is whether you can make it happen from your end," I asked.

He rubbed his eyes and looked at his watch.

"That is actually one of several questions. I'll need 48 hours."

"I can start my end now," I offered.

"I have a better idea. Your courier can leave early tomorrow morning with the instructions hand-delivered to your lawyer. His instructions will be to give an identical copy to Sal Manzo. Is Manzo in town?"

"Yes. Confirmed."

"Good. The courier waits for a response at Las Cabanas and returns to your lawyer. We wait for the phone call tomorrow night and then act." Nando, so far not evincing disagreement with the elements of the plan, was on board.

"Call Panama and your lawyer this evening. I have to make some calls as well. Also, get some cash together. We start tomorrow. Pay the waitress, marika. Your gringo brain may be on the right track." He reached into his bag and pulled out his phone, dialing numbers on its face-plate as he pushed open the front door. With Nando no longer thumping down on my peace of mind like some demented rabbit, I ate my soup and then drove home. My plan was not excellent, but it was enough to entice Nando to act quickly on his end; neither of us had time to entertain significant doubts. Nando had his reasons—his previous ones expressed during Christmas not at all credible in my eyes—and I had a chance to take two million dollars off the top and place it where no one would ever find it.

Amelia took the news about my departure with a resolve to understand the seemingly ridiculous nature of my sudden and unplanned departure. "Fuckin' Nando!" was all she let out emotionally. I held her and promised that I would dance with her on New Year's Eve at any establishment in Cali she chose. "I have some things to do outside, mi amor."

I grabbed my set of keys and took the elevator down into the basement. We had a storage unit with a large steel lock, the kind that locks the fence gate on a large cattle ranch. It could easily absorb a bullet or an axe. I took about twenty thousand dollars out and stuffed them in a bag.

The next part of my plan was to call Cody Pryor in Panama and leave a short message for him, and another for Leo Huff, whom I instructed to call me at his earliest convenience. Nando arrived about an hour later, and after kissing his sister, and peeking at his nieces, sat himself at the kitchen table in silence as he reread, sealed, and handed me two envelopes. He gave me a pen and asked me to sign my name across the fold of them both. I gave him the money.

We went through each step and stage of the plan. "It will work, marika. There are a lot of moving parts, dear brother-in-law, but I see how it takes care of several problems on your end."

Cody Pryor called me in a mild drunken stupor late at night from one of his haunts. I explained that I needed the Cessna tuned up for its high-performance engine's sake, and that I had established relationships with mechanics in Cali.

"I thought it was being tuned up in Panama this week?"

"They didn't have the parts. My mechanic here has a full shop. He is a go-to guy for many of the narco pilots around Cali. It will get done right."

"Ok, boss—if you say so." I apologized for the short notice, but said that it had to be the day after tomorrow at 10:00 a.m. in Cali. I promised him ten thousand dollars plus expenses, since it could be as long as three days. He took the bait. He would be at the Cali airport by 8:00 a.m.

Restless at that point, I walked into the babies' room. They slept on their backs in the bassinet with a few of their fingers entwined in intimate calm. Hi. I'm your father, I thought. I'm not really a team player, I guess. I have killed a man, a terrorist group probably has a price on my head, I am under investigation by a powerful delinquent lawyer in a country without the presumption of innocence, and I have by now a thick DEA file. It would be great if we still are in contact in a few years. Still, I love you and your mother dearly.

I made little noise on the way out. On the balcony, I stared up at the giant cross in the hills above West Cali, and down at the lights of the other high rises in the neighborhood. Nando was right. I accepted the risks, or sold Cadillacs in Miami. Having authored the plan, having directed a great many people how and when to act, I now had to act out my part in order for all the other actors to stay out of jail. I also needed a hot shower and brandy to even get an appointment with sleep that night. I was taking on huge institutions, who had put tougher and cleverer men than Tommy in jail.

Yeah, Nando. I was fucking scared. I knew, if only for a few seconds, how much bullets hurt, and how blood could seemingly flow out of your body until you fell into a cold sleep. Or, being bundled in a plane and dumped in Aruba, and being followed by agents from two governments, I knew many things like that; they didn't come with batteries and easy answers.

Amelia understood that I would be gone about three days. We bathed together in the sunken bath that night. She lay atop me with her head resting on my chest. She seemed to sway nicely to early Stevie Wonder, one of the soulful palace guards of my childhood. She looked so lovely with foam floating on the water and garlanding her breasts.

The slight drop of her breasts, the result of breast milk weighing down the soft tissue, softened the otherwise athletic prowess of her frame, so that she was at least a little human now. In bed, she was braless and warm and fragrant and I held her from behind that night, and listened to her soft, even breath, smelling her hair until I eventually slept.

The day was one of restless inactivity. The courier was already on the island when I woke up. He would make a phone call to Leo Huff's office and then take a taxi there. He would enter and give two envelopes directly to Leo Huff. Leo would read the draft letter Nando wrote, and then the courier would get into another taxi and go to Las Cabanas. He would ask for Sal Manzo at the concierge's desk. Sal would come up from the basement and take the envelope, carefully studying his part of the plan. He would put his response in another sealed envelope and give it back to the courier. The letter would go back to Leo Huff. Finally, around six or seven p.m., Leo would call my home phone and say "Why don't you try one of the other islands for your next vacation? Curacao has a lot to offer." or "I am returning your call on the matter of those investments we discussed." Or, in other words, "Yes" or "No."

Finally, the courier would take a local flight to Maicao and wait for our arrival in two days, thinking this was the best week of his life, and how could he get into Nando's little gang of adventurers, and live a life beyond national police routine tasks and unwanted paperwork. Leo did call that night; I moved out the next morning.

I arrived at Udelva Airport in Jamundi about 07:30. I walked only a few feet into the small terminal before Nando stood at a café table and waved me over. I greeted Red Sox, whom I had not seen in a few months, and introduced myself to "Ramon," our second pilot. He was of the same service generation as Red Sox, probably an ex-air force or marine pilot. Compared to the wiry and alert Red Sox, Ramon seemed to have gone to seed. He was pudgy and pushed his gaze around the inconvenience of a pendulous second neck. He wore jeans under his belly, and a baseball player's colored long sleeve shirt—in this case yellow—partially atop.

The two pilots opened up their newspapers at their café table and read, while Nando and I walked out of the terminal to await the arrival of Cody Pryor. It was 7:57. At 8:11, Cody touched down and parked amidst a small group of 10-12 executive jets. Cody carried his backpack with him, not at all bulging with a change of clothes or even toiletries. We shook hands coldly, and I introduced him to Captain Nando Hernandez of the CNP. "How do you do, Sir," Nando said in cadence-perfect English.

Cody looked him over and finally let out, "Cody Pryor. Good to meet you."

We went inside the terminal and sat down at another café table.

"Nando is my brother-in-law, Cody. I trust him to look after you personally. Rather than a hotel, we found a resort for you. It will have a pool, spa, and a chef. You may be the only guest—I am not sure."

"That's not necessary, Tommy."

"It is my pleasure, Cody. I dragged you here on short notice. I interrupted your holiday. It is the least I can do." He looked at me as if he may have made a mistake accepting my invitation.

"Well, I am much obliged, then. I would like to stretch out for a while in some cleaner air than PC."

"I have to get back to Amelia, Cody. We have a pediatric appointment this afternoon. With two girls, there are a lot of things to do to get them ready."

"I can handle myself—even out here, Tommy." Nando chimed in smoothly, "That is for sure. But there is no reason to be out here all by yourself. We may even be able to arrange some special ladies to keep you company." Cody perked up.

"I am all ears, son."

"This resort has been known to host nice parties around the pool with music and dancing and an open bar—not the kind of atmosphere one might find at a local airport Holiday Inn."

"And these young ladies would be part of the package?"

"You are our guest, Mr. Pryor. We welcome the chance to honor your service to our country. I can't imagine you would need to open your wallet at any time during your stay." Nando—goddamn him—was nearly note perfect in dealing with Cody.

I tried to find some pitch or tone or approach to lull him into acceptance of our offer at face value. "Cody—I have brought business guests to this place. I have never heard a complaint. I got guys begging me to take them back there."

Cody, with a predatory nose for debauchery, was already visualizing what form those treats would take. "I might be persuaded to take a look."

"Of course. If you do not like the setup, we can take you back to a Holiday Inn in Cali," Nando chuckled at his own comment.

"Ok. I'm in. Let's saddle up and take a look." We stood and shook hands again. I asked Nando for some change to call Amelia. He reached into his pocket and gave me some. Cody looked down at the cell phone on Nando's belt.

"I'm gonna call from the lobby then. Enjoy, Cody." Cody waved back to me as Nando led him to the guest parking lot. I walked to the counter of the café and ordered another coffee. I told Red Sox to tell me when Nando's car had left the parking lot. Next, I went to the phone booth and pretended to speak into the phone. I held this position until Red Sox tapped me on the shoulder.

"They are gone, Tommy!"

"Wait five minutes and come back. This guy is a professional. He can always 'lose something on the plane,' and then come back to check if we are still here. If he sees the plane is gone, he will suspect something is not right."

Red Sox went back to the front entrance and stood outside. He pretended to smoke a cigarette. He came back in about ten minutes.

"It's ok, Tommy. They are not coming back."

The planes took off about 45 seconds apart.

We followed the Magdalena River until it was a narrow slit between high mountain crags and then ascended. We went west toward Medellin until the peaks were to the east, and then followed green jungle for several hours. Only during the last hour did desert take over the panorama. Finally, we touched down on a familiar airstrip behind an abandoned air force base near Maicao. We had to park the two planes end to end on the runway. There was a red Renault parked to the right.

The heat was brutal. I stripped down to jeans and a t-shirt and took a big drink of water before deplaning. The layout that befuddled my medicine and wound-addled brain last year was more plausible now. The building to the right—where Nando dressed my wounds—was an abandoned gas station. It was part of a development scheme that probably collapsed when the base shut down. In the distance, there were flat, square parcels cut from the desert floor. The gas station pumps had been yanked out with a view down to their hollows below, but their pedestals remained. The gas station's windows were bare frames now, the glass having succumbed to the wind and occasional vandals. Our runway was a frontage road along the back side of the base. We were using the mostly hidden portion, which was behind a small, craggy bluff of about a hundred yards.

We all got out and stretched.

A young man about my age in my style of jeans, t-shirt and shoes walked out of the gas station door. He had shorter hair in a military cut, but he could pass for me from the distance of a telephoto lens, until you saw that he had brown eyes, instead of green, and two straight eyes, instead of one lagging one. We shook hands.

"You must be Tommy. You can call me Rigo." He gave a glance toward the Renault. "It belongs to him," he said, pointing to Red Sox in the Cessna.

"Do you have any communications for me?"

"Oh yes, Sir! Wait a moment."

He ran back into the gas station and came back with a sealed envelope. I turned and walked away to read it. It was a single page on hotel paper.

"Good plan, Tommy, you are one smart bastard! Emphasis on bastard. Will see you 'underground'!? Be bad, bitch! Sal." I tore it into small bits of paper and released them into the wind.

Red Sox stepped out of the plane with a machine gun in each hand. He handed one to Rigo and Ramon. "We should be gone two or three hours. We'll bring back food and water. Stay in the office. You can sleep in shifts if you want, but keep your guns close." He looked toward me. "Let's get out of this fuckin' heat."

The desert heat dissipated only slightly late in the afternoon. Tactically, there was little to discuss. We just had to wait out the heat in order to lessen the burden on the planes, which we expected to perform much better in the cool Caribbean night air.

Red Sox, Nando and I drove into Maicao to his family restaurant. Red Sox's wife noticed me, my face now human, and my control over Red Sox more pronounced. She gave me a deep embrace.

"My God! It's you! How are you, by God! You have changed so much. It is a miracle."

"I have recovered well, thank you, senora."

"And you, senora? Is everything ok?" I could not mention their daughter's medical problems.

"Gracias a Dios, si, senor!"

She looked briefly at Red Sox, a look lacking comprehension. He returned her glance, as if to say I will tell you about these matters later. She returned her look to me, and in an instance she knew: I was not a victim awaiting airlift back home anymore. I was home, and Red Sox was clearly working for me. I was not a wounded comrade whom she wished to cradle back to life, but in charge of the operation—perhaps a dangerous one for her husband.

I gave Red Sox's wife, Maria, a final hug and left. She did not offer me a cross, or give me a blessing. If I had not been near Red Sox, she probably would have given him a blessing to protect him from me, or whatever instructions I gave him. We drove back to the airstrip and made our final preparations. I changed into a linen suit with black dress shoes. The Piper now contained only my suitcase and the supplies. The Cessna was lighter since most of its cargo was now in the gas station.

We topped off each plane before Red Sox parked the gas truck beside the gas station. He left a plastic container of picadas, a gallon of water, and "alertness" pills for Rigo, who could look forward to a long, sleepless night, or he would never touch the golden ring again in his career as a national policeman in Colombia.

At 20:00, we got in the planes, Red Sox in the Cessna, and Ramon and I in the Piper. Rigo positioned the truck parallel with the runway and flashed it lights down toward the desert wastes on either side of the runway. We turned the planes around on the hard, rocky desert floor and got back on the runway. The Piper was first in formation and took off; Red Sox and the Cessna followed about thirty seconds later.

This was it; the start of a mission that would make our own types of fortunes: enough money to care for Red Sox's daughter; a new farm for Ramon somewhere in the desert where something would grow; two million and a flying, flashing bitchslap across the bow of the DEA, and—as I strongly suspected—new careers for the Hernandez clan, real estate moguls on the eastern shores of Lago Calima.

We flew low over the eastern coast of the peninsula and then over darkness, splitting the distance between Aruba and Curacao. At around 10:45, Ramon, upon schedule, called in a distress signal and a request for an emergency landing at the Aruba airport. The plan called for one of Sal Manzo's guys to call in an anonymous tip of suspicious cargo landing at the airport from Maicao. Sal had greased things so that a courtesy call would be placed to the DEA nearby.

We were about twenty miles southeast of the island. Even during the holidays, I felt that the DEA would have to take the bait. Dutch intelligence, thanks to Sal, even passed along my plane tags to make the obvious connection for them. Behind us, Red Sox kept a minimal but safe distance between us. We all went down to about fifteen hundred feet and slowed so that our separation would be undetectable on radar.

We could see a line of lights a few hundred meters long inside the eastern shore. Ramon flew over the lights and westward toward the airport, while Red Sox plunged right down toward them. Like a rocket leaving the atmosphere, we achieved separation, and went on with our part of the mission, leaving Red Sox to manage his part on the Eastern airstrip in the hills.

I could not see the Cessna land, nor did I see the airstrip lights turn off. Red Sox was on his own now, taking risks he calculated as acceptable to educate his children, and give his daughter the chance to dance at her Quinceanera, or at least climb stairs normally. Within minutes, Ramon and I were parked next at the Aruba airport. In the hills, Sal's men were emptying about half of the thirty million into one of the Las Cabanas vans. Back in Colombia, Rigo was guarding about fifteen million in the ruins of the gas station. As planned, a well-designed hell broke loose at the Aruba airport.

CHAPTER THIRTY

Sal Manzo had paid and rehearsed his police contacts on the island to relate certain things to Dutch Intelligence and the DEA. Convinced by Sal Manzo that something wayward was afoot, they had more than professional curiosity toward our strange arrival that night.

As soon as we landed and parked, Ramon ran back to the engine and caused a plausible malfunction. He wiped his hands on his old baseball shirt and resumed his shut down procedures. We parked with our lights dimming before a phalanx of police, intelligence types and dogs. In silence, we let the propeller sputter to stillness, not at all heeding the dog barks and calls for us to step down.

We had endeavored to protect Ramon as much as possible. He knew and trusted Nando; he had a current pilot's license, a passport and a valid flight plan. He was not associated with Tomlinson, and was experienced on coastal routes. Nor did he look the part of a professional drug smuggler. In Maicao, he had taken off his wool beanie, shaved with an electric razor, and put on a clean oxford cloth shirt. He applied cologne from an expensive personal bag, too. Inside the bag, there was also an ear-marked Bible and photos of his children and a rosary. Finally, he put on gold-rimmed glasses. In front of the locals at the airport, he looked like he worked in a Miami bank.

Down our respective wing doors, we walked toward them briskly as they cautiously approached us. I smiled and extended my hand to the guy whom I believed to be in charge. He neither held a dog in his hand, a flashlight, nor deferred to the obvious DEA agent within the group.

It was not Agent Greg Robinson, and his absence served to minimize the friction. The Dutch agent in charge showed me his VDA credential with a little pocket flashlight. His name was Wilhelm Grodt. He was obviously career security, probably ex-Dutch military intelligence, enjoying the light duties of security affairs on a tourist island where white collar crime had an astounding success rate, and other types of crimes rarely occurred.

He kept the tight haircut—now silvery—atop a black suit and tie. "How can I help you, officer?"

"Your distress call aroused our curiosity about your true course of action this evening…" I kept my smile in place, waving it back and forth to the three policemen and the tall, perturbed DEA agent in back.

"Pardon, do you mean action or heading? We were on our way to Curacao."

"Do I have your permission to examine your plane?"

"Of course, Mr. Grodt. You will have my full cooperation. My name is Tommy Connolly, and my pilot is Ramon Soto of Maicao, Colombia. He can explain his flight plan and instructions if you have a translator."

I stepped back and showed the way with a light arm swing. Two of the policemen stopped in front of us and maintained a position a few yards from the plane. Then they opened up the wing doors and the hatch. One of the dogs put his forelegs on the hitch. He barked and the policeman there gave him a treat. Agent Grodt peered into the plane with his flashlight. He held it constant and asked the policeman to investigate the rear section of the fuselage. He pressed himself up into the hatch and reached back for the flashlight. They exchanged some short comments in Dutch. Agent Grodt turned and walked back to me. "We have found some items in your plane of a suspicious nature. They require further examination. Meanwhile, we will take you both into temporary custody."

I held out my hands to be cuffed with a modest smile, implying an earnest attempt to cooperate.

"That is not necessary, Mr. Connolly. But please follow me to our car."

"Agent Grodt. As I stated, I intend to cooperate fully with your investigation. However, I would like to call my Aruban lawyer upon arrival at your station."

"That will be possible, yes. For now, Mr. Connolly, would you and your pilot please hand over your passports?" I translated for Ramon.

The DEA would insist upon an abrupt treatment of my person since it was their modus operandi to unsettle and confuse a subject in order to break down his defenses. I doubted whether Dutch intelligence would be eager to comply—they were not clients of the DEA like the intelligence agencies in other countries, and did not want to give the DEA more impetus to move onto the island.

I could sense that the DEA was pushing the Dutch to investigate me and the plane thoroughly. This was the "big mistake" that Agent Greg Robinson had confidently predicted I would make, which would lead to my capture and long-term incarceration. The smug diplomat's son had tried to catch the DEA asleep at the wheel during the holiday season; however, the young outlaw had been foiled by a quick response from Dutch Intelligence, who had alerted the local DEA agent in charge. That was exactly what I wanted them to think and how I expected them to respond.

The office was a little north of the compact sprawl of Orangetown. It was about a hundred meters in elevation, but afforded the security service a commanding view of the airport, and coastal littoral. At the front counter, they took the rest of the contents of my pocket, taking the wallet and pen, and cheerfully returning the handkerchief. We were lead into the building and immediately separated. An officer held Ramon by the elbow and another carried his small personal bag. I found myself on a comfortable couch in Agent Grodt's office. Another officer brought me a cup of coffee, for which I thanked him in English.

Agent Grodt returned in a few minutes.

"About your lawyer. What is his name?"

"His name is Leo Huff." I caught a slight slump in his demeanor, which he quickly hid away at the bottom of a pile of courtesy and orderliness.

"You can use this phone."

We all knew that this call would be recorded. Leo picked up the phone at his home after five or six rings.

"Mr. Huff. Good Evening. I apologize for this call at such a late hour. My name is Tommy Connolly."

"Yes. Tommy. Don't worry about the hour. How can I help you?"

"My plane has had engine trouble. My pilot decided to land at the Aruba airport about an hour ago. We were met by Aruban police, and they have detained me."

"I see. Where are you?"

"In VDA headquarters. I have given them my assurance that I will cooperate, but would like legal representation. They have taken my passport."

"Ok, Mr. Connolly. I understand your situation. As you know, I am a commercial contract lawyer, but you need some type of representation. I ask that you make no more statements until I arrive. Is that clear?"

"Yes, Mr. Huff."

"Please hand the phone to the Agent-in-charge."

"He wants to speak with you, Agent Grodt." Mr. Grodt listened to Leo for about a minute and then hung up the phone.

"Wait here, please," he stated unnecessarily and left.

Grodt was by now trying to pressure Ramon into a preemptive confession of some misdeed, one mutually-agreed upon that would land him in a witness's box back in Holland, and me in the box. Ramon's role and legend were both simple and incidental. He picked up a chance to make some money by flying a businessman from Cali to Curacao. It could lead to more lucrative assignments in the future, and help with the down payment on a finca he wanted to buy for his family outside Maicao.

He had never met me before and helped to load the plane himself. His usual routes were between Maicao and the other cities up and down the Magdalena River. Finally, his flight plan was consistent with international standards. Every fact checks out in Colombia; the conversation could not proceed forward much further than that.

I looked at the large, government-issue clock on the wall above me. It was now 2:30 in the morning. Red Sox was by then back at the airstrip in Maicao, having left the first cargo with Sal Manzo and crew, and quickly returned to our air strip, where he would take the next watch so that Rigo could get some rest.

Leo arrived about 3:15 a.m. I stood up and formally shook his hand.

"Please make yourself comfortable, Mr. Huff." Leo sat down on the couch with me and spoke directly to Agent Grodt.

"May I speak to my client alone, please?"

"Of course, Mr. Huff."

We continued in a formal manner when the door closed.

"Mr. Connolly, it may have occurred to you that the security services were waiting for you to land. That means that some government body between Curacao, Aruba and Colombia gave them a tip. It may have been an outside agent from a friendly law-enforcement partner."

"I understand, Mr. Huff."

"You have broken no Aruban laws. The security services are conducting an analysis of the contents of your plane. Under Aruban law, they do not need your cooperation, and they have noted your willingness to cooperate. They would like to ask you some questions. Is that acceptable to you?"

"What is your advice, Mr. Huff?"

"You may answer or not answer as you see fit. But I think that cooperation with them may hasten your departure from this office."

They already knew there was nothing illegal in that plane. This part was just to fill their files with conjecture for use another day. "I will cooperate, Mr. Huff." Leo stood up and left the room. Agent Grodt opened the door and beckoned me to follow him a few minutes later. We went down a central corridor and stepped into a formal interrogation room. Leo sat on the far side. With his legs crossed, I noticed that he wore no socks. The first ten minutes were to establish my nationality, my background, my current employment, and the provenance and ownership of my plane. Agent Grodt noted that the plane had an irregular history of usage. I told him about my ongoing medical condition and that often I was not permitted to fly, nor could I fly for great distances without the need for unexpected stops to relieve pressure on my scull.

Grodt queried the source of these injuries. Leo put his hand on mine. "The injuries my client endured caused significant neurological damage, including long-term memory. He is not fully aware of the cause of his injuries, only that they took place in Cali, Colombia in 1997, and that he was only a bystander at the time."

Agent Grodt stood up with his pen flashlight and flashed it around my head. He spread the hairs behind my ear until he found the scar. He sat back down. "He is unable to make further comment about those events."

"Ok. Let's discuss your plane." Leo spoke again.

"It is owned by Tomlinson, Ltd of Panama City, Panama. Its previous registry was in Aruba. Its home airport is in Maicao, Colombia. My client uses it for personal travel and occasionally for business purposes."

"What is the nature of your business, Mr. Connolly?" I whispered in Leo's ear, and Leo nodded. I spoke.

"I am a transportation consultant under contract with an agency of the United States government."

"Would you care to mention the name of that agency?"

"I am afraid that my client has signed an agreement not to disclose his relationship with this agency until he receives permission from them."

"I see. Is this agency available on our island now?"

"No, Sir. I have never dealt with them on this island."

"What was your business in Curacao, Mr. Connolly."

"My business was to assess opportunities for import and export between Colombia and Curacao."

"And the bags of coffee, the exotic fruits, the cocktail cherries."

"Product samples."

There was a knock on the door, and an officer handed Agent Grodt a folded piece of paper. He read it and carefully folded it.

"We are almost done here, Mr. Connolly. I have a few more questions.

"Are you familiar with a man named Sal Manzo?"

"Yes, I am."

"How long have you known him?"

"Since 1997."

"Is the nature of your relationship one of business or friendship?"

"I attended the University of California at Berkeley. One of my friends at that time was Chiara Manzo. She lived in my neighborhood and we took classes together. I ran into her in Aruba and was introduced to Sal Manzo, with whom I have maintained friendly relations since then."

"How often do you see Mr. Manzo?"

"I have not seen Mr. Manzo in several months. Before then, I saw him once or twice. As I said, during my recuperation, he offered me the use of a room in his resort."

"Why has Mr. Manzo been so kind to you?" I whispered in Leo's ear again. He nodded his guarded approval.

"In the United States, as in Holland, I imagine, there are levels of academic attainment. Miss Manzo needed to take a certain number of non-business courses to graduate. She calculated that she needed an A in her last semester to attain Cum Laude. I helped her with that. She graduated Cum Laude, which enabled her to gain acceptance at more prestigious business schools."

"Which one did she accept?"

"She is in Boston. I assume Harvard or BU."

"Thank you, Mr. Connolly."

He looked at Leo Huff. "I will be back shortly." He left the room for about ten minutes.

Leo and I made awkward small talk. He asked me about my wife. I told him we recently had twin girls. He joked that he would have to run back to the office and update his files. We talked about our condo in Cali and the current real estate conditions. He also made some comments about my medications and any side effects I may be suffering. I told him that dry mouth and numbness behind my eyes were the only remaining side effects. He shook his head in a pitying way.

"Have they offered you any water? Did they take your medicines?"

"They are in the plane, Mr. Huff." He shook his head, eager to add tantalizing details to the letter of complaint which would start with Dutch intelligence, and make its way to the DEA and beyond.

"It should not be much longer now." We sat in silence for several more minutes. At 3:42, the door opened. A policeman spoke Dutch to Leo.

"You can leave now, Mr. Connolly."

"I can never repay you for your assistance, Mr. Huff."

"You may not be so happy when you see my bill, Sir." We laughed, but Agent Grodt, peering in from the hallway, did not see the humor.

Ramon was already in the front office, looking as bored as his initial presence the previous night. An officer handed me a plastic bag with my possessions. We walked out to Leo's car. "I imagine they will follow us until you leave the airport. How about an early breakfast?" We drove up and down the coast a few times. There was definitely a tail on Leo's car. We stopped for gas once and saw it across the street as we ate breakfast in an American style diner.

Ramon sat at the counter at my request. I explained the urgency in Cali, and about the need to respect the spirit of the CIA's warnings about Sal Manzo.

Leo seemed to understand. "Let's get your pilot off the island. As a courtesy, I will inform Agent Grodt that you have taken ill and need a more spacious way off the island to recover in full." While I paid, Leo made a phone call from a phone in the bathroom corridor. We then drove Ramon to the executive airport. Leo confirmed that the tower was informed of our release from custody. I approached the plane with Ramon and grabbed my suitcase from the hatch. We shook hands. "I'll see you in Maicao, Ramon!" I yelled over to him. "Tell Red Sox we meet at his restaurant at 12:00." He nodded, turned, and left.

Leo drove me to the commercial airport. "There is an eight o'clock flight to Maicao. Don't take one before 10:00 a.m." Leo and I shook hands. "Leo, I consider this special billing. You can take yours off the top." He smiled. "I already have."

I bought my ticket at the counter and sat on a bench with a magazine and a Coke. The team was assembled at the airstrip by now. The first stage was complete. So far, the score was Tommy 1, DEA 0 at halftime. The first part of the plan had succeeded according to my careful design. Faulty intelligence caused Aruban intelligence to unnecessarily detain a man in poor health nearly all night long. At the same time, Red Sox made a quick entrance, drop and exit from Aruba without ever having alerted anyone's suspicions, which were attentively and optimistically focused on a nasty piece of work called T. Connolly.

I skimmed through the magazine several times in hasty boredom. At 9:30, a man sat down next to me. He dropped a piece of paper on my magazine and left. I picked it up. "Bathroom. 5 minutes." It was at the end of a row of food kiosks and around a corner. I looked in the mirror. My eyes were purple and my hair matted down, my clothes reeked of tobacco and aircraft fuel. I splashed water on my face. The door opened and the same man handed me an envelope. He turned and left. I sat down in a stall and read.

Sal had evidently pulled an all-nighter in the count room. That, evidently, was why Leo did not want me on the eight a.m. flight—Sal had not finished the count by then. "Tommy, half way done. The count so far is $20,750,000.00. Accounts filled within 36 hours. My love to Amelia, and girls. Sal." I tore up the pieces and flushed them down the toilet.

I flew into Maicao, zigzagged through town a few times in various taxis, and walked a few blocks into Red Sox's restaurant, late for our 12:00 meeting.

As I took swigs of beer and water, Red Sox explained that his part in last night's operation was routine. Sal's team had heard the engines down the coast and turned on the lights on the landing strip. While we flew westward toward the airport, he had landed easily and cruised to the end of the strip. "Their lights went off. Sal Manzo was there with another guy. I stayed in the plane. They quickly unloaded our cargo and then I turned the plane around. The lights went on again briefly, and I sped forward and cleared the runway. I was on the ground about ten minutes, total. I was back on our airstrip by 1:30."

"How was Rigo?"

"Awake and alert. He walked out of the gas station like a villain in a Rambo movie." I laughed.

"Any communication from Nando?"

"Yeah. He said your friend has already taken Ecstasy and fucked two whores."

"It's a long story, Sox."

"I don't think I want to know, Tommy." Ramon was already back at home, having flown the Piper to the Maicao municipal airport, and parked it there. As soon as Red Sox and I were airborne on the second flight into Aruba, Rigo would drive Red Sox's car into Maicao, and take a series of local busses half way across the country back to Cali.

Eight hours later, Red Sox and I flew the same course as last night to the same desert landing strip. We squared up and landed smoothly, coasting to the end of the runway and stopping before the sole model home. There was a panel van, open with three men in the back. Only when our lights lit up their faces could we recognize Sal, who was accompanied by two other unfamiliar men. They stood relaxed on the back of a black sedan, which would not have any business in the middle of the night on the almost uninhabited side of the island, except to serve as a diversion in case of a sudden raid.

We slid down the wing doors and approached the van. While the other two men began to unload the body bags, Red Sox stayed on the plane, anxious to leave and not get devoured by a silly oversight or mistake.

I greeted Sal with a hug and a kiss on the cheek.

"Hello, Big Boy!"

"Fuckin' degenerate."

"All clear?" I asked. He patted me on the shoulder.

"All clear."

It took only three to four minutes to complete the load. One man shut the hatch door, and when both were clear of the propeller, he signaled to Red Sox to take off. I knew Sox liked to leave quickly and without goodbyes in those situations. I gave him a thumbs up, and almost immediately he made a tight circle and squared the plane for takeoff. He gunned his engines and left smoothly. The lights went off at 3:24.

The van ride was slow and bumpy to the basement of Las Cabanes. Rather than sitting in the front seat, I rested my back against seven body bags of cash. When the van stopped in the basement, I dropped my beanie cap over my head like a bank robber, and hopped into one of three laundry bins. Dark arms meanwhile lifted the body bags out of the van hold into the other bins. They covered me with some sheets. I could hear Sal's voice amidst the others.

"Take these two directly to the counting room."

"I'll take the other one." Sal wheeled the bin over a few doorways and then stopped.

"You ok in there, Tommy?"

"Home, James…" I heard an elevator open, close and rise one floor. Sal pushed open some doors and then stopped.

"Alright, Tommy. You can get out now." I pushed the sheets aside. Gripping the side of the bin, I jumped out and embraced Sal.

"I hope to God those sheets didn't come from Lucas's suite."

"Yeah, we'll talk about that." The bar was dark. Its floor was sticky from last night's tourist take. We went up the ramp, through the VIP room, and into Sal's office. Sal signaled for me to remain quiet. He pointed his remote at a stereo system, and loud, pulsating music lit up the silence. I took off my mask while Sal poured some drinks behind his desk. He handed me a small tumbler of brandy and we toasted to one of the most sophisticated operations he could remember on the island. "To more good times."

"To good times," Sal grabbed his desk chair and carried it over the desk next to mine.

Sal poured deep whiskeys that time.

By willingly offering myself to Aruban authorities, which caused them costly overtime, frayed nerves, and above all a dereliction of duties on the other side of the island, we snuck twenty-million dollars into Aruba, and into the counting machines at Las Cabanas. The next night, we did it again—this time relying upon our normal subterfuge of a late-night arrival at our personal air strip while the guy in the tower at the airport went out for a long cigarette break.

"I gotta hand it to you, Tommy, your plan was smooth and a fuckin' poke in the DEA's eye with a hot stick."

"Thanks, let's hope it permanently blinds them."

"Our men in the security police scrambled all resources to the airport. I mean everyone. They couldn't have brought anyone to the other side of the island! They didn't have anyone else on duty!"

"How about air traffic control?"

"Your pilots did a good job. Our tower guy followed a single dot on radar. He didn't pick up the exit flight at all. Nothing to see, nothing to report."

"What about this morning's flight?"

"I'll find out later, but $50,000.00 should buy us all the radar blindness we need. My guy in the VDA said that the whole office went home early to get some sleep. No one but me knows you landed a second time. Pretty good plan, Tommy."

"Tell me about the accounts, Sal. Had you seen those account numbers before?"

"A few. This is mostly for new accounts. You probably know more than I do."

"A little. There was a false raid for the TV cameras at an empty narco mansion in the South of Cali. They hauled out a bunch of worthless computers and mobile phones into one van. Another van came later and scooped up the money. The narco condition of the deal was a safe harbor with a reliable banker. They want a final untraceable score before the perp walk into the DEA jet."

"Here's to them—their money will still be here after their twenty year stretches."

"How is Lukas by the way?" Sal took another sip and leaned forward."

"I had to get rid of him."

"In what sense?"

"I didn't off him, Tommy. But he is no longer welcome on the island."

"What the fuck happened, Sal."

"The DEA approached him."

"How long ago?"

"It was about three months ago."

"So, he could have given them our strip?"

"I don't think so."

"One of the whores is on my payroll. I use her for VIPs. She told me that Lukas was meeting with someone… we had a little sit-down meeting with Lukas."

"What did he give up?"

"He said that they were interested in the names of corrupt police in Aruba. That they were getting tired of tip-offs. He said he told them nothing about you or the strip."

"How can you be sure?"

"Because some of our police friends bugged him during his DEA meets for about a month."

"What did the DEA want?"

"They never mentioned you. They wanted police names and the take through the casino and the bar."

"Did they talk about planting devices?"

"They wanted Lukas to wear a wire. He said it was too dangerous."

"You sweep the place, don't you?"

"Every week, Tommy!"

"Have you ever found a device?"

"No, but DEA technology is way beyond ours."

"What happened to Lukas?"

"He is not welcome on any island where I have contacts… I put him on a plane for Amsterdam a few weeks ago… I also alerted the security police that the DEA was operating behind their backs. After that, they were kind of surprised to see you on the island. The security guys even bought the plane engine ruse." Sal stood up and took my glass.

He filled two more drinks. "And so on and so forth, Tommy. So far, you are beating them at their own game."

"Yeah, but these things usually don't end well."

"You read too many newspapers, Tommy. Crime does pay—enormously. So does corruption. Just stay connected. And keep fuckin' records—everywhere you go, everything you see—tie it all to your business with the CIA. They won't let you fall if it means a secret being revealed."

"Sounds like a plan, Sal. Do I have to wait around for the count to finish?"

"No. Leo will take care of your end. I will set up the new accounts when the second count is complete. If there is any discrepancy, I will call Leo."

"One more thing, Sal. There will be DEA and local intelligence reports on my arrival and detention. I want a copy of the DEA's report, and I want you to tell your intelligence buddies to lay it on thick in their report. Undue pressure, failure to supply me with my medicine, sleeplessness techniques."

"Good thinking. I won't even charge you, your clever little prick."

"Send a messenger, if you don't mind, Sal."

"Ok. Let's get you off the island now."

Sal snuck me on a local flight into Maicao, from where Red Sox and I flew back to Cali in the Cessna.

I arrived back in Jamundi about midnight the same day. I was banged up, constipated, cotton-mouthed and beaten down from spent adrenaline and an overall lack of water and sleep. All my muscles felt like little bristly pipe cleaners. Red Sox taxied and parked the Cessna within the small number of executive planes in the total quiet of a seldom-used airport. We walked to the edge of the field and into Nando's new red Renault.

"Hail the conquering heroes," Nando said in English. He handed Red Sox a small brown-paper bundle.

"Worth all the sacrifice!" Red Sox burst out. There were no taxis available so Nando drove Red Sox to the Hotel Inter. I thought he was going to drive me home. Instead, he drove up near the Cali Zoo and parked.

"You look like shit, marika!"

"Nando, I just want to sleep! Can't this wait?"

"No, I need a debriefing before you sleep." I explained from my perspective the events of the last three days. He was impressed that the DEA, as I predicted, had sent all their men to the airport, and had nothing in reserve for the other side of the island.

Nando told me about events on his side. At last count, Cody Pryor bedded down three prostitutes, singularly or in tandem. One of the women of easy virtue who distastefully lapped up Cody Pryor's attentions was actually a Colombian Army intelligence officer. She feigned menstruation, and this disappointed Cody greatly, and to the point that he offered her a free vacation in Panama for a chance to paw her Panama-style. Nando also said that they bugged Cody's room and that Cody had had hours of interesting conversations with their agent, which Nando's team was now editing. Everyone in the operation was paid well, and would welcome a chance to work with Nando again.

Nando, in retrospect, was not so happy with my decoy landing. "No more games with the DEA, marika. Your plan was creative, but there were too many moving parts. That is not how intelligence operations work. Too many things can go wrong in a foreign location. Intelligence is about limiting risk, not courting it. You had almost no control of events inside that VDA compound. Remember that. From now on, we go directly to the eastern landing strip on Aruba and avoid the airport."

"I got official proof of harassment from the DEA in the form of depriving me of medication and sleep. You got your house, or whatever the fuck you wanted. Now take me home, Nando."

I unlocked the door of the condo at about 02:30. Wobbling on my feet, I had taken only a few naps in the last three days. There was quiet throughout the two floors of the condo and stillness on the streets below. The girls were close together in the bassinet, tucked into a corner with their blankets cast off to the side, tender towards each other like little Renaissance cherubs hovering above Christ in some Italian masterpiece. I moved them back toward the center and covered them, even though it was still steamy in Cali that night. In the kitchen, I drank cup after cup of water, and in the bathroom, under the pulsating beat of the shower, I slumped on the ground, and let water beat down and dissolve the grime of the last few days.

Afterwards, the man in the mirror had a strange leer, the marauding thief's exhausted satisfaction at having landed in darkness on a rocky shore, stolen every lamb on the island, and escaped without hearing even a single warning horn. In those days, such a feat begat mocking and festive celebration offshore among the boatsmen and invaders involved in such an operation. In my case, we all walked away quietly, hoping above all not to be lionized within an island legend about the operation, or even subjects of bar stool gossip.

My little gang of intelligence-agency Argonauts had performed their distinct roles almost to perfection. Cody and the DEA had each succumbed to their own greed, and I now had proof of it. I also had two million dollars of well-earned narco money on my side of the ledger. I was the Captain that night—not the Colonel or Nando.

I slept without dreams and did not wake up until dinner time the next evening. The Colonel was there when I walked out of the bedroom in my college warm-ups and a t-shirt. Careful not to speak within range of Amelia and her mother, he pulled me aside to congratulate me on my efforts. All for the greater good of your real estate portfolio, mi Colonel! I thought. "It went smoothly, Colonel," was all I could think to say.

We watched some soccer on TV, like regular guys with beers and chips, nary a word spoken of the events that transpired between Cali and Aruba over the previous three days. While the Colonel played with his granddaughters, I checked messages on the phone's answering machine that had been blinking for perhaps several days. There were three messages: one from SoCom in Panama, one from Captain Duarte, and one from Virgilio Hastings, the owner-agent of the security firm I hired to watch over Amelia in the University. Each voice described their call as urgent.

Bloody hell, it never ended. The conquering hero could not wait for his guests to leave so he could take his wife like the bad man he was beginning to feel within.

CHAPTER THIRTY-ONE

When I woke up, Amelia had left for school already. The only sound in the house was Costanza's humming to the girls in the bathtub. My first call was to SoCom in Panama, who reminded me that there was a briefing with Dr. Fuller the next day at noon at Howard. My reply was that I would be there for the briefing, but not for any flights, which Cody Pryor could undertake on his own. My next call was to Captain Duarte, with whom I left a coded message that I would call him in an hour from a secure phone to his cell phone. Finally, I called Virgilio Hastings. I agreed to meet in two hours in a midtown mall parking garage. Before I left, I took five thousand dollars out of my secured locker in my garage with the expectation that, whatever he felt obliged to report, it would cost money to remedy with adequate resources. On an impulse, I took out another five thousand for Duarte.

An hour later, I slipped into the back seat of Hastings's car in a basement shopping mall parking lot.

"Hola, Tommy."

"Quibo, Virgilio." He reached his arm back over the seat to shake my hand; otherwise, he did not look back at me or even take a peak in the mirror. He came quickly to the point.

"We may have found something at Amelia's university. We do not know its extent, or whether it concerns senora Amelia, but…."

"Tell me about it, Virgilio."

"First, I need to tell you something about our protocols. As soon as senora Amelia arrives on campus, or exits a building, we make a note of anyone within a certain range—say twenty meters—who approaches her. If we detect a pattern of intrusion, something which is not the product of a consistent relationship, we take note for future reference."

"I understand—continue."

"Senora Amelia does not have many friends at the University. She does not take coffee with classmates or chat on the grounds with any particular person. She will occasionally take out her phone to place a short call. We noted a young male student who has been in our protective zone for senora Amelia three times recently. He does not share any classes with her, and he is not on the staff of the university."

"He has a crush on Amelia? He is scared to talk to her?"

"From the distance he maintains, it would seem his intention is to listen to her phone calls and conversations."

"Ok." I did not like the sound of that. It is what an operative would do.

"We placed the young man under limited surveillance. We followed him for three days before Christmas vacation. My concern, senor Connolly, is that the youth is familiar with counter-surveillance techniques."

"What?"

"Let me give you an example. Once, he sat about ten meters from senora Amelia on the terrace of a cafeteria. She was on the phone, talking with you, I believe. The young man walked across the campus lawn to the avenida. He got in a taxi, which we followed with a driver on a motorcycle."

"What happened?"

"He switched taxis two times, once walking through a shopping mall to the other side in order to switch taxis."

"Did you lose him?"

"No, he entered an apartment building in a neighborhood in the east of Cali."

"What happened next?"

"We do not have the personnel to maintain surveillance on fixed locations."

"What do you think is going on?"

"We placed further surveillance while he was on campus."

"He attends classes, but very irregularly."

"Does he have friends?"

"He does, two other young men."

"Are you following them as well?"

"Senor, our current budget does not permit such a level of surveillance on third parties."

"I understand, Virgilio." I handed him a sack of money. "This will pay for the extra surveillance on the three young men for the next month. Do not tell any police authorities about your suspicions until you talk to me first. If you believe some kind of action is imminent, take immediate action to ensure the safety of Amelia. Understood? After that, call her father if I am not available."

"Of course, senor Connolly."

"I will be back in one week."

This was not bile rising in my throat; it was rage. There was a plot against Amelia. It did not sound like Ivan, either. He would have no reason to rent an apartment to gather intelligence on Amelia. It would suffice to use local police to follow her from school to home. Anyway, Ivan knew where we lived. It was not public record, but Ivan had access to non-public records and unconventional intelligence means.

The M-19 or the FARC were taking another look at Amelia. Between political assassination and kidnapping, the latter seemed more likely. They were using the technique with great success in Bogota, forcing the rich families in the north of the city to travel to small villages in the south to pay ransoms for their children. So far, the practice had not extended to Cali, much of the credit belonging to the Colonel, who had told me that the FARC, no longer in fear of the extensive intelligence network deployed by the Cali Cartel, had more unwatched patches of society within which to move about unnoticed.

It made great sense to alert the Colonel and Nando. They would fold up the cell and disappear the youths and their cell leader. It would be another feather in the cap of the Colonel, and restore some luster to the CNP. But Amelia would have to leave the university, and perhaps the country, which would cause her to expect dangers wherever we decided to hide her. And I would not get any satisfaction. I did not care about some stupid nineteen-year-old revolutionary who was in thrall to his first lecture on Marx. I wanted his cell leader, the older, seasoned revolutionary who wanted to assert his credentials as a major force within the FARC.

CHAPTER THIRTY-TWO

I shook hands with Randy Keuken the next afternoon in the boggy conditions of his office. Outside a low fog covered the base, so that the top of the control tower was invisible most of the morning. We enjoyed a cup of coffee until it was time to drive to the communications link building. Randy asked me about my family and my recovery, but stayed away from command matters. We drove across the base in a jeep within a foggy, muggy air that concealed the jeep's movement. He let me out of the jeep at the grassy curb and drove away.

"Not coming, Randy."

"Beyond my need-to-know, Tommy. You're on your own now."

Both links were quickly established between my end and Tampa. The screen stayed blue with the familiar scrolling sequences of numbers on the bottom of the screen. Then I saw Dr. Fuller in the middle of the screen.

"Tommy, good morning!"

"Good afternoon, Dr. Fuller." He looked at his watch.

"That's right. It's pretty near lunch hour for me, isn't it? How are you these days, Tommy?"

"I am well, Sir."

"And the girls?"

"Growing quickly, thank you."

"Please express my gratitude to your father-in-law for the fine work they undertook in the matter of the seizure last week."

"I shall, Dr. Fuller."

Was I bullshitting him or was he bullshitting me?

"Excellent… well, phase one of our little operation is now complete. We have serviced thirteen brigades in the past year. Each now has a trained intelligence team, dedicated radio and LAN capabilities."

"The last time I was in Cimitarra, I noticed a lot more… I'm guessing here—marines on the base. Are they in a separate program?"

"No, it is our budget, a Directorate of Operations project. It is too conspicuous to bring the Colombians to Panama, so we are training in-house, now."

"What is the nature of the training?"

"It is mostly commando training for the infantry."

"Medio Magdalena is getting crowded, Sir."

"In what way?"

"There are now more than ten paramilitary camps within an hour's drive of Puerto Berrio. There are high-value marine targets the FARC would love to parade in front of cameras." I paused.

"Go on...."

"By now, the FARC know we are planning something big. If they were ever to kidnap even one marine, he would be tortured to reveal what he knows, which is that Cimitarra figures as an important base of operations."

"Meaning?"

"Meaning that you are going to have to clear the FARC about twenty-five miles from the whole area, on their turf... in their mountains."

"How far would you say the FARC are from the base?"

"About five miles, but at night who knows?"

"What is the area like around these bases?"

"Ranges of hills on all sides... Perimeter security... light weaponry... some of the recruits have wooden gun stocks... and the brigade base itself—soldiers go AWOL frequently. It is just something to keep your eye on, Doctor."

"That's why we pay you, Tommy."

"Understood, Dr. Fuller."

"Good observations, Tommy—keep 'em coming."

"These so-called CONVIVIR, Sir. I see their utility. But they are not embedded within the grid command. I like the brigade-umbrella model, if I may, Sir. I think professional control is important since the country is so vast and the population so dispersed. The distribution of weapons is a military command decision. In many places the CONVIVIR are the first drop of ink in a disputed territory... but... there are too many of them, and they are not strong enough to defend themselves if attacked. They should just receive weapons, disband, and be taken over by paramilitary commands. Otherwise, the FARC will pick them off, torture them, and get the names of high-level officials. Most are not operational according to brigade-assisted paramilitaries. And they tend to align themselves with local ranchers—they see themselves as local and not part of the grid. These ranchers have their own interests, Sir."

"Have you shared these views with anyone else?"

"No, Sir."

"Continue."

"And more careful thought has to go into selecting the Commandantes."

"Why?"

"Some are there because they are bored with civilian life, some to get rich, some to get away from their old ladies."

"That's Colombian middle management stuff, Tommy. It is not something we can step in and correct."

"Yes, Sir. But it is worth monitoring at the brigade-intelligence unit level."

"Indeed."

"Any other concerns?"

"The security at the small airports we fly into. Sometimes, we have to wait with a full load until someone shows up. These operations need more security."

"Ok. We'll talk to D-2 about that."

"Will there be a second tranche of weapons, Sir?"

"The upcoming appropriation will be in the $50 million range. That will replace losses. We are looking at about $150 million from our own accounts. So, we will focus on the 13-14 strategic brigades… Congress has convinced themselves once again that giving peace a chance works. They also have a hair up their asses about human rights again. The Colombian Congress is no better."

"The ones near major cities?"

"Correct. We will arm Cali, Medellin, and Bogota to the teeth. The FARC feel the wind at their back. It is a race to the year 2000, in several ways. We are building a professional army, while they are demoralizing a population and undermining governmental authority. They see a real possibility of taking Colombia for their side. That would be disastrous for our national interests. They see control of Bogota by 2002. This comes from their own documents, by the way. They cannot do that of course without massing troops and attacking the army directly, not just guerrilla attacks."

"Where would you place the odds, Doctor?"

"60-40 government side. As soon as they fight in open formation on an open plain, a professional army will wipe them out… Let's talk about the next phase for you…."

"Alright, Sir."

"You don't have to be on every flight now, Tommy. Mr. Pryor is capable of unloading weapons and returning home to his favorite puteria before dark."

"Yes, Sir."

"We would like you to spend more time at the local brigade level, under the brigade-umbrella, as you call it…."

"What sort of things are you interested in, Sir?"

"Well, the performance of the networks, most of all. We have poured tens of millions into these WAN love shacks. We want to know how smoothly and properly information travels through them. We want to know if the design serves the command objective. We want to know about any leaks—or, hell—any sort of thing they would hesitate to tell us directly."

"Do you want me to focus on any of the brigades in particular, Sir?"

"Yes. Brigade 17 in Uraba, Barrancabermeja, and Cimitarra."

"Why those, Sir?"

"The other brigades are more urban and closer to actual army intelligence control. I doubt you will learn a lot there. People speak more freely on the frontier. Get to know the Commandantes, their officers, the local intelligence liaison—even the brigade commanders if you can."

"Will I be operating under any cover, Sir?"

"Good question. What do you suggest, Tommy?"

"They are always greedy for more weapons, Sir. Why don't I travel to assess their command requirements for weapons and uniforms—a sort of auditor."

"Yes, that will work fine."

"Can I have a budget for the beers and hookers bills I seem to get stuck with, Sir?"

"I'll talk to Colonel Keuken about a little something in your stocking this year, ok?"

"Yes, Sir. Dinners for 16 add up, Sir."

"Noted, soldier. Next?"

"Where do we start today, Sir?"

"The infirmary if you have any sense about you. Get some malaria shots. It is time to get down and operational in Uraba, as the young folk would say. We are in the initial phase of plugging up the FARC's strategic rearguard. If we clog their drug routes to Panama, we will severely affect their overall budget for insurrection and mayhem. We want to take the entire coast away from them, but we'll start with Uraba. Are you familiar with the region?

"Only from about 5,000 feet, Sir."

"Get to know the terrain, the people… the paramilitary command. The intelligence units are now fully-operational there. Information will come into D-2 units from Bogota, from us, Tampa, and from other brigades. We will be listening in real-time, but would prefer a little plausible deniability on the ground. We are asking these people to risk careers for us. Report back to me directly if you see any sloppy handling of intelligence, or lapses of security protocol. We have a lot riding on this. Cody will fly you into Carepa, along with about 3000 pounds of goodies for the Comandante there. The Brigade Commander there is something of an anti-communist folk hero. He aims to clear the whole zone of Communists in two years. Some of D-2's best folks have been reassigned there. The comandante and the brigade D-2 leader both know you are coming. Neither is ever to be mentioned or referenced in any communication outside this room. Is that clear?"

"Understood, Sir."

"Good luck, son."

"Thank you, Sir."

It was a Friday morning, the last day of Amelia's school week, meaning she was done by noon and back with her babies shortly thereafter. Hastings had no way of reaching me through a brigade switchboard—firstly, I did not exist, nor would they make an exception, even if I foolishly insisted. That left pay phones, whose utilization would not inspire confidence among the intelligence officers I was surely to encounter in Carepa.

Cody was catching on that TommyLand was a more opaque place than he had heretofore believed. Smiling broadly, he noted that the Cessna not only did not fly any better, but had accumulated a lot of flight hours on its tachometer. I smiled back just as broadly.

We flew low across the shallow seas between Panama and Colombia, and reached Carepa within a half an hour. From the air, it occupied the mostly flat green pastures of a small valley. The open-field landscape became quickly forested on all sides, and bounded by a thin, muddy band of river. It was perfect setup for the FARC, who sat in the thick scrub in the higher ground to the east, and sent down revolutionary tax collectors to the small hamlets of industrious farmers and cow herders down below.

Cody gave a sequence of numbers to the tower that I did not recognize as standard landing requests. For the first time in my aviation consultant career, I heard an airport tower say, without irony, "Tranquilo—adelante!" The airport had a single runway and a long, low terminal building with a faded blue awning. We landed and turned at the end of the runway, coming to a quick stop, which left Cody plenty of room for his departure. He took off his headset and thumped the steering wheel like a bar stool drummer. He pointed down the runway, almost happy that our separation was so near.

"Not long now, Tommy boy. They're coming for you." A military truck—its bed covered in a green half-circle of heavy fabric—and a black Toyota Hilux powered down the runway toward us. Young men stood behind the cab with rifles pointed to the sky like sentinels rushing to keep abreast of a new leader and his pace.

"Stay for a beer?"

"No. I think I'll head back."

"Ok. I'll make my way back to Panama."

"Be careful out here, Tommy… I… oh, hell. You know what you're getting into, don't you son."

Of course, I didn't. The terms of my employment were simple on the surface of things, but not at all clear where official duties duly ended. The transportation of armaments was the official part of my job. The more subtle function, which neither Dr. Fuller nor Randy Kerker ever elucidated, was to report back to them on the willingness of these men to kill indiscriminately and broadly in order to pacify a people into stupefied unwillingness to continue any long-standing tribute-paying and intelligence-sharing arrangements they had made with the FARC.

The writings of Dr. Fuller, which admittedly I skipped through quickly with the intention of showing my colleagues at Howard AFB that I was a speed reader rather than a neo-illiterate, were replete with the metrics of counter-insurgent success. I remember one particular phrase from Dr. Fuller's introduction to his classic Before the Ink Dries: Essays on COIN for the Twenty-First Century: "The local population, either engaged with the revolutionary landlord, or passively enduring his rule, shall equally feel terrorized by the new landlords, 'like shining from shook foil.'"

I knew that phrase from one of my university classes, so I doubted whether Dr. Fuller lifted it from a classic of COIN theory.

Before the Toyota came to a complete stop, five paramilitary soldiers jumped off the truck bed, and encircled the plane, their glares straight ahead and pitiless. They wore the same fatigues as Colombian soldiers, but had red bands on their right forearms. Their glances, while not insolent, told anyone before them that they would kill without hesitation or reflection, and certainly without remorse.

An older, trim mestizo man in his 30s with a thin moustache got out and stood in front of the plane. Evidently, he made some sort of joke since several of the young paramilitaries laughed, brought their hands out before them, and returned to parade rest. The mestizo also wore fatigues and large black boots and a black t-shirt without an arm band. A light-skinned mestizo—also in his early 30s—came around the truck and shook hands with him. They exchanged a few remarks. So far, no one had invited me down from the plane.

"See you down the road, Cody."

The propeller stopped on the Cessna. I stepped down from the passenger seat, looping around the right propeller to join the two officers in front of the plane. The Colombian officer and the paramilitary commander both stepped forward toward me. I extended my hand to the Colombian officer.

"Tommy," I offered. "Nice to meet you, Stamper!" he said in good English. "Capitan Jose-Manuel Mosquera."

"A pleasure, Captain," I replied in Spanish. I turned my gaze to the paramilitary commander.

"Comandante Pedro Flaco."

"A pleasure, Comandante."

"Captain Mosquera, if I could see your military ID, please."

"Certainly, Stamper." While he pulled a chain with his ID out of his dress uniform, Comandante Pedro looked me over; I was, for him and in that climate, a rarity—tall, thin, in a crinkled linen suit and expensive shoes.

"I have heard of your father-in-law in Cali. He has a reputation for brilliance in counter-narcotics there," Captain Mosquera politely offered.

"I know him as a father-in-law, but I share your assessment of his abilities."

"Well, welcome to Carepa. Have you been here before?" he asked.

"I have not been much north of Medellin."

"So, you live in Cali?" the comandante asked. I looked at the Captain before speaking. He gave me a slight downward turn of his head as a gesture that the comandante probably already knew my background.

"I have a house there, yes."

The Captain patted my shoulder.

"How about some lunch, Stamper?"

"That would be nice, Captain."

"We'll meet up at the brigade HQ in an hour, ok?"

Mosquera ordered the men, whom I could not identify as either military or paramilitary now that I stood near them, to transfer the contents of the plane into the bed of the truck. The young soldiers all moved off toward the plane and began to methodically empty its large crates into the rear of their truck. "Captain, my suitcase is also in the cargo hold. Where should I place it?" The comandante spoke. "We'll keep it in the back of the Hilux and drop it off at your hotel."

The comandante waved over two of his men to assist the soldiers, while the others reformed in a triangle around the Cessna. I noticed that all the wooden crates had identifying marks which had been sanded down and painted over. There were about twenty of them. I figured that Cody would deliver about one hundred crates per brigade between Carepa and Cimitarra. Having dealt with the crates, the soldiers and the paramilitaries returned to their formations, peering out with menace once more, even at me.

Our route took us beyond the rear gate of the 17th Brigade Headquarters to a smaller, fenced-in facility of new aluminum-roofed buildings. There were new white gravel paths bordered by painted stones between each building, so that the effect was more like a series of hospital buildings rather than a paramilitary headquarters. We parked on a mixed gravel dirt parking lot and entered the low building which glowed like hot metal under the direct equatorial sun of noontime. There was a single metal desk to the right, but no sentry, and a shotgun-corridor that went all the way to a single door at the back of the building from which pulsating music could be heard.

Pedro Flaco waved me down the long hallway. In each room small groups of men in fatigues and mostly black t-shirts looked over maps and print-outs. Most of them had paramilitary arm bands, but some of them were obviously on-duty military personnel. One room with a computer, printer, and radio set was clearly the communication room for the paramilitaries, who were not part of the D-2 communication network, yet could quickly receive radio orders from the D-2 intelligence officers in the building nearby.

"We have rooms for communications, finance, logistics—even personnel."

"What is the formal name?"

"It doesn't have one. We keep an office in Carepa called the Convivir Costa Bananera. We do our work here though." A tall, black soldier approached us and handed the comandante a sealed envelope. Once he had broken the seal, he read it and then put it in his pocket.

"Despues." Later. We went out the back door and down a muddy, dirt path to an identical building, this one butting up against a grove of cedars within which a creek meandered slowly toward the coast. Several of the paramilitary soldiers smoked or washed their faces in the water, but nearly without a murmur of sound.

The music originated from this back building, almost prohibiting conversation if one were not inclined to scream at others only a short distance away. There was no hallway, or sentry to greet us, or to check our papers—just a smelly cavern with crates and boxes stacked on the walls, hanging metal light covers, and a metal pole at the far end of the concrete floor.

Handcuffed to it—naked and bleeding—were a man and a woman. They were mestizos, but now covered in black and red streaks of grime and excrement. Their fingers were mangled and broken, so they had to lean against each other to stand. Her breast nipples were cut off, and dried blood had formed new red cones. Many of their teeth were pulled out. There were slash marks—probably from a machete—on their backs and legs. They had defecated around themselves repeatedly, which was only one source of the mixture of terrible odors in that room.

I felt suddenly as if somebody had slammed my heart into reverse, sending all the blood in my body back to its source. This was not according to the laws of war, and not really human, as I understood the word at that time. I clenched my teeth in order to steel my jaw so that bile would not rise up my throat and cause me to vomit. This was beyond Dante or anything that I had read or seen, my mother being strict about horror movies when I was a child. This was the last station on the track of humanity toward an apparent goal of expelling these soldiers and that couple from any positive regard for themselves.

Evidently, the paramilitary soldiers felt I was an experienced CIA officer who had a technician's feel about scenes like this, or that I needed to see their world of mayhem, without the words or metaphors or theories.

This was grid zero.

The Liverpool Bar notwithstanding, this was my first view of the enemy. The couple, thin and weak even before their horrific fall into paramilitary clutches, probably could not even fire guns. These were urban guerrillas, the invisible white-collar militia who subverted locally, and sympathized globally for the expected revolution. They were the main target of the new communications networks, rather than the jungle soldier. Having extorted and threatened these parts without government response since the 1970s, their shock from being captured and brought to this place must have represented a total rout of their understanding of the inevitability of revolution in Carepa.

They must have fervently believed in their Marxist eschatology that their enemies, and not themselves, would wind up in these straights. Their type was closing in on my wife, so my sympathies were mitigated somewhat, even though it was otherwise unforgiveable.

Walking slowly toward them as if delivering his final summation in court, the comandante pointed at them and explained the intelligence on the couple: "He is an urban guerrilla. He has lived here in Carepa with his wife for almost fifteen years. He was a school teacher. It makes me sick." He looked like a teacher; there was patience and persistence in his eyes that disclosed that he was more than just a shadow revolutionary. "Luckily, they did not bring any junior communists into the world."

"How did he function as a guerrilla?" I asked quietly to the comandante, who proceeded to repeat my question loudly, so that the couple would know that their case had come to the attention of the CIA.

"They would feed the FARC soldiers who came down from the mountain at their small finca. He handled several bank accounts for them as well. He also provided intelligence on troop movements in his area."

"He told you that?"

The comandante looked at me like I had not grasped something basic. "Satellites, joven. We have seen FARC trucks at their finca. We knew that when he got here. We want to know the names of the other members of his cell."

"What did she do?"

"She? She was a nurse—can you believe that? She had access to medical records on many of our soldiers, including the addresses of their families. She extorted a lot of families in that way."

I wanted to know more, though they would know nothing of a small cell of college freshman at a university in Cali, over four-hundred miles to the south. The comandante got on the radio and called out the names of two men. Putting out his cigarette, he walked past the two guerrillas and grabbed a bucket, which he filled with water from an oil barrel nearby. He splashed them with water, which brought them back to their renewed horror and surprise that their worst fears were true—the CIA was actually the source of anti-guerrilla counter-insurgency and in the person of a tall, handsome and thin young man in a white linen suit with sun glasses hanging outside his coat pocket.

They looked at the Comandante and then at me—he with dull surprise and she with raw terror. They licked water off their own skin; otherwise, they were rendered motionless by dried lacerations and heavy chains. Pedro Flaco turned off the music from a boom box on a chair. He came close to them, taking cautious steps to avoid excrement.

"Here is my friend from the CIA. You remember them. Your propaganda says that they run terror campaigns all over Colombia. You know... you're right! Those bastards are everywhere, running around this country like Pedro through his own house. But they are giving us a lot of guns, so we try not to complain. Here is your devil. Look at him—tall, handsome, reserved—like a gringo actor, maybe Gregory Peck. I would want my daughter to marry him. But he probably has a blond, beautiful gringa wife and children. They live in a house with two cars, and they take a vacation to Disneyland each year. But for now, he has come here to teach me new ways to make you suffer."

The woman exhaled in a low murmur and lowered her head, looking down at her own missing nipples, ruined limbs and runny excrement. Death could not be more than a day or two away, I thought.

"He does not care about dogs like you and your dog dreams of saving the world." The front door flew open, and two more thin black soldiers came in with unrehearsed gusto. The woman looked up at the boys, pulling her chains and her husband closer to the bar as she lagged backwards and yelled for mercy. The male guerrilla just looked up at me with the remains of his dulled and unwinding faculties. How could you countenance this, he seemed to ask from the depths of his cratering mind.

She began to implore me with her eyes to put an end to the horrific passion play they had endured for several days at that point. I looked at her but forced my pity to stand down. The commander put in a new cd, which turned out to be American heavy metal music, which took its imagery from the savageness of Germanic forest tribes.

I felt like I was the deus ex machina of the scene to come—the white devil incarnate, who came from the north in an elegant white suit to issue a statement of approval for the torments of the enemy couple and the triumphal moment of their eventual deaths.

One of the soldiers opened up a chest along the wall and took out a machete. The other approached the woman and kneeled. He unlocked her chains and ripped her upward by her elbows. The comandante pushed a saw horse toward the paramilitary with the machete, who positioned it close to the metal pole and the FARC guerrilla. The soldier bent the woman over the saw horse, so that she looked at her husband. The soldier stretched out each of her hands and tied them to an end of the saw horse. She whimpered, but did not beg for a reprieve.

The couple had decided to die; they were not going to talk. I could not imagine why the comandante introduced humiliation into their deaths. Their terror would never leave this room. Could this ever happen to Amelia, I thought. I would kill with Homeric savagery to prevent her harm. If my life proved little else, it could stand for that.

I looked at the Comandante, questioning him with my eyes. He moved closer to the soldier, who had taken out his penis and was rubbing it up and down her butt. He entered her, and she screamed. The comandante walked near the guerrilla and kneeled down to his level. "This can end with no more pain, comrade. Or it can continue for days or weeks. We can bring in a doctor and make you well and start all over again." The soldier eased in and out of her slowly, listening intently to his comandante in case he would give an order.

The comandante looked at the soldier sharply. The soldier took out his penis and aimed its head toward her anus. "This is probably one of her fantasies, anyway—eh, comrade?"

The soldier pushed his penis into her anus, fighting for more space until he was fully within. She screamed out enraged fear until snot and tears gathered on her lower face. The guerrilla unsheathed the last of his voice. "Just kill us, ¡jueputa capitalista! We are finished with you."

Though I had grown to hate the guerrillas and their pathetic reductions of this huge, complex world to simple Marxist terms, it was a courageous response to his own breaking. The comandante understood his meaning clearly. "I will decide when you die, dog!" The black soldier took out his penis and shoved it back in her vagina and wasted little time before coming inside her. The other black soldier dropped his machete and stepped into position behind her as the satiated, but frightened soldier zipped up his fatigues and returned to attention.

The comandante patted the retiring soldier on the shoulder and whispered in his ear before the soldier exited the rear door. The second soldier walked in front of the woman and steered his penis toward her mouth. She clenched her jaws tightly. He punched on her neck and her mouth opened so she could cough. He put his penis in her mouth, pinching her nose to force her mouth open.

The comandante pointed at the woman as he leaned back toward her husband. "This can go on for weeks, 'comrade.'" We may even keep her alive to have a baby. Then we will kill her." The soldier was whipping his penis in and out of her mouth toward a climax, which he did on her face.

"Wow! What does that tell you, comrade!" The guerrilla looked down and away. The comandante stood up.

"My CIA friend and I will leave you now; he doesn't want his gringo penis anywhere near your dirty guerrilla wife... but he will tell me many new things we can do to your whore wife. Bye, bye—Comrade Harold!"

The second soldier untied the woman and retied her to the pole. She slumped down and cried in horrific wailing.

They had expected me to join in their mayhem like a teen who approaches the edge of the dance floor, already swaying to the rhythm. Instead, I said little, having reached an equilibrium between the horror without and the dismay within. I imagined that Dr. Fuller would reminisce about his first grid during our next satellite chat.

Somehow, there was a drop of blood on my shoe that spread like red ink into the dark leather.

Comandante Pedro Flaco walked me back to the jeep. "He will take you to the Brigade Headquarters. You can ask them questions there." He pointed at another tall, young paramilitary, who walked to the jeep. "After that, we will drive to Turbo." He shook my hand strongly. The soldier drove us out of the paramilitary compound and along a side road to the front of the 17th Brigade entrance. We drove through without questioning. He dropped me off in front of a new building in the rear of the parade ground. It was hidden from view by tall trees on three sides. There was a small complex of radio dishes on a concrete slab off to its side.

The entrance had the standard cheap desk and a sentry, who looked surprised to see me—in a white linen suit, and open collar white shirt—in front of him. I had no visitor's badge.

"I am from U.S. intelligence to see the intelligence director of the brigade."

"Does the senor have any identification?"

"No. Please call the director." Instead, he went down a central corridor that appeared to be about the length of two barracks. He was gone several minutes.

The building was cooler than most military buildings in Colombia. For the first time all day, I did not sweat in my clothing. Finally, the sentry and Captain Mosquera arrived. He extended his hand, noticing the drop of blood on my shoe. Captain Mosquera was short, brown and chunky about the midsection. He was starting to go bald at the top of his military haircut, which gave him a monkish appearance. I told him that this morning I went to "other places" in the area with friends of ours. He nodded in comprehension slowly, but did not say anything in return. We walked down the large central corridor in silence.

I was in need of a bathroom so that I could heave my guts out in privacy.

Instead, Mosquera led me into his intelligence command center. He explained that the building was fully linked to D2 headquarters and 13 other military intelligence commands and 27 smaller tactical units. "It is an impressive technological achievement. Our military has never had these capabilities before."

"The better to dismember you my dear," I thought.

He spoke excellent English and preferred to converse that way. A young female recruit delivered and poured coffee as we sat in silence. She smiled at me as she left the room. He continued with enthusiasm. "The real-time data sharing allows us to track FARC units, couriers, and shipments across the country."

"The technology also requires a considerable change in command," I offered.

"How so? He replied. "Isn't there some contradiction between intelligence compartmentalization and widespread distribution of information?"

"Yes. I see what you mean."

"We are careful to spread information only to authorized agents."

"The decisions about 'actionable' intelligence… how is that decided?"

"That comes from my office or above. We try to limit the scope of friendly actions, so that they serve command objectives." I had failed to note any mitigating factor in the dungeon out back.

"And dedicated personnel interact with friendly forces?"

"Contact is informal. We deal with friendlies on a…" he struggled for the right word. "Handshake-basis," I finished for him.

"Yes. Exactly."

"I am here to learn about your work, Captain. But not to judge it. In that sense, I am not an auditor. We just want to know if you are satisfied with the equipment, the training—that sort of thing."

"I appreciate that, Stamper."

"We also want you to know that regardless of politics in either country, we are here to support you—technically and financially. Our commitment is long-term. Within Colombia, we see no more important work than yours in the 17th Brigade. We realize that with this enemy, only superior intelligence will overcome their advantages. Again, we are not here to judge. I will be here periodically to liaise with friendlies, but only with your permission and guidance. I will make this my first stop when I am in the theater, and will only act with your authorization. We would appreciate your ongoing input concerning the distribution of weapons and supplies to friendly forces. We value the command perspective on the informal military operations. We certainly do not want to cooperate with friendly activities that do not support your objectives." These last comments, though impromptu, covered the main points that Dr. Fuller wanted me to explain to the Captain.

I spoke quickly since my vomit was beginning a second run up my stomach. I began to think if this is legitimate counter-insurgency, who teaches this stuff? What kind of man would write a manual that taught inhumanity in the service of ideology?

"He is out there alone…." said Dr. Fuller. He could have been talking about me.

Captain Mosquera having cancelled at the last moment, Pedro Flaco and I ate at a small table for two under heavy guard who stood nearby in the rear of a local steak restaurant. The morning's ghastly images stayed with me, dulling my appetite for conversation and cuisine, though I had no problem with cold beer and would have accepted whiskey, had it been available.

The comandante divided his attention among his radio and portable phone, and to a lesser extent, our conversation. Radio communication was frequent on what appeared to be a shared frequency. Annoyingly, his phone rang every few minutes. We were able to settle into conversation shortly before the steaks and yucca arrived.

I repeated many of the points from my conversation with Captain Mosquera. Having run out of points from the CIA, I added another.

"I hope these protocols do not limit our cooperation in this theater." He smiled across the table. "There will be plenty of work for everyone."

The Comandante seemed to believe—correctly—that the role of auditor was just a cover for me, and that my real job was to bring panache and credibility to his role as creative director of torture and death. I did not tell him that I had not been in a fight since the 7th grade, nor had I yet adapted my conscience to the murder of defenseless persons. Anyway, in COIN terms, a good producer does not have to share the passion of the director.

He gobbled down food quickly and did not tend to conversational pauses. He spoke to me only in Spanish. We did not speak of his background, nor did I ask about the strength or reach of his command. I knew his story, though: ex-policeman, ex-contrabandista, and finally head of security at a jungle cocaine lab under Pablo Escobar until Los Pepes came calling. He had turned on Pablo, which saved his life, and brought him within the sphere of control of the paramilitary narcos who took over management of Medellin's cocaine routes after 1993.

He wanted to know if I was satisfied with what I had seen. "The proof is in the intelligence thus derived," I said. "Puede ser, si," he countered. "That is probably so."

Mosquera, Pedro Flaco—these guys believed I was a real agent who had authority on the ground, taking my blandishments about a non-judgmental approach to their operations as an example of compensatory gringo humility. I was, after all, the son-in-law of a Lieutenant Colonel in the CNP, and depending on the range of their ken, the son of an ambassador-level official in the United States government. All that stature meant something to them, though it signified next to nothing for me among the heat-baked entrails of the Uraba.

Looking across at Pedro Flaco, I wondered what would be worse: to disappoint these men, or to prove them correct.

CHAPTER THIRTY-THREE

Comandante Flaco paid for our lunch from a stack of money that appeared from somewhere at the end of our meal. Within minutes we were back on the road north to Turbo. There were no pay phones—even if I could contrive a reasonable explanation for the its use amidst paramilitary roadblocks. My cell phone was almost certainly flagged by the DEA for constant surveillance, and the CIA for occasional location monitoring. My best bet was to gain a private audience with the Colonel from a telephone within the brigade.

Who was I kidding, though: there was no such thing as a personal phone call for me anymore.

We headed north on the airport highway with four armed guards in the bed of the truck. The comandante drove with one hand, using the other to dial numbers on his satellite phone every few minutes. He spoke little during these calls, as if agents were reporting their status at pre-appointed times, and then clearing the channel for others to report.

We stopped at our first road block on the highway near prosperous village. While several young soldiers trained their rifles on the occupants of the lead car at the road block, others checked their id cards—probably with brigade intelligence.

"Apartado, the guerrillas control about thirty percent of the territory here."

"Control?"

"… Some local drug sales… mainly extortion of the tradesmen and large ranches on the plains."

"Are they easy to identify?"

"D-2 believes only about 200 FARC control the area. There are no more than ten in the city at any time. The others are in rotation among camps in the higher mountains." It seemed amazing that two hundred men could control an area the size of Southern California.

"The people have been tamed well, then."

I could not tell if he took issue with my phrase concerning the passivity of the people in the region, but he did not let the comment die away. "The government in Bogota gave these lands to the FARC. They have become a corrupt landlord class—hated by everyone-it makes our job easier. We have many people coming forward with intelligence about them."

"Do the ten also rotate?"

"No. They are urban guerrillas—as you saw this morning, they have jobs—usually in important offices of government. They are recruited in the larger universities and told to come to a certain place and take a certain job. The FARC in this way control over 800 municipalities. They decide how budgets are spent—and of course, steal large parts of the funds. Some of them are even in the local police."

"Do you suspect that activity in Carepa and Apartado?"

"And Chigorodo and Turbo and Necocli and most of the villages in between."

"Comandante, I am not a counter-insurgency expert, but I have to ask: don't the road blocks take away the advantage of surprise?"

"There are no surprises, senor. They have counter-intelligence, too. They know we have road blocks and how we have formed ourselves. They know when you arrived and when you will leave. We want them to know we are here. We want them to talk about us and make a small mistake. It is obvious you are gringo and CIA. We want to advertise the fact. They don't fear us, but you are different."

"That couple this morning...."

He cut me off quickly. Pedro Flaco was beginning to zero in on my ambivalence as a potential source of contamination for his men, or as a snide rebuke to his chosen profession. "He was a teacher for God's sake. It makes me sick."

"Which one did you catch?"

"Neither. We are offering guerrillas twice their salaries if they come to our side. So far, we have recruited six new soldiers from their ranks. Their intelligence is obviously highly valuable to us. According to the guerrilla who came to our side, the FARC pick up chemicals for cocaine production in Turbo on the black market. That witch even used government trucks for her trips. They also give some of their pigs and chickens to the rotating FARC patrols. We watched the FARC trucks arrive at their farm a few days ago and take away barrels of chemicals."

"Do you suspect that their co-workers were aware of their activities?"

"Those people will have to answer to us as well."

"Won't the FARC notice that the couple is away from their farm?"

He smiled a little at that moment, apparently happy to bring the conversation back to the enormous technological capabilities that we had bestowed upon D-2, and indirectly, to the paramilitaries.

"We listened to their telephone calls at home and her calls from her office. They also have ham radio. D-2 shares satellite imagery with us as well. Anyway, we sat across the road in the woods from their farm for about two weeks. We saw her truck arrive only once, but it was filled with chemicals. The FARC arrived in a large truck about three nights ago. There were nine of them. They kept four sentries: two at the road, and two with their comandante. We arrived with Special Forces from the brigade and about eight of us. We waited until after four in the morning so that we attacked as they changed sentries. The rest slept in the barn. We used silencers to kill the sentries, and the Special Forces attacked the barn with fragmentation grenades. At the same time, our forces went into the house to make sure the couple did not send out a distress call. We blindfolded them so that they did not see or hear anything. It was a good plan. I felt proud to be a paramilitary that night."

"What happened to their comandante?"

"After we killed all his men and got rid of their bodies, we took him with us. We also took the truck and chemicals. We traced them back to a supplier in Turbo. He works for us now. Every barrel is electronically tagged."

"Needless to say, the FARC are curious about their men, no?"

"We still watch the finca, but no one has shown up."

"How are references to the finca on the radio?"

"That is a matter for Captain Mosquera… one thing more… the lady guerrilla had a notebook with the names of bars where the brigade soldiers relaxed."

"Did they ever speak?"

"No, but they will—just to be allowed to die."

Before the rules of war, before the ancient myths of glory, before the man who issued the first formal call to battle, there was just scattered, chaotic, brutal fear—and then hate, which institutionalized the whole business, like a meaningless star arrangement that leads the Argonaut nowhere.

We drove along the highway into Turbo and then up the coast to Necocli, where the comandante stopped at a pier in the middle of town.

The men fell out on both sides of the Toyota with their guns pointed outward. "This is the prize. If we control the coast between Turbo and Necocli, we shut down their strategic rearguard and their easy access to Panama. We will recruit and place hundreds of men on these roads. It will be a tremendous change in the fortunes of the FARC."

Oily, dark blood pools were the only evidence that the tortured guerrilla couple had ever spent time in the back of the warehouse. At the bottom of the pole now, with splayed legs and flattened and broken fingers, was the FARC comandante from the raid on the couple's finca. One of his eyes was closed over and his nose was badly broken. His fingers were bent at strange angles like strange claws that occasionally flickered wildly without their nails. Somehow, he had not shat himself yet.

He had lost his prestige, livelihood, command, and soon he would have his last moments of life while undergoing hyper-violent rituals of pain and release until death came to him like his mother's warm embrace. There would be hundreds more to come like him. He did not realize that he was the ancient regime in the far-flung provinces of Colombia. The new regime was coming for him in particular—the man who believed ideologically in taking and redistributing and subduing whole regions with their own Marxist grid. There would be no grandeur of the guillotine for him. Death would be slow and drawn-out for the satisfaction of the private audience of counter-intelligence deaths—the troops, who drank it up like a demented tonic.

Two new paramilitaries—I did not recognize them from the morning or the ride up the coast to Turbo—brought in equipment consisting of a small plastic chair, a battery with cables, a voltage meter with a dial, and a hose. They brought plastic chairs for us, too. I took off my jacket and handed it to one of the new paramililtaries, giving him instructions in Spanish to take it back to the Toyota.

Harkening back to military courtesy, perhaps for my sake, since he perceived that I was not a torturer by trade, Pedro Flaco slid his chair close to the comandante and gave him a cup of water. Being unable to use his hands, the career FARC comandante accepted the cup to his lips from his paramilitary counterpart, probably unable to see who had shown him a moment's kindness. He drank and then gulped and finally coughed out some of the water.

"We are going to start in a moment, Comandante. In case you have forgotten, this is the deal. A D-2 intelligence officer—an expert in your communication protocols—will be here soon. He will sit with his hand on the machine. If he hears a coded phrase that you are under duress, he will put high voltage through your body. You know what will happen after that. It will happen before the day ends—I promise you that. Is that clear, comandante? You will issue an exfiltration request. You will say nothing more. We will tell you what to say next."

The FARC comandante raised his head at Pedro Flaco and then lowered it back down further on his chest where it rested in shocked dejection. He had, after all, not only been thrashed with fists in this place, but he had lost his entire squadron at a small, tranquil farm he probably felt to be on safe, unapproachable ground. He had probably spent many nights around camp fires at militants' fincas throughout Uraba, enjoying the good humor and veneration of the local urban guerrillas as if he were a patrician Roman on a provincial inspection tour.

A tall, thin light-skinned soldier in blue jeans and a t-shirt arrived. He was out of uniform, but obviously active military, since he still wore his army belt. We shook hands—odd, considering the setting, but hewing to the protocols of Colombian formality. One of the soldiers said, "Todo listo, mi comandante!"

One soldier wetted down the FARC comandante with a bucket of water, while the other, quite naturally, as if this was little more than a farm chore, ripped open the comandante's trousers, and applied clips to his testicles.

Pedro Flaco, like a provincial garrison captain suddenly in the presence of central command, which in this case were the technicians and communication tools that he had never seen before, talked into his radio more slowly than was required. "Todo listo por aca!" Flaco looked at his watch for nearly a minute, while the comandante settled into his role as a man with not long to live, and whose final actions in life would be ones of betrayal to his unit and his command. One soldier leaned toward the FARC commander with his finger on the transmit button. "Adelante!" said Pedro Flaco.

The FARC guerrilla made a call signal to another FARC post. He identified himself, and then there was a long pause, during which he sunk his head downward until a guard lifted it cautiously back up.

A female voice said, "Quibo comandante, Freddy! A revolutionary salute to you and your men!" The comandante looked at the man with his hand on the dial, who shook his head at the doomed comandante slowly, and held up a small white card with the precise language that a FARC captain would use in those circumstances: "Please transmit the following message to command 647. The six bales got spoiled outside the barn. The barn is now locked. We need two more green bales. The store manager will give you credit today. If you go, also buy three kilos of the chicken feed."

"Understood, comandante. Please hold for response. Out, comandante." Pedro Flaco nodded and a soldier brought the guerrilla commander more water.

"What do you think?" Pedro Flaco asked the army officer.

"That was the latest exfiltration code we are aware of. If there is no response within an hour, then he gave a duress warning. His contacts will expect to see the comandante and two injured men. We just have to wait."

During the next forty-five minutes, the FARC comandante rarely looked at me. A soldier washed him down—to keep his testicles wet in case the FARC called back and he inadvisably gave a warning to his command—and gave him water a few times. The paramilitary and D-2 members shared a couple of canteens, which they passed to me as well. There was almost complete silence in that room until the radio awakened with speech.

"A friendly revolutionary salute from Lake 76 to command 543," a monotone female voice said. We looked at the D-2 officer who monitored FARC codes. He gave a thumbs up to Pedro Flaco, who in turn nodded to the soldier with the radio. The army officer coughed loudly and pointed at his finger on the dial. The FARC comandante spoke again from a text prepared on the spot by the D-2 intelligence officer.

"Command 543 extending a revolutionary salute to Lake 76." There was perhaps a thirty-second pause. "Lake 76 to buy supplies for the account of command 543. How many chickens require feed Command 543? Over." The soldier pulled the radio away. We looked at the army officer. He nodded for the operation to continue.

"We had 20 chickens, but now we have 17. Over."

"Confirm feed for 17, Comandante."

"Command 543 confirms feed for 17. Over."

"Go with our warmest revolutionary regard, Comandante. Over."

The soldier took his finger off transmit and leaned away from the guerrilla.

"It's on for eight o'clock tonight," said the army officer, somewhat convinced of the veracity of the comandante.

Pedro Flaco stood up and approached the guerrilla. "What is the location?"

The Army Officer then spoke. "Let me guess. On 71st Street there is a park. If your take the road east of the park, it leads out of town and into the hills. It is a good spot for exfiltration. The light is very poor there, and there are no shops nearby. There are dirt roads that lead to higher jungle areas."

Pedro Flaco addressed the soldiers in a manner whose charity cost him effort. "Clean him up and give him some food." Without further orders to the soldiers left behind to guard the FARC captain, we went out the front of the building and took a dirt path to the other aluminum-roofed building. Captain Mosquera was waiting for us with some of his men in a large office at the rear of the complex.

Pedro Flaco reviewed the information extracted from the comandante since his ordeal as a doomed captive began. Captain Mosquera sat back on a couch like a satisfied ranch supervisor whose men had saved a calf from some thickets.

I asked a question. "Captain, it is rare for a guerrilla to give information that puts in danger the lives of his comrades? He locked like a tough man to me. What made the difference?"

Pedro Flaco looked at Captain Mosquera in a silent request to field the question himself. "We issued the capture announcement to D-2 in Bogota yesterday. They found his real name and cedula. From that we located the birth documents of his daughter. We located her in Turbo and took surveillance photos. The photos arrived here last night. The comandante understood the message... The operation involved three D-2 units, including naval intelligence. Within eight hours of identifying Comandante Freddy, he was looking at pictures of his daughter on a swing in Turbo... finally, we are a professional army!"

By the end of the day... we will kill your daughter by the end of the day.

Professional was not the word I would use to describe bringing a man face to face with his most basic fear in life, but I did not demur in front of these men. I was supposed to bring good tidings and weapons from their American friends, not question their tactics—or humanity.

There was not much to do in that building until the rendezvous hour. I felt free to wander about and ask questions of the other officers in the building. They seemed to consider serving in that command as the summit of their careers so far. We had given them keys to the most exotic and powerful sports car they had ever seen and not asked them to return it by a certain time or in a similar condition. After I came back to Captain Mosquera's office, there was a knock on the door and a sentry delivered an envelope to him. With a grin, he opened the envelope and spread the pages on Pedro Flaco's desk.

"We placed the radio call exactly at 11:00." Captain Mosquera began to explain the normal pattern and volume of phone activity throughout Carepa and Apartado between 11:00 and 12:00. He explained to Pedro and me that normal call volume is predictable from previous patterns. He said that during this time 96% of the calls were made to other numbers that were routine in length and destination. He said that they were checking on the four percent, but it would take some hours, since though they had the software to detect unusual patterns of communication, they still had to investigate each corresponding residence for signs of probable guerrilla affiliation.

I stayed on the base the rest of the day, pretending to inventory stocks of arms, and actually listening to radio chatter from Bogota, fascinated by the steady flow of information about FARC troop movements or supply requests. Whether from cowardice or respect for the doomed, I avoided several radio calls for me to return to the paramilitary torture room to witness more—for them—fun and games with human flesh.

The room had only been used for interrogation for a month, but it smelled of misery, cruelty, fear, and death. Besides, it was filling with flies.

At 19:45 that night, Captain Mosquera, I, and several officers gathered in large conference room, the senior officers and I comfortable on couches, and the junior officers sitting on wooden tables or nervously upright on the available wall space. As we drank from stacks of bottled water, Mosquera, standing next to a black board, which a sentry had wheeled into the room before departing quickly, introduced the officers to me, a collection of fresh, young lieutenants and sub-lieutenants from Bogota. They had been briefed to address me only as Stamper.

Their enthusiasm and glee came from the knowledge that there were no more rules of war in the armed forces. What the FARC had given, they would now receive, delivered in massive anvil strikes of death and torture in order to shake the FARC's belief in the inevitability of revolution victory at its essential core.

Darkness seemed to be essential to joint army-paramilitary plans, since the comandante's face was beaten down to mush, and would cause his rescuers to suspect a ruse. Radios from the scene reported several perspectives on the same commando-style operation, which they had correctly placed at a roadside restaurant outside of Carepa. As drawn on the blackboard, two brigade soldiers and the FARC comandante waited at a table on the side of the restaurant, which was abandoned and empty. All three were bandaged and wearing FARC uniforms.

One of the young intelligence officers quickly drew the remaining on-the-ground arrangement of forces on the black board. The FARC comandante had been tranquilized into docility, though obviously he had not been given a radio. The young officer drew the main road and the abandoned restaurant, and began his army details in green chalk to show an army sharpshooter 200 yards away and four Special Forces soldiers placed nearby awaiting attack orders. They would all follow instructions in real-time from a Special Forces command nearby, which Mosquera had placed well down the road.

The expectation was that the FARC would send an exfiltration team of four to six and a driver. They would all be armed. The main variable was whether the FARC exfiltration team would send advance scouts. All army units checked in and gave their status, and then there was silence for about two minutes. An engine sound puttered through our receiver. "Van here. 50 meters up the road from the restaurant. Two FARC in formation... running with weapons drawn to the targets. Driver stays in car... two more FARC positioned behind rocks on far side of road with weapons drawn." Another voice spoke. "Car under tree 200 meters up road. Driver 2 positioned there." That was probably a second car in case the van driver was unable to escape. The Special

Forces team leader on the ground nearby spoke again, as Mosquera quickly drew in the FARC positions with red chalk.

The Special Forces leader on the ground spoke quietly, but forcefully. "On my command, Boxer 1 and 2 subdue roadside driver. Boxer 3 and 4 shoot to kill two FARC behind rocks. Boxer 5 place scope on two FARC approaching the decoys. Shoot to stop if they raise weapons." Captain Mosquera drew lines connecting the shooters to their targets to make sure that no one would be caught in a crossfire.

More silence ensued until the sniper spoke. "Two FARC rescue team carrying FARC comandante with limping Boxers 9 and 10… clear shot." There were a few seconds of silence. "All fire. Go!" We heard a few seconds of gunfire crackling through the radio for which we had no way of measuring its efficacy until several voices crowded in. "Scouts behind rocks two dead. Rescue two down. Van driver dead. Escape driver down."

"All Boxers report status." One by one in numerical order the soldiers reported their status as safe. "Boxers 1 through 4 secure area and prepare to depart. Boxers 7 and 8 to position."

The officers around the table pumped their fists and shook hands. FARC propaganda had convinced the country that Bogota would fall to them before the millennium, but out here in their own hinterlands, the tides of war were beginning to turn away from them and the men in that room knew it. I looked at faces eager to take guerrilla war back into FARC territory through their paramilitary surrogates. One of the officers slapped me on the shoulder. "We could never have done that before! This is how a real army performs, no joda!"

The lead voice on the radio spoke again. "Mi capitan. Two enemy dead. Four captured. Scene secure." Captain Mosquera spoke into his radio.

"Boxer Zero. Take all bodies. Process all personal identification and take cadaver finger prints. Get me license numbers on cars when secure."

"Si, Capitan!"

"I will see you at our briefing at 22:00."

"Si, mi capitan!"

"Did the FARC hear any of that?" I asked.

"Not a sound."

"Where is Pablo Flaco?" He and his men are in the truck that arrived. They will handle interrogations of the wounded... this gets better and better!"

They were giddy now, like geeky teens who made their own model rocket and sent it into the sky—beyond what they thought was the safety of their town.

"Captain Mosquera—may I make a suggestion?" I spoke to him in English. Pulling out all the Colombian money I had, I handed it to him.

"It will be a long night. The men doing the interrogations and processing evidence—they will need coffee and water to continue and pizza for energy... a gift from your North American friends."

"I can't believe we are using a million dollar communications system to take pizza requests. Ijueputa!" He broke into English.

"This is unfuckin' real, Stamper!"

The gathered officers dispersed to their own offices for about an hour. I heard several of them reporting the status to their superiors in Bogota, and awaiting additional instructions. Mosquera went to the communications room and logged onto one of the twenty or so PCs there. "I have to write this all up for D-2, Stamper. I will see you in about an hour."

A sentry accompanied me to my guest quarters where I showered, checking and rechecking my skin for blood until there was no more hot water. I shaved a face in the mirror that wanted to shut down all sensory inputs from that place, and then escape through the nearest window. I willed my features back to those that would be at least comprehensible to the officers with whom I would likely spend close courters until dawn the next day.

Someone had already brought my suitcase there, so I changed into blue jeans and a polo shirt and running shoes. We reconvened 20 minutes later in a larger conference room across from the previous one.

CHAPTER THIRTY-FOUR

It was late at night—the time of the cicadas, who tuned their metallic buzzing sound outside every window along the length of the building. I began to sweat even before I returned to the conference room, which only had a small fan for over ten people.

Atop a corner table, there were stacks of empty pizza boxes and gallons of coffee in pots, as well as cans of Colombian soda in a large bucket of ice. This room had a large wall display like the one at Howard AFB. It was divided into eight screens, each vividly describing the denouement of one horror, and the beginning of another.

There were screens for the captured driver, who though wounded, was tied in his chair to keep his wounded torso upright; the two wounded FARC guerrillas, and the tortured comandante each had their own screen. In another screen was a man in civilian clothes, and in another screen a woman nude from the waist upwards. A piece of pizza appeared in one of the screens and then an upward thumb jerked its approval. The officers in the room laughed. I asked about the last two people on the screen. "More fuckin' urban guerrillas," one of the officers punctuated his disgust in English.

I asked an officer next to me, "Who can watch these images?"

"All forty-one commands, as well as D-2 in Bogota, and probably you guys in Panama."

My God! I thought. We are as deep in the mire as these men, but leagues away in terms of deniability. Except for me. Tommy the pizza delivery boy.

The communications officer explained the methodology by which his men tracked down the two additional urban guerrillas. They tracked 126 unusual phone numbers called during and after the morning's interrogation, and the subsequent distress call to the FARC. From that, nine were checked individually. Three matched a profile of guerrilla supporters. They raided all three and made one capture, including a radio unit. He told me that they found intelligence in that apartment that would help them find FARC soldiers in civilian clothes in several nearby villages.

On the screens, there were occasional savage beatings of each person for the next hour. Several of the officers looked through file folders on the couches, and only occasionally looked up at the screen. They came and went as their names were called out down the corridor to exchange intelligence with other commands. Perhaps as a result of the new information gained at the abandoned restaurant, or in the apartment of the FARC urban radio operator, this was evidently not the only operation in motion that night.

The female urban guerrilla suffered the most. Her face, which was pretty and sensual when she arrived in the torture room, became round with the repeated blows to her nose and cheeks. Her breasts became covered with the red gloss of her own blood. There was no volume, but I could see her agony when they pulled out each finger nail with pliers. Captain Mosquera explained the expected outcome to me. "The urban guerrillas only know other cells and perhaps a few names. They are radio operators most of all. They know little about the jungle. Their papers—after D-2 in Bogota analyzes them--will tell us more than they will reveal under torture…."

Why torture the poor woman then? I thought.

"The real intelligence will come from the driver and the two wounded guerrillas. They will tell us everything and kill the others for us. They will make good paramilitaries."

"And become sick, psychotic killers at the employ of other morally unbound characters for the rest of their short, expendable lives," I thought.

It turned out exactly that way. The paramilitaries treated the tied-up FARC soldiers roughly, but within boundaries meant to keep them alive and serviceable, especially for further intelligence work. They were careful to concentrate their damage on soft tissues, since in a short while the guerrillas could be standing beside them in battle, or carrying them away on their backs.

The FARC guerrillas were young, ignorant, and apparently had no loyalty to the comandantes who had kept them cozened with dreams of the grand march in jungle camps for most of their adolescence. Several officers in the room with us radioed questions to individual torturers, who directed the question to their bound victims. The young guerrillas gave up every name and location they could, whether it was a favorite whorehouse or the girlfriend in town of a jungle fighter in a nearby village. They were given morphine for the pain of their beatings, and when there were no more questions to answer, pepperoni pizza. They savored the Coca-Cola, and asked for more, a thirst the paramilitaries were happy to provision at the expense of their own.

When they ran out, we just brought them more.

A brigade doctor looked at their wounds as well. By 04.00 a deal was in place. The eight screens collapsed into one screen, and suddenly the only image was a pole in the middle of the screen. A paramilitary set up four chairs. Other soldiers brought the three urban guerrillas to the chairs and blindfolded them. They were in their street clothes, now caked with their own dried blood that had rolled down their faces and onto their shirts like a frozen waterfall of blood. The boys were silent, but the woman screamed for mercy.

The FARC comandante came last. The three wounded FARC soldiers, who had reached an agreement with Pedro Flaco and his men to save their own skin, slowly limped onto screen. They held daggers in their hands for the task that lay ahead and assumed identical positions behind the chairs of the guerrillas. The former stretched the necks of the latter by pulling back on their hair. Almost in unison, the wounded soldiers slit their FARC colleagues' throats in precise motions. The urban guerrillas gagged on their own blood and shook wildly, topping over their stools onto the ground, where they were soon still.

This was revolutionary justice coming back at the FARC, like a river changing its course after a meteor explosion.

The FARC commander finally yelled out in exasperation at the prospect of an identical death only moments away.

"I have intelligence, but only for the gringo!" Captain Mosquera grabbed his radio.

"Stop. Let him speak."

Pedro Flaco yelled out to his men, "Stop!"

Captain Mosquera put his hand on my knee. "Are you willing to talk to him?"

"Yes, most definitely."

I can do this, I thought—like the way I felt during my first late-inning appearance in a little league baseball game as an eight-year-old.

Captain Mosquera walked me to the rear door of the intelligence building and stopped, thereby maintaining a distance and therefore deniability about the events inside the paramilitary compound. "We did not expect this, Stamper—it is not your function, but any intelligence you can extract would help up us greatly."

"I'll see what I can do." I slowly walked with several guards out the back of the intelligence building, through the gate, and into the paramilitary compound. Once inside, I walked along the wall of the building toward its far end, past the three dead guerrillas, toppled over and resting in mottled puddles of their own blood on the floor. I gasped—thankfully, I did not wretch—and put my chair next to Comandante Freddy, the FARC commander.

He waited until Comandante Freddy was not looking our way. Leaning toward my ear, he spoke in a quiet, worn-out voice that had endured its own invisible knife across its throat. "I don't want to die this way. These men are not soldiers—they are illiterate village butchers." He cast a dismissive glance at the FARC and paramilitary recruits around us. He spoke to me in a manner that morally separated them from us.

"I have intelligence of high-value, but I will only tell you."

"Continue."

"You are from the CIA. You can make things happen, no?"

"It depends... on the quality of the intelligence."

"I understand. Listen, please. My daughter lives with her grandmother. She is a smart girl..."

"What do you want for her, Comandante?"

"I have some money saved for her education. It is hidden. I will give you instructions. I also want your guarantee that no harm will come to her."

He assumed I had this power, which I did not—at least formally.

I looked over my shoulder at the paramilitaries who quaffed down Coke from large plastic bottles.

"I don't need your money, and they will take it, comandante."

"This intelligence is different. The price of the intelligence is the hidden money. That is for my daughter—for her education. Do you understand?"

"Yes, Comandante. Let me speak to the intelligence officers."

I walked back through the chamber of spent lives to Captain Mosquera and explained the opening gambit of Comandante Freddy. "Captain," I explained. "If I give my word to the FARC captain, I intend to honor it." The Captain reluctantly agreed to abide by any terms I would reach with Freddy, as long as they did not touch upon FARC command issues. Mosquera gave me a notebook and a pencil, reminding me that the FARC are treacherous, even when nearing a certain death.

The FARC comandante sat with his head down, unwilling to look at the paramilitary guards, or the dead guerrillas, whose blood had seeped around one of his boots, sealing it off from the rest of his body. I explained that while I had the power to save his daughter, I could not save him.

Freddy proceeded to tell me the names of three companies in Turbo, Carepa, and Chigorodo that were owned by the FARC. He then told me the names of several labor leaders in the area who were active FARC members, and who had stolen large amounts of funds for transfer to the FARC. Finally, he gave me a list of municipal workers in the surrounding villages who were active FARC militants, and the ways in which embezzled funds made their way as capital into FARC-controlled gold mines. He had given me more intelligence in five minutes than the army had been able to ferret out through traditional intelligence operations in ten years.

It was not Tommy who changed his mind; it was the certainty that savagery would reach his daughter as well if he did not deliver a bonanza of information to us.

We gave him pizza and Coca-Cola. I asked Captain Mosquera to allow the comandante to shower and to sleep on a cot under guard that night and he granted my request. The next morning, the FARC captain—with only a few hours to live—was given a fresh uniform. Taking a moment to collect my thoughts, I placed myself in the center of events, not as a belligerent, but someone with unusual powers over life and death that I never sought for myself, and could not imagine deploying in an official manner.

"On a full-time basis, it would lead to madness," I thought.

I had been gone two days and knew nothing of Hastings's surveillance or Amelia's safety. My thoughts about Amelia shriveled to the back of my mind, as if they did not want to share the same space as the sickening images, and the sordid manipulations of human nature the interrogations presented that night. Every depravation was there, so that by nightfall everyone, had they taken a moment to reflect on that torture room, would have to admit that men were capable of nearly anything, properly motivated, or despicably endowed—everyone, including themselves.

But she was still my wife; my love for her felt pure and sweet that night like a flower that grows out of a landfill.

Both Comandante Freddy and I wanted to protect our children, and felt uncertainty whether there was enough time and goodwill in the world to bring this into effect. His only chance at some certainty before his death would be the quality of my promises to him. There would be no other mercy in his world until the end of his time.

Comandante Freddy, Captain Mosquera, a driver and I went to the previously captured couple's finca where we found a shovel in the barn. The Comandante walked us beyond the barn and through a thicket to a group of rocks near a large tree. The Comandante paced out a line from the rocks and said, "Here," pointing to a spot beyond the tree. A soldier dug down about six inches until he hit a hard, metal object, and bent over to scoop the remaining dirt, finally standing up with a large plastic-covered metal box in his hands. The Comandante turned to me.

"Don't open it. Take it to a bank and open an account. Don't give them details. My daughter's grandmother will know what to do." He had obviously planned for this possibility, and with one more spiteful glance at Captain Mosquera, said, "Make sure my daughter gets a good education—as good as his... the rest of the contents of the box are for her."

"I understand, Comandante."

We drove back to the brigade quietly in a one-jeep cortege. Captain Mosquera and I shook hands—the notes from my conversation with Comandante Freddy went into his hands; he gave to me his promise that he would never pursue the comandante's only child, and would allow me to place the funds for her education in a bank account beyond their knowledge. In return, he would possess sole credit for the incredible intelligence cornucopia the comandante had provided.

I walked with Comandante Freddy behind the torture building to a site with stacked hay bales in a hollow between massive trees near the river. "No harm will come to your daughter… the money will go to her education—you have my word." He did not thank me, but spoke to me in a whisper as he brushed past me toward the hay bales where two paramilitary soldiers waited for him. "This savagery is not for you."

Minutes later, after blindfolding him, the paramilitary soldiers formed a firing squad and shot Comandante Freddy dead. Comandante Freddy left no message for his daughter, which I assumed was in a letter in the metal box.

For the next two days Cody landed in Carepa about every six hours during the light of day. The crates went into the local Brigade, out the back door, and quickly up the road to Turbo and Necocli. I was, for the most part, in speed boats inspecting smuggling routes that had now fallen under paramilitary control, and on paramilitary training bases, where the raw intelligence from D-2 arrived from couriers a few times per hour by courier, or by fax according to the code of the day.

Late on my fifth day, unshackled from a paramilitary guard for a few moments, I made a call to Hastings from a pay phone inside a gas station, relating that I needed to speak to my wife about our young children.

"Hastings—this is Tommy—I haven't much time. Do you have anything to report of an urgent nature?"

"Urgent—no. Important, yes. When can you get here?"

"In two days, can it wait?" Hastings told me his news, expecting me to decide how to act upon it, whereupon I asked for a paramilitary driver to take me back to the 17th Brigade.

I asked Captain Mosquera to get me a secure telephone line to the Colonel, and then I went to pack my bags. There were two hundred miles of muddy and unsecured roads to Medellin, the nearest airport that could get me to Cali that day. A jeep ride with two vehicles would have taken until the next morning, with only a moderate probability of ever arriving alive. The sun was setting over Carepa, and Cody Pryor was already off base and probably unable to fly. Even if they could recall him to base, there was no justification for picking me up before my scheduled departure the next day. I was stuck in Carepa while ideological zealots circled closer and closer to my wife and children.

I reached the Colonel in the early evening at his office at the CNP base.

"Tommy—hello—has something happened?"

"I don't know, Colonel. I need to give you some background details, and then we can decide together if we need to act."

"I understand, Tommy. Proceed."

"Colonel—since August I have utilized a private security service for a college student I know. Two weeks ago, in the course of their work, they detected a functioning cell of three members near the target. I spoke with my contact recently. There is a fourth member of the cell—the cell leader. It is operational, but we have not been able to learn its objective."

"I see. I will tend to the student. When can you return to Cali?"

"Tomorrow night."

"In that case, we will speak then. Have a good flight, Tommy. Goodnight."

The Colonel knew that no telephone line was ever completely secure, so he did not ask me for specific information. He knew it involved Amelia, and that the cell was in place for a kidnapping or an assassination. He may have known about the cell, or had infiltrated it. In that case, tomorrow's meeting would serve only to brief me, and ask me to back away from further participation. But somehow I doubted it. The Colonel could not hide his surprise or concern for the life of his daughter, a feeling that was beginning to stake itself in my heart as well.

Thus far, I knew the killer in me only through video, like a movie buff who watches the same scene over and over, and thereby misunderstands the scene and the movie. I had seen the video about five times, but I did not really understand the plot. The bullet in my brain pulverized any knowledge I may have carried away from that night about myself—what I felt, who I thought I was, or why I was able to summon demonic ferocity upon the young sicario, and rendered me unable to know or feel anything about the actor or his purpose throughout the story.

But there was a story. There had to be.

But through the mists of my own mind, I could see him on the other side, pacing, stamping, throwing sticks into the abyss below out of tightly-coiled boredom. He knew Amelia was in danger, and he knew exactly how to make her safe. I had to admit—it was him that Amelia fell in love with that night. She wakes up to me, and goes about her schooling and shopping in Cali, curls under his body at night until deep sleep arrived for her, all the while knowing that he patrols around her at night, and would know what to do whatever befell her.

Things were happening quickly—Ivan, the university cell—and I felt certain that I would need him before the year would end.

CHAPTER THIRTY-FIVE

Amelia greeted the three of us at the door without any real reckoning about the purpose of our arrival together at the door of our home. Her mother had arrived earlier, by taxi from the south of the city, also without foreknowledge about the unusual family gathering. We took light family camaraderie as far as it would stretch. Mrs. Hernandez came to the realization that the men needed to talk seriously during dinner and not just watch a local soccer match. There was of course a game on TV, but at halftime, while Amelia and her mother played with the girls, the Colonel led Nando and me onto the balcony and shut the door.

I retold the story to the Colonel and Nando, but this time with considerable detail about Vigilio Hastings, his detection of the cell and the tracing of one of its members to an eastside apartment.

"Colonel, did you know about this cell?"

"No, we know there are cells operating in the city, but they are mostly for logistical support. This does not fit that profile. Have you been able to penetrate that apartment?"

"No, Hastings has a small firm; he is probably waiting for more cash or authority to conduct more thorough surveillance."

"Does he feel some event is imminent?"

"He didn't say. He probably prefers to talk in person."

"How did he find out about the professor?"

"I don't know. I called him on a pay phone. I called you about an hour later. That's all I know."

Nando looked upward at his father. "Pa, should we take over the operation? I mean, Tommy is out of town a lot… he doesn't have access to secure phone lines."

"Nando is right, Colonel. We need someone to oversee this operation locally, unless we capture them all and roll-up the cell." The Colonel was quick to reply.

"We would lose valuable intelligence that way."

"And Amelia?" I asked, which prompted Nando to pounce.

"Of course, we will protect Amelia!"

"No, Nando, should we tell her?" Like monks of a lower order, who had thought their way to the limits of their understanding of church dogmatics, we instinctively looked to the Colonel for guidance.

"We have the weekend. Tommy, get me the phone number of senor Hastings, please. We will take over the surveillance of the eastside apartment. By the time you leave Sunday night, we will have a plan in place. For now, leave Amelia in the dark. If we need to pull her out of school, Nando will handle those details. Carry on in a normal fashion, Tommy. When do you return to Panama?"

"Sunday night."

"You did the right thing, Tommy. We'll take over and of course keep you abreast of events."

Nando wanted to be part of his father's affirmation.

"Tommy, good work. You probably saved Amelia's life again."

"Colonel, Hastings will want lots of money..." The Colonel cut me off.

"It is our concern now, Tommy. I will bring you into the operation when Amelia needs you."

I trusted the Colonel in matters of security precautions, even those whose aim was the protection of his only daughter; he was offering me a subordinate role in the operation, one that excluded planning—and execution—unfortunately. I wanted—I deserved—a spot on that team. But we all knew that I was feeding a growing monster in the north of the country, whose huge appetite required weekly feedings, so it was not prejudicial of the Colonel to ask me to step down from active management of the operation.

The next week, we transported two-thousand pound loads to Puerto Berrio, Barrancabermeja, and Cimitarra—long flights across hundreds of miles of guerrilla territory. Cody Pryor went back to Panama on the last day, while I remained in Cimitarra. I had decided to fire him, or at least ask for his removal from my team, when I next spoke with Dr. Fuller. I knew two competent pilots who did not drink to excess or present a security risk with their drunken, ill-chosen war stories in Panama whorehouses. After a year, I was beginning to hate him.

The base in Cimitarra had changed noticeably. There were new buildings, a great variety of uniforms, and a lot more Green Beret instructors. Money had also put starch in the strides of the intelligence command. I went into one classroom on the morning after Cody left for Panama's booze-sodden whorehouses.

Comandante Miguelito was projecting slides from his PC to a wall screen. He was still teaching the same introductory counter-insurgency class to fresh recruits and some paramilitary instructors, evidently not having impressed the paramilitary command that he could take on greater responsibilities than teaching. This time he did not interrupt his lesson to greet me, continuing for about ten more minutes before dismissing the class for a break.

We embraced and walked outside.

"Long time, primo!"

"You look good, mi Comandante."

"I have been stuck on this base too long—and without promotion!"

"Be patient. In all of Uraba there are only four real commanders— most of the Middle and Lower Madgalena is unclaimed. You will have too much command, believe me."

"How is it going down there?"

"They are well commanded. The intelligence design is working. Their communications system is first-class. The FARC will not know what to do until it is too late."

A truck pulled onto the road on the other side of the parade grounds.

"That's our load, I believe."

"It won't be here long. The weapons go straight to the paramilitary camps now."

"How many are there now?"

"Five in the valley and more in Puerto Berrio and Barranca-berme a."

We delivered supplies to several basic training bases near to the brigade. The advanced training base for recruits was in the rear of an officers' training camp. Nearly everyone was an officer so that the mood was more like a graduate school seminar than a boot camp. There was no shouting at young boys, and trainers and trainees seemed to help one another hone techniques, rather than learn basic skills. There were no barracks and no mess—it was likely a practicum or a training center for the courses taught within the main Cimitarra base.

We drove down a sloped jeep path to a cattle-crossing manned by two sentries. They waved Miguelito onward with a tired, heavy salute during the intense heat of noon. We drove forward about two hundred yards to a barnyard with a corral. A paramilitary officer with a red armband stood with his right leg on one of the slats of the wooden corral. Inside two recruits with scimitars waited in the direct sun. The officer turned and waved at Miguelito. He walked over and shook hands.

"Quibo, Miguelito!"

"Quibo, Julian!"

He looked at me. "This is a North American friend named 'Stamper.'" That did not fit into his expectation of me, but he did not pursue the matter. We shook hands, and he gladly accepted the gallon of water I extended to him.

"When do we start?"

"The delivery is a little late... these two are about to shit their pants!" The detainees looked at me with fear and terror in their eyes, made worse by the sudden appearance of the white man in clean clothes and dark sun glasses.

"We have doubts about these two—they are probably infiltrators... this is the best way to find out."

"Why are they in the corral?"

"It is the best way to spot a FARC spy. They will start shortly."

Miguelito looked at his watch.

"How often do you do this?"

"About twice a day."

A group of young recruits from another base walked down the path toward us, their marching done in sullen, fearful silence. They halted, and the officer in front gave the instruction for them to disperse around the corral. Miguelito took the water from me and drank deeply.

A tall, thin, tanned officer in military fatigues and white t-shirt walked over and took the radio from Miguelito. He identified himself through his coded name and made his request for the 'training cadaver.'

The radio was silent for several minutes. The recruits passed a five-gallon jug of water around the corral. The voice came back onto the radio. The package was on its way. I put a leg on the corral to watch the beginning of the show. The two recruits in the corral stepped back when they heard the jeep door shut. I took off my sunglasses and wiped my neck with a towel.

I thought to myself: you are inured to this sort of thing. It has always been this way in Colombia. There are just certain countries where they like to kill each other. They need to be blood-slaked. You can't change anything. Stay out of their way. Hundreds are dying each week, either from FARC attacks, the limpieza of the streets of the major cities of drug users and thieves, or paramilitary death squad murder sprees. These thoughts bounced through my mind like insincere advertising slogans. Death was coming to this place whether I could rationalize it or not. It did not offend me anymore, but it still terrified me, the extinguishing of life with such savage calm, and ridiculous staging. They were like children trying to understand and then stage a Wagnerian Opera. They were having too much fun in the costumes to bother with the libretto.

The recruits were mostly quiet; there was no laughing. Most of them wore their caps low over their noses and ignored the flies that settled onto their noses and hands. A jeep entered from the rear and parked next to ours. Two paramilitary soldiers lifted a third boy out of the back of the jeep. He screamed and kicked his legs through the rag taped in his mouth and tried to wriggle free from the rope that tied his hands behind his back. He had wet himself.

The soldiers walked him into the corral and dropped him in the middle. Julian spoke in stentorian blasts of enraged words and dead silences: "Every man here has shown their willingness to follow orders—except you two. You have given your allegiance and taken your oaths. You are now warriors in our great cause…except those two." He opened the gate at that moment, and walked into the corral where the three boys were gathered, addressing his comments to them in a harsh, but less commanding voice. "Now, you have this last chance to prove yourself… this boy is from the FARC. He has killed for them and he will kill again."

The boy shook his head wildly and tried to wriggle free upwardly to his feet. Julian pushed him down. "One man will die in this circle or two will die or three will die. If you are a true paramilitary, you will kill like a paramilitary or you will die like a FARC dog… when you hear the command, you will strike this man down. You will follow orders or you will not leave this corral. You will take his life with the weapons you see or we will take your weapons and take yours. On my command—kill the traitor!"

The most sickening part was that there were no men in that corral. They had all probably been shanghaied from their villages, and wanted just an escape from the heat, hunger, and disease of their village.

The two soldiers whose allegiance was being tested jerked their attention to each other and to the tied-up boy. They did not want to die or kill each other or take pay in the paramilitary army anymore. The captured boy slid backward on his neck and shook his head, imploring the two soldiers to spare him in whimpering gasps through his stuffed mouth. He tried to rise again until Julian stepped forward and tripped him downward. He quickly rolled over and went back to his knees.

One of the two boy-soldiers in the corral now stood in front of the shackled youth, peering down and attempting their juvenile versions of a pitiless stare. With a hesitation that made the blade swivel in his arms, he raised his scimitar and lashed it down across the doomed boy's neck. The cut was about half way into the neck. Upon pulling the scimitar out with twists of his hands upon the handle, blood spurted toward the killer and left a spray on his shirt.

He dropped his scimitar in complete horror, which he hid behind tightly clenched jaws and fists upraised in victory. The other soldier realized his chance to kill was nearly gone. He brought his scimitar down on the other side of the boy, decapitating him. The boy's body fell backward and his head rolled to the side. Blood poured out of his neck stump for a few seconds onto the soft dirt, attracting more flies. Julian approached both boys and lifted their arms like boxing champions. He gave them water from his own canteen, and then led them like children out of the corral and away from the others. I looked at Miguelito. "Otherwise, those two might kill us all."

Before Miguelito's knock on the door for our trip into town for dinner, I paced in my room—more quickly when I felt the surge of more dry heaves. I avoided the mirror in my officer's quarters, not knowing whether to expect a cunning leer or haunted frozen shriek in return. In form, this movement showed no more meaning than middle-aged men forcing their ignorant followers to commit ritualistic murder upon other young boys. It was probably the same on the FARC side. That boy today was not an infiltrator and certainly not FARC. They had sized him up as too scared to be of use in the upcoming massacres of innocents or neutrals, so they formed a ceremonial ring and celebrated his death, thus achieving total fear of disobedience among those boys.

My fingertips were blue. My mind was as blank as I could maintain it, but I was on the verge of puking incessantly. I had been in that small room, ostensibly napping, for two hours, but I could not sleep, or understand the meaning of my stricken face in the mirror. I had seen enough, and it was only the beginning, but I had never objected to the barbarity, or even questioned it as a tactic. The thin man in the white suit who brought gifts to the paramilitaries seldom spoke, as if this were just another job in another messed up client state.

There was nothing that removed these murders from the realm of basic savagery; in fact, they seemed to be teaching the boys to embrace horror more than shoot a gun straight, or understand complex radio signals. They were teaching children to murder other children, a skill that would perpetuate this war for another quarter century. Those boys would never reenter society.

The question remaining was whether I ever would.

That young boy had been born, lived, and died in the dirt of the damned. He was probably illiterate, living his whole life in mild shock with no expectation of relief from the heat, filth, and brutality of life in his village. In death, he was not allowed to explain himself, or reflect upon the road he had travelled to that point. Now, he was deep in a common pit without witnesses to give him a proper farewell, his body slowly dissolving under chemicals for quick bleaching of bones that we probably gave them. There would be no letter from the paramilitaries; his mother would never know the date, place or circumstances of his sickening death. His mother may have only had a photo of her boy for the rest of her own short life.

It was sickening that we did business with such people and gave them tools to cut swathes of dripping blood and sawed bones across tens of thousands of gridded miles. Maybe that was what Cody Pryor saw in me and despised: a quaint moral conscience—a college boy's dim understanding of the way things have got to be in this world... one that had no place among the men that ran these sorts of operations, and settled affairs for countries who were habitual insurgency risks; one that would only lead to trouble for myself and those around me, eventually. For Cody, I was fit for little more than gay porn. Cody did not know anything of the other Tommy. But Cody had sized up the Tommy he dealt with on a day-by-day basis, and rejected him as an inferior grade for most military purposes.

I had lost personal time. How many days had passed since I spoke to the Colonel? Neither had I spoken to Amelia, although there had been many opportunities to call the condo and hear the girls' voices, and bring some calm to my wife. I had stopped showering days ago, and taken on the look and scent of the young thrill-killers who stood in ranks in the paramilitary camps. There had been no further instructions from Panama, only loads of weapons and grenades that landed each day, giving the comandantes confidence that victory was finally near at hand. I tried to nap, but I could not tamp down my own chorus of jackals on the amphitheater of my own exhaustion and horror.

CHAPTER THIRTY-SIX

To take a plane load of guns from Panama into Carepa was a sort of logistical impertinence. It was a waste of flight time and gasoline and runway wear and tear. The flight was about twenty minutes, even with a generous curve over the Pacific Ocean. But mostly due to the fact that there was an industry in place to smuggle goods efficiently, and at a reasonable cost, from the endless coastal jungles of Panama to those of Uraba.

But a plane signified something. It was the utilization of space and metal and speed to make a specific point: the materials and the power and the solutions come from above and beyond. It was the CIA version or riding an elephant between cities during the British Raj. We could have moved—and we probably did behind my back—thousands of pounds a day of weapons via speedboat and small freighter. But a plane signified domain over all that slopped beneath it or lagged behind it.

There was also a tonic effect—for both paramilitaries and soldiers—to await and then unload weapons from factories in other continents, weapons that travelled a long distance, and that were chosen by experts, but that in the end were the same weapons that could have been ordered in Uraba and picked up in any number of shallow inlets in Panama, and speed-boated to Colombia. My huge paychecks owed their providence to such elaborate arrangements and paramilitary choral amazement

Captain Mosquera ordered a caravan to take me up the banana road to Turbo. A major operation, one involving both paramilitary troops and brigade military command was planned for the next day at dawn. "All the parts will come together—military intelligence, the paramilitary commands, and your weapons; we wanted you to see it first-hand."

A damn fool could cultivate these lands or raise a herd of cattle, and pass the whole thing down to his son. The land provided enough for everyone without the need for superior skill or greater than normal luck. But the FARC had sat in the hills above these plains for over twenty years, sending out tax collectors and small teams of insurgents for the occasional murder of reluctant merchants. Like feudal lords, they taxed the smallholders, the ranches, the banana plantations, and the smugglers. Everyone toiled, rather than prospered, but the FARC was the only idle class.

Like Romans, they seldom mingled in the villages, and therefore became provincial and untested. They mostly held onto river and small-road routes to deliver drugs over these plains and west through the watery swamps and channels to Panama. They were living fat off the land, unprepared for the assault to come, reluctant to even believe that there was a force greater then themselves in these lands.

We drove onto a muddy jeep road through dark foliage and into a small, heavily-guarded finca on the hilly slopes to the northeast of Turbo. There were small Renaults and Jeeps parked irregularly in front of them. There were also large stacks of lime, bottled water, and sacks of rice under a black tarp covering in front of the nearest building.

I met Comandante Pollux, who called for us to enter. He was about thirty years old, but carried himself like a much older man. A man of hard work and action, he sat uncomfortably behind the sharp angles of his desk. He was about as tall as I was, but had thirty pounds on me. On the back wall behind his sweat-stained form was a large map of Uraba. There was a grouping of green pins on the names of the coastal cities; eastward, there was a mix of yellow and green and blue ones; and in the mountainous highlands beyond that, there was a mass of red ones.

He stood and stretched out his hand to me from behind his desk.

"Bienvenido, senor!"

"Gracias por la invitacion, Comandante!" He beckoned for both of us to sit.

"Have you eaten, senor?"

"I ate early this morning in Panama, Comandante." I pulled several bottles of Panamanian rum from my backpack and stood to gently hand them to the Comandante. "A gift from my friends to our new friends in Uraba. We look forward to supporting your brave efforts." He smiled and received them graciously. "We are grateful for your friendship."

He placed them on the shelf behind him and continued. "This is the main headquarters for our Bloque. We have another installation in Turbo, but that is mainly for recruiting.

"How is recruiting coming along, Comandante?"

"In the past eight months we have increased our forces from twenty to over six hundred."

"How many of those men have been trained, Comandante?"

"All of them, Senor."

"That is a remarkable increase, Comandante."

"They come from many parts of Colombia. They can make twice as much money with us as with the guerrillas or a banana plantation. A lot of the soldiers come directly to us after their military service."

He grew stronger in his oratory as he progressed. "There is also the matter that most people hate the FARC. They are bandits at heart. They grow nothing, they fix nothing… this part of Colombia has been under their dictatorship for decades. Until your assistance came to us, we could not dream about confronting them in their own territory. They are bastards, senor. They shoot their deserters—they will hunt them across the country to kill them. But they know we will take care of them, and they can move up in our ranks. Word is spreading and more FARC soldiers are joining us each week."

"I have heard similar stories in other commands."

"They are animals. This country will never be worth shit until they are all dead."

"That is why they sent me, Comandante. I am not here to evaluate you or your command. We just want to know how far you have developed as a fighting force and what services we can offer to increase your readiness and capabilities."

"In that case, we can take a tour of the area around Turbo, and I can explain our progress toward the pacification of the region."

We bedded early that night—with each passing day I felt less and less inclined to bathe—and left the next morning before the violet and pink dawn, which we saw before us while driving toward one of those red dots in the low hills in the east of Uraba, one particular dot that the FARC probably considered about as dangerous as Sherwood Forest to Robin Hood.

We drove in a small convoy atop rutty, one-lane roads higher and deeper into the neutral ground between the paramilitary coast and the FARC highlands. We parked our caravan of small Renaults next to two white Range Rovers from the Seventeenth Brigade on the side of the main road into the small, quaint village of San Antonio. Under a sprawling tree beyond our roadblock there was another Range Rover, from which soldiers carried card tables and electronics gear.

We shook hands all around. Comandante Pollux was warm and deferential to the brigade officials, but still represented the main fighting force for this mission. There were two Captains, and a Lieutenant, who seemed to have ultimate control of the events that transpired over the next several days. Several soldiers took off their official brigade shirts and put on paramilitary black shirts and red arm bands in front of me. In the light of dawn, they had acquired black and green face paint that transformed them from protectors of the population into their likely assassins.

Once the roadblock, which consisted of several saw horses and armed soldiers, had been established to the satisfaction of the Lieutenant, the officers and I walked toward the shade of the tree in order to receive—not so much a briefing—as battle orders. The Lieutenant spoke first, his initial remarks concerned with clearly dividing the roles of the army and paramilitaries. The plan was elegant. The army would stop traffic from three directions on all the passable roads into San Antonio, mostly to forestall the interference of human rights observers or neutral government agents, who would eventually hear about the arrival of the paramilitaries from within the village and rush to the scene to collect evidence of atrocities. Overhead, helicopters would patrol, so that the FARC could not enter or escape the village without immediate detection.

Then, the paramilitary troops would enter the village and begin their part of the mission.

"Bienvenidos a San Vicente—el Lugar de Gente Pacifica y Alegre!" Pollux motioned for me to return back to our car. We drove past small businesses and onto the central plaza. There were about three hundred villagers gathered around it, mostly reluctant witnesses to the dans macabre to come. Behind them about twenty masked paramilitaries barked and butted those peasants who would try to leave in order to save themselves or warn others.

Comandante Pollux reminded me to put on my hat and sunglasses to make identification difficult before we got out of his red Renault. "War paint?" He laughed. "You would just look like a gringo with paint on your face." He pointed to a white balcony above the "Commune" sign. Together with four sentries, we ran up two flights of stairs and entered a small office.

Entering, I recognized Captain Mosquera and two of his men. They were in blue jeans and polo shirts and had dark glasses, which they rested on their heads. He quickly explained that paramilitaries had been beating and taunting FARC infiltrators on the plaza below for about an hour. We made our way to the balcony, like observers from Rome in the provinces, where the theater of terror was well underway.

In an open circle were the two infiltrators—badly beaten about their faces, their ribs likely broken—crumpled on the ground, no longer able to struggle to escape the binding of their hands behind their backs.

They did not cry for mercy. Several women in the crowd, however, shouted "Auxilio! Auxilio!" until a paramilitary entered the crowd and hit them with their rifle butts on their noses. Comandante Pollux called a man called Diego Uno on his radio. Down below, one of the paramilitaries touched his finger to his ear plug and looked up.

"Si, Comandante!"

"Adelante, Diego! We are losing precious time, primo!"

Diego Uno—like Oscar, another trusted paramilitary under Pollux's command—had green and yellow face paint that made his cruelty seem from a nearby swamp. Oscar began to scrape a scimitar on the ground in a hunched-over motion farmers use to sharpen their blades or fighters use to frighten their enemies. Diego Uno screamed out like a rapper to the scraping of the scimitar the FARC portion of their village history and in particular, these two men's participation. They were not members of the village, he explained. They did not work in the sun like the good people of San Vicente. They did not suffer when an animal died, or there was not food for the children. They had never helped their neighbors or given money to poor people. They didn't pay taxes to the community. They had no children in the schools. But for the last thirty years they were the most important members of the community. They were FARC tax collectors.

One of the men looked up at Diego Uno, but found that he could not produce sound from his mouth. Diego Uno noticed that and kicked him directly in the mouth. Oscar scraped his scimitar in a circle closer and closer to the men. After each rhythmic phrase from Diego Uno, Oscar would skip his scimitar on the ground and cast a menacing glance at the townspeople. Other paramilitaries shouted and chanted to whip up the crowd, who stayed quiet, unwilling to join the chorus of death.

"How did he do this? How did he collect taxes for thirty years?"

He pointed his scimitar around at the crowd.

"Did you pay willingly? Most of you did not. The truth is that he had friends... in this community! Your friends... your neighbors... maybe even yourself. If you are this kind of friend of the FARC—if you collected money or told them about a neighbor who had a new cow or started raising pigs... if you helped the devil with a favor or a political assignment—you have until sundown to leave San Vicente. Take your clothes and leave. Your car, your animals—they now belong to the poor of San Vicente...."

Diego Uno pointed down at the man he had kicked. "He is not collecting taxes anymore... The FARC is not taking your money anymore. They will not scare you or burn your lands or kill your family members. They will not kidnap your sons for military service. They are not coming to this village again!" He nodded to Oscar, who stepped behind the man. He raised the scimitar high in the air with both hands, and brought it down and through the neck of the man. His head rolled a few feet away and blood spewed toward the crowd in a warm red spume.

Silence took over the entire plaza. "This village is now under official political and military control of the Bloque Urabano. This man will collect no more taxes!" He nodded again, and Oscar took another head. This head rolled closer to the crowd, who backed away, until the soldiers behind them pressed them back. Oscar cleaned his blade on the shirt of one of the headless men.

On the balcony, Captain Mosquera turned toward Comandante Pollux and spoke. "Comandante—have you acted upon the list?" The Comandante radioed down to Diego Uno about the list. Diego took a piece of paper from his pocket and shoved it in the face of some of the cowed men and women in the first row of the crowd. "There is another class of traitor in San Vicente—those that not only support the FARC, but work actively alongside them. They cook food for the FARC... they give them money... or they steal money from you and give it to the FARC. These traitors will not live to see sundown...."

Comandante Pollux turned to Captain Mosquera. "Primo, to city hall?" We all wore dark glasses on the way down the stairs. A soldier named Evers handed me a mask, and Comandante Pollux wore one as well. The crowd had dispersed. The bodies remained on the plaza where flies had begun to gather around the corpses. We walked past them to the other side of the plaza.

The city hall was on a small hill on the eastern side of the plaza. We walked as a small phalanx through the front doors. Two sentries in front of us, painted in frightening stripes of yellow and orange like tigers, pushed a weapon in the face of everyone they saw. We followed their minacious boot rhythm down the corridor to the Mayor's office. Diego Uno was already there. The Mayor, who began muffled explanations from within a gag, was in his underwear and tied to a wooden chair. Two sentries stayed with us, while two stood guard outside.

"My name is Comandante Pollux from the Bloque Urabaro, senor… you are still the mayor of this town. You will receive a salary and control your staff—at least the ones who are not traitors to the nation. The only difference is that you will not make a single decision. He will." He pointed at Diego Uno. "That man controls this town now. The list of your crimes is long—and we may still deal with you as we dealt with those men. But for now, you will stay. But you will do nothing, senor."

He pointed at Captain Mosquera and his men. "These men have been investigating your crimes for a long time. They have enough evidence to convict you of treason, embezzlement, and conspiracy. But we need you to calm your people and convince them that cooperation with us is the best policy. Is that clear?" The petrified man merely grunted through the rag in his mouth, jerking his head from man to man to see who ultimately had to be reckoned with.

A jeep came to an abrupt stop on the edge of the plaza. Two soldiers hopped out and quickly grabbed two women from the back seat. There was commotion from within the mass of observers who had been forced to regroup around the edge of the plaza below. These new accused prisoners entered the main square from within a wide alley in the crowd, made by more gun-wielding soldiers. The women, as soon as they stepped onto the plaza, slipped and rolled in horror on the blood of the decapitated men. Seeking escape, they were pushed back down close to the headless bodies by face-painted men from Pollux's command. Their shrieks intensified, unsubdued by the rifle butts they took to their heads as they tried to waddle away from the blood pool.

Oscar and Evers and their men shot the two women after a short speech about infiltration into local schools. The women were probably forced to teach from a FARC curriculum under threat of a similar punishment. Next, Oscar turned his gun to three farm workers, who knelt with lowered heads as Diego Uno read out their crimes, which amounted to little more than cooking meals for FARC patrols that passed through fincas where the men were property caretakers.

The sun was rising toward its noon zenith above us. The ring of peasants had not been allowed to leave the square, so they sat in the hot sun and begged for water, which the painted faces denied them.

D-2 agents examined the confiscated office files from the mayor's office behind us. While we ate a lunch of sandwiches and Cokes on the cleared-off desk of the mayor, Captain Mosquera summarized events for his commanding Lieutenant on his radio. "Comandante Pollux and his men are collecting the names on the list... Si, Lieutenant, we will burn their houses and businesses... Si Lieutenant, interrogations are taking place now—we are using the fire station on the edge of town... si Lieutenant, as soon as actionable information arrives, we will send it along to you. Gracias, Lieutenant, Captain Mosquera out."

Mosquera and I flew back to the Seventeenth Brigade late in the afternoon in a helicopter, while the other officers remained behind and took high-value suspects to a second, secret interrogation center outside the village. While I was not allowed to leave the base that night, the encirclement of San Vicente continued, which required a team of intelligence officers to stay awake and monitor the radio frequencies of the paramilitary commanders, the CNP, or NGO groups, who would hear of the violence through their contacts in the FARC and rush there in their own caravans.

There being no secure line on the base, I waited for the Colonel to send me a message of any kind about his activities against the cell Hastings discovered. There had been no note, fax or call from him or Nando. I had to trust the Colonel; he would not deprive me of information that touched upon Amelia, especially if it was of an urgent nature. There was nothing more to think about then but the awful deaths in San Vicente.

I rationalized those deaths as well since I did not know what else to do with them. They were now lodged in my mind: visions of some bodies without heads with open eyes and lolling tongues; others with the fear seared into their faces knowing that an absolute end was only moments away; the older fighters left more calm expressions, echoing Virgil's reminder that "The one hope of the doomed is not to hope for safety." None of this applied to the children. I had not seen any small bodies, but I knew the paramilitaries often killed entire families, as it reduced the number of revenges they would have to deal with in the future.

The process of detachment from the day's horror continued as if I could leave the darkness of a movie theater and just walk way. For the most part, the murdered militants were armed combatants out of uniform; they had no rights to due process or fair treatment. They had done the same or worse to innocent villagers who did not pay their war taxes. In fact, it had been ex-FARC soldiers, ones who joined up with Comandante Pollux, who had pointed them out, as well as their girlfriends and family members.

But the school teacher was different. Her death was horrible, looking out at the community to defend her position as an ideological non-combatant, and at the last moment, realizing that the lowered heads in the audience would not raise a whimper to save her. The single bullet entered the back of her brain, casting her brains and blood on the first row of the petrified campesinos. Without showering again, I went to bed and never reached sleep until awoken by a knock on my quarters at 04:00.

"Stamper, it's time to empty the swamp and kill the alligators." I remembered the phrase differently, but I got the point. Captain Mosquera handed me a thermos of coffee. "We leave in fifteen minutes," He paused. "What smells in here?"

We flew at about one thousand feet toward the high plateau of San Vicente. Upon reaching the army checkpoint, we headed south to the ridges of woods and high pastures that afforded a commanding view on the village and its surrounding planes, nearly all the way to the sea.

The village had wisely chosen not to awaken that morning. There were very few fumes of smoke from the small shack houses, or trucks on

373

the roads, or children on their way to school. We heard some radio chatter from the fire station. They had caught almost all the contrabandistas in the village who drove cargo loads of food and medicines to the FARC in the distant woods. Many of the paramilitaries who held the drivers captive until they were shot did not know how to drive, so the paramilitary officers at the fire station requested drivers to take the commandeered contraband trucks to Turbo.

We landed on a meadow below a small hut perched on the side of some woods of thin-trunked trees that rose and fell with the top of the ridge. Four paramilitary troops stood below us, and another four stood in formation near the hut. As we landed, Captain Mosquera tugged at my sleeve. "These men hiked seven miles to secure this spot at dawn. They are each carrying twenty-five kilos. That is what a Colombian soldier can do!"

We stepped downward out of the helicopter onto tall grass and headed quickly away from open spaces toward the small hut above us. There were no cows or chickens or even a family dog, or piles of wood—the bare minimum for an isolated hut. The soldiers saluted Captain Mosquera as he approached them from below. "Stamper, your mask—none of these people will ever talk to anyone."

We stepped onto the dirt floor of the hut. There was no refrigerator or sink, and only a plank for a bed, on which sat two boys of about eighteen or nineteen in dirty, holey jeans and t-shirts. The soldiers had removed their shoes, which were no longer in the hut. They shivered from cold and fear, and did not dare to look at us.

"My little guerillito does not want to talk—is that so?" queried Mosquera, mockingly. They continued to look downward. While there was no radio or TV, there was a generator on the floor of the far wall. I remembered seeing canisters of gasoline outside. "Stamper, that electric line has been cut. We are looking for it now."

"What is 'it,' Captain?"

"This is a FARC radio post. Look." He pointed to one of the few pines in the woods up the hill. There were antennae atop the tree, and I supposed an electric cord running down its trunk, though I could not see one.

"Where is the transmitter?" We spoke in English, which seemed to puzzle and then terrify the boys.

"That is the question that these young guerrillas do not want to answer." Captain Mosquera nodded at one of his soldiers, who brusquely pulled the two boys out the door and onto the meadow. The Captain tried a different approach. "The first one who speaks, lives. He will go to prison, but he will live." The boys did not raise their heads, or even look at one another, the offer being expected and the response purposely mute. Captain Mosquera nodded to the soldier. He quickly lifted his rifle and shot one of the boys on the top of the head. The bullet furrowed through the top of his brain, carrying him about twenty feet down the meadow until his head over heels roll stopped.

"I guess it is your turn, chico." Captain Mosquera raised his radio. "Eagle One to Fox Hole."

"Fox Hole, Eagle One. Are you ready there?"

"Ready Eagle One." Captain Mosquera smiled at me.

"The privations of the young guerrilla." Moments later we heard a young girl's voice.

"Migey, I'm scared. They said they will kill me. Migey, help me please! Migey, please do something!" The guerrilla shot a glance at Captain Mosquera.

"Last offer little guerrilla; tell us where the transmitter is or listen to your girlfriend's death."

The guerrilla spit on the ground, but did not look up. "Fox Hole, shoot the girl now!" Moments later, we heard a shriek and then a single bullet fire. Mosquera had lost whatever hold he had on the boy at the death of his girlfriend. The boy slid his chin further down his chest, and gave a small sigh, one that was as close to a farewell as the Captain would allow. He nodded again at the same soldier, who shot the guerrilla in the same place above his eyes. We watched as the boy lunged downward, coming to a rest near the body of his fellow guerrilla in the tall grass in the lower meadow.

Captain Mosquera spoke to two other soldiers. "Put the bodies in the woods—not too far away—and set the dynamite traps behind the generator." He looked at his watch, and then spoke to me, and gave radio instructions in one running conversation. "We didn't find the transmitter. We don't have much time remaining though—the FARC will realize that we have discovered this site soon. If we had a metal detector and a few more hours, we would find it… shit! This is Mosquera.

send the helicopter to rendezvous point 'Blue-Carlos-Twelve… let's go, Stamper… Fuck!"

We ran down the tall meadow grass to a trail at its edge, which our soldier-guards pointed out to us. After a further mile of down-trail sprinting to the helicopter, we stopped short of the powerful blades. They were spinning so quickly that the helicopter seemed to bounce off the ground and then softly back down every few seconds. We arrived with a final lunge onto its metal floor. As we rose quickly, we looked down at San Vicente from the south. Blocks of houses were aflame, joining their flames in one ugly, black cloud that we avoided by curving around the south of the city.

There was also a long line of cattle on the main road that lead from the village to the roadblock. Captain Mosquera pointed at the strange sight, nudging his binoculars on my arm. There were no cowboys on horseback with them; instead, young paramilitary boys whipped them forward along the shoulder of the road out of town with small branches whittled down to thin flexible whips. "They will eat well this week."

We landed outside an abandoned farm about two miles beyond the road block. For the first time on these trips with Captain Mosquera, I knew what was to come. My stomach turned acidic, and I could feel the early upheavals of vomiting. My stomach began to make noise, which amused Captain Mosquera. Under an oak tree whose canopy provided shade for several vehicles, there was a large truck, shovel, and bags of lime around its trunk, the essential tools to move, bury, and chemically stabilize the remains of untreated corpses.

"Captain Mosquera, the mask?"

"If it makes you feel better, leave it on—the prisoners here aren't going to remember you."

Six paramilitary guards stood around a literal pile of shoeless FARC prisoners, stacked face down in six pairs, so that the feet of one prisoner would be the only thing visible to his companion prisoner. The guards were silent, not bothering to wipe drops of sweat that slid down their cheeks, only registering on their features the incessant hatred that came from deep within their eyes. Captain Mosquera gave each one a bottle of water, which they all drank quickly, crumpling the empty plastic bottle in their hands, and tossing it aside, so that they could return to the duty of watching over the condemned men.

I heard one of the Range Rovers braking outside the barn. Four more soldiers and the Lieutenant from the roadblock stepped into the barn, so that there were now twelve of us, and twelve FARC prisoners on the floor. The paramilitary soldiers stood erect, addressing salutes to him, which he returned promptly, a way of recognizing the friendly forces as valid soldiers. Incessant crackling came through his radio, which he clicked off before addressing his comments to Captain Mosquera and me.

"Captain, is this the whole catch?"

"This is all those who we have managed to capture this week, Lieutenant."

"What is the breakdown?" The men on the ground were soon to be ghosts; they would only hear themselves described briefly, and then would be quickly dispatched.

"Five active-duty soldiers, three government workers who are active urban guerrillas, two…" Captain Mosquera's radio suddenly erupted in quick bursts of requests to speak to him.

"Red Fox."

"Red Fox, four birds cooked in the pot. Repeat, four birds cooked in the pot. Over."

"Excellent, Hawk leader. Return to rendezvous point for evacuation. Over." Mosquera turned to me.

"We blew up that communications cabin and killed four FARC soldiers."

"Two teachers and two that our own ex-FARC mentioned having seen at a FARC camp a few weeks ago."

"Do we have plans to let any of them join Comandante Pollux's men?"

"No. His recruitment numbers are growing. Anyway, these are career FARC. Most of them have over ten years as urban or jungle guerrillas. They don't make very good converts." Thus, their fate was decided.

"Understood. Proceed then, Captain." Mosquera walked over to one of the paramilitaries and whispered in his ear. The paramilitary whispered something in return, and then stepped forward toward the complex of bodies. Captain Mosquera tapped me on the arm. "Let's go, Stamper."

The rest was a paramilitary matter. Officially, the army did not commit human rights abuses, and could scoff at the claims of non-government organizations that military death squads were murdering their way through small villages throughout the countryside. A military check point outside a village currently undergoing a cleansing of guerrillas was a growing coincidence in Uraba, but just that.

The Lieutenant, Mosquera and I walked outside into the bright sun of midday. As I shielded my eyes, I heard the screams and metallic sprays of bullets onto the men on the floor. The sound stopped by the time we reached the white Range Rover, but reinitiated as individual shots, probably to the head, which stopped after twelve bullet shots like a hammer strike coming from a tower belfry.

While we cruised at two thousand feet over verdant green pastures toward the airport at Carepa, Captain Mosquera felt obligated to restore some proportion to the massacre at the San Vicente barn. He spoke in English, as if the argument needed to utilize the words of international law in its most common language to gain some kind of intellectual pedigree. "Stamper, those men were probably responsible for the deaths of over one hundred soldiers—the theft of thousands of cattle—not to mention the enslavement of that entire village. From that stinky, little plateau, they could watch our movements so that we could not get within fifty kilometers without their having time to attack our convoys."

"They are killers, Stamper, not soldiers. Please don't confuse the two things. They do not offer prisoner guarantees, but we are obliged to do so. Our prisons are filled with their soldiers, who recruit from within the prisons, and then leave back to the jungle. This brings their rules into their 'hamlets' and their ranks. This will all end—but not while they sit up in the jungle and demand half from anyone with one hundred pesos in his pocket. Peace will come when they have no one to tax or extort, and they have no coke to sell. Then they will talk—not in good faith—but they will talk, and only then will we listen."

I continued his thoughts in English. "Drain the water to kill the fish."

"Eso! I was close before, wasn't I?" The helicopter dropped onto the end of the runway at the Carepa airport.

"Should I leave a security force with you?" I shook his hands before jumping out.

"No—Captain—you have a lot of intelligence to organize. My plane will arrive in a few minutes. Go take a shower and congratulate your men."

"My country thanks you, Stamper! Take care!"

My roll out of the helicopter onto the hard ground of the runway renewed the acidic confab within my stomach. The moment was about to come. I scampered to the edge of the runway, and crumpled downward while a solid thrust of vomit met the ditch beside the runway. A second, third and fourth volley followed.

I rolled on my side, vomit dangling from my chin toward the ground and beginning to dye my dirty t-shirt; after three days during which I took no more than an occasional nap, lack of sleep took hold. The ground began to stretch away from me and then whip back only inches from my eyes. I fell with my head beside the runway where the hard pavement met the clammy dirt and wet grass of the ditch edge.

I looked at my watch and then turned upward to see Cody standing behind me. My sleep must have lasted only a few minutes since the kick to the back of my feet occurred at the exact hour and minute when Cody Pryor had agreed to land.

"Mess yourself at your first rodeo?" I did not have to present any bona fides to Cody Pryor.

"It's a bug. I have had it a few days now."

Wobbly, mission-drunk, sleep-deprived, mildly in shock—still, I was awake enough to know that my words—ill-chosen or well-considered—would equally be the probative ravings of someone Cody had long ago decided not to respect. The vomit on my face—which I quickly wiped away with my handkerchief—issuing the first guffaw from Cody—made his interrogatories crueler and more enjoyable for him. "So this counter-insurgency stuff is a little too formidable for you, eh Tommy?"

"I told you—it's a bug—it's not mission related. You know as well as anyone the weird waters in these villages."

"Right—but falling asleep in ditch water in an unsecured area would not help the mission much, would it?" Sensing an astounding victory to be near, Cody afforded me one last pitying, wry grin.

"I haven't slept much in the last three days."

"I'll note that in my report."

"Report—what fuckin' report?"

"Someone has to tell Tampa what their million-dollar boy is all about."

"And that someone is you?"

"Always has been."

"But somehow never in the context of an actual debriefing where we discuss real business."

"I get my points across to people that matter."

I vomited again.

"Time to go home, Tommy. Your real home. Let the professionals take over now. Your pappy can get you a job in Washington and a little house for your beauty queen wife." I stood up, staggered a little, and then came up to Cody Pryor so that our noses nearly met.

"Cody, have you ever killed someone? I mean with your own hands? Have you ever seen the brains squeeze out like a live birth?"

"I let the savages handle that."

I thumped him on the chest. "I have. Now get out of my fuckin' sight you cowardly piece of shit."

From the airport lobby, I was able to reach Captain Mosquera, and in forty-five minutes a paramilitary convoy drove me to Turbo. With my nausea came a fever, but Comandante Pollux enjoined festivities for all in the camp outside Turbo, including me. We emptied out several grocery stores of beer and whiskey and raided a suspected pro-FARC beef wholesaler for a few hundred pounds of beef, which weighed down the green Renault on the drive back to camp. Around the campfires in Pollux's camp, where we passed bottles of whiskey as comrades in arms after a rout of our enemies, my sweat and feverishness did not look at all unordinary that night.

A few hours after midnight, one of Pollux's men drove me to an inlet waterway, where I took a choppy ride in a speedboat onto a beach in Panama, and arrived at Howard AFB at dawn. I puked again and drank gallons of water from plastic milk jugs to cool my burning throat. My high fever blocked out most of my range of thought by the time I sat down in front of a monitor and waited for the screen to show Dr. Fuller.

"Tommy, good morning. Might I be allowed to be the first to say that you have never looked worse?"

"It is good to see you too, Dr. Fuller." Without preamble, I galloped through a prepared analysis that had been percolating in my mind for a few weeks. My thoughts, while still quite orderly in the archives I had mentally constructed for this briefing, may have been quite lucid or an incomprehensible outpouring for Dr. Fuller.

"Let's consider three cases, Dr. Fuller. The first is the friendly village scenario. On your map, that would be Pueblo Bello. It is completely occupied. There is an administrative base off the central plaza. They charge a war tax, and people pay willingly. The paramilitaries go where they want and do what they want. They go into the schools and read the lesson plans for god's sake. They trust the locals; in fact, they give away weapons and their phone numbers to the shop owners. They have built a following of young, jobless boys who want to be in uniform. They recruit in a lot from places like this."

"The other scenario is the neutral village scenario. This is the shock attack routine. They arrive in numbers, with face painted and in masks. They order all businesses closed. They beat people up and flash lists of names. They deliver a bellicose speech with prisoners on the ground near the speaker. It is very Roman in its way. The whole time military intelligence is monitoring phone traffic nearby. Meanwhile, they round up their suspects from town office, the schools, and the cooperatives. They shoot them and leave the bodies to be easily found. The climax is a public execution in front of the whole community. They stay in force for a while, but in the end they settle for paid spies and road blocks."

"So far, so good."

"The last scenario is the hostile village scenario: Currulao, Apartado, Carepa, and Chogorodo—all to the south of Turbo. This time, an army patrol arrives early in the morning and grabs priests and police. They show them a list of names and demand that the individuals be apprehended. Usually, the locals have kin or social relationships and do not want to turn their buddies in to the army. The army leaves with the explicit threat that the next visitor will be the paramilitaries. The army sits back and waits for the phone lines to go wild. A few days later the paras arrive. They already know who has left town and who has stayed. They walk into town in formation, breaking windows, spraying graffiti—they want to know where the guerrilla camps are. They probably already know, but they want to see who will tell them—the whole community knows already. The ones who know, but don't talk—they shoot. They can't yet hold these places, but they let people know they don't have much time to get on the right side of God. They usually rotate in about once a week. They shoot about 5-10 people, ask the same questions, and leave."

"Good analysis, Tommy…" He stroked his chin and thought for a moment.

"What do you see as their strengths?"

"Ruthlessness. These guys are ice-cold killers. They come from nothing, and they expect to die or go back to nothing. We used to call them 'thrill killers.'"

"Quite."

"Anything else?"

"The Colombians are incredibly clever people—they are natural hobbyists and tinkerers. They love the technology and integrate it well into command. They also want our respect, Dr. Fuller. They are desperate for someone to take them seriously."

"Weaknesses?"

"They are corruptible. They want to kill the Don to become the Don. They are stealing ranches from innocent people and damaging the brand."

"Excellent stuff—it will be a shame to lose your insights at the level of tactics and objectives."

"What do you mean, Dr. Fuller?"

"I have some good news from the point of view of national interest. We're not shacking up anymore; we've gone legit. Congress has appropriated $180 million for weapons and training. We are 'loud and proud' as they say in 'Gay Paris.' We are going to stock the shelves around the clock from the Amazon to the Caribbean!"

"I gather HQ will be in Cimitarra?"

"In the sense of stockpiles, there is no HQ. In the sense of research and development, Cimitarra is our place."

I began to realize at that moment the basis for the pose that Cody Pryor struck on the runway the previous afternoon. He knew that with appropriations came legitimacy, and no need to utilize talented locals anymore. Cody, I felt sure, would find his way onto the team.

"Do I get my plane back?" Dr. Fuller laughed again.

"Of course. Delivered to the airport of your choice in Panama or Colombia."

"I guess this is goodbye, Sir."

"Not quite goodbye, Tommy. You have insight and flexibility and tact. You can't teach those things. There are some projects you may be interested in, but I have to get some approval. For now, I want you to take some time off. Take your wife to Washington for vacation. Think about what you'd like to do next. I will contact you through your father-in-law. How does that sound?"

"I have been proud to serve my country, Dr. Fuller. That's all I can say for now."

"Rest up, Tommy. We left a nice present for you in an envelope in Randy Keuken's office." I gave him a quick wave and walked away from the camera.

With my clothes having a burnt smell, my hair singed from fire sparks, my own personal odor rather more than repellent to the counter person in the Panama airport, the airline was probably correct not to seat me until I cleaned myself up. I checked into my favorite airport hotel, paying a healthy tip for my clothes to be washed and returned to me in two hours. My fever had abated somewhat, but after I arrived home in Cali late at night, I fell back into a deep fever from which I did not leave my bed without assistance for the next six days.

Every time I pushed my way out of bed toward a robe or a telephone, Amelia intercepted me and gave me pills that sent me way back down into a long sleep. I saw images of the Colonel, Mrs. Hernandez, and Nando, in which Amelia yelled at them both, but it may have been only a dream. Eventually, my fever broke, and I woke up—apparently on a school day—in a sweat-stained and rank bed. Amelia had taken to sleeping in the guest bed. I tried to stand, but felt a strange pull in my arm where a needle was connected to an IV on a metal pole. I had to pee, so I pulled it out of my arm, and wormed my way to the bathroom.

The scale read fifteen pounds below my normal weight. Coming out of the bathroom, I noticed on the opposite wall a new mattress, still in its factory wrapping. The envelope from Randy Keuken's office was on my dresser, and I opened it casually. It was for five hundred thousand dollars. I figured that five thousand was for services rendered and four hundred ninety five thousand to forget everything I saw for the rest of my life. Costanza, alerted to the noise of my waking, walked into our bedroom and screamed at the sight of the nude and bearded anchorite that had snuck into the master bedroom of our exclusive San Vicente condo.

Amelia had hidden my wallet, backpack, and passport. I did not get my usual victor's sex from Amelia that night. Instead, she gave me a quick hug, blunted by her tears and sobs, after which she quickly pulled away from me with a look of pity and alarm. She took me to the bathtub, where she rescrubbed me until I fell asleep.

She put me on a special diet, which included big boxes of protein powder and vitamins, and forbade the porter from calling me a cab. Costanza, apparently, had signed on as her accomplice, calling Amelia on her cell phone to alert her about any attempts I might undertake to put on clothes and leave the building. I still had the key to my cash box in the basement, from which I pulled out a few thousand dollars, and quickly went back to the apartment with a newspaper in my hands.

Later, during my first ambulatory day in the condo, I called Nando to set up a meeting. He informed me that in fact I had not been dreaming, that Amelia in an intense rage gave her father and Nando notice that she would not allow them back in the house. The patio conversation between the Colonel, Nando and me being one of her last memories before I left for Carepa, Amelia had not understood the duality of my employment in the north, of which Nando and his father represented only half of my business.

Nando told me to go to the condo pool in two hours.

I was wrapped in a bathrobe on a chaise lounge chair like a Palm Springs invalid when Nando strode toward me, awakening me with a tap on the bill of my Giants cap. He was dressed in his khaki uniform, accompanied by two guards that stood near the pool gate. For once, there were no sardonic openings or dismissive greetings in his remarks. Instead, he put his hand on my forehead—almost with tenderness— to see if my fever had really gone down enough to make his briefing worthwhile.

He spoke in English. "Hello, Tommy. How do you feel?"

"Weak, but alert. I am only taking vitamins, not sedatives—that's what Amelia tells me."

"You were way out there for a few days—we had our family doctor see you one night when your temperature reached one hundred and three. We called one of our hospitals and had you connected to the IV. Amelia was going crazy. Her mother made her go to school just to remove her from the house. She stayed with you during the day until Amelia got home. You did not eat anything. You took everything from the IV. The doctor even brought some pills for Amelia—she was waking you up with her tantrums."

"I only remember your faces and Amelia yelling."

"That was the only time she has ever raised her voice at her father. She demanded to know where the Colonel had sent you. Of course, he did not know, but she did not believe him."

It was like the Amelia I knew from the military hospital. She placed an "under new management" sign on my early, unreliable attempts at rejoining life in that hospital. I knew that Amelia never wanted to relive those experiences. This brought it all back to her—my incapacity, weakness, and helplessness. It was not how she ever wanted to see me again.

"It's not anyone's fault. Bad water led to lack of hydration, which led to fever. I walked into a drinking party in Turbo and could not say no. Anyway, tell me what is going on in this town."

"You are lucky it was not malaria. Anyway, the cell is M-19. They think the paramilitaries are too extended in the north, and that Cali is open territory. These cells are inexperienced; they want to break into the kidnapping business, more than extend their reach."

"Who is the cell leader?"

"He is a sociology professor at the university. The apartment has a radio—it's at the top of the building and connected to an antenna they put on the roof. Amateurs. That makes our job easier. We are taking the signal from there—we don't need the apartment."

"Are there more cells in the city?"

"No, mostly they talk with the jungle and ask for more funds. The M-19 leadership is losing patience. They want a major kidnapping "

"Why are they hesitating?"

"Besides the fact that we have beaten and tortured each of them, shown them family pictures, and have them under surveillance? Nothing, I guess."

"What do we do then?"

"We tell them what to say and ask on that radio—if they don't, we kill them. For now, it is intelligence gold."

"Have they mentioned Amelia?"

"Amelia—she was not actually the target. You were."

"Me?"

"They have their sources too. You travel in certain circles, etc. etc. They figure capturing an actual CIA agent will boost their terrorist ratings."

"You have not told Amelia?"

"No, those wannabe revolutionaries are not allowed within five hundred meters of Amelia."

It was distinctly possible that Ivan slipped them that information.

I was beginning to feel sleepy, wondering if perhaps Costanza had instructions from Amelia to spike my orange juice with more sleeping pills.

"Is there anything else, Nando?" He registered my fading ability to understand him.

"Yes, I'll be brief. Your father, Ambassador Faraday, is retiring in two weeks. Amelia accepted the invitation to fly to Washington during your incapacity. Hence, her desire to fatten you up for the family appearance. You both—and the girls—will spend a week in Washington as guests of the ambassador."

"In his house?"

"Ask Amelia, marika."

"Ok. What's next?"

"You have to go to court before you leave."

"Why?"

"Ivan strikes back."

"How?"

"First, the timing. It would be too suspicious for you to leave the country while under subpoena, so we had the Fiscalia appointment moved to next week."

"What is the subpoena?"

"It covers your testimony, medical records, including all doctor notes from the night of the Liverpool Bar shooting to the present."

"You are going to have to explain, Nando."

"The bartender's version of events has no factual support—no other witnesses, no forensics, no bodies. The only things that could corroborate his version are your x-rays or your confession. Ivan knows you will not talk. Your medical records would allow Ivan to start telling stories about what happened since it would support the testimony of the bartender. Then, he would file a motion to hold you as a protected witness— probably in a basement cell in Bogota-for an indefinite period of time."

"Shit."

"Almost. Of course, we are going to file motions against the subpoena. The first is that the materials he wants have national security importance. The second is that you are engaged in matters involving national security, which would be harmed by the continuation of this investigation."

"What is the worst that could happen?"

"You leave the country with one of your new speed boat friends, and fight an Interpol warrant that will eventually go away with a change in administration."

"Nando, don't kill the bartender, please." My eyelids wanted closure at that moment more than my mind wanted sense.

The rest of his discourse sounded eerily like the first sounds I awakened to in the military hospital over two years ago. Before sleeping, I felt two pairs of arms drag me away from the pool, up an elevator, and up the stairs to my bed. That night, Amelia screamed at Nando on the phone for "thuggery" and "deception." She told him to stay away from her husband and her house. I was certain of that.

The following Monday, I turned the tables on poor Costanza. I ground into powder two sleeping pills, which I slipped into her morning coffee, putting her in a deep sleep before the introduction to her favorite morning TV gossip programs were over. Dressing quickly, I made it to the federal building in downtown Cali in time to meet my lawyer, Danny Bonilla, who was new to civilian law, but well known to the Colonel as a talented CNP lawyer.

The Colonel had likely briefed him on my current condition, since his only instruction for me was to remain completely quiet during proceedings, and only say the exact words that he would whisper to me. We entered the hearing, formally a request before a judge to seize my medical records from the CNP, so that Ivan could begin thereafter to have solid legal ground on which to issue subpoenas for my testimony under oath. In a purely civilian case, he would already have his hands on my records, but he needed to thwart any defensive moves from the Colonel and the CNP. Another lawyer joined us in our walk into chambers.

Ivan was not part of the team of opposing counsel, but sat in the audience. All refined smugness and sangfroid, which I could not imagine he earned through any work requiring sweat, he would not look at me at all. He looked sharp in his grey suit, but soft and jowly from too much cuisine and too little exercise.

The Cali Fiscalia made their opening argument through a vivid retelling of the facts known to them through their key witness. Throughout the presentation, Ivan, through the voice of his Cali counterpart, keenly avoided any mention of Amelia in the bar, more than likely to prod me toward a confession that would avoid her role in the murders. Indirectly, he credited me with the capacity to do the honorable thing, but only when trapped and without recourse. That was a charitable way of paraphrasing Ivan's view of me. "On that occasion, we have evidence that Mr. Connolly was present in the Liverpool Bar during these acts of murder, and may have had a role in the night's carnage."

The judge seized on this last point. "You wish for Mr. Connolly to testify against himself based only on the testimony of a single witness?" Ivan would not be that sloppy. "No, your honor, we only seek medical records which would prove that Mr. Connolly suffered injuries on that particular night in the Liverpool Bar. We do not regard him as a suspect, but since the Cali police files are almost empty with regard to the night and event in question, it would assist our investigation into these murders to gain access to the only forensic evidence concerning a non-decedent from the criminal acts of that night." That was his plan—to convince a judge that the Fiscalia just wanted to clear up a few details in order to bury the incident for good.

The judge, thankfully not given to letting lawyers indulge in too much palaver, signaled to Danny Bonilla that it was his time to offer rebuttal. "Your honor, the events of that night touch upon matters of national security at the highest levels. It would risk the personal security of Mr. Connolly as well as national security for any details of this event to leave the protection of the CNP medical staff. We cannot divulge the particular role Mr. Connolly has played—and continues to play—in the defense of Colombian national interest, for which he is not a citizen, but still participates in activities involving the highest levels of intelligence and trust."

"I offer the court letters of commendation from the Chief of Army D-2 Intelligence and the Colombian National Police Office of Intelligence—both affirming the role that Mr. Connolly has played and continues to play in the defense of the nation. As counsel, I have advised Mr. Connolly not to offer any testimony, submit to any medical examination, or waive privilege of his medical records from any doctor in Colombia. If I may, your honor." Bonilla handed the clerk the two letters, which the judge perused closely.

I looked over my shoulder at Ivan, and gave him a look that said, "We could have ended this a long time ago."

He looked away the whole time.

"Based on these considerations of national security, as evidenced by supporting affidavits from the leaders of our national security institutions, I place before your honor a writ for protection of constitutional rights, based on the need for absolute secrecy about the role, dates of arrival in Colombia, personal history, physical appearance and any changes thereto, and known whereabouts of Mr. Connolly, who is still actively cooperating of his own free will with organs of national security." Bonilla handed that document over to the clerk as well.

I sat quietly, not making eye contact with anyone, or speaking to Bonilla.

Ivan left the courtroom before the judge spoke without speaking or looking back. The writ complicated matters for him. He could no longer place me in that bar or compel evidence to support his sole witness. He certainly did not want to hear what the judge announced next.

"In light of the serious contribution Mr. Connolly purportedly has made to activities of intelligence in this country, as these letters attest, I will need time to weigh the public's right to inquire into Mr. Connolly's role—if any—in the tragic events in the Liverpool Bar against the likelihood that harm would come to him personally or to the national interest should any information about his person be made in a public forum. Therefore, this court will adjourn in order to consider, firstly the merits of the writ of protection of constitutional rights, and the prosecution's request for the release of Mr. Connolly's private medical records."

Outside on the sidewalk, Nando grabbed my arm before I could get into a cab.

"Congratulations, marika, I hear you won by knock out."

"The judge can still rule for a limited release of my records."

"I wouldn't bet on it."

"You know something, Nando?"

"The judge's assistant and I had an interesting talk during your hearing. I would be surprised if he ever acts on Ivan's request. Of course, he will rule in favor of your writ. But a dual outcome of yes on the writ and no to Ivan was what we were in the market for."

"For fuck's sake, Nando—you bribed him?"

"Not yet. We made the deal when he agreed to hear the motions last week. Since they involved constitutional writs, it gave him a lot of cover to turn down Ivan. Everyone knows what this is about. This just about shuts down Ivan's little operation." He was like a little brother who wanted to impress his big brother by stealing cigarettes from a liquor store.

"How much?"

"A hundred-thousand U.S."

I put my arm up for another cab.

"You pay him, Nando. It should never have come this far. This was sloppy, like the cell at her university." I gave him a moment's pause to defend himself, but he fixed his gaze on mine and would not release it.

"What if Amelia finds out about today? What if Ivan leaks something to a newspaper? This shit is getting too close to her. That's how I manage things, Nando, I keep them the fuck away from Amelia. You saw her reaction to my illness. She's not as tough as she looks, dammit! She needs protection from people like Ivan before he gets this close. Someone did not do his fuckin' job to protect her. You pay!"

Constitutionally, the judge had ten days to approve Bonilla's writ. He probably stamped it minutes after his assistant picked up a thick envelope from one of Nando's guys on a bench in a local park. Amelia and I went to Washington a few days short of the formal limit.

Dr. Fuller had not meant to wish me a happy retirement from service in clandestine operations. He had intimated, though, that the era of rough living was over for me; that under the aegis of my father in Washington, D.C., I would parlay my experience and contacts into a high-level career in informal intelligence work—perhaps as a manager of a CIA front company in the suburbs of Virginia, or a manager of operations from within a U.S. airport. That was my first tropical disease, though. In its aftermath, I lacked the ability to sustain any kind of informed reflection. Its only mercy was that I no longer dwelled on the gruesome deaths I had seen. I was skinny, pale and weak. I would listen to whatever offer came my way in Washington.

But I was a changed man within, though they probably could not see how much that was true.

CHAPTER THIRTY-SEVEN

Apart from those times when they crawled too close to the air conditioner in the condo, our two girls had never known cold before, especially the pure, late-winter freezes in Washington, D.C. Neither Amelia nor I had proper clothes, nor were we able to find clothes in Cali that would suffice the pure cold blasts that we encountered on the sidewalk outside the D.C. airport. We rushed as a family block into our limousine, and with the girls wrapped in extra airline blankets which Amelia had sneaked into her backpack, we went directly to our hotel on 16th Street.

Amelia had arranged most of the details of the trip through frequent telephone conversations with the Ambassador's wife, Celeste, a woman about whom I knew less than Amelia had learned in a few weeks. Convalescing, mostly in the sauna at the club, or over an illicit scotch in the Colonel's office, I did not take part in these arrangements, only raising the issue that Amelia was still a student, which Amelia informed me was not an issue that required T. Connolly's attention. The formal dinner was on Saturday night, and I had no idea what Amelia had planned for the five days until then.

The retirement of an ambassador with nearly forty years of service would attract some of the highest names in policy circles in Washington. This was a chance for a lot of mercenary politicians to play nice, and not spew a narrow set of hate points for the cameras. The Ambassador was not a polemical figure in Washington, and therefore widely-liked and trusted. He was little known outside policy circles, never appeared on political talk shows, or wrote tattle-tale books about any of the Presidents he had served or the major events of recent history in which he had undoubtedly taken part.

He began his career out of Yale during the late Eisenhower Administration. He had served in each administration since then—that I knew--but never shared with me during my boyhood meetings within which department of government he actually carried out his duties. I had some suspicions, though. He had obviously been instrumental to the early and final stages of my CIA-contractor career, and probably knew of my semi-comical mission to Geneva. One did not direct a U.S. embassy without passing the odd undercover agent in the hallways.

Cody Pryor scornfully threw out the idea that my activities there had been a lark, or a favor between high-level players to find a useful occupation for a wayward son whose ideas about himself and the world required some leavening in dangerous, but controlled circumstances. I had no idea whether the Colonel concurred with any of these events or outlooks that I imputed to Cody.

The Colombian side at least took me seriously. They knew the danger out there was real—whether through a sniper's bullet or a surprise attack from a nearby grove of trees. They knew nothing about the absurd sums of money the CIA arranged for me to be paid. Conversely, they almost assuredly knew about my side-business with Stevenson and Nando and my cooperation with the Seventeenth Brigade in Carepa. Those weapon shipments allowed distant bases to defend themselves, and later, helped the paramilitaries take and hold many of the FARC's drug routes in the north of the country. I never had a shipment intercepted, nor was there ever a dispute about the goods I delivered. Word got back to me that I would always be welcome again in their circles. On balance, the Colombians had more reason to appreciate T. Connolly than question his motives.

The story of my departure had to be more complicated than that. Dr. Fuller must have learned about Ivan through his sources in Bogota, and sensed that his ability to shape outcomes in my favor—and keep away scrutiny about their activities in Colombia—was limited. In that sense, he was exfiltrating me from my own growing troubles before they exploded in the middle of his new budget appropriation. Ivan, if he had known what I did in Colombia, would also have known that I could not be the object of subpoenas in Bogota and Cali, and still serve as a contractor for U.S. intelligence.

I had not thought about leaving Colombia, nor had I ever discussed it with Amelia. People like me did not make millions of dollars, albeit somewhat obliquely in the sense of classical crime or virtue, but I had. The Colonel, with all his venal flaws, was someone whose good opinion mattered to me. Caring for his daughter and country far more than he cared for me, he was still straight with me. He was above all a patriot, and even though his corruption enabled narcos to avoid extradition, I had the feeling that they had to contribute in their own way to the war effort as a condition of their checkered liberty.

He was not my father, but he enjoyed my successes; more importantly, he honored my commitment to the safety of his daughter, which was about as close to unalloyed esteem as I ever enjoyed in my life. He also appreciated the small deeds I undertook to crush the insurgency.

Amelia told me the Ambassador had a son, older than I was, who lived in Washington, but was not involved in government or contracting or influence-peddling. I imagined that was what CIA agents or defense contractors or connected lawyers would say to someone outside the business. I imaged him parachuting into the jungle only a few miles from where I was, and departing entirely due to his own jungle aplomb. Apart from that, she said that Celeste had been hesitant to talk about him.

Ambassador and Mrs. Faraday arrived at our hotel a few minutes before noon. The procurement of suitable, warm clothes for Amelia, the girls and me occupied much of the morning, and took place across two downtown malls. Amelia attended to the late-sleeping girls, leaving me the only available resource to do the actual shopping. I had been back in our hotel room only a few minutes when the concierge rang our room and announced that the Ambassador was waiting for us in the lobby. He waited approximately nine minutes, while I ripped price tags off of thick sweaters, parkas, socks, and boots, and Amelia placed the girls in our double-wide stroller for the trip down the elevator to their paternal grandfather.

The last time I saw the Ambassador was during my junior year of college. We had lunch at one of the named hotels in San Francisco during which we briefly discussed the direction of my studies and my plans, which I chose not to divulge to him. Even then I did not want or need his intervention to make great things happen for me. I shared little of my limited outlook on political issues of the day, an attitude that he took in good stride, knowing that they were unformed and jejune anyway. After that, I did not hear from him again, and only knew of him from my early view of his slacks crease in the CNP hospital and Amelia's subsequent reference to his visits.

Amelia and I walked out of the elevator like outdoor catalog cover models. The Ambassador, now in bifocal reading glasses, which he quickly pocketed when he noticed a stroller exiting the elevator, was slower than Celeste to rise and greet us just beyond the elevator door. He was not to be denied, though, the right of first view of his granddaughters. They arrived at the same time and from both sides of the strollers looked down upon the girls and, after moments of calm awe and followed by furtive arrangements of the girls' blankets, finally took full notice of Amelia and me. Celeste gave Amelia a hug, while I settled for handshakes from both.

The girls would not be kept down, informing us with little squeals that they resented being prone on their backs while the rest of the lobby walked and talked freely. Amelia and I held each girl, but in a few moments we transferred the girls to the arms of the Ambassador and Celeste, who were rubbing their fingers to get a feel of baby skin on their cheeks for probably the first time in their lives. They sat back down with a granddaughter on their chests, and took in the coos and grasping of their little hands.

Celeste was in tears, and not having a free hand, Amelia took a towel from the stroller to attend to her eyes. The Ambassador delivered a steady hum and back-patting to a gleeful Bonnie. "They are beautiful, Tommy," Celeste intoned. The Ambassador was transfixed. His face was a few years older than the last time I saw him, but he was still a handsome man, and he looked in command of the tiny creature in his arms. Celeste beamed at the happiness subtly suffusing her husband's face.

I sneezed, which brought peace to an end. Bonnie jerked away from the Ambassador's chest, and began to cry. "Tommy!" Amelia volleyed at me.

"I'm not used to this climate, mi amor." It likely occurred to everyone that she was less familiar than I, but I was still several months away from robust health. Amelia went back to the stroller for two milk bottles from their heated compartments. She handed one to Celeste, and asked the Ambassador if he wanted to give Bonnie her milk.

"Of course, Amelia," who carefully put a bib on the Ambassador's shirt front, and then slipped a bottle nipple in Bonnie's mouth.

Had we allowed him, the Ambassador would have wheeled the girls down the middle of Pennsylvania Avenue. He had thereafter the face of an ambassador examining his own honor guard that day. We decided to eat in the hotel restaurant since the girls would need a full nap soon. In short order, I was acutely aware that I was dining with a professional diplomat, who flawlessly brought ease to the tenor of our mostly pedestrian conversation. He smoothly adhered to the script and did not touch upon US or Columbian politics, my recent employment or my distant role in the life of the Ambassador.

That left baby details, a topic upon which Amelia and Celeste were able to sustain conversation for most of lunch. The Ambassador and I were not cold to each other, but we had not reached terms of address, let alone endearment, that would have made conversation a smooth enterprise. We agreed to meet for dinner the following night.

The next day I made the acquaintance of Andrew Faraday, first child of the Ambassador, lead singer of the local band "The Moolah" and lunch-shift waiter at a restaurant for hurried office workers a few blocks from the federal department office complex. Amelia had evidently received an invitation from Celeste for shopping, though lurking somewhere in her tone must have been some rough sketch of Andy that dissuaded her from accompanying me. So, I traveled alone to his restaurant and arrived after the last of the lunch crowd had returned to work.

He was about ten years older than I, green-eyed, black-curly-haired, with tattoos on his forearms beyond his Black Flag t-shirt. He chain smoked Marlboros throughout our conversation. Instead of getting off his bar stool to shake my hand, he nodded at the chair next to his.

"So, you are the famous Tommy. I'm Andy."

"Tommy." Yeah, I know. Dad mentioned that you would be in town."

"I came for his retirement dinner..." I broke off, as he let out his policy toward formal engagements in a sudden rush of words.

"I don't like to get trapped in that kind of bullshit—all those suits and bullshit speeches. I don't even own a suit." I ordered a whiskey and began to pull out cash, but Andy quickly slid some of his tip money toward the bartender.

It was hard to reckon Andy Faraday as even a distant relative of the Ambassador. There was little physical resemblance, nor was there a shared vocal cadence or syntax, or any verbal commonality for that matter, which would suggest that they sociably took meals together or shared time as a family or even spoke to one another upon occasion. They had no common interests; the Ambassador—in a positive sense— appeared to have made no imprint upon the outlook of his son.

This would have made a normal man feel a deep anguish.

"Tell me about your band."

"We are a ska-punk band—sort of mix between the Dead Kennedies and reggae."

"Do you have any club dates this week?" He took a deep drag from his cigarette which, in the stagnant air, was beginning to make me dizzy. "No—our drummer cut his hand—he will be out six weeks. Gives me time to work on new material, though." He prattled on about his writing technique, his girlfriend, her teenage daughter, but nothing about his illustrious father, or my life, at all.

I learned a little more at that moment about Dr. Fuller's decision to cut me loose. It was an assist to the Ambassador, who though he would not personally mention me during his farewell speech on the dais, could proudly look down on his beautiful daughter-in-law and grandchild-producing illegitimate son, rather than his embittered rocker son who rejected his profession, his social position, and nearly the whole of the man.

His particular tenderness with Bonnie also made sense. It was far from clear if he would ever see them again. The Ambassador knew that while Amelia and Celeste could become email buddies, it was my decision whether to agree to the linking of the two families. Hence, the Ambassador, while incapable of diffidence in the face of difficult circumstances, uncharacteristically lacked confidence; he was in doubt that a future meeting would ever come about. He was an ambassador after all—he either knew something, or he sensed something, but he could not get a read on me.

The Ambassador must have taken quite a few sick days that week. For the next two days, Celeste and he arrived for breakfast with us in the hotel usurping control of the stroller almost immediately. Amelia was anxious to see a bit of D.C and had hoped to tour the sites: the Capitol Building, the White House, and the Smithsonian Museums were at the top of her list. And so we obliged.

Deep cold had blown into the Capitol Mall and stayed that week, and Amelia had lost whatever Latina gloss the Colonel's inheritance had given her. We emerged pale and exhausted, and at last, slumped on the steps of the Lincoln memorial, casting eyes weakened from sandblasting snow on an obliquely falling sun.

"I'm so cold, Tommy!"

"No, mi amor, you may lack interpersonal warmth and harbor deplorable attitudes toward the weak and helpless, but I wouldn't classify you as cold." She took her hand out of her glove and slipped a finger in my ear.

"Quite." I coughed.

"I don't much like this climate, either."

"You could adapt."

"In a matter of years, and at some cost. Are you and Celeste planning something?"

She beamed a mute smile at me. "We can talk seriously after you finish school, Amelia. How did you get in touch with her, anyway?"

"My father forwarded me an email from her. We have been speaking for about two months."

"I see. She is pretty open—despite the fact that I am not her son."

"I think you think about those things more than other people. Besides, your birth made the girls possible. He wants to know his granddaughters—what's the matter with that?"

Instead of replying, I thought of Laura Benitez and little Cecilia. "I think he wants the whole package. Me in a safe career, a nice house, the girls in the back yard playing ball."

"Is that so bad? You can be gloomy in Cali or Washington, Tommy—the rest of us would like to have a little fun." She had gone too far—we both took notice.

"Do you regret it, Amelia?" She leaned over and with her gloved hands gripped my face.

"Not for a second, Tommy. I know you don't tell me things. I'm not stupid. I know you walk around the condo at night. Sometimes, you look like you are afraid someone is going to throw a grenade through our window. They send you to those places with putas and cholera and guerrillas..."

"Don't forget the NGO girls with the hair in their armpits."

"You always save the best for last, Tommy."

She kissed me, a small tear forming and falling down her cheek.

"I know who you are, and what you can do, mi amor. The rest are details I don't want to know. Ok?"

"Sometimes they braid their armpit hair with ribbons. I think about breaking my vows to you."

"You are gross."

"Hah! At least I'm not cold!" I kissed her, the first time our lips had ever come together in such a cold lock, literally warming each other from the lips toward the extremities.

"What do you think of him, Amelia?"

"He is retiring, Tommy. I think he just wants a normal life now. He will lose his power soon. It will happen to my father, too. All the papers come for him to sign, but someday the phone will be quiet, and someone else will have the power. Your father is a little afraid. He doesn't want to be alone in his house. You can understand a little, no?"

"Yes. It is all so sudden though—the emails, the trip here, the girls with someone who is their grandfather, but still kind of a stranger."

"Tommy—you don't understand people sometimes. Why don't you think about NGO girls instead?" Amelia laughed and laughed her way down the Lincoln Memorial steps, toward the pond, and to the street, where we took a taxi back to the hotel, and made love for the first time since my fevered arrival from Uraba.

CHAPTER THIRTY-EIGHT

The Ambassador's retirement party was in the ballroom of our hotel. Amelia and I shared a table on the right side of the dais with three other couples: a Yale classmate turned Wall Street investor, a bookish type from an unidentified agency of government, and a scholar from a prominent think tank. I identified myself as his son, an air transport small business owner in Latin America. This description, which was a coded message in the circles within which I travelled in Colombia, came across as only nefarious, rather than supportive of current policy.

There were no follow up questions. The male contingent at the table was entranced by Amelia. I could have told them that I sold drugs and porno outside an elementary school and received the same casual nods and floating grins from the alphas at the table. While Amelia parried the clichéd questions and remarks about Cali and the narco control of the city, I drifted back to my last conversation with the Ambassador during our Friday lunch, which we took without our spouses.

"Have you given thought to your future plans, Tommy?"

"My immediate plans are for Amelia to finish her studies. Evidently, my contract with the CIA has run its course, but a man with a plane in Colombia can always find work. After that, we'll see."

He gave me one of his weakest nods in the history of our lunches together.

"A young man with your experience could do well in Washington. Companies need men with your insight, not to mention your contacts in Colombia." He was no longer having a conversation with a young, country boy from the Delta. His comments, which floated above the ugliness of the world like a petunia-colored zeppelin, were no longer the old, reliable cues for me to appreciate—and emulate—his high mindedness.

"Most of my contacts are on the far side of the human rights divide, Sir. We greet each other in passing and move on."

"I mean your contacts with official commands, of course."

He meant the Colonel, which I knew, but I enjoyed taking the strand of conversation down to the level at which I actually operated, rather than the more imaginary stratum where things happened because men like him willed them into being with the right sort of rhetoric. "Celeste, Ambassador—this is my good and great friend, Sal Manzo. The bathroom is up the staircase and to the right. You can cut some lines there." I guess I giggled at an inappropriate moment, the guests all beginning to stand for a toast from one of the speakers on the dais.

Though on more equal terms, I could see that that conversation had gone no better than the ones during my college years, and explained why the Ambassador's interest in my affairs petered out to indifference until my hospitalization in Cali and the birth of the girls. He never credited me with having a mature view of myself or the world around me. There never was, nor would there ever be, an intervention to set me upon a firmer path, one in which high character happily finds high calling. And he lacked the familiarity that would allow him to assume a sharper tone with me and lift my responses to the seriousness of purpose, which he prized in men.

He continued with his opening gambits, which I childishly parried, rather than addressed. "Amelia is a wonderful girl, Tommy. You made a wise decision with her." He wanted safe, neutral ground from which I could not summon up petty feelings for no reason, and set them loose on his sweet, reasonable attitude. That angered me, anyway. I paid in blood and brain matter for my wife—I certainly did not need a man who had his handkerchiefs starched to make my decisions something they were not.

"She could certainly finish her degree in any of the Universities in the area." I pondered the thought for a moment. The Ambassador wanted the same family experience as the rest of the class of mortals. His only problem was that he had never earned it, so he decided to arrange it. He would not have to transform Amelia. She could find her way in the upper classes of any society, start a smart career in the field of her choice, and provide the Ambassador and Celeste with more grandchildren.

On weekends, the girls would play in his back yard, while he tended his barbeque in coat and tie. While Amelia and I skied in Vermont, they would have the girls to themselves, speak to them in French, and take them to the Nutcracker during the holidays. It all sounded lovely, except for one small problem: me. I never signed on to the idea of gentry Irishness, had been raised in a milieu of hippies, and did not want to be right with the laws of God and Man as understood by practitioners of empire, the men with their fingers on the tacks of the world's maps, the death hobbyists of other country's misery. His grandpa fantasy was just another attribute of his worldview, one so distant from mine.

I had been, if not transformed, at least mentally and emotionally impressed by the smash of bullets into soft flesh, and the last cries for mercy where there was none forthcoming. I had earned my place in a different brotherhood, and while Sal Manzo could not uphold his end of any serious conversation, he was honest with himself and fair enough to me. I did not want to throw bolts down onto the earth from the higher places, or make death grids before returning home to suburban Virginia.

I liked living on the ground, artfully dodging the same thunder bolts and living another day, scampering freely around the earth's bloody ground as the nemesis of men like Ivan and the vengeful Gods themselves. The Ambassador understood this—at least its puerile orientation, since he would have believed the idea and its formulation to be utter gibberish—just as he thought he could overcome it with sweet family images, the trappings of an upper-class life that would attract Amelia and pull me along in her sensible wake. Or, he sensibly thought that I, a close observer of torture and mayhem, would have outgrown a romantic disposition to field work. I didn't plan on it.

I checked back into the party during the last pre-dinner introductory speech, a warm peroration from the Secretary of State about the Ambassador's many postings abroad, from Italy in the early 1960s to the National Security Council at present. "With his wise counsel, with the breadth of his learning and considerable resources of resilience and fortitude—the essence of statecraft, in my opinion—Ambassador Faraday is our Apollo, a seeker of truth and light, a healer of rented and torn countries."

This was how his class in Washington saw itself—not as a meddling Goliath of questionable aptitude for healing, but as a spiritual entity with only material means at its disposal to bring order to the messy affairs of lesser nations, a caste of practitioners with an almost medicinal interest in the ills of the world. I wondered if the speechwriter was ironic or daft; he was certainly no fan of the classics. Apollo also sent down plague and disease to tribes that displeased him, and was ultimately a God that demanded appeasement as prepayment to forestall his terrible wrath. He would have understood grid-management, though; I had to credit him with that.

The audience was openly moved by the gibberish. The Secretary received warm applause from the politically-mixed audience, including the couples at my table, who looked at me with fondness, and who assumed that the smoke that made my right eye begin to drip was actually the upwelling of a proud son, ready to take up the cause of his father. Amelia knew better, but played along with the charade by leaving her seat to wipe the discharge from my eye and kiss me on the cheek.

The Ambassador spoke last. Thanking nearly half the audience for one reason or another, he was nearly five minutes into his speech before he reached the theme of his address. He spoke of his love of country, and the ideal of service, and the importance of calm deliberation upon matters of state, "far from the maddening crowd of partisan shrillness and press inaccuracy." Amelia whispered in my ear, "You have to forgive him, Tommy."

True. But not croquet with him.

The Ambassador spoke next of the great sacrifices that his class made in the post-war world, and the safer, saner world they left behind as they confronted the mortality of their careers. His final remarks were about his lovely wife, and grandchildren, "with whom I will endeavor to spend those precious moments of life, which service did not allow me to spend with my own children to the extent I greatly desired." The Ambassador paused dramatically until the thought and the moment passed.

He definitely wanted forgiveness, but I did not want to salve his conscience that winter. I am not a penetrating thinker or noble-hearted man. I am clever, a little ruthless, and good at what I do, which usually are not laudable undertakings. My job at times was a self-designed cozening of the various Gods—of airports, revolutions, and cash—and not to scamper up to their forgiving hem for a defense contractor's job. I am a bit of a fool, but not a haughty or silly one. I explained to the Ambassador during our lunch that I still had commitments with the CNP for some ongoing operations, but that my wife could stand for me until they were completed.

The audience, given the chance to applaud themselves within the vanity of the Ambassador's address, gave him a standing ovation. I stood as well.

After I flew back to Cali, Amelia spent two weeks with the girls at the Ambassador's house. She attended some conferences at the State Department, and lunched with several of the defense contractors who controlled pieces of the billion dollars that were to be spent in Colombia. She returned to Colombia with the useful contacts that were meant for me, and immediately opened an office in Cali, where she and Monica began to work on legal issues as "consultants" to the big defense contractors. She had taken to call Ambassador Faraday "Dad." The girls recognized the Ambassador's voice on the phone as that of "Gomba."

How my wife mixed with the Gods was her business. I wanted a drink with Sal Manzo, or an impertinent lecture from Leo Huff. I also had Ivan, Laura Benitez and other vulgar matters on my mind. There was no one from the DEA shadowing me on the plane ride back, perhaps signifying that the word had come down about my sudden retirement. That made the next few months a little easier down below.

CHAPTER THIRTY-NINE

$182,000, $93,000, $129,000, $114,000. After returning to Cali, I told Stevenson to convey to his clients that we were raising prices in light of... certain conditions. We would charge 8% now, 3% of which was mine. I added—not at all to Stevenson's amusement—that if any of our clients expressed reluctance to pay us more, they could speak with me directly.

Gloom leached away the bonhomie of people wherever I went in Cali. There seemed little sense in maintaining a society that most people considered six months away from the guillotine. "What are you doing here?" was the sum of the looks ordinary people gave me around town. Even the guys in the club looked at me with expressions that suggested I should go back to America and forget whatever business I had in Colombia. Several of them even sought advice from me to get their families safely to Miami. I could have filled the Cessna with the wives and children of the guys at the club with daily flights to Aruba and made nearly the same money.

But I had reason for optimism amidst the resignation to collapse that I witnessed around me. Instead of spying on ruthless, near-psychotic comandantes and their suppurating youth brigades, I was back at my old job with Red Sox and the Cessna, enjoying raucous nights of heavy drinking and pirate philosophizing with Sal Manzo, and the occasional thoughtful discussion of risk-reward factors with Leo Huff. Even though the checks were smaller, I was retired from the oily, smelly dens of death, the massacre fields and the lime pits, places that would eventually have turned me into one of them, a monster.

Even if it was due to my position as an ambassador's son, I willingly accepted the pass out of hell.

On March 2nd, we celebrated my birthday at Restaurante Simon Parrilla, where we tended to gather as a family, and to drink too much. The Colonel strode into the restaurant in uniform that night, his four-man security retinue on the lower steps of the entrance behind him. He came directly to his granddaughters and raised them high, twirling and kissing and making the faces they loved. I shook hands with him, and came around the table for a quick pat on Nando's shoulder.

The Colonel was no longer a Lieutenant Colonel. He had become a full Colonel, having assiduously escaped the forced retirements—often disgraceful ones—within the CNP. Someone—actually a great number of somebodies—had to pay for the golden age of Cali Cartel corruption. Allies of the Colonel went to jail for long terms, or moved to Spain or Miami; some even became narco lawyers and hidden partners. The illicit gains possible by pairing up with a narco were still tremendous, but the verve to undertake high crimes in order to access narco riches had passed to a new generation of judges, cops, and army officers. The Colonel was now working with Interpol matters, which gave me some degree of comfort, though it would not be a significant impediment for Ivan if he made serious charges stick against me.

After dinner, we went back to drinking. I stayed with beer, but Nando drank quite a few whiskeys, drawing the occasionally roving and rebuking glance from Monica. Amelia, giving me a pass from the usual abstemiousness she imposed on me in public, helped herself to champagne cocktails she concocted with mango juice, and ignored the rounds of beer Nando, the Colonel and I drank with gusto. She did insist that Nando sat apart from me, so that he could not whisper in my ear, or pull me away from the table for a quick meeting on the sidewalk.

Suddenly, the Colonel's phone rang, and then Nando's, and a brief moment later, Monica's. Stares came to us from the other diners, already predisposed to find us inconsiderate, since our security needs required cordoning off almost half of the prized patio seats. Even after bleating annoyingly more than ten times, neither Nando nor Monica picked up their phones. The Colonel responded to his call with uninterrupted listening until he clicked his phone off. With a glance suggesting his request for a private meeting, he motioned us into the bar.

Nando asked the bartender to turn up the TV news, and to give us some privacy. The security team positioned themselves at each end of the bar, effectively closing it off during our stay. A national news program had begun. A field reporter stood behind a news truck in a hunched, nervous posture, the clacking of gunfire in spurts behind him. Scrolling across the bottom of the screen were the relevant data: the 3rd Mobile Brigade—an elite counter-insurgency unit with CIA training and the army's best weaponry—was attacked by a massed force of over

700 FARC soldiers in an ambush in a small village in disputed territory southeast of Bogota.

It was a rout. We looked at mounds of dirt caused by explosions of mortars, and the jagged chips of the pieces of flattened buildings, and the burning husks of cars in a panorama on the screen. There were no helicopters to remove the wounded or chase after the FARC's retreating forces. I did not see a single medic or Red Cross ambulance on that TV screen. Nando pointed out to me that the damage came from cylinder bombs, ingeniously clever combinations of shrapnel and combustible materials, which blew up and fed off air to burn and suffocate soldiers hiding deeper in the barracks.

"A technological breakthrough from your Irish cousins, marika." He referred, of course, to the IRA, with whom the FARC traded drugs and cash for bomb-making know-how. "Now, they can treat Bogota the way the IRA treats London," he intoned, almost in the form of an accusation.

The Colonel asked for three whiskeys. We watched together and mostly in silence the glimpses of defeat and suffering the small screen captured. Combat was the only part of war I had not experienced. By that time, I could guess what the Colonel and Nando, and military officers within D-2 were thinking that night: guerrilla armies are no longer aptly named when they can gather 700 men in a frontal attack that wipes out a highly-trained army unit, one that was trained and paid for by the CIA. The FARC were coming down from the mountains with the élan of a real army.

While hardly a deserter, there was nothing I could say to bring relief to the Colonel that night.

The country could not take more news of defeat so close to Bogota without a complete nervous collapse. There was good news from the north, but that did not matter to people around Bogota—they lived with bombs, kidnappings, and murder, already.

With whiskeys in our hands, we watched repeated cycles of the same images until the first commercial break. There were no interviews with military spokesman, or even quotes from high officials in the Department of Defense. Everyone seemed to be out of reach in Bogota that night. Yet, I knew that within the U.S. Southern Command and in CIA headquarters someone was asking the relevant questions, mostly in preparation for their prepared statements in front of a closed-door Senate hearing that would likely occur in the next few weeks.

While so many were fighting and dying, I was taking mine off the top. But I was through with war. It was never my fight, anyway.

The big pour of guns and ammo that Cody Pryor and I initiated was now a tropical torrent. Military hardware was still in boxes on every major military base in Colombia. But however much we stuffed the bases and brigades with weapons, the political class felt that a real chance at a lasting agreement with the FARC was possible if we all just believed in peace together. Everyone who had dealt with the FARC directly knew that was a pipe dream, but theirs was an alarmist, minority view.

I had never seen the Colonel look so downcast before.

On the drive home, I kept the radio turned off. Amelia has been so glad to see all her family together and happy. She loved her father dearly, and she had faith in Ambassador Faraday, in American power, and Tommy. She did not sense that our counter-insurgency had perhaps come too late to stop the final rush of the FARC in long, victorious columns into the national capitol. I wanted her to have that feeling of safety—of a motherhood high above it all—at least until the moment we had to rush to the airport and fly out of the country ignominiously, like the Cubans who knew early on that Castro was no democrat.

I told Stevenson to stuff the Cessna to the gills for our flight that week. He understood without the need for an explanation, having watched the news as well that night. Sal Manzo told me that I worried too much. "The medicine is working, Tommy. They are terrorists, not a modern army. If the FARC wants to take on Uncle Sam and the CIA, my money is on the CIA." I was not convinced, since an earlier generation had probably found comfort in the view that the CIA would make short work of that pest in the Cuban mountains.

A phone call from the embassy came for me in the condo a few days later. They gave me a date and a time, with no offer of a free flight or a hotel. Coincidentally, I had business in Bogota that day. A client of Amelia's insisted upon dealing with the principal of the company, which was nominally me.

I woke up early with the first light that took quick steps down the western hills of Cali. There was a large manila envelope that someone had slid under our front door. It was probably last-minute briefing materials of some new information from Nando about our precocious cell at Amelia's university. It could wait. Amelia kissed me deeply on the cheek, issuing an "After you fuck someone up today, mi amor, could you try to come home for dinner by seven?" She rolled onto her side, contentedly hugging her pillow in deep sarcastic sleep.

After taking a taxi from the Bogota airport the short distance to midtown, I approached the front desk of a smaller hotel near the midtown behemoths where airport vans stopped and dropped customers around the clock. This one was older and only about five stories. After I announced myself at the front desk, the clerk made a phone call, and told me I could proceed to a room on the fifth floor. I expected a brief confidence-building meeting in the lobby, but it did not alarm me that a military officer expecting a kickback would want to meet in a more controlled setting.

I knocked on a fifth floor door, and saw when the door opened, not Major Pedro Antonio Murillo, but two smiling men in fashionable civilian clothes. We shook hands, and they offered me a seat on the sofa in front of the window, a request I did not follow through upon. They wanted to seat me exactly where I wanted to sit in the hotel room in Geneva, a place where sound waves could travel the furthest without impediment, and light could make my facial expressions more obvious on video recording. I looked, but they did not appear to be armed.

I asked instead for a chair to be brought away from the light and closer to the door. These guys were pretty good. They had that annoying habit of calling me "guy," an affectation a non-American uses with the idea that we commonly use it in conversation. I asked about the arrival of the Major. "He is a little late, but he said to make you comfortable until he arrives," said the one with the black t-shirt and sunglasses on his forehead. My appointment in the embassy was in two hours, and with traffic, I had not much more than an hour to spend with my new gomelo friends.

The other type sat against the edge of a table in expensive khakis with a blue polo shirt. Someone had briefed them that a jaunty manner was either the way to Tommy's heart, or the manner most inclined to subdue the suspicions of a North American. They peppered me with offers for drinks, lunch from the hotel, cigarettes—all of which I declined. I murmured or mumbled my words, causing them no annoyance at all.

In the background was a radio talk program from the Left about paramilitarism. "You understand Bogota Spanish, eh Stamper?" the first gomelo chimed in. They were raising the stakes. They wanted me to know that they were familiar with my legend, and therefore my job. I became even less interested in meeting Murillo at that moment. The confidence of those two did not have a control button to roll back their attitude toward perhaps mere friendliness. While I thought of something to say, I noticed their interest in my backpack, which held the manila envelope and some other papers. I did not follow their glance.

Between them, they tried four or five other conversational starters—California, the next American president, baseball, and of course that go-to Latin American conversation starter, Miami nightlife. I smiled mostly, or offered a "Yeah, that's right" in return. This was not a business meeting. I spoke in a near whisper in response to their questions, meanwhile casting little glances toward likely video-camera perches. After about twenty minutes, I stood up to leave, which they did not impede at all. We shook hands, and I left, knowing that if Major Pedro Antonio Murillo existed, that someone had just borrowed his name for a short while in order to bring me to that room.

Those guys may have been military, but were definitely intelligence officers. They did not care if I knew, just as Felix Rabinovich did not care about my puny legend during our meeting in Geneva. What could they have wanted? I wiped the door handle off on the way out the door, and never touched the chair. I turned down all their offers of refreshment, the easiest way to grab a fingerprint. They had my voice print, but they could have gotten that from a cell phone call to me. They had my likeness, too, but cameras in the lobby, or surveillance in the airport, would have sufficed.

That left me: they were sizing me up psychologically, perhaps in preparation for an operation against me. They had a short interview in bad light, which a psychologist would watch and rewatch until certain small features loomed large enough to hazard a psychological profile.

They could also have been from the FARC, but in that case I would likely be dead already.

Someone wanted to get to know Tommy a little deeper and had considerable resources with which to carry out the initial sit-down interview. They also were demonstrating a certain bureaucratic prowess, that of showing the ease with which they could eavesdrop on my business and move some furniture around, figuratively. They already knew my personal history, including most of what occurred that night at the Liverpool Bar and during its aftermath. This was to remind me that if I stayed in Colombia, I would never walk alone. I had planned to walk away, but not at the point of their stick.

I called Nando from the taxi uptown to the U.S. Embassy, and explained the basic details of the faux meeting, and my decision to come to Bogota to meet him.

"What did you say the guy's name was?"

"Pedro Antonio Murillo." Nando burst into a relaxed laughter that reached higher and higher peaks of hilarity.

"That is too much, marika!"

"Do you want to explain, Nando?"

"Pedro Antonio Murillo was a Major in the Colombian Army about ten years ago. His wife caught him in bed with a male prostitute and made a public scandal. Murillo was court-martialed and had to leave the country. I think he is in Argentina. He is now a joke. We leave his name on phone messages with friends, so that he gets in trouble with his wife. Someone played a joke on you, a sort of comic entrapment… you didn't mention his name, did you?"

"I think I said something like 'when will Major Murillo be arriving?'"

Nando howled in laughter again. "That was the point of the meeting, marika. To get you to say those words. The joke will spread far and wide in Bogota."

"Ivan?"

"Undoubtedly. He is still angry about getting shut down in Cali."

"What can I do?"

"Nothing. Game, set, match, Ivan. He really fucked you this time, marika." Nando continued to laugh until I hung up.

About an hour later, the taxi let me out on the curb. A throng of about five hundred well-dressed professionals stood in a line leading to the main gate. I walked to the side gate, where a marine with side arm escorted me to the third floor of the embassy, a traditional no-go zone for stampers. The escort handed me off to a military sentry, who then directed me down several more corridors until we came to large double doors. They opened, and I entered.

A woman with rich red lipstick and a revealing white blouse smiled at me and extended her hand.

"You must be Tommy."

"Yes, ma'm."

"I'm Dr. Appleman from the Directorate of Operations," a description that said both a great deal and almost nothing at all. She led me to a group of men reclined on burgundy couches. Dr. Fuller was his normal jaunty, quizzical self. Behind him there was a white board with maps of Colombia and the Magdalena. There were two other men on matching love seats.

I shook hands with Major John Gross from the U.S. Army Green Berets, and Dr. Larry Trammell from the Defense Intelligence Agency. I sat on the only unclaimed space, which was on the sofa near Dr. Fuller. It was frosty in Bogota that day, so I helped myself to coffee.

I had supposed that this was my first informal chat as an "old hand," a younger version of those journalistic adventurers who had shared the toil of the Long March with Chairman Mao, or had known Fidel Castro in the early mountain days, and brought back enough insight to make themselves welcome—briefly—in certain corridors of power, and with enough gleanings to produce two or three volumes of memoirs.

It was Dr. Appleman's meeting; she sat on her own sofa chair apart from the others and thanked me for coming to Bogota on such short notice. She looked the part of the workaholic national security type. I noticed the fading red hair with a few streaks of grey, and the nervous thinness of someone who worked nights, weekends, and holidays, likely tending little to either her own needs, or those of her husband. I doubted whether she ever took more than a week of vacation a year, and never more than a few hundred miles from Washington.

She also thanked me for my services to the United States in the earlier period.

"It is nice to have you back in Colombia, Tommy. I hope that your stay in Washington was restful."

"Pretty close to the comforts of home, thank you." I could not get my mind off Ivan, and only half followed her initial comments and the briefing book synopses that came from each of the analysts in that room.

This time, the matter at hand was the pacification of the Magdalena. They wanted to turn it into a paramilitary toll-road, which was fine with me, since I did not even fly over it on my route from Cali to Aruba. The discussion was dense in national security-speak. As the subordinate clauses piled up, I only saw Ivan and his cool smugness in the back of the courtroom in Cali. He never even looked at me, as apparently I did not deserve to alter his reserve that day.

Dr. Appleman reviewed the current social vox populi in Colombia, which was sending thousands of doctors, lawyers, and business types to the first floor windows of the embassy for a visa to the United States. Even the Colombian government had begun to glumly accept some sort of takeover, or at least an accommodation with the FARC, for which the government was softening up the people for an unannounced type of shared rule.

But for Dr. Appleman, it was merely political petulance from a governing class that was simply corrupt and could not hold up its end of a pretty simple bargain. These were not the Soviets, after all.

I missed the first minute or so of her remarks. What was Ivan thinking? Was this an opening gambit, or just some frat boy prank to impress his friends?

"The FARC appear stronger than their actual operational capacity to seize and hold territory. Their banditry exemplifies the capture of rhetorical space rather than strategic space." Super. The problem, she noted, is that political processes respond to appearances and emotions, rather than statistics and relative factors. She must have made those opening remarks a few hundred times by now, I thought.

My head began to rage and pound with anger. Even Nando laughed at Ivan's joke. What if it made its way down to the brigade level? CIA-connected Tommy P. Connolly was bested by two junior Intel officers during their lunch hour. How could I have let them entice me into that room?

It appeared to Dr. Appleman that there was a strong possibility that the current government, with three more years in power, would sign a lopsided peace treaty, which would inevitably produce greater gains for the FARC than their military strength could ever gain for them. It would also give the moribund Cuban regime a second chance at validation. Strategic logic suggested that if there were a sudden comprehensive ceasefire, a distinct possibility in the next year, it would be advantageous if we held territory to the greatest extent possible prior to signing, regardless of the intentions of the president of the "host country."

She meant Caguan. It was a one-word preview of the FARC's ultimate intentions: by 1999, they would have their own zone in Colombia the size of Switzerland. As Caguan came ever closer, the CIA did not trust the Colombian government to make even a half-decent deal for itself. It did not even bother coordinating its actions with its president, choosing to deal directly with army intelligence. So, we—along with a few thousand paramilitary troops with army intelligence connivance—were going to save the government from making a chump's deal.

I smiled and nodded at the right times, wondering all the while what topic the academic Dr. Appleman would want me to expound upon. What was my expertise? I knew something about the paramilitary mind and the loneliness of the long distance intelligence officer. I could not keep my mind on the topic though.

There was Ivan in the restaurant, blowing smoke in my face, and watching my eyes tear up; next came sartorial Ivan, wearing that ridiculous wool suit in Cali, like a British officer in a high collar suit among the savages—including Tommy—in the British Raj. Finally, came Ivan the jokester. How many cocktails would Ivan share with his friends before slipping the tape into the VCR and topping off drinks for his friends, convulsed in laughter, and in thrall to Ivan's brilliant manner of giving a gringo his comeuppance?

Was he giving up? Was his low theater a signal that all his higher approaches would not find legal purchase, even in friendly courts?

I reentered the flow of presentations after mentally preparing some opening remarks. "Now, we come to the rub," Dr. Fuller summarized his ample remarks. "The paramilitary commanders are not exactly the most trusting souls. They do not trust the CIA, nor do they know what to expect if there is a peace treaty. They are smart enough to have realized that no one has offered them even qualified immunity. The quid pro quo is that army intelligence literally writes nothing down on paper about paramilitary matters, and kills anyone in the ranks who speaks to investigators about them. They also turn a blind eye to the petty larcenies and high crimes of the local commanders. And they leave no witnesses, literally and figuratively speaking."

There are always witnesses, Dr. Fuller. It is just laborious to find and kill them all.

I spoke at last—just a few words, but enough to get a toehold in the conversation. "Do you conceive, Dr. Fuller, of some sort of advisory role for me?" Smiles opened up on all their faces, quaint among military planners, an acknowledgment of naïveté in an almost pure form that must have taken them back to their first jobs in Washington.

Dr. Appleman intervened before my lack of savvy undermined her control of the meeting. "We are facing hard deadlines, Tommy. We are about eight months from the expected signing of Caguan. The FARC are pressing for several Caguans in strategic areas for them, including the crop growing and processing areas around the Sierras of San Lucas. If they hold a strategic area by next Christmas, they will probably demand its inclusion as a safe haven, where we cannot attack or even fumigate. We can't give that to them. Our analysis is that we have to push them back into the mountains before Caguan freezes the status quo perilously in their favor. The military task is simple: we push them back into the Sierras of San Lucas, and then we bomb them into oblivion."

"To achieve this, we will require a risk-taking, motivated paramilitary force. The government troops will not be much help. There is an unofficial stand-down notice along the Magdalena, though we expect a lot of arm bands and dark glasses in their pants pockets. We need people on the ground, Tommy. It's that simple."

I dreaded the unspoken parts to come. "We need you to help them run their routes. Specifically, we want you to run the air operation "

"I could suggest a few names," I offered, looking imploringly at Dr. Appleman. She looked crossly at Dr. Fuller. I obviously had some catching up to do in this conversation.

Dr. Appleman took her tongue out of her cheek just long enough to continue her pitch.

"We are in a pinch, Tommy. The FARC have run the upper Magdalena for over twenty years. We are talking about one hundred miles of control of rivers, tributaries, coca farms, drug-mule routes, river canoe patrols, and civilian support infrastructure. We need to take it all down before Christmas. You are uniquely qualified to carry out this mission. It is why your country needs you now. Is that clear?"

Clear enough, but an undeniable setback to my plans to make Ivan's life hell, move a few more tens of millions of dollars out of the country, and retire rich and young in someplace like Perth, Australia or Sao Paulo, Brazil. In fact, it was far from all right. I liked my work with Stevenson, which did not take up much time, and paid ridiculously well, with a level of risk that I found acceptable, and nights in Sal Manzo's den that were suggestive fun for a married man. It was not at all right—there was still an active terror cell in the immediate vicinity of my wife, which I had planned to attend to as a principal, not an occasional observer. Finally, there was Ivan's smug, superior face in that courtroom, and his new tack toward anti-Tommy mischief.

Dr. Appleman, her hands on her hips, ready to pivot on a single high-heel toward a secure telephone line, did not seem to be entering into negotiations with me.

"I understand, Doctor." The comment felt as lame as it sounded, and signaled my defeat. She watched my features closely for signs of fear or loathing. "What do you have in mind?" As soon as the words came out in that way, I was routed.

"We need to get their product out of the country in the most expeditious manner possible. We need to do it behind the back of most agencies of Colombian government. We need to pay them for their efforts in cash and/or with banking services—something you may know about. We need central coordination between the paramilitary command and this room, and a local, soft touch. Does that sound familiar?"

"Dr. Appleman, my experience is in the north, but the same rules apply. These guys don't need help getting product out of the country. They brought those skills to the paramilitary movement. It is where their hearts are at, not killing guerillas. Most paramilitary cocaine goes to their own ranches on the other side of the San Lucas Mountains, and from there into Panama by speed boat or small aircraft. They are making huge profits on their own routes with their own pilots and middlemen. They are feeding and equipping their troops that way. Why do they need our assistance at something they do rather well on their own? They're narcos for fu… God's sake!"

I got another precious smile from Dr. Appleman, who threw a look of slight exasperation at Dr. Fuller, who spoke in her stead. "Tommy, there are always attendant benefits to intelligence operations and outcomes when one controls the terms of an enterprise. Our carrot is that we can make them more money and our stick is to have considerable influence about how they spend it."

She was right. Those guys could call themselves Comandante Baked Tostada, but they thought like narcos. They attended paramilitary summits as military commanders, and sang the hymns with gusto, but they would shoot the guy on the sofa next to them to make room for another guy who could double their money. That was why the army was stiffing the paramilitaries now. The comandantes had the money to run their operations; they just didn't want to spend it on their own boy-armies.

"So—in essence—we are going to run a parallel drug operation to their own, using our routes out of the country?"

"Precisely."

"The cocaine will be local production from lands taken from the FARC along the Magdalena?"

"Correct."

"And they will withstand the FARC's attempts to take back those crop-growing areas with fresh weaponry?"

"With fresh men, arms, and materials, yes."

"Who will know about this operation?"

"You, your team, Steve Dubrinsky, three or four paramilitary capos, and their security people."

"Randy Keuken?"

"We don't have to talk specifics, Tommy. The point is that little Caguans could sprout up wherever the FARC have something worth protecting in the next six months, and this government appears willing to concede them all if we do not change the facts on the ground in our favor. We need to take the Magdalena away from the FARC before Caguan takes definite shape."

Dr. Appleman had a gift for reducing complexities to their essential elements. Still befogged by Ivan's psychological pre-warfare against me, I merely nodded my head methodically at that point, since her analysis seldom faltered. "We have put together a small team to help you coordinate flights from the Magdalena to Panama. We need you to coordinate shipments and payments, and remind them from time to time that the way is forward, not toward the hammock back at whichever finca they stole that week."

Welcome back to mass slaughter, Tommy. Welcome to disgusting, ruthless men, malaria, putrid canteen water, psychopathic theater in the round, kill-joyful boy-soldiers and their heinous cold looks, instant terror among the simple folk along the river, and now effluent-fed fish and mercury poisoning in the Magdalena.

"I'll have to talk this over with my attorney...."

She looked at Dr. Fuller for some reassurance that I was the seasoned pro—the natural operator who had outwitted Felix Rabinovich—and not the cheeky little shit she perceived nervously holding his coffee cup and saucer on his sofa arm. "Tommy, you are in the club now. We have extended to you enormous trust and support, and we will expect equal amounts of loyalty. The legal types can fashion some sort of document that meets both of our needs, the agency and yourself. Isn't my word sufficient?"

What did she take me for? "Frankly, yes and no. At a minimum I want a contract that explains each service you request from me, signed and delivered to my lawyer. The contract will mention each law I am violating, and that you instructed me to take such actions. Finally, a letter from you, Dr. Appleman—or, better—your legal staff, explaining that you have reviewed my file and find nothing wrong with my conduct in my earlier employment, the word employment amplified to full volume and covering any such action I took to further our interests in Colombia. Please sign off that I took every action under your auspices and guidance. I also want 2.5% of each outgoing cargo, measured by its inward cash value, and 2.5% of each incoming cash load in planes for which we are co-owners, or I am sole proprietor. My lawyer in Aruba must have forty-eight hours to review the contract." She put her pen in her mouth and unconsciously gave it a swirl, perhaps of naughty delight—I couldn't tell.

I would not have put up with such impertinence from a contractor, and I hoped that Dr. Appleman would cancel the deal and give the job to Cody Pryor, or some other career CIA thrill seeker. My nerve silenced the room. I had wonderful images of a perturbed military escort throwing me onto the street outside the embassy. "And don't come back, Commie!" Instead, she took notes as I spoke.

"Is that all?" deadpanned Dr. Appleman.

"That sounds good for now." Dr. Fuller was about to speak, but Dr. Appleman cut him off.

"And if this contract were feasible on both our ends and to our mutual satisfaction, when could you start?" The truth was that all the parts were already in place; it could easily begin by the end of the week.

I was fresh out of gambits, or reasons why I should not help my country in its time of dire need. Finally, I saw Ivan in the court room at Cali, snidely and dismissively turning towards me to speak: "It was inevitable you would leave under some type of cloud, but more than satisfactory for all concerned parties."

"I will wait for my lawyer's opinion." I stood up to leave. "I will see myself out. Nice to meet you all." Dr. Appleman followed me to the door, shaking my hand with both of hers. "Don't fly too close to the sun, Tommy!" she whispered to me. I turned and smiled at her, enjoying a view of her breasts.

"Well, you know, Dr. Appleman, 'Mona tried to tell me to stay away from the train line....'" Dr. Appleman laughed heartily, and spoke the next line of the song: 'she said all the railroad men just drink up your blood like wine.'" At least, she knew her Dylan.

CHAPTER FORTY

I began to pull my hair out during the taxi ride back to the Bogota airport, but the taxi driver's concerned stares caused me to settle down in my seat and get a hold of myself. It would have been an uncomfortable walk along the highway out to the airport. A gathering of jackals was near, which were soon to be turned loose on the small, unfortunate villages along the stagnant stretches of the Magdalena. One of my gleanings from the meeting was that the operation was already several months underway. The Magdalena was sealed off above and below the oil, mining and cocaine regions. The paramilitaries controlled the major highways, and labor leaders and sympathizers from the big cities had already begun to disappear. Small villages along strategic routes had emptied out. Now, it was time for untrustworthy locals—defined by the paramilitary bosses in the broadest possible sense—to enter the lime pits next to real urban guerrillas.

I craved a drink, which I eventually found at a kiosk in the airport lobby. My backpack, which I had not opened, still held the manila envelope I found next to my front door. I also was in need of some cheer or novelty, a contract from a defense contractor, or a letter from Leo Huff, or even better an invitation from Sal Manzo for Amelia and me to visit Las Cabanas. I wanted to see her in Aruba again, frolicking in the water, and dancing in Sal's nightclub, where she would laugh and drink with Sal's prostitutes like they were sorority sisters.

I ripped open the envelope. There were two documents. The first was a section of a Bogota street map with an address affixed by a paper clip at the top of the map. The second document was five-pages of single-spaced paragraphs. The memo, from Ivan to his boss in the Fiscalia, was titled "Request for Subpoena of Target's Spouse in the matter of the Liverpool Bar Incident." Shit. Shit. Shit. He was coming for Amelia. Instinctively, I looked around for prying eyes and stood and walked through the lobby to the bathroom, squatting down on one of the stalls.

Ivan had a nice, smooth style in Spanish, and the argumentation was detailed and informed. I read quickly through the parts about the probable sequence of events at the Liverpool Bar, which were correct in all essential facts, to the extent that Ivan knew that most of the blows to the head of street punk took place when he was prone—and already dead. Next came an argument for the Fiscalia to determine the culpability for the events on that night and not to leave unsolved an incident involving the deaths of three individuals.

His heart was not in the justification; Ivan's real interest was the last part of his brief:

"… subject has near blanket immunity from testimony in open court, and with regards to events of that night, due to his ongoing collaboration with Colombian Army Intelligence in classified activities, for which this office has not been able to gain privileged access. Subject also is an agent or contract employee of the United States Central Intelligence Agency, and known as such by the Colombian National Police, the United States Drug Enforcement Agency, and virtually all internal Colombian security apparatuses. Due to these activities, subject's defense argued successfully in a writ of constitutional protection that the revelation of the subject's role, appearance, and subsequent disappearance in the Liverpool Bar would negatively affect the interests of the nation. As a result, subject will not have to testify in either open or closed proceedings about his presence, role, and trajectory during and after the events in the Liverpool Bar."

"Subject's present wife, a Colombian citizen, was present during the whole of the events in the Liverpool Bar, and possesses information and/or recollections material to our efforts to determine the course of events that night. Our witness states that Amelia Connolly observed the relevant sequence of events, and can corroborate the testimony of said witness in its essential aspects."

"We request the issuance of a subpoena in the name of Amelia Connolly for purposes of discovery of new facts and corroboration of previous testimony with regard to allegations of physical altercations and illicit fire arms discharge that night. We do not believe that such a subpoena contravenes the protections of anonymity given to Mr. Connolly, since we contend that he possesses no such right to avoid the legal consequences for any such violations of Colombian criminal law that he would have perpetrated that night. Nor does Mr. Connolly enjoy the protection to prevent other witnesses from providing testimony that touch upon events for which he may have played a substantial role. We intend to limit the scope of our questioning to the events of that night, and her subsequent dealings with Mr. Connolly that pertain to the events in question. In this manner, we will protect the letter and spirit of Mr. Connolly's constitutional rights, and still substantiate the recollections of our protected witness with regards to any criminality yet unsubstantiated by our offices concerning this matter."

For God's sake, Ivan, your country is under siege, your friends' families are paying ransom to get their children back from communist kidnappers south of Bogota, your middle classes spend their days in front of the U.S. Embassy, your family is probably under surveillance already, and you may not have a country next year. Is defeating me so important to you?

Amelia will never, ever take a stand in front of your gaze, and relive the horror of that night, neither the bullets into the torsos of her friends, nor the hot molasses of my blood on her face and arms, nor the monster in bandages she willed back to life in the hospital.

I found merit in his contrivances of reason and law, and his clever ruses de guerre, since it could have been Ivan himself who sent the envelope to our house, but the intellectual jousting ended there.

Once under oath, he could ask Amelia questions from my bullet holes to my debraining of the first shooter to my disappearance for six months of time after that night in the Liverpool Bar. He could keep her there for days on that stand, watch her weaken and eventually crumble, until he found out what he wanted. The play was simple and effective: he was forcing her to perjure herself or testify against me. Even her father—and mine—could not save her from that.

I had to get to know this guy a little better since he had already begun to figure out a few things about Tommy P. Connolly.

Amelia had already applied for her U.S. passport, which she told me was the last business Ambassador Faraday requested before he stepped down. She would finish her thesis in June, and was already planning to spend the summer in Washington. Once in Washington, it would be doubtful that the United States would support her repatriation to Colombia. But in that case, Amelia could not return to see her parents until Ivan dropped the case, or until someone convinced him to do so.

On the Tommy side, his ploy was to ridicule and isolate me from institutions such as the CNP and the Colombian Army, which knew and trusted me by reputation. I had already handed him a major assist. It was foolish for me to have entered that hotel room, or to have spoken at all. It lent credence to his thesis that I was a dull tool, and not entrusted with major operations along the Magdalena.

I had not told Amelia anything about the Magdalena. Leo approved the contract, which I would sign in Panama, and Red Sox had reenlisted for another stretch. I was due back in Panama in two days. I wanted to go somewhere in the country and tell her, but a social event—one that caused upsurges and slow cascades of bile down my throat—was on our calendar.

Nando and Monica were married in a huge mansion in the south of Cali. Amelia and I walked several blocks to get there since the CNP blocked access to the building in all directions. The guest book at the entrance showed quite a few names I recognized as Majors and Captains of the CNP, though none of them wrote down their titles in the book. The rest of the crowd consisted of colleagues of the Colonel in the DIRAN or Nando in the SAPOL.

I recognized my two "narco" pals from the attempted shakedown at the airport bar. They looked a little embarrassed and waved me over to chat, but I placed Amelia on my arm and walked away. Stevenson probably dressed them down pretty badly for their attempt to cut a side-deal with me. The whole system that Nando and Stevenson set up rested—wobbly, but so far effectively—upon compartmentalization. Free booze at a wedding was no reason to get careless and chatty and stupid about the secret details of our flights or their cargoes.

Monica wore a simple white dress with few creases, but an ample tail. Her hair was high on her head; her red lipstick gleamed brightly. She was still a homely woman. Nando loved her in his own limited way, but the carrier of their relationship would never be sexual heat. I could see a continued role for Laura Benitez in her little apartment well into the new millennium.

Nando wore a classic tuxedo and tails; his grooms—including Red Sox—wore identical suits without the tails. Red Sox and I spoke briefly about his restaurant, but nothing at all about the fact we would rendezvous—he from Maicao with my Cessna—in Panama in two days. Nando and I did not speak that night. He sat and conversed with senior colleagues, not introducing them to his clever brother-in-law, the guy with the Aruban friend who set up the foreign accounts for their children's education at the University of Miami, or that dream finca back in some safe part of pastoral Colombia, or even a pad for their own Laura Benitez.

They dimmed the lights theater-style to draw the crowd onto the main floor. We had seats in the first row on the groom's side. Amelia sat between the Colonel and me. Nando, unusually serious, did not make any of his frat boy antics; rather, he turned martially when Monica arrived on the arm of her father and took her small, bony hands tenderly in his large, white ones. He held his head high, kept a straight posture, and seemed sincere in his appreciation of Monica as his bride. It was always hard to tell with him.

The priest's preamble dealt with holy love that provides certainties that few human feelings, which are not all together trustworthy in God's eyes, can. His central simile was to close the circle of love for protection and unity through God's grace.

Amelia squeezed my hand during the mentions of love and pride. When her time came, Monica spoke almost in a hoarse whisper. It seemed she had finally obtained a long-sought goal, a life-long membership in one of the richest civil service families in Cali. It was a good life inside the Hernandez Clan, unless somehow it all came crumbling downwards, an outcome I seriously doubted. The Colonel trusted few people with the details of his private operations, and left no tracks behind.

Instead of a simple kiss, Monica wrapped her arms around his neck and bent him toward her. There were sarcastic guffaws in the audience about waiting for the hotel, and respecting the priest. Music started on cue, and waiters brought out a half-barrel on a dolly with about 50 bottles of champagne. There were toasts to the couple, the families, and to the CNP. No one thanked one of the most important of the uninvited guests, Sal Manzo.

The photographer marshaled the relevant groupings in a parlor with bouquets of flowers. The Colonel stood proudly when his turn came. The photographer placed Amelia, Monica and Mrs. Hernandez in front of him and Nando. Monica stepped aside then, and the Colonel held Amelia in front of him with his arm around Nando and Mrs. Hernandez. Amelia waved for me to join the photo, but I waited to take a picture of us alone.

Amelia held me close on the dance floor during the first slow song, a maudlin American pop song.

"Did you want a wedding like this, Amelia?"

"When I was a little girl, maybe. I got what I wanted in the end," she added, pinching me on the bottom for emphasis. "You look more rested, mi amor—a lot of people are smiling and waving at you. Do you know them all?"

"They must know me through you or Nando. I only know a few people in this room." Smiling? Considering the risks I took to fatten their overseas accounts, they should have approached me with bowed heads.

"Are you happy now?" Amelia asked.

"I am happy to be with you."

"That's not the same, Tommy."

"It's the top of the heap for me."

"I see. Thank you for placing me above your American black music and Colombian beer."

"I came to the decision slowly. You have made some improvements lately—intestinal gas, broken mobile phones, car dents are all down—you are showing a promising aptitude for U.S. suburban life."

"I am so sorry, mi amor. These ijueputa parking garages in Cali are for little mice on their bicycles, not a Range Rover." She laughed and pressed her cheek on my chest. "My tall, handsome, charming husband…."

"That's not the way to go about these things, Amelia," I warned her ironically.

I had not told her anything—about Ivan, Laura, or the Magdalena— and time was short. Howard AFB expected me in a matter of days, after all. "Mi amor?" She looked up at me from her lean-to on my chest, not at all expecting what I had to tell her.

"I have to go back to work." Clenching her hands tightly into my back, she almost bit her tongue.

"No, mi amor, not to those places—you can't."

"No—not there—it is just airport to airport this time. Maybe ten days a month."

"I thought you quit all that, Tommy."

"I thought I did. I wanted to. But a certain agency of the U.S. government heard I was back in town and called me in for a meeting."

"Was that why you went to Bogota?"

"It was after the contract meeting, yes."

Amelia suddenly squeezed my arms to check for the solidness that six days of high fever had sweated out of me a few months ago.

"Can't you just 'say no', mi amor?"

"Not to these people, Amelia. They know too many ways to make your life crash down on your head. Besides, they think I owe my country my talents. The money will be tremendous... I'll never have to work again." Amelia looked at me with the sort of disappointment I had not ever wished to see from her.

"What kind of goal is that? Do you want to sit around and listen to your black music the rest of your life?"

I looked at her sharply. Through stealth, risk, and cleverness, I earned those moments of calm, those Zen scrubbings of my mind in the wee hours of night, my wife and children wrapped in a high tower of safety of my own making. Apparently, I was made of less firm stuff than the noble office-goer. Fine, I was Irish, anyway. All that Calvinist determination to plow an extra field before the sun went down had no purchase with me anyway.

As a child, I gathered my own walnuts from the groves in town and blew up mounds of them with firecrackers I bought during the 4th of July. I took my money in large sums now, and stuffed it away until the next opportunity to increase my take came to me from those people, including the office-goers at that wedding. I had plenty of walnuts, nicely notated in Bermudan brokerage firms.

I seldom was peeved with Amelia, but the maintenance of her charmed life, whose next venue was likely the more expensive suburbs of Washington, came from me—Tommy the intrepid—taking dangerous flights laden with cargo that many would like to get their hands on, and in small, unstable planes that had a tendency to fall from the sky, one way or another. After that, there was lunch with psychopathic, middle-aged misfits and their security rings of complacent, adoring and dead-eyed boy-killers.

If that was not enough, I had to sup with her repulsive half-brother and court the dignity of her father, a master thief in the disguise of a police colonel. I dealt with a cast of characters that Amelia would never have to encounter, through my design and protection, except in the safe, amusing form of cardboard villains in her American thriller movies.

And then there was Ivan, who at least I could understand. Our town was replete with poor kids who got new school clothes once a year, and put cardboard in the bottom of their shoes to last until the last day of school. There were only a few, rich land-holding families in town with sons like Ivan. They never had to fix their own bikes, or get a whipping when they came home with clothes muddy up to their necks, or wear hand-me-down clothes from a thrift store. They developed differently than we did. They felt comfortable in a world where things are done for you, and you were part of a higher order.

The moment of pique passed, nearly.

"Leo Huff got me a good contract. It is only six months. You will be with the girls in Washington in three months, anyway. By the end of summer, I will be with you. You will be treating parking lots in Washington with the same tender touch as here. Things will be ok, Amelia. It will go by fast." Whenever I did not believe my own words, it came that way, a bunch of topic sentences without further development.

"Your father?"

"He would not ask them to leave me alone, and they probably would not listen anyway—now that the Ambassador is retired."

Her eyes began to tear up. "Tommy, why don't you just call him your father?" I tried to put my hands on her face, but she backed away from me.

"Someday, Amelia. I gave him you and the girls. This is something between father and son. He knows that. You have to leave it at that."

"Tommy, you have to find a way to stop this mierda of jobs for those people; they don't care what it does to you."

She was correct about that. The inner-Tommy and the quality of his emotional well-being would never cross their minds. The national interest was like a high tower. Everything and everyone down below looked like they could be stomped on pretty effortlessly from up there. Its present embodiment was the third floor of the U.S. Embassy in Bogota, where people like me received their orders and were sent out to make right the local varieties of mayhem and disorder, like the takedown of Pablo Escobar or the bloodletting along the Magdalena.

"Everybody works for someone, Amelia. Most people just don't know it." She slunk back, knowing full well that her own business was probably entwined in some way with those people.

"You'll be careful?"

"Of course. There will just be airport runs between Panama and the Magdalena."

Stupidly, I let the word slip out. Amelia's face contorted—it was a frozen image of the horrible things she felt and tried to hide from me during our time in the hospital. It sent me momentarily back there, too. "They are sending you to that place? Ijueputa! No, Tommy! That is the middle of the war. No-with all that cholera and putas and dead fish. How could they do that to you?" Beginning to tear up, Amelia put her hand over her mouth and scampered away from the dance floor toward the bathroom, leaving me alone to stand alone amidst Nando and Monica and a dance floor of other couples.

Nando, reeling on the dance floor with his bride, and not amused at Amelia's departure amidst wall-to-wall good feeling, gave me a look of peeved concern, which I shrugged off, and followed Amelia outside to the street.

Go close your little fuckin' circle of trust, Nando, I thought.

CHAPTER FORTY-ONE

Two days later, Red Sox landed the Cessna, devoid of cargo, and slapped around by updrafts in the intense, muggy heat of midday along the Magdalena at the Barrancabermeja Airport. It was an oil town airport. We saw the tails of large corporate jets within huge hangars in an isolated part of the airport. By the time we unbuckled, two large SUVs and four motorcycles had surrounded us in the small plane lot. Armed men jumped off the runners to help us both out of the plane and into one of the SUVs. It seems paramilitarism had made it uptown at last.

"He stays with the plane," I motioned to Red Sox. The man in charge—a tall black with an Uraba accent—told two men to stay behind to watch Red Sox and the plane, while another armed and menacing boy patted me down on the way into the SUV. He tried to take my backpack, but I would not give it him. His boss told him to stand down. "Tranquilo, chico—el es un amigo."

They evidently had not practiced their protocols for that situation.

Minutes later, I got out of the lead car in a convoy of black Range Rovers and motorcycles on a dusty, potholed street in the southern part of the city. The boy-soldiers wore dark sunglasses atop their pitiless grimaces, and instead of arm bands, wore colored bracelets on their wrists. Smart, I thought—the FARC could not attack in paramilitary uniforms without knowing the bracelet for that day and place. As soon as the cars stopped, the boy-assassins split up and ran in opposite directions to the ends of the street, where orange-vested police officers were already waving traffic away from turning onto the road.

Two boys took me quickly into an empty, nondescript restaurant. I recognized Julian Colorado from the corral outside Cimitarra. We shook hands coolly, whereupon I introduced myself to a Lieutenant Bustamante from D-2 Intelligence. There was no one else in the restaurant but paramilitary or military men, which had a single swamp fan on the ceiling, casting enough coolness for the principals at the table, but not the security, who stood at several angles from our table. The three of us made small talk and ate Bocachico, an anguished fish, raised on industrial and municipal effluent water pumped into the Magdalena from the oil factories north of the city.

Julian Colorado signaled a soldier to bring out our nervous waiter, who came to clear the plates and bring coffee. After that, the room emptied of observers. Julian Colorado seemed at ease, maybe even bored, with the tension caused by rigid attention to security details. He was bespectacled in wire-rimmed glasses and angular of jaw, and wore the clothes of a village teacher, rather than the European labeled-clothes most comandantes affected.

Up close, he looked like a tired man. He was beyond mirth, curiosity, or interest in the lives of other human beings, it seemed. He had survived over ten years in a leadership role in Santander, Bolivar, and Cesar, wiping out the FARC in each area while never facing rebellion from within his command and assassination attempts from the supreme command. He had also brought millions of dollars to the paramilitary movement.

A paramilitary hall of famer, I thought.

I had to remind myself: he was first and foremost a killer of men, women and children.

The purpose of the meeting was to agree upon security protocols for the new mission. Although the paramilitaries had pushed the FARC out of the city, the latter still had eyes and ears, and would want to stop hundreds of millions of dollars from entering paramilitary coffers.

It was my intention, I explained, to leave each night back to Panama, and thereby not to increase risk for anyone by staying unnecessarily on the ground. Julian Colorado agreed; we had to assume that the FARC knew about my person and my role, he noted. Therefore, under no circumstances would the name Stamper or Tommy be uttered by members of this command unit. My operational call sign would be henceforth "El Chofer," the driver.

Lieutenant Bustamante summarized his security concerns. A minimum of twelve fighters would provide security for all landings and transfers of product or cash. Julian Colorado would select one man for communications, and that man would speak directly to Lieutenant Bustamante's command, which in turn would have veto power over all arrivals and departures. I was the only other person who had the right to cancel a flight. In that way, we placed less reliance on unsafe communications on the paramilitary end, and more on safer ones between D-2 and me. It also reminded the paramilitary command who ultimately held the strings and who danced on them.

Julian Colorado was anxious for the operation to begin without further delay, but I had to have my say first. I would be a target too, after all.

"When do we start, 'Chofer'?"

"We are ready to fly a planeload out today, if that is your wish, Comandante. After that, we will return next week with your first payment. Our maximum load will be 3,000 pounds. We can fly twice a day for two days maximum. That limits your export to 12,000 pounds a week. You will be paid for the whole two-day total the following week." I paused to make sure heads were nodding and there were no objections. Neither man wrote down anything.

"We will take out as much cocaine as you can provide… from the coast, Cesar—we don't care. As long as you bring it to this airport and the turn-around is no more than fifteen minutes. If you can manage even five thousand pounds a week, you will have a two-hundred-million-dollar yearly budget. Plus, free Disneyland tickets for wives and girlfriends." Even Julian Colorado raised himself out of his funk and laughed a little at this.

"You will provide us with lading documents concerning the weight of your cargo. Our sponsor will verify their accuracy in Panama and pay you accordingly. When the cash arrives, only Julian Colorado or his appointed agent will sign for it. As previously noted, the whole exchange must take no longer than fifteen minutes. You know my take. Do you have any questions?" Julian Colorado looked at Lieutenant Bustamante and shook his head, dyspeptically.

Lieutenant Bustamante interjected a comment. "That reminds me." He took out a folder and showed me photos. "These are Julian's command leaders. El Maestro—he will sign for Julian." He put down another picture. "Hawkins—intelligence." Another photo looked up from the table. "Taylor—security. El Piloto—recruitment… these are the seconds in command in this Bloque. You may see them from time to time. If you lose contact with me or Julian Colorado, ask for these men. They can be anywhere in the city within an hour with their men."

You mean 'boys', I thought.

The deal having been concluded, Bustamante lifted a bag and placed it on the table. He took out a large box. "Your satellite phone. I will reach you on this phone only, so read the manual closely." He handed me his card, on the back of which was the phone number of his secured line. "Are there any other issues?" asked Bustamante.

"My team?"

"It is you and your pilot," responded Bustamante. "You do your own accounting and scheduling. Call me if there is a change of plans. We will handle the rest."

"Understood. When do you wish to begin?" I looked at Bustamante, and then at Julian Colorado, who scratched his chin. As I expected, Bustamante had the last word on official matters. "Tomorrow. Two flights for two days, as you stated before." Once Bustamante finished these words, he became officially engaged on his end of the operation, handing me a sealed envelope, which I slipped into my front cargo pocket. "These are this week's landing times. There will be no need for a fuel credit card. If there are any problems, reach me on your new phone."

If it was a CIA phone, it would be able to track my movements all over Colombia in real time. I had to think about the meaning of that.

With that, we stood up, shook hands, and went back outside and under the swampy pressure cooker of oil refinery and putrid river smells. Sweat immediately rolled down my face. I had achieved my own personal goals. I would never officially have to leave the airport, mix with more than a few selected boy-killers, or cross the river where the slaughter up and down the river had already begun.

We were about to set off back to the airport with two guards on each flank of the runner of our truck, Uraba style. From the river end of the street, I noticed a frantic white girl held back by a police officer. She struggled to pass by him, yelling out wildly toward our convoy in English. I looked at the boy-killers, who were eager to send her to a lime pit. It was not clear at that moment who was the ultimate authority on the scene. "She says she has a message for the gringo," one of the police yelled down to us. Both Bustamante and Julian Colorado had left in separate cars, so I waved off security, walking down toward the girl alone.

Up close, she looked like a standard west coast university hippy, indignant, sexually-disappointed, surly and petty, and convinced of her superior moral judgment. She was even more hippy than my mother.

NGO teams traveled in caravans to the hot zones to glean evidence of paramilitary rights abuses and verify FARC adherence to international norms. Supposedly, youth all over the country simply dropped their farm tools to join the FARC in their jungle hideouts on a daily basis. Their act played better in Europe than the United States, where most of their funding came from. This one was ugly, with ratty hair, burnt, freckled skin, and a boy's figure that failed to form breast cups beneath a progressive NGO shirt. I stepped close to her. "Do we know each other?"

Luckily for her, we were the only English speakers among the eight or ten men who had by then gathered around us. I looked back at the boy-killers, who had come down from the runners and were walking toward us.

"No, I don't personally know any CIA pigs."

"Ok. We have established you possess a strong sixth sense. Now, what the fuck are you doing here?" Her gambit was the usual litany of accusations, which in her case were more or less correct.

"Did you plan some peasant massacres in there?"

"I had lunch with friends. What business is it of yours?"

"You are going to hell for this—to prison first, but to hell eventually."

"For ordering the Bocachico?"

"Funny. For planning and financing massacres all over this country. Do you sleep well at night? Do you hear the voices of the peasants you kill?"

"Where are you from—Amherst, UMass, University of Oregon, Wisconsin? You have that Peace Studies cheap oregano smell about you."

"Cute. Berkeley—wait… I know you. You used to work at a café near the architecture building." This was not good. I needed an "exit strategy" that did not involve her violent murder where she currently stood.

"You have me confused. I'm from Florida."

"You worked at night—I remember you now. You were that tall, cute boy behind the counter."

She knew me. That was dangerous for me, but far more dangerous for her.

"Sorry, not me, I went to school in the east, but here is a little tourist tip, missy. Take FARC propaganda with a grain of salt. Apply your critical thinking skills to their propaganda as well. When you see a fourteen-year old girl in the next FARC camp you go to, ask her how many abortions she has had, and at what age she had her first one. If she doesn't answer you, the answer is probably twelve. When you talk to a capitalist—you know, a guy who has more than five cows—ask him if the FARC cares whether he can feed his children after paying his revolutionary tax."

"I'll do that, but the FARC do not do those things. They are leading a revolutionary war of conscience." The bystanders did not speak English, but they heard the word FARC come from her mouth, and were anxious to be the first paramilitary on their block to practice basic torture on a white foreign woman. Looking back, I saw that the boy-killers had come even closer to us.

I pulled her aside and lowered my voice to a whisper. "Where do hear such crap? They are the largest drug dealers in the world and own more cattle than the richest Colombian families. They are the worst industrial mineral polluters in the Magdalena. Children on both sides of this river will die from mercury poison from their illegal mining. And their children study in the best European schools."

"They don't exploit people."

"You mean hire them, give them skills. Pay them. Of course, they don't. They enslave them. Listen—this is tiresome. Go to Cuba for the advanced course. You are not going to convince anyone with that patter, especially here."

I began to worry about her security. "Listen, you have got to get out of here. These people don't care about your U.S. passport. They will fuckin' kill you." I turned to the local policeman. "She is fuckin' nuts! She's crazy from the heat! She is just lost and looking for her hotel." The boy-killers began to taunt her in Spanish. She looked at me with recognition of her probable outcome if I did not get her out of there.

I grabbed her by the arm. "Walk away slowly. Get into the first cab you see. Go straight to your hotel. Walk away with a smile. I don't ever want to see you again. Now fuck off—fast!" She half ran down the street. I managed to pacify the boy-guards, who likely thought that more prestige would accrue to them by killing a wild hippie.

We got into the truck. I had no idea who sent her my way, or with what instructions, but somehow she knew the exact time to show up at a highly-classified meeting between the CIA, D-2 and paramilitary leaders. She was a little stupid, but she knew things, which would not sit well with Julian Colorado. I could not imagine that combination leading to good times for her in a city turned over to paramilitary management. But something worried me more than the purpose of her pro-FARC road trip in search of dialectical thrills: a lot of people knew I was back in town.

CHAPTER FORTY-TWO

A few days later, a sentry waved me through the gate at the Colonel's base without a document check. The Colonel was noticeably thinner, or his regulation CNP tie had somehow commandeered more space on his chest. His large shoulders were now like tall masts over the bagginess of his shirt that the Colonel strained to push back down his pants when he rose from his desk to shake my hand. The old firm grasp was lacking—I felt as if something had popped in his hand when I shook it. On his desk, the ash tray had the butts of several packs of cigarettes. His voice had risen and become hoarse above its powerful baritone since the last time I saw him at Lago Calima. He offered me a seat and settled his now bony fingers onto the wooden arms of a stiff, upright chair, almost for support.

The Colonel asked me about life along the Magdalena, as if it were a matter of rafting with Nigger Jim on the Mississippi. "I don't leave the airport, Colonel. Security is at a high level. In fact, I think they close the airport when we arrive." Though I could not tell him more than those details, he was certainly able to imply the rest. Our exchange lagging after that, I reached into my pants pocket and retrieved the memo between Ivan and his boss.

The Colonel read quickly through the first page, knowing full well that the only jeopardy for any of us was in the policy recommendation, not the summary of the crime-filled night several years ago uptown in the night club district of Cali. When he got to the pertinent parts, he stood to retrieve his lighter and cigarettes, and sat back down for a deeper, more thoughtful read of Ivan's master plan. His face did not change expression, but each part of his face sunk just a little at the ravenous hunger for revenge from the man who should have been his son-in-law, protégé, and probably ambassador to a mid-sized European country within the lifetime of the Colonel.

"I understand, Tommy—is there a timeline?"

"This draft came to me anonymously, Colonel. I expect the actual subpoena to arrive as a free sneak peek as well."

"You think that Ivan is sending these drafts to you?"

"It makes sense... I mean... no offense, Colonel, but he is an arrogant sonuvabitch. He probably feels that he is giving me Mulligans on a golf course where I don't belong."

The Colonel nodded appreciatively at the cultural reference, which he had probably declined in his days on Alabama golf courses. "Has there been any other contact with his office?" I repeated the ballad of Pedro Antonio Murillo for him. "What does it mean, Colonel? He goes out of his way to let everyone know he finds me an unworthy opponent. Why the low road?" The Colonel just shook his head and seemed to take a pass on commenting at all, when he put down his cigarette and tried to offer some kind of explanation.

"Ivan comes from a prominent Liberal family, Tommy. They would be Social Democrats in Europe—they do not openly side with the guerrillas, but they would rather come to an agreement with the FARC than cooperate openly with the United States. Ivan suffered multiple shocks—through no fault of yours, mind you—but one of the cruelest was to lose Amelia to what he perceives as an exponent of the imperialism that his family has traditionally decried."

"Why the vulgarity, though?"

"Parody, Tommy. His friends around Bogota would see the video as a satire on Yankee spy craft, or beating a CIA agent at his own game." That made more sense than Nando's explanation; Ivan had a cutting, dismissive wit, and would relish the opportunity to best me at a sport at which he had no prior experience.

"Colonel, where do we stand? How can I beat this off?"

"Firstly, it should be apparent that you are the real target, not Amelia. Ivan expects you to agree to testify voluntarily and under oath in order to save Amelia from possible perjury charges—it is paradoxically, Ivan not able to solve the problem in such a way that does not credit you with valor and conviction. But apart from that, there is not much I can do, Tommy."

"But Colonel, this is your daughter. You must have some influence?"

"Tommy, she is my daughter, but Amelia is your wife. Let me explain. After our civil war, our country, like yours, began anew in a precarious balance between regions and parties. We have always rotated the presidency between parties, and we fill our cabinets with our political enemies to keep that balance. We also do not undercut other agencies of government…"

"But the CNP has been under tremendous pressure from Bogota, Colonel. Your friend's careers have ended because of investigations from the Fiscalia."

He shrugged, began to speak, and then looked out the window again.

"I want Amelia out of the country then, Colonel."

"That does not solve the problem. Flight from justice is a half-admission of guilt."

"She can't testify, Colonel—she will walk either into perjury or obstruction of justice charges to protect you or me."

"Let's worry about you and not Amelia or me for now, Tommy."

He knew something.

"What options do you see, Colonel?"

"Let's discuss parameters instead." He took out another cigarette. "Your objective is that Ivan has a change of heart, and Amelia does not have to testify.

"Yes, and not to have to relive that horror of bloody death again as a young mother of two children."

"So, whatever you plan, it has to have the effect that Ivan decides that it is not worth the effort to carry on to the end of his plan. Is that more or less correct?"

"Yes."

"Then the means have to suffice to achieve those ends, but not more than that, and not less than that."

It was not at all that simple, but the Colonel addressed me like a young case officer who only needed a slight nudge in the direction of an obvious solution for a rather simple problem. The Colonel had his own interests, though: he respected Ivan, and knew that if shotgun blasts came toward his family, they should only hit me. That was probably the implicit agreement beyond the wording of the subpoena.

I went back to my milk runs between Panama and Barranca-bermeja. We flew empty in either direction in an hour and a half, and made it with full loads of cocaine or money in about two hours. In Panama, we sat in an office between flights in the back of an unmarked hangar with the shades drawn down and ate hamburgers that we did not have to order and listened to refueling tanks and men laughing and pneumatic noises, and finally a hard knock on the door. "Fueled and Ready, Sir."

By the time we finished our burgers, the hangar would be empty.

I was still amazed at the deal the paramilitary-narco chiefs had made for themselves. Leo Huff, upon hearing the details of the operation in Aruba before I signed the contract, was astounded. He asked me to explain the numbers a second time so that he could take notes.

"Basically, the comandantes will purchase the finished blocks of coke for $500 a pound in the jungle. We load it and fly it to Panama City. The CIA will pay $2500 per pound. The 'paracos' will clear about twenty million dollars a month. I take about two-hundred twenty-five thousand each way on a weekly basis."

"So, your gross, assuming you fly weekly is 1.8 million dollars a month."

"Correct. It's not unprecedented, Leo. This business pays."

"Go on."

"Minus $100,000.00 in airport 'fees'; minus $200,000.00 in pilot expenses; minus $200,000.00 to the CNP and Colombian Army retirement fund. Plus plane expenses."

Leo held up his hand so that he could review the figures one more time.

"Tommy, you are going to clear around one million two hundred fifty thousand a month."

"It kind of sounds too good to be true, doesn't it?"

"It is a deal which should arouse your strongest suspicions about the risks involved in such an operation, Tommy."

He did explain them to me, and they were substantial, but I knew there was no practical way out of this operation, so walking away with some millions did not seem to be any more risky than doing the same thing for free, or out of love of my country. "Leo, my main concern has not changed. The CIA puts my take in a Panama bank. After that, I transfer it to Sal's bank. Make sure it disappears for good. Only you can know where that money is, ok?"

"As it has been since the beginning of our relationship, Tommy— but thanks for the reminder." I had even managed to piss off my lawyer.

In Barrancabermeja, there was no handoff of cash for drugs on a barely-defensible landing strip between parties who may not have achieved much trust between them. We landed, turned the plane around so that it pointed back down the runway, and opened the cargo door. Then the paracos took control. I lost count at about fourteen soldiers around us. Eight of them surrounded the plane at spaced intervals with their guns pointing outward at head level. Four other soldiers unloaded the blue cash bags and placed them in the hold of a large, black helicopter on the grass just beyond the runway.

Meanwhile, I stood close to El Maestro and Hawkins, who looked at their boy-laborers and their watches, nodding in approval at their own direction and choreography, occasionally remonstrating about a slow pace or lack of concentration among the armed boys.

One morning, about two weeks into the operation, we landed under heavy winds to pick up the day's second load, but during the hand-off maneuvers the sky quickly darkened, and wind and rain lashed the plane. Red Sox would not fly, so we were stuck along the river, at least for a night.

"Chofer, this storm will not let up. We control a nice hotel in town. We have our own men as security—you can stay there."

"Alright, let me get my backpack."

"Sox," I yelled from the cargo up to the front seat.

"Come on, they have a hotel for us!"

"No, Tommy. I stay with the plane. They can leave a few men to stand guard until the storm dies down. Then, I leave."

"But they are not going to fill the plane at night, Sox!"

"I will wait until tomorrow, then. You go on, Tommy!" I related his determination to Maestro, who agreed to leave a team of four to guard the plane overnight.

The hotel was a four-story brick building next to a cavernous mall of small shops and kiosk food stands. The two armed guards in the lobby sported the trademark surliness of the Uraba killer and were not at all surprised or gladdened at our arrival. Two men from our truck ride accompanied me in the elevator to the top floor and briskly led me into a small, spare room that overlooked the busy street below. They looked intently out the window and down to the street below, and then closed the drapes. "Key?" I asked, holding out my hand.

"No, senor, we will be outside at all times until you leave."

"Dinner?"

"We will bring it to you?"

"Beer?" There was not even a chuckle.

"I will tell your request to the comandante."

"Ok, no Bocachica, please."

A bed, a small table, plastic chairs, and a single bulb: yet, I was probably safer there than in my own condo in Cali. No one went in that elevator without a key and a reason. Even if they managed to kill everyone in the lobby, the men outside my door would dispatch them without hesitation as soon as they stepped out of that elevator. So, I napped into the mid-evening, awakening only to loud banging on my door, and a shrill, vulgar female harangue toward the men outside my door.

I stepped out into the hallway. A prostitute in a low-topped miniskirt and high heels was pointing her finger into the chest of one of the guards. "Respect me, illiterate dog fucker!"

"Miss, please, I don't know how you got here, but this is no place for you. Please—for your own good—leave now."

A gift for the wayward traveler from my new friends on the other side of the river, I thought.

"You must be the gringo," she turned and ran a finger down my chest. "Papi, I am your treat for tonight!"

I spoke directly to the boys, who were thinking of the career consequences of beating a prostitute to death outside the room of a secret guest of the paramilitaries.

"Tell El Maestro 'thanks', but I do not want company tonight. Just some dinner." Surprisingly, the prostitute broke into the conversation with some claim of prior authority.

"Yes, the same man who hired me today and told me to come to this place and attend to this gringo! Please--call him!"

"Senor, can we use the phone in your room—we cannot reach our commander."

"It doesn't matter. I do not want this woman with me tonight." She squared up and looked at me.

"The night is still young, gringo. You may change your mind. But someone is going to pay me and buy my dinner."

The other guard began to pat down the prostitute, who told him to get his filthy hands off her. "I will permit the gringo to touch me—you can go through my things." He bent down to examine her rolling suitcase. I felt her legs, and tummy, and quickly her behind for a hidden weapon. "Oh, yes, gringo! Just like that!" she purred insincerely.

They made their call and waited near me until they received a confirmation. The woman looked around the room from her own professional perspective. There was a large single bed with an orange spread centered in the room. There was no desk or couch or closet, only a small white plastic table with a few chairs. She sat down there and began to smoke.

On the far wall, a black mini-fridge sat on the floor. This was a classic money-laundering love hotel, bereft of paying clients, and therefore adequate to store me overnight. We waited in silence until the phone call came. "Senor, she is authorized to attend to you tonight, but you have to pay her." I opened my wallet to grab some Colombian money for her.

"Dinner first, gringo! I have never met one of you before."

I gave some money to the men. "Get some beer and pizza and chicken. One of you, stay outside. Make it fast." They left the room with reluctance, realizing that this was a huge breach of security. At least, she made the room smell better.

I put my eye on the door spyhole and sighed. I certainly did not want to start off with any acts that would make her feel comfortable, or that she could convince me to pay for an all-nighter. A soft voice said in lightly-accented English," thanks, Stamper. I'll take it from here." I whipped around. The prostitute peeled off her wig and flung off her high heels toward the center of the room. "I will clean up that mess, sorry. God, I hate that thing!"

"What the fuck?" I let out in English.

She smiled pleasantly, and walked toward me to shake my hand, pulling her ID out of her bra to show to me. "My name is Patricia. I am a Lieutenant in the Colombian Army. D-2. I am presently attached to the Special Forces Brigade in Medellin. Bustamante sent me."

"Fuck, I am so sorry, Patricia. Would you like a beer?"

"You know—that would be really nice right now! But do you mind if I take a shower and remove all this… mierda?"

"Makeup."

"Right. Maquillaje. Makeup."

"Yeah. Make yourself comfortable. I won't be long."

She came out from a steam aura about fifteen minutes later in military issue shorts and t-shirt. Her hair was pressed to her scalp and divided into two equal parcels by a careful part line. In real life, she was a light-skinned triguena with pretty, but not lovely features. Her eyes were light brown, but still darker than her hair; her nose was straight until the distinctive downward curl of its tip. Her lower lip was full, and her upper lip straight and neat. It was a face constructed of lovely parts that imparted less beauty than would have been the effect through a more classical arrangement. But there was enough there to keep a man around for a while.

She went over to the door. "Eh—hijo de perro. The gringo has paid for all night. Now, hurry with that beer and food, imbecile!"

"Do you have to be so cruel with them?"

"They would expect a puta to speak that way—it is more suspicious if I am not rude." She came back to me at the table, standing just outside my reach, as if she made her first stop before the audience of a beauty pageant.

"Well, what do you think?"

"About what?" It was the wrong thing to say, but if she had been briefed on me, she knew there was a Mrs. Connolly.

"My performance."

"Those guys believed it. You had me fooled."

"I feel so sorry to hurt their feelings that way, but I had to get into this room alone with you."

"You could have come in uniform and presented your credentials."

"You don't mean that, Stamper."

"Yeah, you're right. This town is still shaky from what I hear."

"This is a top-secret mission, Tommy. That does not include bodyguards or desk clerks."

"Patricia, I trust your sincerity, but how far does your authorization extend? I mean, why couldn't Bustamante come here?"

"He works in Medellin, mostly. He is running other operations. The legend is that there is no contact between the paracos and the army.

We have to continue that at all cost. You are young with money and time; it is natural you would order a puta."

"You know me well." She smiled.

"Let's have some dinner first; then we can talk business." I took a shower myself, and we had a nice dinner, and then she laid out her business, whereupon, the other shoe dropped.

"We want you to get closer to the paracos, Tommy. So far, they know very little about you. You bring money and you take away drugs, but they need some picture of you."

"My agreement is to convey 'product' and deliver dollars to the airport. It is in my contract. No one told me that there was a social component to this mission—some kind of paracos outreach program."

She smiled at my description, beside herself. "This is the first time I have used English in an operation before. Please excuse me. But you do not understand business here, Tommy. These men will not trust a cold, distant, numbers-obsessed gringo. That is what they have come to expect from gringos. The sense of ..."

"Standoffishness, we call it."

"Yes, that."

"If they know you, we can influence the relationship more."

"Through me?"

"Yes. You are the one who is making them huge profits. They will listen to you."

"Who wants this... friendship between me and the paracos?"

"You are part of an operation between D-2 and the CIA. But we are the managers on the location." She could tell I did not like the sound of that arrangement.

"We are looking after your security closely, of course."

"So, I should assume that the orders you give to me have been agreed upon by D-2 and Langley?"

"I don't know about Langley, but Bogota, yes."

"Patricia, the security situation is not stable on the other side of that river."

"Yes, but the FARC have no forces within twenty miles of the paracos headquarters. They fly helicopters between the airport and there many times a day. Anyway, you do not have to stay for long—just drink with them, and listen to their stories, and once in a while make a strategic suggestion."

"And you will tell me these strategic instructions."

"Something like that, yes."

We both knew that it would take quite a few visits before I could drop friendly suggestions about how to manage their cocaine empire. After settling the details D-2 wished to impart to the chief paracos, I had one more issue to settle before I settled down to sleep. Opening the door a crack, I whispered to the nearer killer-doorman. "Bring me another mattress, amigo. I want to fuck her again in the morning, but I'm not going to cuddle with her tonight."

I slipped open my left eye the next morning. I saw fully-flexed knees and lightly downed soft thighs and little curls of black pubic hair on the sides of light blue panties. The fingers from one hand jogged in circles into the scalp behind my right ear. A finger on another hand ran over the edges of my back scars.

Not a bad massage, I thought. I looked up. "Good morning, Tommy."

"Good morning, Herr Doktor."

"Have you ever had a plane crash, Tommy? Bad car accident. Skate board accident?" she giggled.

"No. Why do you ask?"

"How did you get those scars on your head and your back?"

"That is more or less classified information."

"In which country?"

"In the one that pays me. Why do you ask? It is not operational."

She hopped off my back and slid down next to me, continuing to run her fingers over the scars on my back. "There is a rumor around the armed forces about a gringo in Cali that stopped a sicario's bullets and saved the life of a Colombian girl. He was very brave, and killed the man, but no one knows what happened to him. He was injured, and almost died, but he just disappeared. There is no body of his victim, and there was nothing in the newspapers, and no witnesses."

There is at least one extant witness now, I thought. "That is pretty common in this country. Not every murder makes the newspapers. There is not enough paper."

"Hmm. Everyone thought he returned to the United States. But later, the girl married a gringo."

"I am not familiar with that case. But we make admirable husbands."

"It was about two and a half years ago. The girl was supposed to be very beautiful with a powerful father. It is thought that her ex-boyfriend will never forgive the gringo and wants revenge on him."

"Sounds like a child's fable."

"Yes, it does. Tell me again how long have you been in Colombia?"

"About six months. I was in a monastery before that."

"Como no, Tommy!"

She looked down my body and smiled. "Does your wife know about that?"

"Hmm?"

Her gaze directed mine down toward an uncovered erection. I pulled the covers back over my waist. "No, but she would not be surprised. Sorry about that."

"I am going to shower again, Chofer. I will leave you two alone."

I met up with Red Sox on the runway the next morning after he returned from Panama with blue bags tucked neatly into U.S. Army body bags. "Nice touch."

"Someone improvised on your end, Tommy." The drug truck came onto the runway and stopped near us.

"Sox—do me a favor. I have to run up to Bogota tonight. Can you run this load down to Panama alone?"

"Yeah, Tommy. 'No sweat'."

"I'll explain to my contact here. I'll meet you here on Saturday morning for the next money run. Call me and tell me your arrival time in code."

"Got it, Tommy. Spend a few days in Cali. You look spooked."

"No. Give my best to the family, Sox. Bye."

My last conversation with the Colonel stayed with me uncomfortably, like a recurring bout of a lasting illness. I had yet to give Ivan any reason to halt his anti-Tommy campaign. I had no plans, and time was no longer—if it ever was—on my side.

I walked into the terminal to catch the next flight to Bogota.

CHAPTER FORTY-THREE

"Tommy!" It was a faint, hoarse whine from the other end of the terminal that seemed to gain force from attentive appreciation within a group of European NGO types. "Christ!" I thought. She broke free from a group of Europeans with local artisan shoulder bags and open-toed shoes and came right up to me, beating the whole group by only seconds. "Tommy!" She bent down over my table, sending my coffee saucer perilously close to the edge of my table, and planted a wet kiss on my cheek.

There were about ten of them, half of whom had cameras with expensive zoom-lenses on their politically-active shirt fronts. "You saved my life last week! If you hadn't come along when those paracos stopped me, I would be dead." I hadn't come along anywhere; she had come to me. The only truthful part is that I did in fact reroute her before someone made a phone call, and drove her away to the last ranch she would ever see. She was playing some sort of game to protect them from me, or me from them. Or maybe it was a simple ugly-girl crush. It was possible that even the open-minded Euros could not bring themselves to share a bed with her.

I stared down the first social justice-tourist who made a furtive, knuckled movement of camera to face. "This is my friend Tommy. He believes in social justice like we do."

"Who are you with, Tommy?" said a woman with long, frizzy hair.

"National Geographic. We are planning a scenic killing fields issue." I stood both of us up. "There are armed men outside the airport. They don't have cameras. They remember faces. Get the fuck out of here. Now." Surprisingly, she spoke directly into my ear. "I need to talk to you. In private."

"We have nothing to talk about."

"Just give me a chance. Here is my number."

She gave me another kiss on the cheek, imparting the image that we were early in a budding courtship of mutual attraction. She also pushed a manila envelope into my hand before turning back to her friends. I looked out toward the runway, which had recovered its business purpose now that the paramilitary trucks were no longer on the runway.

During the handoff, at least one camera from within the European group snapped. I thrust her away from my side as quickly as I could.

I could have sent that particular photographer into a nearby lime pit with a phone call, but I was not that person. I did not do those things.

It was a big night for Ivan in Bogota. The envelope that I picked up just inside the front door of my condo had only a single-page of paper. It gave me the name and address of this restaurant, and the time and date of a dinner reservation which Ivan had made. It was a smart tip. There would be security and cameras near his job, his home and his club. Most malls had cameras, even down to the lower garages, which I had learned in Cali.

Luckily, it was a large Italian trattoria with outdoor seating and a long bar inside where I could choose the most propitious places to watch and not be watched in return. I sat outside in a corner table behind a newspaper, a baseball cap, and dark glasses. It is beginning, I thought. There is no way to avoid this, and I would be a coward if I did not handle things starting now. But this was different. I was not a member of a team, and I was not assisting grids—Ivan was my grid.

The file from NGO girl contained a human rights update from her organization on missing labor leaders, university professors, and peasant organizers along a fifty-mile stretch of the Magdalena. The dates of the disappearances started about a year ago down the river, and slowly moved upwards to Barrancabermeja, which still bore the new paramilitary welcome sign on the incoming highway overpass at the entrance of town: "Under New Management."

I could not afford a troubled moral conscience, nor did I actually feel one. The turpitude of this war was not a one-sided affair. The FARC had recently drugged a small boy to walk a donkey onto a town square in a small village in the north. The boy stopped in front of a police garrison and several police officers came outside to see the boy, who was reported as missing. The donkey-bomb killed mostly children, but also all the police officers in that village. I expected the Europeans to at least lodge a complaint on behalf of the donkey.

In the back of the restaurant the staff had put four tables end to end with chairs for twenty people. The red-checkered table cloth reminded me of the restaurants my mother would take me to in San Francisco after we watched the Sunday matinee symphony. Well-dressed couples entered and sat down at that table, all in the space of about ten minutes. I pulled my newspaper high above my tabletop when Ivan walked toward the restaurant and down the aisle between the outdoor tables.

The table was full when Ivan arrived. He shook hands as he walked down the length of the table and kissed all the women gallantly on the cheek. Stacked on an unused table was a grounding pile of nicely wrapped presents. My attention went sharply back to the entrance of the restaurant. At first, I thought it was Amelia, but quickly changed my mind—like that sensation when you see the wax figure of someone famous, and can see immediately that the features did not align, or did not capture the intangible humanity of the person.

So it was with this woman. She was close in appearance to Amelia, but each feature on the face was dulled by a small imperfection, and the whole appearance was not classic beauty, but earnest prettiness. This was a knock-off of Amelia, like the handbags they sell in Hong Kong in the narrow alley shops of Kowloon. Did she know that Ivan enlisted her to stand-in for Amelia during her extended absence from his life? Even her hair was in the style from the time when I first met Amelia, and when Ivan saw her for the last time.

She was also pregnant, and not at all comfortable-looking in the frigid Bogota cold. I looked over my shoulder as she walked to Ivan's table. He rose and kissed her, rubbing her hands inside his own, and then her belly as he whispered in her ear, in the way that only the father of the baby would presume in public. She reminded me of the characters who are written into movies or plays to tell a single joke, or deliver a pivotal speech. Ivan wrote her into his life to salve the irretrievable loss of Amelia, not to plumb the depths of passionate love or rise to the heights of power he expected to with Amelia at his side.

I can't kill him, I thought. He is not a cutthroat, or a soldier like the FARC captain who knew the rules of war, and only wanted the courtesy of a firing squad. He was a dandy in a land where hard, cruel, merciless types were setting up shop and taking over villages, and rivers and states. Ivan could use the courts for a minor squaring of accounts, or petty revenges such as my case, but in the furious rush toward Caguan, the intelligence officer and his paramilitary killers were the law.

It was problematic to kill a guy who needed a spanking more than anything. Ivan was not worth a bullet to anyone in Colombia that year.

I had to stop him, though. He was close to springing his trap, and I had not even set mine. He was considerably ahead, but I had a knack, even as an amateur, for this sort of thing, as even Nando would concede. I looked at my watch. The last plane to Cali left in an hour, so I paid for my beer and left.

For a few months, I had made it a habit to come and go not through the front door of the building, but through the parking garage rear door. That night I ran down the trail from the upper street where I found taxis to my own personal pirate's chest. I looked over the tools of my constantly evolving trade: a baseball bat, tens of thousands of dollars and pesos, a knife, a small pistol, tape, changes of underwear, and a flash light. The cloth sack was wrapped inside a plastic bag and wedged behind a log under some fallen branches.

I could see the lights of my condo, which meant that Amelia had decided to stay awake and greet me, a treat to Tommy, who usually caught the late-night flights and arrived to quiet stillness. Opening the door, I felt the unwanted crang of some grungy guitar music, not at all what I wanted after the vileness of my business along the Magdalena. I grabbed the nearest remote to turn the music down. Amelia, who had not heard my arrival through the heavy metal rumble, rushed back into the living room, stopping and staring at me, as if still unable to hear me. I approached her for a kiss, but she pulled away to the side, continuing to circle on some drunken, wobbbly path. I turned the music off.

"Amelia, what's the matter?"

"You tell me, Tommy." Instinctively, I looked around for the girls.

"They are upstairs, Tommy."

I dropped my backpack off onto the table, which gave me the opportunity to get a glass of water and check how much alcohol Amelia had poured into herself. I had never seen this before: Amelia in a state where she was either a few drinks or bad memories away from wicked anger. I went up the stairs to check on the girls, who were thankfully asleep, apparently unperturbed by the storm and grind of her music.

She had not moved when I came back down the stairs and approached her, except that now she had some pieces of paper in her hand. I knew what they were, and could not hide my lack of surprise. I saw buzzards now on the railing of our balcony.

"How long have you known about this, Tommy."

"Sit down, Amelia." I poured myself a whiskey and sat down on the smaller leather couch across from her. "Let me see the subpoena."

Being Sunday night and only minutes from Monday, I had exactly two weeks to stymie Ivan, who set such a close date between delivery and execution of the subpoena for maximum distress in my household, and most of all, minimum maneuverability for Tommy. Ivan was saying, "Go ahead, smart guy. Show me what you can do." The document was straightforward—she had to appear and testify under oath with or without counsel. I handed the papers back to her, which sent her sobbing, her head down at the level of the table. "I've known for about.. six months, Amelia."

"Why didn't you tell me anything? Why would you want to keep this a secret? You are my husband, Tommy. Is this what you think about when you are on the couch with your black music?"

"Yes, Amelia. This is what I think about: how to keep you from harm and harm from you. How to make sure you can be a happy mother, and finish school, and leave this country, not under suspicion that would affect your family, but freely, so that you can return. The answer is yes."

"I didn't mean to suggest that you.... "

"I understand, Amelia."

"We have to discuss this, Tommy, from the beginning. I need to know so we can make a plan together." There was only one kind of planning that the situation required at that late stage of Ivan's two-act play, but I told her the whole history, including my meeting with her father. "My father is conflicted, Tommy. He cannot afford their interference so close to his retirement. He does not want you to testify, but if he interfered and failed, it would damage him and the CNP. He would retire in disgrace."

Sometimes, I marveled at how little Amelia knew about the Colonel and Nando and their lucrative side businesses, which constituted enough disgrace for a few years of news headlines. "I don't judge him, Amelia—I decided to bring my family back to this country. That decision carried risks to our security—one of them was that Ivan would take another shot at me."

"What do you mean, 'me,' Tommy?"

"This is not about you, Amelia—his first subpoena got him nowhere, so he is closing the circle around us."

"What do you mean, Tommy—what circle?"

"While you are under subpoena, you cannot leave the country. Ivan knows I will not leave you here alone, and when he learns more about that night from you, he will demand that I testify under oath, or maybe your father, even though I have protection. He can take me into custody as a 'protected witness' or just a plain suspect, and dare the Army and your father to try and set me free. If I leave the country, he can use Interpol to hound me back, or prevent me from returning. I will not be able to leave the States or return here. Meanwhile, you will remain under subpoena and stuck in Cali."

"Ese ijueputa sinverguenza! Can he do that?"

"He is nearly finished, Amelia."

"Get me a drink, Tommy!"

Amelia took a big gulp of whiskey. "Is there anything else you are not telling me about?"

"About Ivan? I followed him this evening in Bogota. He has a girlfriend that looks like you—I would put her at about six months pregnant."

"Then why won't he just leave us alone?"

"We all have our theories, Amelia, but the problem is still there."

"I need to get a lawyer, don't I?"

"Yes. Tomorrow. We both need to speak to him."

"What about your lawyer, Tommy—the one you used in the first court case?"

"I can flee, Amelia—I have no assets here. I can switch the ownership of the condo to the girls. You have assets—your family, your father's remaining years as a Colonel, your ability to come and go freely, and to continue to see your family. You need your own lawyer."

"That's crazy, Tommy!"

"No, it's sensible. It is not about trust. It is beating back a wild animal with your own shield. You will realize it someday."

Amelia stood up and walked back to the balcony. Talked out, I took off my shoes, and stretched out on the small sofa, nearly to the point of dozing off. Amelia shook me awake. "This is bad, Tommy. You are right. The fucker Ivan wants you locked away!"

"The idea is disgrace or separation, Amelia. He has put considerable thought into this project, and it is completely legal." That was not what Amelia wanted to hear—sweet, reasonable, almost complementary words about the man who would bring down her family in one elegant stroke of his pen.

She put my chin in a firm grasp and directed my eyes toward hers. She gave me the look—the one she gave a complete stranger in a bar when, pressed to the wall and about to be shot, she needed help and did not care about restraint and civility, the one she hoped would awaken a man to his job, to his peril, to himself. She sat on her knees on the floor next to me. "Fuck him up, Tommy."

"I can't kill him, Amelia."

"No. You don't understand. My father was right, Tommy. You just didn't understand. Fuck him up so bad that he will never bother us again."

"Are you sure, Amelia?"

"I know who you are and what you can do, Tommy—more than you do."

"I don't have a lot of time, Amelia."

"One thing your mother told me about you, Tommy. She said, 'I love Tommy dearly, but I would never want him for an enemy.'"

"I never had enemies, Amelia. Why should she say that?"

"You can do this, Tommy. You have to. I can't live without you if Ivan keeps you in prison year after year."

The image of a Roman triumphal parade came to mind. Ivan was atop his chariot with a glass of Pinot Grigio in his hand, while I was behind him naked in a cage.

"Amelia, call your father first thing in the morning and get the name of a good civil lawyer in town. Tell him the appointment has to be tomorrow. Tell him it concerns constitutional protection and national security. Mention your father's name. I'll meet you there. But don't say anything about our other plans. Do you have your U.S. passport, yet?"

"No."

"Call my father. Tell him we need it in one week."

"Tommy—you called him 'father.'"

"Yeah."

My mind was already elsewhere. The sorrows of young Tommy were coming to an end. I stood up and cracked my neck with a few forced twists. I needed to think about giving Ivan his just desserts.

"Amelia, I'm going to drive around for a while. Go to bed, mi amor. I need you to be fresh tomorrow." She gave me a deep kiss, the kind she would give me in our early days in Aruba. For Amelia, I was getting back on my steed, where I belonged. "Wake me up when you come home." Muss es sein? Yes, Ivan. I am tired of your trumped up ego, and my own half-hearted deliberations that never arrived at a concrete plan. Es muss sein, motherfucker!

The streets of Cali were like the bottoms of hallow dark basins of blowing leaves and soft raindrops in the first hours of that Monday morning. After an hour of Otis Redding on the CD player and my own lethargic driving, I still had nothing. In Cali, Ivan would be in high towers with security cameras, armed guards, and a locked door. In Bogota, Ivan was unassailable, with no point of interception, unless I pulled him out of his car at a stoplight and pistol-whipped him into jello-brained incapacity. In that case, his friends would make sure I did not see Amelia for twenty years.

I came to a police checkpoint a few miles from the condo: I handed the policeman my license, registration, insurance, and the Colonel's signed business card, which gave me privileges not available to the average tipsy driver. "Out for cigarettes" is how I responded to his query about my wanderings through West Cali. I had not had much to drink, but smelled of whiskey, so the policeman shined the flashlight around the car a little, and was about to click it off and wave me forward when he pointed it at the front window. "You have an envelope on your front window, Sir. Please remove it and drive safely."

I grabbed the matted manila envelope from the front hood, where it had fastened itself. Up ahead, there was an all-night burger stand with white plastic tables under bright florescent lights. I ordered a burger there and opened up the envelope, yet another single page of paper, this one a copy of a faxed hotel confirmation at the Hotel Inter. The name on the reservation was Ivan Moreno.

Someone up there likes me, I thought. The reservation began the Friday before the hearing until the following Tuesday. Ivan evidently wanted to party that weekend in Cali, then break down Amelia's force of will and ruin her husband—all in two days of questioning. Oh, Ivan—you certainly do not lack for confidence.

He would come alone to Cali—I was sure of it. To bring his Amelia lookalike to our town would be to conflate the two women uncomfortably and thereby expose his own brittle mental fault lines.

My burger arrived, and after a few bites a sad, smelly waif appeared in front of my table, and sat down on the other side. It was a girl about twelve or thirteen years old in a man's large t-shirt and panties that had come out of the darkness to beg for food. She was abnormally small, not a midget, but stunted from serious malnutrition. She had yellowed, phosphorescent eyes and brown, moldy teeth, and sticks for arms and legs. Her eyes bulged so much I thought they would fall out of their sockets, and roll across the table to me if she coughed.

The cook came out from behind the oil barrel grill, yelling for the girl to go away. She backed away to the curb near my table with her hand fighting to stay upright, still staring at me with desperate hunger on her face.

"I am so sorry, Sir. It is not a good idea to feed them."

"What is the matter with her?"

"Basuko." He pointed at his own head like he was setting off a pistol. Basuko was the unprocessed cocaine paste sold cheaply on the streets to child-beggars mostly, so they would have the stamina to beg all day and night or perform vile sexual acts in parked cars on side streets. It was like pouring kerosene into the brain, biochemically. Physically, it was five minutes of chemical love that a user would sell his anus to relive.

I wrapped up my remaining hamburger for the girl, and sent her away with some pesos inside the wrapper.

"Do you want another, Sir?"

"Yes. Two of them with lots of fries. And a beer."

I began to move away from the curb to an inside table.

In an instant, the whole plan came to me in a parade of vile imagery that would fit nicely into sequential and easily executable actions. I ran back to my car for my notebook and pen, after which I wrote and wrote for an hour; I also made columns and added dollar amounts and dates and times to them and then reviewed the plan for oversights "A person, a place, a time—these are all variables which you have to control at your peril," said Nando.

It was a good plan; it had an economy of participants, settings, and actions, which would have pleased Nando, had I ever been in a position to brag. Though everyone would know its author, it would be almost impossible to connect me to the events.

At home, I woke Amelia up from her sleep to take her suddenly and strongly in the soft light of morning. Seeing Amelia so happy in the dawn light, I realized that I had become a hunter again, and that I intended to harm Ivan with malice, forethought, and more than a little glee. As much as the paramilitaries liked to see their enemies in lime pits, I wanted Ivan to crawl away from what I had planned for him.

Amelia and I met with Leonardo Diaz in his offices in Ciudad Jardin after he realized his new client was the daughter of Colonel Aurilio Hernandez of the CNP. He reviewed the previous court order, which shielded me from testimony as we sipped coffee in his large office chairs. It took me about twenty minutes to summarize Ivan's attempts to bring me and now Amelia into a courtroom chair, under oath and subject to his questioning. I told him nothing about the actual events that night in the Liverpool Bar, but told him that all events for which Ivan would want to discuss had implications for national security.

His job was simple: to extend my legal protections to Amelia on spousal and constitutional grounds. Ivan had already thought through arguments to counter these basic ones and found a judge willing to follow along. I just needed to keep Diaz busy, and believing he had a real legal dispute on his hands. What Diaz did not need to know was that Ivan would not show up in that courtroom or any courtroom for quite a while. After all, why would I destroy Ivan and pay an expensive lawyer at the same time? I left Amelia in his office since I had made another, more important appointment in a parking garage uptown.

Nando had told me that I should not waste my time with Gregorio Antonio Palanco. He had a dull, puffy, unremarkable face, and for Nando, he represented the short-timer among police officers in Cali—lacking education, finesse, polish, and above all initiative—overall, a rather blunt instrument for serious police work. His type, however, was in high demand among the narco gangs for their martial skills and their insider knowledge of police procedures. Within a few years, they usually quit police work for well-paying narco employment. But Palanco had accumulated three years on the force and was plodding along well enough to be assigned as an evidence collector in some high-priority cases. I knew though that he would never make Captain or gain access to the police circles where high-stakes illicit enrichment took place.

He would be open, in other words, to a risky operation that would make him narco rich.

He remembered me—I had, after all, left him with the choice between collaboration with me and a broken ankle—and showed up before me for our appointment this time. We shook hands, guardedly on both ends.

For months, Captain Duarte had not mentioned my name or asked staff to follow me. As far as he knew, there had been no wire surveillance. He assumed I had taken my winnings and left the country. "The Fiscalia has not forgotten me, and I have certainly not forgotten them. I have a job for you—it could cost you about ten years of your life down a prison shithole. That would be the least of your problems—some very important families would never forget you, and pay for you to die in prison. On the other hand, I will pay you one hundred thousand dollars cash. If you get caught, I will give you another fifty thousand for your silence, and to get you the best lawyer in town."

"You are talking about killing the Fiscalia from Bogota, senor?"

"No, not killing him, and not really beating him. It is more than that."

"You had better explain, senor." I pulled ten thousand dollars out of my backpack and held them before him.

"Not until you take the deposit. When this goes down, you will know it was me—there will be a reward for information, a big one. If you take this money instead, I will explain." He looked at more than his yearly salary and the promise of nine more of them, and coaxed the money into his front pocket. "Tell me, senor."

I told him the beginning, the middle, and the end of the operation. I explained the risks and how to reduce them, and finally how to escape.

"You hate this man deeply, senor."

"What do you think?"

"There is much risk, senor Tommy, especially since I cannot kill any of the witnesses."

"I feel your pain," I believe was the operative expression in Washington political circles that year.

"They will not want to speak ever—it is built into the plan."

"In the police we can make anyone talk—that is a weak point."

"Gregorio, there are things I cannot tell you about the other participant—the point is that his life will not be worth shit if he speaks to anyone."

"Senor Tommy, the plan is too long. Saturday night until the early hours of Monday is better. That will reduce risk considerably."

"Can you deliver the product I want in less time?" He smiled a hard grin, the kind that harkened back to a worse deed he had performed before.

"Leave that to me, senor."

I gave Palanco another two-thousand dollars for some things to quietly purchase, preferably through pawn shops or electronics stores in nearby villages. Under no circumstances would I allow Palanco to do the shopping himself, under penalty of more inoperative limbs. We shook hands. We had to meet again, but only once, as the plan was simple, and I did not want Palanco thinking too much about what he needed to do, beyond some simple acting lessons he would not enjoy, but would be vital to his role.

My end of things was simple: after the plan was in motion, I had no role whatsoever; even if Palanco cried out in terror, I would listen, but not come anywhere near Ivan. Palanco was on his own. Unlike the previous mission, this time I did not write myself into the operation—I could understand now the lives of the Colonel and Nando, Bustamante and Patricia a little better. The number of variables that could topple the stack was incalculable, and many could topple over just due to human factors.

I gave Amelia some pretty strict instructions that evening. None of them sat well with her, but she understood their importance, and prepared well in advance: to have suitcases packed, to have passports in a safe place, to have the girls ready for a sudden departure, and to alert the Ambassador about their sudden arrival no earlier than twelve hours in advance. Amelia left me alone without comment my last two days in Cali, ones in which I did pool laps at the club, or otherwise lay on the couch with Miles Davis and Chick Corea.

There was only a week remaining before my reckoning with Ivan. Only one of us would walk away after that.

CHAPTER FORTY-FOUR

The Magdalena was a good place not to think about pressing matters elsewhere in the country. The newspapers in the airport lobbies were befuddled by Caguan, the word conjuring up such hopes for peace until the reader realized the FARC were on the other side of any peace deal. To the chagrin of my bosses, the government had signed on, and would not be dissuaded from its good will tour into the heart of communism. Nothing in Caguan mattered along the Magdalena, though.

The next day, Red Sox landed with a payload of blue bags that nearly reached the passenger windows of the Cessna.

"Sox, what's going on? This is way too much money for last week's loads."

"I don't know, Tommy, maybe the paracos renegotiated their deal with your bosses. It wouldn't surprise me—it's a business on both ends." Red Sox was able to shrug off these kinds of drastic changes, since they did not change his paycheck or his flight plans, the only things he could control amidst all the blood and death that was taking place all around us on both sides of the Magdalena.

As I expected, there was no truck with armed boys on the runners to take me to my hotel. There was only a single truck to return the men back to their base after the transfer was complete. There were instead two black helicopters parked on the grass beyond the end of the runway. The killer-boys instead loaded the body bags into one of the helicopters in a hustling fashion, considering the extra distance. It reminded me of documentary images from the Vietnam War.

A single grenade launcher from the high grass beyond the runway would explode the gas in the trucks or the Cessna, resulting in the deaths of many men. We usually acted on the runway with these facts in mind. Oddly, that day, El Maestro came to my side with an aplomb that probably took his men by surprise. "Chofer, hombre—we are heading to San Blas—those men over there want to talk to you. They have been waiting for weeks, hombre. They don't take 'no,' so don't bother. Give me your backpack, my son. We take off as soon as the transfer is complete." With a slap on the back, he beckoned me to follow him to the other helicopter.

We flew north over the sluggish brown blot of the Magdalena until we suddenly swerved and dipped, and then shot downward rapidly toward a small village with training camps on the crests of the hills behind its main squares and churches. "Alla-La Casa Verde, Chofer!" he exclaimed, as if showing off a prominent building to a new novitiate on his way to a renowned monastery.

The Green House squatted like a fat, lazy ranch overseer on a shaded porch over the small, busy village of shopkeepers and idlers who kicked up dust on the streets down its steep hills. The seven or eight brick buildings built on its flanks ruined whatever charm it once could claim. The heat was intense and blasted me when I stepped out of the helicopter. I was in a war zone now and things like air conditioning or ice buckets did not warrant discussion. El Maestro showed me to a small guesthouse and left me to see to the arrival of the blue bags.

My guest room had a bed, couch, and bathroom, and a small refrigerator with bottles of water. I told the sentry to not interrupt me for two hours, so I could I nap during the intense heat of the early afternoon beside a small fan, which I pointed at my head.

I was there under orders from D-2, but I had to assume that the CIA knew as well and approved the visit to further some plan known only to them. Precisely two hours later, there was a series of knocks, and then another, followed by the sentry's voice. They were waiting for me in the Green House.

Two men led me out the building in a row, like the last stroll of the condemned. Our destination was one of the masonry failures beyond the Green House, which had become a hive of unexpected activity. Boy-soldiers carried boxes of whiskey, bags of ice, and ice chests filled with steaks into the Green House. There was a huge barbeque on the lawn and long tables with white clothes.

What the fuck are colored balloons doing in a conflict zone? I thought.

As we passed in front of the Green House, I took a quick peak through the open door at a large ballroom floor, which in relevant narco terms could support about fifty prepagos and their patrons. The sentries left me at the bottom door of the last building, only showing me three fingers and walking away.

I walked slowly up to the door and knocked sharply, waiting with the tightest bowels I had ever felt in my life. I knew that these men had brought hell storms of death along the Magdalena, had met in secret with Presidential envoys, and had taken over effective management of over half the country.

Three men sat under a large fan that wrenched cigarette smoke away from their control, and swirled it up to the ceiling for redistribution elsewhere. On the table were bottles of beer, aguardiente, lit cigarettes, radios and satellite phones. I took another step forward, thus far not looking up at their faces, almost nailed to my spot at the edge of the room. Other men, with Israeli or maybe Italian accents, passed quickly out of the room as I entered.

There were three men on that couch, one of whom I knew passably well. One of the men on the couch in a white shirt like mine, extended his hand toward the sofa on the right. I walked towards it and sat down like an unsure tyro. While they chatted, he handed me a beer, pointing toward a tray of food after I had capped it. I shook my head negatively, but smiled.

I fanned a quick glance across the table at all three men, trying to gain some feel for my purpose in that room. The man who offered me beer I recognized as the political boss of the Magdalena region, or the second most powerful man along the Magdalena. The man next to him was Colorado. The man on the sofa across from me—who so far had not spoken or looked in my direction—was the leader of all the paramilitaries in Colombia. He was the man I had seen on several mad television interviews, like a graduate of the Kurtz School of Media Communications. In person, he was small, with a weak torso and rickety arms, but with an undeniable fierceness, as if he were looking for a reason to pick up a knife and drive it through my chest.

The chief comandante neither smiled nor looked at me. He nibbled on pistachios nervously, prying them open with his teeth, and spitting the shells on the ground and grabbing another one as soon as he had deposited the previous one in his mouth. Red veins were splayed across the whites of his eyes. His eye bags were black and yellow and green, like dried chemical stains around the edges of a dying lake. His skin sagged on his bony and worn face. He leaned over for another bottle of water and our eyes met. He was a serious user of something.

Whatever he came for, he took it all in with one instantaneous look into my eyes, as if for him the meeting began and end at that moment. His drug of choice was not Basuko, but something was eating away slowly at his brain, or perhaps his soul.

He was the media-savvy paraco. He preferred live interviews, and always on TV, so that he could speak without interruption for minutes and minutes and show his dominance over the media of the Bogota oligarchy. Standing in front of his tallest, blackest and meanest troops, who glared without motion in the intense heat, he would carefully present his ideological program to the unlucky interviewer, but the real message was torture, control, mayhem and death. His voice was raspy and uncoiled harsh phrases that spit down at the listener like red hot steel.

"Have you had lunch? Can we bring you something to eat?" he spits out in a maniac's attempt at courtesy.

"No, Comandante, but thank you. I am fine. More water would be nice, though."

Colorado came back with bottles of water, which he set on the table. The seething, breathless rasp started up again after Julian sat down. "We can clear out these villages in six months, but the FARC will never leave the San Lucas alive. We will have to smoke them out."

The political director began his presentation. "We want this base to be our national military and political headquarters. We already have our short wave radio in operation. We have hospitals, schools, markets. We even fabricate our own mortars and bullets. Full-time, there are over one hundred officers in charge of over a hundred trainees each month in this facility alone."

"Everyone but a decent mason," I thought.

He made no mention of the obvious reliance on helicopters to overfly hundreds of miles of territory that shifted like dunes between paramilitaries and FARC troops. "How far along is the build-up?"

"We can get most of our armaments now from Turbo or other sources. We are supplying globally now. We have good supply lines now, either from Medellin or down the river. Our problem is that we need to get the product out fast, quietly, and reliably."

"That was the whole point of my flights to Barrancabermeja," I thought.

The raspy voice yanked back the conversation within the orbit of his conspiratorial worldview.

"Why won't our friends give us a fleet of planes and pilots?"

"Well, Comandante, I cannot speak for our friends, but I think they have been warned about driving down the street price of cocaine so much that no one makes any money. They have to unload the product profitably on the other end. There is also the matter of profile. Since the Contra operation, there are more eyes on the CIA. I think they want to keep this operation small and secretive."

The comandante spit out his seeds and did not reach for more. "Listen, Pelao! In 1983, Rafa Cardona moved one-thousand kilos a month into the United States. Fabio Ochoa moved between one point two and one point five thousand kilos. Pablo Escobar moved about the same. And a man named Mejia—who was as rich as the rest combined— he moved two to three thousand kilos a month. What is this mierda about not wanting to change the price of cocaine in New York?"

"I was speculating, Comandante."

The Comandante had taken some sort of measure of me, which did not loosen my gut muscles. "I don't know. Speculating can get you killed, pelao."

My glare met his with my own awakening malice. He breathed out a low, cunning laugh and stood up in a jerky manner, brushing pistachio shells off his jeans. He reached across the table to shake my hand. "Ok, Pelao! I have other business to attend to. Talk to these guys for a while—you will learn a lot." He went through the back door, almost immediately growling orders into his radio.

The political jefe resumed his more measured, objective address. He was a career narco, who had bought himself a share of the new paraco El Dorado along the Magdalena, and had so far had proven himself useful in the almost non-existent duties of paramilitary political affairs. "Chofer, we appreciate your visit to our site. So far, we are very satisfied with the services you have offered to our movement. You have maintained a low profile at the airport, which is important to all our security objectives. You have been on time and on budget always. We appreciate that."

That concluded the travel brochure portion of his comments. "We want you to see the scale of our plans for this region… the political transformation here is already underway. A year ago, we barely had a toe hold on this side of the river. Now, we control most of the territory between Puerto Berrio and Simiti. We look forward to your continued assistance. In fact, there are some modifications to our existing agreements we would like to speak to you about."

Over a hundred miles, I thought—but not all the territory along the Magdalena. There were at least five navigable rivers that began in the Sierras of San Lucas and spilled down into the Magdalena. They did not control a single one. There were over one hundred small villages—each under FARC control—an equal number connecting dirt roads that were unguarded by either side. They were still losing skirmishes to the FARC and did not control all the main roads at night, or have a protected line of troop and supply movement for more than twenty miles. They had no presence in and out of the main routes to the mines and cocaine labs in the Sierras of San Lucas, so they had no share of the enormous profits still made by the ELN there.

But they had the FARC and the ELN scared in their plastic boots that they would find them, out of uniform and in an unguarded moment, when an ex-FARC soldier would point at them. That did not add up to victory for me. But as a guest, I did not feel it appropriate to challenge his assessment of the facts on the ground.

"In this way, you will understand how… as conditions change, our needs as a command change, and our expectations for our partners will change as well." There was a huge request tucked neatly inside that mild formulation, like an explosive device in a mule's pack saddle. "But we have plenty of time for discussion of business conditions and opportunities. Today is a day for enjoyment of the riches this land has brought to us."

He motioned to Colorado. "Why don't you take El Chofer on a tour of our facilities? We will talk again at the party tonight. Ok, Chofer?"

Colorado drove me along alternately rain-slickened and dried-out, bumpy roads that connected several flat parcels on the higher bluffs. Rather than bull dozers, teams of shirtless, young paramilitaries worked the ground with picks and axes, or ground-rollers pulled by a donkey to level out the ground. At one site, a horse, slapped and prodded by troops, struggled with a rope around its neck to pull a tree stump out of the ground. Other troops took siestas under giant black tarps tied to stakes and lifted high by tree trunks denuded of their limbs. Each base had a white-poled, rectangular entrance, but without perimeter fences around them or protected bunkers for the sentries, they all looked like amusement parks that lost their financing.

On the way back, we drove down the rutted part of the jeep trail toward the Green House, a vantage that yielded a view of a small, enclosed community with the Green House at its center, and wings of brick buildings along the ridge. There were about eight helicopters parked on a helipad cut from brush nearby. Armed paramilitaries stood with their guns raised across their chests and stared out at the surrounding hills, or down into San Blas. More troops with binoculars and machine guns guarded the far ends of the bluff behind sand-bagged positions.

We heard lively music and laughter from the Green House, which rolled onto the lawns, a merriment that stopped abruptly at the blank expressions of the boy-killers on the periphery of the grass lawn that overlooked San Blas.

"What's goin' on?"

"A celebration, Chofer—we are entertaining some guests, mostly from the capital. We need political commitment to continue our work here—from many people, so we invited them down to show that we have established more than an outpost here—it is more like a... community."

"It is certainly an excellent spot—you can see all the way down to the Magdalena from the higher bluffs."

"It also is half way on the main route between San Pablo and Simiti. We can bring men and arms to bear on any point in both directions in less than an hour."

The ELN were trained to wipe out a platoon and be back in the mountains in half that time.

I had many questions about his life before he became a comandante, but the rules of the game, at least what I had learned in the field thus far, suggested that he was not going to share anything with me or ask me about myself. He was dour and thoughtful, a forward-thinking man, not at all simple-minded and far more reflective about himself and his predicament than he chose to entrust to anyone, especially a CIA contractor of untested metal. But I did learn that the FARC shot his brother in front of their family for failing to pay their war tax. Shortly after that, he signed on as a paramilitary.

Did he ever tell a woman that she was beautiful or remark to her about the beauty of a lovely sunset? Did he ever tuck a child into bed with a soft kiss? Did he learn simple skills from his father and imitate his ways out of wholesome admiration? Like so many of these paramilitary types, there was a severance which took place, whether through a formal initiation or a slow inurement to brutality, between a previous self and the new paramilitary one. So many of these men knew brutality from early in their lives and expected little more than to rack up some good kills before they slid down before the knife themselves.

"It will be like our Vatican...."

"What?"

"The Green House—it will be like our Vatican." It was an odd comment; if he had a different look in his eyes, it would have been unsettling. But he believed in the power and correctness of his simile. It was a particularly gruesome one since one of its primary functions was to teach skills of torture and murder and displacement.

I had by that time participated in several high-level discussions of COIN theory on closed-circuit TV between Tampa and Panama City. The idea of localized terror and friendly force encampment was to hold a territory until government force returned, not to turn it into a place of middle-aged retreat, where philosopher-murderers reflected on paramilitary ideology in a resort atmosphere; or impressed each other with the depth of their COIN knowledge like ambitious graduate students circling around a professor of renown. Did they snap each other with towels jokingly after an hour or so in the sauna? Camouflaged brethren of brutality and cocaine—it would be easy to go insane along this river, I thought.

"I can't go to that party. I'm here to do a job. I can't show my face down there."

"I know. There is a back entrance to the Green House. We can go straight to the second floor balcony—you can take a look at the crowd for a moment. You will find it interesting."

"I could go for a steak though."

"We'll eat on the second floor in the main dining room there."

After dining, we walked to the edge of the balcony to behold a Shangri-la of perfect female forms in tight, neon dresses and powerful men at their ease in casual, collared shirts. Partnered off, they danced to salsa music, and sipped cocktails delivered by boy soldier-waiters in camouflaged pants and black shirts. For some reason that made sense to him—it made none to me—he drew the curtains wide open and showed me the privileges of the most powerful men in the country.

Within the modest festooning of brightly colored lights and a single disco ball, I saw two governors, several Generals, the Director of D-2, and more than a few Senators. For each man there was a corresponding beauty queen, each tantalizingly close to Amelia in sexiness, but not formal beauty, more Laura Benitez than Sophia Loren.

"Is that really her?"

"Yes. It's her." Alongside the political director was one of the more beautiful television news announcers from a nightly national news program.

"Why is she here?"

"A gift from our supreme commander to himself. He has been seeking a visit from her for months. Tonight, she sleeps with him; tomorrow she interviews him. Like him, she is on a tight schedule." Colorado did not laugh, but he did raise the side of his lip and raise his eyes a little.

"How much?"

"About a shoe box." That could be from one hundred to five hundred thousand, I thought. She and I made eye contact for a brief moment, and she smiled at me, intrigued by the one that did not fit into the obvious categories of celebrants, but I pulled back to hide my face.

In the center of the ballroom, there was a fake Christmas tree with balloons at its base instead of lights on its branches. Even though the light was quite dim, tucked neatly around the tree were stacks of blue bags, now with ribbons and bows on them.

That explained the higher than normal level of money in the Cessna. Julian—probably not with official clearance from the other bosses—was telling me the real function of how the Green House figured in the national plans of the paramilitary movement. Those men below, with their hands on the soft, downy backs of young women, soon to enjoy a coupling with their daughter's college classmate, could give the paramilitary leadership a place at the main dining table of power and control. The paramilitaries and the army not only did not trust the President and his Congress—they were raising funds to vote them out. Danger for me had just increased five hundred percent: by funding the takeover of an entire country's Congress, I was dealing with people who would never forget a favor and would deal with it appropriately—like an enemy planted deep inside their camp. How naïve and stupid I had been. My little contract was null and void on this side of the river.

I did not trust Julian Colorado—he was, after all, the ex-headmaster for the school of killing nearby, as well as having the overall outlook and sensibility of a trained killer—but I felt more comfortable hearing the news from him than the other members of the triumvirate who spoke a language closer to that of the Ambassador, without any mention of blood, money, or fear.

"—thanks for the tour, the wine, the steak… but… why am I here?"

"The plan is not changing—maybe evolving is a better term for what we want to do. The other side of the river has its own command. We are maturing as a community. Eventually, we will want to use our own runways."

"My pilot would never agree to that."

"There are plenty of pilots in Colombia that would, Chofer. Good pilots—patriots—that would work for less just to contribute."

"But I have a contract with him and the CIA. I am not going to pay him for nothing."

"We can always run flights on both sides of the river. His will just be a little light."

"—this is not yet secure territory—you guys still feel more comfortable flying around in helicopters than driving on these roads. As soon as the ELN learn I am on this side of the river, it is just more risk and danger for everyone."

Julian just moved his mouth a little to the side, in the manner he did when there was not an immediate need for a violent response, but there was a need to tamp down dissent.

"You can discuss that more with the supreme comandante."

"Ok. What else do they want?"

"They want to discuss some laundering routes you have."

Of course, fuck. They expect me to carry cash from the supreme comandante of the united paramilitary forces in my Piper onto a small strip on the eastern bluff of Aruba. Word had traveled far and wide.

"I'm not in that business, anymore. I only service my family accounts."

"Like I said, this will be an important topic the next time you arrive. Anyway, these discussions can wait. You are our guest tonight, Chofer—can I get you a girl? I heard a few of our guests want to take their money and leave tonight, so there will be extras."

He already knew the answer. "No—you can have one." He just shook his head. He probably did not need me to extend the courtesy of foregoing a pretty girl so that he could have one, nor did he seem comfortable taking one of the more sought after rewards of high command.

I asked for a helicopter to take me back to Barrancabermeja that night. For the rest of the week, I did not speak a word to Red Sox about the change of plans to come.

CHAPTER FORTY-FIVE

Our condo was about two miles from the Hotel Inter, whose lights I could see at night from my balcony. It was well within range of our radios, but I felt more at ease with a secure, stable line of communication to Palanco, one based on line of sight. Besides, if the plan failed, I would be of more help to Palanco on the street outside the hotel than screaming into a radio in front of Amelia.

Amelia wanted to come with me, or for me to let her know about the progress of my plan. Before I left, I stroked her face before leading her back toward the girls in their room. "You must not take any action out of your routine, Amelia. Nothing that would make an investigator think, 'Hmmm. That's odd.' You know that. I will be back in about two hours. After that, you will be in bed, asleep or watching a movie, and I will be on the patio. It is the way it has to be. If there is something to report, I will tell you. Otherwise, you have to think that I am just out for a jog."

The first coms check with Palanco was at 8:45. He signaled his readiness, which was code for "If there is any break in radio silence over the next hour, abort the mission."

Rather than decoy maneuvers, loud explosions, or gunfire—the stuff of Amelia's movie fare—radio silence was vital to my plan. I jogged for about twenty minutes, and walked back into the condo lobby with my hoody down, squaring my face and looking directly into the security camera in the lobby. I engaged the porter in small talk, letting him know that I would be home with Amelia the rest of the night.

Instead, in a dark jogging outfit—my walkie-talkie in the hand-warmer pocket of my hoody—I ran out the rear garage door into the woods where I kept my tools. Once I landed on pavement on the street above, I began a slow steady jog in the direction of the hotel.

The rest of the night belonged to Palanco: dressed in a dark blue suit with a floral pink tie, wearing thick black-rimmed glasses and a touch of eyeliner, his hair dyed red on top and carrying a bouquet of flowers and champagne against his belly, he was ready to make his delivery with a personal touch. According to my plan, Palanco had to be a credible homosexual—flamboyant and fussy about his looks but not comically portrayed—so that the last person they would seek in a police investigation was a young dullard of a policeman, torpid to the point of imbecility.

During our only planning session in an abandoned finca in the hills above Cali, we spent a half an hour on the walk alone, aguardiente reordering Palanco's macho sensibilities, so that he would give a credible performance for the security cameras, which would record him from multiple angles throughout the hotel. Typical of Palanco, he had bought a pair of black leather shoes, but had not shined them. Nor had he practiced an accent that would convey his eagerness to please. While not a master of sibilance after only an hour or practice, at least he would be credible in the hallway outside Ivan's hotel room.

Uncovering Ivan's hotel room number cost me five thousand dollars, out of which I imagined Hastings kept about half. It was 9:43 when I began to slow my pace. I was still about half a mile from the Hotel Inter. There was nothing more to do than hope that the training session, in which I forced Palanco to repeat again and again the timeline of his operation, still had traction in his mind. I sat back on the lawn beside the riverside road above the hotel and waited. It was all up to Palanco now. Fuck me!

Ivan would hesitate to open the door, so Palanco was instructed to slide Nando's business card under the door and say, "Ay, Dios! It is just champagne and flowers from a friend, senor. Por favor, they are so heavy for me! Please take them from me. Por Dios! Be a gentleman!"

As soon as Ivan unlatched the door lock and moved the door open slightly, Palanco would kick it open. He would take out his gun and subdue every person in the room. From within the flowers, he would take out chloroform, and using the handkerchief in his pocket, knock out Ivan, who would be tied at the hands and feet. From his breast pocket, Palanco would take two Xanex pills and force them down Ivan's throat. He would disrobe Ivan and dress him in provocative underwear, which was in his coat pocket. Next, he would place all of Ivan's work papers in a garbage bag. Finally, he would shut off Ivan's phone and ask the front desk to take messages and not to allow inward calls.

At 9:52, my radio crackled: "Southbound traffic is open with three lanes." South: Palanco was in control of Ivan's room, Ivan was subdued, and there were no other persons in his room. "Continue to monitor and report. Out."

Palanco would return to the task at hand. Inside the bouquet of flowers, there was also a small tripod—the plan was that we would place it atop a chair—and in its pot a video camera. Finally, he took out the small marijuana pipe from the pot as well, and stuffed it with basuko for Ivan's first of many powdery crystalline puffs.

My stomach felt tight, my body alternatively heating up and chilling, which I attributed to nerves. I was placing about as much faith in Palanco as the CIA placed in me during those first few flights. Up the road, I could see our condo lights as a still portrait, while down the hill I counted up thirteen floors from the lobby, and only saw a single light from which there was no sudden motion during the forty minutes I lay on my back and stared at it.

At 11:05, Palanco checked in again. "Eastbound traffic merged into two lanes but without delays." The next phase of my plan had begun without any attempt by Palanco to qualify events with even a slight coded caution flag. East: the thinner, more boyish of the three members of the ELN cell at Amelia's university arrived at room 1402 in the guise of a young, gay hooker.

He had no choice but to arrive. Palanco had beaten him up a bit during our first encounter, convincing him that if his taxi did not go to the Hotel Inter at the date and time we chose for him, he would be dead within the hour. If he left town, his family would die for him. I could not imagine his lasting beyond the first few kidney punches from a tough guy like Palanco.

The boy refused to touch basuko, so we had also prepared some fake joints, ones that just had tobacco inside. Still, I wanted a scene of the boy taking a puff and handing it to Ivan. There would be no need for more than about 45 minutes of filming for the first movie. The boy knew he had to perform recognizable gay sex acts with Ivan if he wanted to live.

By that point, Ivan would have taken enough basuko to render him nearly imbecilic, but the core of his personality would still be recognizable and intact. He would not be able to act upon knowledge that there were such things as sexual preferences or masculine identities. His brain was turning into a compliant, small child's version of its previous self. The scenes I reviewed the next day did not suggest much ardor, more like

Ivan with a new box of masculine toys. The movies were sufficient in technical proficiency to fool the casual viewer, and to end Ivan's career.

Producing the second video would be more difficult. The boy, in post-coital cuddly mode, had to entice Ivan not only to disparage me personally, but also to prompt Ivan to reveal that his investigation had the sole purpose of destroying me, and getting revenge, rather than seeking justice in the matter. It also had to touch upon any pre-trial arrangements that Ivan—or his office—had concluded with the investigative judge.

Palanco could not speak during filming, having strict instructions not to utter a sound or enter into conversation with either subject, or coerce them toward certain actions with gestures the boy would respond to; the onus fell to the boy to extract natural, unrehearsed confessions from the floppy-tongued Ivan, who only lacked a Chinese dungeon to complete the effect of opium-fed degeneracy.

At 12:05, I saw the boy walking slowly up the sidewalk along the Cali River promenade. His work was done, and his life safe—for now. I gave a slight whistle and beckoned him towards me on the sloping grass close to the cement walls along the river, which was quiet after a rainless night.

"Did you do all I asked?"

"Yes."

"If you want to qualify that statement, now is your last chance."

"No, Sir. It went well."

It was all he could say, and in a voice that believed his spiral down into terror had no apparent end that night.

I handed him over a small sack. "The bag has twenty-five thousand dollars. Go home and pack. At dawn, go to Buenos Aires by as many busses as you can string along. Always pay in cash. There, you can bribe a ship captain and get on a ship on the other side of the world. I suggest Australia. Or you can stay in Argentina. I don't care. If I find out you are alive and in this country, even if you speak to no one, our agreement is null and void, and you will die a painful, merciless death. Don't call your girlfriend. There will be people following you after you leave this place, and others will follow you if you try to hide somewhere in this country. Your brothers and sisters will never feel the bullet that blows their brains onto the sidewalk. Do you understand?"

"Yes. I got it. I got it!"

"Leave now, and never speak about this. Stay the fuck away from revolutionaries."

The last bit was some heartfelt advice. The warnings were brutal, sordid words from a man who once championed himself the kind defender of something or another.

He slumped away, his plans for life kneecapped by bad luck and folly and not yet twenty-two years old. He was lucky; my intervention kept him alive far after he had value for the CNP. His personal healing or future odyssey was his business. Maybe it was a mistake to keep him alive, but I was not yet ready to declare people no longer worthy to live.

Palanco told me later that he chewed caffeine tablets after the boy left the hotel room, but otherwise did not eat over the next twenty-eight hours. Neither did Ivan, who could produce little more than gooey slurping noises like an infant by the next morning. It did not matter if he could talk after Palanco called it a rap on our two movies. We just wanted his brain to turn more and more into mush.

Palanco woke him up every hour for a puff or two for the next twenty-eight hours, the finale arriving at precisely 03:00 on Monday, the point at which Palanco would have planted drugs in several places, wiped down all furniture for prints, and ordered a six o'clock wake up call for Ivan. Then, he would heavily perfume himself in cologne and stroll through the lobby with the flowers, tripod camera, and papers, all up the street to me.

We had no radio communication over that period since our protocols were that he would communicate only if he needed to run away quickly and required a place to hand over Ivan's papers and the videos.

At home, I enjoyed a quiet Sunday with Amelia and the girls. Holding our girls with tenderness, occasionally locking our glances in unison on the front door, we both stared for long stretches at the walkie-talkie, knowing its crackle could send her to the lobby with the girls and suitcases, and me into the jungle. Whenever Amelia began to formulate a question, I would change the subject to one that a possible eaves-dropper would never conflate with a conspiracy against Ivan Moreno and the Attorney General's Office in Bogota.

My nerves by then had begun to more strenuously wrench my insides with headaches, strange fevers, and lethargy, which I tried to overcome by napping on the couch downstairs. We went to bed early Sunday night, my walkie-talkie on the bed stand next to me, still in prolonged silence. At 3am Palanco gave his final message: "Not expecting heavy traffic during commute this morning."

I had dressed in chinos and a hoody to bed. I ran and ran through the back woods to escape the lobby security cameras. I again felt hot and flushed with a strong headache that worsened during my jog down toward the hotel. Palanco and I crossed paths on a pedestrian bridge upstream from the hotel over the rushing waters of the Cali River. We exchanged large green garbage bags, his holding Ivan's papers, the DVD player and tape, and any evidence for immediate disposal; mine containing ninety thousand dollars. The sun was still an hour away. He did not pause or speak as we passed quickly in the middle of the bridge in the quiet of the night. I only said to him, "Burn those fuckin' clothes!"

At 4:30am, I handed the DVD materials personally to Hastings, who rushed off in his car since he had only three hours to turn the raw footage into two copies on separate CDs, one of which I would bury in the woods, and one which a courier would take to the judge's chambers. At six o'clock, Palanco would call the local police to complain about drug usage in room 1402 at the Hotel Inter.

The operation ended at that point. Palanco slipped away to take care of his mother for a few weeks of leave. Ivan was likely half-dead and stymied, unable to formulate a serious thought or even dress himself. His War on Tommy was the least of his worries, even if he had any in his sudden, reduced mental state. At noon, according to television news that day, an ambulance took Ivan to a hospital directly from the hotel, which the newspapers tidied up in identical stories about a possible heart attack the next day. I had released all my hounds in one ferocious attack on the heaths of Ivan's prosperity. He was stymied in this particular endeavor, and perhaps ruined for life.

But a lot of people had hounds.

At a later time, when I was able to peruse Ivan's incriminating confessions from my copy of Palanco's tape, it was almost heroic how Ivan husbanded his last spasms of lucidity to describe the plans he and the investigative judge had for me. My earlier suspicions about the extent of Ivan's clever maneuvering were correct. The plan was to steer Amelia toward a confession that she tended to me in the CNP hospital, and to threaten her with obstruction of justice and perjury charges since she failed to remember these details during her first police interview.

Ivan knew that I would make a deal to save Amelia, a weak one due to her precarious position, which would see me in jail for an extended stay. It was bold and ballsy, but small and unimportant compared to the blood-stained abattoirs small villages had become after they were selected for cleaning by the paramilitaries.

Amelia called me at 10:38am, about two hours after Hastings's people got that tape to the judge. "Tommy—it's all over! The judge accepted the tutela! Ivan never showed up at all. His assistants did not know what to do, but the judge would not accept any more delays! I am free to go!" The judge obviously studied that second CD closely.

I told Amelia to rush home so that we could celebrate, but this was not my true intention. I needed her at home to protect her from whatever spasmodic response Ivan's crew would attempt, one that would likely tilt toward the confrontational and violent.

Nando called me a few minutes later to ask me whether I had heard about Ivan's sudden hospitalization.

Nando knew it was a staged overdose. What he did not know was that it was his business card that tricked Ivan into opening that door, a fact that was used to equal effect by some down-on-their-luck, desperate Greeks long ago, and gave me the idea. I gave Nando nothing. Maybe he was trying to tell me to run, but could not break protocol, or maybe he just wanted to see me get my comeuppance once and for all, up close and personal. We left things at mutual ignorance and hung up.

I had to move fast—that at least was clear from his unusual reticence.

I had enough time before Amelia's arrival to prepare her departure: her suitcases at the front door; the girls dressed and their flight bags packed; passports on the kitchen table; my cell phone charged and the charger placed in my backpack, along with as much cash as I had left in the basement.

Sweat now came in steady rivulets down the sides of my face. I ran to the toilet and puked a smelly, yellow stream.

Amelia wanted to celebrate, rushing into my arms for kisses for her conquering, clever husband, but I needed to keep my wits. And rightfully so. Within a few minutes, the dreaded call came from the porter. "Senor Tommy, there are men down here with guns." I did not need to hear the rest, since guns was the only supporting detail that mattered, not whether they were hired killers or plain-clothes cops.

I grabbed Amelia in my arms. "Mi amor, I have to leave. Lock the door behind me. Don't open it for anyone. Call your father and tell him to send a car to take you to the airport. Don't take a taxi. Make it happen now, mi amor."

"Tommy, must it be this way?"

"I will find a way to call you in Washington tomorrow." I kissed her like the first time, and ran outside to meet them head on.

I went down to the lobby, a long scamper down twelve flights of stairs that left me nearly breathless. With my cell phone, I called the porter from the first floor stairwell.

"Where are they?"

"One in front and one in the elevator."

"Count to ten and set the fire alarm. After that, shut down the elevators until Amelia's father or brother arrive. Now!" I continued back down the stairs to the parking garage, putting the key in the back door lock with shaking hands. A strong headache had come back, forcing my brain to operate in separate, iron compartments.

As soon as I heard the fire alarm, I skidded down the grade behind the pool. Looking up, I saw a figure pulling itself from its grip on the pool fence to figure out the quickest way to me. I had a two or three-minute lead since he would need to go back to the street and follow the retaining wall through bushes the entire length of the building to reach my point below the parking garage.

Back in my woods, I dug into my hiding place with both hands, sending leaves and twigs up into the air. I wanted a gun, more cash, and the knife. Ivan's materials were there as well, which made me rush to recover the whole area with branches and leaves. With my backpack weighed down with the tools of my new trade, I jumped down onto the dry gulch trail and over the other side to the thick bushes there.

He came into the woods alone in a Fiscalia light blue jacket, which meant he had a gun, although he kept it on his waist or in a shoulder holster. I had to catch him at the steep part of the trail—the part where it had roots that hugged a steep slope in the trail, so that one had to grab onto the roots and pull oneself up. I moved over to another tree whose roots spilled downward and stood behind it. A few minutes later, I heard the lurching grunt of someone not used to the exertion of pulling his own body weight up a steep slope.

I came around and brought the bat down on his forward hand, and then on his head, after which he slid harmlessly down the slope and into a rapid darkness.

After a few more pounds on his ankle and knee cap, and another to his other hand, I quickly grabbed his id. Groggily, he came around to his predicament. None of his limbs was in shape to provide comfort to any of the others. I kneeled down over him. "Friend—for the record—you never identified yourself as a policeman, and you tried to enter my house without a warrant. I am going to keep your id as a remembrance of our meeting. Get well soon." After throwing his shoes away, I smacked him one more time hard on his knee, which topped off his approaching shock. I ran up the hill and along the edge of the woods for a mile where it straddled the street, emerging far below where I usually caught a taxi. I placed the bat behind a fallen tree. It seemed reasonable that I would need it again someday.

CHAPTER FORTY-SIX

"Amelia. It's me."

"Tommy, where are you?"

"No more questions, mi amor. Are they in the apartment?"

"No, I refused to open the door. They are calling me from downstairs. Daddy is sending a car. There are fire trucks outside."

"Good. Call the portero. Tell him to get your bags and carry them to his desk, but only after your father or his men arrive. Grab the girls and leave directly to the airport. I love you beyond words. You know that, right?"

"Of course, Tommy. Is it bad?"

"It had to be done. Time will tell. Don't tell your father anything. I love you. Bye."

I bought a gallon of water from a tiendecita on a side street across the street from the Hotel Inter. My head now was hot with fever. Something else besides nerves was at play inside me. I spotted a driver eating a hot dog in his taxi at the curb on the side of the store. I walked over to the curb to present him with an offer.

"How far to Medellin?"

"The next bus leaves at 2pm. You will arrive about eight this evening. I can get you there on time. You can get a flight almost every hour from the airport." I was suddenly wobbly, my muscles contorting rather than softening, quite apart from the slow seepage of adrenaline back out of my blood stream after beating a man and escaping in a mad, forward rush.

Gripping the handle of the passenger door, I leaned in closer to muffle my words. My sweat fell on his arm. "I want to arrive quietly. I'll give you five hundred dollars to drive me there. Quietly. Smoothly. I need to rest." By the end of the phrase, I was gasping for breath. At that moment, I could not tell how he sized me up, or whether he knew something about me from his radio dispatch or police contacts. "Ok. Hop in."

For some reason, I strained to get into the back seat due to sudden muscle pains firing in almost sequential order, and the back seat seemed to be swerving back and forth slowly on some invisible axis. I started to wipe away sweat, but my handkerchief was soon completely wet, and drops of sweat continued to fall. There was more than a chance that the police were looking for me, so I tried to stay awake, and follow his course out of town. But my mind just wanted to sneak out the back and fall asleep in a hammock. "Keep the music low for a while, senor." I slid down the seat and soon fell, with aching bones and fading strength, deeply asleep.

The movement of the car slowed, halted and finally stopped. Through aching bones I let out a cough, which propelled me back to consciousness, my eyes opening upward toward gas station awnings and a driverless car. My backpack—and therefore my guns and money—were still on the seat. "Si, primo. Es gringo! Pienso que esta enfermo. Esta durmiendo como nina! Cuanto vale un gringo?" My taxi driver was negotiating my sale, probably to a gang. He thought I was still asleep, so he took the opportunity to find out my value in the market for kidnapped gringos.

There were gangs who made a living locating, taking and delivering high-end kidnapping victims to the lords of the jungles in Colombia. "Tiene plata. No se si tiene pistola, pero sin problema se le dominen." He knew that I had money, but he did not want to subdue me himself, preferring to deliver me to the gang for some easy money and a quick return to Cali by nightfall with enough money to buy a new taxi.

"Si. Ijuemadre—que pesca milagrosa!" The miracle fish—it was a term the FARC used to describe kidnap victims that wonderfully fell into their clutches without a net. The hid them away locally until security eased and then took them into the jungle to slowly rot away.

The taxi driver had given them our present location, which was a highway exit just outside Manizales in the low mountains south of Medellin. I must have been sleeping for about four hours. I continued to feign sleep. Whistling, he circled the car and then reached into the front seat to grab some cigarettes with his right arm. I sprang up with my knife and made a huge gash across his forearm. Blood spurt down his arm before he could yank it back out of the cab. He screamed in pain, holding it aloft to stop the gush of fresh blood that went back down his arm and onto the ground.

"That was stupid, senor. Selling me to the FARC." I jumped out of the back seat, wobbly and feverish, but able to point my knife at his throat. He felt the knifepoint now in the small of his back. "Get me your keys." I stuffed him into the trunk and drove away quickly.

I had no pills to deal with this intense pain, and after a few bumpy miles the demands of diarrhea. Several times I pulled over in the woods and shat near the sides of streams or behind improvised garbage dumps on empty lots. In two hours I was nearing Medellin, so I pulled off the freeway and stopped several blocks behind a busy gas station-estadero where several taxis were parked. With my knife in my hand, I popped the trunk, where the taxi driver had wound his shirt around his forearm like a big red beehive on his forearm. I offered him no assistance as he rolled out of the trunk, his one useful arm unfortunately behind him and not of much use.

"Amigo, time to go back to Cali. Do you have the money I gave you?"

"Si, senor. Please understand."

"Shut up. I know your plan. You can keep the money since you will need it. Go back to Cali."

"I am sorry, Sir. I needed the money. It was nothing personal."

I gave him a last look; there was blood on his face and arms and chest, and his pallor suggested an ample loss of blood. His wife would berate him once again for his lack of smarts.

Inside the trunk, there was a spare tire and a jack, so to keep him busy for a while, and to place myself far away by the time he fixed the tire with his one good arm, I cut into one of his tires with my knife. I gave him another hundred dollars. "Drive safely."

The next driver, whom I picked up at the gas station nearby, was more reasonable, perhaps cognizant that I was going to Barrancabermeja—now under complete paramilitary domination—for a specific reason that he would delay or undermine at considerable peril to himself. Happily showing Captain Bustamante's card at three paramilitary check points, and patient with my frequent bathroom stops, he easily earned the thousand dollars I offered him to drive me directly to my hotel and then forget that he had ever seen me.

There were no guards in the lobby of my hotel, which seemed to have reverted to its normal self, a cheap love motel where the airport road reached the edge of downtown. The front desk clerk expected me to arrive with female company on my arm, instead of disheveled, smelling like shit and alone. He hesitated to permit me to enter until I rudely told him to call Hawkins for approval.

I prepared a list of items and sent him out with instructions to bring them me up to my room on the fourth floor. I could pinch and hold the skin on my arm between my fingers like wax. My thirst was tremendous, and my temperature had shot back to where I could not raise myself off my pillow anymore. The clerk had to respond to my weak voice call to bring the items into the mini-fridge, which I asked him to move next to my bed.

The fever geared up for a long stay. I barely noticed the change from night to day, nor had I much idea how many times the change occurred while I sweated and stank in that room. When I awoke, it was because someone led me to the bathroom for horrid bowel movements, redolent of the swollen dead body smells from Uraba. The arm brought me back to bed, and put towels on my head, speaking in a soft, female voice with reassuring phrases like "It's ok, Tommy, your fever is already going away."

It was not Amelia; I knew that much. Amelia, beloved of the Gods and with similar disdain for the earthly and unhygienic, did not like me to touch her after spending days and days in the field until I had showered and placed my clothes in the washing machine. Amelia, who drove around Cali with boxes of Kleenex on the front and back window dashes, and would not eat food from street vendors—that Amelia was safe and sound in an Olympian palace of taste and refinement in the suburbs of Chevy Chase, Maryland, or would be by the next morning. This woman was carnate to Amelia's etherealness, whether wiping me on the toilet, or lowering me into the shower to scrub me down, or removing my underwear, though probably for disposal.

I finally awoke clear of fever after some number of days. My Girl Friday was gone, but she had left behind an orderliness like my mother's well-prepared lunch boxes when I was in elementary school. There was a new, larger backpack on the small table. Instead of filling it, she had placed the items in small stacks, so that I could arrange them as I saw fit. The gun and ammo I took from Cali were gone. A new gun, cleaned and loaded, took its place. The knife, carefully cleaned of all its fresh blood, was still there. She had charged my cell phone and the satellite one, and wrapped the cords like small garden hoses on a wheel. About twenty-five thousand dollars was also missing, which did not make any sense, unless the front desk clerk was suddenly a budding bandit as well. I still had about half my cash left.

There were also new clothes: underwear, socks, colored shirts, new boots, chinos—the only thing that remained was my belt. I did not know whom to thank, and the card left atop the undershirts did little to clarify her motives: "Tommy—take it easy—you need rest, not more flights!" Did she mean the flights from Panama or the one from Cali, which I began to remember that morning in awful detail.

Ivan's men would be coming for me. It was a question of loyalty, or class solidarity. They saw themselves as the lawgivers in a nation of chaos and lawlessness, infiltration and conspiracy, and I had successfully moved against one of their kind. Not only had I badly outsmarted him, but I had by implication bested them as well. They had lined up a lengthy investigation and a favorable judge for nothing more than humiliation and defeat for their carefully plotted efforts.

I can make movies, too, you arrogant fucks.

I wondered about Palanco, the only card that remained face down on the card table. I hoped he had the smarts to play dumb as the whirlwind of accusations would blow through his office, hopefully landing on the trustworthy and connected Captain Duarte's desk. For me, that was his charm: his apparent inability to count to twelve, rather than a hidden ability to follow a thirteen-step plan.

I had permanently scarred Ivan—that much basuko cut through virgin brain tissue like a good hunting knife through a small rabbit— so that he would live with the effects perhaps for a long time. I may have also busted him mentally for good. It is difficult to determine the survivability after massive trauma among people who have never had to will themselves back from anywhere, and Ivan had a pretty easy existence up in Bogota—no military service, no violent encounters—until he crossed paths with me, and plenty of new tennis balls and favorable court assignments at his club.

It was easy to break down a man in the cheap way I brought down Ivan; lifting himself back up was his business, though I was ambivalent about how much luck I wished him. I had—at least for some time—lost the thrill of the hunt.

Instead of armed guards and a convoy, I took a taxi out to the airport. My head had cleared, but I still had no appetite, and strange-colored urine was my new symptom. The paramilitary flight was due in about twenty minutes, so anyone with authority inside the airport had taken a coffee break, or an early lunch. There were no lines at the airline counters, no incoming flights of passengers milling about, and the kiosk workers sat patiently until the paramilitaries came and went. For me, the absence of policemen was as noticeable as if there had been a platoon of them. No one on either side of the river would tell them about me, unless the money was enough to betray some pretty ruthless killers.

Red Sox arrived within two minutes of his touchdown time with another huge load of cash, one that nearly reached the levels of the windows. "There must be a big party at the Green House tonight," I thought. We shook hands warmly, but he kept etched on his face that look of pity and concern I had become used to sponsoring in others when I was sick, and in this instance tracked the sweat that dripped over my nose and onto the ground.

"Tommy, what's the matter?"

"I'm just a little sick, Sox. It'll pass… anyway, we have to discuss some business." He looked down at the boys who had already emptied about half of the cargo.

"What is it?"

"They are building a runway on the hills over there," I said, pointing toward San Blas.

"They want direct flights."

"I haven't changed my mind, boss. I like the job… the opportunities you gave to me, but I'm not going there, man. In that case, I'm out, Tommy."

I knew that would be his answer, not as a gambit, but simply to protect his family from the danger that prolonged exposure to the paracos could bring. "The ELN have hundreds of trained troops in those mountains, Tommy. They are losing a lot of militants in the villages—to be sure—but that doesn't change their fighting capability. Those guys—" he pointed at the men walking toward us from the helicopter—"are moving too fast. They are losing battles out there, Tommy. They are gaining ground, but not holding it. It is not enough just to terrorize people."

I knew all about it. The talk was that the paramilitaries ordered about fifty caskets a month from the undertakers in Simiti. "They don't have any choice, Sox. They are under orders. If the ELN gets their own Caguan with the only refinery in the country within it, the government will sue them for peace. This is the only way." Sox was insistent. "Anyway, this is working," he said, speaking broadly of the shut-down airport, heavy security, and quick handoffs. "We have never missed a landing since we started. Tell them that." I looked at the men to whom I would futilely relay Red Sox's concerns, but they had already decided on the future direction of our joint mission.

The world knew nothing at all about the massacre factories that we were helping to finance on the Magdalena. They never would, unless someone spoke, which I doubted. Even if they knew, the news-inhaling crowds could only smoke one war at a time, and no journalists were touching this one. Bosnia had used up all the public appetite for war horror. That was the way the CIA liked it.

I could feel my fever rising on that walk to the helicopter—my shadow a stick figure next to those of the men who walked with me on either side away down to the helicopter. I had the notion that this was what the CIA and D-2 wanted. But what was it?

Before I slipped into another delirium that night, Colorado and the political director made their pitch, succinctly and formally: they needed accounts outside the auspices of the CIA to take advantage of the whole global bazaar of arms and expertise. They wanted to move about fifty million, at least for now. They could not write checks against blue bags of cash.

They looked at me as if the CIA had trained me in laundering money, whereas I only knew how to slide a plane around and under radar into a single landing strip under the control of a crooked and under-staffed police force, and wait for the vault count to finish. It would have been perilous to strip down my own legend among these types within their own compound—they were, whether they knew it or not, or whether they wanted me to know it, hiding me until Ivan loomed less important in the greater scheme of things.

I needed sleep and rest; after that, I needed to talk with Sal Manzo. I called Howard AFB to leave a simple message for delivery to Red Sox: "Ramon... Piper... Barranca... Now!" While they ate on the second floor of the Green House, I just sweated and sweated, not at all savoring the smells of food or hanging onto any particular comment they made. "You have to give me a week. Fifty million is a big haul. Meanwhile, our arrangements are the same—my pilot flies into Barrancabermeja on a fixed schedule with guaranteed security. He is not to be questioned or impeded in his work."

They had already agreed to these terms, but they needed to hear them again. "After we conclude this business, we can discuss your other plans."

My head at that point was peeling with non-stop headaches like the first days after I awoke from the Liverpool Bar. Once back in bed, I disgraced my quarters again with awful smells like those in my hotel room across the river. They had to send for a girl from San Blas to swill my room and tend to my sheets and clothes. After her first visit, she wore a mask and cleaned the room from within rubber gloves that reached her elbows. She looked at me like this was the last room I would ever occupy.

Illness was seeping into my lungs, and for all I knew, the major organs keeping me alive. I did not want to see a doctor, or for them to know much about my overall condition. Nothing good could come from their knowing more about me than I knew about myself. On a net basis, I was short of knowledge. A woman had entered my hotel room to nurse me; a taxi driver may or may not have filed a criminal complaint against me for armed assault; Palanco may have been caught and decided to give me up; the CIA may have determined that I was or was not worth keeping around; my wife was either safe and sound in Chevy Chase or detained in Bogota as a flight risk, my children without their mother; the paracos may or may not have heard about Ivan and decided to cut their losses in the Tommy account.

On the plus side, I had the goodwill, sound business judgment and endless cleaning supplies of psychopathic, riverside killers.

A few days later, I took a helicopter over to Barrancabermeja so that Ramon could fly me to Aruba; it looked to the guards on the tarmac more like a medical evacuation of an invalid than an executive transport of an important player. My first night in Las Cabanas, I called for Doctor Hilliard, who still travelled with his black bag to alleviate minor tropical illnesses ailing hotel guests along the coast.

Mine was another kettle of fish. Barely raising my hand to shake his, I explained my illness in Uraba, and my symptoms over the last week. He forbade me to leave the room until the results of my stool and blood samples came back to him. He washed his hands after examining me.

Ignoring doctor's orders, I met with Sal Manzo and Leo Huff the next morning in Leo's office. Like witnesses to a solemn procession, which was how they looked at my awful decline, we kept to a murmured quiet and only spoke at length when necessary. As I expected, fifty million would overwhelm Sal's small operation, apparently raising too many red flags that he could no longer avoid if he wanted to keep his bank away from U.S. Treasury lawyers.

"There is a lot of pressure from the Feds… you either have the smarts and chutzpah to make the new system work for you—like the Russian mafia—or you get caught and your bank goes down with you," Sal begin to explain.

"How is that affecting you?" I asked.

"I have to chop things up in little pieces and send them around Euro and Caribbean banks. It is fuckin' expensive to stay under Uncle Sam's radar… they own Panama. I can't place any money there… I might as well store it in the vault."

Leo provided a more official review of the new Caribbean banking standards: "Formally, it is called the Money Laundering and Financial Crimes Act of 1998. It requires those who take advantage of the Fed wire system to provide more details about the clients for whom they transfer monies."

Sal felt he needed to explain in greater detail why he could no longer take large sums from me. "Chiara told me the Montreal banks are scared shitless. They are closing their doors on all their old Sicilian friends."

"Still, there are billions of dollars being laundered, Sal. It is just a question of finding new ports of call."

Unexpectedly, it was Leo who suggested a possible solution to our problem. "Sal, would you excuse Tommy and me for a few minutes. I need to discuss some confidential aspects of his private banking." After Sal departed, Leo began. "Tommy, your personal funds are in numbered savings and brokerage accounts with old friends of mine in the Bahamas. Your money is growing tremendously. We got you in on the ground floor of something called 'Google' which has proven quite profitable. There might be a solution there. Go back to your hotel and rest—that is, to the extent that I am authorized to direct your affairs-an order. I will call you later today."

Doctor Hilliard was finishing the final taping of the IV into my arm when Leo called, requiring him to stretch the phone cord taut to stretch across the bed. "Tommy, it is all set. A man named Jonathan Overton will be arriving in two days. We will meet in my office. Until then, follow Hilliard's instructions to the letter. If I find out you are living la vida loca with Sal, I will put guards on your door."

That night, I called Amelia, fully aware that the CIA had my voice print, which they would use to record this conversation.

"Hola, mi amor."

"Tommy, where are you?"

"I'm safe."

"Has something happened?"

"No, I am just here for a little rest."

"How are you?"

"Good. What about you? How are the girls?"

She was not hiding anything on her end. No one had attempted to impede her or even asked her down for a friendly chat at the Colombian Embassy. "They are growing, Tommy, and they miss you. They are asking for their Papa."

I made a fist that caused Hilliard's needle to partially slide out of my arm, and which I nearly broke off when I jabbed it back inside. "Tell them we will all meet soon."

"Is there any... resolution, mi amor?"

"I have heard nothing. Work continues, Amelia. That sort of thing."

"Your father is going to open a consulting firm. He and I have been looking for office space while Celeste looks after the girls. They love the house. They put their toys at the bottom of the stairs—the maid pretends to get upset with them, and they move them back when she is gone."

"Essential skills, mi amor, tell them they have my full support."

"How much longer, Tommy?" It was time to break off before I gave away too much of my plans.

"I will call you again, Amelia. I love you." I hung up with literally an aching heart.

The next morning, Doctor Hilliard delivered the news in a matter-of-fact manner through which a little gloating, perhaps to make up for his earlier misconduct with me, registered in his voice. "As I expected, typhoid. You picked it up several months ago, and experienced a near-cure. Two weeks ago, probably due to a poor diet, stress, even alcohol, it came out of hibernation in your system. It is creating havoc with your normal organ functioning, hence the strange smells. It could still kill you—you seem to like living life under a caution flag most of the time—unless you get complete rest and defeat it once and for all this time." The pills were only for a month, but Hilliard promised me more at a later date.

No one told me I picked up typhoid in Uraba. I wondered if Amelia knew at all. It would explain some of her anger with her father and Nando.

Leo Huff did not participate in the meeting between Jonathan Overton, Sal and me in the nightclub office under Las Cabanas. Leo had already taken significant risks over the telephone, ones that could call into question his oaths to the Aruban bar if we were ever caught. Overton was dressed in blue jeans and a polo shirt, tropical business casual in the Caribbean. He looked about fifty years old, in good shape except for a swelled mid-section, sporting the light tan burned into his skin that one sees among whites who live full-time in the tropics. He knew Sal Manzo by reputation, but he knew nothing about me, and only came on Leo Huff's guarantee.

My fever had broken again the night before, and in order to appear less the invalid and more the seasoned operator, I forced myself to eat, and when not eating, to swim in the ocean for a few days. I had told Colorado I needed a week to formulate a plan. Two days remained.

I told Overton the requirements of the placement, not insisting upon anything on his part. Occasionally looking down at his whiskey tumbler, interrupting with only a few questions, none of which touched upon the providence of the funds, Jonathan Overton grasped the essence of our problem quickly, even reaching over to my side to offer some business advice. "You'll need a corporate jet on your end, I believe. Your cargo will be from four to five thousand pounds. You will also need to fly long-hauls. The Caribbean being what it is, a corporate jet is your best bet," he said, almost like he had used the rhyme before to close a similar deal.

The rest of the matter did not seem to arouse much concern for him. He and Sal then spoke using a language of territorial and banking acronyms and nicknames that left me out of the conversation for long stretches. They each took notes—Sal inside a cheap collegiate notebook, Overton in a leather-bound notepad, but not enough to encompass the enormous project that we had agreed to undertake.

Overton also had surprisingly few requests. He wanted the moneys in separate two-hundred-fifty-thousand-dollar containers, preferably sturdy, taped boxes. He wanted a week to plan and organize his end. He wanted Sal Manzo and me to be without other demands on our time for three days. He also wanted a deposit of one hundred thousand dollars, a ten-percent down payment for services, which Sal had delivered from his bank vault to Overton's room in another hotel that night.

"That's it, Tommy. Get a jet, and we are in business." Sal's services did not come cheaply, either; he wanted a half a million dollars, part of which was to provide timely banking services, the other to help me hoodwink anyone who might be checking tail numbers at the Aruba executive airport. I set aside two and a half million for myself.

I had the feeling that it would cost me at least a million in bribes and tributes to turn Ivan from tragic upper class hero to farcical dinner joke in Bogota.

Ramon flew me back to Barrancabermeja on the sixth day. After fueling the plane, Ramon went back to Maicao. He knew better than to spend the night without proper papers in Barrancabermeja.

CHAPTER FORTY-SEVEN

The next morning, Hawkins came over from the helicopter to tell me that the pilot was in the airport bathroom. I had had no communication with D-2 in over a month, during which the paramilitary leaders had ripped up my contract as a flight consultant and pressured me into a deepening role in their internal affairs. I called Bustamante, who was not available, and then Patty, who was tight-lipped about these new events, but promised to get back to me.

Next, I called Nando. It was not the jocular Nando of Christmas vacations or Cali lunches, the prancing pony of mirth that entertained at family events. This was a new guy. He was official to the point of curtness, using phrases I never expected from him. "I will relay your concerns to...."

"Our office currently has no information concerning..." He would not field any questions about Amelia or her father, cutting me off even further from simple matters that I would want to know in a normal life.

"Thanks for your time, Nando." He gave me more official speak as he said his formal farewell, but suddenly broke into English in the middle of his phrase. "Run, marika!"

"Hawkins, can you fly this thing?" He laughed at the thought.

"Yeah, right, Chofer."

"Something is not right. Get that pilot. We have to leave now." Hawkins sprinted into the airport, returning in a sprint with the pilot.

"Get us the fuck out of here now!"

As we rose wobbly into the heavy, swampy air, I could see police cars with revolving sirens arriving at the airport, which I pointed out to Hawkins with a look of admonishment. "No more bathroom breaks. This is a serious breach of security, hombre." He looked at me in a perturbed manner, which perhaps responded to my challenge of his security arrangements, or the insolent manner I assumed in my first day as an outlaw, whereas he had probably spent years that way.

Still fevered, I took a nap in my room within the staff quarters near the Green House. The girl from San Blas had scrubbed all the surfaces of the room, so that its new smell was a strong odor of cleaning supplies. The pills from Doctor Hilliard had some effect. My fever had receded into a few hours of chills at night, and the persistent headaches no longer spiked into brain-frying ones that made speech and movement intolerable. Hilliard said that with rest and a "normal routine," I could expect a full recovery in two weeks.

Hawkins must have known those sirens were for me, but he said nothing at all. There was no ceremonial rite to mark my first night as an outlaw in the Green House. The officers that came and went through the canteen on the second floor, who operated the various schools of torture and dismemberment, and perhaps dentistry, had probably amassed enough crimes against humanity to keep The Hague busy for ten years.

I never expected to end up here, holed up in this place, with my protections from Dr. Appleman now also null and void.

That night I gave my pitch to Colorado and the political director, who it turned out answered to the name of El Mono. The placement would be forty-five million dollars; the overhead, which I declined to specify with line items or amounts, was five million dollars. In two weeks, through coded account names and passwords, they would take control of either lines of credit or personal loans to fictitious companies registered throughout the Caribbean, but only if and when I delivered the codes to them.

I knew they would take the deal, as they had been paying me a million dollars a month already to do essentially nothing but show up occasionally at a local airport. They were also greedy; I figured some of those monies would pay for guns and food, but these guys also were rich and wanted more easy money to come their way.

"What about the corporate jet? Can you order one for arrival next to a war zone?"

"Not to worry, Chofer," replied El Mono.

"We are on good terms with the oil company executives on the other side. We can borrow their jet for a few days for a minor cost."

"In that case, I will leave in a few days."

I stood up to leave. "There is one more thing, Chofer," Colorado began.

"What's that?"

"Your health, hombre."

"I am recovering from a viral infection. I will be able to undertake the mission."

"Yes, but afterwards. We can't have an outbreak here. We can't be seen that way. That is inviting an ELN attack."

"What do you have in mind?"

"After you get back, we'll have our doctor check you out again. For now, he wants to see you tomorrow morning."

Funny: I was a health risk, a threat to camp hygiene for the truckloads of pimply assassins who killed innocent villagers for serving soup to insolent patrols of rebel soldiers. They were comfortable issuing instructions to me, as they knew the balance between us had shifted—badly for me—in the last week. I would never make it through any passport control, and if identified, was looking at years in a cold basement cell in Bogota before the Fiscalia even looked at my file.

I was also cut off from my own command, which apparently did not see fit to pull me from action with a simple satellite phone call and a kindly extraction order. Live bacteria had settled into my bowels and lungs. Rotting from within, I had little choice but to follow their camp rules, taking solace in a clean, sterile room.

I had destroyed two lives, one a boy much like myself, who saw himself capable of heroic deeds for noble reasons, but with awful luck. The other—Ivan—I cut down for essentially smirking at me too many times. I was much closer to a future life as Cody Pryor than Tommy Connolly.

I had no appetite again, so I slept and took pills and supervised walks along the flanks of the Green House until it was time to leave. When I left, Colorado looked at me as if a curse had finally departed from the Green House.

CHAPTER FORTY-EIGHT

We flew low and steady across the Northern plains of Colombia at the tremendous speed of an executive jet into Aruba. This time we taxied directly into an unused hangar in the executive wing of the airport. One of Sal's guys quickly closed the door as soon as the jet's pilot cleared the threshold of the two large sliding doors. Leaning on the far right wall was Sal himself. Seeing him, I signaled to the pilot to shut the engines down.

We embraced as the old friends we had become.

"You ready, Sal?"

"Yeah, let's get on with it."

"When was the last time you left the island?"

"It's been about six years."

"There's not going to be any passport control in the Caymans, I hope."

"No— "

"You know what to do in the Caymans?"

"Jeezus, Tommy—I taught you this business. Now, you want to give me lessons… let's go, already."

"Ok. It's 800 miles—two and a half hours… you got your hemorrhoid cream, Sal?"

"Douche." Sal brought two of his guys with him; unknown to the pilot, who would not have left had he known, all three of them were armed.

We arrived in the Caymans around lunchtime. From the air above the landing strip we could see our armored truck near a back fence apart from the auxiliary roads, and far from the runway or the terminal. This time we did the grunt work. There were five of us—the oil company pilot was a Colombian with dark glasses and few words, who merely watched from his pilot's seat as we unloaded and packed away boxes filled with twenty dollar bills. The armored car guards took note that their clients were well-armed when they bent over to the edge of their truck to push in another box.

The transfer took about twenty minutes in all. When we finished, one of Sal's guys went into the back of the plane and gave me a briefcase.

I shook Sal's hand warmly. Again, he and I had pulled off something irregular in the extreme and still could look each other in the eye with respect.

"Good luck, Sal."

"You too, Tommy."

"See you back at Las Cabanas in a few days." A lot had to happen, though, between now and then.

The first step was refueling. Sal would stay in the Caymans until I picked him up on the return flight from Bermuda. He knew all the island bankers—and therefore how to cajole or entice them into a highly illegal transaction worth around thirty-two million dollars--, which he would empty into the vaults of ten different banks in the Caymans through the back door, and then return through the front door to make sure that the count was honest, and the fake bank paperwork tidy.

The pilot and I touched down about 18.00 in Bermuda with a significantly smaller and more jiggly pile of boxes, a consequence of the plane's trundling side excursion down a dirt road to a set of abandoned small-plane hangars, where we parked behind the furthest one from the tower controller, who was well-paid not to notice, but still might be curious. I loaded the remaining thirteen million into another vault on wheels.

Jonathan Overton agreed to meet me at the first bank on the list. We shook hands warmly and found an empty office where I handed him the brief case from Sal Manzo. I also gave him a file with about twenty pages of paper that he quickly recognized as the agreed-upon loan papers from the Cayman Islands banks.

"I will get started in the morning," Julian casually mentioned.

"Will they call you about the count? I need some sleep."

"We will make our rounds tomorrow afternoon, Tommy. When was the last time you slept by the way?"

"About two days ago."

"Youth. Get some sleep—preferably until about noon tomorrow. I will stop by the hotel and pick you up around then. Stay keen, old sport—you look like a fright."

I taxied to the hotel and fell into sleep in my pants and boots. In the mirror, I fancied myself as one of the first Irish prisoners to wash up on the beach in Australia as a prisoner of Her Majesty. The image fit me, but my crimes were a bit more premeditated than the acts of pocket-picking and drunken brawls whose judicial remedy cleaned out the lower orders of Victorian Ireland.

My face had crevices now—deep and angular ones, capable of casting their own shadows—and my legs were once again bandy. I dreamed that night of gale winds that broke apart small boats and lashed against the rocks of a small lighthouse island. One could take that dream a number of ways, which I did not bother to reflect upon, since I woke suddenly to a loud knock.

My headaches were manageable, but not helped by jet flight around the Caribbean. I gobbled several pills before meeting Jonathan in the lobby.

We met for lunch in the hotel café. Since I wore the same smelly plane clothes—the same ones I had worn since Barrancabermeja, I was seated quickly and at a great distance from other diners. Julian was a gentleman and made no mention of my odor or appearance. "Good news, Tommy! I went for my neighborhood walk this morning and did some banking of my own. It seems your papers are all in order. It looks from afar like small short-term loans to offshore firms—small-scale and ordinary by Caribbean standards. By the time anyone asks questions, the loans will be repaid and the companies will fold up."

I waved down the closest waiter and asked for a double espresso to jumpstart my soggy brain. "Well—your work is done here, Tommy .. I will not be able to give you any definite news until the 19th or 20th, as you can appreciate. It takes a while to get into the system and start moving things around, and this won't happen until the wire transfers are all complete from the banks. But I'm hoping that two days should be adequate time for me to set up the corresponding accounts and start to fill them."

"Jonathan, excellent news. My customers will be pleased to hear this. Your work speaks for itself."

So did mine, but not to my credit according to a growing list of Colombians in Bogota, and now along the Magdalena.

I looked at my watch. We had no need to be out of Bermuda by 16.00, so there was plenty of time for lunch and to get to know my new business associate. We ate lunch in a friendly manner, though watchful when any new table of adult males sat too close to us. I was curious about his life, how he found his niche at a comfortable distance from raw criminality, yet still able to take his share of its winnings, how he enjoyed the pirate's bounty without ever stepping foot onto a pirate ship.

His boarding school and Cambridge mien left an impression of a well-polished and capable businessman, but he was still essentially one of us. At some point, he just walked away from the safe confines of respectable wealth accumulation in England for Bermuda. He explained that Bermuda had been either entrapping or seducing government officials since the time of Cromwell, and he did not see things changing considerably during his career. It was true—one never read about Bermudan banking scandal or the United States Treasury demanding access to its bank records on an "or else" basis. Still, he kept a South African passport.

For the second time since leaving Cali, I swapped clothing—even my belt, which had a lingering odor of tropical illness—and left Bermuda in new chinos, boots and underclothes.

On the flight back from the Caymans to Aruba, Sal wanted to talk and joke and enjoy our latest triumph of piracy over empire, but I was staring at more trouble than I cared to share with my pirate friend, the man who showed me that crime could be both profitable and recreational. I went straight to sleep in my suite that night with sweat-stained sheets interrupting what should have been fruitful sleep.

We met up the next day for lunch in his office in Las Cabanas.

"Jesus, Tommy. You have come a long way since you jumped into the ravine that first night." It was the measuring stick Sal used to chart my rise in the world of crime, like a proud father measuring his son on the kitchen wall with a ruler. Between cycles of fever and chills, I still had little in the way of reserves of mirth.

"I'm ready to retire, Sal. It was never about the thrill or the lawlessness. I can't poke these guys with a small stick forever—eventually, they will hit me with a bigger one."

"So, what are you gonna do with all that money—you are a rich man now, Tommy."

"When I get there, I'll tell you. You'll be my first houseguest."

Sal gave me a look strongly suggesting that he did not believe a word of it. "You have enough money, Sal. Why don't you buy yourself some diplomatic immunity and travel a little? Find a girl from the old country and teach your son crooked banking." Sal took a gulp of whiskey and instead of responding, he looked at his watch.

In all, thirteen banks—eight in the Caymans, four in Bermuda, and Sal's—made loans to holding companies that had no ongoing business until Jonathan Overton willed them into existence through computer keystrokes in his Hamilton, Bermuda office. The loans went to these new companies' accounts immediately, though the money we delivered would unofficially sit in the cooperating banks' vaults for quite a while. Once a month for six-months, the bank managers would take part of the money and introduce it formally into his bank as a loan repayment.

Sal's part was easy. We had in effect taken out pre-paid loans. Sal was the lead banker within a consortium that loaned out forty-five million dollars to a small group of pre-existing and newly-created bogus banking clients. None of the banks had more than a 3-4-million-dollar exposure, which would not cause a Treasury agent to begin a formal investigation. All the banks made exorbitant fee income in a risk-free manner, making the venture worth the risk of U.S. Treasury displeasure. It was rather simple: the paramilitaries took their money as electronic wire transfers to the new accounts; the bankers opened their vaults each month and repaid themselves.

Overton's part was easy, too. He only needed to take the wired money from Sal's bank—on behalf of the loanees—and move the money around the world at dizzying speed, and in and out of the accounts until it became unfeasible for any Treasury investigators to keep track of the original source of funds.

All the money would eventually settle into accounts in banks from the Caymans to Hong Kong; and all the gentleman pirates in the Caribbean slept easily that night, except for me, who had the smarts to keep ahead of government types in low-stakes games, but not in the essential mistake the Colonel had warned me about—never directly take on a state, which in the person of Ivan Moreno I had kicked hard in the balls.

For all I knew, I had worn out my welcome with two governments.

My last meeting before hopping back on the jet for the return to Colombia was with Leo Huff. He seemed to take in with deeply hued sadness the instructions I gave to him in a short discourse in his office.

"I understand, Tommy." Leo continued.

"Are you sure this is what you want to do?"

"Yes, Leo. It makes the most sense. Do you think they will be receptive?"

"As long as the paperwork is in order, they will handle it expeditiously."

"About how long?"

"I would say about six weeks."

"Ok. You have all my signatures, right?"

"I have power-of-attorney, and a little machine that fakes your signature if I am in a spot."

"Good. Leo. Give yourself a nice bonus for this job."

"It keeps me young, Tommy. I don't have many clients that take on narcos and intelligence services."

"Not for long, Leo. Not for long."

I was twenty-eight years old. I had over ten million dollars in banks and accounts under management in island banks throughout the Caribbean. I had just updated my will to give Amelia power-of-attorney over my mother's care needs in perpetuity upon the occurrence of my death or prolonged disappearance. But I was wanted for questioning by the Attorney General's Office in Colombia for obstruction of justice and criminal assault. The CIA had apparently abandoned me to my fate, while the paracos were probably anxious to move on without having to set aside a portion of their profits for my cut.

My smell had started to turn bad again, and I felt achy. In the lobby after my meeting with Sal, the concierge handed me a message from another anonymous friend: "Tommy, Barrancabermeja airport watched by Fiscalia agents. Find alternate route back. A friend."

I slept in warm sweat the rest of the day and into the depths of the night.

"You got a parachute?" the pilot laughed. He had every reason for mirth; his nights in Las Cabanas included free meals, drinks, and Sal's prostitutes. Hawkins also laughed the problem away when I told him about the warning I had received about surveillance of the airport. "Not to worry, Chofer! We'll bring a body bag and carry you out of the plane directly onto a helicopter."

"You're a thoughtful, wonderful and creative human being, Hawkins," I thought, but left the matter alone. At about 05:00 we reached the Colombian coast under a beautiful pink and purple sky, over a point close to our own runway outside Maicao.

It would have been the wiser course to just land there and sit out the rest of the cleaning up of the Magdalena. Small, local little massacres were not making headlines anymore, and they were getting along well without me. The CIA was utilizing my company name, plane, and pilot, enough to fog their involvement in those early months of preparing the Magdalena for the mass slaughter and cocaine production to come. It also would have been wiser, too—as I rummaged faster and faster through my new backpack, banging my fist on my knee in reproach for my stupidity since I had left my pills once again in the hotel room in Las Cabanas.

At the airport in Barrancabermeja, the pilot parked the jet and walked down the stairs on the flank of the plane with his briefcase while I waited within. Hawkins walked up the stairs next, carrying a flattened extra-large body bag: "The army only had one in gringo size," he smirked—and then beckoning me to get inside. I would not give up my backpack, which had my gun, my satellite phone, and more importantly, the bank account codes that I would only hand over to Colorado in person.

He zipped me inside, leaving me in meditative silence for several minutes, the only sound coming from the spinning rotors of the nearby helicopter. I sweated badly in there, whether from fear or premonition or resurgent typhoid, awaiting the bizarre trust walk to come. Two pairs of hands lifted me down the stairs, and toward the helicopter, probably in a mock, solemn cortege for a downed comrade.

Hawkins had put on a show for my arrival at the Green House. Their guns held in their hands in firing position, there were about fifteen soldiers positioned in a large circle at the end of the new dirt runway. Easily three kilometers in length, packed down smoothly, it bore no resemblance to the rough, rocky strip of dirt I saw the previous week. Now, there were barrels of gasoline under black tarp tents—a gift no doubt from the executives across the river for services rendered in Barrancabermeja. There were sandbags stacked in semi-circles for large guns which had not yet arrived.

Though there was still three months remaining on my contract, it was clear my services would not be needed for much longer. Some sort of reckoning was near—that I was sure about—but I doubted that a gentle providence still had me on its caseload. I had become troublesome for too many people.

Once on solid ground, I only wanted water, but Hawkins handed me a satellite phone instead.

"Hello?"

"Chofer, it's Julian. Welcome back!"

"On time and on budget. It is all done."

"Excellent. We have a special surprise for you at the Green House; then you will fly to Santa Rosa."

"That's fine."

"How do you feel now?"

"I saw a doctor. He said I am nearly recovered."

That was hardly the truth, which Hawkins would undoubtedly convey to Colorado when we parted; without the pills, I was weakening again in my bones, and my headaches had returned. "That is good to hear. We will see you in about two hours."

A surprise in the Green House could mean many things; I was too tired, though, to struggle through the implications.

Gripping the edge of the sink, I drank about a gallon of water in the Green House canteen before two sentries came for me. They looked too cheerful to be harbingers of sudden doom, at least mine. Rather, they looked like they were taking me to a mystery date with a famous celebrity. I could hear pairs of boots coming up the stairs, so I gobbled aspirin, and looked for more on the shelves of the canteen. There was a full bottle, so I stuffed it in my backpack.

In the bathroom, after filling the toilet with a dark, copper-colored liquid, I looked at my thinned and worried face in the mirror. I was sliding back down into typhoid; it was clearly circling back for another chance at me. There was no way Colorado and Hawkins would allow me to regain my health within the compound of the Green House, or even on their side of the river. Recuperation on the other side of the river would result in my immediate arrest.

"Senor! Could you come with us for a few minutes? Your helicopter will arrive shortly. But we need you to attend to something first." Their cheerfulness was unnerving. They would gladly—meaningfully—smile and smile until they put a bullet in my head under one of the buildings nearby.

Our destination was the basement of the building next to the Green House. We walked down freshly laid concrete steps to a large black door, where one sentry held me back, while the other opened it with a stiff pull outward. A thick, rusty, and repulsive smell pushed outside for mercy's sake, temporarily overwhelming my own putrid stench. We all reached for our noses.

A string of hanging bulbs lighted up a wet and slimy path between a series of cubicles—more like pig basins with straw flooring and only a bucket in a far corner. There were naked bodies resting on several of the straw mats. The stench was fecal and abhorrent, and made its own headache in the otherwise pain-free parts of my brain.

Was this to be my final resting place? It made sense since no one knew I was there, and no one would come around to ask about me.

I could hear the now familiar murmuring for death or mercy or the reciting of a few distinguishable prayers. We walked along the wet muddy basement path to yet another large door. This one had a chained lock, which the same man opened. I looked back at the sentries, who still smiled as if they wanted to share a moment of wonder and awe that the Gods had put into motion only for me. A new festoon of wretched stench entered my nostrils and impelled a quick round of dry vomiting.

The leader turned on a light. In the back of the room, a boy I recognized was tied to a horizontal wooden bar. "No, God, no!" I thought. This is what Hawkins meant by 'Coronemos,' the word commonly used for the celebration after a successful drug touchdown in a foreign destination. But this was not a party with putas and music and booze. Colorado meant this coronacion for me only. They would not kill me down here. Instead, they had accepted me into their world as a respected comrade, sealing the deal in the only way that made sense to them.

His almost lifeless head dangled over the top of the sawhorse. With the dead weight of his useless legs, he leaned on his knees in his own urine and defecation, pressing his neck on the wood so that breathing was nearly impossible. Someone had cut off several of his fingers.

He did not respond to the sound of our entrance. So, one of the soldiers picked up a bucket of water. He approached the boy, who could not see or lift his head, and splashed him on the face. Simultaneously, the other soldier pointed his flashlight in the boy's face. It was the second shooter from the Liverpool Bar. He was too far gone toward death to recognize me, but that was not essential to the celebration that Julian and Hawkins had planned.

They were thanking me for services rendered to the movement.

In the light, I noticed more ghoulish detail: his eyes were covered with black and purple heavy sacks of skin; his nose was pushed inward, and he was missing most of his teeth. He could not manage speech, so he pushed out a nasal grunt from deep in his throat.

"Do you recognize him, Chofer?"

"Yes… Where did you pick him up?"

"In Cimitarra. The stupid guerrilla came to town to buy supplies for his comrades. He did not know that the storeowners now report unusual purchases to our command. We detained him and later confirmed his identity."

There was a new voice behind me, which I recognized as that of Hawkins, though he was invisible in the near darkness behind me. He spoke to me in the manner of an intelligence colleague. "He found the taxi and drove himself and a local punk to the bar. He sent the boy in to shoot all three girls. He waited until the shots stopped, and entered. His job was to kill the shooter and escape in the taxi. He did not expect to see you, as you were not part of the plan. He only wanted to fulfill his mission. He shot you so that you would fall, but you didn't. You protected the girl with a bullet in your brain. It was his bullet, Chofer." Those last few sentences were for the boy to ponder as much as for me to understand.

"Why?"

Hawkins did not understand my question, but I felt safer not rephrasing it. "Let me talk for our little guerrilla friend. Colonel Hernandez had uncovered several guerrilla cells in Cali. The feeling was that with the decline of the Cali Cartel, Cali was becoming an open city. The FARC wanted to enter the city with a splash. They would begin a campaign of targeted killings of the children of 'the oligarchy.' They would also kidnap others and blame the drug cartels. They hoped to take over Cali this way. Of course, the Colonel learned the location of the cells, and turned their occupants over to us. This is the only one who got away from us, Chofer."

That was not exactly true; I had just turned a young and callow revolutionary loose on Argentinean society so that he would not end up like this.

To all my physical weariness there arrived a moral despair to slosh around in the same ooze of my physical decline. I did not want to harm this boy. I did want to beat to a sodden, bloody pulp the radical professor who enticed him into revolution; the savvy urban recruiter who delivered him into the jungle; and the FARC ideological officer who completed his miseducation. This country was feasting on its children.

They were offering him to me like a birthday cake, or a ten-year service pin. Stupid boy, I thought. Why didn't you run far away and never look back? The truth was that a FARC camp in the jungle probably was his best refuge, as long as he stayed there. Another man poured more water on the faceless young guerrilla. Through a sliver in his eye he looked up toward me.

"That's right, little puchurria. This tall, handsome gringo is going to take your life. He is going to kill you now. We will let him choose the manner of your death. It has to happen now because he has a helicopter to catch. Do you remember the girl in Cali? She survived your attack, little guerrilla. This American was very brave and took bullets in his brain to save her life. That is how men act, little guerrilla. They don't bomb villages or attack soldiers from the bushes. The gringo's wife will be glad you are dead."

That last statement was true.

Hawkins and his men took a last look at his remaining features. They lifted his head, striking their fists down on his cheeks and mouth, careful to step away from plumes of blood that spat out of his face. "What do you think, Chofer? We have a rope, a knife or a gun."

Hawkins muttered something in support of my selection, which caused the sentries to whoop their approval.

I held out my hand for his gun, which Hawkins unholstered and handed to me.

"Would you step outside, please?" All of the men went back toward the door, and left. I cocked the pistol. I walked to the boy, kneeling in front of him, but not lifting his head. I leaned toward his ear. "Can you hear me?" He gave a grunt.

"You have to die now. I am very sorry. I wish you had escaped. I never wanted them to find you. I forgive you for my wife and her friends. You were just a boy. I know it was not your decision. This is not fair—none of this. This is a world of shit. I wish I could have saved you from all of it. I wanted to find you and give you money to escape. Please believe me."

A voice called out to me from the door, which had opened a little. "Chofer—man—you are here for revenge, not for a game of cards!" The other men laughed.

"Give me a little more time." The door closed again.

"I hope there is another life for you with more fairness and kindness and love somewhere. Please forgive me." As I said this last word, I pulled the trigger and sent a bullet into his brain through his ear. His body swung right and then fell backward into his own watery excrement.

The door reopened. "Thank you. I appreciate the courtesy." Hawkins looked at me sharply, not having seen the appreciation he expected on my face. "That was for your father-in-law as well, Chofer."

I was not a hero; I wanted no mercy, anymore. It was that simple. I had a serious quarrel with that boy, but not one I wanted to end with his torture and assassination and lime treatment. I was in the middle of a grid with a satellite phone tracing my movements to within a hundred yards, but I was lost. I had broken a commandment a man should not break.

Mercifully, delirium was coming for me; I had about six hours before I would not be able to lift myself off my bed without assistance, and would be at the mercy of men who had no need for an invalid in their headquarters. But I did not give the gun back to Hawkins. I needed to be judged, but not by anybody I had come to know since the Liverpool Bar—certainly not anyone on that side of the river. Even though he detected that my typhoid had returned, Hawkins shook my hand warmly before I got into the paramilitary helicopter.

About a half an hour after I shot that young man, a new pilot touched down on a soccer field in Santa Rosa, scattering young teenagers to nearby trees to escape the swirling debris and low-swirling blades.

A jeep took us to a four-story hotel only a few blocks from the central police office, which we passed with armed soldiers on our jeep runners.

We walked, exhaustingly for me, to the point where the soldiers pulled me by the elbows up four flights of stairs to the large suite on the top floor. Colorado stood in military fatigues with men I did not recognize, but were clearly at his level or higher in the paramilitary command along the Magdalena. Husbanding my remaining strength, I quickly sat down on a nearby couch without shaking hands with the other comandantes.

"—could I get some water, please." I looked upwards at the ceiling fan for a moment, but it lulled me when I most needed wakefulness. I stood up again, so that Julian could introduce me to other comandantes from Barrancabermeja and Cesar, down river about one hundred miles. They soon left, so that Colorado could query me about the present whereabouts of his money.

I handed Julian the envelope, whereupon he took out the three sheets of paper and read them at a wooden table near the window. I drank three bottles of water while he familiarized himself with the columns of bank names, accounts, and passwords. The deal was now complete. His command now had its own private budget, which he did not need me to empty or fill as command needs dictated.

Only then did he look at me. "You look sick, Chofer." It was an accusation, more than an expression of concern. It was a little cooler in the foothills of the Sierras of San Lucas, but my sweat—bitter and sodden on my face and clothes—made Colorado uncomfortable. "You need a doctor. We will bring one from Barrancabermeja with the appropriate medicines, but we will need to place you in quarantine." My thoughts went out to the poor campesina who would have to clean me when I fell back into delirium, which was about four hours away.

"If that is all, I would like to go back and rest now." I had no other option at hand. Any hospital would check my identification, triggering an order of capture from the Fiscalia. I would, in that case, likely wake up in a hospital in Bogota, my arms handcuffed to the bed. "Thank you for your efforts in this matter, Chofer. We will always appreciate what you have done for us."

It sounded more like a farewell than a compliment, but I was losing the ability to delineate such fine distinctions. He let me pass out of the room without a handshake or pat on the shoulder, though he gave me some bottles of water. Two soldiers kept me from falling over down the four flights of stairs.

One soldier kept me upwards in a crouched position under its blades, while the other opened the door of the helicopter and pushed me inside. The pilot gave me an update on our return flight to the Green House as soon as I buckled into my seat. Pointing to several boxes of armaments in the back of the helicopter, he explained that "We have to drop these off at one of our camps. We will be flying close to the low mountains…" He was trying to tell me that we would be flying over hostile territory, but I just mumbled some sort of reply.

We flew abreast with the foothills of the San Lucas. Down below were small fincas connected by roads that slithered between small hills and over nearly-dried out creeks. I counted three of the rivers that came down from the San Lucas on the way to the Magdalena. Above were the high peaks whose tops were encased in with thick clouds.

We sank downward with a few sways and lurches until the helicopter touched down firmly on tall grass in a large clearing. There was a single tree on the edge of the field where soldiers lounged in the shade. They ran toward us—bent well below the spinning blades above us—with their guns hanging over their shoulders. With their hands on their caps—rather than their rifles—so they would not blow away, they stood outside our side door, impatient to take their supplies and hike back down the nearest trail to a transport, which would take the arms back to their camp.

We would be back at the Green House in ten minutes, I reckoned.

I looked beyond the boys that pressed themselves against the sliding door of the helicopter to the thick woods above us. Coming toward us was a swirling white fume that sank slowly on a smoky line. The impact was mostly against the bodies of the boys next to us, but the hatch door was also hit and began to burn. It was probably an rpg that should have blown us up, but for the anxiety of the boys to conclude the exchange. The force of the explosion scattered the dead bodies of the soldiers on the ground around us, but there was enough remaining force to lift the helicopter upward a few feet, where it began to commence its death spin.

"This is how I will receive my judgment," I thought.

Almost immediately, machine gun fire opened up against the flank of the helicopter. As we spun, bullet holes appeared randomly through the metal skin of the chopper. The pilot and I never spoke. I unbuckled, grabbed my backpack and moved through the smoky chamber to the open hatch. Our spinning now having lost its axis, the blades were coming closer and closer to the ground. I tried to time my jump so that I would hit the ground on the far side of the FARC's bullets. I leaped out and down, immediately crawling, rolling, and finally pitching myself down the side of the hill, where I took cover in thick bushes below the bluff, which had become a smoky FARC shooting gallery of the remaining soldiers.

I had no wounds, but if I stayed there, I would end up in a FARC lime pit. I rubbed oil and smoke off my face, and prepared to run when I heard the huge explosion on the plain behind and above me.

"It is time to move now, Tommy," I thought, "run for your life.'

CHAPTER FORTY-NINE

I ran without looking back through bushes that laced my face with small scratches. The screams of the dying paramilitary boys was faint until the mortar fire stopped completely. Then the wounded, surrounded by guerrillas who came down the hill toward them, screamed until they were silenced by single shots.

My brain had pumped my body with massive amounts of adrenaline, which would delay my delirium by about an hour—two hours at most. My bowels were anxious for relief, but I just ran and ran back toward Santa Rosa. I avoided passing near fincas, which would have telephones, or even radios if they belonged to FARC or ELN militants.

They did not seem to be coming for me, as I heard neither gunfire or voices from my rear. I could not be sure whether they had even seen me, but that sort of optimism was no basis for a successful survival strategy in one of their areas of control. Through woods and over creeks and quickly across dirt roads, I ran with my head low for about ten minutes until I stopped to catch my breath, and to plan some type of logical escape. After drinking about half a canteen, I slid down an embankment onto a broad dirt road. I heard voices from a finca on the lower ground to my right, while to my left was an impossible thicket atop a creek. Up ahead, the road rose with diminishing embankments on both sides.

A motorcycle was slowing down on the road as it approached me. To run would only be suspicious behavior so I stood in the middle of the road and waved my arms to slow down the motorcycle. A young Indian boy geared-down the bike and eventually stopped next to me. He wore jeans and a dirty white tee-shirt, and the tell-tale FARC boots. I was behind enemy lines in his territory, but by the time he reached for the pistol in his waistband, my hands would already be around his neck, which he knew as well.

Keeping the engine on his motorcycle running, he looked me over for weapons bulges. "Hello. I am lost. There is trouble down the road. Can you take me to Santa Rosa Del Sur? I can pay you some money." The mining camps being far away in the mountains to the north, I had no other story to spin to the young guerrilla that would account for my appearance along that road.

The boy, unable to draw a weapon on me at such close quarters, or call for reinforcement, continued to look me over, unable to formulate a solution to his problem. I stood close to him and waited for him to act.

"Sure. I am going there." I hopped on the back of the motorcycle, but without quick access to the gun in my backpack. He sped hard up the grade and then down into the shade between palm groves on both sides of a cut grade. At the bottom, the road had ruts almost a foot deep.

He accelerated again to the top of the next ridge. Below, I could see Santa Rosa Del Sur in the distance, but a road-block about half way there stood in the way. I tapped the boy on the shoulder and yelled above the engine noise, "I appreciate the ride. I recognize the way now. I can walk from here."

"Are you sure, gringo? I can take you easily."

"No. I know where I am now." I gave him a small amount of pesos. He sped forward, down into a dry gulch in the road and up toward the plains around Santa Rosa Del Sur.

My sweat—staining my clothes with a putrid odor—had nearly stopped, inducing my body to just pour dry heat through my pores. I was lucid, but the adrenaline was losing its buttressing effect on my strength and judgment. He would be back. The question was whether he was smart enough to ask and then act upon instructions. If he played the part of the cocky hero, I had a chance, but almost none if he stayed and waited for backup.

Almost immediately after he had sped out of sight, I ran back up the road to a broad curve that limited visibility on both sides. I trudged down a sloped field and came back to the road with a large stick. I made a second trip to drag back a small tree branch, which I placed on the hidden side of a dogleg in the road.

In the distance, I could hear the motorcycle returning. He had apparently stopped and turned around, which meant he was not waiting for instructions. "Keep coming, son—don't wait for backup—he's just a gringo. You can handle him." He gunned his motorcycle and came up the grade hard. He did not stop at the top to look around, but came quickly up the dry gulch and approached the dogleg at full speed.

Pressing myself against the grade, my pistol was in my left hand, and the stick in my right. His motorcycle engine whined higher and higher until his front tire hit the tree branch and he went straight over the top of the motorcycle in a low arc down the slope of the road. Another boy was on the back of the motor cycle with a pistol in his hand. Unable to control his flight through the air, he slammed into the road with his head, breaking his fall only with his extended and now broken neck.

The rest of their team could not be more than a half mile behind.

I picked up the passenger's gun and radio and turned up the volume to hear FARC chatter. The driver, directly ahead of me, was trying to move forward toward his own gun, which had slipped off his waistband during his landing. His right arm appeared smashed, a bloody mess with a stick of bone protruding through his forearm. With that kind of injury, he was only moments from deep shock. I picked up his gun and his helmet. "I need a doctor, gringo," he begged.

I bent down near him.

"What was your plan—to shoot me or take me back to your comandante?"

"My friend told me to bring you back alive—that they had been waiting for you."

"What do you mean—waiting for me?"

"They expected you—that is all I know."

"Your friend is dead."

"You can get me a doctor on the radio. They will come from the roadblock."

"And me?"

"The ELN will take care of you. Someone will pay a lot of money for you. You are a gringo, after all."

"Ok."

Pointing one of the two guns I had just collected at his head, I dragged him to the side of the road, tucking his body into the bottom of the embankment under a tree near the creek. "Help will arrive soon. You'll be OK." Then I removed his friend's body from the road. I did the same with the tree branch and stick. They also had a full canteen, which I put in my backpack.

Nature bequeathed to me a second shot of adrenaline, but smaller this time, and undoubtedly of shorter duration. I had to move; judgment and lucidity were short-timers by that point.

The motorcycle, though on its side, was still running. With my cache of guns and the FARC radio, I walked the motorcycle through a shallow part of the creek until I found a small trail, which headed into the fields on the mountainous side of the road. My head—in fact, my entire body—felt like I had sat next to a large bonfire. The terrain gradually changed to steeper and steeper foothills with bunches of trees above their midlines. I rode for about another ten minutes before I heard the radio crackle. An ELN captain was asking for his men to report to him. There was no reply since the boy had likely passed out from pain and shock. The terrain became more and more difficult to push through on the motorcycle; several times I had to get off and push it up hills made impassible with rock formations or slippery, muddy ruts on its trails.

I was thirsty and wet with sweat—there was no way I could continue without hitting some rocks or a fallen branch, and joining the dead FARC soldier in the annals of "Killed in Action, motorcycle." I guzzled the whole canteen of water and immediately wished I had more.

"Don't look back, Tommy," I thought.

The captain repeated his request for a report from his men. Before he signed off, I heard him say, "Ijueputa! Vayase pa' alla!" I could not ride any higher through the mountains in what remained of the light of day. I stopped to pull out my binoculars. There was no view of Santa Rosa Del Sur due to intervening mountains; toward the south, there was a single grey fume of smoke still rising upwards from the helicopter attack zone. I had only put about two miles between myself and the road below—perhaps four from the black fume that marked the blood-soaked terminus of the helicopter.

It was likely that I would be in their clutches in less than an hour.

The ELN had likely found one dead and one unconscious boy by then; on the other side of the war, I wondered if Julian Colorado had any idea what took place in that clearing, or what the repercussions would be for him.

I rode down a steep hill, half walking and sliding the motorcycle in the soft, rain-soaked dirt. Abandoning the motorcycle behind a complex of fallen trees just above a river, I fell out of the woods at a rocky and sandy fork, where I spotted a cabin set back from the river. I pulled out my pistol and ran low toward it. There was less light at the bottom of the tall peaks on both sides of the river. Empty, its windows broken, there was a musty, dirty bed sheet, which I took with me. I quickly filled my two canteens in the river outside.

My bowels began to squeeze upward and my stomach downward. Even my tongue was blazing hot. I realized I had about ten to fifteen good minutes left before my body would yield no further to another outrageous surge of activity. I was going down, probably for a while. With unsteady hands which made my control of the bottle shaky at best, I opened the bottle of aspirin and gulped down a handful of aspirin with cold river water.

I sat and listened for a moment to the strong current of water pouring down from the higher mountains above me.

Cold was settling into the San Lucas, carried by darkening, rushing water and foggy, thick air that pushed down the canyons. I pushed the motorcycle further back up into the scrub behind the cabin. The water in the river was bitterly cold, so for purposes of a final surge of clear thinking, I dunked my head under it to provide some much needed short-term lucidity.

I—and the ELN team that was most likely searching for me—had about another hour of daylight left. But for me, my fight was against delirium. Before it was completely dark, I managed to pull myself up two more ridges, ensconcing myself near the top of a mountain under a canopy of entwined trees that permitted no light.

I sat for a moment, willing myself not to roll over and sleep for a few more minutes.

Soon, the rain began, softly at first, and then in all-enveloping downpours. I secured the bed sheet from the cabin between two trees and with an improvised stake on the ground below me, formed a redoubt against the lashing rain all around me. Deep sleep was coming for me, but since it could last for days, I used my last few minutes of wakefulness to plan my mountaintop refuge. First, I vacated my bowels down the ridge line, covering my liquid, stinky turds with leaves and branches. In camp, I placed my boots in a dry spot, turned off the radio, gobbled a bunch more aspirin, and using my backpack as a pillow, let delirium finally take me down and away.

During the next few days, I only awoke to drink water, or to crawl down the ridgeline to spew out yellow stool. Whether during the day or at night, it was not difficult to return to sleep. When I was awake, I felt no regrets or fears, no wish to be reunited with my wife and children, no anguish about the warrants out for my arrest, only the dull furnace of my head, which could scarcely manage its tenuous connection with time. I experienced only time in equal parts of hot, sticky days, and damp, cool nights, occasionally lit up by flashes of lightning and heavy rain above my bed-sheeted canopy.

I heard no voices or gunfire the whole time.

One morning, I don't know how many days later, I awoke with some clarity, able to form thoughts and reflect upon my situation, which, as I could see through my binoculars from a large rock on the ridgeline above my camp, was that I was alone, within ELN territory, and more objectively, about seven miles southeast of Santa Rosa Del Sur.

I welcomed the cramping hunger that I awoke to, knowing that it was incompatible with the ravages of typhoid fever. My water was gone, though, making my situation more perilous, since I would have to leave my camp in the daylight to find more. I liked the ELN's chances of finding me better than my chances at escaping them. They probably knew I had escaped further into their territory, where I could count on no one for sustenance or communications. They would probably take their time, listening in to paramilitary radio frequencies to familiarize themselves with my predicament, and the paramilitary response to it. Then they would slowly close the ring around me until I went away with them willingly.

Along with hunger, Amelia came back into my mind that morning for the first time since the Green House. We had last spoken from Leo Huff's office phone late at night about a week ago. She was comfortable in Washington, D.C, girding herself against worry by becoming useful to the Ambassador in his new business, and sharing baby duties with Celeste in their Chevy Chase mansion. Had anyone told her that my helicopter exploded after a missile attack, and that there were no survivors found on the scene?

Did the Ambassador get a courtesy call from Dr. Fuller announcing the loss of his son? Did anyone know I was alive? I needed the ELN to talk about me on as many frequencies as possible, or to blab in an unguarded moment to one of their NGO cheerleaders that a big gringo hunt was underway in the mountains. I put away all these thoughts in order to make my present predicament a puzzle to be solved, rather than a terror to be endured until my eventual capture.

Without maps or intelligence, I had to learn more about the terrain. I travelled down the southern flank of my mountain, crossed a mountain creek, and went up the next. The forests were so dense on the mountains—even at the bottom of the canyons—that I was only visible for brief moments along the rivers. That was information I needed.

I had to descend, though. There would be no food at this level unless I could catch my own kind of pesca milagrosa. Below, there would be yucca or papaya, or at least some coca leaves to numb my hunger. Eventually, I would run into the small-holders who harvested the coca leaves for that day's master. That would not be a pretty death, as they were faster with machetes than I was with my pistol. But I had to find out what the local landholders knew about me.

Again looking through my binoculars, I peered down at a small finca on a mountain mesa with sloping columns of coca plants around it. From the distance I could make out a farm manager standing outside his shack. He stared back toward my location with his binoculars. I quickly slumped down on the ground to avoid detection. On the bottom of this ridge was another creek; I looked again toward the shack. I wasn't detected it appeared, since the mayordomo had begun his morning chores, tossing out chicken feed through the fence of his small coop. Dropping a small bucket, he went back inside his finca. In these parts there were no phone lines, so his dialing for back-up was unlikely. He would likely have a radio, however.

I slithered slowly down the hill thinking that he would be indoors for a spell. But then he came back outside with a cup in his hand. He set it carefully on the railing so that he could wipe his face and swat away flies. Was he expecting someone?

Suddenly, a jeep appeared at the edge of the green plateau of his finca. I could see the insignia of the ELN on its flank. Two soldiers got out and shook hands with the man. The mayordomo went inside, returning shortly with two more mugs, which he handed to the soldiers. I took out my pistol and cocked it, letting it rest beside me while I held the binoculars to my eyes. If they came for me, I would have to fire to pin them down, but not to kill them. So far, I was an unwanted interloper in their mountains; I did not want to become an immediate threat to them.

As they spoke, they pointed toward the mountains from where I had come, and those on the far side of his finca. Having left their guns in the jeep, they obviously knew this man and were comfortable with him. Once they had finished their coffee, the soldiers piled in the jeep and left.

The mayordomo did not go back to his binoculars, and rather unexpectedly looked straight my way. Did he actually know I was up here? How did he see me? Suddenly, without warning he began waving at me, signaling that I should come down from the mountain.

Could I trust him? Was this a set-up and were the soldiers simply hiding at the bottom of the hill, waiting to make an arrest? With my pistol in the waist of my chinos I cautiously walked onto the edge of the clearing of his finca. He met me there.

"Willie, senor!"

"Tommy."

"Come with me, Tommy!"

"Senor, I will stay here. If they return, it will not be a good ending for you or me."

"That is true, senor, but you cannot stay here." I looked around his finca, but failed to locate a better alternative.

"What did you tell them, senor?" I said, motioning toward the gun sticking out of my pants.

"Tranquilo, senor. They are not my friends, senor. They stole two of my sons. My wife left after that. I am all alone here."

"I am sorry, senor. But they are trained military officers. They could return at any moment."

"Ok. Wait here. I will bring you coffee and some fresh eggs."

"Thank you so much, senor. You are very kind. Please be quick."

He walked back to his little shack, while I squatted behind the nearest tree with my pistol cocked. When he came close, I waved to him with a handkerchief. He decided to sit with me under the tree despite the risk of being discovered with a fugitive. He had brought a thermos of coffee, bread, and eggs.

"Thank you, senor. I cannot thank you enough. It has been a long, cold night."

"Call me Willie, por favor." I wasn't sure I heard him correctly at first.

"How did you get the name Willie?"

"My father loved Willie Mays." A baseball fan. A Giants fan. What are the odds, I thought.

"That's pretty incredible, Willie. I am a big fan of the San Francisco Giants baseball team."

"Bueno, senor! Have you been to the stadium in San Francisco?"

"Of course, many times."

"Did you ever see Willie Mays in person?"

"No. That was before my time."

"But you know about Willie Mays. All Gringos must know about him, no?"

"If I had a son, I would name him for Willie Mays."

"I never saw him play, but in the news in the movie theaters, I saw him… is he still alive?"

"Yes, Willie. He trains new players and makes speeches across the country to baseball fans. He is still a hero to many people."

I gulped down coffee and stuffed a couple of eggs in my mouth. "Tranquilo, gringo."

"I have to hurry. They know I am in this area."

"Yes, they told me to report to them if I saw you."

"What are they paying?"

He laughed. "They do not give money, gringo. They take it." I ate the bread while he spoke.

"I have not seen them for several months. The paramilitaries chased them far into the mountains. We began to sell our coca to the paramilitaries. At first, they paid double the ELN, but now it is just a little more. But they leave us alone."

"No more political lectures?"

"No, they just want more yield."

"What happened to bring the ELN back?"

"The paramilitaries are taking the bigger cities, but they take terrible losses when they get closer to the mountains."

That was pretty close to the formulation of the problem Red Sox expressed a few weeks ago to me. With some obvious foresight, he flatly refused to cross to this side of the river.

I drank the rest of my water from the bottle.

"Do you know about the disposition of their forces?"

"Pardon?"

"Do you know where they are?"

"They are about ten miles to the east, higher in the mountains. They have their main camp there. They cook the coca there. Helicopters come there and take it away."

"What about patrols?"

"Close to the camps, they patrol in groups of four or eight. Around here, they patrol in groups of two."

"Do they climb to the top of the ridges?"

"No, that is probably the best place to hide. They will try to catch you when you come down for food or water."

"Why do they think I am still here?"

"Because they know you came in this direction—they think you stole a motorcycle—and that you have not been seen below. They also have informants, as well as the extra men they have watching the roads below."

"Where are the villages near here?"

"They are on the south sides of the lower mountains." He pointed beyond his finca.

"There are about ten of them."

"The ELN has eyes in all of them… when the paramilitaries return, they will kill all the sapos."

"Where can I find food?"

"There is yucca and papaya near the villages. There is not much here, or in the mountains."

I could not ask him to shop for me since someone would ask the right questions in the villages when he shopped for two.

"Do you have water?"

"Yes. Wait here." He walked away with my bottle and canteens to the finca. He came back with a parcel of wrapped newspaper and the water containers.

"Take this, gringo." I put the parcel inside my backpack. I handed him about five-hundred dollars in Colombian pesos. He was reluctant to take the money.

"You took a big risk, Willie."

"Gringo, the next time come in the early morning, look for a plant in a large pot. If it is hanging from the railing, stay away. If it is on the ground, it is safe to approach."

We shook hands. "Willie, one more question—how did you see me up in the coca grove."

"Your skin. You are like a light bulb, gringo. Put some dirt on your skin." He laughed warmly. I turned and walked back up the mountain.

That night the rain fell hard again. I tied the bed sheet to the branches, under which I rested and pondered my circumstances, and my once brilliant life as a part-time associate pirate and CIA delivery boy. There was nothing on the ELN radios which even suggested that a hunt was underway for me. Their parsimony with communications made sense. They would not want the paramilitaries to know whether I was alive or dead. It would be better to capture me, clean me up, help me rehearse my lines, and then make a video in which I recanted my cruel deeds on behalf of the CIA and American Imperialism.

But it also meant that as soon as I turned on my satellite telephone and communicated my predicament to the paramilitaries, the hunt for me would intensify, since the ELN's plan for a surprise rollout of the captive gringo would evaporate. The paramilitaries had pulled back from these parts; they would not be able to mount any rescue unless it was part of an overall campaign to clear out the mountains, which was probably years away from taking place. The army probably did not know I was gone, and Colorado, no fool, would have no incentive to tell them. The Colonel would know—Colorado would feel obligated to tell him--and the Colonel would certainly pass word to the Ambassador that I was reported missing after an ELN ambush.

So, much of my ability to remain a low-priority for them depended on what kind of words Julian Colorado breathed into his radio over the next forty-eight hours.

That left Amelia, a matter the Colonel would hesitate to tell her until he knew more. I forced myself not to think about Amelia since it was too ruinous to any thoughtful attempt to stay alive in these mountains. I put my head on the ground and immediately thought about Amelia until I slept.

No plan had so far taken even rough form in my mind. Even if the army reopened the main roads, I would have at least ten kilometers back to the Magdalena through low hills with few trees in which to hide. If I arrived, it was likely I would be either arrested by the army, or detained—very likely for an indefinite period—by the paramilitaries. The paramilitary leaders certainly would rather silence a reckless arms shipper than explain their camp security failures to the CIA. In fact, my death behind enemy lines would solve quite a few problems for the paramilitaries.

They had the bank codes and the means to fill the accounts; what use did they have for a sickly CIA contractor who apparently was on a streak of terrible luck. Anyway, the helicopter was burned to a crisp; if they only found one body inside, they would not ask many questions before declaring me dead.

The rain sizzled down onto the mountains that night on the flashy knife's blade of jagged lightning strikes. Or, as Dr. Fuller would say, "Like shining from shook foil." As long as the rains continued, we were all grounded, and the real contest could not begin.

I guessed that four days had passed in this makeshift campsite, perhaps three of them in various states of delirium. That morning, I ate another half papaya. I put my guns, knife, guerrilla radio and water in the backpack in preparation for a reconnaissance mission of sorts. To the north, beyond the latrine, I bent down behind a group of rocks to survey the terrain, which sloped downward for several miles to the north. I decided to go in that direction and stayed about a hundred yards from the top of the ridges within the foggy, green canopy of their flanks.

There were no trails or villages, not even a single cottage. After a few miles, the ridge fell downward to small, scrubby hills. I could see now that Santa Rosa Del Sur was about five or six miles away. There was one roadblock in view, and likely many more that I could not see.

There would be plenty of patrols in this area. It was where I would begin my search for a missing gringo.

I soon caught sight of a small mining operation below me on a sloping plain between hills and a dirt road. Its camps consisted of about five tin shacks on stilts, and far up the denuded hillside a cabin. There was no sound of workmen or trucks nearby, so I took a chance and ran for it, flying down the hillside, stopping my acceleration by sliding baseball-style under one of the shacks. I sat quietly for 30 seconds-from what I could tell there were no noises or work hums at all.

I crawled low on the ground, popping up to take a look inside a rear window of what was apparently a kitchen. I slithered over to the biggest shed, which gave off a putrid odor. Its door was locked, but through the window I saw huge vats and, on the far wall, empty barrels.

This was no mining operation, at least one that would ever be profitable; it was a drug kitchen. The ELN probably abandoned it when the paramilitaries forced their way into Santa Rosa Del Sur. Still, it was in usable condition, lacking only the chemical precursors and agricultural products. In another small shed, I absconded with wire-cutters and pliers, but left behind a stack of cylinder bombs in aluminum tanks that was too heavy to carry at once. There was also a small box, which was filled with hand grenades when I opened it, and half-filled when I left.

In four trips, I took eight of the cylinders to the woods above the complex. I put them behind trees and broke the lower branches so that they hung down and covered them. I placed more branches directly on top of the cylinders. As I peered out of the woods, however, I saw two ELN foot-patrollers enter the camp from below. I froze in my tracks. They looked to be on a routine patrol, but they had rifles, which would not be a fair fight for Tommy in case of a long-distance shoot out.

They cackled with laughter, reclining and smoking, wiping away the occasional fly, oblivious to the fact that I had arrived first. They were just kids, seventeen at most, probably the average age of a dead paramilitary or guerrilla soldier in combat. After half an hour, they stood and walked back down the trail.

In the kitchen, there was an empty milk jug. I filled it with water too and went back up to the ridgeline for the long hike back up into the higher mountains. When I got to my camp, I drew a map of all the places I had been in the last two days. As soon as the sky darkened, and the first stars appeared, I slept, but not before forming my favorite image of Amelia—nude, garlanded with suds around her milk-filled breasts, cackling with laughter in the bathtub.

CHAPTER FIFTY

The next day, day five in my mountain hiding-place, it rained hard again in the mountains. I decided to make the trip down to Willie's finca. His plant was on the ground, so I walked down to the bottom of the sloped terrace of coca bushes. Seeing the waving motion of my little handkerchief, he came out with more eggs, coffee and bread. I told him about my previous encounter with the ELN foot patrol. "They are on normal patrol. I spoke with their boss yesterday afternoon. He wanted to know if I had seen any garbage or evidence of you."

"I am hiding my shit pretty well, Willie." He laughed. "Do they think I have left?"

"No. They are going to bring more men into the area. They have alerted all their contacts in the towns, the river crossings, and in Santa Rosa. They think you will coordinate an escape with the paramilitaries in Santa Rosa. So, if you approach by the Santa Rosa road they will be ready for that as well."

"Well, that's insightful because that is my plan."

"They are going to give back the main roads to the army, but keep control of the mountain roads and the rivers. The army will not walk into an ambush."

"Shit, it sounds like I need a new plan."

"I have to go into Santa Rosa tomorrow. I will go to the bars and listen. There will be talk. I will let you know—you better go now." I handed him another five-hundred dollars.

"Be careful how and where you spend this."

"Putas don't care where you get your money, gringo!"

"Willie, what is the name of your finca?"

"El Campo Central."

"Center Field?"

"Yes."

"How many hectares?"

"Twenty-five."

"When was the last time you took a vacation?"

"Probably my honeymoon—to Medellin—thirty years ago."

"No more silly questions, gringo. Go now!"

They were securing the main roads below to the larger cities and closing off the villages to me through threats and rumors. It was a good, solid plan. I still had no idea if the paramilitaries had their own plan.

The next day—day six by my reckoning—I headed northeast to the higher mountains of the Sierras, which I reckoned would place me well beyond the main concentration of the ELN patrols. I filled my backpack with eggs, bread and papayas, atop the water, knife and gun, wire, clippers, binoculars and satellite phone. There was no rain now, but the terrain was soaked and slippery. By dawn, I had covered about three rows of ranges, each subsequent one a little higher and broader. On top of the last ridge, there was a small clearing where the scrub ended just feet below the summit.

With my binoculars, I could see San Blas in the distance. To the north was Santa Rosa Del Sur. Due east beyond the haze would be Barrancabermeja. There was a small mining operation cut into the hillside of the next ridge, but luckily no ELN boys with their own binoculars that I could see. A bulldozer was filling trucks with rock and sediment for processing elsewhere, creating quite a commotion, and a dust screen, which allowed me to observe the operation at closer range. I slid down the six or seven hundred feet of thick foliage with my right leg as rudder, stopping about a hundred feet from the bottom.

There was another small creek between the ridges. The mining operation was now upstream from my position. There were no patrols at that moment, but not wanting to become known in those parts, I slid down the rest of the hill and darted through the creek and into the woods on the other side. I had nothing to gain by making myself known to the mining crews. They were highly taxed guests in these mountains; it would behoove them to report anything they saw to the ELN, rather than take pity on a wayward gringo traveler.

This new ridge was much higher and steeper than the previous one. I had arrived in the high mountains, where the climate on the ground did not change—cold, wet, and without nutrients. On the way up, I often clutched at branches to pull myself up steep grades and keep myself from sliding back down. The air was getting thinner, too. Soon, familiar dollops of fat raindrops began pelting the canopies of trees above me. In two hours I had scaled this mountain as well. It was the tallest peak for the next several miles. Still, I had seen no patrols beyond the teen boys with radios at the cocaine lab.

I drank water sparingly, but gorged on my last slices of papaya. Peering out from the canopy of trees, San Blas was now barely visible in the mountain clouds and hazes. A pattering of rain began, its drops seemingly falling only a few feet from the clouds around me. I had traveled about five miles thus far. Worn down and unaccustomed to the thin air, I stopped for a long midday rest. Sleeping briefly, I awoke to a heavy pounding of rain, and repulsion to my own smell. I believe that I had not bathed in nine days. My hair was now oily and matted. Sweat cut grooves into the dirt covering of my skin. I could feel a thick beard growing on my face.

Suddenly, I heard the cracking of branches and dim voices. I inched downward and away from the peak until I found a rock covering. Through the binoculars, I saw two more boys with rifles about two hundred yards below. They were slowly coming towards my position. I switched off my ELN radio. Reaching into the backpack, I took out my pistol and cocked it. They were now about fifty yards away and following my path up the mountain. There was a large rock beside me. If they picked up their radios, it would be to report a possible gringo sighting—I would have to shoot them first.

Their rifles were slung over their shoulders as they walked directly into my camp and only feet away from my hiding spot. I had no more time; they had spotted my backpack and were reaching for their radios. I leaped up and fiercely struck one boy on the side of the head with the rock. He tumbled down the hill into a motionless crumpled form. The other boy reached for his shouldered weapon, but I caught him on the shoulder, and again on the back of the head, dropping him cold. The other boy down the slope bled profusely from his scalp.

They both had radios, with likely more power than mine, so I swapped my captured radio with one of theirs. I then dragged their unconscious bodies over the rocks to what would become my second mountain outpost. I used the wire to tie their arms and feet together, so that they sat back-to-back with their hands clasped together. They had no food, and I took all the water they had. They awoke from their sleep groggily, surprised to see they had been captured by a white caveman.

"You are the gringo?"

"Yes." Still in their teens, they had seen plenty of death, enough to quiet their features and their fear.

"We have been looking for you."

"In the wrong places, obviously."

"How many men are looking for me?" I showed him my water bottle.

"About twenty."

"For how long?"

"Three days."

"Where?"

"Around the mining camps." He accepted a long swig of water.

"Where else?"

"Around the coca plantations or the mountain streams."

"Where will they search next?"

"They will go into the higher mountains."

I put the canteen to his mouth to reward him for his forthright explanations.

"Who ordered you up here?" I took out my knife and showed it to him.

"My comandante. He told us to explore the peaks in the area."

"Where is your camp?"

"It is about four miles to the west." I gave him more water.

"How many soldiers are there?"

"About a hundred."

"Tell me about the camp. Is it a processing plant for cocaine?"

"Yes, senor."

"So, it is not a camp with comandantes at the higher levels?"

"No, it is for processing cocaine. They can make about five hundred pounds a week there. Helicopters come to carry it away."

That small amount of production would have gotten a paramilitary shot for poor management of resources.

"What is your job there?"

"We are part of security. Now that the paras have been destroyed, we will deal with the coca production."

"How many rings of security?"

"There are men every five hundred meters and mobile patrols starting on the next mountain… is my comrade alive?"

"He will live. He will need a doctor, but he will live."

"What will you do to us?"

"You will stay here for now. If I am caught, they will not spend many days looking for you. I will not admit that I encountered either of you, so you will probably die in that case. If I escape, my friends will start a rumor that you are deserters. So, please tell me how to get close to that camp."

He told me in detail the layout of the camp and the best approach to observe it safely. I unwired one of his hands. They had enough water to last a few days, though his friend would need medical care or he could die from infection before that.

By noon, I had traversed another ridge and was mounting the second one from the north. I had found a mountain stream with water in the gorge and filled my water bottles again. On the side of this ridge, I hid behind an outcropping of rocks, the closest I could get to the ELN without a closer but more reckless approach. The camp was below, about a mile away. There were few visible clues that a major cocaine plant was nearby. But the smell—even from this distance--was putrid. There was little noise as well.

The boy's intel was good; I could easily see the security outposts from my position. I had to expect that there were exploding mines on these slopes, and patrols on the trails on the lower slopes of the ridges to the east and below me to the north. You could attack this place, but only from the air. A ground attack was impossible. RPGs would take out a slow, low-flying helicopter, from which the facility was most like designed to defend itself. A ground attack would be detectable before it got to within ten miles.

It was about time to share my intelligence, but with whom? A cynical process of elimination crossed out each name until there was only one: the Colonel. Hawkins would take credit for any find, and forget any communication with Tommy C; D-2 would not want the Fiscalia to know that we were communicating and planning together. For all I knew, Colorado preferred me out in the wild, as those commissions were taken out of his share as well. So, I called the Colonel, knowing that my satellite phone had modifications from the CIA, and that as soon as it started, they would start recording data and location information.

I spoke in English. "Hello, Colonel." There was no emotion in his voice.

"Hello… friend. How are you?"

"Have you heard about the helicopter ambush?"

"Yes, word came to me shortly afterwards."

"How many days ago was that—I was sick for a few days."

"It was six days ago."

"Colonel—does she know?"

"No. I have not told her anything."

"Tell her I am safe. Just that."

"I understand, friend."

"Colonel, I have been busy up in these mountains. They are crowded, especially at the lower levels."

"I understand. Proceed."

"At this location, where I just turned on my phone, I am about one mile northeast of a major ELN kitchen. 500 pounds a week. It looks like a large flat valley with a thick canopy of trees with mountains on the west, east, and north sides. A ground attack from the south would be suicidal. It is approximately one mile by one mile. We have friends that can tell you the precise point where I turned on my phone and engaged the satellite. Do you understand, Colonel?"

"Yes. Go on."

"You cannot fly low over this place in a helicopter. They are waiting with RPGs. These friends of ours can also share satellite imagery of the surrounding areas. By the time you analyze this information, I will be far away. Please give this information to people who can use it, with my warmest regards. Tell them to aim for any smoke fumes rising out of the trees."

"I understand. Please stay safe."

"I will. Tell them not to fly low. So long, Colonel."

I switched off the phone. The rest of the job was a matter for D-2 in Bogota. But I had announced myself. The ELN would know somehow. The game would get quicker and much more dangerous.

I hiked back to my second camp, arriving just before nightfall. My two ELN hostages were slumped over, anxious for me to unfasten their hands so they could relieve themselves. We shared the water, chatting like war veterans about the war along the Magdalena. The wounded boy had a fever, so I laid him down on some branches and covered him with some more. His wound had dirt in its dried blood. I tore off strips of his t-shirt and bound his head. I fastened the foot of this boy to the hand of the other boy. It was only about six p.m., but I fell into a deep sleep and woke up still wearing my boots at three in the morning.

We marched in a slow column the next morning, stopping only to gather papaya and water, or to let other patrols, which were still following the rivers and the low scrub at the bottoms of the mountains, pass freely. Fording one of the creeks, I stooped over to re-clean the head wound of the more seriously-injured boy. The cut was wide, infected and needed stitching. I also washed some of the oil off my face. The reflection in the water was a wild, bearded and overly wrought man with little time or luck left. Fear and exhaustion bulged out through his eyes like his head could not contain them any longer.

We arrived about noon at my initial camp. The boys were tired. They were used to patrols through creeks and dry gulches, but not tramping over two or three peaks in a day, especially with head wounds and cramped muscles. Once more, I unfastened their hands. We ate slices of papaya again. The boys wanted to sleep, so I cut some branches and spread them behind the rock where I hid. I crept behind a tree and slept, my pistol in my right hand.

The boys slept nearly until sunrise. I checked their arms and legs for proper circulation and woke them up like a thoughtful scout master on a sleep-over in the woods just outside the city. For breakfast, we ate the last of the papaya and drank the last canteen.

I left the redoubt to determine if the patrols had singled out my mountain for special examination. From the next peak, lower than mine to the north, I could see a patrol in a clearing below. There was a mixture of young men and boys in the patrol. They had two radios, and appeared to be actively sharing intelligence with other patrols. I switched on the radio, but kept the volume at its lowest level. "That gringo is like a ghost. We have not seen a single turd or toilet paper. Over."

"How far are you from the road where the gringo attacked the motorcycle?"

"About five kilometers."

"Maybe he left already."

"Doubt it. He has a motorcycle, but the road has been quiet for the last week… he is still here… we are listening to the paracos radios. He has not reported a position or asked for rescue. Over."

"Is there any sign of the two missing soldiers? Over."

"No. He probably killed them and pushed their bodies down the river. You will find them in the Magdalena, probably."

"There is nothing here, capitan! Over."

"Keep moving toward the main road. Go higher in the mountains. He is an experienced CIA intelligence officer. They call him 'El Estamper'! He knows you lazy faggots would prefer to wash your feet in the rivers than climb the higher peaks. He is up there. We have found large gringo footprints above the old processing laboratory. We are slowly surrounding him. If you see him, do not approach. Try to separate and surround him. Now, go out and grab some glory for yourself."

Maybe if I just explained that I was not really a trained CIA officer….

They were less than a mile away. I waited while they pushed south in the direction of the cabin next to the river fork. At any moment, they could begin their ascent toward my camp. I went back to prepare the boy for the trip We north. My radio crackled to life as we put our feet ashore.

"Capitan! Capitan! We have found a camp of the gringo! Over."

"Excellent. What did you find there?"

"There are some papaya skins on the ground. He cut some branches to make a bed. He had a bed sheet. Soldado Perez found it behind some rocks. He also made a latrine. Over."

"Good. We are close."

"He is somewhere between your mountain and ours…" He paused and spoke to me directly. "We are coming for you, gringo! Don't die before we have the honor of interrogating you. Some of our techniques will be familiar to you."

"Soldados. Bring everything but his shit to the cabin at the base of the next range. Over." They were less than a mile from me, but luckily decided not to double-back, as I had effectively slipped behind them on the upper ridges.

It was game time.

We reached the mine shortly before 12.00. I had no food to offer the boys, or to sustain myself. I expected the whole cycle of fever and chills to start up again, but I no longer cared about the staying power of typhoid fever. I tied them to a tree on the far side of the ridge, above the mine and below a cascade of mining tailings. Though they were about five hundred meters from where the ELN commander would arrive, they were hungry and thirsty, and in the direct sun. I cleaned the boy's wound as best I could with the tap water and toilet paper from the cabin.

I went back to the cabin, which had a large, low table with wooden chairs, where I sat and drank water. I turned on my satellite phone, and dialed the number for her office in Langley, Virginia. She answered with a terse greeting; I pressed the transmit button on the ELN radio. "Capitan! Capitan of the ELN forces searching for the North American citizen in the Santa Rosa Mountains. Over." I brought the radio and telephone together in electronic congress.

"This is Captain Sandino. Over."

"This is Tommy Connolly of the United States. I have two of your soldiers in my protective custody. One is badly-injured and needs immediate medical attention. I want to transfer custody of these men to you and leave these mountains. Over."

"Where are my men? Over."

"They are with me, Captain. I kept them with me for their safety. These mountains are dangerous at night. There are men with guns everywhere. They are only boys, after all. Over."

"What is your position, gringo? Over."

"I will disclose that to you last. First, my conditions: bring no more than four men with you. If I see more than four, I will leave upon your arrival. Second, you will not take me into your custody. I am only negotiating my safe passage out of these mountains in exchange for the speedy delivery of your men. Is that clear? Over."

"Gringo. You are a guest in my mountains. Please do not presume to make conditions about your status around here. We are the masters of these territories. It is our pleasure to take you into our custody or release you into someone else's. Over."

For the benefit of our listening audience, I decided to get a little cheeky. "We will have to disagree on that issue, Capitan. Over."

"Please tell me where you are, so that I can recover my men. Over."

"Capitan, in addition to my two previous conditions, here is the third: I am in the abandoned mine approximately two miles north of the site where you found my camp. I will leave here in thirty minutes. I have already selected a safe route back to Santa Rosa Del Sur, but I would like an escort. You can reject these terms. In that case, your men will die while under your command, in your mountains, and it will be my pleasure to announce this fact to your superiors. The clock is now ticking, Capitan! Over."

"I know the place, gringo. I will be there shortly. Please wait for me." I clicked off both apparatuses.

They were coming—and not for a formal diplomatic meeting between equals.

A plan formed, a live-action version of my fantasy life as a boy along the rivers of the Sierra Nevada in California. Instead of taking the higher ground, where I could command the best views and shoot downward, which he would assume, I ran below the camp, across the road, and hid in a drainage pipe at the bottom of a smelly, swampy ravine. The water was up to my waist, nearly reaching my backpack.

The first jeep arrived above my position by about a hundred yards with four men and the captain. He quickly directed two men towards the cabin atop the mine clearing and two to the low hills to the south. That would place me in a crossfire were I so inclined to walk toward the table and chairs I had set up in the middle of the clearing for the pompously demanded meeting of minds I had suggested to the ELN captain.

Fuckin' weird-ass gringos, I hoped he was thinking.

I crept a little closer to the lip of the pipe. From there I had a clear view of the jeeps, and the Captain in my line of sight. Apart from that, I could not follow the movements of the deployed troops or the voiced instructions of the Capitan.

As I expected, another jeep arrived a few minutes later, parking close to the other jeep. Four more men got out and stood at attention behind the jeep. The captain appeared to explain the terrain to them. I estimated that there was no more than an hour of daylight remaining. The men and boys began to reconnoiter the camp buildings. "Capitan! I found a caleta of cylinder bombs about two hundred meters away. They were hidden under some branches."

"Do they have detonators?"

"No, capitan. They were moved here by somebody."

"Very good, soldado."

"Leave them and continue your reconnoiter in the hills above the mine."

There were four soldiers in the hills approximately two hundred yards away, which in that terrain would take at least two minutes to traverse. Two others looked inside the mine shacks. It had to be now, before the Capitan saw the growing disadvantages of a dusk search, and his own vulnerability. I hurried out of the ravine until I was only fifty yards from the Captain, but nearly on the same level as him. I was now a brown cave man, my clothes and bearded face caked with brown, chalky grime.

They would face their sudden attack from a shit-smelling yeti.

Two soldiers, unfortunately, had stayed by his side for personal security, yet fortunately had not positioned themselves far away from him. The bend of the road provided me some cover for the first part of my sprint, but not the final twenty yards, which would be uphill on pebbled rock, which would alert them to my arrival with plenty of time to fire. I ran toward him from behind. He did not turn until I was about ten yards away. "Good afternoon, Capitan!" a frightening, bearded madman greeted him.

My backpack was on my back, a hand grenade was in my left hand, and my cocked pistol in my right hand. "Drop your weapons—all of you." Moving forward quickly, I pointed my pistol directly at the head of the capitan. When I was close enough, I waved it at the soldiers—who dropped their rifles—and hit the Capitan in the side of the head with the bulging side of the grenade.

Flinching toward me, the soldiers watched their captain fall to the ground. The other soldiers followed him to the ground compliantly with their hands on their heads. In the distance, we heard a loud series of booms. "I think the Army found your processing plant, Capitan! Another feather for your stupid cap." I removed the cartridges and guns from all three men and put them in the far jeep. Using the wire and cutters, I began to bind the hands and feet of the two guards.

The radio crackled to transmit. "Capitan! There is no sign of the gringo or the missing soldiers. I think he killed the boys and is tricking us in order to escape. Over!" I directed my comments to the Capitan. "Tell them to hold their positions for ten minutes and then all soldiers are to meet in the cabin above the camp. Tell them there is fresh water there." I put the knife in the neck of the Captain. He repeated the message.

I struggled to carry the two ELN guards into the second jeep. I carried the Captain into the passenger side of his own jeep. I addressed the two young men. "The boys you are looking for are next to the tailings on the other side of the ridge. When your reinforcements arrive, send two men to find them. This is not a trick. They have water, but they have not eaten all day. They need medical attention. The radio started to crackle now. "Capitan! The plant has been attacked with bombs. Repeat: we have been attacked with bombs. There are attack helicopters firing missiles. There are many wounded with casualties. Please report, Capitan!"

"Tell them you have not yet captured the gringo and will wait another fifteen minutes before going back to the high mountain camp." He reluctantly, but convincingly relayed my message, which met with almost distain from his mountain associates.

I found the jeep keys in the capitan's pocket. Before we left, I cut the tires on the other jeep, and, reaching into my backpack, took one more grenade out, showing it to the Capitan before putting it between his legs on the passenger's seat. I let the jeep roll slowly down the slope in reverse until we rested on the main road. The engine responded quickly, and I went about a hundred yards down the road before I turned on the lights. My pistol rested warmly on my lap.

"Where is the next road block, Capitan?" I put my hand on the pistol and cocked it in his direction.

"When we pass onto the valley road, it will be about three kilometers." I put the radio to his ear.

"Tell them that you have to get a syndicate figure who has taken ill away from the troubles in the mountain, and to let us pass. Tell them he is badly injured and requires a doctor." He told me to switch channels. He called the men at the roadblock, who confirmed his instructions. I blinked the car lights three times, but sped through the four-man detail.

"You look like Rasputin, gringo! What will you do to me?"

"Today is a lucky day for you. I am not exactly on good terms with the paramilitary command these days, so you get to decide your fate. I will release you to the local police. You can buy your freedom from them."

"No, I would prefer that you release me to friendly people in Simiti."

"That is possible, Capitan."

"La Gringa Fea told me that you are not a paramilitary, Gringo, that you do not like them, and that you only want the drug money."

"Who is that?"

"The ugly gringa girl from the NGO. She visits us to share intelligence that she gathers in Barrancabermeja. She brought us your backpack with twenty-five thousand dollars. She said that you wanted to cross over to the ELN, but that you had to plan your escape carefully."

If I ever get my hands on her neck, I thought.

It came together in my mind at that moment. NGO girl had sized me up as a collaborator, bringing gifts on my behalf to the mountains, and speaking of me as a burnout within the counter-insurgent ranks. She was the one who cared for me in the hotel during my first delirium. Running her own intelligence operation from within the safe confines of her skin color and her "truth-seeking" credentials, she was far more foolish and dangerous than I had imagined. "When you called, I thought you wanted safe conduct to us, and that your language was just to avoid suspicion from the paracos."

"It is easy to make mistakes, Capitan!"

He did not return my grin.

Once beyond the roadblock, we drove down a single-lane road toward the lights of Santa Rosa Del Sur. I spotted an abandoned finca down a path on the right side of the road. I drove behind it and stopped. "Capitan! It has been ten minutes. Your men are walking toward the jeeps where they will find their comrades tied up with wire. The other two men will be found in a ravine on the other side of the ridge. The jeep is immobilized until four new tires arrive from Santa Rosa or Simiti. They will call to report their status to your superiors. You will not be found to have behaved with military caution, especially towards your men. It would be my honor to report to your superiors that you have joined the paramilitaries. That is one way to make sure you live another year or so. Or, I can turn you into the local police, who will give you to the army, after which you can expect incredible pain and suffering until you succumb to a variety of wounds. Or, I can shoot you… do you follow?"

"Yes, Gringo."

"Good. Where do we go now?"

"If you take me back, they will ask for a ransom, but they will not harm you."

"If we go forward?"

"You can let me out in Simiti. I will find my way back to the mountains." I stood upright with my pistol in my hand.

"Ok, Capitan!" As my arm swung forward, he gave me a look of pure panic that twisted his features into another man's face. I hit him atop his head with a live hand grenade.

I dragged his groggy body over the dusty ground until it slumped against the back door of the finca. Moments later, the radio calls began. "Capitan Sandino—respond please. Over. Capitan Sandino—awaiting instructions. Over." This continued a few more times until they realized they were now on their own. I turned off the radio on the outskirts of Santa Rosa.

I turned on the satellite phone for the last time. "Hello, Colonel. I heard a loud boom in the mountains a few minutes ago. My intelligence is that they scored direct hits. Keep 'em coming, I saw. Listen closely, Colonel… " Speaking slowly, I gave him the name of the finca, and its approximate location south and west of Santa Rosa Del Sur. I told him that behind the main building—gagged and bound—they would find Captain Sandino of the ELN. "He will require a medic. He botched my capture, so he will want to make a deal. One more matter, Colonel. A man or woman will go to a tire store in Simiti or Santa Rosa soon and ask for four jeep tires. He or she will be an ELN urban militant. Please pass that on to our friends. I am signing off now, Colonel." After the Colonel gave me acknowledgment, I turned off the satellite phone.

On the ground, I saw an almost hopeless figure, now with fresh blood on his beard, likely from a head wound. His hands and legs were wired together, his head was pounding with aftershocks of intense pain. I left him to his last moments of freedom before his world turned very dark.

I had escaped from a snare which they in turn had not properly set. High marks for T. Connolly! Drinks all around! I felt on top of things until I further recollected that having escaped the ELN, I had only reduced my troubles by about 33%.

I drove forward—a marauding typhoid carrier in a purloined ELN jeep, covered in industrial effluent, sweat and probably shit, wanted for questioning by a host government, and despised as an unlucky talisman by the paramilitaries—since essentially there was nowhere else to drive.

CHAPTER FIFTY-ONE

Santa Rosa Del Sur had only a few chipped, paved roads in the center of town. The Capitan's hat and the darkness added some much needed ambiguity to my scraggly beard, dissipated condition, and hideous smell. I kept to the speed limit, conscious though that through a series of relayed radio calls, my whereabouts would be a known fact in Santa Rosa and Simiti at any minute.

It was dark on the road to Simiti. There were no police cars or roadblocks as darkness took over the rural roads. Sweat, back in business in the lower, more humid climes closer to the river, cut rivulets through the dry mud on my face. Bugs hit the jeep front window or went into my face. I had no particular Simiti plan. The paracos were there, but spread thinly, and not able to monitor every unusual appearance, among which mine was a chart-topper. Hopefully, they would keep themselves busy torturing tire store owners, and not notice the odd gringo in the stolen jeep.

Simiti was perched on a hill at the edge of a huge swamp. Luckily, my rancid smell and mud pelt kept most of the mosquitoes away from me. What I had in that moment was a human impulse, which I could ill-afford—I just wanted to be clean.

I parked deep in the shadows of an ill-lit street on the edge of town. Sitting low in my jeep, I heard the scraping of a restaurant grill and laughter down the street, which was otherwise empty of lights or noise. There was a single grill estadero on a lit stoop with a few plastic tables and a glassed refrigerator with beer and soft drinks. Two boys drank soda on their small motorcycles on the street in front of its awning.

A tall, white yeti in mud-caked chinos and a t-shirt approached the steps as the boys held their breath, not wanting to breathe in my stench, and suppressing their normal contempt. After all, I was a golden-skinned gringo, apparently taking his mining consulting work a little too seriously by local standards. I held out about fifty dollars in pesos to the man at the grill. "I want two beers, four hamburgers with cheese and French fries. Lots of them." Frightened, he pointed to the bathroom to the rear.

Instead, I walked to the boys at the curb. "Hello."

"You look banged up, senor."

"Yes. I had some trouble in the mine where I work in the mountains."

"Do you need a doctor?"

"No. I am not hurt. Listen. Do you want to earn some money?" They looked at me for signs of perverted intent on my part.

"Yes, senor. But what do you want us to do?"

"For now, get me a pen and paper." One boy stepped off his motorcycle, lifted the seat, and pulled out a notebook and pen.

"Are there any stores open tonight?"

"Yes, senor. In the center of town there are many stores that are still open."

"I will pay each of you a hundred dollars, twenty dollars now, and eighty when you return."

"Listo, Senor. What do we have to do?"

"Go to the stores and buy these items." I wrote down my sizes in jeans, shirts, shoes, a cap, a hoody, a belt, tooth paste and a brush, underwear, t-shirts, a razor and shaving cream, a comb, dark glasses, cologne, and as many maps as they could find. I gave the natural leader between the two boys five hundred dollars.

They smiled when I handed them the money. "No—chico—leave one of your motorcycles here—with the keys. You can carry the bags back with you or take a taxi." They looked at each other. "Alright, senor. We will be back in about an hour."

With typhoid in partial withdrawal, and my time in the mountains, subsisting on papaya for a week, apparently over, my appetite had reasserted itself as primus inter pares among my concerns. I drank the first beer in two gulps, the second one in about four. The cook brought me another without prompting, kicking away the empty cans, so that he would not have to put his nose near to me at ground-level. It took me about three bites to eat each hamburger. The French fries did not have much salt, so I sprinkled on too much, and wolfed them down, too.

The man at the grill told me he did not have coffee. I gave him twenty-dollars to go to a minimart and get me a large one, which I soon realized was a mistake, since he already had my money, and could possibly earn more with a call to either the police or the local paramilitary captain in town.

I was starting to fear that I had already spent too much time in one place, but I wanted those clothes. The Colonel had likely routed my message to his military counterpart, who had made the call to the local brigade in Santa Rosa Del Sur.

The army would be in that finca at any time, and then start looking around for me since the capitan would give up my appearance and my "donation" to the ELN to gain a little good will with his new masters. Otherwise, he would find his way to the cellar next to the Green House before midnight.

The cook came back with two large coffees. I asked for more burgers, French fries and another beer. He did not charge me for the rest.

Scooting myself back into the rear shadows of the estadero, I listened anxiously for slow, furtive car brakes, low radio chatter, or a sudden break to a sprint from the darkness—anything that would suggest that an assault was imminent. After eating, I sat in the darkness of the sidewalk and just listened to the sounds of the night, my head down like a tired street beggar.

Before long the boys on the motorcycle came back, luckily carrying several bags with my supplies.

"Do you know a place—not a motel—where I can shower?" The boys discussed several options.

"You are a gringo, no?"

"It doesn't matter who I am. I will give you another two hundred dollars to take me to a safe place."

"Follow us, gringo. It is not far."

I turned toward the single-grill hamburger vendor. I put a hundred dollars in pesos in his hand. "Wait two days. Then, you can talk to the police or paramilitaries. But for two days say nothing." He nodded. "Do not mention those boys." I followed the boy and his friend through downtown, and then out toward the small fingers of land on the edge of the swamp. We parked around the corner from a small, plaster house with a tin roof.

"This is my mother's house. She is working in the hospital tonight. She will not be back until late. You can use our shower, senor."

"That is acceptable, but I need you both to give me your motorcycle keys while I am in the shower, and stay nearby. Do you understand?"

"Are you in trouble?"

"I cannot speak about that. Do you understand my conditions?"

"Yes, gringo. Relax. We are not going to tell anybody that you are here."

"Sometimes, they find out on their own."

The shower was part of the raised shelf on the laundry room floor meant for a washing machine. A hose came out of the wall.

"Is there hot water?"

"It is not hot, but it is not cold, either." They handed me their motorcycle keys.

"We will sit in the hallway, gringo."

"One of you start a fire outside. I will hand you my clothes. Take them out and burn them."

"Understood, gringo."

I placed my backpack in the corner and took off my clothes. I started with my feet and my hands. I scrubbed and scrubbed in different directions and over and over again. I washed my face and hair and scraped away the crud that had caked behind my ears. A thick, curling line of black water circled down the drain. I shaved, too. While the water spilled onto my legs, I brushed my teeth over and over again. When I finally felt clean, I turned off the water, and started again.

"Chico, can you bring me a towel?" The new clothes did not fit well. They were too short and tight in the crotch, sort of like Pee Wee Herman in backpacking clothes. I combed back my hair. The cologne the boys had bought burned the cuts on my neck and chin from my clumsy shave. The boys stayed in the hallway outside the door as requested. I took a quick inventory of my belongings: in the backpack were the satellite phone, two pistols, the ELN radio, my knife, and some stale papaya. There was also more than half of my dollars and pesos, and a live hand grenade. I emptied it out in the towel.

"Chico, take this mochila outside, please, and wash it thoroughly."

I put on the rest of my clothes. The boy brought back the backpack, which I filled with the rest of the new clothes, the radio, the phone, the knife, the grenade and the gun, all cleaned. I walked out to the living room and sat on the threadbare, orange and yellow couch.

"Chico, can you make some coffee." I handed him back their keys.

"Yes, gringo. Would you like anything to eat?"

"No." I sat back and studied the maps. The boy brought me coffee with dry cream.

"When will your mother return?"

"About four in the morning."

"I will be gone… are you a student, chico?"

"Yes, senor. I study electronics in an institute."

"And your friend?"

"He is studying welding."

"Who controls the city these days?"

"The paracos now run the city, senor. They raid houses sometimes and take people away. They charge a fee to the business owners."

"Do they control the river?"

"Yes. They examine each person who enters or leaves the boats."

"What about the highways?"

"They have men on the roads with radios. They check the id of each person in the car. They ask about your destination."

"Are there any roads they do not control?"

"They are not so strong on the small, country roads. The ELN can attack them there."

"What is the best way out of here?"

"If you are a friend of the ELN, you can go up to the mountains."

"I am not a friend of the ELN, or the FARC, or the paramilitaries. In fact, I want to avoid all of them." They laughed.

"That is the hardest thing of all."

"What can you suggest?"

"Let me take a look at the map."

The quicker boy, the son of the woman who owned the house, watched me attentively. "What time is it, chico?"

"It is about ten o'clock."

"Do the paramilitaries watch the bus station?"

"Yes, they check the cedula of each passenger. They will be there until the last bus arrives or leaves."

"What about the river? Is it possible to cross in a small boat?"

"You would have to pay a lot of money, and still the answer could be 'no.'"

"The map shows that the highways are on the east side of the river. Is that true?"

"Yes. The pueblitos on this side of the river do not connect with anything."

"How are the roads?"

"Some of them are paved, but most are dirt."

"Are there any checkpoints?"

"If you leave after midnight, you should be ok."

"But who controls it?"

"The paracos control the roads, but by midnight they are with their putas."

"How long will it take me on those roads to La Gloria?"

"Maybe five or six hours."

"Will there be gas stations?"

"No, only here in Simiti."

"Do you know a place to buy gasoline and some gas cans?"

"I know a place, yes."

"Let's go."

I filled up the tank of the jeep, its gas can, and several other plastic ones. The boys were on their motorcycles across the street behind a billboard that called for the eradication of communist sympathizers. "Good. Now go home. Do not go back to the estadero where I met you tonight. Do not tell your mother anything. Do not spend this money on putas or whiskey. Do you understand?"

"Yes, gringo."

We shook hands. "Good luck. Be good to your mother. Forget you ever met me." I drove into a darkness of thick, mosquito-clotted air toward the north of the country. There were eight rivers that right between Simiti and La Gloria through which I drove in almost complete darkness. Even after midnight, there was hot, heavy air tamping down on the stagnant delta of the Magdalena. There were no lights in the half–abandoned towns, the police kiosks closed and many of the stores boarded. There were no lights either from the isolated, viable fincas near the river, as if these communities wanted outsiders to pass by without a look. There was paramilitary graffiti though in every village I saw.

By 03:00, I was almost one hundred miles from Simiti. On the other side of the river, on the main toll roads, truckers would be on the roads early. The paramilitaries would be checking for me on each truck bed and car trunk that stopped at one of their road blocks. The Colonel gave me no assurances during our phone calls, which he would have had he possessed any reason for optimism about my case. Here, on the quiet, malarial side of the river, there was nothing and nobody on the rocky, riveted dirt roads between towns, which was the safest place for me.

Driving farther and farther north, implicitly closer to my wife and children, I had to tamp down any visions of Amelia and the girls. If this was my last day on earth, Leo would follow my instructions. It served me better not to see the faces of Amelia and the girls, or to see a safe arrival at the end of this road. Some memories of Sal Manzo and Aruba snuck through. I imagined the condition he found me in for the first time. He never condescended to my vulnerability or ignorance, and he always played fairly with me. There was something to the idea of the outlaw code.

I heard the first chicken crow at about 04.30. That put me about twenty-five miles from La Gloria. This first morning light brought the nearness of the river into relief. The faint light also softened the nighttime swill of putrid river and roadside garbage odors. At times, the road was near the bank of the river; at others, it curved away to accommodate a sandbar or dock. I drove faster now. This was palm country, though each no taller than myself, and stretched in grids that reminded me of San Joaquin Delta farms.

On the road into a small village called Regidor, there were some more abandoned fincas. I parked behind a small house apart from the road. I kicked open the back door. It was abandoned to a degree I had not encountered—there was no mattress, or table, or living room furniture. I had a choice to make: either succumb to sleep or force more coffee down my throat. From the back window I could not see another finca. There were no chicken sounds, or heavy machinery or children walking to school. I rolled my hoody into a pillow and slept in the shade tucked against a wall, uncomfortably in the thick, hot air of the Magdalena.

In another strange place, I did not have enough intelligence upon which to make any sort of decision. But I needed to and fast.

CHAPTER FIFTY-TWO

The hot sticky miasma of noontime awoke me. Sweat pooled where it could, and dripped down my sides annoyingly. There was still no sound of life outside on the street, only the quiet of abandonment. I took a close look at my map. I was between Regidor and Rio Viejo, and along the stagnant swamp that could have been either the Rio Viejo or the Magdalena, depending on the tide.

Hunger hit me. Yesterday's burgers and fries were hardly sufficient to compensate for the 5 days of near starvation I had endured. Luckily there was still water in the back of the jeep. I cocked my pistol and walked slowly out of the back of the shack. There were only a few butterflies navigating the thick compressed air near the river. I drank two bottles of water, relieving myself even before I finished the second bottle. I climbed to the top of the jeep for a better view, and could see clearly enough up and down the river. La Gloria was set with its back to the river, but apart, and surrounded by a dike on three sides.

It was a town of about five thousand people. That meant it would house a small police force and military garrison. The region had been pacified by paramilitaries for about three or four years. There was probably about ten paramilitaries directing the local police forces, and taking orders from Colorado or another commander along the river. Through my binoculars, I could see a good business in flat barges between Regidor and La Gloria, which meant the paramilitaries taxed it, and would shoot anyone who would stupidly let me pass through without calling the higher ups.

I looked down coast toward another village called Gamarra. River traffic consisted mostly of small long canoes. They carried people like taxis with loads of fruits or palm oil balanced in the middle. I decided to walk down toward the river. For a while it was possible to hop from sandbar to sandbar, but then the water became two to six inches of deep, dark sludge. Skipping from dry spot to dry spot, I continued to traverse the river in the manner until I reached the Magdalena after about an hour.

Upstream, about a mile away, was La Gloria. My quick study of the maps the motorcycle boys had provided pointed to La Gloria as the best way to get quickly on the major highways to the east and north. If I stayed on the river, or if I hopped by night on the side roads, my luck would eventually end, badly more than likely.

I took out my binoculars. There were canoe taxis on both banks, idle, swaying, their drivers waiting for cooler weather to bring customers. I snuck back into the foliage of the riverbank and waited. I quickly considered another option–I was a sitting duck and needed to keep moving. An even less enviable task would be to swim out to a flat barge and ride it across. The cooling in the afternoon brought out the irregular formations of mosquitoes—repellant being the one item I failed to add to my list in Simiti last night.

My hunger began to cause me nausea by late afternoon. There were shadows now under the tall palms around me, providing me some relief from the ungodly heat. The tide also rose, causing me to unflex my knees and instead bend over to keep my backpack dry. Unable to sustain a bent-over posture, I walked upstream, keeping inside and under the canopy of palms. There was music starting in the cantinas upstream. I moved slowly and noisily on soggy ground in wet shoes from thicket to thicket, zigzagging quickly to stay out of sight. The music was growing louder up ahead. A plane flew over and landed near La Gloria. I hoped it was a regular flight, and not a paramilitary team acting upon a timely tip.

The tide was rising higher now; in an hour, I would be up to my chest in water. I crept up to the edge of the poor, oft-flooded streets on the south edge of Regidor, lined with shacks on stilts with no windows. Puddles from the previous high tide were in small, shrinking circles in the open spaces between them. There was a small dock with two canoes lounging on the water, each with an outboard motor on it. I walked to a back window and peered inside.

A black man was on a large mattress at which he had pointed a small fan. He appeared to be alone. Through the shack, I could see two black boys playing soccer on a dirt patch between nearby shacks. The boys moved off down the dirt road away from the river.

I slowly and quietly crept into the shack with my pistol drawn. Covering my face with the hoody and glasses, I moved quietly to his side. My hand quickly covered his mouth just as my pistol became firmly rested on his cheek. "Usted es piloto?"

He darted his eyes toward my hand, which was all he could see. "Si, senor."

"Soy, paraco. Se me perdio mi jeep. Entiende usted?" I was a paramilitary who had stupidly lost his jeep. He nodded his head. "If my boss finds out, I am fucked. Can you take me across the river?" He nodded his head again. "You will not look at me or talk to me. You will follow my instructions. Afterwards, if I hear rumors about a paraco who hired a negro to take him across the river, I will know it was you. Do you know how we kill negroes?"

He shook his head negatively. "With their own machetes until their guts fall down to their feet... now stand up!" He stood, careful not to take a glance in my direction. "Walk forward to your canoe, start it, and then whistle. Do not look back—is that clear?"

"Si, Senor."

"Go." He walked out to his canoe without sandals. He started the canoe and moved it so it pointed out toward La Gloria. He whistled.

I walked to the edge of the river and lifted my sore legs into the back of the canoe. "Cross the river to the south. Land about a mile down river from La Gloria. Find a hidden spot. Be friendly if we come across other pilots." I snuck down inside the canoe, which glided smoothly over the river to the other side. He put the boat to shore, still being very careful not to look at me. He pulled the canoe onto a dirt slope under branches that hid our little cove. I gave him about fifty dollars.

"Leave the boat. Go and buy food—lots of it—your favorites, with some water bottles, juice and coffee. If I hear the police, I will sink your boat, and then head back to your place. If you return with someone, I will shoot you both. Do you understand?"

"Si, senor." He walked up a trail and into the thick leafy trees. The sun was setting now in the west. I walked into the jungle myself, positioning myself at an angle to shoot quickly and double back for the boat.

This man was accustomed to being pushed around and humiliated by paramilitary pistoleros. He naturally looked down when he spoke to me, a product of my warning, but in a deeper sense, his inurement to constituting little more than another worthless and poor boatman in those parts.

He came back around an hour later. I followed him down the trail. "Sit in the boat with your back to La Gloria." He dropped the food on the bank and sat down. He did a good job. There were about twenty empanadas, donuts, some tropical fruits whose names I had not mastered, and large, hot coffees. I walked near him. He began to murmur for mercy. I put a few empanadas and some green hot sauce on the boat seat near him.

"Eat. As long as you do not look at me, you will have no trouble from me. Do you understand?" I placed about one hundred dollars in Colombian money in his left hand. "Thank you. I am sure you are a gentle and kind man. I do not want to harm you. But please do not ask me any questions or look at me. For your own good. Do you understand?"

"Si, senor."

"What is your name?"

"Mario, Sir."

"Mario, do you know what day it is?"

"It is early in December, senor. I forgot the date."

"I am sorry that I disturbed your sleep."

"I had to wake up anyway, senor."

"How is your hamburger?"

"Good, senor."

"With whom do you live?"

"My wife and my son."

"How old is he?"

"He is twelve."

"Will they worry about you?"

"No, I work at night many times."

"Tell me about La Gloria—are there many police?"

"There is a small force."

"What about the guerrillas in these parts?"

"They have all left for the mountains. There are many informants who told the paramilitaries their names. The urban guerrillas are all dead now. The people from Uraba killed many local people."

"Is there a place to find a room?"

"Do you mean in a hotel, senor?"

"Si. But not a high-class hotel. One where they cannot see who enters or leaves a room."

"I think so. It is a hotel for truckers and boat captains. They pay and then walk to little cabins. It is near the highway."

"That is too far."

I put a donut on the flattened wrapper of his empanadas.

"What about a cheap hotel for putas? Is there such a thing?"

"Yes. There is one near the waterfront."

"Where do the putas come from?"

"There are two bars that have putas. They serve beer. One bar has a hotel in back. They rent rooms for the putas and their clients."

"Who goes to the bars?"

"River workers. The paramilitaries bring in their putas from up and down the river... they only enter the bars to take away a FARC suspect... or to collect money."

"I need a room on the first floor on the back side with a window. Can you do this for me—I am not FARC or ELN or paramilitary. I am on a government mission. It is important that no one know I am here... do you understand?"

"Si, senor." I handed him another two hundred dollars of Colombian money.

He held in his hand more than his monthly take on the river. "Mario, listen carefully. Get me a room with a back window. Get a business card from the lobby. Enter the room and leave through the window, but leave the window open. Make sure you write down the room number on the card. Can you remember that, Mario?"

"Si, senor. But they will not allow me to enter the hotel in these clothes."

I handed him more money. "Buy yourself jeans, a nice shirt with buttons, and shoes. Keep the store bag. When you check in, do not use your own name or address. Use your father's first name and the name of your favorite soccer player... shift the number of your cedula by one number--do you understand?"

"Si, senor."

"Ok, Mario. Finish your hamburger and go. I will wait for you here."

Mario trampled back through the woods about two hours later. I pulled my cap down low over my head. It was too dark for sunglasses.

He wore a nice pair of jeans, a white cotton shirt with buttons, and new Nike tennis shoes.

"You look good, Mario."

"Thank you, senor."

"Tell me what happened."

"I bought the clothes at a store near the central plaza. I walked back to the river. The puteria with the hotel had several rooms. I asked for one night. I told them to get me a room in a quiet place on the first floor… I wrote the name and the cedula like you told me. I paid cash. The man asked me if I wanted a puta. I told him that maybe later."

"Good. Do you have the card?" He handed it to me out of his shirt pocket.

"Is it in the back?"

"Yes. The window is open."

"Ok. Now take off your new clothes. Hide them under your bed. Do not tell your wife. Is that clear?"

"Si." Mario explained to me the route to the hotel.

"Mario, do you want to earn some more money?"

"Si, senor." I gave him one hundred dollars more in Colombian. He understood my explanation of the route back to the jeep. He also understood that the best time to retrieve it would be in the last hours before dawn. I told him to park the jeep out of sight—no closer than two kilometers from his shack—and not to tell anyone about it. Lastly, I told him that he should check for messages at the hotel tomorrow at noon. If there were no messages, he should come to the back window.

The hotel had a long porch with a railing. River men were drinking beer on the porch, some of them holding their putas with swagger like they were holding their own young girlfriends. I darted toward the garbage cans, hiding behind them in my zipped hoody and sunglasses. There was a slip in the concrete wall where they took out their garbage. I walked until I saw the open window. Throwing my backpack first, I heaved myself into the room, which consisted of only a bed and a small bathroom. There was also a telephone on a small nightstand.

I tried to approximate Mario's accent and rhythm of speech on the telephone. The man at the desk—or the bar—said they did not offer room service. I mentioned a tip large enough to induce him to bring me more fruit juice, some fried chicken, and fresh soap. He changed his mind.

There were used condoms on the floor. I took the old bathroom towel and scrubbed the floor of the room and the bathroom. The shower had hot water, which I did not expect, but to which I succumbed with humble gratitude. There was a lot to clean; I had been squatting in swamp water most of the day. I washed my clothes with the last of the small bar of soap. They would not dry quickly in the swampy air along the river.

Someone knocked on the door. I shut off all the lights. It was probably a slow night at the puteria, since in the opening of the door, a high-heeled leg planted itself.

"Why the darkness, for fuck's sake! I have your food, negro ijueputa desgraciado!"

"Put the food on the bed, nena."

"Why don't you turn on the lights, negro!"

"I have a headache, nena. How much money?" I handed her money only when she retreated back in the hallway through a crease in the door of about an inch.

"Negro bastardo impotente!"

"Gracias, nena!" I wolfed down the fried chicken with some fruit juice I still could not pronounce.

Afterwards, I counted my Colombian and U.S. currency in piles on the bed. There was another knock on the door. "Crazy, black bastard— are you a faggot or what? Open the door you black faggot!" She gave up after a few more guttural deprecations of my alter ego. And then I slept, panting my way into a difficult night of shallow, intermittent sleep.

There was a tap on the window around noon. I opened it and stood back in the shadows, giving Mario room to enter the window. He saw me now, but did not look at all surprised at whom I turned out to be. He sat on the edge of the bed in his grungy blue jeans shorts and dirty wife beater shirt. Since the attack on San Blas, I had spent little time in the sun. I was also pale from lack of vitamins, except for those attributable to papaya consumption. I had lost considerable weight as well.

"Buenos dias, Senor."

"Buenos dias, Mario." He looked down at fried chicken boxes and empty fruit juice cartons on the floor. "Everything but a puta, I guess."

"Si, senor."

"Mario, has anyone followed you or questioned you?"

"No, senor."

"Has your wife asked you about your new clothes?"

"No, I left them under the bed like you said."

"Ok. Mario, do you want to make some more money?"

"Si, senor."

"Ok. Leave through the front door and ask for another night in the hotel. Give a tip, so that they don't care about your clothes. Ask for another towel and soap at the front desk. Tell them to leave them outside the door. Do not let them near the room."

"Do you understand?"

"Si, senor."

"Go get me a bottle of vitamins—do you know what vitamins are?"

"Si."

"Ok. Next, coffee with cream, more fried chicken, and every newspaper you can find from the last week. Do not buy all the newspapers in one place. When you return, tell the man at the front desk you are not to be disturbed in this room. Do you understand?"

"Si, senor. Tip him a second time."

"Come back through the front door. I will have more instructions for you then." Mario stood up to leave.

"Mario, change clothes first."

Mario smartly opened the door without knocking about an hour later. He left the food items on the floor, and the newspapers on the bed. I gave him another two hundred dollars in Colombian money.

"Mario, listen carefully—I want you to buy me a motorcycle. It needs to be at least 250cc. It should be used. I want no paperwork. When you find the best motorcycle, come back to me. Also, go to a bank and open a bank account in your name. Do you understand?"

"Si, senor, I understand everything, but this will take some time. I must return to my shack for my documents. I hope you understand."

"Of course, Mario. But when you come back, bring me something different for dinner and more juice. OK?"

"Si, senor."

"Bueno. Talk to no one. If you are stopped by the police, do not mention me or the hotel."

"Ok, senor." Mario left smartly, putting on some sunglasses he had acquired.

His stack of newspapers went back five days. There was no news about the downed helicopter, a missing gringo, or the explosion in the mountains. It made sense that the paramilitaries did not announce their failures, but not that the army hid their victories. There was a small article about the capture of an ELN captain outside Santa Rosa Del Sur though. The local police had no clues about the source of the police and paramilitary good fortune, only that it was apparently the result of an anonymous tip. There was no mention in the article about the disposition of the criminal, which probably meant he was in army hands for now.

Hours later Mario again entered without knocking, skillfully managing to enter quietly while carrying paper food bags under one arm and more juice bottles in the other. It was late in the afternoon. The music was grown louder in the lounge in the front of the hotel. Mario also brought more newspapers. He had been a lifesaver, Mario. I felt I needed to show him a little more respect. I offered and he agreed to join me on the floor to enjoy some ribs, empanadas, picada and juice.

In between bites he informed me that he had found a 350cc motorcycle in good condition—he even checked the spark plugs, which were almost new. "Brakes?"

"Good."

"Acceleration?"

"Powerful, senor."

"How much?" He mentioned a price of about fifteen hundred dollars in Colombian money. I handed him another hundred dollars in Colombian. "Tell the man you will pay him at noon tomorrow."

I pulled out my notebook. "Let me see your bank statement." I copied down all the relevant information. "Ok, Mario. Go home—out the back. Come back tomorrow before noon. Hide your bank statement inside your mattress. Do you understand?"

"Si, senor. I understand." I shook his hands, pointing toward the back window. That night, several legs—long and smooth, stumpy, in red and black high heels—tried to get through my door. I gave brief apologies, but pleaded for rest and understanding before retiring early. I again awoke late.

Only one plan had seemed feasible: to ride through the night until I reached the Caribbean, and then bribe my way on a freighter bound for Maicao, or directly to Aruba. From there, I would be in a much better position to explain the providence of my actions over the last few weeks, and to an audience less-inclined to imprison or shoot me.

Mario tapped on the window at about 11.00. He was in his jeans and white shirt with his old boatsman's clothes in a bag. I drank his stiff, bitter coffee with sweet rolls and chased them with vitamins and swigs of water. I gave him some final instructions and precautions. He was to buy the motorcycle, drive it around, and not to return until around 18:00. I needed to know all the police stations and road blocks in the area. I told him to bring me back more fast food, water, and coffee. Only then did I give him the money for the motorcycle, adding about five-hundred dollars in Colombian pesos for his trouble—and risk, since poor boatman did not go out for fast food meals every night, or negotiate a motorcycle purchase.

That day, even though I was running no deficit, I slept as much as I could, fearing the next leg of my adventure could be long, hard and probably sleepless. Mario came back around 19.30. He gave me the keys to the motorcycle, along with my food. "Senor, will you leave now?"

"Yes, Mario." I reached into my backpack. I gave Mario about one thousand dollars more in Colombian money.

"Mario, if you want to live, you have to listen closely: do not spend more than ten dollars at any store. Do not go to the same store twice. Do you understand?"

"Si, senor."

"Go back to the bank in about a week. There will be some more money for you. If they ask questions at the bank, say that a relative died and left you money. Take that money and leave this place. Do not tell anyone before you leave. Do not tell your wife and children until you are in the jeep and on the road. Pack for them when they are not in the house. Do not let your wife call anyone. You will have enough to start again in any place you choose. Do you understand?"

"Yes, senor. I understand."

I proceeded to eat the greasy food quickly, after which I brushed my teeth and dressed. "Senor—before you leave, I want to show you something."

"Is it in La Gloria?"

"No, senor. It is in the water. I have the boat nearby."

"Where is the motorcycle?"

"It is in front of the hotel. I told the putas that I will take them all for a ride tonight. They are watching it for me."

"Good." My backpack was packed: satellite and cell phone, pistol, knife, money, and toiletries. Oh, yes, and grenades.

"Ok, Mario. Let's go."

I was courting unnecessary risk, but I owed this to Mario.

He drove his canoe south along the bank of the La Gloria side of the river, gliding along carefully under a half moon. We could barely see the lights of La Gloria when he suddenly stopped the boat. He picked up his flashlight. "We do not come here, senor. If the paramilitaries know that we know about this place, they would kill us."

He put his flashlight in the water. The light bobbed inconsequentially on the dark water until he held the beam on a spot. There were two bodies near the surface of the water. "They take out the intestines so that the bodies sink. Sometimes they are lazy and the bodies rise upwards or float away." It was a woman and a little girl, still in her school uniform. They each had bullet holes in their foreheads.

"I knew the woman. She was a school principal. The FARC forced her to hire FARC teachers, and give some of her budget to them. She had no choice. They threatened to kill her if she told anyone. When the paramilitaries found out, they took her and her daughter away. That was about two weeks ago. She was not a communist. She just wanted to protect her daughter. They probably tortured her in front of her daughter. It is what they do."

"I am truly sorry, Mario."

"My son went to that school—I just wanted you to see that before you left." Mario had no ability to share these images with the world, but he wanted me—a representative of the world outside the Magdalena—a person who flew in planes and could read and write well; who could talk with other people in an international language and explain the horrors with which Mario was forced to live—to share them with him. We all want someone to bear witness, no matter how inconsequential, to our experience of joy or horror. Mario had nothing of joy to share with me.

He turned the canoe around and went back upstream. We soon arrived at our spot south of La Gloria without trouble from other boatmen or paramilitary patrols. "I am sorry for scaring you, Mario. I am not a bad man. I am simply in a very difficult position."

"I know, senor."

"Mario, please be careful. There are people who notice new things—a poor riverman with unexplained money, for example—and report those things. Do not ever go back to that hotel or the places you bought food or the neighborhood you bought the motorcycle. Continue to work and work hard. Dress poorly. Drink with your friends like nothing has changed, but do not spend too much money. Do not tell your wife about your money or your plans. Do not buy her presents. Stay away from that jeep until you decide to leave. If you can, buy some paint and paint the jeep a light color. Do you understand? You must do these things. Promise me you will follow my advice! There are bad men out there. You know what they will do."

One small slip, and Mario would join the principal and her daughter, as he well knew.

"I understand, senor."

We shook hands. "Thank you, Mario. I will always remember your kindness."

"Gracias, senor." From there I walked back to the hotel. My newspapers were in the garbage cans around back. I put one can in the back yard and started a large fire. In a few minutes, the putas and the bar customers emptied out through the front door, and ran around the building to see the growing fire. My diversion complete, I ran to the motorcycle, started it, and sped toward the eastern part of town.

There were only three highway toll stops between La Gloria and Santa Marta, natural places for police and paramilitary to compare notes on the types on drivers whose stories did not quite add up. The roads were windy but paved, and the night was warm but dry. Mario had certainly found a nice motorcycle for my escape. It accelerated nicely on the long straight stretches and braked smoothly when they ended. I was averaging about forty miles per hour, and arrived in Santa Marta at about 05.00. Somehow, I was waved through each toll stop en route.

The view from the ridge overlooking Rodadero Beach on the Caribbean was majestic, the early morning sun pinkening the horizon atop the quiet sea. I drove into Rodadero, the end of the country, a spot where I could bribe my way all the way to Puerto Rico if I needed to. The usually booming tourist industry was still sleeping. A few drunken tourists were asleep on the beach; a few vendors pushed their carts toward the best spots on the beach in preparation for the busy day that lies ahead.

I took off my hoody and parked on a beachside street. Tourist zone or not, amazingly none of the major hotels were serving coffee that early—at least not to me. There was a minimart on one of the side streets that would suffice. I drank the bottle of water, fruit, and coffee on one of the benches near the beach. With nothing better to do, I walked and walked until the city slowly awoke. When the hotels finally began servicing, I opted for a big American breakfast on a terrace restaurant of one of the larger hotels. I ate six eggs with bacon and toast and juice. It was now about 08.00.

From the terrace I could make out the raising of the side panels of a kiosk for international phone calls on the beach. The girl attending the booth accepted enough cash for fifteen minutes of telephone time on her cellular phone.

"Colonel Hernandez, please."

"Who is speaking?"

"A friend from San Lucas."

"I'm sorry to say that the Colonel has taken ill."

"When did this happen?"

"Three nights ago." It happened after I called him from Simiti. As if he did not have enough open cases on his desk, I thought.

"What is his current condition?"

"The Colonel is stable. Unconscious. He is still in intensive care, but he is breathing on his own." It must have been a major heart attack.

"Has anyone called his daughter?"

"Yes. She arrived yesterday. It is my belief she is in the hospital now."

"No message. Thank you."

Shit. Shit. Shit. I had to get to that hospital. The Colonel was not my friend, my business partner, or my blood. But he was my wife's father. And he could have been dead before I arrived. He, more than anyone else, started me in this business. Besides, Amelia needed me. She would not understand, nor could I explain to her, the reasons why I needed to leave the country like a bandit. But for Amelia—I was not a killer, a thief, or a traitor. I was a hero, which narrowed the scope of my possible actions that moment. I was going back to Cali—without protection, guarantees, or even promise of safe passage.

With only short stops for food and coffee, I drove half way across the country, arriving in Cali at about 02:00 the next day. From what I could tell, there had not been anyone on my tail the whole route since Santa Marta the day before. Cali was still hopping that night. I stopped at sidewalk bar I liked near Carrera 80. There were the requisite TV screens for the image-hooked vidiots. The images went too fast for any sort of recall: floating and flipping motorcycles, a crotch shot of a football cheerleader, a group of bicyclists crashing into each other, and then two Latino sportscasters with handsome smiles. I got a double whiskey, took a swig, and then put a coaster on top of the glass. Across the street was a girl at a bridge table and a "100 Peso" sign.

I gave her five hundred pesos for a fifteen-minute phone call to Bogota. I told her that I must dial the number. She handed me the phone and immediately looked at her watch to start counting the minutes. I spoke the proper code word to the first embassy operator that picked up the call and hung up quickly. "They will call back, Nena—keep that phone turned on." The bartender started to fill my drink, stopping assiduously at the line I drew with my finger across the midpoint of the shot glass. After eighteen hours on a motorcycle, I had earned a last moment's respite from the new health regimen that someone would soon impose upon me like an athlete about to enter training camp.

I could see the girl carrying the phone through the loud, honking blasts of Cali traffic to my side of the road; whoever was on the other line would know I was somewhere in Cali, but they did not have men on the ground at this hour to scoop me up. I gave her another two hundred pesos. Thinking that I did not have plans that night, she winked at me and caressed my cheek with a final little wave before she went back to her little card table desk.

It was Dr. Appleman. The embassy had routed the call to Langley, who in turn had woken her at her home.

"Dr. Appleman."

"Tommy Connolly."

"Tommy. Where are you? It does not sound like a secure phone."

"I was in the jungle for a couple of weeks—now I am back."

"Where are you exactly?"

"Safe. That's all."

"When can you come in for a debriefing?"

"I need to see my doctor for a medical clearance. And my father-in-law has had a heart attack. I will call you when I am declared healthy and flight ready."

"We can send a vehicle for you, now."

"That's not necessary. I'll let you know more when I can."

"Where are you staying? How can we get in touch with you?"

"Wait for my call. It will only be a couple of days. That's all for now. Sorry to interrupt your sleep."

"Tommy…" was the last words I heard.

Dr. Appleman was naturally cautious in her speech outside the security of a CIA-controlled phone line. But there was a tell-tale hesitancy in her voice, as if she knew already that I was alive, but had not worked out how to make that fact work best for the CIA. She wanted me in the embassy—soon—to put an end to the mayhem in which I had been squalidly strutting around lately, which had worked out quite well for me, but might not have been in their interests at all.

I waved at the girl across the street. She came back for the phone and another hundred pesos. She stood near me for a moment, expecting me to ask her to spend some time with me, but I sent her away. I felt more relaxed after my whiskey buzz kicked in, so I drove around Cali some more to clear my head until the sun cast a nice orange glow on Cali. I got an old book for the Colonel, and then drove to the hospital to see him, Amelia and my girls.

Though capable of little more than an occasional grin or hoarsely-breathed question, the Colonel enjoyed my stories about derring-do in the mountains of the San Lucas greatly. Taking evident interest and almost showing pride, as he listened to my accounts, I held back nothing from him, including my murder of Oscar. I needed to rehearse the story I would eventually tell over and over inside the walls of the embassy. Oscar, a private matter for the Colonel's family, would not be part of it.

CHAPTER FIFTY-THREE

"You said before that you were in Aruba on personal business. After receiving a message that you were needed in San Blas, you returned to the Magdalena region in an unspecified manner. Please slowly walk up through the next few weeks."

I had—several times over the course of the last few days, in which I had not left the embassy compound or spoken with my family. My medical papers, which I proffered as the trump piece of evidence that I was ready for a long break from agency work, and verified my claims of ill health in the mountains, had little purchase during the discovery period of the apparent upcoming trial of CIA v. Tommy C.

In front of a mixed group of U.S. and Colombian representatives from several spy agencies, I gave them an accounting of my wilderness tour, from San Blas to La Gloria. No one asked me about Oscar. Evidently, my crime would join the thousands of other unsolved murders from the year 1998 along the Magdalena. The rest of the story required no distortions of the actual events, even though I refused to provide them with corroborative names or places.

While the others around the table seemed to follow the written version of my statement carefully, Doctor Appleman took few notes, alternatively observing the facial responses of the meeting's guests, and casting her own features to emphasize her full support of my version of events.

The other Americans were not on board with several details of my journey—clearly—and the Colombians even less so. Doctor Appleman seemed anxious about regaining cooperation from the Colombian side; the pipeline of armaments and aircraft, now filling Colombian bases to the rafters, needed responsible people on the other end to train and equip whole army and air force divisions. Appleman did not want l'affaire Tommy to spill out and over the dam she had endeavored to forge over the last few weeks.

"When you arrived in Santa Marta, what was your intention?"

"Not to be discovered by angry remnants of the paramilitaries who might kill me and ask questions later."

"Why would they do that?"

"Incredulity that I was the lone survivor of an attack which killed twenty of their comrades."

"So, it was your intention to return to Aruba?"

"Yes."

"And then?"

"To get fit and make contact with you."

"Why not the other way around?"

"I returned to Cali because my father-in-law suffered a serious heart attack. My wife was distraught and needed to care for her mother and our children. Those were my priorities. I promised to return for this briefing at the earliest convenience. I have honored that promise. My wife still needs me in Cali, my father-in-law still lives with tubes keeping him alive, but I am here."

It was a snow flurry of self-righteous bullshit that came from somewhere in me, but certainly not my heart. "Because I find you as trustworthy as coiled snakes..."was his honest thought. "We thank you for that, Tommy." Fuckfantabulous, Doctor.

The Green Beret officer across from me began to show a little impatience with my pattern of simple but—according to his understanding of the survival arts—implausible explanations.

"Tell me, Mr. Connolly, you had a satellite phone and an ELN radio in your possession, why didn't you call for recovery as soon as you awoke from your... rather long sleep?"

"Suicide."

"Excuse me? What do you mean by that?"

"That would have been suicide. The ELN suspected that I was in their mountains—making radio contact—which they monitor—would have confirmed that I was some combination of lost, wounded, and nearby.

"How do you know that?"

"Common sense, Sir. In addition, the captured ELN captain can confirm their monitoring of all paramilitary communications. Instead, I provided them with no intelligence about my location while I gathered useful information about their disposition of forces. I also got stronger. In retrospect, I believe I was correct in my assessment."

"Why did you go to the higher peaks?"

"The ELN would expect me to take advantage of local knowledge and language skills to make contact and seek relief with locals. At a basic level, that is where the food is. Experience also confirmed this. They put a price on my head among the locals."

"So, by not leaving, you confirmed for them that you had in fact not left."

"That is one way of describing it. Still, I preferred to hide in their mountains than try my luck crossing rivers and roads under their control."

"You said it rained for three days."

Doctor Appleman spoke up. "We have confirmed that."

"OK. What did you do during those three days?"

"I slept for two days with a high fever brought on by typhoid. After I awoke on the third day, my fever had broken, so I made small forays to look for food, to hide my waste, and to keep my muscles limber. I also made contact with a local farmer who provided me with intelligence."

"What can you tell us about the campesino who supposedly helped you?"

"Nothing. He took enormous risks. I will not say anything which might lead to his exposure. He was a good man."

"And your hostages?"

"We ran into each other on the same mountain. I got the jump on them, and attacked them when escape was not an option. I disarmed them and took their radios. I hurt one of them badly. I tied them up, gagged them, and then continued my reconnaissance in the higher mountains. They became valuable sources of intelligence, as did their radios."

"Did they know who you were?"

"They were part of a search team looking for me. They were getting closer. They also confirmed my suspicion that the ELN were looking for paramilitary strays along the river, and had offered boatmen a price for any soldier. Walking out of their mountains was never an option."

"Why did they give up the ELN processing lab?"

"I made a creditable threat that I had the means and the will to kill them if I was displeased with them."

"You bound them with wire."

"Yes, from the mining camp—their escape would have been impossible."

"You telephoned a source and gave him the location of the processing lab?"

"Yes. I knew my satellite phone had been modified so that you knew my precise location. Turning it on was for your benefit—giving instructions was for D-2's benefit."

"Why didn't you call us directly to report your location?"

"Because the guerrilla intelligence capabilities sometimes exceed those of the army. If I alerted you, there was a good chance someone would alert them. Also, they are not afraid of you in their backyard—they would have welcomed a rescue attempt."

"What caused you to choose the abandoned mining camp for your final escape?"

"Because I had been there before, and knew the layout. I also knew how the ELN would treat the event, and therefore how I could take advantage of my disadvantages. The ELN fanned out their men over the high ground around the camp, once they discovered my hiding places and waste. They did only a cursory search through the high grasses on the lower slopes on the other side of the road. I was in about a foot of watery effluent inside a drainage pipe, and well hidden by fronds. I was willing to attack the captain with as many as six men around him. I had two grenades and two rifles from my captives, and a pistol. When I saw the captain with only two men around him, it seemed my only chance for a clean break with a vehicle."

"You subdued two men?"

"Three, including the captain. The threat of death by grenade paralyzed them. When I cracked the captain on the scull with a live grenade, they panicked. I induced them to tie themselves with wire and keep quiet. I was able to convince the captain to further disperse his troops in the higher woods. My escape with the captain took all of five minutes. Ten minutes later I was in Santa Rosa Del Sur, and in a half an hour I was in Simiti."

"The captain?"

"I left a message with my source as to the location of his live person." There were several moments of silence, trading of glances, notes being scribbled.

"Quite a story!" threw in one of the CIA analysts. I directed my next comments directly to him.

"While under extreme duress, I took appropriate actions to remain alive and provide useful intelligence which resulted in the destruction of a drug factory and the capture of an ELN captain. I did so while malnourished and without command assistance of any sort. If you have evidence to contradict any part of my 'story', please present it, so that I may defend myself and my honor properly."

The room quieted considerably.

The CIA was seeing a different Tommy than in previous debriefs. Having killed a man, beaten several of them, and humiliated a poor river boatman, a sneering analyst from Langley did not register in me as anything more than an annoyance. Oscar was dead and gone, but for me he was a ghost across the river, rowing quietly away, but never taking his eyes off of me. His glance frightened me.

We settled back into our positions after a fifteen-minute break to clear the air. Without greeting anyone, Doctor Appleman marched behind her forwardly-pressing elbows towards the head of the table at precisely 16:30. For a few moments, she beamed a smile at each member of the table, by which she tried to gingerly enforce a good feeling between allies.

"Tommy, the representative of the Fiscalia would like to ask you some questions about your activities before your last visit to the Green House."

"I will of course endeavor to cooperate, Dr. Appleman."

"Under-Secretary Moreno, the floor is yours." The Bogota ruling class at its highest levels was a small club, which important families traded amongst themselves. Could this guy be an actual relation of Ivan's? Was his selection meant to show the depth of their concern with the behavior of an American agent?

Pushing his coffee saucer away from his clip board, he began his questioning without any sort of framing or otherwise introductory remarks.

"Have you ever participated in a conspiracy to harm the person or impede the investigative work of Ivan Moreno?"

"No."

"Have you ever received intelligence from police officers in Cali that alerted you to ongoing investigations touching upon your person?"

"No."

"Are you aware of the circumstances of his abduction, imprisonment, and torture?"

"No."

"Did you leave Cali last month to avoid questioning about the imprisonment of Ivan Moreno in his hotel?"

"No."

"Did you attack an officer of this office in the woods outside your condo building?"

"Yes."

"What reason can you provide for this aggressive action?"

"He did not announce himself as a government agent, although given multiple opportunities to do so. His partner attempted to gain entrance to my condo without a warrant and by force. Neither agent was in uniform, and both were armed. The agent who tried to beat down my front door scared my wife and our children—maybe that is how you fellows do business, but not in my house. At no time did he ask for my detention or attempt to place me under arrest. I thought he was an insurgent, or criminal, and took defensive appropriate action in defense of my family and myself."

"Did you stab a taxi driver on the way to Medellin while at a gas station."

"Yes. I sliced his arm rather badly."

"What was the reason for this crime?"

"He was going to sell me to either the FARC directly, or a local kidnapping crew, which would pass me along to them. If you check the logs of the pay phone at the location, you will find a phone call he made on that date of approximately five minutes. If you further investigate the number he called, you will probably locate an urban FARC militant."

"He said that you refused to pay your fare."

"I paid him five-hundred dollars to take me to Medellin, and a hundred dollars for his tire."

"Have you ever paid anyone to follow Ivan Moreno, or sell you his private work records?"

"No."

He looked crossly at Doctor Appleman, who probably had set a limit to his questioning. His paramount frustration was that in his own country, five miles from his office, he had no power to detain me at all.

Doctor Appleman asked the next question with finality, so that she could permanently shelve the matter of Ivan Moreno.

"Tommy, have you been completely honest with us today?"

"Doctor, I have never ignored an order or violated security, or taken an action inconsistent with what I believe were my instructions, and I consider the idea that I would be disloyal to my country as almost a slander. I further believe that my actions have been of great assistance to the defense of this country. That's about the best answer I can provide to your question."

In other words, "Go fuck yourself!" I took another sip of coffee.

At that moment, I felt like a free man, but the Colombians who had been forced to listen to my insolent rebuttals did not consider the matter as closed as Dr. Appleman had intimated.

I looked back at them with equal spite: Is this how you spend your country's most desperate days? Defending the honor of a useless dandy like Ivan?

I thought the Undersecretary Moreno's head would explode. He looked at the other Colombian dignitaries, who were probably college classmates or tennis partners of Ivan's father, and slowly came to terms with the fact that there would be no justice—as he understood it—for poor Ivan. Appleman had no intention of permitting follow-up questions from the Colombian side. The case of Moreno vs. Connolly died at that table under anesthetic before the surgeon even entered the operating room.

"Boys," I thought, "ditch your foolish pride if you are going to become a client state that accepts a few billion dollars per annum to fight an insurgency that you cannot manage on your own. And maybe get it into your fat heads that your master is therefore going to help himself to a few liberties. Be happy you're in the club—even as a junior member. Membership is easily revocable."

"Tommy, we value your contribution to the counterinsurgency effort. You showed ingenuity and courage beyond what we ever expected. Your locating the ELN camp stopped over ten million dollars a month from enriching their finances. The intelligence we have harvested from

Captain Sandino will also prove quite valuable to the tamping down of pro-FARC social movements. As a result, all political and military manifestations of the campaign to demilitarize the Magdalena to the permanent advantage of the FARC-ELN are greatly compromised."

But I was a murderer. A killer. Character, Identity, Mind, Heart, Soul, Ego: all the modern constructs that cutely attempt to ferret out some sort of reliable human essence all cried out 'murderer' to me like an angry Greek chorus. I had no defense against them. I had no need to be esteemed by the Colombians.

"We will never be able to acknowledge your contribution—nor shall you—but we appreciate your efforts on behalf of Colombia and your loyalty to your country and its interests. We also hope the Colombian Government acknowledges the extraordinary contribution Mr. Connolly has made to their security, and treats him with appropriate consideration."

I stood up and walked around the table to shake hands with the U.S. officials whose faces could not disguise their own disappointment in hearing the rave review I just received. The Colombians stood in unison, marching out in a single, sullen file before they had to endure the final insult of shaking my hand.

The Special Forces like to retail their superhuman strength and courage to a grateful nation. They could even magnanimously accept amateurism from afar, like a father who shoots an intruder in his home to save his children, as long as they remain top dog in the public imagination. In my case, they refused to believe that an amateur— especially one lacking the training that only men such as them could complete—had survived ten days behind enemy lines, evading detection and battling typhoid fever. It presented too many marketing problems for them.

The Colombians had few doubts, though, about what kind of havoc I could wreak. They only had to speak with Ivan's father.

The afternoon clouds began to fall onto Bogota like a cold compress on a feverish patient, but I still had time to catch a flight to Cali—and Amelia, who made all my contractions burn away.

CHAPTER FIFTY-FOUR

I walked out to the hallway with Doctor Appleman at my side, thinking that my end of the presentation helped to achieve satisfactory results for her. The Colombians had been gently reminded about the rules of empire: they might not like the way we conducted ourselves, but they had no legal recourse when we broke their laws, unless they kicked us out of the country. We all knew they liked their new toys too much to countenance that. On the other side of the table, none of the analysts were able to present a counter-theory about my time behind ELN lines that fit the facts and suggested treasonous or cowardly intent.

Any other issues pending between us could wait for the resumption of business after the holidays. Appleman and I each had planes to catch. But instead of turning right, which would have led us to the nearest elevator, she steered me left toward the offices at the far end of the floor.

"You got a minute, Tommy?" was all she said.

That office had no books on the shelves or personal items on the desktop—nothing to suggest that there was a permanent occupant whose domicile we had encroached upon, albeit temporarily. In the ashtray were the butts of about a pack of different types of cigarettes, though I was pretty sure Dr. Appleman did not smoke. She pointed to the guest seat in front of the desk, which I settled into lightly, still desirous to catch a flight to Cali to see Amelia dancing in her tight shorts to Ray Charles, a cocktail held high in her hand as she warmed up some dinner in the microwave with a single dancing finger.

There was a view in that office toward the cloud-garlanded eastern hills of Bogota that we both pondered for a moment.

"Tommy, you handled yourself well in there, considering...."

"Considering what, Doctor? That I am a bullshitter whose growing repute has not earned unanimous acclaim?" I thought.

Smiling, she let the comment drift away, and instead picked up a phone. "Please—no more coffee, Dr. Appleman," I interjected.

"Make it something stiff or just water."

"Yes—this is Dr. Appleman—bring in a drink tray to 326, please. Yes. Hard stuff. Two glasses."

She sat down behind the desk, trying different poses—her hands folded on the desk, and then on each side of her lap, finally sitting back in her chair with both hands resting palms down on her lap.

"Maybe I have time for one drink," I started with some jocularity.

"My father was in the oil industry, Tommy. We lived in many places when I was growing up, like Iran and Kuwait, other locales in the Middle East, and even Nigeria. My mother refused to live in Angola, so we lived in Washington, D.C. during my high school years. Of all the languages I picked up, I liked Farsi the best. I fell in love with the poetry and the literature of pre-Islamic Persia. I stayed in Washington, D.C. for college. I picked up degrees in Middle Eastern studies and Arabic, though my Farsi was much better. I went to Georgetown for law school, met a man from the World Bank, and got a job at an international law firm. We got married before I was thirty, very proper and Washingtonian."

Super! You are a member in good standing of the permanent governing class with the added cachet of being licensed to wreak havoc in the country of your choice.

"Then, one day an assignment came my way. It involved agricultural credits for the Iraqi government during the Iraq-Iranian war. My job was to present the credit offer on behalf of a consortium of U.S. banks to the Iraqi Agricultural Department. We flew over to Iraq on a Defense Department airplane. I met with navy, army, and air force officials, but no one from the Agricultural Department. I met with Iraqi bankers too. We discussed credits and tranches and wiring, but not agriculture. I even took a jeep ride to the Iranian border, an unexpected detour considering my assignment."

She stopped abruptly, so a young consular officer could bring us a tray of whiskey, which she placed on the table behind me. I wheeled around to make myself a drink even before the clerk had left the room. "Do you know what a cluster bomb is, Tommy?"

As a holiday conversation starter, that fell far from a traditional harbinger of good cheer. I wanted to end the year with fewer conversations of this sort. I stared at the telephone, wondering briefly if I could get an outside line to our condo. Amelia would give me one of her special kisses—that pecked me about ten times on the way to the shower, which she would run while disrobing me. I sat back down.

"My impression is that it is the battle-field equivalent of a land mine. Its purpose is to spread itself outward and maim."

"That is correct… the Iraqi Army Command wanted to show me the utility of cluster bombs in their defensive operations against the Iranian counter-offensive. The Iranians used 'human wave' attacks. They were just young peasant boys—drugged, promised a comfortable toy pen in heaven, and then sent through mine fields to clear a path for soldiers and tanks. The Iraqis needed an edge, so to speak. We arranged for shipments of cluster bombs and missiles under cover of agricultural credits. The intermediaries were Israeli, which also added a layer of secrecy."

"On that day, we sat under a tent-like cover with tea, cookies, and binoculars, while we watched teenage boys get cut in half by the hundreds until the day's wave activity was called from the Iranian side. There were a few boys who made it through a mile of cluster mines that were shot down by snipers at the end of the field. It was truly a slaughter of the innocents. Under the dim yellow lights of Iranian flairs, Iraqi special forces just placed more cluster bombs to replace the discharged ones."

"Excellent eggnog, Doctor. I wouldn't mind a second cup at all," I thought.

"However, those weapons probably shaved four of five years off of what was shaping up to be a Middle Eastern version of World War One. It saved untold numbers of billions of dollars. It weakened perennial belligerents for twenty years. It saved the world economy, since it was the Iranian intention to lift oil prices to pay for its expensive war. Therefore, it met our objectives, which I did not know at the time, of course."

Can we just get to the part where we wish each other a happy holiday?

I took a sip of whiskey that turned into a strong gulp through some sort of unconscious appreciation that Dr. Appleman was still in the early stages of a long explanation of something or another. I took a surreptitious look at my watch.

It came to me. This was her own subtle rebuke of the spy craft of Tommy C. But there was something deeper that disturbed her.

It was Tommy's ambivalence. Cody had long been a student of it; Leo Huff, unable to directly confront a client, had made frequent though circuitous references to it. Unchecked, it could become diffused within an operation. She needed Tommy to act in concert with other agents with fidelity to common aims—and ideology. It was almost like the terms of a love affair; Appleman wanted me to put my heart in my work.

She wanted me to love the CIA in the way she loved it.

"So, I got back to Washington, had a debriefing similar to this one, and was thanked for my service to our nation."

"So you knew you were working for the agency, then, I presume? Did you sign anything? Was your assignment on record?"

"I signed a standard non-disclosure document... Of course I knew what was going on. I took the business card from the man who did the debriefing. They called me back a few weeks later—I had interviews in English, Arabic, and Farsi, security checks, psychological exams, and went to work in a new non-descript building off the mall. I have been with the agency for over fifteen years now."

"Why aren't you attached to the Middle Eastern Division?"

"When things get hot again, I probably will be."

Having sipped my whiskey to its last, it was time to go.

Doctor Appleman gave me a look, which registered that she was through both with CIA small talk, and her earnest attempts to talk me down from sort of rashness.

"Tommy, I need you to go back to work." We had had this conversation before, though on each occasion I had lost; I felt quite capable though of deflecting Appleman's attempts to lure me back into the field that day.

"In the Magdalena?" I scoffed. "Sorry, Dr., I am not going back there. As you suggested, I set them back years. It's someone else's career opportunity to turn the Magdalena red." She glanced at the telephone briefly, but brought her glance down to the desk, and then back to me.

"Tommy, that is quite correct. Your recent heroics rendered you without suitable employment along the Magdalena. You have a face and a legend that are too recognizable."

"What then?"

A terrible pause lingered for an uncomfortable stretch of time.

"I mean your other job—I need you to go back to Aruba."

My hand trembling slightly, I put my glass down carefully on the edge of her desk so that I would not crush it in my hand. It was as if each time she dealt a card, she pulled it from a new deck.

"I don't understand, Dr.; I don't have any business in Aruba." She took more than a sip that time, all the while fixing her eyes on me with her trademark look of concern for Tommy. "It's ok, Tommy. We've known from the beginning."

Oh, Good God! I thought. They have been running me the whole time. I have been their agent since the beginning.

I was not going to corroborate her statements without hearing some more facts, which after a brief pause, she carefully laid out before me.

"We designed the operation with the CNP in mind, Tommy. We needed secrecy, local knowledge—we knew about your father-in-law and his track record negotiating with the cartels in Cali. His was a name that was more trustworthy to the narcos than ours or the DEA. We pitched him the plan in Cali, and he agreed. This was about the time you set foot in Colombia. The maiden flight was scheduled for the beginning of March, 1997."

I looked at my glass, holding it up to the light to look for imperfections in the pellucid brown water. My instincts were at least correct about the contents of the plane—it was narco money, and probably high-grade cocaine that Sal Manzo could retail on the island, and spritz up his guest's nostrils.

"What exactly was the plan?" Perhaps from the whiskey, but I suddenly felt tired.

"To nudge reluctant narcos to go into permanent retirement on our terms. There was a lot of interest on their side, but not a lot of trust, since while they greeted us through the back door; the DEA was kicking in their front doors. In addition, all the narcos suspected their socios of being rats for the DEA, and therefore were killing each other off. That is not a terrible outcome for us, but we don't exactly gain useful intelligence if they are killing each before we can strike a deal."

"Of course, it goes without saying, Dr."

"We decided on a second track—reduced sentences, permanent retirement—either in Colombian prisons or short stretches in Florida and fresh intelligence in exchange for a going away present that the

DEA could not offer, an untraceable bank account that they would never have to report to the Federal Courts or the Colombian Fiscalia."

They had made fools of the DEA. The whole time they were dealing from the bottom of the deck with a fellow federal agency, and to a lesser extent, with Tommy P. Connolly. But in my case it was mutual deception, which they secretly encouraged. I needed off that merry-go-round of psychotic agency scheming before I began to think like them.

"Who knew about this?"

"My assistant and I—you'll meet her in a few minutes—your father-in-law, your brother-in-law, and a team Colonel Hernandez put together."

Stevenson, I thought. He kept the circle of trust small to avoid leaks about a plane taking off weekly with over ten million dollars in its belly.

"Your hospitalization set back our plans—we agreed to postpone the flight part of the operation for three months, but your father was spread thin in Cali due to your slow recovery, which you decided to spend back in Colombia."

It almost sounded like an accusation, but I let it pass.

"Did Sal Manzo know he was part of a CIA operation?"

"No-as far as he knew, he was dealing with crooked officers from the CNP who were cashing in their winnings from the new cartels in Cali. Your unexpected medical crisis in Aruba during your exfiltration added to the legend of wayward Colombians looking to hide their own little stacks of flight capital; it also caused us to take a look at you since Sal Manzo was boxed in by his sister."

"Family," I joked, though I knew otherwise. No one boxed Sal Manzo in unless it served his interests to appear that way. He knew more than they thought, profiting handsomely and in a risk-free manner under the aegis of the biggest narco of them all.

"This past year Congress passed new laws directed toward Caribbean banks; specifically, with a mandate to force them to identify their customers by name in all their wire transactions, ninety-nine percent of which are international, and from numbered accounts. That just about puts an end to secret accounts among the island banking community. Due to our pressure, the Caribbean banks are already closing their windows to numbered accounts. The only exception to that rule is

Sal Manzo. He took advantage of that unique monopolistic opportunity to make millions of dollars, without asking any of the more intelligent sorts of questions, which would have led him to us and our operation."

Had Sal really been that simple-minded? It struck me that they underestimated the talented Mr. Manzo, who was able to rally half of the major banks in the Cayman Islands in the matter of a few days to put together a syndicate for laundering all the paramilitary money.

What had they seen in T.P. Connolly?

"Why bring me in?"

"You fell into it more than anything. Sal Manzo thought of you as a protégé. You lulled him into the operation with your own suspicion and anger toward the Colombians. He saw something in you. And, over time, he liked dealing with you and only you. We were quite happy if his trust reposed solely in you, as long as his counting machines worked as requested. In fact, thanks to you, they ran better than we ever expected."

Sal could see the obvious insurance policy benefits in dealing with the son of a U.S. ambassador. He didn't need a blinking traffic sign to point it out.

Dr. Appleman took another uncomfortable sip of whiskey. "You also put your father-in-law—and the agency—in an uncomfortable position, Tommy."

"How so?"

"That was our two million dollars you took off the table and put into your own pocket."

I was skimming money from people I did not even know were my employers. Those were CIA operational funds I walked away with. I had not taken that money from men with fewer scruples than myself; nor had I redeemed anything. I just arrived late and maneuvered clumsily through an operation that did not require me, and compromised with my greed.

Maybe Dr. Appleman's story about her day under the tent near the Iranian border had another meaning: maybe she knew that I had acted recklessly, but had I been in possession of the facts, I would have been more of a team player.

My father-in-law was not crooked, then. He was more of a patriot than I had ever been. He just wanted to clear as many narcos from Cali as he could in the most bloodless manner that circumstances within the cartels would allow.

I had to get back to Cali. Not just to support my wife, but to tell the Colonel that I had misjudged him—without any right to do so—while I still had time. I knew the nurses in the CNP hospital; they would let me see him that night, even after normal visiting hours. I looked at my watch, and this caused Dr. Appleman to yank the reins a little in her address to me.

"That was the money we agreed to place for one of our most important narco turncoats. Your father-in-law would not ask you for the money, but he was quite amenable to the idea of putting you to work in the operation—within a limited scope, and closely-protected. He felt that you would return the money in time."

But I scorned him, keeping it in my own pirate's cove in Bermuda. Later, I took his daughter, and to add to my list of injuries to him, had secured visas for Laura Benitez and her daughter to the United States. Even Nando came out cleaner than I had; in fact, I had more proof of my own corruption than anyone else involved.

I looked out the window and into the distance, where I saw Tommy as an old man, sitting in a park, watching a statue of classical Tommy crashing to the ground. Observing my budding yet obvious anguish, Dr. Appleman spoke up for me.

"You did a remarkable job, Tommy. You provided both the agency and the CNP with plausible deniability. The Colonel's reputation took a hit, with his son-in-law up to no good under protection of a powerful man, but he accepted the loss of face to take narcos out of commission. Over time, with some carefully-planted rumors, the CNP was able to recoup much of its lost reputation due to the number of 'voluntary' retirements from the ranks of the cartels."

"Why not retire me?"

"You showed a certain aptitude for the work, Tommy, which we never expected. It is not easy to find someone who had time on their hands, and a willingness to jump into murky ethical waters based solely on trust."

Trust of whom, I thought.

"Besides—you paid yourself."

"What do you mean?" I nervously picked up her whiskey glass—almost off her lap—and refilled it, along with my own, hurrying back to the conversation like a teen stumbling in the dark into a movie theater in the middle of a good film.

Except that I was the plot of the movie.

"Your flights made enormous profits—we charged the narcos a fifteen percent fee."

"But I only got 2.5!"

Dr. Appleman laughed. "Do you remember all those bonuses and commissions? After buying arms for the buildup from our Aruba profits, we had enough money left over to fatten your bank account on an ongoing basis—especially as you decided to stay with us. We also repaid ourselves the lost two million. After all, we had to pay you for the risks you took in that small plane, the possible loss of livelihood for your wife in case you died, and the toll in bad health it cost you."

At a minimum, two bouts of typhoid fever, a concussion and a few actual brushes with death. But who was keeping track. That was just the small print; I was more than just the money-man. I had morphed into their source of mayhem, torture and death across hundreds of miles of Colombia. It could have easily been someone else, but I was the linkman with the brigades and their good friends who milled around the back gates to fill their trucks. I had caused death by the planeload.

I am Air Tommy, bringer of death.

"Your father found out about your illness—evidently Colonel Hernandez felt obliged to inform him of any significant changes to your health. He wanted you back in Washington for good. He was quite upset that we had taken advantage of your innocence." She gave me a coquettish wink whose meaning was obvious… I guess he never heard seen the videos from the Liverpool Bar.

"But you decided to come back here, Tommy. No one forced you. Your father wanted you safe and prosperous inside the Beltway, but you wanted something else—something more. You could have walked out of the embassy at any time. Calling you back into action was one of the easiest pitches I ever made to an asset, Tommy. Even knowing everything you learned in the Uraba, you decided to stay and play."

She had reached her summation. My ambivalence was an issue that had caused her some pains, but would never be allowed to threaten operational security again. My little Prometheus act had worn out its audience.

Fine. I lack gravitas. I still have ten million dollars and Amelia Hernandez though. Enjoy your flight back to Washington.

"Where does that leave us, Dr. Appleman?"

I regretted those words as soon as I spoke them.

"You won't be going back to Cali for a while I am afraid, Tommy."

"Pardon?"

I must have heard you incorrectly, Dr., You just banned me from my wife and children during the holidays.

"We are going to expand both routes—the Cali route and the Magdalena flights. Two planes this time—all registered in Panama to Tomlinson—one attached to the Cali route, and the other one for the new Green House landing strip. If anything needs to be discussed, it will be in Panama on the big screen. As promised, you do not have to enter the Colombian theater this time—just keep Sal Manzo fat, drugged and able to count massive amounts of cash in short periods of time. Under your own discretion you can create more consortiums in the Caymans, if such an arrangement is required. Get another plane and register it—a bigger one. We start January 1. Pretty easy stuff for a man of your experience."

That stung: the only question was whether she meant it to. Dr. Appleman was still acting as if I had returned to active duty, none of which I agreed to in the conference room around the corner. Why was she so blatantly confident, almost giddy about my signing back on for active duty?

"Where is this going, Dr.? What's the catch?"

"There is no catch, Tommy—we are recalling you."

"She's good," I thought.

But I had reached the end of the era of good feeling with Dr. Appleman. "Let me remind you—I am not an active agent—you CAN'T recall me, Dr. We have a contract, and it is mostly finished. Anyway, I would prefer to take my chances out on my own. My father-in-law is ill and my wife needs me. Happy Holidays!"

I stood up to shake her hand, but her voice sharpened decisively. "Tommy, sit down!" she said, like a high school teacher to a rebellious student whose insolence was pushing past regrettable and toward punishable behavior.

I sat down. Power thus reestablished between us, she changed her tone back to her other standby—one of feminine and sympathetic worry.

"Christ, Tommy, you'll never make it to the airport alive. Those men in that room—they are dying to get their hands on you, and, honestly, this is a scenario from which we cannot protect you. You're not... You're fucked if you leave this building without a guard."

Agency, she meant—I am not fully agency.

"Are you talking about serious threats?"

"Did you see their faces? They did you... us... a favor—probably out of respect for Colonel Hernandez—but you are persona non grata in Colombia as of midnight tonight. Then the guns come out."

"I thought that term was just for diplomats."

"Close enough. Their request was something between a frank warning and a credible threat. Anyway, either way you have to leave, Tommy. There are no more negotiations and no sincere apologetic niceties to try to make this right. You leave tonight."

"Come one, Dr., are you kidding me? This is just CIA asset-management. You are just inventing all this danger to get me to go back to work—to force me to do something for you again. The Colombians are not that angry about...."

"Yes, Tommy, you were saying?"

I said nothing.

"Ivan Moreno..." she began. "It has been almost three weeks now. There is great news. He can walk unassisted... he no longer needs help brushing his teeth. His parents expect him to begin speaking soon—at least, they're hopeful. His stroke after all was very minor. All his therapies appear to be on schedule. There is a strong possibility that he will be able to hold his child someday."

I said nothing and held back a nearly overwhelming urge to break into a smile.

"You know—the Fiscalia in Bogota sent ten investigators to Cali to locate clues about that incident in the Hotel Inter. They still cannot locate the man who entered the hotel, not from fifteen different camera angles. They never found the video camera, nor the actor, nor his clothing, nor the courier, nor the 'autor intelectual' of the whole sordid affair. The presiding judge in your case refuses to comment. They estimate that the intruder spent over thirty hours in that room, but he left no trace of himself—no prints, no cell phone communication, no getaway car."

Fuckin' half-wit Palanco—I was worried about candy wrappers more than anything else. Still, he did a crackup job. My only mistake was giving him all the money at once—the pig has probably already bought himself a candy factory.

She looked at me like I was a dog who might have to be put down soon.

"What a desperate, vivid imagination someone must have possessed to plan and oversee such a high-risk operation."

My chorus of interrogators would agree with you there, Dr.

Bringing down Ivan was kind of like a battle of the bands—only this time with video equipment, I thought. Ivan made his video and I made mine. Let history judge whose movie made the greatest impact on its target audience.

"How did you ever survive for three days on that mountain with typhoid, Tommy?"

The words fell out clumsily before I had a chance to retrieve them, since they suggested the source of all of my ambivalence, and my liability as an agency asset. "I wanted to see Amelia again. I didn't want to die. I love her."

Let me out of this fucking room! Your concern for the inner-Tommy is noted, now call the first floor and tell them to reopen the front gate.

Slumping deeply into my chair, I said no more, looking at the invisible attorney next to me who would tell Appleman that his client would answer no further questions. Beyond him, I took note of the grey and fading daylight of Bogota, on the last Friday before Christmas, 1998. Dr. Appleman picked up the phone and dialed four numbers. "It's time, Bernadette."

There was a shy knock on the door, whereupon a pair of black shiny shoes and grey stockings with tiny silver spangles, which held tightly around a pair of long porcelain-white legs, were visible at the door. Dr. Appleman smiled at the face that came around the door.

"He's here, Bernadette."

Of course. Now it all made sense. Subjects were objects which became subjects until they were needed as objects once again.

Slowly peering around the door, in a blue velvet dress, with red, shimmering hair, full lips, deep green eyes, and large breasts was NGO girl. She stepped besides Dr. Appleman's desk, holding a folder on her chest defensively, as if the manner in which they compressed her breasts under her NGO t-shirt was a closely-guarded CIA secret.

She was beautiful.

"Hi, Tommy, glad to see you are better."

"Hi—I don't remember your name—it was probably fake anyway." Bernadette did not dwell on the waning powers of my sarcasm.

"Yes—it was. My name is Bernadette."

"For real?"

"For real, this time."

"You look dressed to kill."

"Not part of tonight's agenda, but thanks for the compliment."

She was like Steve Dubrinsky's little Midwestern sister—all earnestness, and character and forthrightness. She was quite an upgrade from the pro-FARC harpy that followed me around Barrancabermeja for what I perceived to be the interleaved goals of hippie sex and ideological reorientation.

We both looked down at her dress. "A big embassy party tonight before I fly back to Washington."

"I have never seen you without your disguise. My compliments to the makeup crew... and thanks for taking care of me in the hotel."

"You are welcome. You had me worried there for a few days."

"Sorry about the mess."

"I grew up with brothers, Tommy—pretty standard stuff."

Nor had I ever suspected that NGO girl was part of the operation. I was too busy sizing up opportunities for greed of one sort or another. But they knew that; in retrospect, they encouraged it. They wanted Tommy to be Tommy. They counted on it.

"Pull up a chair, Bernadette," Dr. Appleman said, offering her the chair near mine. I looked at her deeply—all shapeliness and loveliness and health, showing no sunburn or imperfections or wear on her face from the heat and stench and miasma along the Magdalena, while I would never fully recover from my two bouts of typhoid.

"You ran me." She looked briefly at Dr. Appleman with the right amount of reticence about exposing too many operational details. "Officially, this building did. But you ran yourself pretty well—I have to admit. I was there to make sure that our investment in you was protected."

"Until the mountains."

"Yes. Until then. That put a monkey wrench in things. But since you brought Sandino down the mountain to us so quickly, there isn't much more for me to do there."

"He was a bit of an ass."

"I heard that— " she lied. She had met him in those mountains—I was sure about that. She had taken my money and presented it to Sandino as a good will gesture from a regretful, burned out agent that could possibly be turned. That explained why Sandino was so sluggish in his responses. He thought I was joining up with him.

"Did the paramilitaries suspect anything?"

"I'm sorry, Tommy—that is all I can say on that topic." I was no longer part of the operation, which brought me a moment's gratification. She felt that she had not shown adequate appreciation of my sacrifices though, and was eager to prod the conversation away from operational details and back to my great works in the field. "You really did break their bank, Tommy. They are going to be cash-short for quite a few years."

"I suppose you are right." I wanted to go home to Amelia, not listen to another take on my dirty deeds done well, or receive compliments about killing young boys who had as much right as I did to cash, travel, a beautiful wife, or just simple dignity. I could not imagine that either of them had put a gun—even with tenderness—to the head of a young boy, whose last weeks of life were unabated agony and cruelty, and then pulled the trigger; or, had called in coordinates to blow up a camp that mostly contained child-soldiers.

What would Oscar have become under different circumstances? He had more guts than Ivan Moreno. He would have made something of himself, I was sure. But he was forever somewhere in the hills behind the Green House in a pauper's cemetery with hundreds of ex-boy soldiers.

I bolted toward the drink table, but once there kept my glance moving across the outer walls and patio of the embassy complex, which I subjected to a quick surveillance. Street lights outside the compound lent almost no auxiliary light on the courtyard below. Out of sight, there were armed marines on the first floor, which I could not pass through without Appleman's approval. Unarmed, and in fading light, it was too dark to bust out of the embassy without taking someone else's gun, which would have consequences I could not begin to imagine, let alone control.

"Bernadette—why don't you give Tommy an overview of the Irish project."

"Irish project?"

"How much time do I have?" Bernadette queried Dr. Appleman.

"His plane leaves at eight."

"Plane? What fuckin' plane?" I shot a sinister look at Dr. Appleman, one that bounced like a BB off the plating of her regard for my ability to deter her preset plans for me.

"You have to go slowly with Tommy, Bernadette. He is prone to little temper tantrums when surprised."

I wondered at that moment if Dr. Appleman had ordered a psych analysis of me.

Appleman never mentioned anything about a plane. Time was short if I was to get back to Amelia that night. I also had to see the Colonel in case he succumbed to his weak, ailing exhausted heart, brought down in large part by the chaos his son-in-law had introduced to his country, command, and family.

"None of this is going to happen, Dr., consider this breach of contract—and an apology. I'll see myself out." I went quickly towards the door and opened it, where I saw two armed marines glaring at nothing in particular in the hallway. As I turned back, Bernadette and Dr. Appleman sat with their heads held down out of respect for my shame, or in recognition of their own. I could never be sure about those things.

I yawned, but not from the whiskey. They had fed me something.

Bernadette looked me over for a moment, trying to see whether her previous take on Tommy P. Connolly required any significant modification. Away from the field, I did not seem to have all the answers after all.

I took a hard look at Appleman. She was not enjoying this situation—neither the decision to keep me away from my family in the narrow sense, nor to drag me back into more sordid adventures in the larger context. In that moment, she seemed to be reliving her own seduction somehow.

She probably walked into the agency with the nobler virtues of her class as her personal beacon: the betterment of relations with troubled nations; the chance to lift societies out of predicaments from which they would be unable to extricate themselves; to give millions of people a better life; to riff in two rare languages and be back home before the News Hour began. And now she was in the American Embassy in Bogota on the last Friday before Christmas, babysitting a reluctant spy who can't seem to admit that he understands the game, is good at it, and derives some pleasure from it.

The whiskey now sat uneasily in my stomach; suddenly, I wanted to spew up the whole sordid, brackish life back in their faces.

"Dr., if I go along with all this—when do I get to see my wife and daughters." I phrased it as if Appleman herself held them for ransom in the embassy basement.

She fielded the question, however reluctantly, since I had learned that these people prided themselves on their long-distance willingness to treat their own families as mission-undertaking obstacles.

"My guess, is, Tommy, that as soon as your father-in-law stabilizes, I am sure that she will want to join you in Aruba or Washington."

"Can I at least call her before I go?"

"No calls until you are outside Colombia, Tommy. The Colombians have our equipment now, which they can use for their own purposes."

Appleman was just acting on behalf of empire. There were hundreds of officers like her, deputized to seize a guy like Tommy, and pretty much seal him off from civil liberties or even a simple phone call to his wife if he proved uncooperative to some master scheme. It could have been worse for me—I could have been in that room because I had spilled a dark secret.

My eyes felt heavy, like my first night on the mountain when I succumbed to delirium.

I remember one autumn Saturday when I was about ten years old. I was in the back shed at the house of my friend Bobby Sandrich. He and I watched his father as he sat patiently beneath the light of his work bench, first putting oil on the blade of his chain saw, which he had used to cut some oak trees into fire wood in his back yard; next, he slowly poured oil on the chain, which he pulled around its track. Meanwhile, he picked out little pieces of wood until the chain moved without impediment.

He wrapped that chain saw in cloth, and put it in its container. Then, he put it on a shelf, and shut the lights. It was an important tool, one for which he felt pride of ownership, and gave it quite touching care. But it still went up on the cold shelf and spent the winter there.

I looked at the evening shadow on the window behind me, as I slumped into my chair, defeated. I began to turn my anger inward.

You should never have walked into this trap, Tommy. You knew there was a reason they wanted you back in the embassy. You have always lived on emotional bread and water with these people. You never want to hear their compliments or praises for the dirty deeds you undertake for them—lest you admit you fit in with them or belong with them—as if that guy doing the killing and plotting is someone else like a roommate in your own soul that is getting the chicks you deserve while you read comics in your bedroom.

It's you, Tommy—you are that guy—you are the one Dr. Appleman introduced to the Colombians as one badass agent that they could not touch upon penalty of a ruptured political relationship. You survived on your wits on that mountain, brought down Ivan Moreno, and walked away with Amelia Hernandez. Start savoring it—before these people take it all away from you, and leave you with less than what you arrived with in this damned country. Because they will—and not shed any more tears than the one that Dr. Appleman carelessly let drop. They could find a crooked judge, and doctor enough evidence to put you behind bars for twenty years. And they would if they ever considered you a threat to any number of their concerns.

"Fat fuckin' chance that'll happen!" I said aloud in the hillbilly intonation I grew up with, so that Dr. Appleman and Bernadette harkened to my strange, oracular remark.

"What did you say, Tommy?"

"Nothing. I was talking to myself." Bernadette looked again at Dr. Appleman, though this time with a grin.

"Ok! With that in mind, let's talk Real vs. Provisional IRA."

That night, they carried me out of the back of the embassy in a diplomatic car with my jacket over my head. I could just make out the low bass of the opening dance music at the embassy Christmas reception above.

Before I put an end to his ambitious career, Ivan predicted I would leave the country in this manner, alone and discredited. Your enemies do sometimes know you best.

They are not going to put me on the payroll; I won't be playing in weekly pickup basketball games in the Langley gym. I won't deliver briefing books to the White House. I won't run my own Tommy and make an occasional appearance in the kill zone, like Bernadette.

Instead, they will provision me to make a go at some new reconfiguration of the basic CIA quartet of guns, cash, drugs, and sex. Appleman was right about one thing: my father offered me security well within empire; I turned him down, though, for life on its edges.

Two huskier, more mature versions of Tommy—with ridiculous matching grey ponytails and gold earrings over the collars of their leather jackets—were eyeing me from the front of a dark, sleek sedan that ran quietly over the highway to an airbase south and east of Bogota. Apparently having heard that Tommy C. was quite nimble in situations such as that one, they each made a point to show me the pistols hanging from their inside holsters.

I won't forget you guys—at this Christmas or any subsequent one, for that matter. I was asleep before they dumped me on the plane and signaled to the pilot to depart.